FROM THE PAGES OI
SENTIMENTAL EDUCATIC

Never before had he seen more lustrous dark skin, a ive figure, or more delicately shaped fingers than those through which the sunlight gleamed. He stared with amazement at her work-basket, as if it were something extraordinary. What was her name, her home, her life, her past? (page 9)

"Without ideas, there is no greatness; without greatness there is no beauty. Olympus is a mountain. The most astonishing monument will always be the Pyramids. Exuberance is better than taste; the desert is better than a sidewalk, and a savage is better than a hairdresser!" (page 54)

The dinners started again; and the more visits he paid at Madame Arnoux's, the more his lovesickness increased. The contemplation of this woman had an enervating effect upon him, like the use of a perfume that is too strong. It penetrated into the very depths of his nature, and became almost a kind of habitual sensation, a new mode of existence. (page 78)

He displayed high spirits on the occasion. Madame Arnoux was now with her mother at Chartres. But he would soon come across her again, and would end by being her lover. (page 98)

"What are you to do in an age of decadence like ours? Great painting has gone out of fashion!" (page 126)

There was a look of peculiar sadness in Madame Arnoux's face. Was it to keep him from further reference to the memories they shared? (page 152)

Then began for Frédéric a miserable existence. He became the parasite of the house. (page 191)

"So happiness is impossible?" (page 223)

Then, forgetting his own troubles, he talked about the affairs of the nation, the crosses of the Légion d'honneur wasted at the Royal Fête, the question of a change of ministry, the Drouillard case and the Bénier case—scandals of the day—denounced the middle class, and predicted a revolution. (page 243)

And they pictured a life entirely devoted to love, sufficiently rich to fill up the most vast solitude, surpassing all other joys, defying all sorrows; in which the hours would glide away in a continual outpouring of their own emotions, and which would be as bright and glorious as the shimmering splendour of the stars. (page 303)

"Spare nothing, ye rich; but give! give!" (page 337)

Four barricades at the ends of four different routes formed enormous sloping ramparts of paving-stones. Torches were glimmering here and there. In spite of the rising clouds of dust he could distinguish infantrymen and National Guards, all with their faces blackened, disheveled, and haggard. (page 373)

This event was a calamity which, in the first place, put off their separation, and, next, upset all his plans. The notion of being a father, moreover, appeared to him grotesque, unthinkable. (page 402)

"Have you twelve thousand francs to lend me?" (page 452)

"I would have liked to make you happy!" (page 473)

SENTIMENTAL EDUCATION

GUSTAVE FLAUBERT

Translated by D. F. Hannigan and revised throughout by Kathleen Rustum

With an Introduction and Notes by Claudie Bernard

GEORGE STADE
CONSULTING EDITORIAL DIRECTOR

BARNES & NOBLE CLASSICS
NEW YORK

Barnes & Noble Classics
New York

Published by Barnes & Noble Books
122 Fifth Avenue
New York, NY 10011

www.barnesandnoble.com/classics

L'Éducation Sentimentale was first published in 1869.
D. F. Hannigan's English translation appeared in 1898.

Published in 2006 by Barnes & Noble Classics with new Introduction, Notes, Biography, Chronology, Inspired By, Comments & Questions, and For Further Reading.

Sentimental Education
ISBN-10: 1-59308-306-8
ISBN-13: 978-1-59308-306-9
LC Control Number 2005907805

Produced and published in conjunction with:
Fine Creative Media, Inc.
322 Eighth Avenue
New York, NY 10001

Michael J. Fine, President and Publisher

Printed in the United States of America

QM

1 3 5 7 9 10 8 6 4 2

FIRST PRINTING

GUSTAVE FLAUBERT

Gustave Flaubert was born in 1821 in Rouen, France. His father, a respected surgeon, raised his family in quarters near the hospital where he worked. Gustave was a deeply romantic young man, and he developed an early and permanent disdain for the life of the French bourgeoisie. Its banalities and exigencies trapped him for a time, as he was encouraged to study law, like many a respectable bourgeois son. However, in 1844 his schooling in Paris came to an abrupt halt when he had a series of health problems resulting in seizures and a coma. These attacks, now thought to be symptoms of epilepsy, required Flaubert to leave school and return to the provinces. Established on his estate in Croisset, he dedicated himself to his true passion—literature.

Flaubert's convalescence was soon disrupted. His father died in January 1846, and his beloved sister, Caroline, who had recently given birth, died six weeks later. In his mid-twenties, Flaubert became head of a household that now included his mother and his sister's daughter. Although the three lived a placid country life together for many years, Flaubert often visited Paris, where he fell in love with Louise Colet, cultivated a friendship with writer and photographer Maxime du Camp, and witnessed the Revolution of 1848. He worked for many years on a novel, *The Temptation of Saint Anthony* (finally published in 1874), that in its early drafts was criticized by his friends for being overly romantic.

Upon returning in 1851 from a tour of the Near East, he began a novel in which he experimented with a new narrative style. Working tirelessly for almost five years, taking great care over each sentence, Flaubert composed his masterpiece, *Madame Bovary*, the story of a disenchanted provincial wife. When it was published (in installments in 1856, in book form in 1857) *Madame Bovary* caused a sensation; its frank depiction of adultery landed Flaubert in the courts on charges of moral indecency. Exonerated, the author became a respected frequenter of the Parisian salons, was awarded the French Legion of Honor, and formed friendships with George Sand, Émile Zola, and Guy de Maupassant.

Although he continued to visit Paris frequently, Flaubert lived for most of the year in Croisset, where he wrote and revised his works, and amassed an astonishing body of correspondence. He is also remembered for his novels *Salammbô* (1862) and *Sentimental Education* (1869) and for the collection *Three Stories* (1877). Financial troubles beset him late in his life, and he spent his final years somewhat isolated and impoverished. Gustave Flaubert died on May 8, 1880, in Croisset.

TABLE OF CONTENTS

THE WORLD OF GUSTAVE FLAUBERT AND *SENTIMENTAL EDUCATION*

1821 Gustave Flaubert is born on December 12 in Rouen, France. His father is a surgeon and medical professor; his mother is from a distinguished provincial bourgeois family.

1824 Flaubert's sister, Caroline, is born.

1829 Honoré de Balzac publishes *Les Chouans*, his first literary success and the earliest of his works to be included in what he later will call *La Comédie humaine* (*The Human Comedy*).

1830 Victor Hugo's *Hernani* appears, as does Stendhal's *Le Rouge et le Noir* (*The Red and the Black*). The July Revolution results in the abdication of King Charles X and the establishment of the "citizen king" Louis-Philippe.

1831 Hugo's *Notre-Dame de Paris* (*The Hunchback of Notre Dame*) is published.

1832 Gustave enters school at the Collège Royal in Rouen; he studies the ancient Greeks and Romans, and favors such Romantic writers as Goethe, Byron, Chateaubriand, and Hugo.

1833 George Sand's *Lelia* appears. Jules Michelet publishes the first volume of his monumental *Histoire de France* (*History of France*); the seventeen-volume work will be completed in 1867.

1836 Flaubert falls deeply in love with Elisa Schlésinger, eleven years his senior; he later will take her as his model for several of his literary heroines.

1837 An avid writer from an early age, Flaubert publishes two stories.

1840–1841 He begins studying law in Paris.

1844 Flaubert has his first "nervous" attack, probably an epileptic seizure. The resulting coma and further illness cause him to abandon his legal studies for the life of a writer at his estate in Croisset, on the River Seine between Paris and Rouen. *Le Comte de Monte Cristo* (*The Count of Monte Cristo*), by Alexandre Dumas (père), is published.

1845 Flaubert completes the first version of *L'Éducation sentimentale* (*Sentimental Education*). His beloved sister, Caroline, marries.

1846 Flaubert's father dies in January, and Caroline dies in March. Devastated, Flaubert sets up house in Croisset with his mother and Caroline's infant daughter—a living arrangement that will persist for the next twenty-five years. During a visit to Paris, Flaubert meets the poet Louise Colet, who becomes his mistress.

1847 Flaubert and writer and photographer Maxime du Camp take a walking tour along the River Loire and the Brittany coast. The journal Flaubert keeps during this tour will be published posthumously (1886) as *Par les champs et par les grèves* (*Over the Fields and Over the Shores*).

1848 In Paris, Flaubert witnesses the Revolution and the establishment of the French Second Republic. After some months of political turmoil, Louis-Napoléon Bonaparte is elected president.

1849 The manuscript of *La Tentation de Saint Antoine* (*The Temptation of Saint Anthony*) is criticized by Flaubert's friends for its overly Romantic style. Later in the year, Flaubert journeys to the Near East with du Camp.

1850 Eugène Delacroix paints the ceiling of the Louvre's Galerie d'Apollon (Gallery of Apollo).

1851 Back in Croisset, Flaubert begins writing *Madame Bovary*—a painstaking process that will last almost five years. Gérard de Nerval's *Voyage en Orient* (*Voyage to the East*) is published.

1852 Having staged a coup late in 1851, Louis-Napoléon Bonaparte seizes the monarchy as Napoléon III and establishes the French Second Empire.

1853 Georges Haussmann begins redesigning the streets, parks, and other physical aspects of Paris.

1855 Flaubert and Louise Colet end their relationship.

1856 Late in the year, *Madame Bovary* appears in installments in the *Revue de Paris*.

1857 Flaubert is brought to trial for the novel's alleged moral indecency but is exonerated. *Madame Bovary* is published in book form. Charles Baudelaire's *Les Fleurs du Mal* (*The Flowers of Evil*) is published; Baudelaire is tried and fined for the content of his work.

1858 A trip to Tunisia provides Flaubert with inspiration for *Salammbô*, a novel about ancient Carthage.

1862 *Salammbô* is published. Flaubert begins to spend more time in Paris, cultivating friendships with George Sand, Émile Zola, and Ivan Turgenev. Hugo's *Les Misérables* is published.

1866 Respected by the court of Napoléon III, Flaubert is made a knight in the French Legion of Honor.

1867 The mother of the young Guy de Maupassant is a friend of Flaubert and introduces her son to the author.

1869 *Sentimental Education* is published.

1870–1871 The Franco-Prussian War leads to the end of the French Second Empire and establishment of the Third Republic. When de Maupassant returns from military service in the war, he begins a literary apprenticeship with Flaubert, who coaches him in his writing and introduces him to other leading writers.

1872 Flaubert's mother dies.

1873 Arthur Rimbaud's *Une Saison en Enfer* (*A Season in Hell*) and Jules Verne's *Le Tour du monde en quatre-vingt jours* (*Around the World in Eighty Days*) are published.

1874 The production of Flaubert's play *Le Candidat* (*The Candidate*) is a failure. *La Tentation de Saint Antoine* is published.

1877 *Trois Contes* (*Three Stories*) is published. Émile Zola's *L'Assommoir* (*The Dram Shop* or *The Drunkard*) is published.

1880 Gustave Flaubert dies, suddenly and unexpectedly, in Croisset on May 8.

1881 The novel *Bouvard et Pécuchet*, unfinished when Flaubert died, is published.

INTRODUCTION

The year 1848 can be considered a landmark in nineteenth-century French history. It was a landmark, first, in political history. Since the storming of the Bastille in 1789 and the establishment of the first Republic in 1792, France had lived through a succession of regimes—the Directory, the Consulate, the Empire of Napoléon I, the Bourbon Restoration in 1815, and finally, following the revolution of July 1830, the constitutional monarchy of the "bourgeois king" Louis-Philippe d'Orléans. During his reign (1830–1848), known as the July Monarchy, the industrial revolution took root in France, although more slowly than it did across the Channel. The land-based aristocracy lost ground; the power of a capitalist middle class—the principal beneficiary of the previous revolutions and the key player in a very restrictive electoral system—soared; and there emerged a working class whose exploitation created urban poverty. The confrontation typical of the Restoration, between Legitimists (partisans of the Old Regime) and Liberals (Bonapartist or Orleanist), gave way to a new and enduring split between the conservatives who, under the ministry of François Guizot, favored a "golden mean," and the democrats who, often influenced by a widespread utopian socialism, preached liberty, equality, and fraternity between rich and poor, a set of ideals inspired by the motto of the French Revolution as well as by Christian thinking.

This new split became apparent in the revolution of 1848. Over the course of three days, February 22–24, Louis-Philippe was overthrown and the Second Republic was proclaimed. The 1848 revolution helped spark rebellious movements all over Europe, from Italy to Germany and Hungary, from Vienna to Prague. Unfortunately, this "Spring of the Peoples"—with "Peoples" having the double meaning of "plebeians" and "patriots"—was short-lived. In France, Romantic poet and statesman Alphonse de Lamartine and his friends, heads of the provisional government installed at the Hôtel de Ville, soon faced enormous difficulties. They had instituted universal male suffrage, but the legislative elections favored the conservatives. The national workshops created by the socialist Louis Blanc to counter unemployment proved a failure. Between June 23 and June 26, more than a thousand working-class insurgents were killed by government troops led by General Louis Cavaignac. In December 1848, the presidential election was won by the nephew of Napoléon the Great, Louis-Napoléon Bonaparte, an opportunist who had been sympathetic to the impoverished class but would soon throw in his lot with the "Party of Order." On December 2, 1851, Bonaparte led a coup d'état, followed by a wave of extremely repressive measures and a plebiscite in his favor, and in 1852 he established the Second Empire. Until its collapse during the Franco-Prussian War of 1870–1871, the Second Empire proved a period of economic prosperity, reinforcement of the upper middle class, and clericalism and authoritarianism that gradually gave way to a more parliamentary and socially responsible regime. It was during the war-time occupation of Paris by Prussian troops that the last revolution of the nineteenth century and the first authentic proletarian revolution took place: the Commune of 1871. The Third Republic, the dawning of France's modern democracy, could then really get underway.

Although it is difficult to assign dates to cultural trends, 1848 appears as a landmark in the literary realm too. Since the Restoration, Romanticism (a word borrowed from the German that initially designated a literature inspired by chivalric times) had dominated the scene, first in its aristocratic, nostalgic, and Catholic incarnation, best represented by François de Chateaubriand and Alfred de Vigny, and then with a liberal and humanitarian leaning, exemplified by the bourgeois Victor Hugo and George Sand and the historian Jules Michelet. In 1848, faithful to their ideas, a large number of the Romantic writers took to the streets, or at least to their pens. The ensuing ferocious repression contributed to their withdrawal into the ivory tower of "Art for Art's Sake," while Realism, which was to flourish in the second half of the century with the brothers Edmond and Jules de Goncourt, Émile Zola, and Guy de Maupassant, started to assert itself.

A reaction against Old Regime Classicism, Romanticism celebrated nature in its picturesque or sublime aspects; exalted the sensibility, passions, and genius of the ego; explored history as the struggle of major forces incarnated by heroes and led by Providence; and, in its later tendency, glorified "the people" and "woman" as the regenerating forces of humanity. Romanticism favored imagination and cultivated poetry, drama, and even the epic. Realism retrieved the inheritance of Enlightenment—rationality, materialism, anticlericalism, and a critical spirit—but gave it a more pessimistic spin. After 1848 the dominant classes seemed to have lost the ascendant and dynamic spirit of the decades following the Great Revolution, and the individual lost the confidence he had derived from the recognition of his new rights and his new dignity. Linked to the consolidation of capitalism, of urbanism, and of middle-class values, Realism held a more sober conception of the ego and led to a cynical reevaluation of history; it explored the people as repulsive masses, and woman as a biological and psychological case. To do so, Realism chose the novel, a form it was to bring to perfection.

Midway between the noble genres of tragedy, poetry, and epic, and low genres like farce, satire, and pamphlet, the novel proved the most appropriate tool to describe the predicaments of the class situated between the nobility and the people, the bourgeoisie. Just as the bourgeoisie depends on private property, private interests, and domesticity to ensure the proper functioning of public life, the novel seeks, by concentrating on private matters, to illuminate the public sphere. Devoid of any aristocratic legitimacy, the novel is free of the canons that govern high literature as well as of the archetypes that constrain popular literature, and it has the same diversity and openness as the bourgeoisie. A genre still considered minor when first taken up by Honoré de Balzac, and primarily conceived as the reading matter of women and persons of leisure, the novel was to become—thanks to technological improvements in the printing process, the serialization of novels in periodicals, and increased literacy and the broadening of readership—the dominant form in Zola's time.

Under the July Monarchy, the precursors of Realism, Stendhal and Balzac, were still suffused with Romanticism. Balzac, who gave himself the mission of representing, explaining, and even modifying

contemporary history, expressed the post-revolutionary rapport between the ego, a society in mutation, and the universe at large in terms of action; whether successful or not, his characters, impressed by the Napoleonic myth, take action and try to change the world while advancing their careers or their destinies. Similarly, Stendhal's heroes, male or female, are defined by their energy. While highly dramatic, as the title of Balzac's series, *La Comédie humaine* (*The Human Comedy*), suggests, Stendhal's and Balzac's novels also lay claim to the seriousness of the emergent social sciences, and their authors do not refrain from offering an authoritative or challenging opinion. Under the Second Empire, things change. The (often female) protagonists see their actions blocked, distorted, or weakened; exterior, and sometimes interior, forces overcome even their desire to act. Determinism according to race (that is, genealogy), milieu, and moment—to borrow the concepts of the philosopher Hippolyte Taine (1828–1893)—limits the characters' freedom. The esthetics of the "slice of life" tend to diminish the importance of plot, descriptions, and inventories compete with narration, as do tableaux with adventures. (Let's not forget that the word "Realism" was first applied to painters, most notably Gustave Courbet [1819–1877].) Finally, under the triumphant influence of Positivism, which helped social sciences come into their own, Naturalism (a term coined by Zola for its scientific connotations) substitutes documentation for observation, experimentation for invention, demonstration for representation, and objectivity, invisibility, and even infallibility for authorial interventions. Stendhal compared the realistic novel to a mirror carried along the way, reflecting mud as well as flowers; Zola uses the image of a glass pane, so transparent that the reality is reproduced as such, as if without any mediation.

Like Romanticism at its beginning, Realism created a scandal, not so much because its intellectual enterprise rested on an illusion, but because of its alleged preference for the ugly, the vulgar, the lowly, and the vicious. Courbet's painting *L'Enterrement à Ornans* (*Funeral at Ornans)* shocked the public and in 1855 his canvas *The Artist's Studio* was rejected for display at the Exposition Universelle (International Exposition). In 1857 Charles Baudelaire, the author of the collection of poems *Les Fleurs du Mal* (*The Flowers of Evil*),

and Flaubert, who had published the novel *Madame Bovary*, were put on trial for immorality. What the prosecutor found objectionable in *Madame Bovary* was not the depiction of adultery per se, a traditional topic in fiction, but the absence of condemnation by a "positive" character or by the author.

With *Madame Bovary*, Flaubert, whose precocious works in the 1830s and 1840s were heavily Romantic, was hailed as a champion of Realism. Yet he never felt at ease in either camp.

> There are in me, literarily speaking, two distinct sorts of fellows: one who is fond of mouthing off, of lyricism, of vast eagle soars, of all the resonance of a sentence and the pinnacles of an idea; and another one who digs and scours the truth as much as he can, who likes to highlight the little authentic fact with as much conviction as the big one, who would have you feel almost physically the things he reproduces (January 1852, *Correspondance*, vol. 2, p. 30 [unless indicated otherwise, excerpts from the correspondence are translated by the author]; see "For Further Reading").

Similarly, he wrote in a letter from October 1856: "People think that I love reality, while I abhor it . . . But I hate just as much false idealism, which makes fools of us all in the present times" (*Correspondance*, vol. 2, p. 643). Although he could empathize with his characters, declare that "Madame Bovary is myself," and actually feel the symptoms of poisoning when describing her death by arsenic, he stuck to the positivistic credo: "It is one of my principles, that one must not *write oneself.* The artist must be in his work like God in his creation, invisible and omnipotent. Let him be sensed everywhere, but not seen" (March 1857, *Correspondance*, vol. 2, p. 691). And later: "I even think that a novelist *hasn't the right to express his opinion* on anything whatsoever. Has God ever expressed his opinion?" (December 1866; *The Letters of Gustave Flaubert*, translated by Francis Steegmuller, p. 94). In *L'Éducation sentimentale* (1869; *Sentimental Education*), Charles Deslauriers aspires to be like Balzac's seductive opportunist Rastignac and greatly admires the league of superior men depicted in Balzac's *Histoire des treize* (1833–1835; *History of the Thirteen*), while Frédéric dreams of a great passion and favors Lord Byron, Chateaubriand, and Walter Scott: Flaubert proves them both wrong.

Flaubert's most typical posture was of bitter irony. In his correspondence, he admitted that he laughed at everything—facts, people, feelings, and even those matters dearest to his heart, as a method to test them. His sarcasm did not spare current events. In March 1848 he told his mistress Louise Colet:

> You ask my opinion about all that has just been done. Well! It is all quite droll. . . . I profoundly delight in the contemplation of all the flattened ambitions. I don't know if the new form of government and the social state that will come of it will be favorable to Art (*Correspondance*, vol. 1, p. 492).

His mockery denounced all ideological as well as esthetic clichés—all the discourses that speak through us without our control. He compiled a spicy *Dictionnaire des idées reçues* (1913; *Dictionary of Received Ideas*). And his last and unfinished book, *Bouvard et Pécuchet* (1881), an encyclopedic satire of contemporary practices and knowledge, ends up with the two false scholars returning to their original jobs, that of copyists.

Flaubert's major preoccupation transcended any school; he called it "style," in the larger sense of artistic creation. Style for him was as much behind the words as in the words, as much the soul as the flesh of a work. It was not contingent on a topic: "There are neither beautiful nor ugly subjects, and one could almost establish as an axiom, if one adopts the point of view of pure Art, that there is no subject at all, style being in itself an absolute way of seeing things." He toyed with the notion of composing "a book about nothing, a book without any exterior attachment, which would hold together by the internal force of its style, like the earth holds up in the air without being supported; a book that would have almost no topic, or at least whose topic would be almost invisible, if that is possible" (January 1852, *Correspondance*, vol. 2, p. 31).

While Baudelaire searched for the flowers, the beauty of evil, Flaubert assigned himself the task of extracting the beauty of the mediocre, the ordeal of resuscitating ancient Carthage in *Salammbô* (1862), and the challenge of following two idiots, Bouvard and Pécuchet. A recluse in his house at Croisset, in Normandy, like the saints he liked to describe, he experienced the "throes of style": the

anxiety of cutting all banalities, the painful pursuit of the proper word, the trial of oral recitation, and the endless corrections and accumulated drafts. The final manuscript of *Sentimental Education* is 500 pages long, but the first drafts comprise no less than 2,350 sheets written front and back.

In 1836, at the age of fifteen, Flaubert, the son of a prestigious surgeon from Rouen, visited the Channel beach at Trouville and met a young lady, Elisa Schlésinger, with whom he fell in love at first sight; the two had a quasi-platonic relationship for many years. Her husband, Maurice Schlésinger, a music publisher in Paris, was an exuberant bon vivant and a womanizer. Such is the anecdotal source of the sentimental—that is, amorous—theme of *Sentimental Education*. In the years following his meeting Elisa, the young and ultra-Romantic Flaubert composed two autobiographical texts: *Mémoires d'un fou* (drafted in 1838; *Memoirs of a Madman*), which tells of the narrator's encounter with the brunette angel Maria, and *Novembre* (drafted in 1842; *November*), in which the same event is followed by the narrator's move to Paris to study law—Flaubert and later, his fictional character, Frédéric Moreau, did the same—his affair with a married woman, and finally his death as a result of ennui. In 1845, definitively established in Croisset, Flaubert finished a novel entitled *Sentimental Education*, which presents two friends—Jules, the artist dear to the author's heart, and Henry the climber—who are both in love with a married woman. They prefigure the heroes of the present work, a second and quite different *Sentimental Education*, Moreau and Deslauriers.

Flaubert was in Paris at the onset of the revolution of February 1848. He disapproved both of the popular excesses and of the pitiless repression by the conservatives. He scoffed at the naïveté of Lamartine and at the sophisms of Pierre Joseph Proudhon, but was no less disgusted by the vindictive republican Adolphe Thiers and by the opportunists who hailed Bonaparte. In 1849 he left Paris on a journey to Egypt and the Orient in the company of his friend Maxime du Camp (who shared many a trait with Deslauriers). He came back in time to witness the coup of December 2, 1851. Less than two years later he observed in September 1853: " '89 demolished the royalty and the nobility, '48 the bourgeoisie and '51 the people. There is *nothing* left, but a crooked and stupid rabble.—We have all sunk into the same level of common mediocrity" (*Correspondance*, vol. 2, p. 437). Yet he too came round to the new regime, and stayed on good terms with the Tuileries court, especially Princess Mathilde, the Emperor's cousin, until the end of the reign.

Upon his return from Egypt, Flaubert set to work on *Madame Bovary*, which was issued in book form in 1857. In 1862, after a trip to Algeria and Tunisia to visit the ruins of Carthage, he published *Salammbô*, a historical novel that takes place in the third century B.C. The writing of the second *Sentimental Education* lasted from 1864 to 1869, almost until the collapse of the Empire and the upheaval of the Commune, during which Flaubert served in the National Guard. Following the appearance of *Sentimental Education*, Flaubert went back to a manuscript that he had first completed in 1849 but was never satisfied with, *La Tentation de Saint Antoine* (1874; *The Temptation of Saint Anthony*). In 1875 he faced financial ruin while supporting his niece, whom he had raised, and her husband. He published *Trois Contes* (*Three Stories*) in 1877. And he had almost wrapped up *Bouvard et Pécuchet* when he died of a cerebral hemorrhage in 1880. Critics have often noted in Flaubert's fiction an alternation of narratives set in the realistic here and now and narratives set in a distant space or time: After *Madame Bovary* came the historical novel *Salammbô*; after *Salammbô, Sentimental Education*; then *Saint Anthony* moves into the fantastic mode. Among the tales in *Three Stories*, "Un Coeur simple" ("A Simple Heart") takes place in contemporary Normandy, while "La Légende de Saint Julien l'Hospitalier" ("The Legend of Saint Julian the Hospitaler") and "Hérodias" cultivate the exotic and anachronistic. Finally, the characters Bouvard and Pécuchet bustle around in dangerously close proximity to their public.

This alternation is one symptom of Flaubert's perpetual uncertainty in regard to his work. As for *Sentimental Education*, he was not sure about the title—a title Marcel Proust would admire later for its "solidity" while noting in it a grammatical indeterminacy. About his book, Flaubert explained:

> I want to write the moral history of the men of my generation—or, more accurately, the history of their *feelings*. It's a book about love,

> about passion; but passion such as can exist nowadays—that is to say, inactive . . . Facts, drama, are a bit lacking; and then the action is spread over a too extended period (October 1864; *The Letters of Gustave Flaubert*, translated by Steegmuller, p. 80).

In October 1867 he confessed to George Sand: "I am afraid the conception is faulty, which is irremediable. Will such flabby characters interest anybody?" (*Correspondance*, vol. 3, p. 697). And in July 1868: "The patriots won't forgive me this book, nor the reactionaries either! So much the worse: I write things as I feel them—that is, as I believe they exist" (*The Letters of Gustave Flaubert*, translated by Steegmuller, p.116).

Indeed, *Sentimental Education* was unfavorably received by the press. The book was deemed unreadable because of the thinness of plot and the lack of defined personalities of its characters: Was this still a novel? One of the most virulent journalists, the Catholic and Decadent Jules Barbey d'Aurevilly, attacked it as a perfect example of Realism, deprived of heroes and panache; others criticized the impassiveness of the narrator in the face of the immorality of his subject. The book was simply a faithful depiction of the times, retorted Taine and Sand. A few years later, the Naturalists, Zola foremost among them, extolled *Sentimental Education* as Flaubert's masterpiece, precisely for its avoidance of romance and for the impartiality of the author. After Flaubert's death, Proust and Franz Kafka were equally enthusiastic, but on very different grounds: They liked Flaubert's style. While Henry James and Jean-Paul Sartre rather preferred *Madame Bovary*, the Nouveaux Romanciers (New Novelists) of the 1960s, led by Alain Robbe-Grillet and Nathalie Sarraute, saw in this book a forerunner of their own deconstruction of traditional novelistic character, time, structure, and rhetoric.

Here is how Karl Marx characterized the atmosphere in France around 1848: "passions without truth, truths without passion; heroes without heroic deeds, history without events; development, whose sole driving force seems to be the calendar, wearying with constant repetition of the same tensions and relaxations" (*The Eighteenth Brumaire of Louis Bonaparte*, p. 43). On the triple plane of "passions," "heroes," and "history," Marx says the "development" gets bogged down in the reiteration of the same phenomena and gives the impression of going round in circles, implying an enormous loss of energy, an entropy. Flaubert would agree. Circularity and entropy affect the three elements that, following Marx's suggestion, I will successively examine in Flaubert's novel: the hero's evolution, his passions, and France's turmoil. For *Sentimental Education* is at once an educational novel, a sentimental novel, and a political novel.

The *Story of a Young Man*, as the book is subtitled, is an educational novel, or more specifically a bildungsroman, a subgenre that depicts a generally masculine hero on the threshold of adulthood, whose development results in the acquisition not only of knowledge and skills, but of a certain wisdom. This genre had been popular since the eighteenth century, with the rise of a bourgeoisie that aspired to grow through personal improvement (the nobility only "took the pain of being born," and the lower classes had no hope to get on in life). Noteworthy examples of the genre include Johann Wolfgang von Goethe's *Wilhelm Meisters Lehrjahre* (1795–1796; *Wilhelm Meister's Apprenticeship*); Stendhal's *Le rouge et le noir* (1830; *The Red and the Black*); Balzac's *Le Père Goriot* (1834; *Father Goriot*), in which Rastignac starts his social climbing through the influence of women; and Charles Dickens's *Great Expectations* (1860–1861). "Education" presupposes something to learn, several masters or models, a malleable and fecund recepient, a regularity of practice, and unimpeded continuity of time: All these factors are problematic in *Sentimental Education*. Consequently, at the book's end, no success has been achieved nor experience gained—and yet, contrary to what happens in Balzac's bildungsroman *Les Illusions perdues* (1837; *Lost Illusions*), Flaubert's characters, illusions lost, nevertheless endure.

The novel comprises three parts, the first two divided into six chapters each, and the third one into seven. The first part, which starts *in medias res*, covers the span of time from September 1840 to December 1845. It opens with Frédéric Moreau's return to his hometown of Nogent-sur-Seine and ends with his move to Paris—a necessary step for all provincials who intended to "make it" in France. In Paris, Frédéric hopes to study law, become a writer or an artist, and conquer his sweetheart Madame Arnoux. The second part takes us from December 1845 to the beginning of February 1848; in addition to his debut in life and his sexual initiation, Frédéric also has a political experience, in the ferment preceding the riots. The third part runs from February 1848 to December 2, 1851, the date of Bonaparte's coup: This event puts an end to the protagonist's political ambitions. The last two chapters form an epilogue; in the first, dated 1867, we witness the unhappy end of Frédéric's love story with Madame Arnoux; in the second, dated 1869 (the year of the narration), we measure the impasse of his existential trajectory.

As Flaubert was well aware, the unfolding of narrative time provides no plot advancement, no character development, no building of effect. Frédéric's career, which suffers from "not having kept to a ready course" (p. 477), is like a journey that goes nowhere. In the introductory chapter, the young man embarks on a boat trip back home to his mother and his high-school friend Deslauriers, in a regressive move up the Seine from Paris to Nogent; in the second-to-last chapter, he wanders, over the course of a few lines, through exotic places before coming back, a little more blasé, to his point of departure. In between these two expeditions, he roams endlessly in the capital, to the rhythm of his mediocre law studies, diminishing fortune, and abandoned ideas and aborted projects. Circularity and entropy frame his whole biography. At the beginning, he "found that the happiness that he deserved by virtue of his sensitive soul was slow in coming" (p. 6); at the end, "he endured the idleness of his intelligence and the inertia of his heart" (p. 469). In the concluding words of the book, Frédéric and Deslauriers evoke, in 1869, the memory of a visit they took as boys to a Nogent bordello in 1837, three years before the start of the story, which at the time proved a fiasco and a scandal: "That was the best we ever got!" (p. 479). Ultimately, the "best" amounts to a miserable episode the account of which appears only as an afterthought in the novel.

The problem is not just that time has passed, but that the two comrades are older and disenchanted: Time has constantly slipped out of their grasp. Their conversation in the epilogue offers a sobering echo of their optimistic exchanges at the outset of their existences and of the book.

> Deslauriers longed for riches, as a means for gaining power over men. He was anxious to possess an influence over a vast number of people, to create a great stir, to have three secretaries under his command, and to give a big political dinner once a week. Frédéric would have furnished for himself a palace in the Moorish fashion, to spend his life reclining on cashmere divans, to the murmur of a fountain, attended by negro pages (p. 62).

The dynamism of the former and the musing of the latter will prove equally useless. Deslauriers, the social climber with leftist leanings, petit-bourgeois manners, naïve arrogance, and little money, will not live up to the "laurels" (*lauriers*) promised by his name; he will not rise "by a series of actions deducing themselves from one another" (p. 90), as occurs in the hyperactive universe of *The Human Comedy*; he will never launch one of those newspapers that, as Balzac in *Lost Illusions* and later Maupassant in *Bel-Ami* (1885) have shown, constitute a new and unstoppable force in bourgeois society. Frédéric, for his part, hesitates between professions, artistic pursuits, and opinions. He studies without motivation and makes a living through an inherited income. When he considers presenting himself as a candidate for the legislative elections, it is too late. When, like Goethe's Werther, Chateaubriand's René, and even Madame Bovary, he attempts suicide, the bridge parapet proves too wide. His dream—already somewhat out of fashion in the 1840s—was to become the French Walter Scott. But the narrative relating "How Messire Brokars de Fenestranges and the Bishop of Troyes attacked Messire Eustache d'Ambrecicourt" (p. 477) is forever torn between the past (the Middles Ages inspired by the fourteenth-century chronicler Jean Froissart) and the future (the perpetual postponement of the task of writing). Unlike Lucien de Rubempré in *Lost Illusions*, Frédéric does not produce a historical novel. And the romance he envisions—a series of wonderful adventures set in Venice, which would transpose his great love—discourages him by its triteness.

In their youth, Charles Deslauriers, a little older than his friend and a bit imperious by nature, poses as Frédéric's master. He ends up being more like his double, a double oscillating between sensual intimacy, economic parasitism, and erotic rivalry. Frédéric imagines that "a man of this sort was worth all the women in the world" (p. 50). Deslauriers is sensitive to his comrade's "quasi-feminine charm," and they plan to share their existence. But their social status stands in the way: Deslauriers lives off his roommate, while the latter prefers to pay Arnoux's debts rather than help found a newspaper. Competition prevails in relation to women: Deslauriers becomes an adviser to Madame Dambreuse, tries to seduce Madame Arnoux, tastes Rosanette's charms, and finally supplants Frédéric in marrying Louise Roque in Nogent. Yet friendship—an important element in Flaubert's own life—survives the two characters' rifts and their long separation. When they are reunited in the last pages, Frédéric has squandered most of his fortune and lives as a petit-bourgeois; whatever wisdom this "man prone to every foible" (p. 336) has gleaned is negative: to not trust people, to not believe in ideas, to stay away from politics. Deslauriers has followed a more scattered and declining trajectory: He has renounced his former convictions and fallen from a prefect to a secretary of a pasha to a publicist and petty employee. Betrayed by Louise, he remains alone, like Frédéric. But then, all the characters who achieve success are despicable, most of all Baptiste Martinon, a fellow student of peasant origin and pliable character, who weds the banker Dambreuse's illegitimate daughter and is promoted to senator under the Empire. Humbled, isolated, and yet lucid, the two aging friends are not that far from the satirical pair of Bouvard and Pécuchet.

In his sentimental novel, Frédéric fluctuates among four women: a Romantic idol, a well-endowed heiress, an upper-class socialite, and a prostitute. He courts one for lack of the other, is loved by one while thinking of another—and lets them all escape. Significantly, Madame Arnoux, the idol, occupies the beginning and the end of the text. The second in order of appearance, and the last but one to disappear, is heiress Louise Roque, the provincial neighbor who at first seems unacceptable because of her father's questionable morals, but then is highly desirable because of her father's fortune; the only one candidly to confess her love for Frédéric, Louise nevertheless marries Deslauriers, before running off with yet another man. Further along in the plot appear two courtesans: Rosanette, a professional, and the socialite Madame Dambreuse, who hides behind a sham respectability and proves less difficult to conquer than the prostitute; the frivolous Rosanette takes on Frédéric's sexual education, while the greedy, cold-hearted, and well-connected Madame Dambreuse should insure Frédéric's worldly success. In the end, he sacrifices them both to Madame Arnoux's memory.

Madame Arnoux's first name is Marie, the name of the Virgin Mother. The theme of the young man in love with a maternal figure, often with children of her own, who provides him with both a sentimental and a social education, appeared in the eighteenth century and is not rare in Romantic literature—one thinks of Stendhal's *The Red and the Black*, Balzac's *Le Lys dans la Vallée* (1836; *The Lily in the Valley*), or Charles Sainte-Beuve's *Volupté* (1834; *Sensual Pleasure*). In all these novels, the older woman is in competition with one or several younger females, and her child's disease holds her back from adulterous, and symbolically incestuous, temptation. In our text as in those, Marie is the object of the deepest, and the most forbidden, desire. When Frédéric meets her on the boat on his way back to Madame Moreau's, she sits like a Madonna with child; in the epilogue, she kisses him "on the forehead, like a mother" (p. 474). No one may emulate her in that role: Whereas her maternity is sublime—as when she sacrifices her first and only rendezvous with Frédéric to look after her sick child, and the child survives—Rosanette's unwanted maternity, which she uses to retain Frédéric, is slightly grotesque, and her baby dies.

Starting with the initial "apparition" of the Beloved on the boat, the sentimental novel recycles the clichés of courtly and Romantic love. This love, however, entails neither chivalric prowess nor grandiose despair, not even suicide, as in the case of Madame Bovary. Madame Arnoux resembles "the women of whom he had read in romances" (p. 13)—but bears the prosaic patronymic of Arnoux, a name that sounds like that of the famous demimondaine Sophie Arnould. She looks wonderfully Andalusian, but she is from Chartres, not far from Paris. She represents an ethereal figure, but she is soiled by money problems and conjugal squabbles. She becomes the "center" of Frédéric's existence; the Paris of his perambulations, his daily occupations, the people he frequents—everything revolves around her. For her sake he arranges his attire, his apartments, his activities. For her sake he associates with her husband and his vulgar acquaintances, squandering his financial resources. He projects her image everywhere: "All women brought her to mind, either from the effect of their resemblance to her or by the violent contrast" (p. 78). Frédéric stands in ecstasy before a lighted window—but it is not hers! He elaborates words, gestures, scenarios—which do not come to pass. When, while being posted to the National Guard in 1848 at the same time as Jacques Arnoux, he fathomed that the sleeping Arnoux could be disposed of by an accidental bullet, "images passed through his mind in endless succession. He saw himself with her at night in a coach, then on a river's bank on a summer's evening, and under the reflection of a lamp at home in their own house. . . . Frédéric brooded over this idea like a playwright in the creative act" (p. 354). But whereas Madame Bovary was poisoned by books before poisoning herself with arsenic, Madame Arnoux "did not display much enthusiasm about literature" (p. 163). What she represents is, in fact, a vacuous center, around which the mesmerized suitor turns in vain. The final formula of the sentimental novel is "we will have loved each other so much" (p. 471)—a phrase in the future perfect tense in which the present of love has evaporated in the conjunction of posteriority and anteriority, expectation, and nostalgia. Here too, circularity and entropy dominate.

In the second to last chapter, which can be considered a first epilogue, after years of paralyzed adoration at the foot of Madame Arnoux's "immovable skirt," and more years of episodic and always unsatisfying affairs with stand-ins, Frédéric is surprised finally to see his beloved come to his house. This visit is an echo of a previous one, which also had a pecuniary motive. On her first visit, Madame Arnoux solicits his help; this time, she pays back a loan. Then it was day, now night falls. Marie's intentions are not quite clear: Is she offering herself? She has discovered literature: " 'When I read love passages in books, it is as if you were here before me' " (p. 471). However, whereas Frédéric gave her a rose during the first visit, she now cuts a lock of hair for him as a token of love, but it is white. In part repulsed by a quasi-incestuous contract, in part attempting to preserve his ideal, and in part because of prudence—"what an inconvenience it would be!" (p. 473)—Frédéric lets Marie go. She who "appeared" at the beginning finally "disappears" in a cab: "And that was all" (p. 474).

Madame Arnoux is constantly perceived through her admirer's eyes, which gives her an enigmatic character and a mysterious aura. Frédéric often refers to her as to "the Other": How could such a magnified third person be incarnated as a "you"? Always unattainable, she propels an infinite desire, stimulated less by her presence than by imagination and memory. No mistress can rival her; Frédéric cries during his first night with Rosanette, and his engagement to Madame Dambreuse satisfies primarily his vanity. Yet is this "Other" so incommensurate with all "others"? Are not all "others" somehow the same; are not all women somehow interchangeable?

> If Madame Arnoux happened merely to touch him with her finger, the image of the other [Rosanette] immediately presented itself as an object of desire, because in her case his chances were better, and, when his heart happened to be touched while in Rosanette's company, he remembered his great love (pp. 163–164).

This confusion is prompted by the similarity of the two women's furniture and knickknacks, provided by Madame Arnoux's husband, who is also Rosanette's lover. Later, the reminiscence of his "old love" helps Frédéric court Madame Dambreuse. And he sarcastically cultivates the confusion between Madame Dambreuse and Rosanette: "He would repeat to one the oath which he had just uttered to the other, send them both identical bouquets, write to them at the same time . . . and the more he deceived one of the two, no matter which, the fonder of him she grew" (p. 434). The four women are gathered only once, at a Dambreuse reception not all that different in its formality from the Arnoux dinners and even the orgies at Rosanette's, since many male guests are the same; the courtesan is represented only by her portrait—but Frédéric spends the night with her, while dreaming of the Other.

To reassert the difference and superiority of that Other, Frédéric finally rejects all her rivals. At the auction following Arnoux's bankruptcy and Madame Arnoux's departure from Paris, Rosanette and Madame Dambreuse compete for the spoils of the vanished idol: a Renaissance casket metaphorically linked to her person. It evokes her beauty, her thrift, her chastity (for the casket is closed, like her body), and perhaps the emptiness of her phantasmagoric figure. Frédéric forgets that he saw it in Rosanette's apartment and that it contained Arnoux's extravagant bills. Buying it is tantamount to profaning his Beloved. When Madame Dambreuse places the highest bid, Frédéric breaks up with her: This one magnanimous gesture and decisive action in his sentimental life leaves him annihilated.

The Story of a Young Man is also, according to Flaubert, "the moral history of the men of my generation." Hence his deliberately selective and sketchy (albeit extremely precise) recording of the events of the 1848 period. Flaubert was in Paris in February with his friend Maxime du Camp, who took notes, and he apprehended the riots "from the point of view of art." Later, pushing the realist taste for exact documentation to its limit, he spent long hours in libraries; consulted and annotated entire volumes and collections of newspapers about the revolution; read the socialist thinkers; informed himself about engraving, crockery, horse racing, restaurant menus, and the Lyons working class; picked his friends' memories; contacted the revolutionary Armand Barbès; took trips to Nogent and other relevant towns around Paris; and went to Fontainebleau and rectified his notions on transportation between Fontainebleau and Paris in June 1848.

He was well aware of the difficulties of the historical novel, as expressed by Alessandro Manzoni in his essay *On the Historical Novel* (*Del romanzo storico*), published in 1850. Manzoni contends that such a text either blurs the distinction between the factual and the fictional, and the reader, who wants to learn something certain about the past, is disappointed; or it expressly distinguishes the factual from the fictional, and the reader, who demands unity from a work of art, is again disappointed. Thus neither the realist nor the aesthete is satisfied. The fact is, Manzoni concludes, the separation of truth and invention, or veracity and verisimilitude, is impossible in the historical novel, but neither does this subgenre have any unified form; consequently, it can never be fully satisfactory.

"Historical" means true, or at least veracious, but it also means worthy to be recorded, memorable. "And then, what to choose among the real Facts?" Flaubert asked in a letter of March 1868 (*Correspondance*, vol. 3, p. 734). This was a crucial question, all the more so because he was dealing with a period still present in the minds of his contemporaries, a period rich in events that threatened to obfuscate the imaginary plot. "I have a very hard time embedding my characters in the political events of '48!" he deplored in the same passage. "I am afraid the background will absorb the foreground. Here is the defect of the historical genre. The historical characters are more interesting than the fictional ones. . . . The public will take less interest in Frédéric than in Lamartine?" This is why Flaubert was very careful not to let Lamartine and his famous, or infamous, partisans and adversaries take to the stage, and focused instead on made-up, albeit highly representative, actors.

Finally, though "historical" normally implies "public," the novel concentrates on individual matters. Since the "novel" of "historical novel" is the substantive and "historical" only the attribute, the latter has to remain subordinate to the former. A way to negotiate this tense relationship is to hint at a secret correspondence between the general turmoil and the private tribulations. In *Sentimental Education*, there is an interconnectedness, sometimes an analogy, or, more often, an ironic link between the major scenes of collective life and those of the personal, especially amorous, life. In an unpublished note, Flaubert expressed his wish to "show that Sentimentalism (its development since 1830) follows Politics and reproduces its phases." When Frédéric, having hired a hotel room for his first rendezvous, waits for Madame Arnoux, who does not show up, the February insurrection and its ambiguous promises start rumbling. When he falls back on Rosanette, he proclaims: " 'I am following the fashion! I'm reforming myself!' " (p. 316), "reform" being the slogan of the day. When he takes Rosanette to his hotel room, he notes: " 'Ah! They're killing off some bourgeois' " on the Boulevard des Capucines (p. 317). Frédéric and Rosanette try to escape to Fontainebleau during the June repression. And the auction sale of the Arnoux property, at which Frédéric drops Madame Dambreuse, takes place on the eve of Bonaparte's coup.

At Fontainebleau, Frédéric and Rosanette try to flee from their contemporary history into their sentimental novel. In the forest of Fontainebleau, the linear time of the calendar, punctuated by dates, is superseded by the cyclical and hazy time of the idyllic mode. The idyll resists history thanks to the combined forces of eternal Nature and intimate Love. The fresh and sensuous Rosanette can be assimilated to Nature—to these woods, in fact, as contaminated as she is by civilization. As for Love, Rosanette is an expert. But as such—as a whore, as a "public" woman—she is deprived of any intimacy, bereft of her life, her bed, her body, and her soul. And when she, the daughter of silk workers in Lyons, divulges her own sentimental education—"to what lover did she owe her education?" (p. 369)—she evokes public evils: poverty, exploitation, child prostitution, and implicitly, popular revolt (that of the silk-workers of Lyons in 1831). As a whole, the story of the couple, full of delays and cheating, presents many similarities with history. In the end, Frédéric decides to leave Rosanette behind and, alleging a civic sense that does not encroach on his private interests, goes back to the embattled capital.

Fontainebleau, the site of a François I castle, offers the lovers a flight into past history. While monarchy is being abolished in Paris, the Fontainebleau domain maintains the "impassiveness of royalty" (p. 359); while the Tuileries are ransacked, the Renaissance palace remains severely sumptuous. Paris is a prey to urgency, in Fontainebleau an "emanation of the centuries, overwhelming and funereal, like the scent of a mummy" prevails (p. 362). Yet the tourists penetrating the remote apartments and scrutinizing the furniture and the portraits with a lascivious titillation are not without a certain similarity to the mob invading the Tuileries and the princesses' bedrooms, with an obscene and desecrating curiosity.

As a museum, Fontainebleau could complement the pair's educational trajectory, were it not that the two tend to reduce past history to private, sentimental details. The illiterate Rosanette interprets the deeds of the grandees according to her own petty preoccupations; did Christine of Sweden have her favorite assassinated at Fontainebleau? " 'No doubt it was jealousy? Better watch out!' " (p. 359). The well-read Frédéric relates more accurately to those who haunted these rooms, Emperor Charles V, the Valois kings, Henri IV, Jean-Jacques Rousseau, Voltaire. Their trysts arouse him, and the evocation of Diane de Poitiers, mistress of Henri II, fills him with a "mysterious feeling of retrospective lust" (p. 360).

In a way, before abandoning Rosanette for the happenings of his time, he is unfaithful to her by his lust for bygone times. In *Sentimental Education*, history, past and present, is contaminated by the private; conversely, the private is contaminated by history.

Just like Frédéric's destiny and his great passion, the revolution as reconstructed in the book is tossed off according to chance, sudden inspirations, and weaknesses. Like Frédéric's destiny and passion, it appears split between the future (here the socialist utopia) and its past references: " 'A new '89 is in preparation' " (p. 20). Yet 1789 is a detrimental precedent: "Every person at that time modeled himself after someone, one copied Saint-Just, another Danton, another Marat"; another one "tried to be like Blanqui, who imitated Robespierre" (p. 340). The repetition, noted by Marx, does not end there. Consider, for instance, the mystery of the "calf's head," an English import:

> In order to parody the ceremony which the Royalists celebrated on the thirtieth of January [anniversary of Charles I's execution], some Independents threw an annual banquet, at which they ate calves' heads . . . while toasting the extermination of the Stuarts. After Thermidor, some Terrorists organized a brotherhood of a similar description, which proves how contagious stupidity is (pp. 476–477).

Flaubertian "folly," which amounts to uncontrolled reiteration, does not spare the sequels of revolutions: that of Cromwell, that of the Jacobins, that of 1848, the epigones imitating with reverence what the predecessors imitated as a mockery. And the coup of December 1851 reiterates that of Napoléon Bonaparte in 1799, with a nephew who is but a shadow of his monumental uncle. The course of history also betrays circularity and entropy.

Who is Louis-Napoléon Bonaparte? A Napoléon with a touch of the royal Louis, a prince elected president before usurping power, an adventurer who garners the benefits of autocracy, republic, and military populism. Even though he accepted the new regime, Flaubert shows how this amalgam is in sync with the ideological confusion and the recantations of almost all the characters in *Sentimental Education*: from Dambreuse, an ex-noble turned speculator who always sides with the victor, to Martinon, an opportunist who sleeps with Madame Dambreuse and marries her husband's daughter; from Sénécal, a Jacobin with fascistic tendencies, to Regimbart, a protestor and a drunkard; from the self-righteous Madame Dambreuse to la Vatnaz, a procuress and feminist full of envy; and even Dussardier, the honest republican misled into serving the forces of repression. The exasperation of the revolution reduces them all to "an equality of brute beasts, a same level of bloody turpitude; for the fanaticism of self-interest balanced the frenzy of the poor, aristocracy had the same fits of fury as the mob, and the cotton cap did not prove less hideous than the red cap" (pp. 377–378).

This messy history is largely apprehended from a private perspective, that of Frédéric. As a consequence, even though the narrator never intervenes, history is not described in an impartial way. Of course, Frédéric is neutral, and even too much so; yet his is not the neutrality of the historian who is above any partisanship but rather that of the idler, who gets excited briefly and then leaves. The historian scrutinizes the complexity of the situation, the idler sees surfaces; the historian discerns links and proposes syntheses, the idler catches glimpses; the historian looks for reasons, the idler is stopped by a detail or an image. Frédéric, a quick-to-be-enthused witness, and his comrade Hussonnet, whose nose is more delicate, attend the February events as though they were a spectacle that the one finds sublime and the other nauseating, and in which the People becomes flux, whirlwind, beast—undifferentiated, indefinite, elusive. The interposition of the fictional character, himself a prey to the vertigo of history, has the unexpected consequence of rendering unreal the very experiences he has a chance to live: "The wounded who sank to the ground, the dead lying at his feet, did not seem like persons really wounded or really dead" (p. 323). This is all the more the case because the inexhaustible discourses on the facts obfuscate the facts themselves. Flaubert lets his characters chatter, more or less banally, foolishly, sometimes unintelligibly: At the Club of Intelligence (what a misnomer!), a militant speaks Spanish, and the author does not translate; another one talks chivalric jargon. The collision of half-cooked ideas, deceitful statements, worn-out slogans, broken declamations, and obscure allusions results in the same magma in the political gatherings as in the banquets and orgies, and proves no more efficacious than the stereotypical love rhetoric.

While the characters' existences give a sense of reiteration, circularity, and entropy, Flaubert's mode of composition, in its meandering and occasionally enigmatic complexity, remains highly controlled. If in the epilogue Frédéric and Deslauriers "blamed bad luck" (p. 477), Flaubert calls the shots. If his descriptions are fragmented, he has an overarching aesthetic objective. If his protagonist's perspective, which largely dominates, is not enlightening, he intends it to be so: For only idiots, whose received ideas regularly, although not always visibly, punctuate the text, believe in the certainty of meaning.

Frédéric never completes his artistic education; he becomes neither a writer nor a painter, hardly even an amateur. A similar degradation affects Arnoux's endeavors. He goes from the thriving enterprise of "L'Art industriel" (an oxymoron for Flaubert) to a crockery factory to the commerce of religious knickknacks; this degradation parallels his descent from his wife to the fashionable Rosanette to a nameless working girl. As for the painter Pellerin, he is an uninspired artist, and a pompous theoretician who merely echoes contemporary trends. Neoclassical during the Restoration, he turns eclectic under Louis-Philippe, and his portrait of Rosanette can be dubbed an old Italian piece. In 1848 he represents the Republic in the guise of Jesus Christ conducting a locomotive! Later he shouts, "Down with Realism," and renders Rosanette's dead baby as a grotesque still life, before finishing as a photographer. Like everything else, art is compromised by money, politics, and enormous egos, such as that of the ham comedian Delmar, who changes names and allegiances to hide his lack of substance. All these figures serve as foils to the author's creative ideal. Transcending the stereotypes of the accursed Romantic genius as well as of the Realist laborer or expert, Flaubert would rather remain a secular monk persisting in the cult of style, prey to the pangs of perpetual doubt and self-derision.

Claudie Bernard is a professor of French at New York University. A specialist in nineteenth-century French literature and history of ideas, she is the author of two books, *Le Chouan Romanesque, Balzac,*

Barbey d'Aurevilly, Hugo (1986) and *Le Passé recomposé, le roman historique français au dix-neuvième siècle* (1996), and of many articles. She also edited *Les Chouans* by Balzac, and two volumes of critical essays, *Balzac paterfamilias* (2001) and *George Sand, Families and Communities* (2005).

SENTIMENTAL EDUCATION

The Story of a Young Man

PART ONE

CHAPTER I

On the 15th of September, 1840,[1] about six o'clock in the morning, the *Ville de Montereau*, just about to sail, was sending forth great whirlwinds of smoke, in front of the Quai St. Bernard.[2]

People came rushing on board in breathless haste. Barrels, ropes, and baskets of linen lying around were in everybody's way. The sailors would answer no enquiries. People jostled one another. Between the two paddlewheels was piled up a heap of baggage; and the uproar was drowned out by the loud hissing of the steam, which, escaping through iron plates, enveloped everything in a white cloud, while the bell at the prow rang incessantly.

At last, the vessel set out; and the two banks of the river, lined with warehouses, yards, and factories, opened out like two huge ribbons being unrolled.

A young man of eighteen, with long hair, holding a sketchbook under his arm, stood motionless near the helm. Through the haze he surveyed steeples, buildings of which he did not know the names; then, gave a parting glance, to the Île St. Louis, the Cité, Nôtre Dame; and soon, as Paris disappeared from his view, he heaved a deep sigh.

Frédéric Moreau, having just received his Bachelor's degree, was returning home to Nogent-sur-Seine, where he would have to lead an idle existence for two months, before going back to begin his legal studies. His mother had sent him, with enough to cover his expenses, to Le Havre to see an uncle, in the hopes of his receiving an inheritance.[3] He had returned from that place only yesterday; and to compensate for not having the opportunity of spending a little time in the capital he took the longest possible route to reach his own part of the country.

The hubbub had subsided. The passengers had all taken their places. Some of them stood warming themselves around the machinery, and the chimney spat forth with a slow, rhythmic rattle its plume of black smoke. Little drops of dew trickled over the copper plates; the deck quivered with the vibration from within; and the two paddlewheels, rapidly turning round, lashed the water.

The edges of the river were covered with sand. The vessel swept past rafts of wood which began to oscillate under the rippling of the waves, or a boat without sails in which a man sat fishing. Then the wandering haze cleared off; the sun appeared; the hill which ran along the course of the Seine to the right dropped from view little by little, and another rose up closer on the opposite bank.

The hill was crowned with trees, which surrounded low-built houses, covered with roofs in the Italian style. They had sloping gardens divided by new walls, iron railings, lawns, green-houses, and vases of geraniums, at regular intervals on the terraces with balustrades to lean on. More than one spectator longed, on beholding those attractive residences which looked so peaceful, to be the owner of one of them, and to dwell there till the end of his days with a good billiard-table, a sailboat, and a woman or some other dream. The agreeable novelty of a journey by water made such outpourings natural. Already the practical jokers on board were beginning their gags. Many began to sing. Gaiety prevailed, and glasses were being filled.

Frédéric was thinking about the room which he would live in there, about an idea for a play about subjects for paintings about future love affairs. He found that the happiness that he deserved by virtue of his sensitive soul was slow in coming. He recited some melancholy verses. He walked with rapid steps along the deck. He went on till he reached the end where the bell was; and, in the centre of a group of passengers and sailors, he saw a gentleman whispering sweet nothings to a country-woman, while fingering the gold cross which she wore over her bosom. He was a jovial fellow of forty with frizzy hair. His stocky frame was encased in a jacket of black velvet, two emeralds sparkled in his fine linen shirt, and his wide, white trousers fell over odd-looking red boots of Russian leather set off with blue designs.

Frédéric's presence did not bother him. He turned round and glanced several times at the young man giving him conspiratorial winks. He next offered cigars to all who were standing around him. But getting tired, no doubt, of their company, he moved away from them and took a seat further up. Frédéric followed him.

The conversation, at first, centered around various kinds of tobacco, then quite naturally it glided into a discussion about women. The gentleman in the red boots gave the young man advice; he expounded theories, told anecdotes, quoted himself as an example, all in a paternal tone, with a shameless wickedness that was amusing.

He was a Republican. He had travelled; knew all about the theatre, restaurants, and newspapers, and knew all the theatrical celebrities, whom he called by their Christian names. Frédéric told him confidentially about his projects; and the elder man took an encouraging view of them.

But he stopped talking to take a look at the funnel, then he went mumbling rapidly through a long calculation in order to ascertain "how much each stroke of the piston at so many times per minute would come to," etc., and having come up with the number, he spoke about the scenery, which he admired immensely. Then he proclaimed his delight at having escaped from business.

Frédéric regarded him with a certain amount of respect, and politely expressed his desire to know his name. The stranger, without a moment's hesitation, replied:

"Jacques Arnoux, proprietor of *L'Art Industriel*, Boulevard Montmartre."

A servant with gold-braid on his cap came up and said:

"Would Monsieur please go below? Mademoiselle is crying."

L'Art Industriel was a hybrid establishment, wherein the functions of an art-journal and a paintings dealer were combined. Frédéric had seen this title several times in the bookseller's window in his native part of the country, on big leaflets, on which the name of Jacques Arnoux displayed itself prominently.

The sun's rays fell perpendicularly, shedding a glittering light on the iron bands around the masts, the plates of the rails, and the surface of the water, which, at the prow, was sliced into two furrows that surged out towards the banks of the meadows. At each winding of the river, the same curtain of pale poplars came into view. The surrounding country at this point had an empty look. In the sky there were little white clouds which remained motionless, and the sense of boredom, which vaguely diffused itself over everything, seemed to retard the progress of the steamboat and to add to the insignificant appearance of the passengers.

Putting aside a few people of high society who were travelling first class, they were artisans or shopmen with their wives and children. As it was customary at that time to wear old clothes when travelling, they nearly all had their heads covered with shabby Greek caps or discoloured hats, thin black coats that had become quite threadbare from constant rubbing against writing-desks, or frock-coats with the casings of their buttons loose from continual service in the shop. Here and there some roll-collar waistcoat afforded a glimpse of a calico shirt stained with coffee. Gilt pins were stuck into tattered cravats. List slippers were held up by stitched straps. Two or three rough-types who held in their hands bamboo canes with leather loops, kept looking askance at their fellow-passengers; and family men opened their eyes wide as they asked questions. People chatted either standing up or squatting over their luggage; some went to sleep in various corners of the vessel; several occupied themselves by eating. The deck was soiled with walnut shells, buttends of cigars, peelings of pears, and the droppings of pork-butchers' meat, which had been carried wrapped up in paper. Three cabinet-makers in smocks stood in front of the bar; a harp-player in rags was resting with his elbows on his instrument. Now and then could be heard the sound of falling coals in the furnace, a shout, or a laugh; and the captain kept walking on the bridge from one paddlebox to the other without ever stopping.

Frédéric, to get back to his place, pushed forward the gate leading into the part of the vessel reserved for first-class passengers, and in so doing disturbed two sportsmen with their dogs.

What he then saw was like an apparition:

She was seated in the middle of a bench all alone, or, at any rate, he could see no one else, dazzled as he was by her eyes. At the moment when he was passing, she raised her head; his shoulders bowed involuntarily; and, when he had seated himself, some distance away, on the same side, he glanced towards her.

She wore a wide straw hat with pink ribbons which fluttered in the wind behind her. Her black tresses, curving around the edges of her thick eyebrows, swept down very low, and seemed to lovingly caress the oval of her face. Her robe of pale, spotted muslin spread out in numerous folds. She was in the act of embroidering something; and her straight nose, her chin, her entire person was silhouetted against the background of the luminous air and the blue sky.

As she remained in the same position, he took several turns to the right and to the left to hide from her manoeuvres; then he placed himself close to her parasol which lay against the bench, and pretended to be looking at a sloop on the river.

Never before had he seen more lustrous dark skin, a more seductive figure, or more delicately shaped fingers than those through which the sunlight gleamed. He stared with amazement at her work-basket, as if it were something extraordinary. What was her name, her home, her life, her past? He longed to become familiar with the furniture in her room, all the dresses that she had worn, the people whom she visited; and the desire of physical possession yielded to a deeper yearning, a painful curiosity that knew no bounds.

A negress, wearing a silk kerchief tied round her head, made her appearance, holding by the hand a little girl already tall for her age. The child, whose eyes were swimming with tears, had just awakened. The lady took the little one on her knees. "Mademoiselle was not good, though she will soon be seven; her mother will not love her any more. She has been pardonned too often for being naughty." And Frédéric heard those things with delight, as if he had made a discovery, an acquisition.

He assumed that she must be of Andalusian descent, perhaps a creole: had she brought this negress across with her from the West Indian Islands?

Meanwhile his attention was directed to a long shawl with violet stripes thrown behind her back over the copper support of the bench. She must have, many a time, out at sea wrapped it around her body; drawn it over her feet, gone to sleep in it! Frédéric suddenly noticed that being dragged down by its fringe it was slipping off, and it was on the point of falling into the water when, with a bound, he caught it. She said to him:

"Thank you, Monsieur."

Their eyes met.

"Are you ready, my dear?" cried Arnoux, appearing at the hood of the companion-way.

Mademoiselle Marthe ran over to him, and, clinging to his neck, she began pulling at his moustache. The strains of a harp were heard—she wanted to see the music played; and soon the musician, led forward by the negress, entered the section reserved for saloon passengers. Arnoux recognized him as a man who had formerly been an artists' model, and spoke to him in a familiar tone to the astonishment of the bystanders. Finally the harpist, flinging back his long hair over his shoulders, stretched out his arms and began playing.

It was an Oriental ballad all about daggers, flowers, and stars. The man in rags sang it in a piercing voice; the thumping of the engine broke the rhythm of the song unevenly. He played more vigorously: the chords vibrated, and their metallic sounds seemed to send forth sobs, and, as it were, the plaint of a proud and vanquished love. On both sides of the river, woods extended as far as the edge of the water. A current of fresh air swept past them, and Madame Arnoux gazed vaguely into the distance. When the music stopped, she fluttered her eyelids several times as if she were starting out of a dream.

The harpist approached them humbly. While Arnoux was searching his pockets for money, Frédéric stretched out towards the cap his closed hand, and then, opening it discreetly he deposited in it a louis d'or. It was not vanity that had prompted him to offer such charity in her presence, but the idea of a blessing in which he thought she might share—an almost religious impulse of the heart.

Arnoux, pointing out the way, cordially invited him to go below. Frédéric declared that he had just had lunch; on the contrary, he was nearly dying of hunger; and he had not a single centime in his purse.

After that, it seemed to him that he had a perfect right, as much as anyone else, to remain in the cabin.

Ladies and gentlemen were seated at round tables, lunching, while an attendant went about serving coffee. Monsieur and Madame Arnoux were in the far corner to the right. He took a seat on the long bench covered with velvet, having picked up a newspaper which he found there.

They would have to take the stagecoach at Montereau for Châlons. Their tour in Switzerland would last a month. Madame Arnoux blamed her husband for his weakness in dealing with his child. He whispered in her ear something endearing, no doubt, for she smiled. Then, he got up to close the window curtain at her back.

Under the low, white ceiling, a harsh light filled the cabin. Frédéric, sitting opposite her, could distinguish the shadow of her eyelashes. She sipped from her glass and broke a crust of bread between her fingers. The lapis-lazuli locket fastened by a little gold chain to her wrist made a ringing sound, every now and then, as it touched her plate. Those present, however, did not appear to notice it.

From time to time one could see, through the small port-holes, a boat pulling up to take passengers on or off. Those at the tables stooped to see through the openings, and called out the names of the various places they passed along the river.

Arnoux complained about the cooking. He grumbled particularly at the amount of the bill, and got it reduced. Then, he led the young man towards the front of the boat to drink a glass of grog with him. But Frédéric speedily came back again under the awning where Madame Arnoux had seated herself. She was reading a thin, grey-covered volume. From time to time, the corners of her mouth curled and a gleam of pleasure lit up her face. He felt jealous of the inventor of those things which appeared to interest her so much. The more he contemplated her, the more he felt that there were yawning abysses between them. He was reflecting that he should very soon part from her forever, without having extracted a few words from her, without leaving her even a souvenir!

On the right, a plain stretched out. On the left, a strip of pastureland rose gently to meet a hillock where one could see vineyards, groups of walnut-trees, a mill nestled in the grassy slopes, and, beyond that, little paths zigzagged across the white rocks that seemed to reach up towards the sky. What bliss it would have been to ascend side by side with her, his arm around her waist, while her gown would sweep the yellow leaves, listening to her voice and gazing into her eyes! The steamboat might stop, and all they would have to do was to step out of it; and yet this thing, simple as it might be, was no less difficult than it would have been to move the sun.

A little further on, a château appeared with pointed roof and square turrets. A flower garden spread out in the foreground; and avenues ran, like dark archways, under the tall linden trees. He pictured her passing along by this group of trees. At that moment a young lady and a young man appeared on the steps in front of the house, between the trunks of the orange trees. Then the entire scene vanished.

The little girl kept skipping playfully around the place where he had stationed himself on the deck. Frédéric wished to kiss her. She hid herself behind her nurse. Her mother scolded her for not being nice to the gentleman who had rescued her shawl. Was this an indirect overture?

"Is she going to speak to me?" he asked himself.

Time was flying. How was he to get an invitation to the Arnoux's house? And he could think of nothing better than to draw her attention to the autumnal hues, adding:

"We are close to winter—the season of balls and dinner-parties."

But Arnoux was entirely occupied with his luggage. They had arrived at the point of the river's bank facing Surville. The two bridges drew nearer. They passed a rope-works, then a range of low-built houses, inside which there were pots of tar and wood chips; and children ran along the sand turning cartwheels. Frédéric recognised a man with a sleeved waistcoat, and called out to him:

"Hurry!"

They were at the landing-place. He looked around anxiously for Arnoux amongst the crowd of passengers, and the other came and shook hands with him, saying:

"A pleasant time, dear Monsieur!"

When he was on the quay, Frédéric turned around. She was standing beside the helm. He cast a look towards her into which he tried to put his whole soul. She remained motionless, as if he had done nothing. Then, without paying the slightest attentions to his man-servant's greeting:

"Why didn't you bring the trap down here?"

The man apologized.

"What a fool you are! Give me some money."

And after that he went off to get something to eat at an inn.

A quarter of an hour later, he felt an inclination to turn into the coachyard, as if by chance. Perhaps he would see her again.

"What's the use of it?" said he to himself.

The vehicle carried him off. The two horses did not belong to his mother. She had borrowed one of M. Chambrion, the tax-collector, in order to have it yoked alongside of her own. Isidore, having set forth the day before, had taken a rest at Bray until evening, and had slept at Montereau, so that the animals, with restored vigour, were trotting briskly.

Fields on which the crops had been cut stretched out endlessly and gradually Villeneuve, St. Georges, Ablon, Châtillon, Corbeil, and the other places—his entire journey—came back to him with such vividness that he could now call to mind fresh details, more intimate particulars. . . . Under the lowest flounce of her gown, her foot peeked out encased in a dainty brown silk boot. The awning made of ticking formed a wide canopy over her head, and the little red tassels of the edging perpetually trembled in the breeze.

She resembled the women of whom he had read in romances. He would have wanted to add nothing to the charms of her appearance, nor take anything away. His universe had suddenly expanded. She was the luminous point towards which all things converged; and, rocked by the movement of the vehicle, with half-closed eyelids, and his face turned towards the clouds, he abandoned himself to a dreamy, infinite joy.

At Bray, he did not wait till the horses had gotten their oats; he walked on along the road by himself. Arnoux had, when he spoke to her, addressed her as "Marie." He now loudly repeated the name "Marie!" His voice pierced the air and was lost in the distance.

The western sky was one great mass of flaming purple. Huge stacks of wheat, rising up in the midst of the stubble fields, projected giant shadows. A dog began to bark on a farm in the distance. He shivered, with a sense of uneasiness for which he could find no cause.

When Isidore returned, he jumped up into the front seat to drive. His moment of weakness had passed. He had firmly made up his mind to gain an introduction into the Arnoux's home, however he could, and to befriend them. Their house should be amusing; besides, he liked Arnoux; then, who could tell? At that moment a wave of blood rushed up to his face; his temples throbbed; he cracked his whip, shook the reins, and set the horses going at such a pace that the old coachman repeatedly exclaimed:

"Easy! easy now, or they'll get winded!"

Gradually Frédéric calmed down, and he listened to what the man was saying. Monsieur's return was impatiently awaited. Mademoiselle Louise had cried in her insistence to go in the trap to meet him.

"Who, pray, is Mademoiselle Louise?"

"Monsieur Roque's little girl, you know."

"Ah! I had forgotten," replied Frédéric, casually.

Meanwhile, the two horses could keep up the pace no longer. They were both limping; and nine o'clock struck on the bell of St. Laurent when he arrived on the Place d'Armes in front of his mother's house. This house, large and spacious, with a garden looking out on the open countryside, added to the social importance of Madame Moreau, who was the most respected lady in the district.

She came from an old noble family, of which the male line was now extinguished. Her husband, of plebeian origin whom her parents forced her to marry, was killed by the thrust of a sword, during her pregnancy, leaving her an estate much in debt. She received visitors three times a week, and from time to time, gave fashionable dinners. But the number of wax candles was calculated beforehand, and she looked forward with some impatience to the payment of her rents. Such embarrassments, concealed as if there were some guilt attached to them, imparted a certain seriousness to her character. Nevertheless, without prudery, or sourness, she practiced her virtue. Her most trifling acts of charity seemed like generous alms-giving. She was consulted about the selection of servants, the education of young girls, and the art of making preserves, and Monseigneur used to stay at her house on the occasion of his episcopal visitations.

Madame Moreau cherished lofty ambitions for her son. Through a sort of anticipatory prudence, she did not care to hear the Government criticized. He would need patronage at the start; then, with its aid, he might become a councillor of State, an ambassador, a minister. His triumphs at the college of Sens warranted this proud anticipation; he had carried off there the prize of honour.

When he entered the drawing-room, all present rose noisily to their feet; he was embraced; and the chairs, large and small, were drawn up in a big semi-circle around the fireplace. M. Gamblin immediately asked him his opinion about Madame Lafarge.[4] This case, the sensation of the day, did not fail to lead to a heated discussion. Madame Moreau stopped it, much to the regret, however, of M. Gamblin. He deemed it useful to the young man as a future lawyer, and, annoyed at what had occurred, he left the drawing-room.

Coming from a friend of Père Roque, nothing would have surprised them. The reference to Père Roque led them to talk of M. Dambreuse, who had just become the owner of the La Fortelle estate. But the tax-collector had drawn Frédéric aside to know what he thought of M. Guizot's latest work.* They were all anxious to get some information about his private affairs, and Madame Benoît cleverly inquired about his uncle with that objective in mind. How was that worthy relative? They no longer heard from him. Had he not a distant cousin in America?

The cook announced that Monsieur's soup was served. The guests discreetly withdrew. Then, as soon as they were alone in the dining-room, his mother said to him in a low tone:

"Well?"

The old man had received him in a very cordial manner, but without disclosing his intentions.

Madame Moreau sighed.

"Where is she now?" he mused dreamily.

The carriage was rolling along the road, and, wrapped up in the shawl, no doubt, she was leaning against the cloth upholstery, her beautiful head nodding off to sleep.

Frédéric and his mother were just going up to their rooms when a waiter from the Swan of the Cross brought him a note.

"What is that, pray?"

"It is Deslauriers, who needs me," said he.

"Ah! your old chum!" said Madame Moreau, with a disapproving laugh. "He picks his time well, I must say!"

Frédéric hesitated. But friendship was stronger. He got his hat.

"At least don't be long!" said his mother to him.

---

*François Guizot (1787–1874), a historian and influential conservative minister under Louis-Philippe, had just published a life of Washington.

CHAPTER II

Charles Deslauriers' father, a former infantry officer, who had left the service in 1818, had come back to Nogent, where he had married, and with the amount of the dowry bought up the business of a process-server, which brought him barely enough to live on. Embittered by a long course of unjust treatment, suffering still from the effects of old wounds, and, still harking back to the days of the Emperor, he took out on those around him the rage that seemed to choke him. Few children received so many beatings as his son. In spite of blows, however, the boy did not yield. His mother, when she tried to intervene, was also abused. Finally, the captain planted the boy in his office, and all day long kept him bent over his desk copying documents, with the result that his right shoulder was noticeably higher than his left.

In 1833, on the invitation of the president, the captain sold his post. His wife died of cancer. He then went to live in Dijon. After that he established himself as an army recruiter at Troyes;[5] and, having obtained a small scholarship for Charles, placed him at the college of Sens, where he crossed paths with Frédéric. But one was twelve years old, while the other was fifteen; besides which a thousand differences in character and background separated them.

Frédéric had in his chest of drawers all sorts of useful things—luxurious objects, such as a dressing-case. He liked to lounge in bed all morning, looking at the swallows, and reading plays; and, missing the comforts of home, he thought college life rough.

To the process-server's son it seemed a pleasant life. He worked so hard that, at the end of the second year, he had gotten into the third form. However, due to his poverty or to his quarrelsome disposition, he was disliked intensely. But when on one occasion, in the middle-school yard, a servant openly called him a beggar's child, he sprang at the fellow's throat, and would have killed him if three of the school monitors had not intervened. Frédéric, filled with admiration, threw his arms around him and hugged him. From that day forward they became fast friends. The affection of an older boy no doubt flattered the vanity of the younger one, and the other accepted the good fortune of this devotion freely offered to him.

During the holidays Charles's father allowed him to remain in the college. A translation of Plato which he opened by chance filled him with enthusiasm. Then he became smitten with metaphysical studies; and he made rapid progress, for he approached the subject with all the energy of youth and the self-confidence of a now independent intellect. Jouffroy, Cousin, Laromiguière, Malebranche, and the Scotch metaphysicians[6]—everything that could be found in the library dealing with this branch of knowledge passed through his hands. He found it necessary to steal the key in order to get the books.

Frédéric's intellectual interests were of a less serious nature. He made sketches of the genealogy of Christ carved on a post in the Rue des Trois Rois, then of the gateway of a cathedral. After a mediæval drama course, he took up memoirs—Froissart, Comines, Pierre de l'Estoile, and Brantôme.*

The impressions made on his mind by this kind of reading took such a hold of it that he felt a need within him of reproducing those pictures of bygone days. His ambition was to be, one day, the Walter Scott of France.[7] Deslauriers dreamed of formulating a vast system of philosophy, which might have the most far-reaching applications.

They chatted over all these matters during recess, in the playground, in front of the moral inscription painted under the clock. They kept whispering to each other about them in the chapel, even with St. Louis staring down at them. They dreamed about them in the dormitory, which looked out on a cemetery. On school walks they lagged behind the others, and talked non-stop.

They spoke of what they would do later, when they had finished college. First of all, they would set out on a long voyage with the

---

*Jean Froissart, Philippe de Comines, Pierre de l'Estoile, and Pierre de Brantôme were authors of historical chronicles in the fourteenth through the sixteenth centuries.

money which Frédéric would take out of his own fortune upon reaching adulthood. Then they would come back to Paris; they would work together, and would never part; and, as a relaxation from their labours, they would have love-affairs with princesses in boudoirs lined with satin, or dazzling orgies with famous courtesans. Their rapturous expectations were followed by doubts. After a spell of verbose gaiety, they would often lapse into profound silence.

On summer evenings, when they had been walking for a long time over stony paths which bordered on vineyards, or on the highroad in the open country, and when they saw the wheat waving in the sunlight, while the air was filled with the fragrance of angelica, a sort of suffocating sensation took possession of them, and they stretched themselves on their backs, dizzy, intoxicated. Meanwhile the other lads, in their shirt-sleeves, were playing tag or flying kites. Then, as the school monitor called in the two companions from the playground, they would return, taking the path which led along by the gardens watered by brooks; then they would pass through the boulevards overshadowed by the old city walls. The deserted streets echoed under their steps. The gate flew back; they climbed the stairs; and they felt as sad as if they had indulged in wild debauchery.

The proctor claimed that they egged on each other. Nevertheless, if Frédéric worked his way up to the higher forms, it was through the encouragement of his friend; and, during their vacation in 1837, he brought Deslauriers home to his mother's house.

Madame Moreau disliked the young man. He had an enormous appetite. He refused to go to church on Sunday. He was fond of making republican speeches. Finally, she got it into her head that he had been leading her son into unsavory places. She kept an eye on their relationship. This only made their friendship grow stronger, and they said good-bye to each other with great sadness when, in the following year, Deslauriers left college in order to study law in Paris.

Frédéric anxiously looked forward to the time when they would meet again. For two years they had not seen each other; and, when their embraces were over, they walked over the bridges to talk more at ease.

The captain, who now ran a billiard-room at Villenauxe, reddened with anger when his son called to ask for an account of his trusteeship of his mother's fortune, and even cut the allowance for his living expenses. Since he intended to become a candidate at a later period for a professor's chair at the school, and as he had no money, Deslauriers accepted the post of principal clerk in an attorney's office at Troyes. Through sheer self-deprivation he hoped to save four thousand francs; and, even if he could not draw upon the sum which came to him through his mother, he would have enough to enable him to work freely for three years while he was waiting for a better position. It was necessary, therefore, to abandon their former plans to live together in the capital, at least for the moment.

Frédéric hung his head. This was the first of his dreams which had crumbled into dust.

"Cheer up," said the captain's son. "Life is long. We are young. We'll meet again. Think no more about it!"

He shook his hand warmly, and, to distract him, asked questions about his journey.

Frédéric had nothing to say. But, at the thought of Madame Arnoux, his sadness disappeared. He did not mention her, restrained by a feeling of bashfulness. He made up for it by talking about Arnoux, recalling his stories, his manners, his connections; and Deslauriers urged him strongly to cultivate this new acquaintance.

Frédéric had of late written nothing. His literary opinions were changed. Passion was now above everything else in his estimation. He was equally enthusiastic about Werther, René, Franck, Lara, Lélia,* and other more mediocre works. Sometimes it seemed to him that music alone was capable of giving expression to his troubles. So, he dreamed of symphonies; or else the appearance of things seized hold of him, and he longed to paint. He had, however, composed verses. Deslauriers considered them beautiful, but did not ask for more.

As for himself, he had given up metaphysics. Social economy and the French Revolution absorbed all his attention. He was now a tall

---

*Famous Romantic heroes of, respectively, Johann Wolfgang von Goethe (1749–1832), François de Chateaubriand (1768–1848), Alfred de Musset (1810–1857), Lord Byron (1788–1824), and George Sand (1804–1876).

fellow of twenty-two, thin, with a wide mouth, and a resolute look. On this particular evening, he wore a shabby wool cardigan; and his shoes were white with dust, for he had come all the way from Villenauxe on foot for the express purpose of seeing Frédéric.

Isidore arrived while they were talking. Madame begged Monsieur to return home, and, for fear of his catching cold, she had sent him his cloak.

"Wait a bit!" said Deslauriers.

And they continued walking from one end to the other of the two bridges which rest on the narrow island formed by the canal and the river.

When they were walking on the side towards Nogent, they had, directly in front of them, a block of houses which leaned a little. At the right the church could be seen behind the wooden watermills, whose sluices had been closed up; and, at the left, the hedges, all along the river bank, formed a boundary for the gardens, which were barely visible. But on the side towards Paris the high road formed a sheer descending line, and the meadows lost themselves in the distance under the mists of the night. Silence reigned along this road, whose stark whiteness clearly showed itself through the surrounding gloom. The odour of damp leaves rose up towards them. The waterfall, where the stream had been diverted from its course a hundred feet away, murmured with that deep soft sound which waves make in the night.

Deslauriers stopped, and said:

" 'Tis funny that these good people are sleeping so peacefully! Patience! A new '89 is in preparation. People are tired of constitutions, charters, evasions, lies! Ah, if I had a newspaper, or a platform, how I would shake up all these things! But, in order to undertake anything whatsoever, one needs money. What a curse it is to be a tavern-keeper's son, and to waste one's youth on a quest for bread!"

He hung down his head, bit his lips, and shivered under his threadbare overcoat.

Frédéric flung half his cloak over his friend's shoulder. They both wrapped themselves up in it; and, with their arms around each other, they walked down the road side by side.

"How do you think I can live over there without you?" said Frédéric. The bitter tone of his friend had brought back his own sadness. "I might have done something if I had a woman who loved me. What are you laughing at? Love is the feeding-ground, and, as it were, the air of genius. Extraordinary emotions produce sublime works. As for seeking the woman of my dreams, I give that up! Besides, if I should ever find her, she will reject me. I belong to the race of the disinherited, and I shall die without knowing whether the treasure within me is of rhinestone or of diamond."

Somebody's shadow fell across the road, and at the same time they heard these words:

"Excuse me, gentlemen!"

The person who had uttered them was a little man attired in an ample brown frock-coat, and with a cap under whose peak could be seen a sharp nose.

"Monsieur Roque?" said Frédéric.

"The very man!" returned the voice.

This local gentleman explained his presence by stating that he had come back to inspect the wolf-traps in his garden near the water's edge.

"And so you are back again in our part of the country? Very good! I ascertained the fact through my little girl. Your health is good, I hope? You are not going away again?"

Then he left them, undoubtedly put off, by Frédéric's chilly reception.

Madame Moreau, indeed, was not on visiting terms with him. Père Roque lived in peculiar circumstances with his servant-girl, and was held in very low esteem, although he was electoral registrar, and the steward of the Dambreuses' estate.

"The banker who resides in the Rue d'Anjou," observed Deslauriers. "Do you know what you ought to do, my fine fellow?"

Isidore once more interrupted. He was ordered definitively not to go back without Frédéric. Madame was worried by his absence.

"Well, well, he will go back," said Deslauriers. "He's not going to stay out all night."

And, as soon as the man-servant had disappeared:

"You ought to ask that old chap to introduce you to the Dambreuses. There's nothing so useful as to be a frequent visitor at a rich man's house. Since you have a black coat and white gloves, make use of them. You must get yourself into that world. You can introduce me into it later. Just think!—a man worth millions! Do all you can to make him like you, and his wife, too. Become her lover!"

Frédéric exclaimed in protest.

"All I'm saying to you is in the best tradition! Remember Rastignac in the *Comédie humaine.*[8] You will succeed, I have no doubt."

Frédéric had so much confidence in Deslauriers that he felt shaken, and forgetting Madame Arnoux, or including her in the prediction made with regard to the other woman, he could not keep from smiling.

The clerk added:

"A last piece of advice: pass your examinations. It is always a good thing to have a title added to your name: and, give up your Catholic and Satanic poets, whose philosophy is as old as the twelfth century! Your despair is silly. The very greatest men have had more difficult beginnings, as in the case of Mirabeau.* Besides, our separation will not be so long. I will make that pickpocket of a father of mine pay up. It is time for me to be going back. Farewell! Have you got a hundred sous to pay for my dinner?"

Frédéric gave him ten francs, what was left of those he had gotten that morning from Isidore.

Meanwhile, some forty yards away from the bridges, a light shone from the garret-window of a low-built house.

Deslauriers noticed it. Then he said emphatically, as he took off his hat:

"Your pardon, Venus, Queen of Heaven, but Poverty is the mother of Wisdom. We have been slandered enough for that—so have mercy."

This allusion to an adventure in which they had both taken part, put them into a jovial mood. They laughed loudly as they passed through the streets.

Then, having settled his bill at the inn, Deslauriers walked back with Frédéric as far as the crossroads near the Hôtel-Dieu, and after a long embrace, the two friends parted.

---

*An orator and politician at the time of the French Revolution, Honoré-Gabriel Mirabeau (1749–1791) had had a stormy youth.

CHAPTER III

Two months later, Frédéric, having gotten off a coach one morning on the Rue Coq-Heron, immediately thought of paying his important visit.

Luck was on his side. Père Roque had brought him a roll of papers and requested him to deliver them himself to M. Dambreuse; and the good gentleman included with the package an open letter of introduction on behalf of his young fellow-countryman.

Madame Moreau appeared surprised at this proceeding. Frédéric concealed the delight that it gave him.

M. Dambreuse's real name was the Count d'Ambreuse; but since 1825, gradually abandoning his title of nobility and his party, he had turned his attention to business; and with his ears open in every office, his hand in every enterprise, on the lookout for every opportunity, as subtle as a Greek and as laborious as a native of Auvergne, he had amassed a fortune which might be called considerable. Furthermore, he was an officer of the Légion d'honneur, a member of the General Council of the Aube,* a representative, and one of these days would be a peer of France. However, affable as he was in other respects, he wearied the Minister with his continual applications for subsidies, for decorations, and licences for tobacconists' shops; and in his complaints against the establishment he was inclined to join the Left Centre. His wife, the pretty Madame Dambreuse, of whom mention was made in the fashion journals, presided at charitable functions. By flattering the duchesses, she appeased the rancour of the aristocratic faubourg,† and led the

---

*Aube is the *département* (administrative territory) in which Nogent-sur-Seine is situated. Today continental France comprises ninety-five such *départements*.

†The Faubourg Saint-Germain in Paris, where the old aristocracy still lived.

residents to believe that M. Dambreuse might yet repent and render them some services.

The young man was nervous when he called on them.

"I should have taken my dress-coat with me. No doubt they will give me an invitation to next week's ball. What will they say to me?"

His self-confidence returned when he reflected that M. Dambreuse was only a person of the middle class, and he sprang out of the cab briskly on the pavement of the Rue d'Anjou.

When he had pushed open one of the two gates, he crossed the courtyard, mounted the steps in front of the house, and entered a vestibule paved with coloured marble.

A straight double staircase, with red carpet, fastened with brass rods, rested against the high walls of shining stucco. At the end of the stairs there was a banana-tree, whose wide leaves fell down over the velvet banister. Two bronze candelabra, with porcelain globes, hung from little chains; the large radiator vents exhaled warm, heavy air; and all that could be heard was the ticking of a big clock standing at the other end of the vestibule, under a suit of armour.

A bell rang; a valet made his appearance, and led Frédéric into a small room, where one could observe two safes, as well as cabinets filled with folders. In the centre of it, M. Dambreuse was writing at a roll-top desk.

He ran his eye over Père Roque's letter, tore open the canvas in which the papers had been wrapped, and examined them.

From a distance, he had an appearance of youth, because of his slim build. But his thin white hair, his feeble limbs, and, above all, the extraordinary pallor of his face, betrayed a decrepit constitution. There was a merciless expression in his sea-green eyes, colder than eyes of glass. His cheek-bones were prominent, and his knuckles were knotted.

Finally, he arose and asked the young man a few questions about common acquaintances in Nogent and also with regard to his studies, and then dismissed him with a bow. Frédéric went out through another lobby, and found himself at the lower end of the courtyard near the coach-house.

A blue brougham, to which a black horse was yoked, stood in front of the steps before the house. The carriage door was opened, a lady stepped in, and the vehicle, with a rumbling noise, went rolling along the gravel.

Frédéric reached the main gate from the other side at the same moment as the brougham. As there was not enough room to allow him to pass, he was forced to wait. The young lady, with her head thrust forward past the carriage blind, talked to the concierge in a very low voice. All he could see was her back, covered with a violet cape. He glanced into the interior of the carriage, lined with blue fabric, with silk lace and fringe. The lady's ample robes filled up the space within. He pulled away from this little padded box with its perfume of iris, a scent of feminine elegance. The coachman slackened the reins, the horse brushed abruptly past, and they disappeared.

Frédéric returned on foot, along the boulevards.

He regretted not having been able to get a proper view of Madame Dambreuse.

A little higher than the Rue Montmartre, a jumble of carriages made him turn his head, and on the opposite side, facing him, he read on a marble plate:

'JACQUES ARNOUX'

How was it that he had not thought about her sooner? It was Deslauriers' fault; and he approached the shop, but did not enter. He was waiting for *her* to appear.

The high, transparent plate-glass windows displayed statuettes, drawings, engravings, catalogues and issues of *L' Art Industriel*, arranged in a skillful fashion; and subscription fees were listed on the door, which was decorated in the centre with the publisher's initials. Against the walls could be seen large paintings whose finish had a glossy look, two chests laden with porcelain, bronze, alluring curiosities; a little staircase separated them, closed off at the top by a carpeted landing; and an antique Saxon chandelier, a green carpet on the floor, with an inlaid table, gave to this interior the appearance rather of a drawing-room than of a shop.

Frédéric pretended to be examining the drawings. After hesitating for a long time, he went in.

A clerk opened the door, and in reply to a question, said that Monsieur would not be in the shop before five o'clock. But if a message could be conveyed—

"No I'll come back," Frédéric answered casually.

The following days were spent in search of housing; and he settled on an apartment in the second story of a furnished town-house in the Rue Sainte-Hyacinthe.

With fresh blotting-paper under his arm, he set forth to attend the opening lecture of the course. Three hundred young men, bare-headed, filled an amphitheatre, where an old man in a red gown lectured in a monotone voice. Quill pens went scratching over the paper. In this hall he found once more the dusty odour of the school, a reading-desk of similar shape, the same wearisome monotony! For a fortnight he regularly continued his attendance at law lectures. But he left off studying the Civil Code before getting as far as Article *3*, and he gave up the Institutes at the *Summa Divisio Personarum.*[9]

The pleasures that he had promised himself did not come to him; and when he had exhausted the resources of a circulating library, gone over the collections in the Louvre, and been at the theatre a great many nights in succession, he sank into the lowest depths of idleness. A thousand new things added to his depression. He had to keep track of his linens and put up with the concierge, who reminded him of a male hospital nurse who came in the morning to make up his bed, smelling of alcohol and grunting. He did not like his room, which was decorated with an alabaster clock. The walls were thin; he could hear the students making punch, laughing and singing.

Tired of this solitude, he sought out one of his old schoolfellows named Baptiste Martinon; and he discovered this boyhood friend in a middle-class boarding-house on the Rue Saint-Jacques, cramming legal procedure before a coal fire.

A woman in a print dress sat opposite him darning his socks.

Martinon was what people call a good looking fellow—tall, plump with regular features, and blue eyes. His father, an extensive landowner, had destined him for law; and wishing already to present a serious exterior, he wore his beard trimmed in a fringe.

As there was no rational foundation for Frédéric's complaints, and as he could not give evidence of any misfortune, Martinon was unable in any way to understand his lamentations about existence. As for him, he went every morning to the school, after that took a walk in the Luxembourg gardens, in the evening swallowed his half-cup of coffee; and with fifteen hundred francs a year, and the love of this working woman, his companion, he felt perfectly happy.

"What happiness!" was Frédéric's internal comment.

At the school he had formed another acquaintance, a youth from an aristocratic family, who on account of his dainty manners, was like a girl.

M. de Cisy devoted himself to drawing, and loved the Gothic style. They frequently went together to admire the Sainte-Chapelle and Nôtre Dame. But the young patrician's status and airs covered an intellect of the feeblest order. Everything took him by surprise. He laughed wildly at the most trifling joke, and displayed such utter simplicity that Frédéric at first took him for a jokester, and finally regarded him as an imbecile.

The young man found it impossible, therefore, to be open with anyone; and he was constantly looking for an invitation from the Dambreuses.

On New Year's Day, he sent them visiting-cards, but received none in return.

He made his way back to the office of *L'Art Industriel.*

A third time he returned to it, and at last saw Arnoux carrying on an argument with five or six people around him. He scarcely responded to the young man's bow; and Frédéric was wounded by this reception. None the less he still sought the best means of finding his way to her side.

His first idea was to come frequently to the shop on the pretext of getting paintings at low prices. Then he conceived the notion of slipping into the letter-box of the journal a few "very strong" articles, which might lead to friendly relations. Perhaps it would be better to get straight to the point at once, and declare his love? Acting on this impulse, he wrote a 12-page letter, full of lyrical phrases and exclamations but he tore it up, and did nothing, attempted nothing—immoralized by a fear of failure.

Above Arnoux's shop, there were, on the first floor, three windows which were lighted up every evening. Shadows might be seen moving about behind them, especially one; this was hers; and he went very far out of his way in order to gaze at these windows and to contemplate this shadow.

A negress who crossed his path one day in the Tuileries, holding a little girl by the hand, reminded him of Madame Arnoux's negress. She was sure to come there, like the others; every time he passed through the Tuileries, his heart began to beat with the anticipation of meeting her. On sunny days he continued his walk as far as the end of the Champs-Élysées.

Women seated with careless ease in open carriages, and with their veils floating in the wind, filed past close to him, their horses advancing at a steady walking pace, and with a barely see-saw detectable motion that made the varnished leather of the harness crackle. The vehicles became more numerous, and, slowing after they had passed the circle where the roads met, they took up the entire lane. The horses' manes came close to each other and the carriage lamps near to other lamps. The steel stirrups, the silver curb-chains and the brass rings, cast shining spots here and there, in the midst of the short breeches, the white gloves, and the furs, falling over the emblems of the carriage doors. He felt as if he were lost in some far-off world. His eyes wandered along the rows of female heads, and certain vague resemblances brought back Madame Arnoux to his mind. He pictured her, in the midst of the others, in one of those little broughams like that of Madame Dambreuse. The sun was setting, and the cold wind raised whirling clouds of dust. The coachmen let their chins sink into their neckcloths; the wheels began to revolve more quickly; the gravel crackled; and all the horse-drawn carriages descended the long sloping avenue at a quick trot, touching, sweeping past one another, getting out of one another's way; then, at the Place de la Concorde, they went off in different directions. Behind the Tuileries, there was a patch of slate-coloured sky. The trees of the garden formed two enormous masses violet-hued at their highest branches. The gas-lamps were lighted; and the Seine, green all over, was torn into strips of silver moiré, near the pillars of the bridges.

He got his dinner for forty-three sous in a restaurant in the Rue de la Harpe.

He glanced disdainfully at the old mahogany counter, the soiled napkins, the dingy silver-plate, and the hats hanging up on the wall. Those around him were students like himself. They talked about their professors, and about their mistresses. He couldn't care less about professors! Had he a mistress?! To avoid their high spirits, he came as late as possible. The tables were all strewn with remnants of food. The two waiters, worn out with serving customers, lay asleep, each in a corner of his own; and a smell of cooking, of an oil lamp, and of tobacco, filled the deserted dining-room.

Then he slowly set out on the streets again. The gas lamps vibrated, casting on the mud long yellowish shafts of flickering light. Shadowy forms under umbrellas glided along the sidewalks. The pavement was slippery: the fog grew thicker, and it seemed to him that the moist gloom, wrapping around him, descended into the depths of his heart.

He was overwhelmed with remorse. He returned to his lectures. But as he was entirely ignorant of the subjects being taught, the simplest things puzzled him.

He set about writing a novel entitled *Sylvio, the Fisherman's Son*. The setting for the story was Venice. He was the hero, and Madame Arnoux was the heroine. She was called Antonia; and, in order to have her, he assassinated a number of noblemen, and burned a portion of the city; after which he sang a serenade under her balcony, where the red damask curtains of the Boulevard Montmartre fluttered in the breeze.

The reminiscences, far too numerous, on which he dwelt disheartened him; he went no further with the work, and his lack of motivation intensified.

After this, he begged Deslauriers to come and share his apartment. They might make arrangements to live together with the aid of his allowance of two thousand francs; anything would be better than this intolerable existence. Deslauriers could not yet leave Troyes. He urged his friend to find some means of distracting himself, and, to that end, suggested that he call on Sénécal.

Sénécal was a mathematical tutor, a hard-headed man with republican convictions, a future Saint-Just, according to the clerk. Frédéric ascended the five flights, up which he lived, three times in succession, without getting a visit from him in return. He did not go back to the place.

He now went in for amusing himself. He attended the masquerade balls at the Opera House. These exhibitions of riotous gaiety froze him the moment he had passed the door. Besides, he was restrained by the fear of being insulted on the subject of money, his notion being that a supper with a woman dressed up as a domino, entailing considerable expense, was too much of an adventure.

It seemed to him, however, that he must be loved. Sometimes he used to wake up with his heart full of hope, dressed himself carefully as if he had a *rendez-vous*, and started on interminable excursions all over Paris. Whenever a woman was walking in front of him, or coming in his direction, he would say: "Here she is!" Every time it was only a fresh disappointment. The idea of Madame Arnoux strengthened these desires. Perhaps he might find her on his way; and he conjured up dangerous circumstances, extraordinary perils from which he would save her, in order to get near her.

So the days slipped by with the same tiresome repetition, and enslavement to his usual habits. He leafed through pamphlets under the arcades of the Odéon, went to read the *Revue des Deux Mondes* at the café,* entered the hall of the Collége de France, and for an hour stopped to listen to a lecture on Chinese or political economy. Every week he wrote long letters to Deslauriers, dined from time to time with Martinon, and occasionally saw M. de Cisy.

He rented a piano and composed German waltzes.

One evening at the theatre of the Palais-Royal,† he noticed, in one of the loge-boxes, Arnoux with a woman by his side. Was it she? The screen of green taffeta, pulled over the side of the box, hid her face. Finally, the curtain rose, and the screen was drawn aside. She was a tall woman of about thirty, rather washed out, and, when she laughed, her full lips revealed a row of magnificent teeth. She chatted familiarly with Arnoux, giving him, from time to time, taps, with her fan, on the fingers. Then a fair-haired young girl with eyelids a little red, as if she had just been weeping, seated herself between them. Arnoux after that remained stooped over her shoulder, pouring forth a stream of talk to which she listened without replying. Frédéric tried to figure out the social position of these

*The *Revue des Deux Mondes* was an important journal devoted to literature, philosophy, science, and politics.

†Monumental site near the Louvre, where the Comédie Française and the Théâtre du Palais-Royal are located.

women, modestly attired in gowns of sober hue with flat, turned-up collars.

At the close of the play, he made a dash for the exit. The crowd of people going out filled up the passageway. Arnoux, just in front of him, was descending the staircase step by step, with a woman on each arm.

Suddenly a gas-lamp shed its light on him. He wore a crape hat-band. She was dead, perhaps? This idea tormented Frédéric's mind so much, that he hurried, next day, to the office of *L'Art Industriel*, and paying, without a moment's delay, for one of the engravings shown in the window for sale, he asked the shop-assistant how was Monsieur Arnoux.

The shop-assistant replied:

"Why, quite well!"

Frédéric, growing pale, added:

"And Madame?"

"Madame, also."

Frédéric forgot to take his engraving with him.

The winter drew to an end. He was less melancholy in the spring time, and began to prepare for his examination. Having passed it with mediocre results, he departed immediately afterwards for Nogent.

He refrained from going to Troyes to see his friend, in order to escape his mother's comments. Then, on his return to Paris at the end of the vacation, he left his lodgings, and took two rooms on the Quai Napoléon which he furnished. He had given up all hope of getting an invitation from the Dambreuses. His great passion for Madame Arnoux was beginning to die out.

CHAPTER IV

One morning, in the month of December, while going to attend a law lecture, he thought he observed more than the usual animation in the Rue Saint-Jacques. The students were rushing precipitately out of the cafés, where, through the open windows, they were calling out to one another from one house to the other. The shop keepers in the middle of the sidewalk were looking about them anxiously; the window-shutters were fastened; and when he reached the Rue Soufflot, he perceived a large gathering around the Panthéon.[10]

Young men in groups numbering from five to a dozen walked along, arm in arm, and accosted the larger groups, which had stationed themselves here and there. At the lower end of the square, against the iron railings, men in smocks were holding forth, while policemen, with their three-cornered hats drawn over their ears, and their hands behind their backs, were strolling up and down beside the walls making the cobblestones echo under the tread of their heavy boots. All wore a mysterious, puzzled look; they were evidently expecting something to happen. Each held back a question which was on the tip of his tongue.

Frédéric found himself close to a fair-haired young man with a pleasant face and a moustache and a tuft of beard on his chin, like a dandy of Louis XIII's time. He asked the stranger the cause of the disorder.

"I haven't the least idea," replied the other, "nor have they, for that matter! It's a phase at the moment. What a good joke!"

And he burst out laughing.

The petitions for Reform, which had been signed at the quarters of the National Guard, together with the census implemented by the finance minister, Humann and some other events,[11] had, for the past six months, led to inexplicable gatherings of riotous crowds in

Paris, and so frequently had they broken out, that the newspapers had ceased to refer to them.

"This lacks shape and colour," continued Frédéric's neighbour. "I am convinced, sire, that we have degenerated. In the good epoch of Louis XI, and even, in that of Benjamin Constant, there were more mutinies amongst the students. I find them as docile as sheep, as dumb as doornails, and only fit to be grocers. Yikes! And these are what we call the youth of the schools!"

He spread his arms wide apart like Frédéric Lemaître in *Robert Macaire*.[12]

"Youth of the schools, I give you my blessing!"

After this, addressing a rag picker, who was moving a heap of oyster-shells up against the wall of a wine-merchant's house:

"Do you belong to them—the youth of the schools?"

The old man lifted up his hideous face in which one could trace, in the midst of a grey beard, a red nose and two dull eyes, bloodshot from drink.

"No, you appear to me rather one of those men with sinister faces whom we see, in various groups, liberally scattering gold. Oh, scatter it, my patriarch, scatter it! Corrupt me with the treasures of Albion!* Are you English? I do not reject the presents of Artaxerxes![†] Let us have a little chat about the customs union!"

Frédéric felt a hand laid on his shoulder. It was Martinon, looking exceedingly pale.

"Well!" said he with a big sigh, "another riot!"

He was afraid of having his reputation compromised, and couldn't help but lament. Men dressed in smocks especially made him feel uneasy, suggesting a connection with secret societies.

"You mean to say there are secret societies," said the young man with the moustache. "That is a worn-out ploy of the Government to frighten the middle-class folk!"[‡]

---

*"Albion" is an archaic name for Great Britain.

[†]Given to Athenian general Themistocles by Artaxerxes I, king of Persia. Themistocles, who had vanquished the Persians at Salamis in 480 B.C., was subsequently a victim of political intrigue in Athens and took refuge at Artaxerxes' court.

[‡]Secret societies of opponents to the current regimes flourished under the Restoration (1814–1830, when the Bourbon kings returned to rule after the fall of Napoléon I) and the July Monarchy (1830; the July Revolution forced Charles X to abdicate and Louis-Philippe became king in his place).

Martinon urged him to speak in a lower voice, for fear of the police.

"You believe still in the police, do you? As a matter of fact, how do you know, Monsieur, that I am not myself a police spy?"

And he looked at him in such a way, that Martinon, in his upset, was, at first, unable to see the joke. The people pushed them on, and they were all three compelled to stand on the little staircase which led, by one of the passages, to the new amphitheatre.

The crowd soon broke up of its own accord. A number of people bared their heads and bowed towards the esteemed Professor Samuel Rondelot, who, wrapped in his big frock-coat, with his silver spectacles held up high in the air, and breathing hard from his asthma, was advancing at an easy pace, on his way to deliver his lecture. This man was one of the judicial glories of the nineteenth century, the rival of the Zachariæs and the Ruhdorffs. His new status of peer of France had in no way modified his external demeanour. He was known to be poor, and was treated with profound respect.

Meanwhile, at the lower end of the square, some persons cried out:

"Down with Guizot!"

"Down with Pritchard!"[13]

"Down with the ones who sold out!"

"Down with Louis Philippe!"

The crowd swayed to and fro, and, pressing against the gate of the courtyard, which was shut, prevented the professor from going further. He stopped in front of the staircase. He stood on the lowest of three steps. He spoke; the loud murmurs of the throng drowned his voice. Although at another time they might love him, they hated him now, for he was the representative of authority. Every time he tried to make himself understood, the outcries began anew. He gestured with great energy to induce the students to follow him. He was answered by protests from all sides. He shrugged his shoulders disdainfully, and plunged into the passage. Martinon took advantage of the situation and disappeared at the same moment.

"What a coward!" said Frédéric.

"He was prudent," returned the other.

There was an outburst of applause from the crowd, who saw the professor's retreat as a victory. From every window, faces, filled with curiosity, looked out. Some of those in the crowd struck up the "Marseillaise;" others proposed to go to Béranger's house.

"To Laffitte's house!"

"To Chateaubriand's house!"

"To Voltaire's house!" yelled the young man with the fair moustache.[14]

The policemen tried to circulate, saying in the mildest way:

"Move on, messieurs! Move on!"

Somebody exclaimed:

"Down with the slaughterers!"

This was a regular out cry since the troubles of September. Everyone echoed it. The guardians of the law were hooted and hissed. They began to grow pale. One of them could endure it no longer, and, seeing a short young man approaching too closely, laughed in his face, and pushed him back so roughly, that he tumbled over on his back some five yards away, in front of a wine-merchant's shop. All made way; but almost immediately afterwards the policeman rolled on the ground himself, felled by a blow from a species of Hercules, whose hair hung down like a bundle of tow under an oilskin cap.

Having stopped for a few minutes at the corner of the Rue Saint-Jacques, he had very quickly laid down a large case, which he had been carrying, in order to make a spring at the policeman, and, holding down the officer, punched his face unmercifully. The other policemen rushed to the rescue of their comrade. The terrible shop-assistant was so powerfully built that it took four of them at least to get the better of him. Two of them shook him, while keeping a grip on his collar; two others pulled his arms; a fifth dug his knee in his ribs; and all of them called him "brigand," "assassin," "rioter." With his chest bare, and his clothes in rags, he protested that he was innocent; he could not, in cold blood, look at a child receiving a beating.

"My name is Dussardier. I'm employed at Messieurs Valincart Brothers' lace and fancy warehouse, in the Rue de Cléry. Where's my case? I want my case!" He kept repeating:

"Dussardier, Rue de Cléry. My case!"

However, he became quiet, and, with a stoical air, allowed himself to be led towards the guard-house in the Rue Descartes. A flood of people came rushing after him. Frédéric and the young man with the moustache walked immediately behind, full of admiration for the shopman, and indignant at the violence of power.

As they advanced, the crowd became less thick.

The policemen from time to time turned round, with threatening looks; and the rowdies, no longer having anything to do, and the spectators not having anything to look at, all drifted away little by little. The passers-by, who met the procession, as they came along, stared at Dussardier, and in loud tones, made abusive remarks about him. One old woman, at her own door, bawled out that he had stolen a loaf of bread from her. This unjust accusation increased the wrath of the two friends. At length, they reached the guard-house. Only about twenty persons were now left in the crowd, and the sight of the soldiers was enough to disperse them.

Frédéric and his companion boldly asked to have the man who had just been imprisoned set free. The sentinel threatened, if they persisted, to throw them into jail too. They said they had to see the commander of the guard-house, and stated their names, and the fact that they were law-students, declaring that the prisoner was one also.

They were ushered into a room perfectly bare, in which, amid an atmosphere of smoke, four benches lined the roughly-plastered walls. At the far end a window slid open. Then appeared the sturdy face of Dussardier, who, with his hair all tousled, his honest little eyes, and his broad snout, suggested to one's mind in a confused sort of way the appearance of a good dog.

"Don't you recognise us?" said Hussonnet.

This was the name of the young man with the moustache.

"Why—" stammered Dussardier.

"Don't play the fool any further," returned the other. "We know that you are, just like ourselves, a law-student."

In spite of their winks, Dussardier failed to understand. He appeared to be collecting his thoughts; then, suddenly:

"Has my case been found?"

Frédéric raised his eyes, feeling discouraged.

Hussonnet, however, said promptly:

"Ah! your case, in which you keep your lecture notes? Yes, yes, don't worry about it!"

They made further pantomimic signs with greater energy, till Dussardier at last realised that they had come to help him; and he held his tongue, fearing that he might get them into trouble. Besides, he experienced a kind of shame at seeing himself raised to the social rank of student, and to an equality with those young men who had such white hands.

"Do you wish to send any message to anyone?" asked Frédéric.

"No, thanks, to nobody."

"But your family?"

He lowered his head without replying; the poor fellow was a bastard. The two friends stood quite astonished at his silence.

"Have you anything to smoke?" was Frédéric's next question.

He felt about, then drew forth from the depths of one of his pockets the remains of a pipe—a beautiful pipe, made of white talc with a shank of blackwood, a silver cover, and an amber mouthpiece.

For the last three years he had been engaged in completing this masterpiece. He had been careful to keep the bowl of it constantly thrust into a kind of sheath of chamois, to smoke it as slowly as possible, without ever letting it lie on any cold stone surface, and to hang it up every evening over the head of his bed. And now he shook out the fragments of it into his hand, the nails of which were covered with blood, and with his chin sunk on his chest, his pupils fixed and dilated, he contemplated the ruins of the object that had yielded him such delight with a look of unutterable sadness.

"Suppose we give him some cigars, eh?" said Hussonnet in a whisper, making a gesture as if he were reaching for them.

Frédéric had already laid down a cigar-holder, which was full, on the edge of the hatch.

"Pray take this. Good-bye! Cheer up!"

Dussardier flung himself on the two hands that were held out towards him. He pressed them frantically, his voice choked with sobs.

"What? For me!—for me!"

The two friends tore themselves away from the effusive display of gratitude which he made, and went off to lunch together at the Café Tabourey, in front of the Luxembourg gardens.

While cutting up the beefsteak, Hussonnet informed his companion that he did work for the fashion journals, and created catchphrases for *L'Art Industriel.*

"At Jacques Arnoux's establishment?" said Frédéric.

"Do you know him?"

"Yes!—no!—that is to say, I have seen him—I have met him."

He carelessly asked Hussonnet if he sometimes saw Arnoux's wife.

"From time to time," the Bohemian replied.

Frédéric did not venture to follow up his enquiries. This man henceforth would occupy an important place in his life. He paid the lunch-bill without any protest on the other's part.

There was a bond of mutual sympathy between them; they gave one another their respective addresses, and Hussonnet cordially invited Frédéric to accompany him to the Rue de Fleurus.

They had reached the middle of the garden, when Arnoux's clerk, holding his breath, twisted his features into a hideous grimace, and began to crow like a cock. Thereupon all the cocks in the vicinity responded with prolonged "cock-a-doodle-doos."

"It is a signal," explained Hussonnet.

They stopped close to the Théâtre Bobino, in front of a house to which they had to find their way through an alley. In the skylight of a garret, between the nasturtiums and the sweet peas, a young woman showed herself, bare-headed, in her stays, her two arms resting on the edge of the roof-gutter.

"Good-day, my angel! good-day, my pet!" said Hussonnet, sending her kisses.

He made the barrier fly open with a kick, and disappeared.

Frédéric waited for him all week long. He did not venture to call at Hussonnet's residence, lest it might look as if he were in a hurry to get a lunch in return for the one he had paid for. But he sought the clerk all over the Latin Quarter. He came across him one evening, and brought him to his apartment on the Quai Napoléon.

They had a long chat, opening their hearts to each other. Hussonnet yearned after the glory and the profits of the theatre. He collaborated in the writing of vaudeville shows which were not accepted, "had heaps of plans," could turn a couplet; he sang out for Frédéric a few of the verses he had composed. Then, noticing on one of the shelves a volume of Hugo and another of Lamartine, he broke out into sarcastic criticisms of the romantic school.[15] These poets had neither good sense nor correct grammar, and, above all, were not French! He prided himself on his knowledge of the language, and analysed the most beautiful phrases with that snarling severity, that academic taste which persons of playful temperament exhibit when they are discussing serious art.

Frédéric's sensibilities were wounded, and he felt a desire to cut the discussion short. Why not risk asking the question on which his happiness depended? He asked this literary youth whether it would be possible to get an introduction into the Arnoux's house.

It was declared to be quite easy, and they settled on the following day.

Hussonnet failed to keep the appointment, and on three subsequent occasions he did not turn up. One Saturday, about four o'clock, he made his appearance. But, taking advantage of the cab into which they had got, he drew up in front of the Théâtre Français to get a box-ticket, stopped at a tailor's shop, then at a dressmaker's, and wrote notes in the concierge's lodge. At last they came to the Boulevard Montmartre. Frédéric passed through the shop, and went up the staircase. Arnoux recognised him through the glass-partition in front of his desk, and while continuing to write he stretched out his hand and laid it on Frédéric's shoulder.

Five or six persons, standing up, filled the narrow room, which was lighted by a single window looking out on the yard, a sofa of brown damask wool occupying the interior of an alcove between two door-curtains of similar material. Upon the mantelpiece, covered with old papers, there was a bronze Venus. Two candelabra, garnished with rose-coloured candles, flanked it, one at each side. At the right, near a filing cabinet, a man, seated in an armchair, was reading the newspaper, with his hat on. The walls were hidden from view beneath an array of prints and pictures, precious engravings or sketches by contemporary masters, adorned with dedications testifying the most sincere affection for Jacques Arnoux.

"You've been getting on well all this time?" said he, turning round to Frédéric.

And, without waiting for an answer, he asked Hussonnet in a low tone:

"What is your friend's name?" Then, raising his voice:

"Take a cigar out of the box on the filing cabinet."

The office of *L'Art Industriel*, situated in the center of Paris, was a convenient meeting place, a neutral ground wherein rivalries elbowed each other familiarly. On this day among those present were Anténor Braive, who painted portraits of kings; Jules Burrieu, who by his sketches was beginning to familiarize people with the wars in Algeria;* the caricaturist Sombary, the sculptor Vourdat, and others. And not a single one of them corresponded with the student's preconceived ideas. Their manners were simple, their talk free and easy. The mystic Lovarias told an obscene story; and the inventor of Oriental landscape, the famous Dittmer, wore a knitted shirt under his waistcoat, and went home on the omnibus.

The first topic that came up was the case of a girl named Apollonie, formerly a model, whom Burrieu alleged that he had seen on the boulevard in a carriage with four horses and two postilions. Hussonnet explained this metamorphosis through the succession of persons who had loved her.

"How well this sly dog knows the girls of Paris!" said Arnoux.

"After you, if there are any of them left, sire," replied the Bohemian, with a military salute, in imitation of the grenadier offering his flask to Napoleon.

Then they talked about some paintings for which Apollonie had sat for the female figures. They criticised their absent brethren, expressing astonishment at the sums paid for their works; and they were all complaining of not having been sufficiently remunerated themselves, when the conversation was interrupted by the entrance of a man of medium height, who had his coat fastened by a single button, and whose eyes glittered with a rather wild expression.

"What a bunch of shopkeepers you are!" said he. "God bless my soul! What does that signify? The old masters did not trouble their heads about the money—Correggio, Murillo—"

"Add Pellerin," said Sombary.

---

*The conquest of Algeria lasted from 1830 to 1871.

But, without taking the slightest notice of this witticism, he went on talking with such vehemence, that Arnoux was forced to repeat twice to him:

"My wife needs you on Thursday. Don't forget!"

This remark brought Madame Arnoux back to Frédéric's thoughts. No doubt, one might be able to reach her through the little room near the sofa. Arnoux had just opened the door leading into it to get a pocket-handkerchief, and Frédéric had seen a wash-stand at the far end of the room. But at this point a kind of muttering sound came from the corner by the fireplace; it was caused by the person who sat in the armchair reading the newspaper. He was a man of five feet nine inches in height, with rather droopy eyelids, a head of grey hair, and an imposing appearance; and his name was Regimbart.

"What's the matter now, citizen?" said Arnoux.

"Another rotten trick on the part of Government!"

The thing that he was referring to was the dismissal of a schoolmaster.

Pellerin again took up his parallel between Michael Angelo and Shakespeare. Dittmer was departing when Arnoux pulled him back in order to put two bank notes into his hand. Thereupon Hussonnet said, considering this an opportune time:

"Couldn't you give me an advance, my dear master—?"

But Arnoux had resumed his seat, and was administering a severe reprimand to an old disheveled man who wore a pair of blue spectacles.

"A nice fellow you are, Père Isaac! Here are three works discredited, finished! Everybody is laughing at me! People know what they are now! What do you want me to do with them? I'll have to send them off to California—or to the devil! No, shut up!"

The specialty of this old fellow consisted in attaching the signatures of the great masters to the bottom of these pictures. Arnoux refused to pay him, and dismissed him in a brutal fashion. Then, with an entire change of manner, he bowed to a gentleman of affectedly grave demeanour, with whiskers, a white tie and the cross of the Légion d'honneur over his chest.

With his elbow resting on the window-latch, he kept talking to him for a long time in honeyed tones. At last he burst out:

"Ah! well, it does not bother me to use brokers, Count."

The nobleman gave way, and Arnoux gave him a reduction of twenty-five louis. As soon as he had gone out:

"What a plague these big lords are!"

"A lot of wretches!" muttered Regimbart.

As it grew later, Arnoux was much more busily occupied. He classified articles, tore open letters, set out accounts in a row; at the sound of hammering in the warehouse he went out to look after the packing; then he went back to his ordinary work; and, while he kept his steel pen running over the paper, he indulged in sharp witticisms. He had an invitation to dine with his lawyer that evening, and was starting next day for Belgium.

The others chatted about the topics of the day—Cherubini's portrait, the hemicycle of the Fine Arts, and the next Exhibition. Pellerin railed at the Institute. Scandalous stories and serious discussions got mixed up together. The room with its low ceiling was so much stuffed up that one could scarcely move; and the light of the rose-coloured candles was obscured in the smoke of their cigars, like the sun's rays in a fog.

The door near the sofa flew open, and a tall, thin woman entered with abrupt movements, which made all the trinkets of her watch rattle under her black taffeta gown.

It was the woman of whom Frédéric had caught a glimpse last summer at the Palais-Royal. Some of those present, addressing her by name, shook hands with her. Hussonnet had at last managed to extract from his employer the sum of fifty francs. The clock struck seven. All rose to go.

Arnoux told Pellerin to remain, and accompanied Mademoiselle Vatnaz into the dressing-room.

Frédéric could not hear what they said; they spoke in whispers. However, the woman's voice was raised:

"I have been waiting ever since the job was done, six months ago."

There was a long silence, and then Mademoiselle Vatnaz reappeared. Arnoux had again promised her something.

"Oh! oh! later, we shall see!"

"Good-bye! happy man," said she, as she was going out.

Arnoux quickly re-entered the dressing-room, rubbed some pomade over his moustache, raised his braces to tighten his trouser-straps; and, while he was washing his hands:

"I would require two over the door panels at two hundred and fifty apiece, in Boucher's style. Is that understood?"

"So be it," said the artist, his face reddening.

"Good! and don't forget my wife!"

Frédéric accompanied Pellerin to the top of the Faubourg Poissonnière, and asked his permission to come to see him sometimes, a favour which was graciously granted.

Pellerin read every work on æsthetics, in order to find out the true theory of Beauty, convinced that, when he had discovered it, he would produce masterpieces. He surrounded himself with every imaginable accessory—drawings, plaster-casts, models, engravings; and he kept searching about, and agonizing. He blamed the weather, his nerves, his studio, went out into the street to find inspiration there, quivered with delight at the thought that he had caught it, then abandoned the work in which he was engaged, and dreamed of another which would be more beautiful. Thus, tormented by the desire for glory, and wasting his days in discussions, believing in a thousand absurdities—in systems, in criticisms, in the importance of a regulation or a reform in the domain of Art—he had at fifty as yet turned out nothing save mere sketches. His robust pride prevented him from experiencing any discouragement, but he was always irritated, and in a state of excitement, at the same time artificial and natural, which is characteristic of comedians.

On entering his studio one's attention was directed towards two large paintings, in which the first tones of colour laid on here and there made spots of brown, red, and blue on the white canvas. A network of lines in chalk stretched overhead, like stitches of thread repeated twenty times; it was impossible to understand what it meant. Pellerin explained the subject of these two compositions by pointing out with his thumb the portions that were lacking. The first was intended to represent "The Madness of Nebuchadnezzar," and the second "The Burning of Rome by Nero." Frédéric admired them.

He admired academies of women with dishevelled hair, landscapes in which trunks of trees, twisted by the storm, abounded, and above all ink sketches, imitations from memory of Callot, Rembrandt, or Goya, of which he did not know the models.

Pellerin no longer placed any value on these works of his youth. He was now all in favour of the grand style; he pontificated eloquently about Phidias and Winckelmann. The objects around him strengthened the force of his language; one saw a death's head on a prie-dieu, Turkish daggers, a monk's habit. Frédéric put it on.

When he arrived early, he surprised the artist in his pathetic folding-bed, which was hidden from view by a strip of tapestry; for Pellerin went to bed late, being an assiduous theatre-goer. An old woman in tatters attended to him. He dined in cheap restaurants, and lived without a mistress. His knowledge, picked up in the most irregular fashion, rendered his paradoxes amusing. His hatred of the vulgar and the "bourgeois" overflowed in sarcasm, marked by a superb lyricism, and he had such religious reverence for the masters that it raised him almost to their level.

But why had he never spoken about Madame Arnoux? As for her husband, at one time he called him a decent fellow, at other times a charlatan. Frédéric was waiting for some disclosures on his part.

One day, while leafing through one of the portfolios in the studio, he thought he could trace in the portrait of a female Bohemian some resemblance to Mademoiselle Vatnaz; and, as he felt interested in this lady, he desired to know what was her exact social position.

She had been, as far as Pellerin could ascertain, originally a schoolmistress in the provinces. She now gave lessons in Paris, and tried to write for the small journals.

According to Frédéric, one would imagine from her manners with Arnoux that she was his mistress.

"Pshaw! he has others!"

Then, turning away his face, which reddened with shame as he realised the baseness of the suggestion, the young man added, with a swaggering air:

"Very likely his wife pays him back for it?"

"Not at all; she is virtuous."

Frédéric again experienced a feeling of remorse, and the result was that his attendance at the office of the art journal became more regular than before.

The big letters which formed the name of Arnoux on the marble plate above the shop seemed to him quite peculiar and full of meaning, like some sacred writing. The wide sidewalk, by its descent, facilitated his approach; the door almost turned of its own accord; and the handle, smooth to the touch, gave him the sensation of friendly and, as it were, intelligent fingers clasping his. Unconsciously, he became quite as punctual as Regimbart.

Every day Regimbart seated himself in the corner by the fireplace, in his armchair, got hold of the *National*, and kept possession of it, expressing his thoughts by exclamations or by shrugs of the shoulders. From time to time he would wipe his forehead with his pocket-handkerchief, rolled up in a ball, which he usually stuck in between two buttons of his green frock-coat. He had pleated trousers, shoe-boots, and a long cravat; and his hat, with its turned-up brim, made him easily recognisable, at a distance, in a crowd.

At eight o'clock in the morning he descended the heights of Montmartre, in order to imbibe white wine in the Rue Nôtre Dame des Victoires. A late breakfast, following several games of billiards, brought him on to three o'clock. He then directed his steps towards the Passage des Panoramas, where he had a glass of absinthe. After the sitting in Arnoux's shop, he entered the Bordelais café, where he swallowed some vermouth; then, in place of returning home to his wife, he preferred to dine alone in a little café in the Rue Gaillon, where he desired them to serve up to him "household dishes, natural things." Finally, he made his way to another billiard-room, and remained there till midnight, in fact, till one o'clock in the morning, up till the last moment, when, the gas being put out and the window-shutters fastened, the master of the establishment, worn out, begged him to go.

And it was not the love of drinking that attracted Citizen Regimbart to these places, but the inveterate habit of talking politics. With advancing age, he had lost his vivacity, and now exhibited only a silent moroseness. One would have said, judging from the serious look on his face, that he was turning over in his mind the affairs of the whole world. Nothing, however, came from it; and nobody, even amongst his own friends, knew him to have any occupation, although he gave himself out as being up to his eyeballs in business.

Arnoux appeared to have very great esteem for him. One day he said to Frédéric:

"He knows a lot, I assure you. He is an able man."

On another occasion Regimbart spread over his desk papers relating to the kaolin mines in Brittany. Arnoux referred to his own experience on the subject.

Frédéric showed himself more ceremonious towards Regimbart, going so far as to invite him from time to time to take a glass of absinthe; and, although he considered him a stupid man, he often remained a full hour in his company solely because he was Jacques Arnoux's friend.

After pushing forward some contemporary masters in the early portions of their career, the art-dealer, a man of progressive ideas, had tried, while clinging to his artistic ways, to extend his meagre profits. His objective was to emancipate the fine arts, the sublime at a popular price. Over every industry associated with Parisian luxury he exercised an influence which proved fortunate with respect to little things, but harmful with respect to great things. With his mania for pandering to public opinion, he made clever artists swerve from their true path, corrupted the strong, exhausted the weak, and got distinction for those of mediocre talent; he set them up with the assistance of his connections and of his magazine. Young painters were ambitious to see their works in his shop-window, and upholsterers took inspiration from his home decoration. Frédéric regarded him, at the same time, as a millionaire, as a *dilettante*, and as a man of action. However, he found many things that filled him with astonishment, for my lord Arnoux was rather sly in his commercial transactions.

He received from the very heart of Germany or of Italy a painting purchased in Paris for fifteen hundred francs, and, exhibiting an invoice that brought the price up to four thousand, sold it over again, as a favor, for three thousand five hundred. One of his usual tricks with painters was to demand a small-scale copy of their painting, under the pretext that he would bring out an engraving of it. He always sold the copy; but the engraving never appeared. To those who complained that he had taken an advantage of them, he would reply with a playful slap on the stomach. Generous in other ways, he squandered money on cigars for his acquaintances, "spoke familiarly" to people whom he did not know, displayed enthusiasm about a work or a man; and, after that, sticking to his opinion, and, regardless of consequences, spared no expense in journeys, correspondence, and advertising. He looked upon himself as very upright, and, yielding to an irresistible impulse to pour his heart out, naïvely told his friends about certain indelicate acts of which he had been guilty.

Once, in order to annoy a member of his own trade who inaugurated another art journal with a big banquet, he asked Frédéric to write out in front of him, a little before the hour it was to begin, letters to the guests recalling the invitations.

"This impugns nobody's honour, do you understand?"

And the young man did not dare to refuse the service.

Next day, on entering M. Arnoux's office with Hussonnet, Frédéric saw through the door (the one opening on the staircase) the hem of a lady's dress disappearing.

"A thousand pardons!" said Hussonnet. "If I had known that there were women—"

"Oh! as for that one, she is my own," replied Arnoux. "She just came in to pay me a visit as she was passing."

"What?!" said Frédéric.

"Why, yes; she is going back home again."

The charm of the things around him was suddenly withdrawn. That which had seemed to him to be diffused vaguely through the place had now vanished—or, rather, it had never been there. He experienced an infinite amazement, and, as it were, the painful sensation of having been betrayed.

Arnoux, while rummaging about in his drawer, began to smile. Was he laughing at him? The clerk laid down a bundle of damp papers on the table.

"Ah! the posters," exclaimed the art-dealer.

"It's going to be a while before I can go to dinner tonight."

Regimbart took up his hat.

"What, are you leaving me?"

"Seven o'clock," said Regimbart.

Frédéric followed him.

At the corner of the Rue Montmartre, he turned round. He glanced towards the windows of the first floor, and he laughed internally with self-pity as he recalled to mind with what love he had so often contemplated them. Where, then, did she reside? How was he to meet her now? Once more around the object of his desire a solitude opened more immense than ever!

"Are you coming along to have some?" asked Regimbart.

"To have what?"

"Absinthe."

And, yielding to his obsession, Frédéric allowed himself to be led towards the Bordelais café. Whilst his companion, leaning on his elbow, was staring at the decanter, he was looking around. But he caught a glimpse of Pellerin's profile on the sidewalk outside; the painter gave a quick tap at the window-pane, and he had scarcely sat down when Regimbart asked him why they no longer saw him at the office of *L'Art Industriel.*

"I'd rather die than go back there again. The fellow is a brute, a bourgeois, a scoundrel, a criminal!"

These insulting words matched Frédéric's angry mood. Nevertheless, he was wounded, for it seemed to him that they reflected on Madame Arnoux.

"Why, what has he done to you?" said Regimbart.

Pellerin stamped his foot on the ground, and his only response was a heavy sigh.

He had been devoting himself to artistic work of a kind that he did not care to connect his name with, such as chalk and charcoal portraits, or pasticcios from the great masters for amateurs of limited knowledge; and, as he felt humiliated by these inferior productions, he preferred to hold his tongue on the subject as a general rule. But "Arnoux's dirty conduct" exasperated him too much. He had to express his feelings.

In accordance with an order, which had been given in Frédéric's very presence, he had brought Arnoux two pictures. Thereupon the dealer took the liberty of criticising them. He found fault with the composition, the colouring, and the drawing—above all the drawing; he would not, in short, take them at any price. But, finding himself in difficulties over a bill falling due, Pellerin had to give them to the Jew Isaac; and, a fortnight later, Arnoux himself sold them to a Spaniard for two thousand francs.

"Not a sou less! What a filthy trick! and, faith, he has done many other things just as bad. One of these mornings we'll see him in court!"

"How you exaggerate," said Frédéric, in a timid voice.

"So I exaggerate, do I?!" exclaimed the artist, giving the table a great blow with his fist.

This violence had the effect of completely restoring the young man's self-command. No doubt he might have behaved better; still, if Arnoux thought these two pictures——

"Were bad! say it! Are you a good judge of them? Is this your profession? Now, you know, my young man, I don't accept this sort of thing from mere amateurs."

"Ah! well, it's not my business," said Frédéric.

"Then, what interest have you in defending him?" returned Pellerin, coldly.

The young man faltered:

"But—since I am his friend——"

"Go, and give him a hug for me. Good night!"

And the painter rushed away in a rage, and, of course, without paying for his drink.

Frédéric, whilst defending Arnoux, had convinced himself. In the heat of his eloquence, he was filled with tenderness towards this man, so intelligent and kind, whom his friends maligned, and who had now to work all alone, abandoned by them. He could not resist a strange impulse to go at once and see him again. Ten minutes afterwards he pushed open the door of the art shop.

Arnoux was preparing, with the assistance of his clerks, some huge posters for an exhibition of paintings.

"Hello! what brings you back again?"

This question, simple though it was, embarrassed Frédéric, and, at a loss for an answer, he asked whether they had happened to find a notebook of his—a little notebook with a blue leather cover.

"The one that you put your letters to women in?" said Arnoux.

Frédéric, blushing like a school girl, protested against such an assumption.

"Your verses, then?" returned the art-dealer.

He handled the pictorial specimens that were to be exhibited, discussing their form, colour, and borders; and Frédéric felt more and more irritated by his air of deliberation, and particularly by the appearance of his hands—large hands, rather soft, with flat nails. At length, M. Arnoux arose, and saying, "That's that!" he chucked the young man familiarly under the chin. Frédéric was offended at this liberty, and recoiled a pace or two; then he made a dash for the shop-door, and passed through it, as he imagined, for the last time in his life. Madame Arnoux herself had been lowered by the vulgarity of her husband.

During the same week he got a letter from Deslauriers, informing him that the clerk would be in Paris on the following Thursday. In a violent reaction, he fell back on this affection as one of a more solid and lofty nature. A man of this sort was worth all the women in the world. He would no longer have any need of Regimbart, of Pellerin, of Hussonnet, of anyone! In order to provide his friend with as comfortable lodgings as possible, he bought an iron bedstead and a second armchair, and stripped off some of his own bed-covering to make up this one properly. On Thursday morning he was dressing himself to go to meet Deslauriers when there was a ring at the door. Arnoux entered.

"Just one word. Yesterday I got a lovely trout from Geneva. We expect you this evening—at seven o'clock sharp. The address is the Rue de Choiseul 24 *bis*. Don't forget!"

Frédéric was obliged to sit down; his knees were tottering under him. He repeated to himself, "At last! at last!" Then he wrote to his tailor, to his hatter, and to his bootmaker; and he dispatched these three notes by three different messengers. The key turned in the lock, and the concierge appeared with a trunk on his shoulder.

Frédéric, on seeing Deslauriers, began to tremble like an adulteress under the glance of her husband.

"What has happened to you?" said Deslauriers.

"Surely you got my letter?"

Frédéric had not enough energy left to lie.

He opened his arms, and flung his arms around on his friend's neck.

Then the clerk told his story. His father had avoided giving an account of his guardianship thinking that the period for rendering such accounts was ten years; but, well versed in legal procedure, Deslauriers had managed to get the share coming to him from his mother into his clutches—seven thousand francs clear—which he had there with him in an old wallet.

" 'Tis a reserve fund, in case of misfortune. I must think over the best way of investing it, and find quarters for myself to-morrow morning. To-day I'm perfectly free, and am entirely at your service, my old friend."

"Oh! don't put yourself out," said Frédéric.

"If you had anything of importance to do this evening——"

"Come, now! I would be a selfish wretch——"

This epithet, flung out at random, touched Frédéric to the quick, like a reproachful allusion.

The concierge had placed on the table close to the fire some chops, cold meat, a large lobster, some sweets for dessert, and two bottles of Bordeaux. Deslauriers was touched by these excellent preparations to welcome his arrival.

"Upon my word, you are treating me like a king!"

They talked about their past and about the future; and, from time to time, they grasped each other's hands across the table, looking at each other with affection for a moment.

A messenger came with a new hat. Deslauriers, in a loud tone, remarked that this head-gear was very showy.

Next came the tailor himself to fit on the coat, to which he had given a touch-up with the iron.

"One would imagine you were going to be married," said Deslauriers.

An hour later, a third individual appeared on the scene, and drew forth from a big black bag a pair of shiny patent leather boots. While Frédéric was trying them on, the bootmaker slyly drew attention to the shoes of the young man from the country.

"Does Monsieur require anything?"

"No, thanks," replied the clerk, pulling behind his chair his old shoes fastened with strings.

This humiliating incident annoyed Frédéric. At length he exclaimed, as if an idea had suddenly taken possession of him:

"Good heavens! I was forgetting."

"What is it, pray?"

"I have to dine in the city this evening."

"At the Dambreuses'? Why did you never say anything to me about them in your letters?"

"It is not at the Dambreuses', but at the Arnoux's."

"You should have let me know beforehand," said Deslauriers. "I would have come a day later."

"Impossible," returned Frédéric, abruptly. "I only got the invitation this morning, a little while ago."

And to redeem his error and distract his friend's mind from the occurrence, he proceeded to unfasten the tangled cords round the trunk, and to arrange all his belongings in the chest of drawers, expressed his willingness to give him his own bed, and offered to sleep in the dressing-room bed himself. Then, as soon as it was four o'clock, he began his preparations to get dressed.

"You have plenty of time," said the other.

At last he was dressed and off he went.

"That's the way with the rich," thought Deslauriers.

And he went to dine in the Rue Saint-Jacques, at a little restaurant kept by a man he knew.

Frédéric stopped several times while going up the stairs, so violently did his heart beat. One of his gloves, which was too tight, ripped open, and, while he was fastening back the torn part under his shirt-cuff, Arnoux, who was mounting the stairs behind him, took his arm and led him in.

The hall, decorated in the Chinese fashion, had a painted lantern hanging from the ceiling, and bamboo plants in the corners. As he was passing into the drawing-room, Frédéric stumbled against a tiger's skin. The candelabra had not yet been lit, but two lamps were burning in the boudoir in the far corner.

Mademoiselle Marthe came to announce that her mamma was dressing. Arnoux raised her up in order to kiss her; then, as he wished to go to the cellar himself to select certain bottles of wine, he left Frédéric with the little girl.

She had grown much larger since the trip in the steamboat. Her dark hair fell in long ringlets, which curled over her bare arms. Her dress, more puffed out than the petticoat of a *danseuse*, allowed her rosy calves to be seen, and her pretty childlike form had all the fresh scent of a bunch of flowers. She received the young gentleman's compliments with a coquettish air, fixed on him her large, dreamy eyes, then slipping in between the furniture, disappeared like a cat.

After this he no longer felt ill at ease. The globes of the lamps, covered with a paper lace-work, sent forth a white light, softening the colour of the walls, hung with mauve satin. Through the bars of the fireguard which resembled a big fan, the coal could be seen in the fireplace, and close beside the clock there was a little chest with silver clasps. Here and there things lay about which gave the place a look of home—a doll in the middle of the sofa, a fichu against the back of a chair, and on the work-table a knitted woollen vest, from which two ivory needles were hanging with their points downwards. It was altogether a peaceful spot, suggesting propriety and innocent family life.

Arnoux returned, and Madame Arnoux appeared at the other doorway. As she was enveloped in shadow, the young man could at first distinguish only her head. She wore a black velvet gown, and in her hair she had fastened a long Algerian cap, in a red silk net, which coiling round her comb, fell over her left shoulder.

Arnoux introduced Frédéric.

"Oh! I remember Monsieur perfectly well," she responded.

Then the guests arrived, nearly all at the same time—Dittmer, Lovarias, Burrieu, the composer Rosenwald, the poet Théophile Lorris, two art critics, colleagues of Hussonnet, a paper manufacturer, and in the rear the illustrious Pierre Paul Meinsius, the last representative of the grand school of painting, who blithely carried along with his fame his forty-five years and his big paunch.

When they were passing into the dining-room, Madame Arnoux took his arm. A chair had been left vacant for Pellerin. Arnoux, though he took advantage of him, was fond of him. Besides, he was afraid of his terrible tongue, so much so, that, in order to soften him, he had given a portrait of him in *L'Art Industriel*, accompanied by exaggerated praise; and Pellerin, more sensitive about distinction than about money, made his appearance about eight o'clock quite out of breath. Frédéric imagined that they had been reconciled for a long time.

He liked the company, the food, everything. The dining-room, which resembled a mediæval parlour, was hung with embossed leather. A Dutch what-not faced a rack for chibouks, and around the table the Bohemian glasses, variously coloured, had, in the midst of the flowers and fruits, the effect of illuminations in a garden.

He had to make his choice between ten sorts of mustard. He partook of daspachio, of curry, of ginger, of Corsican blackbirds, and of Roman lasagna; he drank extraordinary wines, lip-fraeli and tokay. Arnoux indeed prided himself on entertaining people in good style. With an eye to the procurement of fine foods, he was on friendly terms with the mail-coach drivers, and with the cooks of great houses, who communicated to him the secrets of rare sauces.

But Frédéric was particularly amused by the conversation. His taste for travelling was tickled by Dittmer, who talked about the East; he gratified his curiosity about theatrical matters by listening to Rosenwald's chat about the opera; and the atrocious Bohemian existence assumed for him a droll aspect when seen through the gaiety of Hussonnet, who related, in a picturesque fashion, how he had spent an entire winter with no food except Dutch cheese. Then, a discussion between Lovarias and Burrieu about the Florentine School gave him new ideas with regard to masterpieces, widened his horizons, and he found difficulty in restraining his enthusiasm when Pellerin exclaimed:

"Don't bother me with your hideous reality! What does it mean—reality? Some see things black, others blue—the multitude sees them stupidly. There is nothing less natural than Michael Angelo; there is nothing more powerful! The anxiety about external truth is a mark of contemporary baseness; and art will become, if things go on that way, a sort of poor joke as much below religion as it is below poetry, and as much below politics as it is below business. You will never reach its goal—yes, its goal!—which is to create within us an impersonal exaltation, with minor works, in spite of all your fine execution. Look, for instance, at Bassolier's pictures: they are pretty, coquettish, neat, and by no means dull. You might put them into your pocket, bring them with you when you are travelling. Notaries buy them for twenty thousand francs, while the ideas they contain are only worth three sous. But, without ideas, there is no greatness; without greatness there is no beauty. Olympus is a mountain. The most astonishing monument will always be the Pyramids. Exuberance is better than taste; the desert is better than a sidewalk, and a savage is better than a hairdresser!"

Frédéric, while listening to these things, glanced towards Madame Arnoux. They sank into his soul like pieces of metal falling into a furnace, added to his passion, and supplied the material of love.

His chair was three seats down from hers on the same side. From time to time, she bent forward a little, turning aside her head to address a few words to her little daughter; and as she smiled on these occasions, a dimple took shape in her cheek, giving to her face an expression of delicate good-nature.

As soon as the time came for the gentlemen to have their wine, she disappeared. The conversation became more free and easy. M. Arnoux shone in it, and Frédéric was astonished at the cynicism of men. However, their preoccupation with women established between them and him, a certain equality, which raised his own self-esteem.

When they had returned to the drawing-room, he took up, to keep himself in countenance, one of the albums which lay about on the table. The great artists of the day had illustrated them with drawings, had written in them snatches of verse or prose, or their signatures simply. In the midst of famous names he found many that he had never heard of before, and original thoughts appeared only underneath a flood of nonsense. All these entries contained a more or less direct expression of homage towards Madame Arnoux. Frédéric would have been afraid to write a line beside them.

She went into her boudoir to look at the little chest with silver clasps which he had noticed on the mantelpiece. It was a present from her husband, a work of the Renaissance. Arnoux's friends complimented him, and his wife thanked him. His tender emotions were aroused, and before all the guests he gave her a kiss.

After this they all chatted in groups here and there. The worthy Meinsius was with Madame Arnoux on an easy chair close beside the fire. She was leaning forward towards his ear; their heads were just touching, and Frédéric would have been glad to become deaf, infirm, and ugly if, instead, he had an illustrious name and white hair—in short, if he only happened to possess something which would install him in such intimate association with her. He began once more to eat his heart out, furious at the idea of being so young a man.

But she came into the corner of the drawing-room in which he was sitting, asked him whether he was acquainted with any of the guests, whether he was fond of painting, how long he had been a student in Paris. Every word that came out of her mouth seemed to

Frédéric something entirely new, an exclusive appendage of her personality. He gazed attentively at the fringe on her head-dress, the ends of which caressed her bare shoulder, and he was unable to take his eyes off of her; he plunged his soul into the whiteness of that feminine flesh, and yet he did not venture to raise his eyelids to look up at her, face to face.

Rosenwald interrupted them, begging Madame Arnoux to sing something. He played a prelude, she waited, her lips opened slightly, and a sound, pure, long-continued, silvery, ascended into the air.

Frédéric did not understand a single one of the Italian words.

The song began with a grave measure, something like church music, then in a more animated strain, with a crescendo, it broke into repeated bursts of sound, then suddenly subsided, and the melody came back again in a tender fashion with a wide and easy swing.

She stood beside the keyboard with her arms at her sides and a far-off look on her face. Sometimes, in order to read the music, she blinked her eyes and bent her head for a moment. Her contralto voice in the low notes took a mournful intonation which had a chilling effect on the listener, and then her beautiful face, with those great brows of hers, tilted over her shoulder; her bosom swelled; her arms stretched out; her throat, from which trills made their escape, fell back as if under aërial kisses. She flung out three sharp notes, came down again, cast forth one higher still, and, after a silence, finished with a flourish.

Rosenwald did not leave the piano. He continued playing, to amuse himself. From time to time a guest stole away. At eleven o'clock, as the last of them were going off, Arnoux went out along with Pellerin, under the pretext of seeing him home. He was one of those people who say that they are ill when they do not "take a turn" after dinner.

Madame Arnoux had made her way towards the hall. Dittmer and Hussonnet bowed to her. She stretched out her hand to them. She did the same to Frédéric; and he felt, as it were, something penetrating every particle of his skin.

He took leave of his friends. He wished to be alone. His heart was overflowing. Why had she offered him her hand? Was it a thoughtless act, or an encouragement? "Come now! I am mad!" Besides, what did it matter, when he could now visit her entirely at his ease, live in the very atmosphere she breathed?

The streets were deserted. Now and then a heavy wagon would roll past, shaking the pavement. The houses came one after another with their grey fronts, their closed windows; and he thought with disdain of all those human beings who lived behind those walls without having seen her, and not one of whom dreamed of her existence. He had no consciousness of his surroundings, of space, of anything, and striking the ground with his heel, rapping with his walking-stick on the shutters of the shops, he kept walking on continually at random, in a state of excitement, carried away by his emotions. Suddenly he felt himself surrounded by damp air, and found that he was on the edge of the quays.

The gas-lamps shone in two straight lines, which ran on endlessly, and long red flames flickered in the depths of the water. The waves were slate-coloured, while the sky, which was of clearer hue, seemed to be supported by vast masses of shadow that rose on each side of the river. The darkness was intensified by buildings whose outlines the eye could not distinguish. A luminous haze floated above the roofs further on. All the noises of the night had melted into a single monotonous hum.

He stopped in the middle of the Pont Neuf, and, taking off his hat and opening his chest, he drank in the air. And now he felt as if something that was inexhaustible were rising up from the very depths of his being, a surge of tenderness that flooded him, like the motion of the waves under his eyes. A church-clock slowly struck one, like a voice calling out to him.

Then, he was seized with one of those shuddering sensations of the soul in which one seems to be transported into a higher world. He felt, as it were, endowed with some extraordinary talent, the aim of which he could not determine. He seriously asked himself whether he would be a great painter or a great poet; and he decided in favour of painting, for the exigencies of this profession would bring him into contact with Madame Arnoux. So, then, he had found his vocation! The object of his existence was now perfectly clear, and there could be no mistake about the future.

When he had shut his door, he heard some one snoring in the dark closet near his room. It was his friend. He no longer gave him a thought.

His own face presented itself to him in the mirror. He thought himself handsome, and for a minute he remained there gazing at himself.

CHAPTER V

Before twelve o'clock next day he had bought a box of paints, brushes, and an easel. Pellerin agreed to give him lessons, and Frédéric brought him to his lodgings to see whether anything was wanting among his painting utensils.

Deslauriers had come back, and the second armchair was occupied by a young man. The clerk said, pointing towards him:

"Here he is! Sénécal!"

Frédéric disliked this young man. His forehead was heightened by the way in which he wore his hair, cut straight like a brush. There was a certain hard, cold look in his grey eyes; and his long black coat, his entire costume, smacked of the pedagogue and the ecclesiastic.

They first discussed topics of the hour, amongst others Rossini's *Stabat*. Sénécal, in answer to a question, declared that he never went to the theatre. Pellerin opened the box of paints.

"Are these all for you?" said the clerk.

"Why, certainly!"

"Well, really! What a notion!"

And he leaned across the table, at which the mathematical tutor was turning the pages of a volume of Louis Blanc.[16] He had brought it with him, and was reading passages from it in a low voices, while Pellerin and Frédéric were examining together the palette, the knife, and the bladders; then the talk came round to the dinner at Arnoux's.

"The art-dealer, is it?" asked Sénécal. "A fine gentleman, truly!"

"Why do you say that?" said Pellerin.

Sénécal replied: "A man who makes money by political maneuvres!"

And he went on to talk about a well-known lithograph, in which the Royal Family was all represented as being engaged in edifying occupations: Louis Philippe had a copy of the Code in his hand; the

Queen had a Catholic prayer-book; the Princesses were embroidering; the Duc de Nemours was girding on a sword; M. de Joinville was showing a map to his young brothers; and in the background could be seen a bed with two compartments. This picture, which was entitled "A Good Family," was a source of delight to commonplace middle-class people, but of grief to patriots. Pellerin, in a tone of vexation, as if he had been the producer of this work himself, observed that every opinion had some value. Sénécal protested: Art should aim exclusively at promoting morality amongst the masses! The only subjects that ought to be reproduced were those which impelled people to virtuous actions; all others were harmful.

"But that depends on the execution," cried Pellerin. "I might produce masterpieces."

"So much the worse for you, then; you have no right——"

"What?"

"No, monsieur, you have no right to excite my interest in matters of which I disapprove. What need have we of laborious trifles, from which it is impossible to derive any benefit—those Venuses, for instance, with all your landscapes? I see there no instruction for the people! Show us rather their miseries! arouse enthusiasm in us for their sacrifices! Ah, my God! there is no lack of subjects—the farm, the workshop——"

Pellerin stammered forth his indignation at this, and, imagining that he had found an argument:

"Molière, do you accept him?"

"Certainly!" said Sénécal. "I admire him as the precursor of the French Revolution."

"Ha! the Revolution! What art! Never was there a more pitiful period!"

"None greater, Monsieur!"

Pellerin folded his arms, and looking at him straight in the face:

"You have the appearance of a member of the National Guard!"*

His opponent, accustomed to discussions, responded:

"I am not, and I detest it just as much as you. But with such principles we corrupt the crowd. This sort of thing, however, is

---

*The civic militia created during the French Revolution to maintain public order; it was abolished in 1871.

profitable to the Government. It would not be so powerful but for the complicity of rogues like Arnoux."

The painter took up the defence of the art-dealer, for Sénécal's opinions exasperated him. He even went so far as to maintain that Arnoux was really a man with a heart of gold, devoted to his friends, deeply attached to his wife.

"Oho! if you offered him a good sum, he would not refuse to let her serve as a model."

Frédéric turned pale.

"So then, has he done you some great injury, Monsieur?"

"Me? no! I saw him once at a café with a friend. That's all."

Sénécal had spoken truly. But he had his teeth daily set on edge by the announcements in *L'Art Industriel.* Arnoux was for him the representative of a world which he considered fatal to democracy. An austere Republican, he suspected that there was something corrupt in every form of elegance, since he wanted for nothing and was inflexible in his integrity.

They found some difficulty in resuming the conversation. The painter soon recalled his appointment, the tutor his pupils; and, when they had gone, after a long silence, Deslauriers asked a number of questions about Arnoux.

"You will introduce me there later, will you not, old fellow?"

"Certainly," said Frédéric.

Then they thought about settling their living arrangements. Deslauriers had without much trouble obtained the post of second clerk in a solicitor's office; he had also entered his name for the terms at the Law School, and bought the necessary books; and the life of which they had dreamed now began.

It was delightful, thanks to their youth, which made everything seem beautiful. As Deslauriers had said nothing as to any financial arrangement, Frédéric did not refer to the subject. He paid all the expenses, kept the cupboard well stocked, and looked after all the household requirements; but if the concierge needed to be reprimanded, the clerk took that on his own shoulders, still playing the part, which he had assumed in their college days, of protector and senior.

Separated all day long, they met again in the evening. Each took his place at the fireside and set about his work. But ere long it would be interrupted. Then would follow endless outpourings, unaccountable bursts of merriment, and occasional disputes about the lamp flaring too much or a book being mislaid, momentary quarrels which subsided in hearty laughter.

While in bed they left open the door of the little room where Deslauriers slept, and kept chattering to each other from a distance.

In the morning they walked in their shirt-sleeves on the terrace. The sun rose; light vapours passed over the river. From the flower-market close beside them the noise of shouting reached their ears; and the smoke from their pipes whirled round in the clear air, which was refreshing to their eyes still puffy from sleep. While they inhaled it, their hearts swelled with great expectations.

When it was not raining on Sunday they went out together, and, arm in arm, they sauntered through the streets. The same reflection nearly always occurred to them at the same time, or else they would go on chatting without noticing anything around them. Deslauriers longed for riches, as a means for gaining power over men. He was anxious to possess an influence over a vast number of people, to create a great stir, to have three secretaries under his command, and to give a big political dinner once a week. Frédéric would have furnished for himself a palace in the Moorish fashion, to spend his life reclining on cashmere divans, to the murmur of a fountain, attended by negro pages. And these things, of which he had only dreamed, became in the end so real that they made him feel as dejected as if he had lost them.

"What is the use of talking about all these things," said he, "when we'll never have them?"

"Who knows?" returned Deslauriers.

In spite of his democratic views, he urged Frédéric to get an introduction into the Dambreuses' house.The other, by way of objection, pointed to the failure of his previous attempts.

"Bah! go back there. They'll give you an invitation!"

Towards the close of the month of March, they received amongst other large bills that of the restaurant-keeper who supplied them with dinners. Frédéric, not having the entire amount, borrowed a hundred crowns from Deslauriers. A fortnight afterwards, he renewed the same request, and the clerk lectured him on the extravagant habits which he acquired in the Arnoux's society.

As a matter of fact, he had no restraint in this respect. A view of Venice, a view of Naples, and another of Constantinople occupying the centre of three walls respectively, equestrian subjects by Alfred de Dreux here and there, a group by Pradier over the mantelpiece, issues of *L'Art Industriel* lying on the piano, and works in folders in the corners of the flour, encumbered the apartment which he occupied to such an extent that it was hard to find a place to lay a book on, or to move one's elbows about freely. Frédéric maintained that he needed all this for his painting.

He pursued his art-studies under Pellerin. But when he called on the artist, the latter was often out, being accustomed to attend every funeral and public occurrence of which an account was given in the newspapers, and so it was that Frédéric spent entire hours alone in the studio. The quietude of this spacious room, which nothing disturbed save the scampering of the mice, the light falling from the ceiling, or the hissing noise of the stove, made him sink into a kind of intellectual ease. Then his eyes, wandering away from the task at which he was engaged, roamed over the chipped paint on the wall, around the objects on the whatnot, along the torsos on which the dust that had collected made, as it were, shreds of velvet; and, like a traveller who has lost his way in the middle of a wood, and whom every path brings back to the same spot, continually, he found underlying every idea in his mind the recollection of Madame Arnoux.

He selected days for calling on her. When he had reached the second floor, he would pause on the threshold, hesitating as to whether he ought to ring or not. Steps drew nigh, the door opened, and the announcement "Madame is gone out," a sense of relief would come upon him, as if a weight had been lifted from his heart.

Yet there were moments when he met her. On the first occasion there were three other ladies with her; the next time it was in the afternoon, and Mademoiselle Marthe's writing-master came on the scene. Besides, the men who were invited to Madame Arnoux's dinner parties did not pay her visits. For the sake of prudence he deemed it better not to call again.

But he did not fail to present himself regularly at the office of *L'Art Industriel* every Wednesday in order to get an invitation to the Thursday dinners, and he remained there after all the others, even longer than Regimbart, up to the last moment, pretending to be looking at an engraving or to be running his eye through a newspaper. At last Arnoux would say to him, "Are you free to-morrow evening?" and, before the sentence was finished, he would give an affirmative answer. Arnoux appeared to have taken a fancy to him. He showed him how to become a good judge of wines, how to make hot punch, and how to prepare a woodcock ragoût. Frédéric meekly followed his advice, feeling an attachment to everything connected with Madame Arnoux—her furniture, her servants, her house, her street.

During these dinners he scarcely uttered a word; he kept gazing at her. She had a little mole close to her temple. Her head-bands were darker than the rest of her hair, and were always a little damp at the edges; from time to time she stroked them with only two fingers. He knew the shape of each of her nails. He took delight in listening to the rustle of her silk skirt as she swept past doors; he stealthily inhaled the perfume that came from her handkerchief; her comb, her gloves, her rings were for him things of special interest, important as works of art, almost endowed with life like people; all took possession of his heart and strengthened his passion.

He had not been sufficiently self-contained to conceal it from Deslauriers. When he came home from Madame Arnoux's, he would wake up his friend, as if inadvertently, in order to have an opportunity of talking about her.

Deslauriers, who slept in the little room, close to where they had their water-supply, would give a great yawn. Frédéric seated himself on the side of the bed. At first, he spoke about the dinner; then he referred to a thousand petty details, in which he saw marks of contempt or of affection. On one occasion, for instance, she had refused his arm, in order to take Dittmer's; and Frédéric vented his humiliation:

"Ah! how stupid!"

Or else she had called him her "dear friend."

"Then go after her!"

"But I dare not do that," said Frédéric.

"Well, then, think no more about her! Good night!"

Deslauriers thereupon turned on his side, and fell asleep. He felt utterly unable to comprehend this love, which seemed to him the last weakness of adolescence; and, as his own company was apparently not enough to satisfy Frédéric, he conceived the idea of bringing together, once a week, those whom they both recognised as friends.

They came on Saturday about nine o'clock. The three Algerine curtains were carefully drawn. The lamp and four candles were burning. In the middle of the table the tobacco-jar, filled with pipes, displayed itself between the beer-bottles, the tea-pot, a flagon of rum, and some fancy biscuits. They discussed the immortality of the soul, and drew comparisons between the different professors.

One evening Hussonnet introduced a tall young man, attired in a frock-coat which was too short in the sleeves, and with a look of embarrassment on his face. It was the young fellow whom they had gone to release from the guard-house the year before.

As he had not been able to restore the box of lace which he had lost in the scuffle, his employer had accused him of theft, and threatened to prosecute him. He was now a clerk in a wagon-office. Hussonnet had come across him that morning at the corner of the street, and brought him along, for Dussardier, in a spirit of gratitude, had expressed a wish to see "the other."

He held out towards Frédéric the cigar-holder, still full, which he had religiously preserved, in the hope of being able to give it back. The young men invited him to pay them a second visit; and he was not slow in doing so.

They all had common interests. At first, their hatred of the Government reached the height of unquestionable dogma. Martinon alone attempted to defend Louis Philippe. They overwhelmed him with the commonplaces scattered through the newspapers—the "Bastillization" of Paris, the September laws, Pritchard, Lord Guizot[17]—so that Martinon held his tongue for fear of giving offence to somebody. During his seven years at college he had never incurred a single penalty, and at the Law School he knew how to make himself agreeable to the professors. He usually wore a big frock-coat of the colour of putty, with india-rubber goloshes; but one evening he presented himself arrayed like a bridegroom, in a velvet roll-collar waistcoat, a white tie, and a gold chain.

The astonishment of the other young men was greatly increased when they learned that he had just come away from M. Dambreuse's house. In fact, the banker Dambreuse had just bought a portion of an extensive woodland from Martinon senior; and, when the gentleman introduced his son, the other had invited them both to dinner.

"Was there a good supply of truffles there?" asked Deslauriers. "And did you take his wife by the waist between the two doors, *sicut decet?*"

Hereupon the conversation turned on women. Pellerin would not admit that there were beautiful women (he preferred tigers); besides the human female was an inferior creature in the æsthetic hierarchy:

"What fascinates you is just the very thing that degrades her as an idea; I mean her breasts, her hair——"

"Nevertheless," urged Frédéric, "long black hair and large dark eyes——"

"Oh! we know all about that," cried Hussonnet. "Enough of Andalusian beauties.* Those things are out of date; no thank you! For the fact is a fast woman is more amusing than the Venus of Milo. Let us be lusty for Heaven's sake, and in the style of the Regency,† if we can!

'Flow, generous wines; ladies, deign to smile!'

We must pass from brunettes to blondes. Is that your opinion, Father Dussardier?"

Dussardier did not reply. They all pressed him to ascertain what his tastes were.

"Well," said he, blushing, "for my part, I would like to love the same one always!"

This was said in such a way that there was a moment of silence, some of them being surprised at this candour, and others finding in his words, perhaps, the secret yearning of their souls.

Sénécal placed his glass of beer on the mantelpiece, and declared dogmatically that, as prostitution was tyrannical and marriage immoral, it was better to practice abstinence. Deslauriers regarded

---

*The Romantics Alfred de Musset (1810–1857), Victor Hugo (1802–1885), and Théophile Gautier (1811–1872) had rendered Spain fashionable.

†The regency of Philippe d'Orléans (1715–1723) was a time of moral laxity.

women as a source of amusement—nothing more. M. de Cisy looked upon them full of fear.

Brought up under the eyes of a grandmother who was devout, he found the society of those young fellows as alluring as a house of ill-repute and as instructive as the Sorbonne.* They gave him lessons without limit; and so much zeal did he exhibit that he even wanted to smoke in spite of the nausea that upset him every time he tried it. Frédéric paid him the greatest attention. He admired the shade of this young gentleman's cravat, the fur on his overcoat, and especially his boots, as thin as gloves, and so very neat and fine that they had a look of insolent superiority. His carriage used to wait for him below in the street.

One evening, after his departure, when there was a fall of snow, Sénécal began to feel sorry for his coachman. He criticized the kid-gloved exquisites at the Jockey Club. He had more respect for a workman than for these fine gentlemen.

"For my part, anyhow, I work for my livelihood! I am a poor man!"

"That's quite evident," said Frédéric, finally losing patience.

The tutor developed a grudge against him for this remark.

But, as Regimbart said he knew Sénécal pretty well, Frédéric, wishing to be civil to a friend of the Arnoux, asked him to come to the Saturday meetings; and the two patriots were glad to be brought together in this way.

However, they took opposite views of things.

Sénécal—who had a skull of the angular type—fixed his attention merely on systems, whereas Regimbart, on the contrary, saw in facts nothing but facts. The thing that chiefly troubled him was the Rhine frontier. He claimed to be an authority on the subject of artillery, and got his clothes made by a tailor of the Polytechnic School.†

The first day, when they offered some cakes, he disdainfully shrugged his shoulders, saying that these might suit women; and on the next few occasions his manner was not much more gracious.

---

*The ancient Faculty of Theology of Paris had then become a public university.

†The École Polytechnique, founded in 1794, a very prestigious school of science and engineering.

Whenever speculative ideas had reached a certain point, he would mutter: "Oh! no Utopias, no dreams!" On the subject of Art (though he used to visit the studios, where he occasionally gave fencing lessons) his opinions were not remarkable for their excellence. He compared the style of M. Marast to that of Voltaire, and Mademoiselle Vatnaz to Madame de Staël, on account of an Ode on Poland in which "there was some spirit." In short, Regimbart bored everyone, and especially Deslauriers, for the Citizen was a friend of the Arnoux family. Now the clerk was most anxious to visit those people in the hope that he might make the acquaintance of some people there who would be an advantage to him. "When are you going to take me there with you?" he would ask Frédéric. Arnoux was either overburdened with business, or else on a journey. Then it was not worth while, as the dinners were coming to an end.

If he had been called on to risk his life for his friend, Frédéric would have done so. But, as he was desirous of making as good a figure as possible, and with this view was most careful about his language and manners, and so attentive to his clothes that he always presented himself at the office of *L'Art Industriel* irreproachably gloved, he was afraid that Deslauriers, with his shabby black coat, his attorney-like exterior, and his inappropriate remarks, might make a poor impression on Madame Arnoux, and thus compromise him and lower him in her estimation. The others would have been bad enough, but Deslauriers would have embarrassed him a thousand times more. The clerk saw that his friend did not wish to keep his promise, and Frédéric's silence only added to the insult.

He would have liked to exercise absolute control over him, to see him develop in accordance with the ideal of their youth; and his inactivity aroused the clerk's indignation as a breach of duty and a lack of loyalty towards himself. Moreover, Frédéric, with his thoughts full of Madame Arnoux, frequently talked about her husband; and Deslauriers now began an intolerable game of repeating the name a hundred times a day, at the end of each remark, like an idiot's nervous tic. When there was a knock at the door, he would answer, "Come in, Arnoux!" At the restaurant he asked for a Brie cheese "in imitation of Arnoux," and at night, pretending to wake up from a bad dream, he would rouse his comrade by howling out,

"Arnoux! Arnoux!" At last Frédéric, worn out, said to him one day, in a piteous voice:

"Oh! leave me alone with your Arnoux!"

"Never!" replied the clerk:

> "He is here, he's there, he's everywhere, burning or icy cold,
> The image of Arnoux—"*

"Hold your tongue, I tell you!" exclaimed Frédéric, raising his fist.

Then less angrily he added:

"You know well this is a painful subject to me."

"Oh! forgive me, old fellow," returned Deslauriers with a very low bow. "From this time forth we will be considerate towards Mademoiselle's nerves. Again, I say, forgive me. A thousand pardons!"

And so this little joke came to an end.

But, three weeks later, one evening, Deslauriers said to him:

"Well, I have just seen Madame Arnoux."

"Where, pray?"

"At the Palais, with Balandard, the solicitor. A dark woman, is she not, of medium height?"

Frédéric made a gesture of assent. He waited for Deslauriers to speak. At the least expression of admiration he would have been most effusive, and would have hugged him. However, Deslauriers remained silent. At last, unable to contain himself any longer, Frédéric, with assumed indifference, asked him what he thought of her.

Deslauriers considered that "she was not so bad, but still nothing extraordinary."

"Ha! That's what you think!" said Frédéric.

They soon reached the month of August, the time when he was to present himself for his second examination. According to the prevailing opinion, a fortnight was enough time to prepare. Frédéric, having full confidence in his own powers, swallowed up in one go the first four books of the Code of Procedure, the first three of the Penal Code, many bits of the system of criminal

---

*This is a parody of a poem about Napoléon I by Victor Hugo in *Les Orientales* (1829; *Oriental Poems*).

investigation, and a part of the Civil Code, with the annotations of M. Poncelet. The night before, Deslauriers made him run through the whole course, a process which did not finish till morning, and, in order to take advantage of even the last quarter of an hour, continued questioning him while they walked along together.

As several examinations were taking place at the same time, there were many persons in the precincts, and amongst others Hussonnet and Cisy: young men never failed to come and watch these ordeals when the fortunes of their comrades were at stake. Frédéric put on the traditional black gown; then, followed by the throng, with three other students, he entered a spacious room, into which the light penetrated through uncurtained windows, and which was garnished with benches arranged along the walls. In the centre, leather chairs were drawn round a table adorned with a green cover. This separated the candidates from the examiners in their red gowns and ermine shoulder-knots, the head examiners wearing gold-braided caps.

Frédéric found himself the last but one in the group—an unfortunate place. In answer to the first question, as to the difference between a convention and a contract, he defined the one as if it were the other; and the professor, who was a fair sort of man, said to him, "Don't be agitated, Monsieur! Compose yourself!" Then, having asked two easy questions, which were answered in a doubtful fashion, he passed on at last to the fourth candidate. This wretched beginning demoralized Frédéric. Deslauriers, who was facing him amongst the spectators, made a sign to him to indicate that it was not a hopeless case yet; and at the second batch of questions, dealing with the criminal law, he came out tolerably well. But after the third, with regard to sealed wills, while the examiner remained impassive the whole time, his mental distress doubled; for Hussonnet brought his hands together as if to applaud, whilst Deslauriers shrugged his shoulders. Finally, the moment was reached when it was necessary to be examined on Procedure. The professor, displeased at listening to theories opposed to his own, asked him in a brusque tone:

"And so this is your view, monsieur? How do you reconcile the principle of article 1351 of the Civil Code with this application by a third party to set aside a judgment by default?"

Frédéric had a great headache from not having slept the night before. A ray of sunlight, penetrating through one of the slits in a Venetian blind, fell on his face. Standing behind the seat, he kept wriggling about and tugging at his moustache.

"I am still awaiting your answer," the man with the gold-braided cap observed.

And as Frédéric's movements, no doubt, irritated him:

"You won't find it in that moustache of yours!"

This sarcasm made the spectators laugh. The professor, feeling flattered, relented. He put two more questions with reference to adjournment and summary jurisdiction, then nodded his head by way of approval. The examination was over. Frédéric retired into the vestibule.

While an usher was taking off his gown, to draw it over some other person immediately afterwards, his friends gathered around him, and succeeded in bothering him with their conflicting opinions as to the result of his examination. Presently the announcement was made in a sonorous voice at the entrance of the hall: "The third candidate was—referred back!"

"Sent packing!" said Hussonnet. "Let us be on our way!"

In front of the concierge's lodge they met Martinon, flushed, excited, with a smile on his face and the halo of victory around his brow. He had just passed his final examination without any impediment. All he had now to do was the thesis. Before a fortnight he would be a licentiate. His family enjoyed the acquaintance of a Minister; "a beautiful career" was opening before him.

"He's got you beaten, hasn't he?" said Deslauriers.

There is nothing so humiliating as to see blockheads succeed in undertakings in which we fail. Frédéric, filled with vexation, replied that he did not care a straw about the matter. He had higher pretensions; and as Hussonnet made a show of leaving, Frédéric took him aside, and said to him:

"Not a word about this to them, mind you!"

It was easy to keep it secret, since Arnoux was leaving the next morning for Germany.

When he came back in the evening the clerk found his friend singularly changed: he danced about and whistled; and the other was astonished at this capricious change of mood. Frédéric declared that he did not intend to go home to his mother, as he meant to spend his holidays working.

At the news of Arnoux's departure, a feeling of delight had taken possession of him. He might present himself at the house whenever he liked without any fear of having his visits broken in upon. The consciousness of absolute security would make him self-confident. At last he would not have to be aloof, he would not be separated from her! Something more powerful than an iron chain attached him to Paris; a voice from the depths of his heart called out to him to remain.

There were certain obstacles in his path. These he got over by writing to his mother: he first of all admitted that he had failed to pass, owing to alterations made in the course—a mere mischance—an unfair thing; besides, all the great lawyers (he referred to them by name) had been rejected at their examinations. But he calculated on presenting himself again in the month of November. Now, having no time to lose, he would not go home this year; and he asked, in addition to the quarterly allowance, for two hundred and fifty francs, to get coached in law by a private tutor, which would be of great assistance to him; and he threw around the entire epistle a garland of regrets, condolences, expressions of endearment, and protestations of filial love.

Madame Moreau, who had been expecting him the following day, was doubly grieved. She threw a veil over her son's misadventure, and in answer told him to "come all the same." Frédéric would not give way, and the result was a falling out between them. However, at the end of the week, he received the amount of the quarter's allowance together with the sum required for the payment of the private tutor, which helped to pay for a pair of pearl-grey trousers, a white felt hat, and a gold-headed switch.

When he had procured all these things he thought:

"Perhaps this is only a silly whim!"

And a feeling of considerable hesitation took possession of him.

In order to make sure as to whether he ought to call on Madame Arnoux, he tossed three coins into the air in succession. On each occasion luck was in his favour. So then Fate must have ordained it. He hailed a cab and drove to the Rue de Choiseul.

He quickly ascended the staircase and pulled the bell-cord, but without effect. He felt as if he were about to faint.

Then, with fierce energy, he shook the heavy silk tassel. There was a resounding peal which gradually died away till no further sound was heard. Frédéric got rather frightened.

He pasted his ear to the door—not a breath! He looked in through the key-hole, and only saw two reeds on the wall-paper in the midst of designs of flowers. At last, he was on the point of going away when he changed his mind. This time, he gave a timid little ring. The door flew open, and Arnoux himself appeared on the threshold, with his hair all in disorder, his face crimson, and his features distorted by an expression of sullen embarrassment.

"Hello! What the devil brings you here? Come in!"

He led Frédéric, not into the boudoir or into the bed-room, but into the dining-room, where on the table could be seen a bottle of champagne and two glasses; and, in an abrupt tone:

"There is something you want to ask me, my dear friend?"

"No! nothing! nothing!" stammered the young man, trying to think of some excuse for his visit.

At last, he said to Arnoux that he had called to know whether they had heard from him, as Hussonnet had announced that he had gone to Germany.

"Not at all!" returned Arnoux. "What a feather-headed fellow that is to take everything in the wrong way!"

In order to conceal his agitation, Frédéric kept walking around the dining-room. Happening to come into contact with a chair, he knocked down a parasol which had been laid across it, and the ivory handle broke.

"Good heavens!" he exclaimed. "How sorry I am for having broken Madame Arnoux's parasol!"

At this remark, the art-dealer raised his head and smiled in a very peculiar fashion. Frédéric, seizing the opportunity thus offered to talk about her, added shyly:

"Could I see her?"

No. She had gone to the country to see her sick mother.

He did not venture to ask any questions as to the length of time that she would be away. He merely enquired what region Madame Arnoux' came from.

"Chartres. Does this astonish you?"

"Astonish me? Oh, no! Why should it! Not in the least!"

After that, they could find absolutely nothing to talk about. Arnoux, having made a cigarette for himself, kept walking round the table, puffing. Frédéric, standing near the stove, stared at the walls, the whatnot, and the floor; and delightful pictures flitted through his memory, or, rather, before his eyes. Then he decided to leave.

A piece of a newspaper, rolled up into a ball, lay on the floor in the hall. Arnoux snatched it up, and, raising himself on the tips of his toes, he stuck it into the bell, in order, as he said, that he might be able to go and finish his interrupted siesta. Then, as he shook Frédéric's hand:

"Kindly tell the concierge that I am not in."

And he shut the door after him with a bang.

Frédéric descended the staircase step by step. The failure of this first attempt discouraged him as to the possible results of those that might follow. Then began three months of absolute boredom. As he had nothing to do, his melancholy was only aggravated by his inactivity.

He spent whole hours gazing from the top of his balcony at the river as it flowed between the quays, with their bulwarks of grey stone, blackened here and there by the seams of the sewers, with a pontoon of washerwomen moored close to the bank, where some children were amusing themselves by making a water-spaniel swim in the slime. His eyes, turning away from the stone bridge of Nôtre Dame and the three suspension bridges, continually directed their glance towards the Quai-aux-Ormes, resting on a group of old trees, resembling the linden-trees of the Montereau wharf. The Saint-Jacques tower, the Hôtel de Ville, Saint-Gervais, Saint-Louis, and Saint-Paul, rose up in front of him amid a confused mass of roofs; and the genius of the July Column glittered at the eastern side like a large gold star, whilst at the other end the dome of the Tuileries showed its outlines against the sky in one great round mass of blue.[18] Madame Arnoux's house must be on this side in the rear!

He went back to his bedchamber; then, throwing himself on the sofa, he abandoned himself to a confused succession of thoughts—work plans, schemes dreams of the future. At last, in order to shake off his broodings, he went out into the fresh air.

He wandered at random into the Latin Quarter, usually so noisy, but deserted at this particular time, for the students had gone back to join their families. The huge walls of the colleges, which the silence seemed to lengthen, looked that much more melancholy. All sorts of peaceful sounds could be heard—the flapping of wings in cages, the noise made by the turning of a lathe, or the strokes of a cobbler's hammer; and the old-clothes men, standing in the middle of the street, looked up at each house fruitlessly. In the interior of a solitary café the barmaid was yawning between her two full decanters. The newspapers were left undisturbed on the tables of reading-rooms. In the ironing establishments linen quivered under the gusts of tepid wind. From time to time he stopped to look at the window of a secondhand book-shop; an omnibus which grazed the sidewalk as it came rumbling along made him turn round; and, when he found himself before the Luxembourg gardens,* he went no further.

Occasionally he was drawn towards the boulevards in the hope of finding something there that might amuse him. After he had passed through dark alleys, where his nostrils were greeted by fresh moist odours, he reached vast, desolate, open spaces, dazzling with light, in which monuments cast dark shadows at the side of the pavement. But once more the wagons and the shops appeared, and the crowd had the effect of stunning him, especially on Sunday, when, from the Bastille to the Madeleine, it kept swaying in one immense flood over the asphalt, in the midst of a cloud of dust, in an incessant clamour. He felt disgusted at the meanness of the faces, the silliness of the talk, and the idiotic self-satisfaction that seeped through these sweaty brows. However, the consciousness of being superior to these individuals mitigated the weariness which he experienced in gazing at them.

Every day he went to the office of *L'Art Industriel*; and in order to ascertain when Madame Arnoux would be back, he made elaborate enquiries about her mother. Arnoux's answer never varied—"the change for the better was continuing"—his wife, with his little daughter, would be returning the following week. The longer she delayed in coming back, the more uneasiness Frédéric exhibited, so

---

*The Luxembourg palace and gardens are in the Latin Quarter.

that Arnoux, touched by so much affection, brought him five or six times a week to dine at a restaurant.

In the long talks which they had together on these occasions Frédéric discovered that the art-dealer was not a very intellectual man. Arnoux might take notice of his cooler manner; and now Frédéric deemed it advisable to pay back, in a small way, his kindness.

So, being anxious to do things nicely the young man sold all his new clothes to a secondhand clothes-dealer for the sum of eighty francs, and having added to it a hundred more francs which he had left, he called at Arnoux's house to bring him out to dine. Regimbart happened to be there, and all three of them set forth for Les Trois Frères Provençaux.

The Citizen began by taking off his frock-coat, and, knowing that the two others would defer to his gastronomic tastes, drew up the *menu*. But in vain did he make his way to the kitchen to speak to the *chef*, go down to the cellar, with every corner of which he was familiar, and send for the master of the establishment, who he blew up at. He was not satisfied with the dishes, the wines, or the attendance. At each new dish, at each fresh bottle, as soon as he had swallowed the first mouthful, the first draught, he threw down his fork or pushed his glass some distance away from him; then, leaning on his elbows on the table-cloth, and stretching out his arms, he declared in a loud tone that he could no longer dine in Paris! Finally, not knowing what to put into his mouth, Regimbart ordered haricots dressed with oil, "quite plain," which, though only a partial success, slightly appeased him. Then he had a talk with the waiter all about the latter's predecessors at the "Provençaux":—"What had become of Antoine? And a fellow named Eugène? And Théodore, the little fellow who always used to attend down stairs? There was much finer fare in those days, and Burgundy vintages the like of which they would never see again."

Then there was a discussion as to the value of property in the suburbs, Arnoux having speculated in that way, and looked on it as a safe thing. In the meantime, however, he was losing interest on his money. As he did not want to sell out at any price, Regimbart would find out some one; and so these two gentlemen proceeded at the close of the dessert to make calculations with a lead pencil.

They went out to get coffee in the bar on the ground-floor in the Passage du Saumon. Frédéric had to remain on his feet while interminable games of billiards were being played, drenched in innumerable glasses of beer; and he lingered on there till midnight without knowing why, through lack of energy, through sheer senselessness, in the vague expectation that something might happen which would give a favourable turn to his love.

When, then, would he next see her? Frédéric was in a state of despair about it. But, one evening, towards the close of November, Arnoux said to him:

"My wife, you know, came back yesterday!"

Next day, at five o'clock, he made his way to her house. He began by congratulating her on her mother's recovery from such a serious illness.

"Why, no! Who told you that?"

"Arnoux!"

She let out a slight "Ah!" then added that she had grave fears at first, which, however, had now been dispelled. She was seated close beside the fire in an upholstered easy-chair. He was on the sofa, with his hat between his knees; and the conversation was difficult to carry on, as it was broken off nearly every minute, so he had no chance of voicing his sentiments. But, when he began to complain of having to study legal quibbles, she answered, "Oh! I understand—business!" and she let her face fall, buried suddenly in her own reflections.

He was eager to know what they were, and could not bestow a thought on anything else. The twilight shadows gathered around them.

She rose, having to go out about some shopping; then she reappeared in a bonnet trimmed with velvet, and a black mantle edged with gray fur. He plucked up courage and offered to accompany her.

It was now so dark that one could scarcely see anything. The air was cold, and had an unpleasant odour, due to a heavy fog, which partially blotted out the fronts of the houses. Frédéric inhaled it with delight; for he could feel through the wadding of his coat the form of her arm; and her hand, cased in a chamois glove with two buttons, her little hand which he would have liked to cover with kisses, leaned on his sleeve. Because of the slipperiness of the pavement, they lost their balance a little; it seemed to him as if they were both rocked by the wind in the midst of a cloud.

The glitter of the lamps on the boulevard brought him back to the realities of existence. The opportunity was a good one, there was no time to lose. He gave himself as far as the Rue de Richelieu to declare his love. But almost at that very moment, in front of a china-shop, she stopped abruptly and said to him:

"Here we are. Thanks. On Thursday—night?—as usual."

The dinners started again; and the more visits he paid at Madame Arnoux's, the more his lovesickness increased.

The contemplation of this woman had an enervating effect upon him, like the use of a perfume that is too strong. It penetrated into the very depths of his nature, and became almost a kind of habitual sensation, a new mode of existence.

The prostitutes whom he brushed past under the gaslight, the female singers breaking into song, the ladies rising on horseback at full gallop, the shopkeepers' wives on foot, the grisettes at their windows, all women brought her to mind, either from the effect of their resemblance to her or by the violent contrast. As he walked along by the shops, he gazed at the cashmeres, the laces, and the jewelled eardrops, imagining how they would look draped around her figure, sewn in her corsage, or lighting up her dark hair. In the flower-girls' baskets the bouquets blossomed for her to choose one as she passed. In the shoemakers' show-windows the little satin slippers with swan's-down edges seemed to be waiting for her foot. Every street led towards her house; the hackney-coaches stood in their places to carry her home the more quickly; Paris became associated with her, and the great city, with all its noises, roared around her like an immense orchestra.

When he went into the Jardin des Plantes the sight of a palm-tree carried him off into distant countries. They were travelling together on the backs of dromedaries, under the awnings of elephants, in the cabin of a yacht amongst the blue archipelagoes, or side by side on mules with little bells attached to them who went stumbling through the grass over broken columns. Sometimes he stopped in the Louvre before old paintings; and, his love embracing her even in vanished centuries, he substituted her for the figures in the paintings. Wearing a hennin on her head, she was praying on bended knees before a stained-glass window. Lady Paramount of Castile or Flanders, she remained seated in a starched ruff and a boned bodice with big puff sleeves. Then he saw her descending some wide porphyry staircase in the midst of senators under a daïs of ostrich feathers in a gown of brocade. At another time he dreamed of her in yellow silk trousers on the cushions of a harem—and all that was beautiful, the twinkling of the stars, certain melodies the turn of a phrase, the outlines of a face, led him to think about her suddenly and unconsciously.

As for trying to make her his mistress, he was sure that any such attempt would be futile.

One evening, Dittmer, on his arrival, kissed her on the forehead; Lovarias did the same, observing:

"You give me leave—don't you?—as it is a friend's privilege?"

Frédéric stammered out:

"It seems to me that we are all friends."

"Not all old friends!" she returned.

This was a way of rebuffing him beforehand indirectly.

Besides, what was he to do? To tell her that he loved her? No doubt, she would refuse to listen to him or else she would feel indignant and turn him out of the house. But he preferred to submit to even the most painful ordeal rather than run the horrible risk of seeing her no more.

He envied pianists for their talents and soldiers for their scars. He longed for a dangerous attack of sickness, hoping in this way to make her take an interest in him.

One thing astonished him, that he felt in no way jealous of Arnoux; and he could not picture her in his imagination undressed, so natural did her modesty appear, and so far did her sexuality recede into a mysterious background.

Nevertheless, he dreamed of the happiness of living with her, of speaking familiarly with her, of passing his hand lingeringly over her hair or remaining in a kneeling posture on the floor, with both arms clasped round her waist, so as to drink in her soul through his eyes. To accomplish this it would be necessary to conquer Fate; and so, incapable of action, cursing God, and accusing himself of being a coward, he kept moving restlessly within the confines of his passion just as a prisoner keeps moving about in his dungeon. The pangs which he was perpetually enduring were choking him. For hours he would remain quite motionless, or else he would burst into tears; and one day when he had not the strength to restrain his emotion, Deslauriers said to him:

"Why, for goodness sake! what's the matter with you?"

Frédéric's nerves were unstrung. Deslauriers did not believe a word of it. At the sight of so much mental anguish, he felt all his old affection reawakening, and he tried to cheer up his friend. A man like him to let himself be depressed, what folly! It was all very well in one's youth; but, as one grows older, it is only loss of time.

"You are spoiling my Frédéric for me! I want the old one back. The same boy as ever! I liked him! Come, smoke a pipe, old chap! Shake yourself up a little! You'll drive me mad!"

"It is true," said Frédéric, "I am a fool!"

The clerk replied:

"Ah! old troubadour, I know well what's troubling you! A little affair of the heart? Confess it! Bah! One lost, four found instead! We console ourselves for virtuous women with the other sort. Would you like me to introduce you to some women? You have only to come to the Alhambra." (This was a dance-hall recently opened at the top of the Champs-Elysées, which had gone out of business after its second season due to premature spending on excessive luxuries.) "That's a place where there seems to be good fun. You can take your friends, if you like. I can even get Regimbart in for you."

Frédéric did not invite the Citizen. Deslauriers deprived himself of the pleasure of Sénécal's society. They took only Hussonnet and Cisy along with Dussardier; and the same hackney-coach let the group of five off at the entrance of the Alhambra.

Two Moorish galleries extended on the right and on the left, parallel to one another. The wall of a house opposite occupied the entire background; and the fourth side (that in which the restaurant was) ressembled a Gothic cloister with stained-glass windows. A sort of Chinese roof floated above the platform reserved for the musicians. The ground was covered all over with asphalt; the Venetian lanterns fastened to posts formed, at regular intervals, a crown of many-coloured flames above the heads of the dancers. A pedestal here and there supported a stone basin, from which rose a thin streamlet of water. In the midst of the foliage could be seen plaster statues, and Hebes and Cupid, sticky with oil paint; and the numerous walkways, garnished with sand of a deep yellow, carefully raked, made the garden look much larger than it was in reality.

Students were walking with their mistresses up and down; shop clerks strutted about with canes in their hands; lads fresh from college were smoking their cigars; old men had their dyed beards smoothed out with combs. There were English, Russians, men from South America, and three Orientals in tarbooshes. Lorettes, grisettes,* and loose women had come there in the hope of finding a protector, a lover, a gold coin, or simply for the pleasure of dancing; and their dresses, with tunics of water-green, cherry-red, or violet, swept along, fluttered between the ebony-trees and the lilacs. Nearly all the men's suits were of a check fabric; some of them had white trousers, in spite of the coolness of the evening. The gas lamps were lit.

Hussonnet was acquainted with a number of the women through his connection with the fashion-journals and the smaller theatres. He sent them kisses with the tips of his fingers, and from time to time he left his friends to go and chat with them.

Deslauriers felt jealous of these playful familiarities. He aggressively approached a tall, fair-haired girl, in a yellow costume. After looking at him with an air of sullenness, she said: "No! I wouldn't trust you, my good fellow!" and turned on her heel.

His next attack was on a stout brunette, who apparently was a little mad; for she jumped at the very first word he spoke to her, threatening, if he went any further, to call the police. Deslauriers made an effort to laugh; then, coming across a little woman sitting by herself under a gas-lamp, he asked her to be his partner in a quadrille.

The musicians, perched on the platform like apes, kept scraping and blowing away with intensity. The conductor, standing up, kept beating time mechanically. The dancers were crowded together and enjoyed themselves thoroughly. The bonnet-strings, getting loose, rubbed against the cravats; boots disappeared under petticoats; and

---

**Lorettes* and *grisettes* were working girls of easy mores.

all this bouncing went on to the accompaniment of the music. Deslauriers hugged the little woman, and, seized with the delirium of the cancan, whirled about, like a big marionnette, in the midst of the dancers. Cisy and Deslauriers were still promenading up and down. The young aristocrat kept ogling the girls, and, in spite of the clerk's exhortations, did not venture to talk to them, having an idea in his head that in the rooms of these sorts of women there was always "a man hidden in the armoire with a pistol who would come out of it and force you to sign a check over to him."

They came back and joined Frédéric. Deslauriers had stopped dancing; and they were all asking themselves how they were to finish up the evening, when Hussonnet exclaimed:

"Look! Here's the Marquise d'Amaëgui!"

The person referred to was a pale woman with a turned up nose, mittens up to her elbows, and big black curls hanging down the sides of her cheeks, like two dog's ears. Hussonnet said to her:

"We ought to organise a little fête at your house—a sort of Oriental rout. Try to collect some of your friends here for these French cavaliers. Well, what is annoying you? Are you going to wait for your hidalgo?"

The Andalusian hung her head: being well aware of the penny-pinching habits of her friend, she was afraid of having to pay for any refreshments he ordered. When, finally, she let the word "money" slip from her, Cisy offered five napoleons—all he had in his purse; and so it was settled. But Frédéric had disappeared.

He thought he had recognised the voice of Arnoux, and got a glimpse of a woman's hat; and accordingly he hastened towards a grove which was not far off.

Mademoiselle Vatnaz was alone there with Arnoux.

"Excuse me! Am I in the way?"

"Not in the least!" returned the art-dealer.

Frédéric, from the closing words of their conversation, understood that Arnoux had come to the Alhambra to talk over a pressing matter of business with Mademoiselle Vatnaz; and it was evident that he was not completely reassured, for he said to her, with some uneasiness:

"Are you quite sure?"

"Perfectly certain! You are loved. Ah! what a man you are!"

And she assumed a pouting look, pushing out her big lips, so red that they seemed tinged with blood. But she had wonderful eyes, of a tawny hue, with specks of gold in the pupils, full of vivacity, love and sensuality. They illuminated, like lamps, the rather yellow tint of her thin face. Arnoux seemed to enjoy her refusals. He stooped over her, saying:

"You are sweet—give me a kiss!"

She took him by the ears, and pressed her lips against his forehead.

At that moment the dancing stopped; and in the conductor's place appeared a handsome young man, rather portly, with a waxen complexion. He had long black hair, which he wore in a Christ-like fashion and a blue velvet waistcoat embroidered with large gold palm-branches. He looked as proud as a peacock, and as stupid as a turkey; and, having bowed to the audience, he began a little song. A villager was supposed to be giving an account of his journey to the capital. The singer used the dialect of Lower Normandy, and played the part of a drunken man. The refrain—

"Ah! How I laughed, how I laughed,
In that racy city of Paris!"

was greeted with enthusiastic stampings of feet. Delmas, "a vocalist who sang with expression," was too shrewd to let the excitement of his listeners cool. A guitar was quickly handed to him and he wailed a ballad entitled "The Albanian Girl's Brother."

The words recalled to Frédéric those which had been sung by the man in rags between the paddle-wheels of the steamboat. His eyes involuntarily focused on the hem of a dress spread out before him. After each couplet there was a long pause, and the blowing of the wind through the trees resembled the sound of the waves.

Mademoiselle Vatnaz, pushing aside with one hand the branches of a privet that was blocking her view of the platform, gazed fixedly at the singer, her nostrils flaring, eyes half-closed, and as if lost in rapture.

"Ah!" said Arnoux. "I understand why you are at the Alhambra tonight! Delmas appeals to you, my dear!"

She would admit nothing.

"Oh! What modesty!"

And pointing to Frédéric:

"Is it because of him? You would be mistaken. No young man could be more discreet."

The others, looking for their friend, came into the arbour. Hussonet introduced them. Arnoux distributed cigars and treated the group to water-ices.

Mademoiselle Vatnaz blushed the moment she saw Dussardier. She soon rose, and stretching out her hand towards him:

"You do not remember me, Monsieur Auguste?"

"How do you know her?" asked Frédéric.

"We used to live in the same house," he replied.

Cisy pulled him by the sleeve; they went out; and, scarcely had they disappeared, when Madame Vatnaz began to sing his praises. She even went so far as to add that he possessed "genius of the heart."

Then they chatted about Delmas, admitting that as a mimic he might be a success on the stage; and a discussion followed covering Shakespeare, Censorship, Style, the People, the receipts of the Porte Saint-Martin,* Alexandre Dumas, Victor Hugo, and Dumersan.

Arnoux had known many celebrated actresses; the young men inclined their heads to hear what he had to say about these ladies. But his words were drowned out by the noise of the music; and, as soon as the quadrille or the polka was over, they all squatted round the tables, called the waiter, and laughed. Bottles of beer and of effervescent lemonade opened with a pop amid the foliage; women clucked like hens; now and then, two gentlemen started to fight; and a thief was arrested.

The dancers soon spilled over onto the walks. Panting, with flushed, smiling faces, they were caught up in a whirlwind which lifted up the gowns with the coat-tails. The trombones brayed more loudly; the rhythmic movement became more rapid. Behind the mediæval cloister could be heard crackling sounds; fireworks went off; artificial suns began turning round; the gleam of the Bengal fires, like emeralds in colour, lighted up the entire garden for a minute; and, with the last rocket, a great sigh escaped from the assembled throng.

---

*Melodramas and Romantic dramas were performed at the Porte Saint-Martin Theater.

It slowly died away. A cloud of gunpowder floated into the air. Frédéric and Deslauriers were walking step by step through the midst of the crowd, when they happened to see something that made them suddenly stop: Martinon was in the act of paying some money at the cloakroom and he was accompanying a woman of fifty, ugly, magnificently dressed, and of questionable social rank.

"That sly dog," said Deslauriers, "is not as simple as we imagine. But where in the world is Cisy?"

Dussardier pointed out to them the bar, where they perceived the noble youth, with a bowl of punch before him, and a pink hat by his side, to keep him company. Hussonnet, who had been away for the past few minutes, reappeared at the same moment.

A young girl was leaning on his arm, and addressing him in a loud voice as "My little cat."

"Oh! no!" he said to her—"not in public! Call me rather 'Vicomte.' That gives one a cavalier style—Louis XIII. and floppy leather boots—the sort of thing I like! Yes, my good friends, this is an old flame—nice, isn't she?"—and he took her by the chin—"Salute these gentlemen! they are all the sons of peers of France. I keep company with them in order that they may get an appointment for me as an ambassador."

"How insane you are!" sighed Mademoiselle Vatnaz. She asked Dussardier to see her as far as her own door.

Arnoux watched them going off; then, turning towards Frédéric:

"Did you like Vatnaz? At any rate, you're not quite frank about these affairs. I believe you keep your amours hidden."

Frédéric, turning pale, swore that he kept nothing hidden.

"Can it be possible you don't know what it is to have a mistress?" said Arnoux.

Frédéric felt a longing to mention a woman's name at random. But the story might be repeated to her. So he replied that as a matter of fact he had no mistress.

The art-dealer reproached him for this.

"This evening you had a good opportunity! Why didn't you do like the others, each of whom went off with a woman?"

"Well, and what about yourself?" said Frédéric, provoked by his persistency.

"Oh! myself—that's quite a different matter, my lad! I go home to my own one!"

Then he called a cab, and disappeared.

The two friends walked towards their own destination. An east wind was blowing. They did not exchange a word. Deslauriers was regretting that he had not succeeded in making an impression before a certain newspaper-manager, and Frédéric was lost once more in his melancholy broodings. Finally, breaking the silence, he said that this ball appeared to him a stupid affair.

"Whose fault is it? If you had not left us, to join that Arnoux of yours——"

"Bah! anything I could have done would have been utterly useless!"

But the clerk had theories of his own. All that was necessary in order to get a thing was to desire it strongly.

"Nevertheless, you yourself, a little while ago——"

"I don't care a straw about that sort of thing!" returned Deslauriers, cutting short Frédéric's allusion.

"Am I going to get entangled with women?"

And he expressed his distaste for their affectations, their silly ways—in short, he disliked them.

"Don't be pretending, then!" said Frédéric.

Deslauriers became silent. Then, suddenly:

"Will you bet me a hundred francs that I won't 'make out' with the first woman that passes?"

"Yes—it's a bet!"

The first who passed was a hideous-looking beggar-woman, and they were giving up all hope of an opportunity presenting itself when, in the middle of the Rue de Rivoli, they saw a tall girl with a little box in her hand.

Deslauriers accosted her under the arcades. She turned abruptly by the Tuileries, and soon diverged into the Place du Carrousel. She glanced to the right and to the left. She ran after a hackney-coach; Deslauriers overtook her. He walked by her side, talking to her with expressive gestures. After a while, she accepted his arm, and they went on together along the quays. Then, when they reached the hill in front of the Châtelet, they strolled up and down for at least twenty minutes, like two sailors keeping watch. Then, all of a sudden, they passed over the Pont-au-Change, through the Flower Market, and along the Quai Napoléon. Frédéric came up behind them. Deslauriers gave him the impression that he would be in their way, and had only to follow his own example.

"How much have you got still?"

"Two hundred sous."

"That's enough—good night to you!"

Frédéric was seized with the astonishment one feels at seeing a practical joke succeed.

"He's just pulling my leg," was his thought. "Suppose I went back again?"

Perhaps Deslauriers imagined that he was envious of this love! "As if I had not one a hundred times more rare, more noble, more absorbing." He felt a sort of angry feeling propelling him onward. He arrived in front of Madame Arnoux's door.

None of the outer windows belonged to her rooms. Nevertheless, he remained with his eyes glued to the front of the house—as if he could, by his contemplation, break open the walls. No doubt, she was now deep in repose, tranquil as a sleeping flower, with her beautiful black hair resting on the lace of the pillow, her lips slightly parted, and one arm under her head. Then Arnoux's head rose before him, and he rushed away to escape this vision.

The advice which Deslauriers had given to him came back suddenly. It only filled him with horror. Then he walked about the streets.

When a pedestrian approached, he tried to distinguish the face. From time to time a ray of light passed between his legs, tracing a great quarter of a circle on the pavement; and in the shadows a man appeared with his basket and his lantern. The wind, here and there, made the sheet-iron flue of a chimney shake. Distant sounds reached his ears, mingling with the buzzing in his brain; and it seemed to him that he was listening to the indistinct flourish of quadrille music. His movements as he walked on perpetuated his feeling of intoxication. He found himself on the Pont de la Concorde.

Then he recalled that evening the previous winter, when, as he left her house for the first time, he was forced to stand still, so rapidly did his heart beat with the hopes that clasped it. And now they had all withered!

Dark clouds were drifting across the face of the moon. He gazed at it, musing on the vastness of space, the wretchedness of life, the nothingness of everything. The day dawned; his teeth began to chatter, and, half-asleep, wet with the morning mist, and bathed in tears, he asked himself, Why should I not make an end of it? All that was necessary was a single movement. The weight of his forehead dragged him along—he imagined his own dead body floating in the water. Frédéric stooped down. The parapet was rather wide, and it was through pure weariness that he did not make the attempt to leap over it.

Then fear swept over him. He reached the boulevards once more, and sank down upon a seat. He was aroused by some police-officers, who were convinced that he had been indulging a little too freely.

He resumed his walk. But, as he was exceedingly hungry, and as all the restaurants were closed, he went to get a "snack" at a tavern by the fish-markets; after which, thinking it too soon to go in yet, he kept sauntering about the Hôtel de Ville till a quarter past eight.

Deslauriers had long since gotten rid of his little tart; and he was writing at the table in the middle of his room. About four o'clock, M. de Cisy came in.

Thanks to Dussardier, he had enjoyed the society of a lady the night before; and he had even accompanied her home in the carriage with her husband to the very threshold of their house, where she had suggested meeting again. He had just left her. They had never heard her name before.

"And what do you propose that I do?" said Frédéric.

Thereupon the young gentleman began to ramble; he mentioned Mademoiselle Vatnaz, the Andalusian, and all the rest. Finally, with much circumlocution, he stated the object of his visit. Trusting in the discretion of his friend, he came to ask him for his assistance in taking an important step, after which he might definitely consider himself to be a man; and Frédéric showed no reluctance. He told the story to Deslauriers without explaining his part in it.

The clerk was of the opinion that he was now doing very well. This respect for his advice increased his good humour. It was through good humour that he had seduced, on the very first night, Mademoiselle Clémence Daviou, embroideress of military uniforms, the sweetest creature that ever lived, as slender as a reed, with large blue eyes, perpetually wide with wonder. The clerk had taken advantage of her simplicity to such an extent as to make her believe that he had been decorated. When they were alone together he wore his frock-coat adorned with a red ribbon, but did not wear it in public in order, as he put it, not to humiliate his employer. However, he kept her at a distance, allowed himself to be fawned upon, like a pasha, and, as a joke called her "daughter of the people." Every time they met, she brought him little bunches of violets. Frédéric would not have cared for a love affair of this sort.

Meanwhile, whenever they went out arm-in-arm to dine at Pinson's or Barillot's, he experienced a strange depression. Frédéric did not realise how much pain he had made Deslauriers endure for the past year, while brushing his nails before going out to dine in the Rue de Choiseul!

One evening, when from his balcony, he had just watched them as they went out together, he saw Hussonnet, some distance off, on the Pont d'Arcole. The Bohemian began calling him by making signals, and, when Frédéric had descended the five flights of stairs:

"Here is the thing—it is next Saturday, the 24th, Madame Arnoux's feast-day."

"How is that, when her name is Marie?"

"And Angèle also—no matter! They will entertain their guests at their country-house at Saint-Cloud. I was told to give you due notice about it. You'll find a carriage at the magazine-office at three o'clock. That's settled then! Excuse me for having disturbed you! But I have such a number of calls to make!"

Frédéric had scarcely turned round when his concierge placed a letter in his hand:

"Monsieur and Madame Dambreuse beg of Monsieur F. Moreau to do them the honour to come and dine with them on Saturday the 24th inst.—R.S.V.P."

"Too late!" he said to himself. Nevertheless, he showed the letter to Deslauriers, who exclaimed:

"Ha! at last! But you don't look as if you were pleased. Why?"

After some little hesitation, Frédéric said that he had another invitation for the same day.

"Do me the favor of sending the Rue de Choiseul packing! I'm not joking! I'll answer this for you if it embarrasses you."

And the clerk wrote an acceptance of the invitation in the third person.

Having seen nothing of the world save through the fever of his desires, he pictured it as an artificial creation functioning by virtue of mathematical laws. A dinner in the city, a meeting with a man in high office, a smile from a pretty woman, might, by a series of actions deducing themselves from one another, have gigantic results. Certain Parisian drawing-rooms were like those machines which take a material in the rough and render it a hundred times more valuable. He believed in courtesans advising diplomats, in wealthy marriages brought about by intrigues, in the cleverness of criminals, in the capacity of strong men for getting the better of fortune. In short, he considered it so useful to visit the Dambreuses, and talked about it so plausibly, that Frédéric was at a loss to know what was the best course to take.

The least he ought to do, as it was Madame Arnoux's feast-day, was to get her a present. He naturally thought of a parasol, in order to make reparation for his clumsiness. Now he came across a shot-silk parasol with a little carved ivory handle, which had come all the way from China. But the price of it was a hundred and seventy-five francs, and he had not a sou, having in fact to live on the credit of his next quarter's allowance. However, he wished to get it; he was determined to have it; and, in spite of his repugnance to doing so, he turned to Deslauriers.

Deslauriers answered Frédéric's first question by saying that he had no money.

"I need some," said Frédéric—"I need some very badly!"

As the other made the same excuse over again, he flew into a fit.

"You might find it to your advantage some time——"

"What do you mean by that?"

"Oh! nothing."

The clerk understood. He took the sum required out of his reserve-fund, and when he had counted out the money, coin by coin:

"I am not asking you for an IOU, since I'm living off of you!"

Frédéric threw his arms around his friend with a thousand affectionate protestations. Deslauriers received this display of emotion frigidly. Then, next morning, noticing the parasol on the top of the piano:

"Ah! it was for that!"

"I will send it, perhaps," said Frédéric, weakly.

Good fortune was on his side, for that evening he got a note with a black border from Madame Dambreuse announcing to him that she had lost an uncle, and excusing herself for having to defer till a later time the pleasure of making his acquaintance. At two o'clock, he reached the office of the art journal. Instead of waiting for him in order to drive him in his carriage, Arnoux had left the city the night before, unable to resist his desire to get some fresh air.

Every year it was his custom, as soon as the leaves were budding forth, to start early in the morning and to remain away several days, making long journeys across the fields, drinking milk at the farmhouses, romping with the village girls, asking questions about the harvest, and carrying back home with him lettuce wrapped in his handkerchief. Finally, realising a long-cherished dream of his, he had bought a country-house.

While Frédéric was talking to the art-dealer's clerk, Mademoiselle Vatnaz suddenly made her appearance, and was disappointed at not seeing Arnoux. He would, perhaps, be remaining away two days longer. The clerk advised her "to go there"—she could not go there; to write a letter—she was afraid that the letter might get lost. Frédéric offered to be the bearer of it himself. She rapidly scribbled off a letter, and implored him to let nobody see him delivering it.

Forty minutes afterwards, he found himself at Saint-Cloud.* The house, which was about a hundred yards from the bridge, stood half-way up the hill. The garden-walls were hidden by two rows of linden-trees, and a wide lawn descended to the bank of the river. The gate was open, and Frédéric went in.

Arnoux, stretched on the grass, was playing with a litter of kittens. This amusement appeared to absorb him completely. Mademoiselle Vatnaz's letter drew him out of his sleepy idleness.

"Darn it all!—what a bore! She is right, though; I must go."

Then, having stuck the missive into his pocket, he showed the young man through the grounds with manifest delight. He pointed

---

*Small town in the suburbs of Paris.

out everything—the stable, the cart-house, the kitchen. The drawing-room was at the right, on the side facing Paris, and looked out on a veranda with a trellis, covered over with clematis. Suddenly a few harmonious notes rang out above their heads: Madame Arnoux, thinking that there was nobody near, was singing to amuse herself. She executed scales, trills, arpeggios. There were long notes which seemed to remain suspended in the air; others fell in a rushing shower like the spray of a waterfall; and her voice passing out through the Venetian blind, cut its way through the deep silence and rose towards the blue sky. She ceased all at once, when M. and Madame Oudry, two neighbours, arrived.

Then she appeared herself at the top of the steps in front of the house; and, as she descended, he caught a glimpse of her foot. She wore little open shoes of reddish-brown leather, with three straps criss-crossing each other so as to draw over her stockings a lattice of gold.

Those who had been invited arrived. With the exception of Maître Lefaucheur, a lawyer, they were the same guests who came to the Thursday evening dinners. Each of them had brought a present—Dittmer a Syrian scarf, Rosenwald a scrap-book of ballads, Burieu a water-colour painting, Sombary one of his own caricatures, and Pellerin a charcoal-drawing, representing a kind of dance of death, a hideous fantasy, the execution of which was rather poor. Hussonnet dispensed with the formality of a present.

Frédéric was waiting to offer his, after the others.

She thanked him very much for it. Thereupon, he said:

"Why, 'tis almost a debt. I have been so much annoyed——"

"At what, pray?" she returned. "I don't understand."

"Come! dinner is waiting!" said Arnoux, catching hold of his arm; then in a whisper: "You are not very sharp, are you!"

Nothing could have been prettier than the dining-room, painted in sea-green. At one end, a nymph of stone was dipping her toe in a basin formed like a shell. Through the open windows the entire garden could be seen with the long lawn flanked by an old Scotch fir, three-quarters bare; groups of flowers filled it out in uneven beds; and at the other side of the river extended in a wide semicircle the Bois de Boulogne, Neuilly, Sèvres, and Meudon. Before the railed gate in front, a canoe with sail outspread was tacking about.

They chatted first about the view in front of them, then about the countryside in general; and they were beginning to plunge into discussions when Arnoux, at half-past nine o'clock, ordered the horse to be put to the carriage. His cashier had sent him a letter calling him back to Paris.

"Would you like me to go back with you?" said Madame Arnoux.

"Why, certainly!" and, making her a graceful bow: "You know well, madame, that it is impossible to live without you!"

Everyone congratulated her on having so good a husband.

"Ah! it is because I am not the only one," she replied quietly, pointing towards her little daughter.

Then, the conversation having turned once more to painting, there was some talk about a Ruysdaël, for which Arnoux expected a big sum, and Pellerin asked him if it were true that the celebrated Saul Mathias from London had come over during the past month to make him an offer of twenty-three thousand francs for it.

" 'Tis a fact!" and turning towards Frédéric: "That was the very same gentleman I brought with me a few days ago to the Alhambra, much against my will, I assure you, for these English are by no means amusing companions."

Frédéric, who suspected that Mademoiselle Vatnaz's letter contained some reference to an intrigue, was amazed at the facility with which Arnoux found a way of passing it off as a perfectly honourable transaction; but his new lie, which was quite needless, made the young man open his eyes in speechless astonishment.

The art-dealer added, with an air of simplicity:

"What's the name, by-the-by, of that young fellow, your friend?"

"Deslauriers," said Frédéric quickly.

And, in order to repair the injustice which he felt he had done to his comrade, he praised him as one who possessed remarkable ability.

"Ah! indeed? But he doesn't look such a fine fellow as the other—the clerk in the wagon-office."

Frédéric cursed Dussardier. She would now be taking it for granted that he associated with the common herd.

Then they began to talk about the improvements in the capital—the new districts of the city—and the worthy Oudry happened to refer to M. Dambreuse as one of the big speculators.

Frédéric, taking advantage of the opportunity to make an impression, said he was acquainted with that gentleman. But Pellerin launched into a harangue against tradesmen—he saw no difference between them, whether they were sellers of candles or of money. Then Rosenwald and Burieu talked about old china; Arnoux chatted with Madame Oudry about gardening; Sombary, a comical character of the old school, amused himself by poking fun at her husband, referring to him sometimes as "Odry," as if he were the actor of that name, and remarking that he must be descended from Oudry, the dog-painter, seeing that the bump of the animals was visible on his forehead. He even wanted to feel M. Oudry's skull; but the latter excused himself on account of his wig; and the dessert ended with loud bursts of laughter.

When they had had their coffee, while they smoked, under the linden-trees, and strolled about the garden for some time, they went out for a walk along the river.

The party stopped in front of a fishmonger's shop, where a man was washing eels. Mademoiselle Marthe wanted to look at them. He emptied the box in which he had them out on the grass; and the little girl threw herself on her knees in order to catch them, laughed with delight, and then began to scream with terror. They all got spoiled, and Arnoux paid for them.

He next took it into his head to go out for a sail in the cutter.

One side of the horizon was beginning to grow pale, while on the other side a wide strip of orange showed itself in the sky, deepening into purple at the summits of the hills, which were steeped in shadow. Madame Arnoux seated herself on a big stone with this glittering splendour at her back. The other ladies sauntered about here and there. Hussonnet, at the lower end of the river's bank, skimmed stones over the water.

Arnoux returned, followed by a weather-beaten long boat, into which, in spite of their prudent objections, he packed his guests. The boat began to sink, and they had to get out again.

By this time candles were burning in the drawing-room, covered in chintz, and with crystal sconces on the walls. Mère Oudry was sleeping comfortably in an armchair, and the others were listening to M. Lefaucheux expounding the glories of the Bar. Madame Arnoux was sitting by herself near the window. Frédéric came over to her.

They chatted about the remarks which were being made in their vicinity. She admired oratory; he preferred the renown gained by authors. But, she ventured to suggest, it must give a man greater pleasure to move crowds directly by addressing them in person, face to face, than it does to infuse into their souls by his pen all the sentiments that animate his own. Such triumphs as these did not tempt Frédéric much, as he had no ambition.

"Ah, why?" she said. "One must have a little!"

They were standing close to one another in the window recess. Before them, the night spread out like an immense dark veil, speckled with silver. It was the first time they did not talk about trivial things. He even came to know her likes and dislikes. Certain scents made her feel ill, history books interested her, she believed in dreams.

Then he broached the subject of sentimental exploits. She spoke pityingly of the havoc wrought by passion, but expressed indignation at hypocritical vileness, and this rectitude of spirit harmonised so well with the beauty of her face that it seemed indeed as if her physical attractions were the outcome of her moral nature.

She smiled, every now and then, letting her eyes rest on him for a minute. Then he felt her glances penetrating his soul like those great rays of sunlight which descend into the depths of the water. He loved her without mental reservation, without any hope of his love being returned, unconditionally; and in those silent transports, which were like outbursts of gratitude, he would have happily covered her forehead with a rain of kisses. However, an inspiration from within carried him beyond himself—he felt moved by a longing for self-sacrifice, an imperative impulse towards immediate self-devotion, and all the stronger from the fact that he could not gratify it.

He did not leave along with the rest. Neither did Hussonnet. They were to go back in the carriage; and the vehicle was waiting just in front of the steps when Arnoux rushed down and hurried into the garden to gather some flowers there. Then the bouquet having been tied round with a thread, as the stems fell down unevenly, he searched in his pocket, which was full of papers, took out a piece at random, wrapped them up, completed his handiwork with the aid of a strong pin, and then offered it to his wife with a certain amount of tenderness.

"Look here, my darling! Excuse me for having forgotten you!"

But she uttered a little scream: the pin, having been clumsily inserted, had pricked her, and she hastened up to her room. They waited nearly a quarter of an hour for her. At last, she reappeared, carried off Marthe, and threw herself into the carriage.

"And your bouquet?" said Arnoux.

"No! no—it is not worth while!" Frédéric was running off to fetch it for her; she called out to him:

"I don't want it!"

But he speedily brought it to her, saying that he had just put it into the paper again, as he had found the flowers lying on the floor. She thrust them behind the leather apron of the carriage close to the seat, and off they started.

Frédéric, seated by her side, noticed that she was trembling frightfully. Then, when they had passed the bridge, as Arnoux was turning to the left:

"Why, no! you are making a mistake!—that way, to the right!"

She seemed irritated; everything annoyed her. Finally, Marthe having closed her eyes, Madame Arnoux drew forth the bouquet, and flung it out through the carriage-door, then caught Frédéric's arm, making a sign to him with the other hand to say nothing about it.

After this, she pressed her handkerchief against her lips, and sat quite motionless.

The two others, on the box, kept talking about printing and about subscribers. Arnoux, who was driving recklessly, lost his way in the middle of the Bois de Boulogne. Then they plunged down narrow lanes. The horse proceeded along at a walking pace; the branches of the trees grazed the hood. Frédéric could see nothing of Madame Arnoux save her two eyes in the dark. Marthe lay stretched across her lap while he supported the child's head.

"She is tiring you!" said her mother.

He replied:

"No! Oh, no!"

Whirlwinds of dust rose up slowly. They passed through Auteuil. All the houses were closed up; a gas-lamp here and there lighted up the angle of a wall; then once more they were surrounded by darkness. At one time he noticed that she was crying.

Was this remorse or passion? What in the world was it? This grief, of whose exact nature he was ignorant, interested him like a personal matter. There was now a new bond between them, as if, in a sense, they were accomplices; and he said to her in the most caressing voice he could assume:

"Are you ill?"

"Yes, a little," she returned.

The carriage rolled on, and the honeysuckle and the syringas trailed over the garden fences, sending forth waves of perfume into the night air. Her gown fell around her feet in numerous folds. It seemed to him as if he were in communication with her entire person through the medium of this child's body which lay stretched between them. He stooped over the little girl, and spreading out her pretty brown tresses, kissed her softly on the forehead.

"You are good!" said Madame Arnoux.

"Why?"

"Because you are fond of children."

"Not all children!"

He said no more, but he let his left hand hang down her side wide open, fancying that she would follow his example perhaps, and that he would find her palm touching his. Then he felt ashamed and withdrew it. They soon reached the paved road. The carriage went on more quickly; the number of gas-lights vastly increased—it was Paris. In front of the storehouse, Hussonnet jumped down from his seat. Frédéric waited till they were in the courtyard before alighting; then he lay in ambush at the corner of the Rue de Choiseul, and saw Arnoux slowly making his way back to the boulevards.

Next morning he began working as hard as he could.

He pictured himself in an Assize Court, on a winter's evening, at the defense's closing arguments, when the jurymen are looking pale, and when the breathless audience is overflowing the partitions of the courtroom; and after speaking for four hours, he was recapitulating his proof, feeling with every phrase, with every word, with every gesture, the blade of the guillotine suspended behind him, rising up; then in the tribune of the Chamber, an orator who bears on his lips the safety of an entire people, drowning his opponents under his rhetoric, crushing them under his repartee, with thunder and music in his voice, ironic, pathetic, fiery, sublime. She would be there somewhere in the midst of the others, hiding beneath her veil her enthusiasm of tears. After that they would meet again, and he would be unaffected by discouragement, slander and insults, if she would only say, "Ah, that was beautiful!" while drawing her hand lightly across his brow.

These images flashed, like beacons, on the horizon of his life. His intellect, thereby excited, became more active and more vigorous. He buried himself in study till the month of August, and was successful at his final examination.

Deslauriers, who had found it so troublesome to coach him once more for the second examination at the close of December, and for the third in February, was astonished at his ardour. Then the great expectations of former days returned. In ten years it was probable that Frédéric would be a representative; in fifteen a minister. Why not? With his inheritance, which would soon come into his hands, he might, at first, start a newspaper; this would be the opening step in his career; after that they would see what the future would bring. As for himself, his ambition was to obtain a chair in the Law School; and he defended his doctoral thesis in such a remarkable fashion that it won for him the professors' complements.

Three days afterwards, Frédéric received his own degree. Before leaving for his holidays, he conceived the idea of organizing a picnic to bring to a close their Saturday reunions.

He displayed high spirits on the occasion. Madame Arnoux was now with her mother at Chartres. But he would soon come across her again, and would end by being her lover.

Deslauriers, admitted the same day to the debating society, at Orsay, had made a speech which was greatly applauded. Although he was sober, he drank a little more wine than was good for him, and said to Dussardier at dessert:

"You are an honest fellow!—and, when I'm a rich man, I'll make you my manager."

All were in a state of delight. Cisy was not going to finish his law-course. Martinon intended to remain in the provinces during the period before his admission to the Bar, where he would be nominated assistant prosecutor. Pellerin was devoting himself to the production of a large painting representing "The Genius of the Revolution." Hussonnet was, in the following week, about to read for the Director of Public Amusements the outline of a play, and had no doubt as to its success:

"As for the framework of the drama, they may leave that to me! As for passion, I have knocked about enough to understand that thoroughly; and as for witticisms, they're entirely up my alley!"

He took a leap, fell on his two hands, and proceeded to march around the table with his legs in the air. These childish antics did not improve Sénécal's mood. He had just been dismissed from the boarding-school, in which he had been a teacher, for having given a whipping to an aristocrat's son. His financial troubles worsened: he laid the blame on the inequalities of society, and cursed the wealthy. He poured out his grievances to the sympathetic Regimbart, who had become every day more and more disillusioned, saddened, and disgusted. The Citizen had now turned his attention towards the issue of the national Budget, and blamed Guizot's entourage for the loss of millions in Algeria.

As he could not sleep without having paid a visit to the Alexandre tavern, he disappeared at eleven o'clock. The rest departed some time afterwards; and Frédéric, as he was parting with Hussonnet, learned that Madame Arnoux was supposed to have come back the night before.

He accordingly went to the coach-office to change his ticket to the next day; and, at about six o'clock in the evening, presented himself at her house. Her return, the concierge said, had been put off for a week. Frédéric dined alone, and then wandered about the boulevards.

Rosy clouds, scarf-like in shape, stretched beyond the roofs; the shops were beginning to roll up their awnings; water-carts were letting a shower of spray fall over the dusty pavement; and an unexpected coolness was mingled with café smells, as one got a glimpse through their open doors, between some silver plate and gilt ware, of bouquets of flowers, which were reflected in large mirrors. The crowd moved on at a leisurely pace. Groups of men were chatting in the middle of the sidewalk; and women passed along with a weary expression in their eyes and that camelia tint in their complexions which intense heat imparts to feminine flesh. Something immeasurable in its vastness seemed to pour itself out and envelope the houses. Never had Paris looked so beautiful. He saw nothing before him in the future but an interminable series of years full of love.

He stopped in front of the theatre of the Porte Saint-Martin to look at the poster; and, for want of something to occupy him, paid for a seat and went in.

An old-fashioned spectacular was playing. There was a very small audience; and through the skylights of the top gallery the vault of the sky seemed cut up into little blue squares, whilst the stage lamps above the orchestra formed a single line of yellow illuminations. The scene represented a slave-market at Peking, with hand-bells, tomtoms, sweeping robes, sharp-pointed caps, and clownish jokes. Then, as soon as the curtain fell, he wandered into the foyer all alone and gazed out with admiration at a large green landau which stood on the boulevard outside, before the front steps of the theatre, yoked to two white horses, while a coachman with short breeches held the reins.

He had just gotten back to his seat when, in the balcony, a lady and a gentleman entered the first box in front of the stage. The husband had a pale face with a narrow strip of grey beard round it, the rosette of the Légion d'honneur, and that frigid look which is supposed to characterise diplomats.

His wife, who was at least twenty years younger, and who was neither tall nor short, neither ugly nor pretty, wore her fair hair in corkscrew curls in the English fashion, and displayed a flat-bodiced dress and a large black lace fan. To make people of such high society come to the theatre during such a season one would imagine either that it was by chance, or that they had gotten tired of spending the evening in one another's company. The lady kept nibbling at her fan, while the gentleman yawned. Frédéric could not call to mind where he had seen that face.

In the next interval between the acts, while passing through one of the lobbies, he came face to face with them. As he made a vague greeting, M. Dambreuse, at once recognising him, came up and apologised for having treated him with unpardonable neglect. It was an allusion to the numerous visiting-cards he had sent following the clerk's advice. However, he confused the periods, supposing that Frédéric was in the second year of his law-course. Then he said he envied the young man for the opportunity of going to the country. He needed a little rest himself, but business kept him in Paris.

Madame Dambreuse, leaning on his arm, nodded her head slightly, and the agreeable sprightliness of her face contrasted with its gloomy expression a short time before.

"One finds charming diversions in it, nevertheless," she said, after her husband's last remark. "What a stupid play that was—was it not, Monsieur?" And all three of them remained there chatting about the theatre and new plays.

Frédéric, accustomed to the grimaces of provincial ladies, had not seen in any woman such ease of manner, that simplicity which is the essence of refinement, and in which unsophisticated souls perceive the expression of instantaneous sympathy.

They would expect to see him as soon as he returned. M. Dambreuse told him to give his kind remembrances to Père Roque.

Frédéric, when he reached his lodgings, did not fail to inform Deslauriers of their hospitable invitation.

"Grand!" was the clerk's reply; "and don't let your mamma sweet-talk you! Come back without delay!"

On the day after his arrival, as soon as they had finished lunch, Madame Moreau brought her son out into the garden.

She said she was happy to see him in a profession, for they were not as rich as people imagined. The land brought in little; the people who farmed it were slow in paying. She had even been compelled to sell her carriage. Finally, she brought their financial situation out in the open.

During the first difficulties which followed the death of her late husband, M. Roque, a man of great cunning, had made her loans which had been renewed, and left long unpaid, in spite of her desire to clear up her debts. He had suddenly made a demand for immediate payment, and she had gone beyond the strict terms of the agreement by giving him, at a ridiculous price, the farm of Presles. Ten years later, her capital disappeared through the failure of a bank at Melun. Out of a distaste for mortgages, and to keep up appearances, which might be necessary in view of her son's future, she had, when Père Roque presented himself again, listened to him once more. But now she was free from debt. In short, there was left them an income of about ten thousand francs, of which two thousand three hundred belonged to him—his entire inheritance.

"It isn't possible!" exclaimed Frédéric.

She nodded her head, as if to declare that it was perfectly possible.

But his uncle would leave him something?

That was by no means certain!

And they took a turn around the garden without exchanging a word. At last she pressed him to her heart, and in a voice choked with rising tears:

"Ah! my poor boy! I have had to give up my dreams!"

He seated himself on a bench in the shadow of the large acacia.

Her advice was that he should become a clerk to M. Prouharam, solicitor, who would assign over his office to him; if he increased its value, he might sell it again and find a good practice.

Frédéric was no longer listening to her. He was gazing blankly across the hedge into the garden opposite.

A little girl of about twelve with red hair happened to be there all alone. She had made earrings for herself with the berries of the sorb-tree. Her bodice, made of grey linen, allowed her shoulders, slightly tanned by the sun, to be seen. Her short white petticoat was spotted with the stains made by sweets; and there was the grace of a young wild animal about her entire person, at the same time, nervous and delicate. Apparently, the presence of a stranger astonished her, for she had stopped abruptly with her watering-pot in her hand darting glances at him with her clear, blue-green eyes.

"That is M. Roque's daughter," said Madame Moreau. "He has just married his servant and legitimised the child that he had by her."

CHAPTER VI

Ruined, stripped of everything, undermined! He remained seated on the bench, as if stunned by a shock. He cursed Fate; he would have liked to beat somebody; and, intensifying his despair, he felt a kind of outrage, a sense of disgrace, weighing down upon him; for Frédéric had been under the impression that the fortune coming to him through his father would mount up one day to an income of fifteen thousand francs, and he had so informed the Arnoux's in an indirect sort of way. So then he would be looked upon as a braggart, a rogue, a scoundrel, who had introduced himself to them in the expectation of profiting somehow! And as for her—Madame Arnoux—how could he ever see her again now?

That was completely impossible when he had only a yearly income of three thousand francs. He could not always lodge on the fourth floor, have the concierge as a servant, and make his appearance with wretched black gloves turning blue at the ends, a greasy hat, and the same frock-coat for a whole year. No, no! never! And yet without her, his existence was intolerable. Many people were well able to live without any fortune, Deslauriers amongst them; and he thought himself a coward to attach so much importance to matters of trifling consequence. Need would perhaps multiply his talents a hundredfold. He grew excited thinking on the great men who had worked in garrets. A soul like that of Madame Arnoux ought to be touched at such a spectacle, and she would be moved by it to sympathetic tenderness. So, after all, this catastrophe was a piece of good fortune; like those earthquakes which unveil treasures, it had revealed to him the hidden wealth of his nature. But there was only one place in the world where this could be turned to account—Paris; for to his mind, art, science, and love (those three faces of

God, as Pellerin would have said) were associated exclusively with the capital. That evening, he informed his mother of his intention to go back there. Madame Moreau was surprised and indignant. She regarded it as a foolish and absurd course. It would be better to follow her advice, namely, to remain near her in an office. Frédéric shrugged his shoulders, "Come now"—looking on this proposal as an insult to himself.

Thereupon, the good lady adopted another plan. In a tender voice broken by sobs she began to dwell on her solitude, her old age, and the sacrifices she had made for him. Now that she was more unhappy than ever, he was abandoning her. Then, alluding to the anticipated close of her life:

"A little patience—good heavens! you will soon be free!"

These lamentations were renewed twenty times a day for three months; and at the same time the luxuries of home seduced him. He found it enjoyable to have a softer bed and napkins that were not torn, so that, weary, worn down, overcome by the terrible force of comfort, Frédéric allowed himself to be brought to Maître Prouharam's office.

He displayed there neither knowledge nor aptitude. Up to this time, he had been regarded as a young man of great ability who ought to be the shining light of the Department. All were disappointed.

At first, he said to himself:

"It is necessary to inform Madame Arnoux about it;" and for a whole week he kept formulating in his own mind rhapsodic letters and short notes, eloquent and sublime. The fear of avowing his actual position restrained him. Then he thought that it was far better to write to the husband. Arnoux knew life and could understand the true state of the case. At length, after a fortnight's hesitation:

"Bah! I ought not to see them any more: let them forget me! At any rate, I shall be cherished in her memory without having sunk in her estimation! She will believe that I am dead, and will miss me—perhaps."

As extravagant resolutions cost him little, he swore in his own mind that he would never return to Paris, and that he would not even make any enquiries about Madame Arnoux.

Nevertheless, he missed the very smell of the gas and the noise of the omnibuses. He mused on the things that she might have said to him, on the tone of her voice, on the light of her eyes—and, regarding himself as a dead man, he no longer did anything at all.

He arose very late, and looked through the window at the passing teams of wagoners. The first six months especially were hateful.

On certain days, however, he was possessed by a feeling of indignation even against her. Then he would go forth and wander through the meadows, half covered in winter time by the flooding of the Seine. They were separated by rows of poplar-trees. Here and there arose a little bridge. He tramped about till evening, crushing the yellow leaves under his feet, inhaling the fog, and jumping over the ditches. As his arteries began to throb more vigorously, he felt himself carried away by a desire to do something wild; he longed to become a trapper in America, to serve a pasha in the East, to set off as a sailor; and he vented his melancholy in long letters to Deslauriers.

The latter was struggling to get on. The slothful conduct of his friend and his eternal jeremiads appeared to him simply stupid. Soon, their correspondence dwindled to almost nothing. Frédéric had given all his furniture to Deslauriers, who stayed on in the same lodgings. From time to time his mother spoke to him. Finally he one day told her about the present he had made, and she was berating him for it, when a letter was placed in his hands.

"What is the matter now?" she said, "you are trembling?"

"There is nothing the matter with me," replied Frédéric.

Deslauriers informed him that he had taken Sénécal under his protection, and that for the past fortnight they had been living together. So now Sénécal was lounging in the midst of things that had come from the Arnoux's shop. He might sell them, criticise, make jokes about them. Frédéric felt wounded in the depths of his soul. He went up to his room. He wanted to die.

His mother called him to consult him about a planting in the garden.

This garden was, in the fashion of an English park, cut in the middle by a wooden fence; and half of it belonged to Père Roque, who had another for vegetables on the bank of the river. The two neighbours, having fallen out, abstained from making their appearance there at the same hour. But since Frédéric's return, the old gentleman used to walk about there more frequently, and was not cheap with his courtesies towards Madame Moreau's son. He pitied the young man for having to live in a country town. One day he told him that Madame Dambreuse had been anxious to hear from him. On another occasion he expatiated on the custom in Champagne, where noble titles could be passed on through the mother.

"At that time you would have been a lord, since your mother's name was De Fouvens. People can say what they like—never mind them! there's something in a name. After all," he added, with a sly glance at Frédéric, "that depends on the Keeper of the Seals."

These aristocratic pretensions contrasted strangely with his personal appearance. As he was small, his big chestnut-coloured frock-coat exaggerated the length of his torso. When he took off his hat, he revealed a face almost like that of a woman with an extremely sharp nose; his hair, which was of a yellow colour, resembled a wig. He saluted people with a very low bow, brushing against the wall.

Up to his fiftieth year, he had been content with the services of Catherine, a native of Lorraine, of the same age as himself, whose face was pock-marked. But in the year 1834, he brought back with him from Paris a handsome blonde with a passive sheep-like expression and a "queenly carriage." Ere long, she was observed strutting about with large earrings; and everything was explained by the birth of a daughter who was introduced to the world under the name of Elisabeth Olympe-Louise Roque.

Catherine, in her jealousy, expected that she would hate this child. On the contrary, she became fond of the little girl, and treated her with the utmost care, consideration, and tenderness, in order to supplant her mother and make the child dislike her—an easy task, inasmuch as Madame Éléonore entirely neglected the little one, preferring to gossip at the tradesmen's shops. On the day after her marriage, she went to pay a visit at the Sub-prefecture, no longer spoke familiarly to the servants, and took it into her head that, as a matter of good form, she ought to exhibit a certain severity towards the child. She was present while the little one was at her lessons. The teacher, an old clerk who had been employed at the Mayor's office, did not know how to go about the work of instructing the girl. The pupil rebelled, got her ears boxed, and rushed away to shed tears on the lap of Catherine, who always took her side. After this the two women wrangled, and M. Roque ordered them to hold their tongues. He had married only out of tender regard for his daughter, and did not wish to be annoyed by them.

She often wore a tattered white dress, and pantalettes trimmed with lace; and on great feast days she would leave the house attired like a princess, in order to mortify a little the matrons of the town, who forbade their brats to associate with her on account of her illegitimate birth.

She passed her life nearly always by herself in the garden, went see-sawing on the swing, chased butterflies, then suddenly stopped to watch the beetles swooping down on the rose-trees. It was, no doubt, these habits which gave her face an expression both bold and dreamy. She was, moreover, the same height as Marthe, so that Frédéric said to her, at their second meeting:

"Will you permit me to kiss you, mademoiselle?"

The little girl lifted up her head and replied:

"I will!"

But the fence separated them from one another.

"We must climb over," said Frédéric.

"No, lift me up!"

He stooped over the fence, and raising her off the ground with his hands, kissed her on both cheeks; then he put her back on her own side; and this performance was repeated on later occasions when they found themselves together.

Without more reserve than a child of four, as soon as she heard her friend coming, she jumped up to meet him, or else, hiding behind a tree, she began barking like a dog to frighten him.

One day, when Madame Moreau had gone out, he brought her up to his own room. She opened all the perfume-bottles, and pomaded her hair plentifully; then, without the slightest embarrassment, she lay down on the bed, where she remained stretched out at full length, wide awake.

"I'm imagining that I'm your wife," she said to him.

Next day he found her all in tears. She confessed that she had been "weeping for her sins;" and, when he wished to know what they were, she hung down her head, and answered:

"Ask me no more!"

The time for first communion was at hand. She had been brought to confession in the morning. The sacrament scarcely made her wiser. Occasionally, she worked herself into a real tantrum; and Frédéric was sent to calm her.

He often brought her with him on his walks. He day-dreamed as they walked along, while she would gather wild poppies at the edges of the corn-fields; and, when she saw him more melancholy than usual, she tried to console him with her pretty childish prattle. His heart, bereft of love, fell back on this friendship inspired by a little girl. He gave her sketches of funny old men, told her stories, and devoted himself to reading books to her.

He began with the *Annales Romantiques*, a collection of prose and verse celebrated at the time. Then, forgetting her age, so much was he charmed by her intelligence, he read for her in succession, *Atala*, *Cinq-Mars*, and *Les Feuilles d'Automne*.* But one night (she had that very evening heard *Macbeth* in Letourneur's simple translation) she woke up, exclaiming:

"The spot! the spot!" Her teeth chattered, she shivered, and, fixing terrified glances on her right hand, she kept rubbing it, saying:

"Still a spot!"

At last a doctor was brought, who recommended that she be kept free from violent emotions.

The townsfolk saw in this only an unfavourable prognossis for her morals. It was said that "young Moreau" wished to make an actress of her later.

Soon another event became the subject of discussion—namely, the arrival of uncle Barthélemy. Madame Moreau gave up her bedroom for him, and was so gracious as to serve meat to him on fast-days.

The old man was not very agreeable. He was perpetually making comparisons between Le Havre and Nogent, the air of which he considered heavy, the bread bad, the streets ill-paved, the food

---

*Romantic novels, by François de Chateaubriand and Alfred de Vigny (1797–1863), respectively, and a collection of lyrical poems by Victor Hugo.

mediocre, and the inhabitants very lazy. "How poor business is here!" He blamed his deceased brother for his extravagance, pointing out by way of contrast that he had himself accumulated an income of twenty-seven thousand francs a year. At last, he left at the end of the week, and on the footboard of the carriage he spoke these by no means reassuring words:

"I am very glad to know that you are comfortably off."

"You will get nothing," said Madame Moreau as they re-entered the dining-room.

He had come only at her urgent request, and for eight days she had been seeking, on her part, for an opening—only too clearly perhaps. She repented now of having done so, and remained seated in her armchair with her head bent down and her lips tightly pressed together. Frédéric sat opposite, staring at her; and they were both silent, as they had been five years before on his return home by the Montereau steamboat. This coincidence, which suddenly struck him, made him think of Madame Arnoux.

At that moment the crack of a whip outside the window reached their ears, while a voice was heard calling out to him.

It was Père Roque, who was alone in his tilted cart. He was going to spend the whole day at La Fortelle with M. Dambreuse, and cordially offered to drive Frédéric there.

"You have no need of an invitation as long as you are with me. Don't be afraid!"

Frédéric felt inclined to accept this offer. But how would he explain his extended sojourn at Nogent? He had not a proper summer suit. Finally, what would his mother say? He accordingly decided not to go.

From that time, their neighbour was less friendly. Louise was growing tall; Madame Éléonore fell dangerously ill; and the intimacy broke off, to the great delight of Madame Moreau, who feared lest her son's prospects of being settled in life might be affected by association with such people.

She was thinking of purchasing for him the clerkship of the Court of Justice. Frédéric raised no particular objection to this scheme. He now accompanied her to mass; in the evening he took a hand in a game of cards. He became accustomed to provincial habits of life, and allowed himself to slide into them; and even his love had assumed a character of mournful sweetness, a kind of soporific charm. Having poured out his grief in his letters, confused it with everything he read, vented it during his walks through the country, he had almost exhausted it, so that Madame Arnoux was for him, like a dead woman whose tomb he was surprised he did not know, so tranquil and resigned had his affection for her now become.

One day, the 12th of December, 1845, about nine o'clock in the morning, the cook brought up a letter to his room. The address, which was in big letters, was written in a hand he was not acquainted with; and Frédéric, feeling sleepy, was in no great hurry to break the seal. Finally, when he did so, he read:

"Justice of the Peace at Le Havre, IIIrd Arrondissement.

"MONSIEUR,—

Monsieur Moreau, your uncle, having died intestate——"

He was the heir! As if a fire had suddenly broken out on the other side of the wall, he jumped out of bed in his shirt, with his feet bare. He passed his hand over his face, doubting the evidence of his own eyes, believing that he was still dreaming, and in order to make his mind more clearly conscious of the reality of the event, he flung the window wide open.

There had been a snow fall; the roofs were white, and he even recognised in the yard outside a washtub which had caused him to stumble after dark the evening before.

He read the letter over three times in succession. Could there be anything more certain? His uncle's entire fortune! A yearly income of twenty-seven thousand francs! And he was overwhelmed with joy at the idea of seeing Madame Arnoux once more. With the vividness of a hallucination he saw himself beside her, at her house, bringing her a present in silver paper, while at the door stood a tilbury—no, a brougham rather!—a black brougham, with a servant in brown livery. He could hear his horse pawing the ground and the noise of the curb-chain mingling with the murmur of their kisses. And every day this was renewed indefinitely. He would receive them in his own house: the dining-room would be furnished in red leather; the boudoir in yellow silk; sofas everywhere! and such a variety of whatnots, china vases, and carpets! These images came in so tumultuous a fashion into his mind that he felt his head spinning. Then he thought of his mother; and he descended the stairs with the letter in his hand.

Madame Moreau made an effort to control her emotion, but could not keep herself from swooning. Frédéric caught her in his arms and kissed her on the forehead.

"Dear mother, you can now buy back your carriage—so laugh! shed no more tears! be happy!"

Ten minutes later the news had travelled as far as the faubourgs. Then M. Benoist, M. Gamblin, M. Chambion, and other friends hurried towards the house. Frédéric got away for a minute in order to write to Deslauriers. Then other visitors turned up. The afternoon passed in congratulations. They had forgotten all about "Roque's wife," who, however, was declared to be "very low."

When they were alone, the same evening, Madame Moreau said to her son that she would advise him to set himself up as a lawyer at Troyes. As he was better known in his own part of the country than in any other, he might more easily find there an advantageous match.

"Ah, it is all too much!" exclaimed Frédéric. He had scarcely grasped his good fortune in his hands when they wanted to take it away from him. He announced his express determination to live in Paris.

"And what are you going to do there?"

"Nothing!"

Madame Moreau, astonished at his manner, asked what he intended to become.

"A minister," was Frédéric's reply. And he declared that he was not at all joking, that he meant to plunge at once into diplomacy, and that his studies and his instincts impelled him in that direction. He would first enter the Council of State under M. Dambreuse's patronage.

"So then, you know him?"

"Oh, yes—through M. Roque."

"That's astonishing!" said Madame Moreau. He had awakened in her heart her former dreams of ambition. She internally abandoned herself to them, and said no more about other matters.

If he had yielded to his own impatience, Frédéric would have set off that very instant. Next morning every seat in the coaches was taken; and so he fretted and fumed till seven o'clock the following evening.

They had sat down to dinner when there were three prolonged tolls of the church-bell; and the housemaid, coming in, informed them that Madame Éléonore had just died.

This death, after all, was not a misfortune for anyone, not even for her child. The young girl would only be the better for it later on.

As the two houses were close to one another, a great coming and going and a clamor of voices could be heard; and the idea of this corpse being so near them threw a certain funereal gloom over their parting. Madame Moreau wiped her eyes two or three times. Frédéric felt a heaviness in his heart.

When the meal was over, Catherine stopped him between two doors. Mademoiselle absolutely had to see him. She was waiting for him in the garden. He went out, jumped over the hedge, and knocking into the trees, made his way towards M. Roque's house. Lights were glittering through a window in the second story; then a form appeared in the midst of the darkness, and a voice whispered:

" 'Tis I!"

She seemed to him taller than usual, because of her black dress, no doubt. Not knowing what to say to her, he contented himself with holding her hands, and sighing:

"Ah! my poor Louise!"

She did not reply. She gazed at him for a long time with a profound look of sadness.

Frédéric was afraid of missing the coach; he thought that he could hear the rolling of wheels some distance away, and, in order to put an end to their encounter without delay:

"Catherine told me that you had something——"

"Yes—'tis true! I wanted to tell you——"

He was astonished to find that she addressed him in a formal manner; and, as she again relapsed into silence:

"Well, what?"

"I don't know. I forget! Is it true that you're going away?"

"Yes, very shortly."

She repeated: "Ah! now?—for good?—we'll never see one another again?"

She was choking with sobs.

"Good-bye! good-bye! embrace me then!"

And she flung her arms around him.

PART TWO

CHAPTER I

When he had taken his place behind the other passengers in the front of the stage-coach, and when the vehicle began to shake as the five horses started into a brisk trot all at the same time, he allowed himself to plunge into an intoxicating dream of the future. Like an architect drawing up the plan of a palace, he mapped out his life beforehand. He filled it with luxuries and with splendours; it rose up to the sky; a profuse display of alluring objects could be seen there; and so deeply was he buried in the contemplation of these things that he lost sight of the world around him.

At the foot of the hill at Sourdun his attention was directed to the stage which they had reached in their journey. They had travelled only about five kilometres at the most. He was annoyed at this slow pace. He pulled down the coach-window in order to get a view of the road. He asked the conductor several times at what hour they would reach their destination. However, he eventually calmed down, and remained seated in his corner of the vehicle with eyes wide open.

The lantern, which hung from the postilion's seat, threw its light on the hindquarters of the horses. In front, only the manes of the other horses could be seen undulating like white billows. Their breathing caused a kind of fog at each side of the team. The little iron chains of the harness rang; the windows shook in their frames; and the heavy coach went rolling at an even pace over the pavement. Here and there could be distinguished the wall of a barn, or else an inn standing by itself. Sometimes, as they entered a village, a baker's oven threw out gleams of light; and the gigantic silhouettes of the horses kept rushing past the walls of the opposite houses. At every change of horses, when the harness was unfastened, there was a great silence for a minute. Someone could be heard stamping around on top under the canvas cover, while a woman standing in the doorway shielded her candle with her hand. Then the conductor jumped on the footboard, and the vehicle started on its way again.

At Mormans, the striking of the clocks announced that it was a quarter past one.

"So it's today," he thought, "I shall see her this very day!"

But gradually his hopes and his recollections, Nogent, the Rue de Choiseul, Madame Arnoux, and his mother, all got mixed up together.

He was awakened by the dull sound of wheels passing over planks: they were crossing the Pont de Charenton—it was Paris. Then his two travelling companions, the first taking off his cap, and the second his silk neck-kerchief, put on their hats, and began to chat.

The first, a big, red-faced man in a velvet frock-coat, was a merchant; the second was coming up to the capital to consult a physician; and, fearing that he had disturbed this gentleman during the night, Frédéric spontaneously apologised to him, so much had the young man's heart been softened by the feelings of happiness that possessed it. The wharf-side station being flooded, no doubt, they went straight ahead; and once more they could see green fields. In the distance, tall factory-chimneys were sending forth their smoke. Then they turned into Ivry. Then drove up a street: all at once, he saw before him the dome of the Panthéon.

The plain, in ruins, seemed a waste land. The enclosing wall of the fortifications made a horizontal ridge there; and, on the unpaved paths, on the ground at the side of the road, little branchless trees were protected by slats bristling with nails. Establishments for chemical products and timber-merchants' yards made their appearance alternately. High gates, like those seen in farmhouses, afforded glimpses, through their openings, of wretched yards within, full of filth, with puddles of dirty water in the middle of them. Large taverns whose facades were as red as ox blood, displayed in the first floor, between the windows, two billiard-cues crossing one another, with a wreath of painted flowers. Here and there might be noticed a half-built plaster hut, which had been allowed to remain unfinished. Then the double row of houses was continuous; and over their bare fronts enormous tin cigars showed themselves at some distance from each other, indicating tobacconists' shops. Midwives' signboards portrayed a matron in a cap rocking a baby wrapped in a quilt trimmed with lace. The corners of the walls were covered with posters, which, three-quarters torn, were quivering in the wind like rags. Workmen in smocks, brewers' drays, laundresses' and butchers' carts passed along. A thin rain was falling. It was cold. There was a pale sky; but two eyes, which to him were as precious as the sun, were shining behind the haze.

They had to wait a long time at the barrier, for vendors of poultry, wagoners, and a flock of sheep caused an obstruction there. The sentry, with his great-coat thrown back, walked to and fro in front of his box, to keep himself warm. The clerk who collected the tolls* clambered up to the roof of the coach and a cornet sent forth a flourish. They went down the boulevard at a quick trot, the whipple-trees clapping and the traces hanging loose. The lash of the whip went cracking through the moist air. The conductor uttered his sonorous shout:

"Look alive! look alive! oho!" and the scavengers stood aside, the pedestrians sprang back, the mud gushed against the coach-windows; they crossed carts, cabs, and omnibuses. Finally, the iron gate of the Jardin des Plantes came into sight.

The Seine, which was of a yellowish colour, almost reached the platforms of the bridges. A cool breath of air issued from it. Frédéric inhaled it with his utmost energy, drinking in this good air of Paris, which seems to contain the essence of love and the emanations of the intellect. He was touched with emotion at the first glimpse of a hackney-coach. He gazed with delight on the thresholds of the winemerchants' shops garnished with straw, on the shoeblacks with their boxes, on the lads who sold groceries as they shook their coffee roasters. Women trotted along under umbrellas. He bent forward to see whether he could distinguish their faces—chance might have led Madame Arnoux to come out.

The shops displayed their wares. The crowd grew more dense; the noise in the streets grew louder. After passing the Quai Saint-Bernard, the Quai de la Tournelle, and the Quai Montebello, they drove along the Quai Napoléon. He was anxious to see the windows

---

*At the time, an excise tax was collected on certain merchandise brought into Paris.

there; but they were too far away from him. Then once more they crossed the Seine over the Pont-Neuf, and descended in the direction of the Louvre; and, having crossed the Rues Saint-Honoré, Croix des Petits-Champs, and Du Bouloi, he reached the Rue Coq-Héron, and entered the courtyard of the hotel.

To make his enjoyment last the longer, Frédéric dressed himself as slowly as possible, and even walked as far as the Boulevard Montmartre. He smiled at the thought of beholding once more the beloved name on the marble plate. He cast a glance upwards; there was no longer a trace of the display in the windows, the pictures, or anything else.

He hastened to the Rue de Choiseul. M. and Madame Arnoux no longer resided there, and a woman next door was keeping an eye on the concierge's lodge. Frédéric waited to see the concierge himself. After some time he made his appearance—it was no longer the same man. He did not know their address.

Frédéric went into a café, and, while having lunch consulted the Commercial Directory. There were three hundred Arnoux in it, but no Jacques Arnoux. Where, then, were they living? Pellerin ought to know.

He made his way to the very top of the Faubourg Poissonnière, to the artist's studio. As the door had neither a bell nor a knocker, he rapped loudly on it with his knuckles, and then called out—shouted. But the only response was the echo of his voice from the empty house.

After this he thought of Hussonnet; but where could he discover a man of that sort? On one occasion he had waited on Hussonnet when the latter was paying a visit to his mistress's house in the Rue de Fleurus. Frédéric had just reached the Rue de Fleurus when he became conscious of the fact that he did not even know the lady's name.

He tried Police Headquarters. He wandered from staircase to staircase, from office to office. He found that the Information Office was closed for the day, and was told to come back again next morning.

Then he called at all the art-dealers' shops that he could find, and enquired whether they could give him any information as to Arnoux's whereabouts. The only answer he got was that M. Arnoux was no longer in the trade.

At last, discouraged, weary, sickened, he returned to his hotel, and went to bed. Just as he was stretching himself between the sheets, an idea flashed upon him which made him leap up with delight:

"Regimbart! what an idiot I was not to think of him before!"

Next morning, at seven o'clock, he arrived in the Rue Notre Dame des Victoires, in front of a liquor-shop, where Regimbart was in the habit of drinking white wine. It was not yet open. He walked about the neighbourhood, and at the end of about half-an-hour, presented himself at the place once more. Regimbart had left it.

Frédéric rushed out into the street. He imagined that he could even see Regimbart's hat some distance away. A hearse and some mourning coaches intercepted his progress. When they had got out of the way, the vision had disappeared.

Fortunately, he recalled that the Citizen lunched every day at eleven o'clock sharp, at a little restaurant in the Place Gaillon. All he had to do was to wait patiently till then; and, after sauntering about from the Bourse to the Madeleine, and from the Madeleine to the Gymnase Theatre, so long that it seemed unending, Frédéric entered the restaurant on the Rue Gaillon just as the clocks struck eleven, certain of finding Regimbart there.

"Don't know!" said the restaurant-keeper, in an unceremonious tone.

Frédéric persisted: the man replied:

"I have no longer any acquaintance with him, Monsieur"—and, as he spoke, he raised his eyebrows majestically and shook his head mysteriously.

But, in their last interview, the Citizen had referred to the Alexandre Café. Frédéric quickly swallowed a brioche, jumped into a cab, and asked the driver whether there happened to be anywhere in the vicinity of Sainte-Geneviève a certain Café Alexandre. The cabman drove him to the Rue des Francs Bourgeois Saint-Michel, where there was an establishment of that name, and in answer to Frédéric's question "M. Regimbart, if you please?" the keeper of the café said with an unusually gracious smile:

"We have not seen him as yet, Monsieur," while he threw his wife, who sat behind the counter, a knowing look. And the next moment, turning towards the clock:

"But he'll be here, I hope, in ten minutes, or at most a quarter of an hour. Celestin, hurry with the newspapers! What would Monsieur like?"

Though he did not want anything, Frédéric threw down a glass of rum, then a glass of kirsch, then a glass of curaçoa, then several glasses of grog, both cold and hot. He read through that day's *Le Siècle*, and then read it over again; he examined the caricatures in the *Charivari* down to the very tissue of the paper. When he had finished, he knew the advertisements by heart. From time to time, the sound of boots on the sidewalk outside reached his ears—it must be him! and a figure would cast its profile on the window-panes; but it invariably passed on.

In order to get rid of the sense of weariness he experienced, Frédéric kept changing his seat. He took a seat at the far end of the room; then at the right; after that at the left; and he remained in the middle of the bench with his arms stretched out. But a cat, daintily picking at the velvet on the back of the seat, startled him by suddenly leaping down, in order to lick up the spots of syrup on the tray; and the child of the house, an insufferable brat of four, played noisily with a rattle on the bar steps. His mother, a pale-faced little woman, with decayed teeth, was smiling in a stupid sort of way. What in the world could Regimbart be doing? Frédéric waited for him in an exceedingly miserable frame of mind.

The rain clattered like hail on the covering of the cab. Through the opening in the muslin curtain he could see the poor horse in the street more motionless than a horse made of wood. The stream of water, becoming enormous, trickled down between two spokes of the wheels, and the coachman was nodding drowsily with the horsecloth wrapped round him for protection, but fearing his fare might give him the slip, he opened the door every now and then, with the rain dripping from him as if falling from a mountain torrent; and, if things could get worn out by looking at them, the clock ought to have by this time been utterly dissolved, so frequently did Frédéric rivet his eyes on it. However, it kept going. Alexandre walked up and down repeating, "He'll come! Cheer up! he'll come!" and, in order to divert his thoughts, talked politics at some length. He even carried his hospitality so far as to propose a game of dominoes.

Finally when it was half-past four, Frédéric, who had been there since about twelve, sprang to his feet, and declared that he would not wait any longer.

"I can't understand it at all myself," replied the café-keeper, in a tone of straightforwardness. "This is the first time that M. Ledoux has failed to come!"

"What! Monsieur Ledoux?"

"Why, yes, Monsieur!"

"I said Regimbart," exclaimed Frédéric, exasperated.

"Ah! a thousand pardons! You are making a mistake! Madame Alexandre, did not Monsieur say M. Ledoux?"

And, questioning the waiter: "You heard him yourself, just as I did?"

No doubt to pay his master off for old scores, the waiter just smiled.

Frédéric drove back to the boulevards, indignant at having his time wasted, raging against the Citizen, but craving his presence as if for that of a god, and firmly resolving to drag him out, if necessary, from the depths of the most remote cellars. The cab he was driving in began to irritate him, and he accordingly got rid of it. His mind was in a state of confusion. Then all the names of the cafés which he had heard pronounced by that idiot burst forth at the same time from his memory like the thousand fireworks—the Café Gascard, the Café Grimbert, the Café Halbout, the Bordelais, the Havanais, the Havrais, the Bœuf à la Mode, the Brasserie Allemande, and the Mère Morel; and he made his way to all of them in succession. But in one he was told that Regimbart had just gone out; in another, that he might perhaps call at a later hour; in a third, that they had not seen him for six months; and, in another place, that he had the day before ordered a leg of mutton for Saturday. Finally, at Vautier's, Frédéric, on opening the door, knocked into the waiter.

"Do you know M. Regimbart?"

"What, monsieur! do I know him? 'Tis I who have the honour of waiting on him. He's upstairs—he is just finishing his dinner!"

And, with a napkin under his arm, the proprietor of the establishment himself accosted him:

"You're asking him for M. Regimbart, monsieur? He was here a moment ago."

Frédéric cursed loudly, but the proprietor stated that he would find the gentleman as a matter of certainty at Bouttevilain's.

"I assure you, on my honour, he left a little earlier than usual, for he had a business appointment with some gentlemen. But you'll find him, I tell you again, at Bouttevilain's, in the Rue Saint-Martin, No. 92, the second row of steps at the left, at the end of the courtyard—first floor—door to the right!"

At last, he saw Regimbart, in a cloud of tobacco-smoke, by himself, at the lower end of the refreshment-room, near the billiard-table, with a glass of beer in front of him, and his chin lowered in a thoughtful attitude.

"Ah! I have been a long time searching for you!"

Without rising, Regimbart extended towards him only two fingers, and, as if he had seen Frédéric the day before, he made a few commonplace remarks about the opening of the parliamentary session.

Frédéric interrupted him, saying in the most natural tone he could assume:

"How is Arnoux?"

The reply was a long time coming, as Regimbart was gargling the liquor in his throat:

"All right."

"Where is he living now?"

"Why, in the Rue Paradis Poissonnière," the Citizen returned with astonishment.

"What number?"

"Thirty-seven—Good lord! what a funny fellow you are!"

Frédéric rose.

"What! are you going?"

"Yes, yes! I have to make a call—some business matter I had forgotten! Good-bye!"

Frédéric went from the tavern to the Arnoux's residence, as if carried along by a warm wind, with the extraordinary ease one experiences in dreams.

He soon found himself on the second floor in front of a door, whose bell was ringing; a servant appeared. A second door was flung open. Madame Arnoux was seated near the fire. Arnoux jumped up, and rushed across to embrace Frédéric. She had on her lap a little boy not quite three years old. Her daughter, now as tall as herself, was standing up at the opposite side of the mantelpiece.

"Allow me to present this gentleman to you," said Arnoux, taking his son up in his arms. And he amused himself for a few minutes in throwing the child up in the air, and then catching him as he came down.

"You'll kill him!—ah! good heavens, stop!" exclaimed Madame Arnoux.

But Arnoux, declaring that there was not the slightest danger, still kept tossing up the child, and even addressed him in words of endearment such as nurses use in the Marseillaise dialect, which he grew up with:

"Ah! my sweet little one! my little chickadee!"

Then, he asked Frédéric why he had been so long without writing to them, what he had been doing in the country, and what brought him back.

"As for me, I am at present, my dear friend, a dealer in ceramics. But let us talk about yourself!"

Frédéric gave as reasons for his absence a protracted lawsuit and the state of his mother's health. He laid special stress on the latter subject in order to make himself interesting. He ended by saying that this time he was going to settle in Paris for good; and he said nothing about the inheritance, lest it cast a bad light on his past.

The curtains, like the furniture upholstery, were of maroon damask wool. Two pillows lay close beside one another against the bolster. On the coal-fire a kettle was boiling; and the shade of the lamp, which stood near the edge of the chest of drawers, darkened the apartment. Madame Arnoux wore a blue merino dressing-gown. With her face turned towards the fire and one hand on the shoulder of the little boy, she unfastened the child's vest with the other. The youngster in his shirt began to cry, while scratching his head, like the son of M. Alexandre.

Frédéric expected to feel spasms of joy; but the passions grow pale when we find ourselves in an altered situation; and, as he no longer saw Madame Arnoux in the environment wherein he had known her, she seemed to him to have lost some of her fascination; to have been diminished in some way that he could not comprehend—in fact, not to be the same. He was astonished at the serenity of his own heart. He made enquiries about some old friends, about Pellerin, amongst others.

"I don't see him often," said Arnoux. She added:

"We no longer entertain as we used to!"

Was the object of this to let him know that he would get no invitation from them? But Arnoux, continuing to exhibit the same cordiality, reproached him for not having come to dine with them uninvited; and he explained why he had changed his business.

"What are you to do in an age of decadence like ours? Great painting has gone out of fashion! Besides, we may incorporate art into everything. You know that, for my part, I am a lover of beauty. I must bring you one of these days to see my earthenware workshop."

And he wanted to show Frédéric immediately some of his productions in the store which he had between the ground-floor and the first floor.

Dishes, soup-tureens, and washhand-basins covered the floor. Against the walls were laid out large tiles for bathrooms and dressing-rooms, with mythological subjects in the Renaissance style; whilst in the centre, a pair of whatnots, rising up to the ceiling, supported ice-buckets, flower-pots, candelabra, little plant-stands, and large statuettes of many colours, representing a negro or a shepherdess in the Pompadour fashion. Frédéric, who was cold and hungry, was bored with Arnoux's display of his wares. He hurried off to the Café Anglais, where he ordered a sumptuous supper, and while eating, said to himself:

"How silly I was back home with my lovesickness! She scarcely knew who I was! How like an ordinary house-wife she is!"

And in a sudden burst of healthy energy, he resolved to be utterly selfish. He felt his heart as hard as the table on which his elbows rested. So then he could by this time plunge fearlessly into the vortex of society. The thought of the Dambreuses came to mind again. He would make use of them. Then he remembered Deslauriers. "Ah! well, too bad!" Nevertheless, he sent him a note by a messenger, in order to arrange to meet for lunch the next day.

Fortune had not been so kind to Deslauriers.

He had presented himself at the examination for a fellowship with a thesis on the law of wills, in which he maintained that this power of law ought to be restricted as much as possible; and, as his adversary provoked him in such a way as to make him say foolish things, he came out with many absurdities, without any reaction for his examiners. Then, as such would have it, he drew by lot, as the subject for his lecture, the statute of limitations. Thereupon, Deslauriers put forth some lamentable theories: old claims ought to be treated like new; why should a proprietor be deprived of his property because he could not furnish his deed until thirty-one years have elapsed? This was giving the security of the honest man to the inheritor of the enriched thief. Every injustice was consecrated by extending this law, which was a form of tyranny, the abuse of force! He had even exclaimed: "Abolish it; and the Franks will no longer oppress the Gauls,[1] the English oppress the Irish, the Yankee oppress the Redskins, the Turks oppress the Arabs, the whites oppress the blacks, Poland——"

The President interrupted him: "Well! well! Monsieur, we have nothing to do with your political opinions—you can present yourself for re-examination at a later date!"

Deslauriers did not wish to try again; but this unfortunate Title XX. of the Third Book of the Civil Code had become a sort of mountain over which he stumbled. He was writing an extensive work on "Prescription considered as the Basis of the Civil Law and of the Law of Nature amongst Peoples"; and he got lost in Dunod, Rogerius, Balbus, Merlin, Vazeille, Savigny, Traplong, and other weighty authorities on the subject. In order to have more leisure time for the purpose of devoting himself to this task, he had resigned his post as head-clerk. He lived by giving private tuitions and preparing theses; and at the meetings of the debating society to rehearse legal arguments he frightened by his virulence those who held conservative views, all the young doctrinaires trained by M. Guizot—so that in a certain set he had gained a sort of celebrity, mingled, to a slight degree, with distrust.

He came to their *rendez-vous* in an overcoat, lined with red flannel, like the one Sénécal used to wear.

Out of respect for the passers-by they restrained themselves from prolonging their friendly embrace; and they made their way to Véfour's arm-in-arm, laughing pleasantly, though with tears lingering in the depths of their eyes. Then, as soon as they were free from observation, Deslauriers exclaimed:

"By gosh! we'll have a good time now!"

Frédéric was not quite pleased to find Deslauriers all at once associating himself in this way with his own newly-acquired inheritance. His friend exhibited too much pleasure on account of them both, and not enough on his account alone.

After this, Deslauriers gave details about his failure, and gradually told Frédéric all about his occupations and his daily existence, speaking of himself stoically, and of others with a tone of intense bitterness. He found fault with everything; there was not a man in office who was not an idiot or a rascal. He flew into a passion against the waiter for having a glass badly rinsed, and, when Frédéric uttered a reproach with a view to mitigating his wrath: "As if I were going to annoy myself with such numbskulls, who, you must know, can earn as much as six and even eight thousand francs a year, who are electors, perhaps eligible as candidates.[2] Ah! no, no!"

Then, with a sprightly air, "But I've forgotten that I'm talking to a capitalist, to a Mondor, for you are a Mondor now!"

And, coming back to the question of the inheritance, he expressed this view—that collateral succession (a thing unjust in itself, though in the present case he was glad it was possible) would be abolished one of these days at the approaching revolution.

"Do you believe in that?" said Frédéric.

"Be sure of it!" he replied. "This sort of thing cannot last. There is too much suffering. When I see the wretchedness of men like Sénécal——"

"Always Sénécal!" thought Frédéric.

"But, as for the rest, tell me the news? Are you still in love with Madame Arnoux? Is it all over—eh?"

Frédéric, not knowing what answer to give him, closed his eyes and bowed his head.

With regard to Arnoux, Deslauriers told him that the journal was now the property of Hussonnet, who had transformed it. It was called "*L'Art*, a literary institution—a company with shares of one hundred francs each; capital of the firm, forty thousand francs," each shareholder having the right to put into it his own contributions; for "the company has for its object to publish the works of beginners, to spare writers of talent, perhaps of genius, sad overwhelming crises," etc.

"You know how it goes!" There was, however, something to be effected by the change—the tone of the journal could be raised;

then, without any delay, while retaining the same writers, and promising a continuation of the series, to supply the subscribers with a political journal: the capital required would not be much.

"What do you think of it? Come! would you like to have a hand in it?"

Frédéric did not reject the proposal; but he pointed out that it was necessary for him to straighten out his affairs first.

"After that, if you require anything——"

"Thanks, my boy!" said Deslauriers.

Then, they smoked cigars, leaning with their elbows on the ledge covered with velvet beside the window. The sun was shining; the air was balmy. Flocks of birds, fluttering about, swooped down into the garden. The statues of bronze and marble, washed by the rain, were glistening. Nursery-maids wearing aprons were seated on chairs, chatting together; and the laughter of children could be heard mingling with the continuous splash that came from the fountain.

Frédéric was troubled by Deslauriers' irritability; but under the influence of the wine which circulated through his veins, half-asleep, in a state of torpor, with the sun shining full on his face, he was no longer conscious of anything save a profound sense of comfort, a kind of voluptuous feeling that stupefied him, as a plant is saturated with heat and moisture. Deslauriers, with half-closed eyelids, was staring vacantly into the distance. His chest swelled, and he broke out in the following strain:

"Ah! those were better days when Camille Desmoulins, standing below there on a table, drove the people on to the Bastille.[3] Men really lived in those times; they could assert themselves, and prove their strength! Simple lawyers commanded generals. Kings were beaten by beggars; whilst now——"

He stopped, then added all of a sudden:

"Never mind! the future is full of promise!"

And, drumming a battle-march on the window-panes, he spoke some verses of Barthélemy,* which ran thus:

> " 'That dreaded Assembly shall again appear,
> Which, after forty years, fills you with fear,

---

*Auguste Barthélemy (1796–1867) was a satirical poet of the time.

A fearless Colussus marching with giant strides'

—I don't know the rest of it! But 'tis late; suppose we go?"

And he went on preaching his theories in the street.

Frédéric, without listening to him, was looking at certain materials and articles of furniture in the shop-windows which would be suitable for his new residence in Paris; and it was, perhaps, the thought of Madame Arnoux that made him stop before a second-hand dealer's window, where three plates made of fine porcelain were exposed to view. They were decorated with yellow arabesques with metallic reflections, and were worth a hundred crowns apiece. He had them put aside.

"If I were in your place," said Deslauriers, "I would buy silver," revealing by this love of lavish things a man of humble origins.

As soon as he was alone, Frédéric proceeded to the establishment of the celebrated Pomadère, where he ordered three pairs of trousers, two dress coats, a coat trimmed with fur, and five waistcoats. Then he called at a bootmaker's, a shirtmaker's, and a hatter's, giving them directions in each shop to make the greatest possible haste. Three days later, on the evening of his return from Le Havre, he found his complete wardrobe awaiting him in his Parisian abode; and impatient to make use of it, he resolved to pay an immediate visit to the Dambreuses. But it was too early yet—scarcely eight o'clock.

"Suppose I went to see the others?" said he to himself.

He came upon Arnoux, all alone, in the act of shaving in front of his glass. The latter proposed to drive him to a place where they could amuse themselves, and when M. Dambreuse was referred to, "Ah, that's lucky! You'll see some of his friends there. Come on, then! It will be good fun!"

Frédéric asked to be excused. Madame Arnoux recognised his voice, and wished him good-day, through the partition, for her daughter was indisposed, and she was also rather unwell herself. The noise of a spoon against a glass could be heard from within, and all those rustling sounds made by things being lightly moved about, which are usual in a sickroom. Then Arnoux left his dressing-room to say good-bye to his wife. He enumerated the reasons for going out:

"You know well that it is a serious matter! I must go there; 'tis a case of necessity. They'll be waiting for me!"

"Go, go, my dear! Amuse yourself!"

Arnoux hailed a hackney-coach:

"Palais Royal, No. 7 Montpensier Gallery." And, as he let himself sink back in the cushions:

"Ah! how tired I am, my dear fellow! It will be the death of me! However, I can tell it to you—to you!"

He bent towards Frédéric's ear in a mysterious fashion:

"I am trying to discover again the red of Chinese copper!"

And he explained the nature of the glaze and the little fire.

On their arrival at Chevet's shop, a large basket was brought to him, which he stowed away in the hackney-coach. Then he chose for his "poor wife" some grapes, pineapples and various delicacies, and directed that they should be sent early next morning.

After this, they called at a costumer's establishment; it was to a masquerade ball they were going.

Arnoux selected blue velvet breeches, a vest of the same material, and a red wig; Frédéric a domino; and they went down the Rue de Laval towards a house the second floor of which was illuminated by coloured lanterns.

At the foot of the stairs they heard violins playing above.

"Where the devil are you bringing me to?" said Frédéric.

"To see a sweet girl! don't be afraid!"

The door was opened for them by a footman; and they entered the hall, where overcoats, cloaks, and shawls were thrown together in a heap on some chairs. A young woman in the costume of a dragoon of Louis XIV's reign was passing by at that moment. It was Mademoiselle Rosanette Bron, the mistress of the house.

"Well?" said Arnoux.

" 'Tis done!" she replied.

"Ah! thank you, my angel!"

And he wanted to kiss her.

"Be careful, you fool! You'll spoil my make-up!"

Arnoux introduced Frédéric.

"Step inside, Monsieur; you are quite welcome!"

She drew aside a door-curtain, and cried out with a certain emphasis:

"Here's my lord Arnoux, kitchen boy, and a princely friend of his!"

Frédéric was at first dazzled by the lights. He could see nothing save some silk and velvet dresses, naked shoulders, a mass of colours swaying to and fro to the accompaniment of an orchestra hidden behind green foliage, between walls hung with yellow silk, with pastel portraits here and there and crystal chandeliers in the style of Louis XVI's period. High lamps, whose globes of frosted glass resembled snowballs, looked down on baskets of flowers placed on small tables in the corners; and opposite through a second smaller room, one could see a third room containing a bed with twisted posts, over which hung a Venetian mirror.

The dancing stopped, and there were bursts of applause, a hubbub of delight, as Arnoux was seen advancing with his basket on his head; the food stuffs contained in it made a lump in the centre.

"Watch out for the chandelier!"

Frédéric raised his eyes: it was the old Saxon chandelier that had adorned the shop attached to the office of *L'Art Industriel*. The memory of former days came back to him. But a foot-soldier in undress uniform, with that silly expression traditionally attributed to conscripts, planted himself right in front of him, spreading out his two arms to express his astonishment, and, in spite of the hideous black extra-pointing moustache, disfiguring his face, Frédéric recognised his old friend Hussonnet. In a half-Alsatian, half-negro kind of gibberish, the Bohemian showered him with congratulations, calling him his colonel. Frédéric, overwhelmed by all these people, was at a loss for an answer. At a tap on the desk from a fiddlestick, the partners in the dance fell into their places.

They were about sixty in number, the women being for the most part dressed either as village-girls or marquises, and the men, who were nearly all middle-aged, in costumes of wagoners, 'longshore-men, or sailors.

Frédéric, having taken up his position close to the wall, stared at those who were going through the quadrille in front of him.

An old buck, dressed like a Venetian Doge in a long gown of purple silk, was dancing with Mademoiselle Rosanette, who wore a green coat, laced breeches, and boots of soft leather with gold spurs. The pair in front of them consisted of an Albanian laden with Turkish daggers and a Swiss girl with blue eyes and skin white as milk, who looked as plump as a quail in shirt-sleeves and a red corset to show off her hair, which fell down to her hips; a tall blonde, an extra in the opera, had assumed the part of a female savage, and over her brown body-suit she wore nothing but a leather loin-cloth, glass bracelets, and a tinsel diadem, from which rose a large spray of peacock's feathers. In front of her, a gentleman who had intended to be Pritchard, in a ridiculously big black coat, was beating time with his elbows on his snuff-box. A little Watteau shepherd in blue-and-silver, like moonlight, dashed his crook against the thyrsus of a Bacchante crowned with grapes, who wore a leopard's skin over her left side, and buskins with gold ribbons; on the other side, a Polish lady, in a short red velvet jacket, made her gauze petticoat flutter over her pearl-gray stockings, which rose above her fashionable pink boots bordered with white fur.

She was smiling at a big-paunched man of forty, disguised as a choir-boy, who was skipping about, lifting up his surplice with one hand, and with the other his red clerical cap. But the queen, the star, was Mademoiselle Loulou, a star of the dance halls. As she had now become wealthy, she wore a large lace collar over her vest of smooth black velvet; and her wide trousers of poppy-coloured silk, clinging closely to her figure, and drawn tight round her waist by a cashmere scarf, had all over their seams little natural white camellias. Her pale face, a little puffy, and with a slightly turned up nose, looked all the more pert from the disordered appearance of her wig, over which she had clapped a man's grey felt hat, cocked over her right ear; and, with every leap she made, her pumps, adorned with diamond buckles, nearly kicked in the nose her neighbour, a big mediæval baron, who was quite entangled in his steel armour. There was also an angel, with a gold sword in her hand, and two swan's wings over her back, who kept rushing up and down, every minute losing her partner who appeared as Louis XIV, bewildered among the figures and confusing the quadrille.

Frédéric, as he gazed at these people, experienced a sense of forlornness, a feeling of uneasiness. He was still thinking of Madame Arnoux and it seemed to him as if he were taking part in some plot that was being hatched against her.

When the quadrille was over, Mademoiselle Rosanette accosted him. She was slightly out of breath, and her gorget, polished like a mirror, rose up under her chin.

"And you, Monsieur," said she, "don't you dance?"

Frédéric excused himself; he did not know how to dance.

"Really! but with me? Are you quite sure?" And, poised on one hip, with her other knee a little drawn back, while she stroked with her left hand the mother-of-pearl pommel of her sword, she kept staring at him for a minute with a half-beseeching, half-teasing air. At last she said "Good night!" then made a pirouette, and disappeared.

Frédéric, dissatisfied with himself, and not knowing what to do, began to wander through the ball-room.

He entered the boudoir padded with pale blue silk, with bouquets of flowers from the fields, whilst on the ceiling, in a circle of gilt wood, Cupids emerging out of an azure sky, played over the pillowy clouds. This display of luxury, which would to-day be nothing to people like Rosanette, dazzled him, and he admired everything—the artificial morning glories which adorned the surface of the mirror, the curtains over the fireplace, the Turkish divan, and a sort of tent in an alcove made of pink silk with a covering of white muslin overhead. Furniture made of dark wood with inlaid copper work filled the bedroom, where, on a platform covered with swan's-down, stood the large canopied bedstead trimmed with ostrich-feathers. Pins, with heads made of precious stones, stuck into pincushions, rings trailing over trays, circular gold medallions, and little silver chests, could be distinguished in the dim light shed by a Bohemian urn suspended from three chains. Through a little door, which was slightly ajar, could be seen a green-house occupying the entire breadth of a terrace, with an aviary at the other end.

Here were surroundings specially calculated to charm him. In a sudden revolt of his youthful blood he swore that he would enjoy such things; he grew bold; then, coming back to the place opening into the drawing-room, where there was now a larger gathering—everything kept moving about in a kind of luminous haze—he stood to watch the quadrilles, squinting his eyes to see better, and inhaling the soft perfumes of the women, which floated through the atmosphere like an immense kiss.

But, close to him, on the other side of the door, was Pellerin—Pellerin, in full dress, his left arm over his chest and with his hat and a torn white glove in his right hand.

"Hello! 'Tis a long time since we saw you! Where the devil have you been? Gone to travel in Italy? 'Tis a commonplace country enough—Italy, eh? not so unique as people say it is? No matter! Will you bring me your sketches one of these days?"

And, without giving him time to answer, the artist began talking about himself. He had made considerable progress, having definitely satisfied himself as to the stupidity of line. We ought not to look so much for beauty and unity in a work as for character and diversity of subject.

"For everything exists in nature; therefore, everything is legitimate; everything is plastic. It is only a question of striking the right note, mind you! I have discovered the secret." And giving him a nudge, he repeated several times, "I have discovered the secret, you see! Just look at that little woman with the headdress of a sphinx who is dancing with a Russian postilion—that's neat, cut and dried, fixed, all in flats and in stiff tones—indigo under the eyes, a patch of vermilion on the cheek, and sepia on the temples—pif! paf!" And with his thumb he drew, as it were, brush-strokes in the air. "Whilst the big one over there," he went on, pointing towards a fishwife in a cherry gown with a gold cross hanging from her neck, and a linen cape fastened round the back, "is nothing but curves. The nostrils are spread out just like the borders of her cap; the corners of the mouth are rising up; the chin sinks: all is fleshy, melting, abundant, tranquil, and radiant—a true Rubens! Nevertheless, they are both perfect! Where, then, is the type?" He was warming up to this subject. "What is a beautiful woman? What is beauty? Ah! the beautiful—tell me what that is——"

Frédéric interrupted him to enquire who was the Pierrot with the face of a goat, who was in the very act of blessing all the dancers in the middle of a quadrille.

"Oh! he's not much!—a widower, the father of three boys. He leaves them without trousers, spends his whole day at the club, and lives with his servant!"

"And who is that dressed like a bailiff talking in the recess of the window to a lady in the style of the Marquise Pompadour?"*

"The Marquise is Mademoiselle Vandael, formerly an actress at the Gymnase, the mistress of the Doge, the Comte de Palazot. They

*The influential mistress of Louis XV in the eighteenth century.

have now been together twenty years—nobody can tell why. Hadn't she fine eyes at one time, this woman! As for the citizen by her side, his name is Captain d'Herbigny, a man of the old guard with nothing in the world except his Cross of the Legion d'honneur and his pension. He acts as uncle of the grisettes at festival times, arranges duels, and dines in the city."

"A rascal?" said Frédéric.

"No! An honest man!"

"Ah!"

The artist went on to mention the names of many others, when, perceiving a gentleman who, like Molière's physician, wore a big black serge gown opening very wide as it descended in order to display all his trinkets:

"The person who presents himself there before you is Dr. Des Rogis, who, full of rage at not having made a name for himself, has written a book of medical pornography, and is a boot-licker in high society, while he is at the same time discreet. The ladies adore him. He and his wife (that scrawny châtelaine in the grey dress) flit about together to every public occasion—and at other places too. In spite of their shabby home, they have *a day*—artistic teas, at which verses are recited. Look out!"

In fact, the doctor came up to them at that moment; and soon the three of them formed, at the entrance to the drawing-room, a group of talkers, which was then augmented by Hussonnet, then by the lover of the female savage, a young poet who displayed, under a court cloak of Francis I's reign, the most pitiful of anatomies, and finally a sprightly youth disguised as a Turk. But his gold-braided vest had travelled so much on the backs of itinerant dentists, his wide trousers full of creases were of so faded a red, his turban, rolled up like an eel Tartar, was so poor in appearance—in short, his entire costume was so wretched and made-up, that the women did not attempt to hide their disgust. The doctor consoled him by singing the praise of his mistress, the lady in the dress of a 'longshorewoman. This Turk was a banker's son.

Between two quadrilles, Rosanette advanced towards the mantelpiece, where an obese little old man, in a maroon coat with gold buttons, had seated himself in an armchair. In spite of his withered cheeks, which fell over his white cravat, his hair, still fair, and curling naturally like that of a poodle, gave him an air of frivolity.

She was listening to him with her face bent close to his. Presently, she accommodated him with a little glass of syrup; and nothing could be more dainty than her hands under their laced sleeves, which passed over the facings of her green coat. When the old man had swallowed it, he kissed them.

"Why, that's M. Oudry, a neighbor of Arnoux!"

"He has lost her!" said Pellerin, laughing.

"Pardon?"

A Longjumeau postilion* caught her by the waist. A waltz was beginning. Then all the women, seated round the drawing-room on benches, rose up quickly at the same time; and their petticoats, their scarfs, and their head-dresses went whirling round.

They whirled so close to him that Frédéric could see the beads of perspiration on their foreheads; and this circular movement, more and more lively, regular, dizzying, communicated to his mind a sort of intoxication, which made other images surge up within it, while every woman passed with the same dazzling effect, and each with her own unique excitement, according to her style of beauty.

The Polish lady, surrendering herself languidly to the dance, inspired in him a longing to clasp her to his heart while they were both speeding forward on a sleigh along a plain covered with snow. Horizons of tranquil pleasures in a châlet at the side of a lake emerged under the footsteps of the Swiss girl, who waltzed with her torso erect and her eyelids lowered. Then, suddenly, the Bacchante, bending back her head with its dark locks, made him dream of devouring caresses in oleander groves, in the midst of a storm, to the confused accompaniment of drums. The fishwife, who was panting from the rapidity of the music, burst out laughing, and he would have liked, while drinking with her in some tavern in the "Porcherons," to rumple her cape with both hands, as in the good old days. But the 'longshorewoman, whose light feet barely skimmed the floor, seemed to conceal under the suppleness of her limbs and the seriousness of her face all the refinements of modern love, which combines the exactitude of a science and the mobility of a bird. Rosanette was whirling around with one hand on her hip; her wig, bobbing over her collar, flung iris-powder around her; and, at

---

*Reference to a popular operetta, *Le Postillon de Longjumeau.*

every turn, she nearly caught Frédéric with the ends of her gold spurs.

During the closing bar of the waltz, Mademoiselle Vatnaz made her appearance. She had an Algerian kerchief on her head, a number of coins dangling on her forehead, black kohl at the edges of her eyes, with a kind of coat made of black cashmere falling over a silver lathé skirt and in her hand she held a tambourine.

Behind her back came a tall fellow in the classical costume of Dante, who happened to be—she no longer concealed it—the ex-singer of the Alhambra, and who, though his name was Auguste Delamare, had first called himself Anténor Delamarre, then Delmas, then Belmar, and at last Delmar, thus modifying and perfecting his name, as his celebrity increased, for he had forsaken the dance-hall concert for the theatre, and had even just made his splashy *début* at the Ambigu in *Gaspardo le Pêcheur*.

Hussonnet, on seeing him, knitted his brows. Since his play had been rejected, he hated actors. It was impossible to conceive the vanity of individuals of this sort, and above all of this fellow. "What a poser! Just look at him!"

After a light bow towards Rosanette, Delmar leaned back against the mantelpiece; and he remained motionless with one hand over his heart, his left foot thrust forward, his eyes raised towards heaven, with his wreath of gilt laurels around his hood, while he strove to put into the expression of his face a considerable amount of poetry in order to fascinate the ladies. They made, at some distance, a great circle around him.

But Vatnaz, having given Rosanette a prolonged embrace, came to beg of Hussonnet to revise, with a view to the improvement of the style, an educational work which she intended to publish, under the title of "The Young Ladies' Garland," a collection of literature and moral philosophy.

The man of letters promised to assist her in the preparation of the work. Then she asked him whether he could not in one of the papers to which he had access give her friend a little publicity, and even assign to him, later, some part. Hussonnet had forgotten to take a glass of punch on account of her.

It was Arnoux who had brewed the beverage; and, followed by the Comte's footman carrying an empty tray, he offered it to the ladies with a self-satisfied air.

When he came to pass in front of M. Oudry, Rosanette stopped him.

"Well—and this little business?"

He reddened slightly; finally, addressing the old man:

"Our fair friend tells me that you would have the kindness——"

"Why, neighbour of course! I am quite at your service!"

And M. Dambreuse's name was spoken. As they were talking to one another in low tones, Frédéric could only hear indistinctly; and he made his way to the other side of the mantelpiece, where Rosanette and Delmar were chatting together.

The entertainer had a vulgar look to him, made, like the scenery of the stage, to be viewed from a distance—coarse hands, big feet, and a heavy jaw; and he disparaged the most distinguished actors, spoke of poets with patronising contempt, made use of the expressions "my organ," "my physique," "my powers," peppering his conversation with words that were scarcely intelligible even to himself, and for which he had quite an affection, such as "*morbidezza*," "analogue," and "homogeneity."

Rosanette listened to him with little nods of approval. One could see her enthusiasm bursting out under the make-up on her cheeks, and a touch of mist passed like a veil over her bright eyes of an indefinable colour. How could such a man as this fascinate her? Frédéric internally worked himself up to even greater contempt for him, in order to banish, perhaps, the sort of envy which he felt with regard to him.

Mademoiselle Vatnaz was now with Arnoux, and, while laughing from time to time very loudly, she cast glances towards Rosanette, of whom M. Oudry did not lose sight.

Then Arnoux and Vatnaz disappeared. The old man began talking in a subdued voice to Rosanette.

"Well, yes, 'tis settled then! Leave me alone!"

And she asked Frédéric to go and give a look into the kitchen to see whether Arnoux happened to be there.

A battalion of glasses half-full covered the floor; and the saucepans, the pots, the turbot-kettle, and the frying-pan were all simmering and sizzling. Arnoux was giving directions to the servants, whom he "spoke to familiarly," beating the rémoulade, tasting the sauces, and joking with the housemaid.

"All right," he said; "tell them 'tis ready! I'm going to have it served up."

The dancing had ceased. The women came and sat down; the men were walking about. In the centre of the drawing-room, one of the curtains was billowing in the wind; and the Sphinx, in spite of the observations of everyone, exposed her sweaty arms to the current of air.

Where could Rosanette be? Frédéric went on further to find her, even into her boudoir and her bedroom. Some, in order to be alone, or to be in pairs, had retreated into the corners. Whisperings intermingled with the shadows. There were little laughs stifled under handkerchiefs, and at the sides of women's corsages one could catch glimpses of fans quivering with slow, gentle movements, like the beating of a wounded bird's wings.

As he entered the green-house, he saw under the large leaves of a caladium near the fountain, Delmar lying on his face on the linen-covered sofa. Rosanette, seated beside him, ran her fingers through his hair; and they were gazing into each other's faces. At the same moment, Arnoux came in at the opposite side—near the aviary. Delmar sprang to his feet; then he went out at a rapid pace, without turning round; and even paused close to the door to gather a hibiscus flower, with which he adorned his button-hole. Rosanette lowered her head; Frédéric, who caught a sight of her profile, saw that she was in tears.

"I say! What's the matter with you?" exclaimed Arnoux.

She shrugged her shoulders without replying.

"Is it on account of him?" he went on.

She threw her arms round his neck, and kissing him on the forehead, slowly:

"You know well that I will always love you, big fellow! Think no more about it! Let us go to supper!"

A copper chandelier with forty candles lit up the dining-room, the walls of which were covered with fine old china plates; and this bright light, rendered still whiter, amid the side-dishes and the fruits, a huge turbot which occupied the centre of the table, with plates all round filled with crayfish soup. With a rustle of garments, the women, having arranged their skirts, their sleeves, and their scarfs, took their seats beside one another; the men, standing up, posted themselves at the corners. Pellerin and M. Oudry were placed near Rosanette, Arnoux was facing her. Palazot and his female companion had just left.

"Good-bye to them!" said she. "Now let us begin the attack!"

And the choir-boy, a joker, making a big sign of the cross, said grace.

The ladies were scandalised, and especially the fishwife, the mother of a young girl she was raising to be a respectable woman. Neither did Arnoux like "that sort of thing," as he considered that religion ought to be respected.

A German clock, adorned with a rooster, chimed out the hour of two, gave rise to a number of jokes about the cuckoo. All kinds of talk followed—puns, anecdotes, bragging remarks, bets, lies taken for truth, improbable assertions, a tumult of words, which soon became dispersed in the form of chats between particular individuals. The wines went round; the dishes succeeded each other; the doctor carved. An orange or a cork would every now and then be flung from a distance. People would quit their seats to go and talk to some one at another end of the table. Rosanette turned round towards Delmar, who sat motionless behind her; Pellerin kept babbling; M. Oudry smiled. Mademoiselle Vatnaz ate, almost alone, a group of crayfish, and the shells crackled under her long teeth. The angel, poised on the piano-stool—the only place on which her wings permitted her to sit down—was placidly chewing without ever stopping.

"What an appetite!" the choir-boy kept repeating in amazement, "what an appetite!"

And the Sphinx drank brandy, screamed out with her throat full, and wriggled as if possessed by a demon. Suddenly her cheeks swelled, and no longer being able to keep down the blood which rushed to her head and nearly choked her, she pressed her napkin against her lips, then threw it under the table.

Frédéric had seen her: " 'Tis nothing!" And at his entreaties to be allowed to go and look after her, she replied slowly:

"Pooh! what's the use? That's no worse than anything else. Life is not so amusing!"

Then, he shivered, a feeling of icy sadness taking possession of him, as if he had caught a glimpse of whole worlds of wretchedness and despair—a charcoal heater beside a folding-bed, the corpses of the Morgue in leather aprons, with the tap of cold water that flows over their heads.

Meanwhile, Hussonnet, squatted at the feet of the female savage, was howling in a hoarse voice in imitation of the actor Grassot:

"Be not cruel, O Celuta! this little family fête is charming! Intoxicate me with delight, my loves! Let us be merry! let us be merry!"

And he began kissing the women on the shoulders. They quivered under the tickling of his moustache. Then he conceived the idea of breaking a plate against his head by tapping it there lightly. Others followed his example. The broken earthenware flew about in bits like slates in a storm; and the 'longshorewoman exclaimed:

"Don't bother yourselves about it; these cost nothing. We get a present of them from the merchant who makes them!"

Every eye was riveted on Arnoux. He replied:

"Ha! about the invoice—allow me!" desiring, no doubt, to pass for not being, or for no longer being, Rosanette's lover.

But two angry voices here made themselves heard:

"Idiot!"

"Rascal!"

"I am at your command!"

"As am I at yours!"

It was the mediæval knight and the Russian postilion who were disputing, the latter having maintained that armour dispensed with bravery, while the other regarded this view as an insult. He wanted to fight; all intervened, and in the midst of the uproar the captain tried to make himself heard.

"Listen to me, messieurs! One word! I have some experience, messieurs!"

Rosanette, by tapping with her knife on a glass, succeeded eventually in restoring silence, and, addressing the knight, who had kept his helmet on, and then the postilion, whose head was covered with a hairy cap:

"Take off that saucepan of yours! and you, there, your wolf's head! Are you going to obey me, damn you? Pray show respect to my epaulets! I am your commanding officer!"

They complied, and everyone present applauded, exclaiming, "Long live the Maréchale! long live the Maréchale!" Then she took a bottle of champagne off the stove, and poured out its contents into the cups which they then extended towards her in a toast. As the table was very large, the guests, especially the women, came over to her side, and stood on tiptoe on the slats of the chairs, so as to form, for the space of a minute, a pyramid of headdresses, naked shoulders, extended arms, and stooping bodies; and over all these objects sprays of wine spurted in the air, for the Pierrot and Arnoux, at opposite corners of the dining-room, each letting fly the cork of a bottle, splashed the faces of those around them.

The little birds of the aviary, the door of which had been left open, broke into the room, quite scared, flying round the chandelier, knocking into the windows and the furniture, and some of them, alighting on the heads of the guests, looked like large flowers.

The musicians had gone. The piano had been drawn out of the entrance-hall. The Vatnaz seated herself before it, and, accompanied by the choir-boy, who shook his tambourine, she made a wild dash into a quadrille, striking the keys like a horse pawing the ground, and wriggling her waist about, the better to mark the time. The Maréchale dragged Frédéric away; Hussonnet did cartwheels; the 'longshorewoman bent her joints like a circus-clown; the Pierrot manœuvred like an orang-outang; the female savage, with outspread arms, imitated the swaying motion of a boat. At last, unable to go on any further, they all stopped; and a window was flung open.

The broad daylight penetrated the room with the cool breath of morning. There was an exclamation of astonishment, and then came silence. The yellow flames flickered, making the drip glass of the candlesticks crack from time to time. The floor was strewn with ribbons, flowers, and pearls. The pier-tables were sticky with the stains of punch and syrup. The wall hangings were soiled, the dresses rumpled and dusty. The women's hair hung loose over their shoulders, and their make-up, trickling down with the perspiration, revealed pale faces and red, blinking eyelids.

The Maréchale, fresh as if she had come out of a bath, had rosy cheeks and sparkling eyes. She flung her wig some distance away, and her hair fell around her like a fleece, allowing none of her outfit to be seen except her breeches, the effect thus produced being both comical and pretty.

The Sphinx, whose teeth chattered as if she had a fever, wanted a shawl.

Rosanette rushed up to her own room to look for one, and, as the other came after her, she quickly shut the door in her face.

The Turk remarked, in a loud tone, that M. Oudry had not been seen going out. Nobody noticed the maliciousness of this observation, so worn out were they all.

Then, while waiting for their carriages, they managed to put on their broad-brimmed hats and cloaks. The clock struck seven. The angel was still in the dining-room, seated at the table with a plate of sardines and fruit stewed in melted butter in front of her, and close beside her was the fishwife, smoking cigarettes, while giving her advice as to the right way to live.

At last, the cabs having arrived, the guests made their departure. Hussonnet, employed as correspondent for the provinces, had to read through fifty-three newspapers before his breakfast. The female savage had a rehearsal at the theatre; Pellerin had to see a model; and the choir-boy had three appointments. But the angel, attacked by the preliminary symptoms of indigestion, was unable to rise. The mediæval baron carried her to the cab.

"Look out for her wings!" cried the 'longshorewoman through the window.

At the top of the stairs, Mademoiselle Vatnaz said to Rosanette:

"Good-bye, darling! That was a very nice party you threw."

Then, bending close to her ear: "Take care of him!"

"Till better times come," returned the Maréchale, as she turned her back.

Arnoux and Frédéric returned together, just as they had come. The ceramics dealer looked so gloomy that his companion wished to know if he were ill.

"I? Not at all!"

He bit his moustache, knitted his brows; and Frédéric asked him, was it his business that annoyed him.

"By no means!"

Then all of a sudden:

"You know him—Père Oudry—don't you?"

And, with a spiteful expression on his face:

"He's rich, the old scoundrel!"

After this, Arnoux spoke about an important piece of pottery, which had to be finished that day at his works. He wanted to see it; the train was leaving in an hour.

"Meantime, I must go and kiss my wife."

"Ha! his wife!" thought Frédéric. Then he made his way home to go to bed, with his head aching terribly; and, to quench his thirst, he drank a whole carafe of water.

Another thirst had come to him—the thirst for women, for licentious pleasure, and all that Parisian life permitted him to enjoy. He felt somewhat stunned, like a man coming out of a ship, and in the visions that haunted his first sleep, he saw the shoulders of the fishwife, the back of the 'longshorewoman, the calves of the Polish lady, and the hair of the female savage flying past him and coming back again continually. Then, two large black eyes, which had not been at the ball, appeared before him; and, light as butterflies, burning as torches, they came and went, ascended to the cornice and descended to his very mouth.

Frédéric made desperate efforts to recognise those eyes, without succeeding in doing so. But already the dream had taken hold of him. It seemed to him that he was yoked beside Arnoux to the pole of a hackney-coach, and that the Maréchale, astride of him, was disembowelling him with her gold spurs.

CHAPTER II

Frédéric found a little townhouse at the corner of the Rue Rumfort, and he bought it along with the brougham, the horse, the furniture, and two flower-stands which were taken from the Arnoux's house to be placed on each side of his drawing-room door. In the rear of this apartment were a bedroom and a closet. The idea occurred to him to put up Deslauriers there. But how could he receive her—*her*, his future mistress? The presence of a friend would be an obstacle. He knocked down the partition-wall in order to enlarge the drawing-room, and converted the closet into a smoking-room.

He bought the works of the poets whom he loved, travel books, atlases, and dictionaries, for he had innumerable study plans. He urged the workmen to hurry, rushed about to the different shops, and in his impatience to enjoy his new home, carried off everything without even holding out for a bargain.

From the tradesmen's bills, Frédéric ascertained that he would have to pay out very soon forty thousand francs, not including the succession duties, which would exceed thirty-seven thousand. As his fortune was in landed property, he wrote to the notary at Le Havre to sell a portion of it in order to pay off his debts, and to have some money at his disposal. Then, anxious to become acquainted at last with that vague entity, glittering and indefinable, which is known as "society," he sent a note to the Dambreuses to know whether he might be at liberty to call upon them. Madame, in reply, said she would expect a visit from him the following day.

This happened to be their reception-day. Carriages were standing in the courtyard. Two footmen rushed forward under the marquée, and a third at the head of the stairs led him in.

He was conducted through an anteroom, a second room, and then a drawing-room with high windows and a monumental mantelpiece supporting a clock in the form of a sphere, and two enormous porcelain vases, in each of which bristled, like a golden bush, a cluster of sconces. Pictures in the style of lo Spagnoletto* hung on the walls. The heavy tapestry door hangings fell majestically, and the armchairs, the consoles, the tables, all of the furnishings, in the style of the Second Empire, had a certain imposing and diplomatic air.

Frédéric smiled with pleasure in spite of himself.

At last he reached an oval room panelled in rosewood, filled with dainty furniture, and letting in the light through a single window, which looked out on a garden. Madame Dambreuse was seated at the fireside, with a dozen people gathered round her in a circle. With a polite greeting, she made a sign to him to take a seat, without, however, exhibiting any surprise at not having seen him for so long a time.

Just at the moment when he was entering the room, they had been praising the eloquence of the Abbé Cœur. Then they deplored the immorality of servants, a topic suggested by a theft which a *valet-de-chambre* had committed, and they began to indulge in gossip. Old Madame de Sommery had a cold; Mademoiselle de Turvisot had gotten married; the Montcharrons would not return before the end of January; neither would the Bretancourts, now that people remained in the country longer. And the triviality of the conversation was intensified by the luxuriousness of the surroundings; but what they said was less stupid than their way of talking, which was aimless, disconnected, and utterly devoid of animation. And yet there were men present who were well-versed in life—an ex-minister, the curé of a large parish, two or three Government officials of high rank. They adhered to the most hackneyed and commonplace topics. Some of them resembled weary dowagers; others had the appearance of horse-jockeys; and old men accompanied their wives, who could have passed for their granddaughters.

Madame Dambreuse received all of them graciously. When it was mentioned that anyone was ill, she knitted her brows with a

---

*Spanish painter José de Ribera (1591–1652).

painful expression on her face, and when balls or evening parties were discussed, assumed a joyous air. She would ere long be compelled to deprive herself of these pleasures, for she was going to take in from boarding-school her husband's niece, an orphan. The guests extolled her devotedness: this was behaving like a true mother of a family.

Frédéric gazed at her attentively. Her matte skin looked as if it had been stretched tightly, and there was a freshness but with no glow; like that of preserved fruit. But her hair, which was in corkscrew curls, in the English fashion, was finer than silk; her eyes of a sparkling blue; and all her movements were dainty. Seated at the lower end of the apartment, on a small sofa, she kept stroking the red tassels on a Japanese screen, no doubt in order to let her hands be seen to greater advantage—long narrow hands, a little thin, with fingers tilting up at the points. She wore a grey moiré gown with a high-necked bodice, like a Puritan lady.

Frédéric asked her whether she intended to go to La Fortelle this year. Madame Dambreuse was unable to say. He was sure, however, of one thing, that one would be bored to death in Nogent.

Then the visitors thronged in more quickly. There was an incessant rustling of dresses on the carpet. Ladies, seated on the edges of chairs, let out little giggles, said two or three words, and at the end of five minutes left along with their young daughters. It soon became impossible to follow the conversation, and Frédéric withdrew when Madame Dambreuse said to him:

"Every Wednesday, is it not, Monsieur Moreau?" making up for her previous display of indifference by these simple words.

He was pleased. Nevertheless, he took a deep breath when he got out into the open air; and, needing a less artificial environment, Frédéric remembered that he owed the Maréchale a visit.

The door of the entrance-hall was open. Two Havanese lapdogs rushed forward. A voice exclaimed:

"Delphine! Delphine! Is that you, Felix?"

He stood there without advancing a step. The two little dogs kept yelping continually. At length Rosanette appeared, wrapped up in a sort of dressing-gown of white muslin trimmed with lace, and with her stockingless feet in Turkish slippers.

"Ah! excuse me, Monsieur! I thought it was the hairdresser. One minute; I am coming back!"

And he was left alone in the dining-room. The Venetian blinds were closed. Frédéric, as he cast a glance round, was beginning to recall the hubbub of the other night, when he noticed on the table, in the middle of the room, a man's hat, an old felt hat, squashed, greasy, dirty. To whom did this hat belong? Impudently displaying its torn lining, it seemed to say:

"What do I care?! I am the master!"

The Maréchale suddenly reappeared on the scene. She took up the hat, opened the conservatory, flung it in there, shut the door again (other doors flew open and closed again), and, having brought Frédéric through the kitchen, she brought him into her dressing-room.

It could at once be seen that this was the most frequented room in the house, and, so to speak, its true centre. The walls, the armchairs, and a big divan were adorned with a chintz pattern on which was traced a great deal of foliage. On a white marble table stood two large washhand-basins of fine blue earthenware. Crystal shelves, were laden with bottles, brushes, combs, cosmetic sticks, and powder-boxes. The fire was reflected in a full length mirror. A shower curtain was hanging outside the bath, and odours of almond-paste and balsam filled the air.

"Please excuse the disorder. I'm dining in the city this evening."

And as she turned on her heel, she almost crushed one of the little dogs. Frédéric declared that they were charming. She lifted up the pair of them, and raising their black snouts up to her face:

"Come on! give us a smile— kiss the nice man!"

A man dressed in a dirty overcoat with a fur collar entered abruptly.

"Felix, my worthy fellow," said she, "you'll have that business of yours disposed of next Sunday without fail."

The man proceeded to coif her hair. Frédéric told her he had heard news of her friends, Madame de Rochegune, Madame de Saint-Florentin, and Madame Lombard, every woman being nobility, as if it were at the mansion of the Dambreuses. Then he talked about the theatres. An extraordinary performance was to be given that evening at the Ambigu.

"Shall you go?"

"Faith, no! I'm staying at home."

Delphine appeared. Her mistress gave her a scolding for having gone out without permission.

The other vowed that she was just "returning from the market."

"Well, bring me your list. I assume you have no objection?"

And, reading the entries in a low tone, Rosanette made remarks on every item. The different sums were not added up correctly.

"Hand me over four sous!"

Delphine handed the amount over to her, and, when she had sent the maid away:

"Ah! Holy Virgin! could I be more unfortunate than I am with these creatures?"

Frédéric was shocked by this complaint. It reminded him too vividly of the others, and established between the two houses a kind of irritating similarity.

When Delphine came back again, she drew close to the Maréchale's side in order to whisper something in her ear.

"Ah, no! I won't!"

Delphine presented herself once more.

"Madame, she insists."

"Ah, what a plague! Throw her out!"

At the same moment, an old lady, dressed in black, pushed open the door. Frédéric heard nothing, saw nothing. Rosanette rushed into the room to meet her.

When she reappeared her cheeks were flushed, and she sat down in one of the armchairs without saying a word. A tear fell down her face; then, turning towards the young man, softly:

"What is your Christian name?"

"Frédéric."

"Ha! Federico! It doesn't annoy you when I address you in that way?"

And she gazed at him in an affectionate sort of way that was almost amorous.

All of a sudden she uttered an exclamation of delight at the sight of Mademoiselle Vatnaz.

The lady-artist had no time to lose before presiding at her *table d'hôte* at six o'clock sharp; and she was panting for breath, being completely exhausted. She first took out of her pocket a watch on a chain and a piece of paper, then various objects that she had bought.

"You should know that there are in the Rue Joubert splendid suede gloves at thirty-six sous. Your dyer wants eight days more. As for the lace, I told you that they would dye it again. Bugneaux has received the instalment you paid. That's all, I think. You owe me a hundred and eighty-five francs."

Rosanette went to a drawer to get ten napoleons. Neither of the pair had any money. Frédéric offered some.

"I'll pay you back," said Vatnaz, as she stuffed the fifteen francs into her handbag. "But you are a naughty boy! I don't love you any longer—you didn't get me to dance with you even once the other evening! Ah! my dear, I came across a case of stuffed humming-birds which are absolutely divine at a shop in the Quai Voltaire. If I were in your place, I would make myself a present of them. Look here! What do you think of it?"

And she exhibited an old remnant of pink silk which she had purchased at the Temple to make a mediæval doublet for Delmar.

"He came to-day, didn't he?"

"No."

"That's strange."

And, after a minute's silence:

"Where are you going this evening?"

"To Alphonsine's," said Rosanette, this being the third version she gave as to the way she was going to pass the evening.

Mademoiselle Vatnaz went on: "And what news about the Old Man of the Mountain?"*

But, with an abrupt wink, the Maréchale bade her hold her tongue; and she accompanied Frédéric out as far as the entrance-hall to ascertain from him whether he would soon see Arnoux.

"Pray ask him to come—not in front of his wife, mind!"

At the top of the stairs an umbrella was placed against the wall near a pair of goloshes.

"Vatnaz's goloshes," said Rosanette. "What a foot, eh? My little friend is rather strongly built!"

---

*Name given to the chiefs of the eleventh- through thirteenth-century Shiite sect the Hashshashin (Assassins), known for murdering their enemies; here, it refers to M. Oudry.

And, in a melodramatic tone, making the final letter of the word roll:

"Don't tru-us-st her!"

Frédéric, emboldened by a confidence of this sort, tried to kiss her on the neck.

"Oh, go ahead! It costs nothing!"

He felt rather light-hearted as he left her, having no doubt that ere long the Maréchale would be his mistress. This desire awakened another in him; and, in spite of the resentment he had towards Madame Arnoux, he felt a longing to see her.

Besides, he would have to call at her house in order to deliver Rosanette's message.

"But now," thought he (it had just struck six), "Arnoux is probably at home."

So he put off his visit till the following day.

She was seated in the same position as on the day before, and was sewing a little boy's shirt.

The child, at her feet, was playing with a wooden toy menagerie. Marthe, a short distance away, was writing.

He began by complimenting her on her children. She replied without any exaggeration of maternal silliness.

The room had a tranquil atmosphere. A glow of sunshine stole in through the window-panes, lighting up the angles of the different pieces of furniture, and, as Madame Arnoux sat close beside the window, a ray of sun, falling on the curls over the nape of her neck, penetrated with liquid gold her amber skin.

Then he said:

"This young lady here has grown very tall during the past three years! Do you remember, Mademoiselle, when you slept on my knees in the carriage?"

Marthe did not remember.

"One evening, returning from Saint-Cloud?"

There was a look of peculiar sadness in Madame Arnoux's face. Was it to keep him from further reference to the memories they shared?

Her beautiful shining black eyes, moved gently under their somewhat drooping lids, and her pupils revealed in their depths an inexpressible kindness of heart. He was seized with a love stronger than ever, a passion that knew no bounds. The idea of it paralyzed him; however, he shook off this feeling. How was he to make the most of himself? by what means? And, having turned the matter over thoroughly in his mind, Frédéric could think of none that seemed more effective than money.

He began talking about the weather, which was less cold than it had been at Le Havre.

"Were you there?"

"Yes; about a family matter—an inheritance."

"Ah! I am very glad," she said, with an air of such genuine pleasure that he felt quite touched, just as if she had done him a great service.

She asked him what he intended to do, as it was necessary for a man to occupy himself with something.

He remembered his lie, and said that he hoped to reach the Conseil d'Etat with the help of M. Dambreuse, the representative.[4]

"You are acquainted with him, perhaps?"

"Merely by name."

Then, in a low tone:

"*He* brought you to the ball the other night, did he not?"

Frédéric remained silent.

"That was what I wanted to know; thanks!"

After that she put two or three discreet questions to him about his family and the part of the country he was from. It was very kind of him not to have forgotten them after having lived so far away from Paris.

"But could I do so?" he rejoined. "Have you any doubt about it?"

Madame Arnoux arose: "I believe that you entertain towards us a true and solid affection. Until we meet again!"

And she extended her hand towards him in a sincere and masculine fashion.

Was this not an engagement, a promise? Frédéric felt a sense of delight at merely living; he had to restrain himself to keep from singing. He wanted to burst out, to do generous deeds. He looked around him to see if there were anyone near whom he could help. No wretch happened to be passing by; and his generosity of spirit evaporated, for he was not a man to go out of his way to find opportunities for benevolence.

Then he remembered his friends. The first of whom he thought was Hussonnet, the second, Pellerin. The lowly position of Dussardier naturally called for consideration. As for Cisy, he was glad to let that young aristocrat get a slight glimpse as to the extent of his fortune. He wrote accordingly to all four to come to a house-warming the following Sunday at eleven o'clock sharp; and he told Deslauriers to bring Sénécal.

The tutor had been dismissed from his third boarding-school for being opposed to the distribution of prizes—a custom which he looked upon as dangerous to equality. He was now working for an engine-builder, and for the past six months had not been living with Deslauriers. There had been nothing painful about their parting.

Sénécal had been visited by men in smocks—all patriots, all workmen, all honest fellows, but at the same time men whose society seemed distasteful, to the lawyer. Besides, he disliked certain of his friend's ideas, excellent though they might be as weapons of warfare. He held his tongue on the subject out of ambition, paying deference to him in order to control him, for he looked forward to a shake-up in which he hoped to make a place for himself and have an impact.

Sénécal's convictions were more disinterested. Every evening, when his work was finished, he returned to his garret and sought in books for something that might justify his dreams. He had annotated the *Contrat Social*; he had crammed himself with the *Revue Indépendante*; he was acquainted with Mably, Morelly, Fourier, Saint-Simon, Comte, Cabet, Louis Blanc[5]—the heavy cartload of Socialistic writers—those who would reduce humanity to the level of barracks, to those who would amuse themselves in a brothel or labor bent over a counter; and from all these things he constructed an ideal of virtuous democracy, with the double identity of a farm and a factory, a sort of American Sparta, in which the individual would only exist for the benefit of society, which was to be more omnipotent, absolute, infallible, and divine than the Dalai Lamas and the Nebuchadnezzars. He had no doubt as to the approaching realisation of this ideal; and Sénécal raged against everything that he considered hostile to it with the reasoning of a geometrician and the zeal of an Inquisitor. Titles of nobility, crosses, plumes, keeping servants above all, and even overly important reputations scandalised him, his studies as well as his sufferings intensifying every day his essential hatred of every kind of distinction and every form of social superiority.

"What do I owe to this gentleman that I should be polite to him? If he wants me, he can come to me."

Deslauriers, however, forced him to go to Frédéric's reunion.

They found their friend in his bedroom. Spring-roller blinds and double curtains, Venetian mirrors—nothing was lacking there. Frédéric, in a velvet vest, was lying back on an easy-chair, smoking cigarettes of Turkish tobacco.

Sénécal wore the gloomy look of a Puritan arriving in the midst of a party.

Deslauriers gave him a single comprehensive glance; then, with a very low bow:

"My lord, allow me to pay my respects to you!"

Dussardier threw his arms around him. "So you are a rich man now. Ah! upon my soul, so much the better!"

Cisy made his appearance with a black band on his hat. Since the death of his grandmother, he was enjoying a considerable fortune, and was less bent on amusing himself than on being distinguished from others—not being the same as everyone else—in short, on "having the proper stamp." This was his favourite phrase.

However, it was now midday, and they were all yawning.

Frédéric was waiting for some one.

At the mention of Arnoux's name, Pellerin made a wry face. He looked on him as a renegade since he had abandoned the fine arts.

"Suppose we forget him—what do you say to that?"

They all approved of this suggestion.

The door was opened by a man-servant wearing spats; and the dining-room could be seen with its lofty oak plinths with gold details, and its two sideboards laden with plates.

The bottles of wine were heating on the stove; the blades of new knives were glittering beside oysters. In the milky tint of the enamelled glasses there was a kind of alluring softness; and the table disappeared from view under its load of game, fruit, and meats of the rarest quality.

These attentions were lost on Sénécal. He began by asking for homemade bread (as dense as possible), and in connection with this subject, spoke of the murders of Buzançais and the crisis arising from a shortage of food.[6]

Nothing of this sort could have happened if agriculture had been better protected, if everything had not been given up to competition, to anarchy, and to the deplorable maxim of "Laissez faire! Vive the free market!"* It was in this way that the feudalism of money was established—the worst form of feudalism. But let them take care! The people in the end will get tired of it, and may make the capitalist pay for their sufferings either by bloody proscriptions or by the plunder of their houses.

Frédéric saw, as if by a lightning-flash, a flood of men with bare arms invading Madame Dambreuse's drawing-room, and smashing the mirrors with blows of pikes.

Sénécal went on to say that the workman, owing to the insufficiency of wages, was more unfortunate than the slave, the negro, and the pariah, especially if he has children.

"Should he get rid of them by asphyxiation, as some English doctor,—a disciple of Malthus—would suggest?"

And, turning towards Cisy: "Are we to follow the advice of the infamous Malthus?"[7]

Cisy, who was ignorant of the infamy and even of the existence of Malthus, said by way of reply, that after all, much was being done to help the less fortunate, and that the higher classes——

"Ha! the higher classes!" said the Socialist, with a sneer. "In the first place, there are no higher classes. 'Tis the heart alone that makes anyone higher than another. We want no charity, understand! but equality, the fair division of goods."

What he demanded was that the workman might become a capitalist, just as the soldier might become a colonel. The trade-guilds, at least, in limiting the number of apprentices, prevented workmen from growing inconveniently numerous, and the sentiment of fraternity was kept up by means of the fêtes and the banners.

Hussonnet, as a poet, missed the banners; so did Pellerin,—a predilection which had taken possession of him at the Café Dagneaux, while listening to the Phalansterians talking. He expressed the opinion that Fourier was a great man.[8]

---

*Slogan of the proponents of total liberty in trade and economic matters.

"Come now!" said Deslauriers. "An old fool who sees in the overthrow of governments the effects of Divine vengeance. He is just like my lord Saint-Simon and his church, with his hatred of the French Revolution[9]—a set of buffoons who would re-establish Catholicism."

M. de Cisy, no doubt in order to get information or to make a good impression, broke in with this remark, which he uttered in a mild tone:

"These two men of science are not, then, of the same way of thinking as Voltaire?"

"That fellow! You can have him!"

"What?" "Why, I thought——"

"Oh! no, he did not love the people!"

Then the conversation came down to contemporary events: the Spanish marriages, the squanderings of Rochefort, the new chapter of Saint-Denis, which had led to taxes being doubled. Nevertheless, according to Sénécal, people were already paying more than enough!

"And why are they paid? My God! to erect the palace for apes at the zoo in the Jardin des Plantes,* to make showy staff-officers parade along our squares, or to maintain out-dated etiquette amongst the servants of the Château!"

"I have read in *La Mode*," said Cisy, "that at the Tuileries ball on the feast of Saint-Ferdinand, everyone was disguised as dandies."

"How pitiful!" said the Socialist, with a shrug of his shoulders, as if to indicate his disgust.

"And the Museum of Versailles!" exclaimed Pellerin. "Let us talk about that! These idiots have cropped a Delacroix and lengthened a Gros!† At the Louvre they have restored, scratched, and roughed up the canvases so much, that in ten years probably not one will be left. As for the errors in the catalogue, a German has written a whole volume on the subject. Upon my word, the foreigners are laughing at us."

---

*The Paris botanical garden, Le Jardin des Plantes, included a zoo and a natural history museum, Le Muséum national d'histoire naturelle.

†The Museum of Versailles was created by Louis-Philippe. Eugène Delacroix (1798–1863) and Antoine-Jean, Baron Gros (1771–1835), were famous Romantic painters.

"Yes, we are the laughing-stock of Europe," said Sénécal.

" 'Tis because Art is subject to the Crown."

"As long as you don't have universal suffrage——"

"Let me speak!"—for the artist, having been rejected at every *salon* for the last twenty years, was filled with rage against Authority.

"Ah! let them not bother us! As for me, I ask for nothing. Only the Chambers ought to pass enactments in the interests of Art. A chair of æsthetics should be established with a professor who, being an artist as well as a philosopher, would succeed, I hope, in uniting the masses. You would do well, Hussonnet, to touch on this matter with a word or two in your newspaper?"

"Are the newspapers free? are we ourselves free?" said Deslauriers in an angry tone. "When one reflects that there might be as many as twenty-eight different formalities to keep a boat on the river, it makes me feel a longing to go and live amongst the cannibals! The Government is eating us up. Everything belongs to it—philosophy, law, the arts, the very air we breathe; and France, weakened and groaning, lies under the gendarme's boot and the priest's cassock.

The future Mirabeau thus poured out his bile in abundance. Finally he took his glass in his right hand, raised it, and with his other hand on his hip, and his eyes flashing:

"I drink to the utter destruction of the existing order of things—that is to say, of everything included in the words Privilege, Monopoly, Regulation, Hierarchy, Authority, State!"—and in a louder voice—"which I would like to smash as I do this!" dashing the beautiful wine-glass on the table, which broke into a thousand pieces.

They all applauded, and especially Dussardier.

The spectacle of injustices made his heart pound with indignation. Barbès had his sympathy.[10] He was one of those men who would fling himself under a carriage to help a fallen horse. His learning was limited to two works, one entitled *Crimes of Kings*, and the other *Mysteries of the Vatican*. He had listened to the lawyer with open-mouthed delight. At length, unable to stand it any longer:

"For my part, the thing I blame Louis Philippe for is abandoning the Poles!"[11]

"One moment!" said Hussonnet. "In the first place, Poland does not exist; 'tis an invention of Lafayette! The Poles, as a general rule, all belong to the Faubourg Saint-Marceau, the real ones having been drowned with Poniatowski."[12] In short, "he no longer believed in all that;" he had "gotten over all that sort of thing; it was just like the sea-serpent, the revocation of the Edict of Nantes, and that antiquated nonsense about the Saint-Bartholomew massacre!"[13]

Sénécal, while he did not defend the Poles, extolled the latest remarks made by the man of letters. The Popes had been slandered, and after all they, defended the people, and he called the League* "the dawn of Democracy, a great egalitarian movement against Protestant individualism."

Frédéric was a little surprised at these views. They probably bored Cisy, for he changed the conversation to the *tableaux vivants* at the Gymnase Theatre, which at that time attracted a great number of people.[14]

Sénécal regarded them with disfavour. Such exhibitions corrupted the daughters of the proletariat. Afterwards, it was noticeable that they showed off with shameless luxury. Therefore, he approved of the conduct of the Bavarian students who insulted Lola Montès.† Like Rousseau, he showed more esteem for the wife of a coal-burner than for the mistress of a king.

"You spit on pearls!" retorted Hussonnet in a majestic tone. And he took up the defense of ladies of this class in order to praise Rosanette. Then, as he happened to make an allusion to the ball at her house and to Arnoux's costume, Pellerin remarked:

"People say that he is in trouble."

The art-dealer had just been involved in a lawsuit with reference to his property at Belleville, and he was actually in a kaolin company in Lower Brittany with other jokers of his sort.

Dussardier knew more about him, for his own master, M. Moussinot, having made enquiries about Arnoux from the banker, Oscar Lefébvre, the latter had said in reply that he considered him by no means solvent, as he knew about extensions of credit he had requested.

---

*Ultra-Catholic association active during the sixteenth-century French Wars of Religion.

†Lola Montez was an Irish adventuress whose seduction of King Ludwig I of Bavaria forced him to abdicate in 1848.

The dessert was over; they passed into the drawing-room, which was covered, like that of the Maréchale, in yellow damask in the style of Louis XVI.

Pellerin found fault with Frédéric for not having chosen the Neo-Greek style; Sénécal struck matches against the wall hangings; Deslauriers did not make any remarks. He did make one in the library, which he called "a little girl's library." The principal contemporary writers were to be found there. It was impossible to speak about their works, for Hussonnet immediately began relating anecdotes with reference to their personal characteristics, criticising their faces, their habits, their dress, glorifying fifth-rate intellects and disparaging those of the first; and all the while making it clear that he deplored modern decadence. Such-and-such a country ditty had more poetry in it than all the lyrics of the nineteenth century. He went on to say that Balzac was overrated, that Byron was discredited, and that Hugo knew nothing about the theatre, etc.

"Why, then," said Sénécal, "do you not have the volumes of the worker poets?"

And M. de Cisy, who devoted his attention to literature, was astonished at not seeing on Frédéric's table some of those new physiological studies—the physiology of the smoker, of the angler, of the toll-keeper.

They went on irritating him to such an extent that he felt a longing to shove them out the door.

"But I'm being silly!" And then he drew Dussardier aside, and asked him if there was anything he could do for him.

The honest fellow was moved. He answered that with his cashier job he needed nothing.

After that, Frédéric led Deslauriers into his bedroom, and took out of his secretary two thousand francs:

"Look here, old boy, put this money in your pocket. 'Tis the balance of my old debts to you."

"But—what about the journal?" said the lawyer. "You are, of course, aware that I spoke about it to Hussonnet."

And, when Frédéric replied that he was "a little short of cash just now," the other smiled in a sinister fashion.

After the liqueurs they drank beer, and after the beer, grog; and then they lighted their pipes once more. At last they left, at five o'clock in the evening, and they were walking along at each others' side without speaking, when Dussardier broke the silence by saying that Frédéric had entertained them in excellent style. They all agreed with him on that point.

Then Hussonnet remarked that the lunch was too heavy. Sénécal found fault with the trivial character of the interior decoration. Cisy took the same view. It was absolutely devoid of "cachet."

"For my part, I think," said Pellerin, "he might have had the grace to give me a commission for a painting."

Deslauriers held his tongue, as he had the bank-notes that had been given to him in his pants' pocket.

Frédéric was left by himself. He was thinking about his friends, and it seemed to him as if a huge ditch surrounded with shade separated him from them. He had nevertheless held out his hand to them, and they had not responded to his sincerity of heart.

He remembered what Pellerin and Dussardier had said about Arnoux. Undoubtedly it must be a slanderous invention. But why? And he had a vision of Madame Arnoux, broke, weeping, selling her furniture. This idea tormented him all night long. Next day he presented himself at her house.

At a loss to find any way of communicating to her what he had heard, he asked her, as if in casual conversation, whether Arnoux still held possession of his building grounds at Belleville.

"Yes, he has them still."

"He is now, I believe, a shareholder in a kaolin company in Brittany."

"That's true."

"His earthenware-works are doing very well, are they not?"

"Well—I suppose so——"

And, as he hesitated:

"What is the matter with you? You frighten me!"

He told her the story about the credit extensions. She lowered her head, and said:

"I thought so!"

In fact, Arnoux, in order to make a good speculation, had refused to sell his properties, had borrowed money extensively on them, and finding no purchasers, had thought of rehabilitating himself by establishing the earthenware manufactory. The expense of this had exceeded his calculations. She knew nothing more about it. He evaded all her questions, and declared repeatedly that it was going very well.

Frédéric tried to reassure her. These in all probability were mere temporary troubles. However, if he got any information, he would impart it to her.

"Oh! yes, will you not?" said she, clasping her two hands with an air of charming supplication.

So then, he had it in his power to be useful to her. He was now entering into her existence—finding a place in her heart.

Arnoux appeared.

"Ah! how nice of you to come to take me out to dine!"

Frédéric was silent on hearing these words.

Arnoux spoke about general topics, then informed his wife that he would be returning home very late, as he had an appointment with M. Oudry.

"At his house?"

"Why, certainly, at his house."

As they went down the stairs, he confessed that, as the Maréchale was free, they were going on a secret pleasure-party to the Moulin Rouge; and, as he always needed somebody to confide in, he got Frédéric to accompany him as far as the door.

Instead of entering, he walked about on the sidewalk, looking up at the windows on the second floor. Suddenly the curtains parted.

"Ah! bravo! Père Oudry is no longer there! Good evening!"

Frédéric did not know what to think now.

From this day forth, Arnoux was still more cordial than before; he invited the young man to dine with his mistress; and ere long Frédéric frequented both houses at the same time.

Rosanette's abode furnished him with amusement. They used to call there on their way back from a club or a play. They would have a cup of tea there, or play a game of lotto. On Sundays they played charades; Rosanette, more boisterous than the rest, became known for her funny tricks, such as running on all-fours or sticking a cotton cap on her head. In order to watch the passers-by through the window, she wore a hat of waxed leather; she smoked cigars; she sang Tyrolean yodeling songs. In the afternoon, to kill time, she cut flowers out of a piece of chintz and pasted them on the windows, put rouge on her two little dogs, burned incense, or drew cards to tell her fortune. Incapable of resisting a desire, she became infatuated about some trinket which she happened to see, and could not sleep till she had gone and bought it, then bartered it for another, sold costly dresses for little or nothing, lost her jewellery, squandered money, and would have sold her chemise for a loge-box at the theatre. Often she asked Frédéric to explain to her some word she came across when reading a book, but did not pay any attention to his answer, for she jumped quickly to another idea, while heaping questions on top of each other. After spasms of gaiety came childish outbursts of rage, or else she sat on the ground dreaming before the fire with her head down and her hands clasping her knees, more inert than a torpid snake. Without minding it, she dressed in his presence, drew on her silk stockings, then washed her face with great splashes of water, throwing her body backwards as if she were a shivering water nymph; and her laughing white teeth, her sparkling eyes, her beauty, her gaiety, dazzled Frédéric, and made his nerves tingle under the lash of desire.

Nearly always he found Madame Arnoux teaching her little boy how to read, or standing behind Marthe's chair while she played her scales on the piano. When she was doing a piece of sewing, it was a great source of delight to him to pick up her scissors now and then. In all her movements there was a tranquil majesty. Her little hands seemed made to scatter alms and to wipe away tears, and her voice, naturally rather soft, had a caressing tone and a sort of breezy lightness.

She did not display much enthusiasm about literature; but her intelligence exercised a charm by the use of a few simple and penetrating words. She loved travelling, the sound of the wind in the woods, and a walk with uncovered head in the rain.

Frédéric listened to these confidences with rapture, fancying that he saw in them the beginning of a certain self-abandonment on her part.

His association with these two women made, as it were, two different strains of music in his life, the one playful, passionate, diverting, the other serious and almost religious, and vibrating at the same time, they grew louder and gradually blended with one another; for if Madame Arnoux happened merely to touch him with her finger, the image of the other immediately presented itself as an object of desire, because in her case his chances were better, and, when his heart happened to be touched while in Rosanette's company, he immediately remembered his great love.

This confusion was, in some measure, due to a similarity which existed between the interiors of the two houses. One of the trunks which was formerly to be seen in the Boulevard Montmartre now adorned Rosanette's dining-room. The same courses were served up for dinner in both places, and even the same velvet cap was to be found lying on an easy-chair; then, a heap of little presents—screens, boxes, fans—went to the mistress's house from the wife's and returned again, for Arnoux, without the slightest embarrassment, often took back from the one what he had given to her in order to make a present of it to the other.

The Maréchale laughed with Frédéric at the utter disregard for propriety which his habits exhibited. One Sunday, after dinner, she led him behind the door, and showed him in the pocket of Arnoux's overcoat a sac of cakes which he had just pilfered from the table, in order, no doubt, to surprise his little family with at home. M. Arnoux gave in to some little tricks which bordered on dishonesty. It seemed to him a duty to practise fraud with regard to the city dues; he never paid when he went to the theatre, or if he took a ticket for the upper level seats always tried to make his way into the orchestra seats; and he used to relate as an excellent joke that it was a custom of his at the cold baths to put into the attendants' collection-box a trouser-button instead of a ten-sous piece—and this did not prevent the Maréchale from loving him.

One day, however, she said, while talking about him:

"Ah! he's getting on my nerves! I've had enough of him! Too bad—I'll find another!"

Frédéric believed that the other had already been found, and that his name was M. Oudry.

"Well," said Rosanette, "what does it matter?"

Then, in a voice choked with tears:

"I ask very little from him, and yet he won't do it, the animal! He just won't do it. As for his promises, well . . ."

He had even promised a fourth of his profits in the famous kaolin mines. No profit made its appearance any more than the cashmere with which he had been luring her for the last six months.

Frédéric immediately thought of offering it to her as a present. Arnoux might regard it as a lesson for himself, and be annoyed by it.

For all that, he was good-natured, his wife herself said so, but so foolish! Instead of bringing people to dine every day at his house, he now entertained his acquaintances at a restaurant. He bought things that were utterly useless, such as gold chains, timepieces, and household articles. Madame Arnoux even pointed out to Frédéric in the lobby an enormous supply of tea-kettles, foot-warmers, and samovars. Finally, she one day confessed that a certain matter caused her much anxiety. Arnoux had made her sign a check payable to M. Dambreuse.

Meanwhile Frédéric still cherished his literary projects as if it were a point of honour with himself to do so. He wished to write a history of æsthetics, a result of his conversations with Pellerin; next, to write dramas dealing with different epochs of the French Revolution, and to compose a great comedy, an idea traceable to the indirect influence of Deslauriers and Hussonnet. In the midst of his work the face of one or the other of the two women passed before his mental vision. He struggled against the longing to see her, but was not long ere he yielded to it; and he felt sadder as he came back from Madame Arnoux's house.

One morning, while he was brooding over his melancholy thoughts by the fireside, Deslauriers came in. The incendiary speeches of Sénécal had filled his employer with uneasiness, and once more he found himself without any income.

"What do you want me to do?" said Frédéric.

"Nothing! I know you have no money. But it will not be much trouble for you to get him a post either through M. Dambreuse or else through Arnoux. The latter ought to have need of engineers in his establishment."

Frédéric had an inspiration. Sénécal would be able to let him know when the husband was away, carry letters for him and assist him on a thousand occasions when opportunities presented themselves. Services of this sort are always rendered between men. Besides, he would find means of employing him without arousing any suspicion on his part. Chance offered him an auxiliary; it was a circumstance that was a good omen for the future, and he hastened to take advantage of it; and, feigning indifference, he replied that the thing was feasible perhaps, and that he would devote his attention to it.

And he did so at once. Arnoux took a great deal of pains with his earthenware works. He was endeavouring to discover the copper-red of the Chinese, but his colours evaporated in the process of baking. In order to avoid cracks in his ware, he mixed lime with his potter's clay; but the articles got broken for the most part; the enamel of his paintings on the raw material boiled away; his large plates had bubbles in them; and, attributing these mischances to the inferior equipment in his factory, he was anxious to order new grinding-mills and install drying-rooms. Frédéric recalled some of these things, and, when he met Arnoux, said that he had discovered a very able man, who would be capable of finding his famous red. Arnoux gave a jump; then, having listened to what the young man had to tell him, replied that he didn't want assistance.

Frédéric spoke in a very laudatory style about Sénécal's extensive knowledge, pointing out that he was at the same time an engineer, a chemist, and an accountant, being a mathematician of the first rank.

The ceramics-dealer consented to see him.

But Arnoux and Sénécal squabbled over the terms. Frédéric intervened, and, at the end of the week, succeeded in getting them to come to an agreement.

But as the works were situated at Creil, Sénécal could not assist Frédéric in any way. This thought alone was enough to make him discouraged, as if he had met with some misfortune. His notion was that the more Arnoux was kept apart from his wife the better would be his own chances with her. Then he proceeded to make repeated apologies for Rosanette. He referred to all the wrongs she had sustained at his hands, told of the vague threats which she had made a few days before, and even spoke about the cashmere without concealing the fact that she had accused Arnoux of cheapness.

Arnoux, stung by the word (and, furthermore, feeling some uneasiness), brought Rosanette the cashmere, but scolded her for having made any complaint to Frédéric. When she told him that she had reminded him a hundred times of his promise, he pretended that, due to the pressure of business, he had forgotten all about it.

The next day Frédéric presented himself at her abode, and found the Maréchale still in bed, though it was two o'clock, with Delmar beside her finishing a *pâté de foie gras* at the little round table. She cried out to him: "I've got it! I've got it!" Then she seized him by the ears, kissed him on the forehead, thanked him profusely, spoke to him endearingly, and even wanted to make him sit down on the bed. Her fine eyes, full of tender emotion, were sparkling with pleasure. There was a smile on her moist lips. Her two round arms emerged through the sleeveless opening of her night-dress, and, from time to time, he could feel through the filmy cotton the firm contours of her body.

All this time Delmar kept rolling his eyes.

"But really, my dear, my pet . . ."

It was the same way when he saw her next. As soon as Frédéric entered, she sat up on a cushion in order to embrace him with more ease, called him a darling, a "dearie," put a flower in his button-hole, and fixed his cravat. These delicate attentions were exaggerated when Delmar happened to be there. Were they advances on her part? So it seemed to Frédéric.

As for deceiving a friend, Arnoux, in his place, would not have had many scruples on that score, and he had every right not to adhere to rigidly virtuous principles with regard to this man's mistress, seeing that his relations with the wife had been strictly honourable, for so he thought—or rather he would have liked Arnoux to think so, in any event, as a sort of justification of his own tremendous cowardice. Nevertheless he felt somewhat bewildered; and he made up his mind to lay siege boldly to the Maréchale.

So, one afternoon, just as she was stooping down in front of her chest of drawers, he approached her, and his unambiguous overtures made her stand up immediately and she blushed.

He renewed his advances and thereupon, she began to cry, saying that she was very unfortunate, but that people should not treat her badly because of it.

He only repeated his attempts. She now adopted a different plan, namely, to laugh like mad at his attempts. He thought it a clever thing to answer her sarcasms with retorts in the same vein in which there was even a touch of exaggeration. But he made too great a display of gaiety to convince her that he was sincere; and their comradeship was an impediment to any expression of serious feeling. At last, when she said one day, in reply to his amorous whispers, that she would not take another woman's left-overs, he answered.

"What other woman?"

"Ah! yes, go and meet Madame Arnoux again!"

For Frédéric used to talk about her often. Arnoux, for his part, had the same mania. At last she lost patience at always hearing this woman's praises sung, and this insinuation of hers was a kind of revenge.

Frédéric resented it. However, Rosanette was beginning to excite his love to an unusual degree. Sometimes, assuming the attitude of a woman of experience, she spoke ill of love with a sceptical smile, that made him feel inclined to slap her. A quarter of an hour afterwards, it was the best thing in the world, and, with her arms crossed over her chest, as if she were holding some one close to her: "Oh, yes! It's wonderful! It's so wonderful!" and her eyelids would quiver in a kind of rapturous swoon. It was impossible to understand her, to know, for instance, whether she loved Arnoux, for she made fun of him, and yet seemed jealous of him. So like-wise with Vatnaz, whom she would sometimes call a wretch, and at other times her best friend. In short, there was about her entire person, even to the very arrangement of her chignon over her head, an inexpressible something, which seemed like a challenge; and he desired her for the satisfaction, above all, of conquering her and being her master.

How was he to accomplish this? for she often sent him away unceremoniously, appearing only for a moment between two doors in order to say in a subdued voice, "I'm busy—for the evening;" or else he found her surrounded by a dozen people; and when they were alone, so many impediments arose one after the other, that one would have sworn there was a bet to keep matters from going any further. He invited her to dinner; as a rule, she declined the invitation. On one occasion, she accepted it, but did not come.

A Machiavellian idea popped in to his brain.

Having heard from Dussardier about Pellerin's complaints against him, he thought of giving the artist an order to paint the

Maréchale's portrait, a life-sized portrait, which would necessitate a good number of sittings. He would not fail to be present at all of them. The habitual unpunctuality of the painter would facilitate their private conversations. So then he would urge Rosanette to have the painting executed in order to make a present of her face to her dear Arnoux. She consented, for she saw herself in the midst of the Grand Salon* in the most prominent position with a crowd of people staring at her picture, and the newspapers would all talk about it, which at once would "launch her."

As for Pellerin, he eagerly jumped at the offer. This portrait ought to place him in the position of a great man; it ought to be a masterpiece. He reviewed in his mind all the portraits by great masters with which he was acquainted, and decided finally in favour of a Titian, which would be set off with ornaments in the style of Veronese. Therefore, he would carry out his design without artificial backgrounds in a bold light, which would illuminate the flesh-tints with a single tone, and which would make the accessories glitter.

"Suppose I were to put on her," he thought, "a pink silk dress with an Oriental bournous? Oh, no! the bournous is cheap-looking! Or suppose, rather, I were to make her wear blue velvet with a grey background, richly coloured? We might likewise give her a white lace collar with a black fan and a scarlet curtain behind." And thus, searching as such, he expanded his concept with every passing day, and marvelled at it.

He felt his heart beating when Rosanette, accompanied by Frédéric, called at his house for the first sitting. He placed her standing up on a sort of platform in the middle of the room, and, finding fault with the light and expressing regret at the loss of his former studio, he first made her lean on her elbow against a pedestal, then sit down in an armchair, and, drawing away from her and coming near her again in order to adjust with a flick the folds of her dress, he looked at her with eyes half-closed, and consulted Frédéric's taste with a passing word.

"On second thought, no," he exclaimed; "I'll return to my first idea. I will set you up in the Venetian style."

---

*Exhibition in Paris of the works of living artists.

She would have a poppy-coloured velvet gown with a silver belt; and her wide sleeve lined with ermine would afford a glimpse of her bare arm, which was to touch the balustrade of a staircase rising behind her. At her left, a large column would mount as far as the top of the canvas to meet certain structures so as to form an arch. Underneath one would vaguely distinguish groups of orange-trees almost black, through which the blue sky, with its streaks of white clouds, would seem cut into fragments. On the carpeted balustrade, there would be, on a silver dish, a bouquet of flowers, an amber rosary, a dagger, and a little chest of antique ivory, rather yellowed with age, which would appear to be overflowing with old Venetian gold coins. Some of them, falling on the ground here and there, would form brilliant splashes, as it were, in such a way as to direct one's glance towards the tip of her foot, for she would be standing on the second to last step in a natural position, and in full light.

He went to look for a picture-crate, which he laid on the platform to represent the step. Then he arranged as accessories, on a stool in the role of the balustrade, his jacket, a shield, a sardine-box, a bundle of feathers, and a knife; and when he had flung in front of Rosanette a dozen coins, he made her assume the pose he required.

"Just try to imagine that these things are riches, magnificent presents. The head a little on one side! Perfect! and don't move! This majestic posture exactly suits your style of beauty."

She wore a plaid dress and carried a big muff, and only kept from laughing outright by an effort of self-control.

"As regards the headdress, we will mingle with it a circle of pearls. It always produces a striking effect with red hair."

The Maréchale burst out into an exclamation, remarking that she did not have red hair.

"Nonsense! The red of painters is not that of ordinary people."

He began to sketch the main outlines; and he was so much preoccupied with the great artists of the Renaissance that he kept talking about them persistently. For a whole hour he went on musing aloud on those splendid lives, full of genius, glory, and sumptuous displays, with triumphal entries into the cities, and galas by torchlight among half-naked women, beautiful as goddesses.

"You were made to live in those days. A creature of your calibre would have deserved a prince."

Rosanette thought the compliments he paid her very kind. The day was fixed for the next sitting. Frédéric took it on himself to bring the accessories.

As the heat of the stove had dazed her a little, they went home on foot through the Rue du Bac, and reached the Pont Royal.

It was fine weather, piercingly bright and warm. Some windows of houses in the city shone in the distance, like plates of gold, whilst behind them at the right the towers of Nôtre Dame showed their outlines in black against the blue sky, softly bathed at the horizon in a grey haze.

The wind began to blow; and as Rosanette declared that she felt hungry, they entered the "Patisserie Anglaise."

Young women with their children stood eating in front of the marble counter, where plates of little cakes had glass covers over them. Rosanette ate two cream-tarts. The powdered sugar formed moustaches at the sides of her mouth. From time to time, in order to wipe it, she drew out her handkerchief from her muff, and her face, under her green silk hood, resembled a rose blooming amidst its leaves.

They resumed their walk. In the Rue de la Paix she stood before a goldsmith's shop to look at a bracelet. Frédéric wished to make her a present of it.

"No!" said she; "keep your money!"

He was hurt by these words.

"What's the matter now with my pet? Is he melancholy?"

And, when the conversation resumed, he began making the same declarations of love to her as usual.

"You know well 'tis impossible!"

"Why?"

"Ah! because——"

They went on side by side, she leaning on his arm, and the flounces of her gown kept flapping against his legs. Then, he remembered one winter twilight when on the same sidewalk Madame Arnoux walked thus by his side, and he became so much absorbed in this recollection that he no longer saw Rosanette, and stopped thinking of her.

She kept looking straight ahead in a careless fashion, lagging a little, like a lazy child. It was the hour when people had just come back from their promenade, and carriages were making their way at a quick trot over the hard pavement.

Pellerin's flatteries having undoubtedly come to mind, she heaved a sigh.

"Ah! there are some lucky women in the world. Decidedly, I was made for a rich man!"

He replied, with a certain brutality in his tone:

"But you already have one!" for M. Oudry was looked upon as a man that could count a million three times over.

She asked for nothing more than to be free of him.

"What prevents you from doing so?" And he made bitter jokes about this old bourgeois in his wig, pointing out to her that such a relationship was unworthy of her, and that she ought to break it off.

"Yes," replied the Maréchale, as if talking to herself. " 'Tis what I shall end by doing, no doubt!"

Frédéric was charmed by this disinterestedness. She slackened her pace, and he imagined that she was fatigued. She obstinately refused to let him take a cab, and she parted with him at her door, blowing him a kiss with her finger-tips.

"Ah! what a pity! and to think that some fools take me for a wealthy man!"

He reached home in a gloomy frame of mind.

Hussonnet and Deslauriers were awaiting him. The Bohemian, seated before the table, made sketches of Turks; and the lawyer, in dirty boots, lay asleep on the sofa.

"Ah! at last," he exclaimed. "But how sullen you look! Can you listen to what I have to say?"

His popularity as a tutor had fallen off, for he crammed his pupils with unfavourable theories for their examinations. He had appeared in two or three cases in which he had been unsuccessful, and each new disappointment flung him back with greater force on the dream of his earlier days—a journal in which he could show himself off, avenge himself, and spit forth his bile and his opinions. Fortune and reputation, moreover, would follow as a necessary consequence. It was with this hope in mind that he had persuaded the Bohemian, Hussonnet happening to be the possessor of a press.

At present, he printed it on pink paper. He invented hoaxes, composed puzzles, tried to start controversies, and even intended, in spite of the premises, to put concerts together. A year's subscription entitled the subscriber to an orchestra seat in one of the principal theatres of Paris. In addition, the board of management took on itself to furnish foreigners with all necessary information, artistic and otherwise. But the printer was making threats; there were three quarters' rent due to the landlord. All sorts of difficulties arose; and Hussonnet would have allowed *L'Art* to perish, were it not for the exhortations of the lawyer, who encouraged him every day. He had brought Frédéric along with him, in order to give more weight to his appeals.

"We've come about the journal," he said.

"What! are you still thinking about that?" said Frédéric, in an absent tone.

"Certainly, I am thinking about it!"

And he explained his plan anew. By means of reports on the stock exchange, they would get into communication with financiers, and would thus obtain the hundred thousand francs needed as security. But, in order that the print might be transformed into a political journal, it was necessary beforehand to have a large *clientèle*, and for that purpose to make up their minds to go to some expense—so much for the cost of paper and printing, and for outlay at the office; in short, a sum of about fifteen thousand francs.

"I have no funds," said Frédéric.

"And what are we to do, then?" said Deslauriers, with folded arms.

Frédéric, hurt by the attitude which Deslauriers was assuming, replied:

"Is that my fault?"

"Ah! very fine. A man has wood in his fire, truffles on his table, a good bed, a library, a carriage, every kind of comfort. But let another man shiver under the slates, dine at twenty sous, work like a convict, and wallow in the mire—is it the rich man's fault?"

And he repeated, "Is it the rich man's fault?" with a Ciceronian irony which smacked of the law-court.

Frédéric tried to speak.

"However, I understand one has certain wants—aristocratic wants; for, no doubt, some woman——"

"Well, even if that were so? Am I not free——?"

"Oh! quite free!"

And, after a minute's silence:

"Promises are so convenient!"

"Good God! I don't deny that I gave them!" said Frédéric.

The lawyer went on:

"At college we take oaths; we are going to set up a phalanx; we are going to imitate Balzac's Thirteen.* Then, on meeting a friend after a separation: 'Good night, old fellow! Go about your business!' For he who might help the other carefully keeps everything for himself alone."

"How is that?"

"Yes, you have not even introduced me to the Dambreuses."

Frédéric cast a scrutinising glance at him. With his shabby frock-coat, his spectacles of rough glass, and his sallow face, the lawyer seemed to him such a typical specimen of the penniless pedant that he could not prevent his lips from curling with a disdainful smile.

Deslauriers perceived this, and reddened.

He had already taken his hat to leave. Hussonnet, filled with uneasiness, tried to mollify him with appealing looks, and, as Frédéric was turning his back on him:

"Look here, my boy, become my Mæcenas!† Protect the arts!"

Frédéric, with an abrupt movement of resignation, took a sheet of paper, and, having scrawled some lines on it, handed it to him. The Bohemian's face lighted up.

Then, passing across the sheet of paper to Deslauriers:

"Apologise, my fine fellow!"

Their friend was asking his notary to send him fifteen thousand francs as quickly as possible.

"Ah! That's the old friend I used to know," said Deslauriers.

"On the faith of a gentleman," added the Bohemian, "you are a noble fellow, you'll be placed in the gallery of useful men!"

The lawyer remarked:

"You'll lose nothing by it, it's an excellent investment."

---

*Balzac's *Histoire des treize* (1833–1835; *History of the Thirteen*) comprises three novels, all dealing with secret associations of superior men.

†Protector of arts and letters under the Roman emperor Augustus (63 B.C.—A.D. 14).

"Faith," exclaimed Hussonnet, "I'd stake my head on its success!"

And he said so many foolish things, and promised so many fantastic things, in which perhaps he believed, that Frédéric did not know whether he did this in order to laugh at others or at himself.

The same evening he received a letter from his mother. She expressed astonishment at not seeing him yet a minister, while at the same time joking a bit. Then she spoke of her health, and informed him that M. Roque had now become one of her visitors.

"Since he is a widower, I thought there would be no objection to inviting him to the house. Louise is greatly changed for the better." And in a postscript: "You have told me nothing about your fine acquaintance, M. Dambreuse; if I were you, I would make use of him."

Why not? His intellectual ambitions had left him, and his fortune (he saw it clearly) was insufficient, for when his debts had been paid, and the sum agreed on remitted to the others, his income would be diminished by four thousand at least! Moreover, he felt the need of giving up this sort of life, and attaching himself to some pursuit. So, next day, when dining at Madame Arnoux's, he said that his mother was tormenting him in order to make him take up a profession.

"But I was under the impression," she said, "that M. Dambreuse was going to get you into the Council of State? That would suit you very well."

So, then, she wished him to take this course. He considered her wish a command.

The banker, as on the first occasion, was seated at his desk, and, with a gesture, intimated that he wait a few minutes; for a gentleman who was standing at the door with his back turned had been discussing some serious topic with him.

The subject of their conversation was the proposed amalgamation of the different coal-mining companies.

On each side of the mirror hung portraits of General Foy* and Louis Philippe. Filing cabinets rose along the paneled walls up to the ceiling, and there were six straw chairs, M. Dambreuse not requiring a more fashionably-furnished room for the transaction of

*Liberal figure of the Restoration whose funeral in 1825 attracted an enormous crowd.

business. It resembled those gloomy kitchens in which great banquets are prepared.

Frédéric noticed particularly two chests of prodigious size which stood in the corners. He asked himself how many millions they might contain. The banker unlocked one of them, and as the iron plate revolved, it disclosed to view nothing inside but blue paper books full of entries.

At last, the person who had been talking to M. Dambreuse passed in front of Frédéric. It was Père Oudry. The two bowed to one another, their faces reddening—a circumstance which surprised M. Dambreuse. However, he exhibited the utmost affability, observing that nothing would be easier than to recommend the young man to the Keeper of the Seals. They would be too happy to have him, he added, concluding his polite attentions by inviting him to an evening party which he would be giving in a few days.

Frédéric was stepping into a carriage on his way to this party when a note from the Maréchale reached him. By the light of the carriage-lamps he read:

"Darling, I have followed your advice: I have just expelled my savage. After to-morrow evening, liberty! Now tell me I am not brave!"

Nothing more. But it was clearly an invitation to him to take the vacant place. He uttered an exclamation, squeezed the note into his pocket, and set forth.

Two municipal guards on horseback were stationed in the street. A row of lamps burned on the two front gates, and some servants were calling out in the courtyard to have the carriages brought up to the end of the steps in front of the house under the marquée.

Then suddenly the noise in the vestibule ceased.

Large trees filled up the space in front of the stair-case. The porcelain globes shed a light which waved like white moiré satin on the walls.

Frédéric rushed up the steps in a joyous frame of mind. An usher announced his name. M. Dambreuse extended his hand. Almost at the very same moment, Madame Dambreuse appeared. She wore a mauve dress trimmed with lace. The ringlets of her hair were more abundant than usual, and she was not wearing a single jewel.

She complained of his coming to visit them so rarely, and seized the opportunity to exchange a few words with him.

The guests began to arrive. In their different ways of bowing they twisted their bodies to one side or bent in two, or merely lowered their heads a little. Then, a married pair, and a family passed by and all scattered themselves about the drawing-room, which was already filled. Under the chandelier in the centre, an enormous ottoman supported a plant-stand, the flowers of which, bending forward, like plumes, hung over the heads of the ladies seated all around in a ring, while others occupied the easy-chairs, which formed two straight lines symmetrically interrupted by the large velvet curtains of the windows and the lofty bays of the doors with their gilded lintels.

The crowd of men who remained standing on the floor with their hats in their hands seemed, at some distance, like one black mass, into which the ribbons in the button-holes introduced red points here and there, and rendered all the more dull the monotonous whiteness of their cravats. With the exception of the very young men just starting to grow beards, all appeared to be bored. Some dandies, with sullen expressions, were balancing on their heels. There were numbers of men with grey hair or wigs. Here and there glistened a bald pate; and the faces of many of these men, either purple or exceedingly pale, showed the traces of immense fatigues: for they were persons who devoted themselves either to political or commercial pursuits. M. Dambreuse had also invited a number of scholars and magistrates, two or three celebrated doctors, and he protested with an air of humility their praises of his hospitality and wealth.

An immense number of men-servants, with fine gold-braided livery, kept moving about on every side. The large candelabra, like bouquets of flame, threw a glow over the hangings which were reflected in the mirrors; and at the back of the dining-room, which was adorned with a jasmine trellis, the side-board resembled the high altar of a cathedral or an exhibition of jewellery, there were so many dishes, bells, knives and forks, silver and silver-gilt spoons in the midst of crystal ware glittering with iridescence.

The three other reception-rooms overflowed with artistic objects—landscapes by great masters on the walls, ivory and porcelain at the sides of the tables, and Chinese ornaments on the consoles. Lacquered screens were displayed in front of the windows, clusters of camelias filled the fireplaces, and a light music vibrated in the distance, like the humming of bees.

The quadrilles were not numerous, and the dancers, judged by the indifferent fashion in which they dragged their pumps after them, seemed to be performing a duty.

Frédéric heard some phrases, such as the following:

"Were you at the last charity fête at the Hôtel Lambert, Mademoiselle?" "No, Monsieur." "It will soon be intolerably warm here." "Oh! yes, indeed; quite suffocating!" "Whose polka, pray, is this?" "Good heavens, Madame, I don't know!"

And, behind him, three greybeards, who had positioned themselves in a window alcove, were whispering some *risqué* remarks. A sportsman told a hunting story, while a Legitimist carried on an argument with an Orléanist. And, wandering about from one group to another, he reached the card-room, where, in the midst of grave-looking men gathered in a circle, he recognised Martinon, now a member of the Paris Bar.

His big face, with its waxen complexion, filled up the space encircled by his collar-like beard, which was a marvel with its evenly trimmed black hair; and, striking a balance between the elegance which his age called for and the dignity which his profession required, he kept his thumbs stuck under his armpits, according to the custom of dandies, and then put his hands into his waistcoat pockets after the manner of learned men. Though his boots were polished to excess, he kept his temples shaved in order to have the forehead of a thinker.

After he had addressed a few chilly words to Frédéric, he turned once more towards those who were chatting around him. A landowner was saying: "This is a class of men that dreams of turning society upsidedown."

"They are calling for the organisation of labour," said another: "Can this be conceived?"

"What could you expect," said a third, "when we see M. de Genoude giving his assistance to *Le Siècle?*"[15]

"And even Conservatives call themselves Progressives. To lead us to what? To the Republic! as if such a thing were possible in France!"

Everyone declared that the Republic was impossible in France.

"No matter!" remarked one gentleman in a loud tone. "People take too much interest in the Revolution. A heap of histories, of different kinds of works, are published concerning it!"

"Without taking into account," said Martinon, "that there are probably subjects of far more importance which might be studied."

A gentleman occupying a ministerial office laid the blame on the scandals associated with the stage:

"Thus, for instance, this new drama of *La Reine Margot* really goes beyond the proper limits. What need was there for telling us about the Valois?* All this exhibits royalty in an unfavourable light. 'Tis just like your press! There is no use in talking, the September laws are altogether too mild.† For my part, I would like to have court-martials, to gag the journalists! At the slightest display of insolence, drag them before a council of war, and then make an end of the business!"

"Oh, be careful, Monsieur! Be careful!" said a professor. "Don't attack the precious gains of 1830! Respect our liberties!" It would be better, he contended, to adopt a policy of decentralisation, and to distribute the surplus populations of the towns through the country districts.

"But they are rotten to the core!" exclaimed a Catholic. "Let religion be more firmly established!"

Martinon hastened to observe:

"As a matter of fact, it is a restraining force."

All the evil lay in this modern longing to rise above one's class and to possess luxuries.

"However," urged a manufacturer, "luxury aids commerce. Therefore, I approve of the Duc de Nemours' action in insisting on having short breeches at his evening parties."

"M. Thiers‡ came to one of them in a pair of trousers. You know his joke on the subject?"

---

*The *La Reine Margot* (1845; *Queen Margot*) of Alexandre Dumas (*père*) unfavorably depicted the Valois kings of the Renaissance.

†See endnote 17 to part one.

‡Historian and politician Adolphe Thiers (1797–1877) was a left-center minister for Louis-Philippe (1773–1850) until his replacement by right-winger François Guizot (1787–1874); later he became a conservative republican.

"Yes; charming! But he turned round to the demagogues, and his speech on the division of power was not without its influence in bringing about the insurrection of the twelfth of May."

"Oh, nonsense!"

"Oh, yes!"

The circle had to make a little opening to give a passage to a man-servant carrying a tray, who was trying to make his way into the card-room.

Under the green shades of the candles the tables were covered with two rows of cards and gold coins. Frédéric stopped beside one corner of the table, lost the fifteen napoleons which he had in his pocket, whirled lightly about, and found himself on the threshold of the boudoir in which Madame Dambreuse happened to be at that moment.

It was filled with women sitting close to one another in little groups on seats without backs. Their long skirts, swelling round them, seemed like waves, from which their waists emerged; and their breasts were revealed by their low-cut bodices. Nearly every one of them had a bouquet of violets in her hand. The dull shade of their gloves showed off the whiteness of their arms. Over the shoulders of some of them hung fringe or flowers, and, every now and then, as they shivered, it seemed as if their bodices were about to fall down.

But the respectability in their faces tempered the provocative effect of their dresses. Several of them had a placidity almost like that of animals; and this gathering of half-naked women made him think of the interior of a harem—indeed, a more vulgar comparison came into the young man's mind.

Every variety of beauty was to be found there—some English ladies, with the profile familiar in "keepsakes"; an Italian, whose black eyes flashed, like a Vesuvius; three sisters, dressed in blue; three Normans, fresh as apple trees in April; a tall red-head, with a set of amethysts. And the bright scintillation of diamonds, which shimmered in sprays worn in their hair, the luminous facets of precious stones laid over their bosoms, and the delightful radiance of pearls framing their faces mingled with the glitter of gold rings, as well as with the lace, powder, the feathers, the vermilion of dainty mouths, and the mother-of-pearl hue of teeth. The ceiling, rounded like a cupola, gave to the boudoir the form of a flower-basket, and a current of perfumed air circulated under the flapping of their fans.

Frédéric, standing behind them, with his monocle in his eye scanned their shoulders, not all of which did he consider faultless. He thought about the Maréchale, and this dispelled the temptations that beset him or consoled him for not yielding to them.

He gazed, however, at Madame Dambreuse, and he considered her charming, in spite of her mouth being rather large and her nostrils too dilated. But she was remarkably graceful in appearance. There was, as it were, a passionate softness in the ringlets of her hair, and her forehead, which was the color of agate, seemed to contain a great deal of ideas, and indicated a masterful intelligence.

She had placed beside her her husband's niece, a rather unattractive young lady. From time to time she left her seat to receive those who had just come in; and the murmur of feminine voices, made, as it were, a cackling like that of birds.

They were talking about the Tunisian ambassadors and their costumes. One lady had been present at the last reception of the Academy. Another referred to Molière's *Don Juan*, which had recently been performed at the Théâtre Français.

But with a significant glance towards her niece, Madame Dambreuse laid a finger on her lips, while the smile which escaped from her contradicted this display of austerity.

Suddenly, Martinon appeared at the door directly in front of her. She arose at once. He offered her his arm. Frédéric, in order to watch the progress of these gallantries on Martinon's part, walked past the card-table, and joined them in the large drawing-room. Madame Dambreuse very soon left her cavalier, and began chatting with Frédéric himself in a very familiar tone.

She understood that he did not play cards, and did not dance.

"Young people have a tendency to be melancholy!" Then, with a single comprehensive glance around:

"Besides, this sort of thing is not amusing—at least for some people!"

And she stopped in front of the row of armchairs, uttering a few polite remarks here and there, while some old men with double eyeglasses came to pay court to her. She introduced Frédéric to some of them. M. Dambreuse touched him lightly on the elbow, and led him out on the terrace.

He had seen the Minister. The thing was not easy to manage. Before he could be qualified for the post of auditor to the Council of State, he should pass an examination. Frédéric, seized with an inexplicable self-confidence, replied that he had a knowledge of the subjects required for it.

The financier was not surprised at this, given how M. Roque had praised his abilities.

At the mention of this name, a vision of little Louise, her house and her room, passed through his mind, and he remembered how he had on nights like this stood at her window listening to the wagoners driving past. This recollection of his unhappiness brought back the thought of Madame Arnoux, and he relapsed into silence as he continued to pace up and down the terrace. The windows shone amid the darkness like slabs of flame. The buzz of the ball gradually grew fainter; the carriages were beginning to leave.

"Why in the world," M. Dambreuse went on, "are you so anxious to be attached to the Council of State?"

And he declared, in the tone of a man of broad views, that public service led to nothing—he could speak with some authority on that point—business was much better.

Frédéric pointed out the difficulty of learning all the details of business.

"Nonsense! I could teach you all about it in a very short time."

Would he like to be a partner in any of his own undertakings?

The young man saw, as by a lightning-flash, an enormous fortune coming into his hands.

"Let us go back in," said the banker. "You are staying for supper with us, are you not?"

It was three o'clock. They left the terrace.

In the dining-room, a table at which supper was served up awaited the guests.

M. Dambreuse noticed Martinon, and, drawing near his wife, in a low tone:

"Is it you who invited him?"

She answered dryly:

"Yes, of course."

The niece was not present.

The guests drank a great deal of wine, and laughed very loudly; and risqué jokes did not give any offence, all present experiencing that sense of relief which follows a somewhat prolonged period of constraint.

Only Martinon looked serious. He refused to drink champagne, as he thought this good form, and, moreover, he assumed an air of tact and politeness, for when M. Dambreuse, who was narrow-chested, complained of being out of breath, he repeatedly asked about the gentleman's health, and then let his blue eyes wander in the direction of Madame Dambreuse.

She questioned Frédéric in order to find out which of the young ladies he liked best. He had noticed none of them in particular, and besides, he preferred women of thirty.

"There, perhaps, you show your sense," she returned.

Then, as they were putting on their cloaks and overcoats, M. Dambreuse said to him:

"Come and see me one of these mornings and we'll have a chat."

Martinon, at the foot of the stairs, was lighting a cigar, and, as he puffed it, he presented such a rough hewn profile that his companion allowed this remark to escape from him:

"Upon my word, what a fine head you have!"

"It has turned a few other heads," replied the young magistrate, with a mix of conviction and annoyance.

As soon as Frédéric was in bed, he went over the party in his mind. In the first place, his own appearance (he had looked at himself several times in the mirrors), from the cut of his coat to the bows of his pumps left nothing to find fault with. He had spoken to influential men, and seen wealthy ladies up close. M. Dambreuse had shown himself to be an admirable type of man, and Madame Dambreuse an almost bewitching type of woman. He weighed one by one her slightest words, her looks, a thousand indescribable yet meaningful things. It would be a right good thing to have such a mistress. And, after all, why should he not? He would have as good a chance with her as any other man. Perhaps she was not so hard to win? Then he remembered Martinon; and, as he fell asleep, he smiled with pity for this worthy fellow.

He woke up with the thought of the Maréchale in his mind. Those words of her note, "After tomorrow evening," were in fact an appointment for the very same day.

He waited until nine o'clock, and then hurried to her house.

Some one who had been going up the stairs before him shut the door. He rang the bell; Delphine came out and told him that "Madame" was not there.

Frédéric persisted, begging her to let him in. He had something of a very serious nature to tell her; just a word would suffice. At length, the hundred-sous-piece argument proved successful, and the maid let him into the hall.

Rosanette appeared. She was in a negligée, with her hair loose, and, shaking her head, she waved her arms when she was some paces away from him to indicate that she could not receive him now.

Frédéric descended the stairs slowly. This caprice was worse than any of the others. He could not understand it at all.

In front of the concierge's lodge Mademoiselle Vatnaz stopped him.

"Has she received you?"

"No."

"You've been put out?"

"How do you know that?"

" 'Tis quite plain. But come on; let's go. I can't breathe!"

She made him accompany her along the street; she panted for breath; he could feel her thin arm trembling against his own. Suddenly, she broke out:

"Ah! the wretch!"

"Who?"

"Why, he—he—Delmar!"

This revelation humiliated Frédéric. He next asked:

"Are you quite sure of it?"

"Why, when I tell you I followed him!" exclaimed Vatnaz. "I saw him going in! Now do you understand? I ought to have expected it for that matter—'twas I, in my stupidity, that introduced him to her. And if you only knew all; my God! Why, I took him in, supported him, clothed him! And then all the paragraphs I got into the newspapers about him! I loved him like a mother!"

Then, with a sneer:

"Ha! Monsieur wants velvet robes! As an investment, you understand! And as for her!—to think that I knew her when she was making her living as a seamstress! If it were not for me, she would have fallen into the mire twenty times over! But I will plunge her into it yet! Let her die in a hospital—and everyone will know the truth!"

And, like a torrent of dirty water from a vessel full of refuse, her rage poured out in a tumultuous fashion into Frédéric's ear the recital of her rival's disgraceful acts.

"She has slept with Jumillac, with Flacourt, with little Allard, with Bertinaux, with Saint-Valéry, the pockmarked fellow! No, 'twas the other! They are brothers—it makes no difference. And when she was in difficulty, I settled everything. She is so stingy! And then, you will agree with me, 'twas nice and kind of me to go to see her, for we are not persons of the same class! Am I a fast woman—I? Do I sell myself? Without taking into account that she is as stupid as a head of cabbage. She writes 'category' with a 'th.' After all, they are well suited. They make a precious couple, though he styles himself an artist and thinks himself a man of genius. But, my God! if he only had intelligence, he would not have done such a thing! Men don't, as a rule, leave a superior woman for a hussy! What do I care about him after all? He is getting ugly. I hate him! If I met him, mind you, I'd spit in his face." She spat out as she uttered the words. "Yes, this is what I think about him now. And Arnoux, eh? Isn't it abominable? He has forgiven her so often! You can't conceive the sacrifices he has made for her. She ought to kiss his feet! He is so generous, so good!"

Frédéric was delighted at hearing Delmar disparaged. He had accepted Arnoux as a rival. This betrayal on Rosanette's part seemed to him an abnormal and inexcusable thing; and, infected with this spinster's emotion, he felt a sort of tenderness towards her. Suddenly he found himself in front of Arnoux's door. Mademoiselle Vatnaz, without his attention having been drawn to it, had led him down towards the Rue Poissonnière.

"Here we are!" said she. "As for me, I can't go up; but you, surely there is nothing to prevent you?"

"From doing what?"

"From telling him everything, faith!"

Frédéric, as if waking up with a start, saw the baseness towards which she was urging him.

"Well?" she said after a pause.

He raised his eyes towards the second floor. Madame Arnoux's lamp was burning. In fact there was nothing to prevent him from going up.

"I am going to wait for you here. Go on, then!"

This command had the effect of cooling the sympathy he had felt towards her and he said:

"I shall be a long time up there; you would do better to return home. I will call on you to-morrow."

"No, no!" replied Vatnaz, stamping with her foot. "Take him with you! Bring him there! Let him catch them together!"

"But Delmar will no longer be there."

She hung her head.

"Yes; that's true, perhaps."

And she remained without speaking in the middle of the street, with vehicles all around her; then, fixing on him her wild-cat's eyes:

"I may rely on you, may I not? There is now a sacred bond between us. Do what you say, then; we'll talk about it to-morrow."

Frédéric, in passing through the lobby, heard two voices responding to one another.

Madame Arnoux's voice was saying:

"Don't lie! don't lie, pray!"

He went in. The voices suddenly ceased.

Arnoux was walking from one end of the room to the other, and Madame was seated on the little chair near the fire, extremely pale and staring straight before her. Frédéric stepped back, and was about to leave, when Arnoux grasped his hand, glad that some one had come to his rescue.

"But I am afraid——" said Frédéric.

"Stay here, I beg of you!" he whispered in his ear.

Madame remarked:

"You must make some allowance for this scene, Monsieur Moreau. Such things sometimes unfortunately occur in households."

"They do when we introduce them there ourselves," said Arnoux in a jolly tone. "Women get crazy ideas in their heads, I assure you. This, for instance, is not a bad one—see! No; quite the contrary. Well, she has been amusing herself for the last hour by teasing me with a lot of stories."

"They are true," retorted Madame Arnoux, losing patience; "for, in fact, you bought it yourself."

"I?"

"Yes, you yourself, at the Persian House."

"The cashmere," thought Frédéric.

He was filled with guilt and fear.

She quickly added:

"It was on Saturday, the fourteenth."

"The fourteenth," said Arnoux, looking up, as if he were searching in his mind for a date.

"And, furthermore, the clerk who sold it to you was a fair-haired young man."

"How could I remember what sort of man the clerk was?"

"And yet it was at your dictation he wrote the address, 18 Rue de Laval."

"How do you know?" said Arnoux in amazement.

She shrugged her shoulders.

"Oh! 'tis very simple: I went to get my cashmere altered, and the superintendent of the millinery department told me that they had just sent another of the same sort to Madame Arnoux."

"Is it my fault if there is a Madame Arnoux in the same street?"

"Yes; but not Jacques Arnoux," she returned.

Thereupon, he began to talk incoherently, protesting that he was innocent. It was some misapprehension, some accident, one of those things that happen in some way that is utterly unaccountable. Men should not be condemned on mere suspicion, vague indications; and he referred to the case of the unfortunate Lesurques.

"In short, I say you are mistaken. Do you want me to take an oath on it?"

" 'Tis not worth while."

"Why?"

She looked him straight in the face without saying a word, then stretched out her hand, took down the little silver chest from the mantelpiece, and handed him a bill which was spread open.

Arnoux coloured up to his ears, and his distorted features puffed up betraying his confusion.

"But," he said in faltering tones, "what does this prove?"

"Ah!" she said, with a peculiar ring in her voice, in which sorrow and irony were blended. "Ah!"

Arnoux held the bill in his hands, and turned it round without removing his eyes from it, as if he were going to find in it the solution to a great problem.

"Ah! yes, yes; I remember," said he at length. " 'Twas a commission. You ought to know about that matter, Frédéric." Frédéric remained silent. "A commission that Père Oudry entrusted to me."

"And for whom?"

"For his mistress."

"For your own!" exclaimed Madame Arnoux, springing to her feet.

"I swear to you!"

"Don't begin over again. I know everything."

"Ah! quite right. So you're spying on me!"

She returned coldly:

"Perhaps that wounds your delicacy?"

"Since you are carried away," said Arnoux, looking for his hat, "and can't be reasoned with——"

Then, with a big sigh:

"Don't marry, my poor friend, don't, take my advice!"

And he went off, finding it absolutely necessary to get some air.

Then there was a deep silence, and it seemed as if everything in the room had become more motionless than before. A luminous circle above the lamp whitened the ceiling, while the corners were shadowy as if covered by black gauze. The ticking of the clock and the crackling of the fire were the only sounds that disturbed the stillness.

Madame Arnoux had just seated herself in the armchair at the opposite side of the fireplace. She bit her lip and shivered. She drew her hands up to her face; a sob broke from her, and she began to weep.

He sat down on the little couch, and in the soothing tone in which one addresses a sick person:

"You don't suspect me of having anything to do with——?"

She made no reply. Then, speaking her thoughts out loud, she said:

"I leave him perfectly free! He did not need to lie!"

"That is quite true," said Frédéric. No doubt, it was the result of Arnoux's way of life; he had acted thoughtlessly, but perhaps in matters of greater importance——

"What do you see, then, that can be more important?"

"Oh, nothing!"

Frédéric bent his head with a smile of acquiescence. Nevertheless, he urged, Arnoux possessed certain good qualities; he was fond of his children.

"Yes, and he does all he can to spoil them!"

Frédéric urged that this was due to an excessively easy-going disposition, for indeed he was a good fellow.

She exclaimed:

"But what is the meaning of that—a good fellow?"

And he proceeded to defend Arnoux in the vaguest kind of language he could think of, and, while expressing his sympathy with her, he rejoiced, he was delighted, at the bottom of his heart. Through retaliation or need of affection she would fly to him for refuge. His hope, which had now grown immeasurably, reinforced his love.

Never had she appeared to him so captivating, so perfectly beautiful. From time to time a deep breath made her bosom swell. Her two eyes, gazing fixedly into space, seemed dilated by a vision in the depths of her consciousness, and her lips were slightly parted, as if to let her soul escape through them. Sometimes she pressed her handkerchief over them tightly. He would have liked to be this dainty little piece of linen moistened with her tears. In spite of himself, he cast a look at the bed at the end of the alcove, picturing to himself her head lying on the pillow, and he saw this so clearly in his imagination that he had to restrain himself to keep from taking her in his arms. She closed her eyes, and now she appeared soothed and still. Then he drew closer to her, and, bending over her, he eagerly scanned her face. At that moment, he heard the noise of boots in the lobby outside—it was Arnoux. They heard him shutting the door of his own room. Frédéric made a sign to Madame Arnoux to ascertain from her whether he ought to go there.

She replied "Yes," in the same voiceless fashion; and this mute exchange of thoughts between them was, as it were, an assent—the preliminary step in adultery.

Arnoux was just taking off his coat to go to bed.

"Well, how is she?"

"Oh! better," said Frédéric; "this will pass."

But Arnoux was in an anxious state of mind.

"You don't know her; she is upset now! Idiot of a clerk! This is what comes of being too good. If I had not given that cursed shawl to Rosanette!"

"Don't regret having done so. Nobody could be more grateful to you than she is."

"Do you really think so?"

Frédéric had not a doubt of it. The best proof of it was her dismissal of Père Oudry.

"Ah! poor little thing!"

And in the excess of his emotion, Arnoux wanted to rush off to her.

"It isn't worth while. I just saw her. She is unwell."

"All the more reason for my going."

He quickly put on his coat again, and took up his candlestick. Frédéric cursed his own stupidity, and pointed out to him that for decency's sake he ought to remain this night with his wife. He could not leave her; it would be very bad of him.

"I tell you candidly you would be doing wrong. There is no hurry over there. You will go tomorrow. Come; do this for my sake."

Arnoux put down his candlestick, and, embracing him, said:

"What a good fellow you are!"

CHAPTER III

Then began for Frédéric a miserable existence. He became the parasite of the house. If anyone were indisposed, he called three times a day to know how the patient was, went to the piano-tuner's, contrived to do a thousand acts of kindness; and he endured with an air of contentment Mademoiselle Marthe's poutings and the caresses of little Eugène, who was always drawing his dirty hands over the young man's face. He was present at dinners at which Monsieur and Madame, facing each other, did not exchange a word, unless it happened that Arnoux provoked his wife with the absurd remarks he made. When the meal was over, he would play about the room with his son, conceal himself behind the furniture, or carry the little boy on his back, walking about on all fours, like the Bearnais.* At last, he would go out, and she would at once plunge into her eternal subject of complaint—Arnoux.

It was not his misconduct that excited her indignation, but her pride appeared to be wounded, and she did not hide her repugnance towards this man, who showed an absence of delicacy, dignity, and honour.

"Or rather, he is mad!" she said.

Frédéric artfully appealed to her to confide in him. Ere long he knew all the details of her life. Her parents were people who lived a humble life in Chartres. One day, Arnoux, while sketching on the bank of the river (at the time he believed himself to be a painter), saw her leaving church, and made her an offer of marriage.

*Henri IV of France (1553–1610), prince of Béarn, in the Pyrenees.

On account of his wealth, he was unhesitatingly accepted. Besides, he was desperately in love with her. She added:

"Good heavens! he loves me still, in his own way!"

They spent the few months immediately after their marriage travelling through Italy.

Arnoux, in spite of his enthusiasm at the sight of the scenery and the masterpieces, did nothing but complain about the wine, and, to find some kind of amusement, organised picnics along with some English people. The profits which he had made by reselling some pictures tempted him to go into the art business. Then, he became infatuated with pottery. Now other types of commerce attracted him, which were becoming more and more vulgar, and he adopted coarse and extravagant habits. It was not so much for his vices she had to reproach him as for his entire conduct. No change could be expected in him, and her unhappiness was irreparable.

Frédéric declared that his own life in the same way was a failure.

He was still a young man, however. Why should he despair? And she gave him good advice: "Work! and marry!" He answered her with a bitter smile; for instead of revealing the real cause of his grief, he pretended that it was of a different, more sublime nature, and he assumed the part of an Antony to some extent, the man accursed by fate*—language not far from his true feelings.

For certain men action becomes more difficult as desire becomes stronger. They are embarrassed by self-doubt, and terrified by the fear of being disliked. Besides, deep feelings of affection are like virtuous women: they are afraid of being discovered, and go through life with downcast eyes.

Though he was now better acquainted with Madame Arnoux (for that very reason perhaps), he was even more faint-hearted than before. Each morning he swore in his own mind that he would make a bold move. He was prevented from doing so by an unconquerable feeling of bashfulness; and he had no example to guide him, inasmuch as she was different from other women. From the force of his dreams, he had placed her outside the ordinary pale of

*This is a reference to Antony, protagonist of a drama of the same name by Alexandre Dumas, and prototype of the somber Romantic lover.

humanity. At her side he felt himself of less importance in the world than the sprigs of silk that escaped from her scissors.

Then he thought up some monstrous and absurd ideas, such as surprising her at night, using drugs and skeleton keys—anything was easier than to face her disdain.

Besides, the children, the two maids, and the relative position of the rooms caused insurmountable obstacles. So then he made up his mind to possess her himself, and to bring her to live with him far away in total isolation. He even asked himself what lake would be blue enough, what seashore would be delightful enough for her, whether it would be in Spain, Switzerland, or the East; and expressly choosing days when she seemed more irritated than usual, he told her that it would be necessary for her to leave the house, to find out some grounds to justify such a step, and that he saw no way out of it but a separation. However, for the sake of the children whom she loved, she would never resort to such an extreme course. So much virtue only increased his respect for her.

He spent each afternoon thinking about the visit he had paid the night before, and longing for the evening to come in order that he might call again. When he did not dine with them, he posted himself about nine o'clock at the corner of the street, and, as soon as Arnoux had slammed the hall-door behind him, Frédéric quickly ascended the two flights of stairs, and innocently asked the servant:

"Is Monsieur in?"

Then he would exhibit surprise at finding that Arnoux had gone out.

The latter frequently came back unexpectedly. Then Frédéric had to accompany him to the little café in the Rue Sainte-Anne, which Regimbart now frequented.

The Citizen began by airing some fresh grievance which he had against the monarchy. Then they would chat, pouring out friendly abuse on one another, for the earthenware manufacturer took Regimbart for a thinker of a higher order, and, annoyed at seeing him waste his talent, teased the Citizen about his laziness. It seemed to Regimbart that Arnoux was a man full of heart and imagination, but decidedly too immoral, and therefore he treated him without indulgence, refusing even to dine at his house on the grounds that "such formality was a bore."

Sometimes, at the moment of parting, Arnoux would be seized by hunger. He found it necessary to order an omelet or some roasted apples; and, as there was never anything to eat in the place, he sent out for something. They waited. Regimbart did not leave, and ended by consenting in a grumbling fashion to have something himself. He was nevertheless gloomy, for he remained for hours seated before a half-filled glass. As Providence did not arrange things according to his ideas, he was becoming a hypochondriac, no longer cared even to read the newspapers, and at the mere mention of England began to bellow with rage. On one occasion, referring to a waiter who gave him bad service, he exclaimed:

"Have we not had enough insults from foreigners?"

Except during these crises, he remained taciturn, contemplating "a foolproof business scheme that would make the shop take off."

Whilst he was lost in these reflections, Arnoux in a monotonous voice and with a slight look of intoxication, related incredible anecdotes in which he was always the star, thanks to his savoir-faire; and Frédéric (this was, no doubt, due to some basic similarities) felt drawn towards him. He reproached himself for this weakness, believing that on the contrary he ought to hate this man.

Arnoux, in Frédéric's presence, complained of his wife's ill-temper, her obstinacy, her unjust accusations. She had not been like this in former days.

"If I were you," said Frédéric, "I would make her an allowance and live alone."

Arnoux made no reply; and the next moment he began to sound her praises. She was good, devoted, intelligent, and virtuous; and, moving on to her personal beauty, he made some revelations on the subject like those careless people who display their treasures in taverns.

The equilibrium of his life was upset by a catastrophe.

He had been appointed to the Board of Directors in a kaolin company. But placing faith in everything that he was told, he had signed inaccurate reports and approved, without verification, the annual inventories fraudulently prepared by the manager. The company had now failed, and Arnoux, being legally responsible, was, along with the others who were liable under the guaranty, condemned to pay damages, which meant a loss to him of thirty thousand francs, not to speak of the costs of the judgment.

Frédéric read the report of the case in a newspaper, and at once hurried off to the Rue de Paradis.

He was ushered into Madame's room. It was breakfast-time. A round table close to the fire was covered with bowls of *café au lait*. Slippers were strewn over the carpet, and clothes over the armchairs. Arnoux was attired in trousers and a knitted vest, with his eyes bloodshot and his hair in disorder. Little Eugène was crying at the pain caused by an attack of mumps, while nibbling at a slice of bread and butter. His sister was eating quietly. Madame Arnoux, a little paler than usual, was waiting on all three of them.

"Well," said Arnoux, heaving a deep sign, "you know all about it?"

And, as Frédéric gave him a pitying look: "There, you see, I have been the victim of my own trusting nature!"

Then he relapsed into silence, and so great was his despair, that he pushed his breakfast away from him. Madame Arnoux raised her eyes with a shrug of the shoulders. He wiped his hand across his forehead.

"After all, I am not guilty. I have nothing to blame myself for. It's unfortunate, but we'll pull through."

He took a bite of a cake, however, in obedience to his wife's appeals.

That evening, he wished that she should go and dine with him alone in a private room at the Maison d'Or. Madame Arnoux did not at all understand this impulse, taking offense, in fact, at being treated as if she were a loose woman. Arnoux, on the contrary, meant it as a show of affection. Then, as he was beginning to feel bored, he went to pay the Maréchale a visit in order to amuse himself.

Up to the present, he had been pardoned for many things due to his good nature. His lawsuit placed him amongst men of bad character. No one visited his house.

Frédéric, bound by honour, thought he should go there more frequently than ever.

He took a box at the Italian opera, and brought them there with him every week. Meanwhile, the pair had reached that period in ill-matched unions when an invincible weariness springs from concessions which people make, and which render existence intolerable. Madame Arnoux restrained her pent-up feelings from breaking out;

Arnoux became gloomy; and Frédéric grew sad at witnessing the unhappiness of these two ill-fated beings.

She had imposed on him the obligation, since she had placed her trust in him, of making enquiries as to the state of her husband's affairs. But shame prevented him from doing so. It was painful to him to reflect that he coveted the wife of this man, at whose dinner-table he constantly sat. Nevertheless, he continued his visits, excusing himself on the grounds that he was bound to protect her, and that an occasion might present itself for being of service to her.

Eight days after the ball, he had paid a visit to M. Dambreuse. The financier had offered him twenty shares of stock in his coal-mining company; Frédéric did not go back there again. Deslauriers had written letters to him, which he left unanswered. Pellerin had invited him to go and see the portrait; he always put it off. He gave way, however, to Cisy's persistent appeals to be introduced to Rosanette.

She received him very nicely, but without throwing her arms around him as she used to do. His comrade was delighted at being received by a woman of easy virtue, and above all at having a chat with an actor. Delmar was there when he called. A drama in which he appeared as a peasant lecturing Louis XIV and prophesying the events of '89 had made him so conspicuous, that the same part was continually assigned to him; and now his function consisted of attacks on the monarchs of all nations. As an English brewer, he inveighed against Charles I; as a student at Salamanca, he cursed Philip II; or, as a sensitive father, he expressed indignation against the Marquise de Pompadour—this was the most beautiful bit of acting! The street urchins used to wait at the stage-door in order to see him; and his biography, sold between the acts, described him as taking care of his aged mother, reading the Bible, assisting the poor, in fact, comparing him to Saint Vincent de Paul with a dash of Brutus and Mirabeau.[16] People spoke of him as "Our Delmar." He had a mission; he became another Christ.

All this had fascinated Rosanette; and she had got rid of Père Oudry, without caring one bit about the consequences, as she was not a greedy person.

Arnoux, who knew her, had taken advantage of her nature for quite some time, spending very little money on her. The old man had appeared on the scene, and all three of them carefully avoided any candid conversations. Then, thinking that she had gotten rid of the other solely on his account, Arnoux increased her allowance. But she made frequent demands for more which was curious since she was living less extravagantly. She had even sold her cashmere in her anxiety to pay off her old debts, as she said; and he was continually giving her money, while she bewitched him and imposed upon him pitilessly. Therefore, bills and writs rained all over the house. Frédéric felt that a crisis was approaching.

One day he called to see Madame Arnoux. She had gone out, Monsieur was at work downstairs in the shop. In fact, Arnoux, in the midst of his Japanese vases, was trying to con a newly-married pair who happened to be well-to-do people from the provinces. He talked about wheel-moulding and fine-moulding, about spotted porcelain and glazed porcelain; not wishing to appear utterly ignorant of the subject, they listened with nods of approbation, and made purchases.

When the customers had gone out, he told Frédéric that he had that very morning been engaged in a little altercation with his wife. In order to prevent any remarks about expenses, he had declared that the Maréchale was no longer his mistress. "I even told her that she was yours."

Frédéric was annoyed at this; but to make reproaches might only betray him. He faltered: "Ah! you were in the wrong—greatly in the wrong!"

"What does that signify?" said Arnoux. "Where is the disgrace of passing for her lover? After all, I am! Would you not be flattered at being in that position?"

Had she spoken? Was this a hint? Frédéric hastened to reply:

"No! not at all! on the contrary!"

"Well, what then?"

"Yes, 'tis true; it makes no difference."

Arnoux next asked: "And why don't you call there more often?"

Frédéric promised that he would make it his business to go there again.

"Ah! I forgot! you ought, when talking about Rosanette, to let out in some way to my wife that you are her lover. I can't suggest how you can best do it, but you'll find a way. I ask this of you as a special favour—eh?"

The young man's only answer was an equivocal smile. This slander had undone him. He even called on her that evening, and swore that Arnoux's accusation was false.

"Is that really so?"

He appeared to be speaking sincerely, and, when she had taken a long breath of relief, she said to him:

"I believe you," with a beautiful smile. Then she lowered her head, and, without looking at him:

"Besides, nobody has any claim on you!"

So then she suspected nothing; and she despised him, seeing that she did not think he could love her enough to remain faithful to her! Frédéric, forgetting his overtures towards the other, looked on her tolerant attitude as an outrage.

After this she suggested that he ought now and then to pay Rosanette a visit, to get a little glimpse of what she was like.

Arnoux arrived, and, five minutes later, wished to take him off to Rosanette's.

The situation was becoming intolerable.

His attention was diverted by a letter from a notary, who was going to send him fifteen thousand francs the following day; and, in order to make up for his neglect of Deslauriers, he went straight away to tell him this good news.

The lawyer was lodging in the Rue des Trois-Maries, on the fifth floor, over a courtyard. His study, a little tiled room, chilly, and with grey wallpaper, had as its principal decoration a gold medal, the prize awarded him on the occasion of receiving his Doctor of Laws, which was set in an ebony frame near the mirror. A mahogany bookcase enclosed under its glass front a hundred volumes, more or less. The writing-desk, covered with leather, occupied the centre of the room. Four old armchairs upholstered in green velvet were placed in the corners; and a heap of wood shavings made a blaze in the fireplace, where there was always a bundle of sticks ready to be lighted as soon as he rang the bell. It was his consultation-hour, and the lawyer had on a white cravat.

The announcement as to the fifteen thousand francs (he had, no doubt, given up all hope of getting the amount) made him chuckle with delight.

"That's right, old fellow, that's right—that's quite right!"

He threw some wood into the fire, sat down again, and immediately began talking about the journal. The first thing to do was to get rid of Hussonnet.

"I'm quite tired of that idiot! As for officially professing opinions, my own notion is that the most equitable and forcible position is to have no opinions at all."

Frédéric appeared astonished.

"Why, the thing is perfectly plain. It is time that politics should be dealt with scientifically. The old men of the eighteenth century began it when Rousseau and the men of letters introduced into the political sphere philanthropy, poetry, and other nonsense, to the great delight of the Catholics—a natural alliance, however, since the modern reformers (I can prove it) all believe in divine revelation. But, if you sing high masses for Poland, if, in place of the God of the Dominicans, who was an executioner, you take the God of the Romanticists, who is an upholsterer, if, in fact, you have not a wider conception of the Absolute than your ancestors, Monarchy will penetrate underneath your Republican forms, and your red cap will never be more than a priest's skull cap. The only difference will be that the solitary confinement will take the place of torture, the outrageous treatment of Religion that of sacrilege, and the European Concert that of the Holy Alliance;* and in this beautiful order which we admire, composed of the wreckage of the followers of Louis XIV, the last remains of the Voltaireans, with some Imperial white-wash on top, and some fragments of the British Constitution, you will see the municipal councils trying to annoy the Mayor, the general councils their Prefect,[17] the Chambers the King, the Press Power, and the Administration everybody. But simple-minded people get enraptured about the Civil Code, a work fabricated—let them say what they like—in a mean and tyrannical spirit, for the legislator, in place of doing his duty to the State, which simply means to observe customs in a regular fashion, claims to model

---

*Pact established between Russia, Austria, and Prussia in 1815.

society like another Lycurgus. Why does the law impede fathers of families with regard to the making of wills? Why does it place shackles on the compulsory sale of real estate? Why does it punish vagrancy as a misdemeanour, which ought not even to be regarded as a technical contravention of the Code. And there are other things! I know all about them! and so I am going to write a little novel, entitled 'The History of the Idea of Justice,' which will be amusing. But I am infernally thirsty! And you?"

He leaned out through the window, and called to the porter to go and fetch them two glasses of grog from the tavern across the way.

"To sum up, I see three parties—no! three groups—in none of which do I take the slightest interest: those who have, those who have nothing, and those who are trying to have. But all agree in their idiotic worship of Authority! For example, Mably recommends that the philosophers should be prevented from publishing their doctrines; M. Wronsky, the geometrician, describes censorship as the 'critical expression of speculative spontaneity'; Père Enfantin gives his blessing to the Hapsburgs for having stretched a hand across the Alps in order to keep Italy down; Pierre Leroux wishes people to be compelled to listen to an orator; and Louis Blanc inclines towards a State religion[18]—so much rage for government have these vassals whom we call the people! Nevertheless, there is not a single legitimate government, in spite of their eternal principles. But 'principle' signifies 'origin.' It is always necessary to go back to a revolution, to an act of violence, to a transitory fact. Thus, our principle is the national sovereignty embodied in the Parliamentary form, though the Parliament does not assent to this! But in what way could the sovereignty of the people be more sacred than the Divine Right? They are both fictions. Enough of metaphysics; no more phantoms! There is no need of dogmas in order to get the streets swept! It will be said that I am turning society upside down. Well, after all, where is the harm in that? It is, indeed, a nice thing—this society of yours."

Frédéric could have given many answers. But, seeing that his theories were far from those of Sénécal, he was full of indulgence. He contented himself with arguing that such a system would make them universally hated.

"On the contrary, as we should have given to each party a pledge of hatred against his neighbour, all will support us. You're going to get down to work too, and furnish us with some transcendent criticism!"

It was necessary to attack accepted ideas—the Academy, the École Normale, the Consérvatoire, the Comédie Française, everything that resembled an institution.[19] It was in that way that they would give uniformity to the doctrines taught in their review. Then, as soon as it had been thoroughly well-established, the journal would suddenly be converted into a daily publication. Thereupon they could find fault with individuals.

"And they will respect us, you may be sure!"

Deslauriers touched upon that old dream of his—the position of editor-in-chief, so that he might have the unutterable happiness of directing others, of entirely cutting down their articles, of ordering them to be written or declining them. His eyes twinkled behind his spectacles; he got into a state of excitement, and drank a few glasses of brandy, one after the other, in a mechanical fashion.

"You'll have to give a dinner party once a week. That's indispensable, even though you would have to spend half your income on it. People would feel pleasure in going to it; it would be a centre for the others, a boost for yourself; and by manipulating public opinion at its two ends—literature and politics—you will see how, before six months have passed, we shall occupy the first rank in Paris."

Frédéric, as he listened to Deslauriers, experienced a sensation of rejuvenation, like a man who, after having been confined in a room for a long time, is suddenly transported into the open air. The enthusiasm of his friend had a contagious effect upon him.

"Yes, I have been an idler, an imbecile—you are right!"

"All in good time," said Deslauriers. "I have found my Frédéric again!"

And, putting his fist under Frédéric's chin:

"Ah! you have made me suffer! Never mind, I am fond of you all the same."

They stood there gazing into each other's faces, both deeply affected, and were on the point of embracing each other.

A woman's cap appeared on the threshold of the anteroom.

"What brings you here?" said Deslauriers.

It was Mademoiselle Clémence, his mistress.

She replied that, as she happened to be passing, she could not resist the desire to go in to see him, and in order that they might have a little treat together, she had brought some cakes, which she laid on the table.

"Watch out for my papers!" said the lawyer, sharply. "Besides, this is the third time that I have forbidden you to come during my consultation-hours."

She wished to embrace him.

"That's enough! Go away! Make yourself scarce!"

He pushed her away; she let out a great sob.

"Ah! you tire me!"

"Only because I love you!"

"I don't ask to be loved, but for people to do what I want!"

This harsh remark stopped Clémence's tears. She planted herself in front of the window, and remained there motionless, with her forehead against the pane.

Her attitude and her silence had an irritating effect on Deslauriers.

"When you have finished, you will order your carriage, will you not?"

She turned round with a start.

"You are sending me away?"

"Exactly."

She fixed on him her large blue eyes, no doubt as a last appeal, then drew the two ends of her tartan shave across each other, lingered for a minute or two, and went away.

"You ought to call her back," said Frédéric.

"Come, now!"

And, as he wished to go out, Deslauriers went into the kitchen, which also served as his dressing-room. On the stone floor, beside a pair of boots, were to be seen the remains of a meagre breakfast, and a mattress with a blanket was rolled up on the floor in a corner.

"This will show you," he said, "that I receive few marquises. 'Tis easy to get enough of them, ay, faith! and some others, too! Those who cost nothing take up your time—'tis money under another form. Now, I'm not rich! And then they are all so silly, so silly! Can you converse with a woman yourself?"

As they parted, at the corner of the Pont Neuf, Deslauriers said: "It's agreed, then; you'll bring the thing to me to-morrow as soon as you have it!"

"Agreed!" said Frédéric.

When he awoke next morning, he received through the post a cheque from the bank for fifteen thousand francs.

This scrap of paper represented to him fifteen big bags of money; and he said to himself that, with such a sum he could, first of all, keep his carriage for three years instead of selling it, as he would soon be forced to do, or buy for himself two beautiful suits of armour, which he had seen on the Quai Voltaire, then many other things, pictures, books and what a quantity of bouquets of flowers, presents for Madame Arnoux! anything, in short, would have been preferable to risking losing everything in that journal! Deslauriers seemed to him presumptuous, his insensitivity the night before having cooled Frédéric's affection for him; and the young man was wallowing in these feelings of regret, when he was quite surprised by the sudden appearance of Arnoux, who sat down heavily on the side of the bed, like a man overwhelmed with trouble.

"What is the matter now?"

"I am ruined!"

He had to deposit that very day at the office of Maître Beaumont, notary, in the Rue Saint-Anne, eighteen thousand francs lent him by one Vanneroy.

" 'Tis an unspeakable disaster. I have, however, given him a mortgage, which ought to keep him quiet. But he threatens me with a writ if it is not paid this afternoon promptly."

"And what next?"

"Oh! the next step is simple enough; he will take possession of my real estate. Once the thing is publicly announced, it means ruin to me—that's all! Ah! if I could find anyone to advance me this cursed sum, he might take Vanneroy's place, and I should be saved! You don't happen to have it yourself?"

The cheque had remained on the night-table near a book. Frédéric took up a volume, and placed it on the cheque, while he replied:

"Good heavens, my dear friend, no!"

But it was painful to him to say "no" to Arnoux.

"What, don't you know anyone who would——?"

"Nobody! and to think that in eight days I should be getting in money! There is probably fifty thousand francs due to me at the end of the month!"

"Couldn't you ask some of the people that owe you money to make you an advance?"

"Ah! well, so I did!"

"But have you any bills or promissory notes?"

"Not one!"

"What is to be done?" said Frédéric.

"That's what I'm asking myself," said Arnoux.

" 'Tisn't for myself, my God! but for my children and my poor wife!"

Then, letting each phrase fall from his lips in a broken fashion:

"In fact—I could rough it—I could pack off all I have—and go and seek my fortune—I don't know where!"

"Impossible!" exclaimed Frédéric.

Arnoux replied with an air of calmness:

"How do you think I could live in Paris now?"

There was a long silence. Frédéric broke it by saying:

"When could you pay back this money?"

Not that he had it; quite the contrary! But there was nothing to prevent him from seeing some friends, and making an application to them.

And he rang for his servant to get himself dressed.

Arnoux thanked him.

"The amount you want is eighteen thousand francs—isn't it?"

"Oh! I could manage easily with sixteen thousand! For I could make two thousand five hundred out of it, or get three thousand on my silver plate, if Vanneroy would give me till to-morrow; and, I repeat to you, you may inform the lender, give him a solemn undertaking, that in eight days, perhaps even in five or six, the money will be reimbursed. Besides, the mortgage will be security for it. So there is no risk, you understand?"

Frédéric assured him that he thoroughly understood the state of affairs, and added that he was going out immediately.

He stayed at home, cursing Deslauriers, for he wished to keep his word, and at the same time, help Arnoux.

"Suppose I applied to M. Dambreuse? But on what pretext could I ask for money? 'Tis I, on the contrary, that should give him some for the shares I took in his coal-mining company. Ah! let him go hang himself—his shares! I am really not liable for them!"

And Frédéric applauded himself for his own independence, as if he had refused to do some service for M. Dambreuse.

"Ah, well," said he to himself afterwards, "since I'm going to meet with a loss there—for with fifteen thousand francs I might gain a hundred thousand! such things sometimes happen on the stock market—well, then, since I am breaking my promise to one of them, am I not free? Besides, so what if Deslauriers has to wait? No, no; that's wrong; I must go there."

He looked at his watch.

"Ah! there's no hurry. The bank does not close till five o'clock."

And, at half-past four, when he had cashed the cheque:

" 'Tis useless now; I will not find him in. I'll go this evening." Thus giving himself the opportunity of changing his mind, for there always remain in the conscience some of those sophisms which we pour into it ourselves. It preserves the after-taste of them, like that of a bad liquor.

He walked along the boulevards, and dined alone at a restaurant. Then he took in one act of a play at the Vaudeville, in order to divert his thoughts. But his bank-notes caused him as much uneasiness as if he had stolen them. He would not have been very sorry if he had lost them.

When he reached home again he found a letter containing these words:

"What news? My wife joins me, dear friend, in the hope, etc.—Yours."

And then there was a flourish after his signature.

"His wife! She is asking me!"

At the same moment Arnoux appeared, to find out whether he had been able to obtain the sum so sorely needed.

"Yes, here it is," said Frédéric.

And, twenty-four hours later, he gave this reply to Deslauriers:

"I have no money."

The advocate came back three days, one after the other, and urged Frédéric to write to the notary. He even offered to take a trip to Le Havre in connection with the matter.

At the end of the week, Frédéric timidly asked the worthy Arnoux for his fifteen thousand francs. Arnoux put it off till the following day, and then till the day after. Frédéric ventured out late at night, fearing that Deslauriers would catch him.

One evening, somebody knocked against him at the corner of the Madeleine. It was he.

And Deslauriers accompanied Frédéric as far as the door of a house in the Faubourg Poissonnière.

"Wait for me!"

He waited. At last, after three quarters of an hour, Frédéric came out, accompanied by Arnoux, and made signs to him to have patience a little longer. The earthenware merchant and his companion went up the Rue de Hauteville arm-in-arm, and then turned down the Rue de Chabrol.

The night was dark, with gusts of tepid wind. Arnoux walked on slowly, talking about the Galleries of Commerce—a succession of covered passages which would have led from the Boulevard Saint-Denis to the Châtelet, a marvellous speculative venture, into which he was very anxious to invest; and he stopped from time to time in order to have a look at the grisettes' faces in front of the shop-windows, and then, raising, his head again, resumed the conversation.

Frédéric heard Deslauriers' steps behind him like reproaches, like blows falling on his conscience. But he did not dare ask for his money, out of shame, and also fear that it would be fruitless. Deslauriers was drawing nearer. He made up his mind to ask.

Arnoux, in a very flippant tone, said that, as he had not got in his outstanding debts, he was really unable to pay back the fifteen thousand francs.

"You have no need of the money, I imagine?"

At that moment Deslauriers came up to Frédéric, and, taking him aside:

"Be honest. Have you got the amount? Yes or no?"

"Well, then, no," said Frédéric; "I've lost it."

"Ah! and in what way?"

"Gambling."

Deslauriers, without saying a single word in reply, made a very low bow, and went away. Arnoux had taken advantage of the opportunity to light a cigar in a tobacconist's shop. When he came back, he wanted to know from Frédéric "who was that young man?"

"Oh! nobody—a friend."

Then, three minutes later, in front of Rosanette's door:

"Come on up," said Arnoux; "she'll be glad to see you. What a savage you are these days!"

A gas-lamp, which was directly opposite, threw its light on him; and, with his cigar between his white teeth and his air of contentment, there was something intolerable about him.

"Ah! now that I think of it, my notary has been at your place this morning about that mortgage-registry business. 'Tis my wife reminded me about it."

"A wife with brains!" returned Frédéric automatically.

"I'd say so!"

And once more Arnoux began to sing his wife's praises. There was no one like her for spirit, tenderness, and thrift; he added in a low tone, rolling his eyes about: "And a woman with so many charms, too!"

"Good-bye!" said Frédéric.

Arnoux made a step closer to him.

"Hold on! Why are you going?" And, with his hand half-stretched out towards Frédéric, he stared at the young man, quite taken aback by the look of anger in his face.

Frédéric repeated in a dry tone, "Good-bye!"

He hurried down the Rue de Bréda like a stone rolling headlong, raging against Arnoux, swearing in his own mind that he would never see the man again, nor her either, so broken-hearted and desolate did he feel. Instead of the break-up which he had anticipated, here was the other, on the contrary, exhibiting towards her a most perfect attachment from the ends of her hair to the inmost depths of her soul. Frédéric was exasperated by the vulgarity of this man. He had it all! He found Arnoux again at his mistress's door; and the upset of their disagreement added to his rage at his own powerlessness. Besides, he felt humiliated by the other's display of integrity in offering him guaranties for his money. He would have liked to strangle him, and over the pangs of disappointment floated in his conscience, like a fog, the sense of his cowardly behavior towards his friend. Rising tears nearly suffocated him.

Deslauriers descended the Rue des Martyrs, swearing aloud with indignation; for his project, like an obelisk that has fallen, now assumed extraordinary proportions. He considered himself robbed, as if he had suffered a great loss. His friendship for Frédéric was dead, and he experienced a feeling of joy at it—it was a sort of compensation to him! A hatred of all rich people took possession of him. He leaned towards Sénécal's opinions, and resolved to make every effort to propagate them.

All this time, Arnoux was comfortably seated in an easy-chair near the fire, sipping his cup of tea, with the Maréchale on his knee.

Frédéric did not go back there; and, in order to distract his attention from his disastrous passion, he determined, to write a "History of the Renaissance." He piled up confusedly on his table the humanists, the philosophers, and the poets, and he went to inspect some engravings of Mark Antony, and tried to understand Machiavelli. Gradually, the serenity of intellectual work had a soothing effect upon him. While his mind was steeped in the personality of others, he lost sight of his own—which is the only way, perhaps, of getting rid of suffering.

One day, while he was quietly taking notes, the door opened, and the man-servant announced Madame Arnoux.

It was she, indeed! and alone? Why, no! for she was holding little Eugène by the hand, followed by a nurse in a white apron. She sat down, and after a preliminary cough:

"It is a long time since you came to see us."

As Frédéric could think of no excuse at the moment, she added:

"It was very tactful of you!"

He asked in return:

"Tactful about what?"

"About what you have done for Arnoux!" said she.

Frédéric made a significant gesture. "What do I care about him, indeed? It was for your sake I did it!"

She sent off the child to play with his nurse in the drawing-room. Two or three words passed between them as to their state of health; then the conversation stalled.

She wore a brown silk gown, which had the colour of Spanish wine, with a coat of black velvet bordered with sable. This fur made him yearn to pass his hand over it; and her tresses, so long and so exquisitely smooth, seemed to draw his lips towards them. But something was bothering her and, turning her eyes towards the door:

" 'Tis rather warm here!"

Frédéric understood what her discreet glance meant.

"Ah! excuse me! the two leaves of the door are merely drawn together."

"Yes, that's true!"

And she smiled, as much as to say:

"I'm not a bit afraid!"

Then he asked her the reason for her visit.

"My husband," she replied with an effort, "has urged me to call on you, not venturing to take this step himself!"

"And why?"

"You know M. Dambreuse, don't you?"

"Yes, slightly."

"Ah! slightly."

She fell silent.

"No matter! finish what you were going to say."

Thereupon she told him that, two days before, Arnoux had found himself unable to meet four bills of a thousand francs, made payable at the banker's order and with his signature attached to them. She felt sorry for having compromised her children's fortune. But anything was preferable to dishonour; and, if M. Dambreuse stopped the proceedings, they would certainly pay him soon, for she was going to sell a little house which she had at Chartres.

"Poor woman!" murmured Frédéric. "I will go. You can rely on me!"

"Thank you!"

And she arose to go.

"Oh! there is nothing to hurry you yet."

She remained standing, examining the trophy of Mongolian arrows suspended from the ceiling, the bookcase, the bindings, all the utensils for writing. She lifted up the bronze bowl which held his pens. Her feet rested on different portions of the carpet. She had visited Frédéric several times before, but always accompanied by Arnoux. They were now alone together—alone in his own house. It was an extraordinary event—almost a stroke of luck.

She wished to see his little garden. He offered her his arm to show her his property—thirty feet of ground enclosed by some houses, adorned with shrubs at the corners and flower-beds in the middle. The early days of April had arrived. The leaves of the lilacs were already turning green. A breeze stirred the air, and the little birds chirped, their song alternating with the distant sound that came from a coachmaker's forge.

Frédéric went to look for a fire-shovel; and, while they walked on side by side, the child kept making sand-pies on the walk.

Madame Arnoux did not believe that, as he grew older, he would have a great imagination; but he had a winning disposition. His sister, on the other hand, possessed a caustic humour that sometimes wounded her.

"That will change," said Frédéric. "We must never despair."

She returned:

"We must never despair!"

This automatic repetition of the phrase he had used appeared to him a sort of encouragement; he plucked a rose, the only one in the garden.

"Do you remember a certain bouquet of roses one evening, in a carriage?"

She blushed a little; and, with an air of bantering pity:

"Ah, I was very young then!"

"And this rose," went on Frédéric, in a low tone, "will it be the same way with it?"

She replied, while turning about the stem between her fingers, like the thread of a spindle:

"No, I will preserve it."

She called the nurse, who took the child in her arms; then, on the threshold of the door in the street, Madame Arnoux sniffed the flower, leaning her head on her shoulder with a look as sweet as a kiss.

When he had gone up to his study, he gazed at the armchair in which she had sat, and every object which she had touched. Something of her swirled around him. The caress of her presence lingered there still.

"So, then, she came here," he said to himself.

And his soul was bathed in waves of infinite tenderness.

Next day, at eleven o'clock, he presented himself at M. Dambreuse's house. He was received in the dining-room. The banker was seated opposite, his wife at lunch. Beside her sat her niece, and at the other side of the table appeared the governess, an English woman, whose face was heavily pock-marked.

M. Dambreuse invited his young friend to take a seat among them, and when he declined:

"What can I do for you?"

Frédéric confessed, while affecting indifference, that he had come to make a request on behalf, of one Arnoux.

"Ah! Ah! the ex-art-dealer," said the banker, with a noiseless laugh which exposed his gums. "Oudry used to act as his guarantor; they have since had a falling-out."

And he proceeded to read the letters and newspapers which lay close beside him on the table.

Two servants attended without making the least noise on the parquet; and the high-ceilinged room, which had three door-curtains of richest tapestry, and two white marble fountains, the polish of the chafing-dish, the arrangement of the hors-d'oeuvres, and even the crisp folds of the napkins, all this sumptuous comfort impressed Frédéric's mind with the contrast between it and another lunch at the Arnouxs' house. He did not take the liberty of interrupting M. Dambreuse.

Madame noticed his embarrassment.

"Do you occasionally see our friend Martinon?"

"He will be here this evening," said the young girl in a lively tone.

"Ah! so you know him?" said her aunt, fixing on her a freezing look.

At that moment one of the men-servants, bending forward, whispered in her ear.

"Your dressmaker, Mademoiselle—Miss John!"

And the governess, in obedience to this summons, left the room along with her pupil.

M. Dambreuse, annoyed at the disarrangement of the chairs by this movement, asked what was the matter.

" 'Tis Madame Regimbart."

"Wait a moment! Regimbart! I know that name. I have come across his signature."

Frédéric finally broached the subject. Arnoux deserved some consideration; he was even going, for the sole purpose of fulfilling his obligations, to sell a house belonging to his wife.

"She is considered very pretty," said Madame Dambreuse.

The banker added, with a display of good-nature:

"Are you an intimate friend of theirs?"

Frédéric, without giving an explicit reply, said that he would be very much obliged to him if he considered the matter.

"Well, if it makes you happy so be it; we will wait. I have some time to spare yet; suppose we go down to my office. Would you mind?"

They had finished lunch. Madame Dambreuse bowed slightly towards Frédéric, smiling in an odd fashion, with a mixture of politeness and irony. Frédéric had no time to reflect on it, for M. Dambreuse, as soon as they were alone:

"You did not come to get your shares?"

And, without permitting him to make any excuses:

"Well! well! 'tis right that you should know a little more about the business."

He offered Frédéric a cigarette, and began his statement.

The General Union of French Coal Mines had been constituted. All that they were waiting for was the order for its incorporation. The mere fact of the merger had diminished the cost of administration and of manual labour, and increased the profits. Besides, the company had conceived a new idea, which was to give the workmen an interest in the enterprise. It would build houses for them, with hygenic living conditions; finally, it would constitute itself the purveyor of its *employés*, and would have everything supplied to them at net prices.

"And they will gain by it, Monsieur: that's true progress! that's the way to reply effectively to certain Republican grumblings. We have on our Board"—he showed the prospectus—"a peer of France, a scholar who is a member of the Institute, a retired senior-officer of the engineers, well-known names, such elements reassure the timid capitalists, and appeal to intelligent capitalists!"

The company would have in its favour the sanction of the State, then the railways, the steam service, the iron works, the gas companies, and ordinary households.

"Thus we heat, we light, we penetrate to the very hearth of the humblest home. But how, you will say to me, can we be sure of selling? By the aid of protective laws, dear Monsieur, and we shall get them!—that is a matter that concerns us! For my part, however, I am a downright prohibitionist! The country before anything!"

He had been appointed a director; but he had no time to occupy himself with certain details, amongst other things with the editing of their publications.

"I find myself rather muddled with my authors. I have forgotten my Greek. I am in need of someone who can interpret my ideas."

And suddenly: "Will you be the man to perform those duties, with the title of general secretary?"

Frédéric did not know what reply to make.

"Well, what is there to prevent you?"

His functions would be confined to writing a report every year for the shareholders. He would find himself day after day in communication with the most notable men in Paris. Representing the company with the workmen, he would ere long be worshipped by them as a natural consequence, and by this means he would be able, later, to push him into the General Council, and into the position of a representative.

Frédéric's ears tingled. Whence came this good-will? He thanked M. Dambreuse profusely. But it was important, the banker said, that he not be dependent on anyone. The best course was to take some shares, "a splendid investment besides, for your capital guarantees your position, as your position does your capital."

"About how much should it amount to?" said Frédéric.

"Oh, well! whatever you please—from forty to sixty thousand francs, I suppose."

This sum was so miniscule in M. Dambreuse's eyes, and his authority was so great, that the young man resolved immediately to sell a farm.

He accepted the offer. M. Dambreuse would fix an appointment one of these days in order to finish their arrangements.

"So I can say to Jacques Arnoux——?"

"Anything you like—the poor chap—anything you like!"

Frédéric wrote to the Arnouxs' to make their minds easy, and he dispatched the letter by his servant, who brought back the letter: "Good!" His efforts deserved better recognition. He expected a visit, or, at least, a letter. He did not receive a visit, and no letter arrived.

Was it forgetfulness on their part, or was it intentional? Since Madame Arnoux had come once, what was to prevent her from coming again? The sort of hint, of confession of which she had made him the recipient on the occasion, was nothing more, then, than a selfish manœuvre.

"Are they playing me? and is she an accomplice of her husband?" A sort of shame, in spite of his desire, prevented him from returning to their house.

One morning (three weeks after their meeting), M. Dambreuse wrote to him, saying that he expected him the same day in an hour's time.

On the way, the thought of Arnoux oppressed him once more, and, not having been able to discover any reason for their conduct, he was seized with anguish, a grim presentiment. In order to shake it off, he hailed a cab, and drove to the Rue de Paradis.

Arnoux was away travelling.

"And Madame?"

"In the country, at the works."

"When is Monsieur coming back?"

"To-morrow, without fail."

He would find her alone; this was the opportune moment. An imperious voice seemed to cry out in the depths of his consciousness: "Go, then, and meet her!"

But M. Dambreuse? "Ah! well, too bad, I'll say that I was ill."

He rushed to the railway-station, and, as soon as he was in the rail car:

"Perhaps I have done wrong. Oh, what does it matter?"

Green plains stretched out to the right and to the left. The train rolled on. The little station-houses glistened like stage-scenery, and the smoke of the locomotive kept constantly sending forth on the same side its big fleecy masses, which danced for a little while on the grass, and were then dispersed.

Frédéric, who sat alone in his compartment, gazed at all this out of boredom, lost in that weariness which is produced by the very excess of impatience. Finally cranes and warehouses appeared. They had reached Creil.

The town, built on the slopes of two low-lying hills (the first of which was bare, and the second crowned by woods), with its church-tower, its houses of different sizes, and its stone bridge, seemed to him a mix of gaiety, reserve, and wholesomeness. A long flat barge floated on the water's current, which surged up under the lash of the wind.

Hens were pecking around in the straw at the foot of a crucifix erected on the spot; a woman passed with some wet linen in a basket on her head.

After crossing the bridge, he found himself on an island, where he beheld on his right the ruins of an abbey. A mill with its wheels revolving barred up the entire width of the second arm of the Oise, which the factory overlooked. Frédéric was greatly surprised by the imposing character of this structure. He felt more respect for Arnoux on account of it. Three steps further on, he turned up an alley, which had an iron gate at its far end.

He went in. The concierge called him back, exclaiming:

"Have you a permit?"

"For what purpose?"

"For the purpose of visiting the establishment."

Frédéric said in a rather curt tone that he had come to see M. Arnoux.

"Who is M. Arnoux?"

"Why, the chief, the master, the proprietor, in fact!"

"No, monsieur! These are MM. Lebœuf and Milliet's works!"

The good woman was surely joking! Some workmen arrived; he came up and spoke to two or three of them. They gave the same response.

Frédéric left the premises, staggering like a drunken man; and he had such a look of perplexity, that on the Pont de la Boucherie an inhabitant of the town, who was smoking his pipe, asked if he was looking for something. This man knew where Arnoux's factory was. It was situated at Montataire.

Frédéric asked where he could find a carriage and was told that the only place was at the station. He went back there. A shaky-looking calash, to which was yoked an old horse, with torn harness hanging over the shafts, stood all alone in front of the luggage office. A street-urchin who was looking on offered to go and find Père Pilon. In ten minutes' time he came back, and announced that Père Pilon was having his breakfast. Frédéric, unable to stand this any longer, walked away. But the gates of the thoroughfare across the train tracks were closed. He would have to wait till two trains had passed. At last, he walked off into the countryside.

The monotonous greenery made it look like the cover of an immense billiard-table. The scoriæ of iron lined both sides of the track, like heaps of stones. A little further on, some factory chimneys were smoking close beside each other. In front of him, on a round hillock, stood a little turreted château, with the quadrangular belfry of a church. At a lower level, long walls formed irregular lines past the trees; and, further down again, the houses of the village spread out.

They had only a single story, with staircases consisting of three steps made of uncemented blocks. Every now and then the bell in front of a grocery-shop could be heard tinkling. Heavy steps sank into the black mire, and a light shower was falling, which cut the pale sky with a thousand hatchings.

Frédéric made his way along the middle of the street. Then, he saw on his left, at the opening of a pathway, a large wooden arch, whereon was traced, in letters of gold, the word "Faïences."

It was not for nothing that Jacques Arnoux had selected the vicinity of Creil. By placing his works as close as possible to the other works (which had long enjoyed a high reputation), he had created a certain confusion in the public mind, with a favourable result so far as his own interests were concerned.

The main body of the building rested on the same bank of a river which flows through the meadowlands. The master's house, surrounded by a garden, could be distinguished by the steps in front of it, adorned with four vases, bristling with cactuses.

Heaps of white clay were drying under sheds. There were others in the open air; and in the midst of the yard stood Sénécal with his everlasting blue overcoat lined with red.

The ex-tutor extended towards Frédéric his cold hand.

"You've come to see the master? He's not here."

Frédéric, nonplussed, replied in a stupefied fashion:

"I know." But the next moment, correcting himself:

" 'Tis about a matter that concerns Madame Arnoux. Can she see me?"

"Ah! I have not seen her for the last three days," said Sénécal.

And he broke into a long string of complaints. When he accepted the post of manager, he understood that he would have been allowed to reside in Paris, and not be forced to bury himself in the country, far from his friends, deprived of newspapers. No matter! he had overlooked all that. But Arnoux appeared to pay no attention to his merits. He was, moreover, shallow and old fashioned—no one could be more ignorant. Instead of making artistic improvements, it would have been better to introduce firewood instead of coal and gas. The master was going under—Sénécal laid stress on the last words. In short, he disliked his present occupation, and he all but appealed to Frédéric to say a word on his behalf in order that he might get an increase of salary.

"Don't worry!" said the other.

He met nobody on the staircase. On the first floor, he pushed his way head-first into an empty room. It was the drawing-room. He called out at the top of his voice. There was no reply. No doubt, the cook had gone out, and so had the housemaid. Finally, having reached the second floor, he pushed a door open. Madame Arnoux was alone in this room, in front of a mirrored armoire. The belt of her dressing-gown hung down her hips; one entire half of her hair fell in a dark wave over her right shoulder; and she had raised both arms in order to hold up her chignon with one hand and to put a pin through it with the other. She gave a cry and disappeared.

Then, she came back again properly dressed. Her waist, her eyes, the rustle of her dress, her entire appearance, charmed him. Frédéric felt it hard to keep from covering her with kisses.

"I beg your pardon," said she, "but I could not——"

He had the boldness to interrupt her with these words:

"Nevertheless—you looked very nice—just now."

She probably thought this compliment a little coarse, for her cheeks reddened. He was afraid that he might have offended her. She went on:

"What lucky chance has brought you here?"

He did not know what reply to make; and, after a slight chuckle, which gave him time for reflection:

"If I told you, would you believe me?"

"Why not?"

Frédéric informed her that he had had a frightful dream a few nights before.

"I dreamt that you were seriously ill—near dying."

"Oh! my husband and I are never ill."

"I have dreamt only of you," said he.

She gazed at him calmly: "Dreams are not always realised."

Frédéric stammered, sought to find appropriate words with which to express himself, and then plunged into a long discourse on the affinity of souls. There existed a force which could, through the intervening bounds of space, bring two persons into communication with each other, make known to each the other's feelings, and enable them to reunite.

She listened to him with bowed head, while she smiled with that beautiful smile of hers. He watched her out of the corner of his eye with delight, and poured out his love all the more freely with the help of clichés.

She offered to show him the factory; and, as she persisted, he made no objection.

In order to divert his attention with something amusing, she showed him the sort of museum that decorated the staircase. The specimens, hung up against the wall or laid on shelves, bore witness to the efforts and the successive fads of Arnoux. After seeking vainly for the red of Chinese copper, he had wished to manufacture majolicas, faenza, Etruscan and Oriental ware, and had, in fact, attempted all the improvements which were realised at a later period.

So it was that one could observe in the series big vases covered with figures of mandarins, bowls of an irridescent bronze, pots adorned with Arabian inscriptions, pitchers in the style of the Renaissance, and large plates on which two personages were outlined as it were in a sort of red chalk. He now made letters for signboards and wine-labels; but his intelligence was not high enough to attain to art, nor commonplace enough to look merely to profit, so that, without satisfying anyone, he had ruined himself.

They were both looking over these things when Mademoiselle Marthe passed.

"So, then, you do not recognise him?" said her mother to her.

"Yes, I do," she replied, bowing to him, while her clear and sceptical glance—the glance of a virgin—seemed to say in a whisper: "What are you coming here for?" and she rushed up the steps glancing back over her shoulder.

Madame Arnoux led Frédéric into the courtyard, and then explained to him in a grave tone how different clays were ground, cleaned, and sifted.

"The most important thing is the preparation of pastes."

And she brought him into a hall filled with vats, in which a vertical axis with horizontal arms kept turning. Frédéric felt some regret that he had not flatly declined her offer before.

"These things are merely the drabblers," said she.

He thought the word grotesque, and, in a measure, unbecoming on her lips.

Wide straps ran from one end of the ceiling to the other, so as to roll themselves round the drums, and everything kept moving continuously with a provoking mathematical regularity.

They left the spot, and passed close to a ruined hut, which had formerly been used as a repository for gardening implements.

"It is no longer of any use," said Madame Arnoux.

He replied in a tremulous voice:

"Happiness might be found there!"

The clacking of the fire-pump drowned his words, and they entered the workshop where rough drafts were made.

Some men, seated at a narrow table, placed each in front of himself on a revolving disc a lump of paste. Then each man with his left hand scooped out the insides of his own piece while smoothing its surface with the right; and vases could be seen bursting into shape like blossoming flowers.

Madame Arnoux showed him the moulds for the more difficult pieces.

In another part of the building, the bands, grooves, and the raised lines were being added. On the floor above, they removed the seams, and the little holes that had been left by the preceding operations were stopped up with plaster.

At every opening in the walls, in corners, in the middle of the corridor, everywhere, earthenware vessels had been placed side by side.

Frédéric began to feel bored.

"Perhaps these things are tiresome to you?" said she.

Fearing that he might have to end his visit there and then, he affected, on the contrary, a tone of great enthusiasm. He even expressed regret at not having devoted himself to this branch of industry.

She appeared surprised.

"Certainly! I would have been able to live near you."

And as he tried to catch her eye, Madame Arnoux, in order to avoid him, took off a table little balls of paste, which had come from unsuccessful repairs, flattened them out into a thin cake, and pressed her hand over them.

"Might I carry these away with me?" said Frédéric.

"Good heavens! What a child you are!"

He was about to reply when in came Sénécal.

The sub-manager, upon crossing the threshold, had noticed a breach of the rules. The workshops should be swept every week. This was Saturday, and, as the workmen had not done what was required, Sénécal announced that they would have to remain an hour longer.

"Too bad for you!"

They stooped over the work assigned to them unmurmuringly, but their rage could be divined by the hoarse sounds of their breathing. They were, moreover, very easy to manage, having all been dismissed from the big factory. The Republican had shown himself a hard taskmaster to them. A mere theorist, he considered only the masses, and exhibited an utter absence of pity for individuals.

Frédéric, annoyed by his presence, asked Madame Arnoux in a low voice whether they could have an opportunity of seeing the kilns. They descended to the ground-floor; and she was just explaining the use of cases, when Sénécal, who had followed close behind, placed himself between them.

He continued the explanation of his own motion, expatiated on the various kinds of combustibles, the process of placing in the kiln, the pyroscopes, the cylindrical furnaces; the instruments for rounding, the glazes, and the metals, making a prodigious display of chemical terms, such as "chloride," "sulphuret," "borax," and "carbonate." Frédéric did not understand a single one of them, and kept turning round every minute towards Madame Arnoux.

"You are not listening," said she. "M. Sénécal, however, is very clear. He knows all these things much better than I."

The mathematician, flattered by this eulogy, proposed to show the way in which colours were laid on. Frédéric gave Madame Arnoux an anxious, questioning look. She remained impassive, not caring to be alone with him, very probably, and yet unwilling to leave him.

He offered her his arm.

"No—many thanks! the staircase is too narrow!"

And, when they had reached the top, Sénécal opened the door of a room full of women.

They were handling brushes, phials, shells, and plates of glass. Along the cornice, close to the wall, extended boards with figures engraved on them; scraps of thin paper floated about, and a melting-stove sent forth fumes that made the temperature oppressive, while there mingled with it the odour of turpentine.

The workwomen had nearly all dirty clothes. It was noticeable, however, that one of them wore a Madras head scarf, and long earrings. Of slight frame, and, at the same time, plump, she had large black eyes and the fleshy lips of a negress. Her ample bosom projected from under her chemise, which was fastened round her waist by the string of her petticoat; and, with one elbow on the board of the work-table and the other arm hanging down, she gazed vaguely at the open country side. Beside her were a bottle of wine and some pork chops.

The regulations prohibited eating in the workshops, a rule intended to secure cleanliness at work and good hygiene among the workers.

Sénécal, through a sense of duty or a desire to exercise despotic authority, shouted out to her as he came near her, while pointing towards a framed notice:

"I say, you, girl from Bordeaux over there! read out for me Article 9!"

"And then what?"

"Then what, mademoiselle? You'll have to pay a fine of three francs."

She looked him straight in the face with an air of insolence.

"What do I care? The master will cancel your fine when he comes back! You can go to the devil, you silly man!"

Sénécal, who was walking with his hands behind his back, like a monitor in the study-room, contented himself with smiling.

"Article 13, insubordination, ten francs!"

The girl from Bordeaux resumed her work. Madame Arnoux, through a sense of propriety, said nothing; but her brows contracted. Frédéric murmured:

"You are very severe for a democrat!"

The other replied in a magisterial tone:

"Democracy is not the unbounded license of individualism. It is the equality of all belonging to the same community before the law, the distribution of work, order."

"You are forgetting humanity!" said Frédéric.

Madame Arnoux took his arm. Sénécal, perhaps offended by this mark of silent approbation, went away.

Frédéric experienced an immense relief. Since morning he had been looking out for the opportunity to declare his love; now it had arrived. Besides, Madame Arnoux's spontaneous movements seemed to him to contain promises; and he asked her, as if on the pretext of warming their feet, to come up to her room. But, when he was seated close beside her, he began once more to feel embarrassed. He was at a loss for a starting-point. Sénécal, luckily, suggested an idea to his mind.

"Nothing could be more stupid," said he, "than this punishment!"

Madame Arnoux replied: "There are certain severe measures which are indispensable!"

"What! you who are so good! Oh! I am mistaken, for you sometimes take pleasure in making other people suffer!"

"I don't understand riddles, my friend!"

And her stern look, still more than the words she used, checked him. Frédéric was determined to go on. A volume of De Musset happened to be on the chest of drawers; he turned over some pages, then began to talk about love, its highs and its lows.

All this, according to Madame Arnoux, was criminal or fictitious. The young man felt wounded by this rebuff and, in order to combat it, he cited, by way of proof, the suicides which they read about every day in the newspapers, extolled the great literary lovers, Phèdre, Dido, Romeo, Desgrieux. He talked as if he meant to do away with himself.

The fire was no longer burning on the hearth; the rain lashed against the windows. Madame Arnoux, without stirring, remained with her hands resting on the sides of her armchair. The flaps of her cap fell like the head bands of a sphinx. Her pure profile traced out its clear-cut outlines in the midst of the shadows.

He was anxious to cast himself at her feet. There was a creaking sound in the hallway, and he did not venture to carry out his intention.

He was, moreover, restrained by a kind of religious awe. Her dress, mingling with the surrounding shadows, appeared to him boundless, infinite, incapable of being removed; and for this very reason his desire became intensified. But the fear of doing too much, and, again, of not doing enough, robbed him of all judgment.

"If she dislikes me," he thought, "let her drive me away; if she cares for me, let her encourage me."

He said, with a sigh:

"So, then, you don't admit that a man may love—a woman?"

Madame Arnoux replied:

"Assuming that she is at liberty to marry, he may marry her; when she belongs to another, he should keep away from her."

"So happiness is impossible?"

"No! But it is never to be found in falsehood, mental anxiety, and remorse."

"What does it matter, if one is compensated by the enjoyment of supreme bliss?"

"The experience is too costly."

Then he used irony.

"Would not virtue in that case be merely cowardice?"

"Say rather, clear-sightedness. Even for those women who might forget duty or religion, simple good sense is sufficient. A solid foundation for wisdom may be found in self-love."

"Ah, what bourgeois maxims these are of yours!"

"I don't boast of being a fine lady."

At that moment the little boy rushed in.

"Mamma, are you coming to dinner?"

"Yes, in a moment."

Frédéric arose. At the same instant, Marthe made her appearance.

He could not make up his mind to go, and, with a look of entreaty:

"These women you speak of are very unfeeling, then?"

"No, but deaf when it is necessary to be so."

And she remained standing on the threshold of her room with her two children beside her. He bowed without saying a word. She mutely returned his salutation.

What he first experienced was an unspeakable astonishment. He felt crushed by this mode of impressing on him the emptiness of his hopes. It seemed to him as if he were lost, like a man who has fallen to the bottom of an abyss and knows that no help will come to him, and that he must die. He walked on, however, but at random, without looking where he was going. He tripped over stones; he lost his way. A clatter of wooden shoes sounded close; it was caused by some of the working-girls who were leaving the foundry. Then he realised where he was.

The railway lamps traced on the horizon a line of fire. He arrived just as the train was about to leave, let himself be pushed into a rail-car, and fell asleep.

An hour later on the boulevards, the gaiety of Paris by night made his journey all at once recede into an already far-distant past. He resolved to be strong, and relieved his heart by vilifying Madame Arnoux with insults.

"She is an idiot, a beast; let us not bestow another thought on her!"

When he got home, he found in his study a letter of eight pages on blue glazed paper, with the initials "R. A."

It began with friendly reproaches.

"What has become of you, my dear? I am getting quite bored."

But the handwriting was so abominable, that Frédéric was about to fling away the sheets, when he noticed in the postscript the following words:

"I count on you to come to-morrow and drive me to the races."

What was the meaning of this invitation? Was it another trick of the Maréchale? But a woman does not make a fool of the same man twice without some reason; and, seized with curiosity, he read the letter over again attentively.

Frédéric was able to distinguish "Misunderstanding—to have taken a wrong path—disillusions—poor children that we are!—like two rivers that join each other!" etc.

He kept the pages for a long time between his fingers. They had the scent of irises; and there was in the form of the characters and the irregular spaces between the lines something suggestive, as it were, of a carelessness in dressing, that excited him.

"Why should I not go?" he said to himself at length. "But if Madame Arnoux were to know about it? Ah! let her know! So much the better! and let her feel jealous over it! In that way I shall be avenged!"

CHAPTER IV

The Maréchale was prepared for his visit, and had been waiting for him.

"This is nice of you!" she said, fixing a glance of her fine eyes on his face, with an expression at the same time tender and joyful.

When she had fastened her bonnet-strings, she sat down on the divan, and remained silent.

"Shall we go?" said Frédéric. She looked at the clock on the mantelpiece.

"Oh, no! not before half-past one!" as if she had imposed this limit to her indecision.

At last, when the hour had struck:

"Ah! well, *andiamo, caro mio*!" And she gave a final touch to her hair, and left directions for Delphine.

"Is Madame coming home to dinner?"

"Why should we, indeed? We shall dine together somewhere—at the Café Anglais, wherever you wish."

"All right!"

Her little dogs began barking around her.

"We can bring them with us, can't we?"

Frédéric carried them himself to the vehicle. It was a hired berlin with two horses and a postilion. He had put his man-servant in the back seat. The Maréchale appeared satisfied with his attentions. Then, as soon as she had seated herself, she asked him whether he had been at the Arnouxs' lately.

"Not for the past month," said Frédéric.

"As for me, I met him the day before yesterday. He would have even come to-day, but he has all sorts of troubles—another lawsuit—I don't know what. What a strange man!"

Frédéric added with an air of indifference:

"Now that I think of it, do you still see—what's his name?—that ex-vocalist—Delmar?"

She replied dryly:

"No; that's all over."

So it was clear that there had been a rupture between them. Frédéric derived some hope from this circumstance.

They descended the Quartier Bréda at an easy pace. As it happened to be Sunday, the streets were deserted, and some citizens' faces could be seen at their windows. The carriage went on more rapidly. The noise of wheels made the passers-by turn round; the leather of the hood, which had slid down, was shining. The manservant doubled himself up, and the two Havanese, beside one another, seemed like two ermine muffs laid on the cushions. Frédéric gave himself up to the rocking of the carriage. The Maréchale turned her head right and left with a smile on her face.

Her hat of pearly straw was trimmed with black lace. The hood of her bournous floated in the wind, and she sheltered herself from the rays of the sun under a parasol of lilac satin pointed at the top like a pagoda.

"What pretty little fingers!" said Frédéric, softly taking her other hand, her left being adorned with a gold bracelet in the form of a curb-chain.

"I say! that's pretty! Where did it come from?"

"Oh! I've had it a long time," said the Maréchale.

The young man did not challenge this hypocritical answer in any way. He preferred to profit by the circumstance. And, still keeping hold of the wrist, he pressed his lips on it between the glove and the cuff.

"Stop! People will see us!"

"Pooh! What does it matter?"

After passing by the Place de la Concorde, they drove along the Quai de la Conférence and the Quai de Billy, where might be noticed a cedar in a garden. Rosanette believed that Lebanon was in China; she laughed at her own ignorance, and asked Frédéric to give her lessons in geography. Then, leaving the Trocadéro at the right, they crossed the Pont d'Iéna, and finally stopped in the middle of the Champ de Mars, near some other vehicles already drawn up in the Hippodrome.[20]

The grassy slopes were covered with common people. Some spectators could be seen on the balcony of the École militaire, and the two pavilions outside the paddock, the two stands contained within its enclosure and a third in front of that of the royal box were filled with a fashionably dressed crowd whose behavior showed their regard for this still novel form of amusement.

The race-going public around the course, more select during this period, had a less vulgar look. It was the era of trouser-straps, velvet collars, and white gloves. The ladies, attired in showy colours, displayed gowns with long waists; and seated on the tiers of the stands, they formed, so to speak, immense groups of flowers, spotted here and there with black by the men's costumes. But every glance was directed towards the celebrated Algerian Bou-Maza, who sat, impassive, between two staff officers in one of the private stands. That of the Jockey Club contained none but grave-looking gentlemen.

The more enthusiastic part of the throng were seated underneath, close to the track, protected by two lines of posts which supported ropes. In the immense oval formed by the track, cocoanut-sellers were shaking their rattles, others were selling programmes of the races, others were hawking cigars, with loud cries. On every side there was a great murmur. The municipal guards passed to and fro. A bell, hung from a post covered with numbers, began ringing. Five horses appeared, and the spectators in the stands resumed their seats.

Meanwhile, big clouds touched with their winding outlines the tops of the elms opposite. Rosanette was afraid that it was going to rain.

"I have umbrellas," said Frédéric, "and everything that we need to keep us happy," he added, lifting up the chest, in which there was a stock of provisions in a basket.

"Bravo! we understand each other!"

"And we'll understand each other still better, shall we not?"

"That may be," she said, blushing.

The jockeys, in silk jackets, were trying to align their horses, and were holding them back with both hands. Somebody lowered a red flag. Then all five bent over the bristling manes, and off they went. At first they remained pressed close to each other in a single mass;

it quickly stretched out and broke up. The jockey in the yellow jacket was close to falling in the middle of the first lap; for a long time it was uncertain whether Filly or Tibi should take the lead; then Tom Pouce appeared in front. But Clubstick, who had been in the rear since the start, came up with the others and outran them, so that he was the first to reach the winning-post, beating Sir Charles by two lengths. It was a surprise. There was a shout of applause; the planks shook with the stamping of feet.

"What fun!" said the Maréchale. "I love you, darling!"

Frédéric no longer doubted that his happiness was secure. Rosanette's last words were a confirmation of it.

A hundred feet away, in a four-wheeled cabriolet, a lady could be seen. She stretched her head out of the carriage-door, and then quickly drew it in again. This movement was repeated several times. Frédéric could not distinguish her face. He had a strong suspicion, however, that it was Madame Arnoux. And yet this seemed impossible! Why would she have come there?

He stepped out of his own vehicle on the pretence of strolling round the paddock.

"You are not very gallant!" said Rosanette.

He paid no heed to her, and went on. The four-wheeled cabriolet, turning back, broke into a trot.

Frédéric at the same moment, found himself button-holed by Cisy.

"Hello, my dear boy! how are you? Hussonnet is over there! Are you listening to me?"

Frédéric tried to shake him off in order to catch up to the four-wheeled cabriolet. The Maréchale beckoned to him to come round to her. Cisy saw her, and obstinately persisted in bidding her good-day.

Since the termination of the regular period of mourning for his grandmother, he had realised his ideal, and succeeded in "acquiring a certain cachet." A Scotch plaid waistcoat, a short coat, large bows over the pumps, and an entrance-card stuck in the ribbon of his hat; nothing, in fact, was wanting in producing what he described himself as his *chic*—a *chic* characterised by Anglomania and the swagger of the musketeer. He began by finding fault with the Champ de Mars, which he referred to as an "execrable turf," then spoke of the

Chantilly races, and the droll things that had occurred there, swore that he could drink a dozen glasses of champagne while the clock was striking midnight, offered to make a bet with the Maréchale on it, softly caressed her two lapdogs; and, leaning against the carriage-door on one elbow, he kept talking nonsense, with the handle of his walking-stick in his mouth, his legs wide apart, and his back stretched out. Frédéric, standing beside him, was smoking, while endeavouring to make out what had become of the cabriolet.

The bell having rung, Cisy took off, to the great delight of Rosanette, who said he had been boring her to death.

The second race had nothing special about it; neither had the third, except that a man was taken away on a stretcher. The fourth, in which eight horses competed for the City Stakes, was more interesting.

The spectators in the stands had clambered on top of their seats. The others, standing up in the vehicles, followed with opera-glasses in their hands the movements of the jockeys. They could be seen starting out like red, yellow, white, or blue spots across the entire space occupied by the crowd that had gathered around the ring of the hippodrome. At a distance, their speed did not appear to be very great; at the opposite side of the Champ de Mars, they seemed even to be slackening their pace, and to be merely slipping along in such a way that the horses' bellies touched the ground without their outstretched legs bending at all. But, coming back at a more rapid stride, they looked bigger; they cut the air in their wild gallop. The sun's rays quivered; pebbles went flying about under their hoofs. The wind, blowing out the jockeys' jackets, made them flutter like veils. Each of them lashed the animal he rode with great blows of his whip in order to reach the winning-post—that was the goal they aimed at. The numbers were taken down, another was hoisted up, and, in the midst of a burst of applause, the victorious horse dragged his feet to the paddock, all covered with sweat, his knees stiffened, his neck and shoulders bent down, while his rider, looking as if he were expiring in his saddle, clung to the animal's flanks.

The final start was delayed by a dispute which had arisen. The crowd, getting tired, began to scatter. Groups of men were chatting at the foot of the stands. The talk was free-and-easy. Some fashionable ladies left, scandalised by seeing fast women in their immediate vicinity.

There were also some ladies who appeared at the dance-halls, some light-comedy actresses of the boulevards, and it was not the best-looking portion of them that got the most appreciation. The elderly Georgine Aubert, she whom a writer of vaudevilles called the Louis XI of prostitution, horribly made-up, and every now and then letting out a laugh resembling a grunt, remained reclining at full length in her big calash, covered with a sable fur-tippet, as if it were midwinter. Madame de Remoussat, who had become fashionable by means of her notorious trial, sat enthroned on the seat of a brake in company with some Americans; and Thérèse Bachelu, with her look of a Gothic virgin, filled with her dozen flounces the interior of a carriage which had, in place of an apron, a flower-stand filled with roses. The Maréchale was jealous of these magnificent displays. In order to attract attention, she began to make grand gestures and to speak in a very loud voice.

Gentlemen recognised her, and bowed to her. She returned their salutations while telling Frédéric their names. They were all counts, viscounts, dukes, and marquises, and he carried his head high, for in all eyes he could read a certain respect for his good fortune.

Cisy looked equally happy in the midst of the circle of mature men that surrounded him. Their faces wore cynical smiles above their cravats, as if they were laughing at him. Finally he shook hands with the oldest of them, and made his way towards the Maréchale.

She was eating, with an affectation of gluttony, a slice of *pâté de foie gras*. Frédéric, in order to make himself agreeable to her, followed her example, with a bottle of wine on his knees.

The four-wheeled cabriolet reappeared. It *was* Madame Arnoux! Her face was startlingly pale.

"Give me some champagne," said Rosanette.

And, lifting up her glass, full to the brim, as high as possible, she exclaimed:

"Look over there! Good health to virtuous women and to my protector's wife!"

There was a great burst of laughter all round her; and the cabriolet disappeared from view. Frédéric tugged impatiently at her dress, and was on the point of losing his temper. But Cisy there, in the same position as before, and, with increased confidence, invited Rosanette to dine with him that very evening.

"Impossible!" she replied; "we're going together to the Café Anglais."*

Frédéric, as if he had heard nothing, remained silent; and Cisy left the Maréchale with a look of disappointment on his face.

While he had been talking to her at the righthand door of the carriage, Hussonnet presented himself at the opposite side, and, catching the words "Café Anglais":

"It's a nice establishment; suppose we had a bite there, eh?"

"Just as you like," said Frédéric, who, sunk down in the corner of the berlin, was gazing at the horizon as the four-wheeled cabriolet vanished from his sight, feeling that an irreparable thing had happened, and that he had lost his great love. And the other woman was there beside him, the joyful and easy love! But, worn out, full of conflicting desires, and no longer even knowing what he wanted, he was possessed by a feeling of infinite sadness, a longing to die.

A great noise of footsteps and of voices made him raise his head. The little ragamuffins assembled round the track sprang over the ropes and came to stare at the stands. Thereupon their occupants rose to go. A few drops of rain began to fall. The crush of vehicles increased, and Hussonnet got lost in it.

"Well! so much the better!" said Frédéric.

"We like to be alone better—don't we?" said the Maréchale, as she placed her hand in his.

Then there swept past them with a glimmer of copper and steel a magnificent landau drawn by four horses driven in the Daumont style by two jockeys in velvet vests with gold fringe. Madame Dambreuse was by her husband's side, and Martinon was on the other seat facing them. All three of them gazed at Frédéric in astonishment.

"They have recognised me!" he said to himself.

---

*Elegant café in the center of Paris.

Rosanette wished to stop in order to get a better view of the people driving away from the course. But Madame Arnoux might reappear! He called out to the postilion:

"Go on! go on! forward!" And the berlin dashed towards the Champs-Élysées in the midst of the other vehicles—calashes, britzkas, wurths, tandems, tilburies, dog-carts, tilted carts with leather curtains, in which workmen in a jovial mood were singing, or one-horse chaises driven by fathers of families. In victorias crammed with people some young fellows seated on the others' feet let their legs hang down over the side. Large broughams, which had their seats lined with cloth, carried dowagers fast asleep, or else a splendid machine passed with a seat as simple and coquettish as a dandy's black coat.

The shower grew heavier. Umbrellas, parasols, and mackintoshes were brought out. People cried out at some distance away: "Good-day!" "Are you quite well?" "Yes!" "No!" "Bye-bye!"—and face after face went by with the rapidity of a magic lantern.

Frédéric and Rosanette did not say a word to each other, feeling a sort of dizziness at seeing all these wheels continually revolving close to them.

At times, the rows of carriages, too closely pressed together, stopped all at the same time in several lines. Then they remained side by side, and their occupants scanned one another. Over door panels adorned with coats-of-arms indifferent glances were cast on the crowd. Eyes full of envy gleamed from the interiors of hackney-coaches. Sneering smiles responded to the haughty manner in which some people carried their heads. Mouths gaping wide expressed idiotic admiration; and, here and there, some pedestrian, in the middle of the road, jumped back with a bound, in order to avoid a rider who had been galloping through the middle of the vehicles, and had succeeded in getting away from them. Then, every thing set itself in motion once more; the coachmen let go of the reins, and lowered their long whips; the horses, excited, shook their bits, and flung foam around them; and the cruppers and the harness getting moist, were smoking with the watery evaporation, through which struggled the rays of the sinking sun. Passing under the Arc de Triomphe, there stretched out head-high, a reddish light, which shed a glittering lustre on the wheel hubs, the handles of the carriage-doors, the ends of the shafts, and the saddle-rings; and on the two sides of the great avenue—like a river in which manes, garments, and human heads were undulating—the trees, all glittering with rain, rose up like two green walls. The blue of the sky overhead, reappearing in certain places, had the soft hue of satin.

Then, Frédéric recalled the days, already far away, when he yearned for the inexpressible happiness of finding himself in one of these carriages by the side of one of these women. He had attained this bliss, and yet he was not thereby one bit happier.

The rain had ceased falling. The pedestrians, who had sought shelter between the columns of the Public Storerooms, made their departure. People who had been walking along the Rue Royale, went up again towards the boulevard. In front of the residence of the Minister of Foreign Affairs a group of onlookers loitered on the steps.

When they had gotten up as far as the Chinese Baths, because of holes in the pavement, the berlin slackened its pace. A man in a hazel-coloured overcoat was walking on the edge of the sidewalk. A splash of mud spurted out from under the springs, and splattered across his back. The man turned round in a rage. Frédéric grew pale; he had recognised Deslauriers.

At the door of the Café Anglais he sent away the carriage. Rosanette had gone in before him while he was paying the postilion.

He found her subsequently on the stairs chatting with a gentleman. Frédéric took her arm; but in the lobby a second gentleman stopped her.

"Go on," said she; "just a minute and I am all yours."

And he entered the private room alone. Through the two open windows people could be seen in the window of the houses opposite. Large puddles quivered on the pavement as it began to dry, and a magnolia, placed on the side of a balcony, shed a perfume through the room. This fragrance and freshness had a relaxing effect on his nerves. He sank down on the red divan underneath the mirror.

The Maréchale entered the room, and, kissing him on the forehead:

"Poor pet! there's something annoying you!"

"Perhaps so," was his reply.

"You are not alone; take heart!"—which was as much as to say: "Let us each forget our own concerns in a bliss which we shall enjoy together."

Then she placed the petal of a flower between her lips and extended it towards him so that he might peck at it. This movement, full of grace and of almost voluptuous gentleness, had a softening influence on Frédéric.

"Why do you cause me pain?" said he, thinking of Madame Arnoux.

"I cause you pain?"

And, standing before him, she looked at him with her eyes half closed and her two hands resting on his shoulders.

All his virtue, all his resentment sank into a bottomless cowardice.

He continued:

"Because you won't love me," and he pulled her on to his knees.

She gave way to him. He pressed his two hands round her waist. The crackling sound of her silk dress inflamed him.

"Where are they?" said Hussonnet's voice in the lobby outside.

The Maréchale arose abruptly, and went across to the other side of the room, where she sat down with her back to the door.

She ordered oysters, and they seated themselves at the table.

Hussonnet was not at all amusing. Writing every day as he did on all sorts of subjects, reading many newspapers, listening to a great number of discussions, and uttering paradoxes for the purpose of dazzling people, he had in the end lost the exact idea of things, blinding himself with his own feeble fireworks. The difficulties of a life which had formerly been frivolous, kept him in a state of perpetual agitation; and his literary impotence, which he did not wish to admit, rendered him grumpy and sarcastic. Referring to a new ballet entitled *Ozaï*, he made a violent attack on the dancing, and then, when the opera was in question, he put down the Italians, now replaced by a company of Spanish actors, "as if people had not quite enough of Castilles already!" Frédéric was shocked at this, because of his romantic attachment to Spain, and, with a view to diverting the conversation, he enquired about the College of France, from which Edgar Quinet and Mickiewicz had been barred.[21] But Hussonnet, an admirer of M. de Maistre,* declared himself on the

*Joseph de Maistre (1753–1821), a Legitimist and Catholic thinker of the post-revolutionary era.

side of Authority and Spiritualism. Nevertheless, he had doubts about the most well-established facts, contradicted history, and disputed things whose certainty could not be questioned; so that at the mention of the word "geometry," he exclaimed: "What a joke this geometry is!" All this he intermingled with imitations of actors. Sainville was specially his model.

Frédéric was quite bored by these quibbles. In an outburst of impatience he caught one of the little dogs with his boot under the table.

Thereupon both animals began barking horribly.

"You ought to have them sent home!" said he, abruptly.

Rosanette did not know anyone to whom she could intrust them.

Then, he turned round to the Bohemian:

"Look here, Hussonnet; be a good fellow!"

"Oh! yes, my dear! That would be very sweet of you!"

Hussonnet set off, without further appeals.

In what way could they repay him for his kindness? Frédéric did not give it a thought. He was even beginning to rejoice at finding himself alone with her, when a waiter entered.

"Madame, somebody is asking for you!"

"What! again?"

"I'll have to see who it is," said Rosanette. He was thirsting for her; he wanted her. This disappearance seemed to him an act of disloyalty, bordering on rudeness. What, then, did she mean? Was it not enough to have insulted Madame Arnoux? So much for the latter, all the same! Now he hated all women; and he felt the tears choking him, for his love had been misunderstood and his desire eluded.

The Maréchale returned, and presented Cisy to him.

"I have invited Monsieur. I have done right, have I not?"

"How is that! Oh! certainly."

Frédéric, with the smile of a criminal about to be executed, beckoned to the gentleman to take a seat.

The Maréchale began to run her eye over the menu, stopping at every fantastic name.

"Suppose we eat a turban of rabbits *à la Richeliéu* and a pudding *à la d' Orléans?*"

"Oh! not Orléans, pray!" exclaimed Cisy, who was a Legitimist, and thought of making a pun.

"Would you prefer a turbot *à la* Chambord?"[22] she next asked.

Frédéric was disgusted with this display of politeness.

The Maréchale made up her mind to order a simple steak, some crayfish, truffles, a pineapple salad, and vanilla ices.

"After that we'll see. Go on for now! Ah! I was forgetting! Bring me a sausage!—without garlic!"

And she called the waiter "young man," struck her glass with her knife, and flung up the crumbs of her bread to the ceiling. She wished to drink some Burgundy immediately.

"You don't drink that at the beginning of a meal," said Frédéric.

This was sometimes done, according to the Vicomte.

"Oh! no. Never!"

"Yes, indeed; I assure you!"

"Ha! you see!"

The look with which she accompanied these words meant: "This is a rich man—pay attention to what he says!"

Meantime, the door was opening constantly; the waiters kept shouting; and on an infernal piano in the adjoining room some one was playing a waltz. Then the races led to a discussion about horsemanship and the two rival systems. Cisy was upholding Baucher and Frédéric the Comte d'Aure when Rosanette shrugged her shoulders:

"Enough—my God!—he is a better judge of these things than you are—come now!"

She kept nibbling on a pomegranate, with her elbow resting on the table. The wax-candles of the candelabra in front of her were flickering in the wind. This white light penetrated her skin with mother-of-pearl tones, gave a pink hue to her lids, and made her eyes glitter. The red colour of the fruit blended with the purple of her lips; her thin nostrils flared; and there was about her entire person an air of insolence, intoxication, and recklessness that exasperated Frédéric, and yet filled his heart with wild desires.

Then, she asked, in a calm voice, who owned that big landau with chestnut-coloured livery.

Cisy replied that it was "the Comtesse Dambreuse."

"They're very rich—aren't they?"

"Oh! very rich! although Madame Dambreuse, who was merely a Mademoiselle Boutron and the daughter of a prefect, had a very modest fortune."

Her husband, on the other hand, must have inherited several estates—Cisy enumerated them: as he visited the Dambreuses, he knew their family history.

Frédéric, in order to make himself disagreeable to the other, took a pleasure in contradicting him. He maintained that Madame Dambreuse's maiden name was De Boutron, which proved that she was of a noble family.

"No matter! I'd like to have her carriage!" said the Maréchale, throwing herself back on the armchair.

And the sleeve of her dress, slipping up a little, showed on her left wrist a bracelet adorned with three opals.

Frédéric noticed it.

"Look here! Why——"

All three looked into one another's faces, and reddened.

The door was cautiously half-opened; the brim of a hat could be seen, and then Hussonnet's profile appeared.

"Excuse me if I disturb the lovers!"

But he stopped, astonished at seeing Cisy, and that Cisy had taken his own seat.

Another place setting was brought; and, as he was very hungry, he snatched up at random from what remained of the dinner some meat which was in a dish, fruit out of a basket, and drank with one hand while he helped himself with the other, all the time telling them the result of his mission. The two bow-wows had been taken home. Nothing new at the house. He had found the cook in the company of a soldier—a fictitious story which he had especially invented for the sake of effect.

The Maréchale took down her cloak from the peg. Frédéric made a rush towards the bell, calling out to the waiter, who was some distance away:

"A carriage!"

"I have one of my own," said the Vicomte.

"But, Monsieur!"

"Nevertheless, Monsieur!"

And they stared into each other's eyes, both pale and their hands trembling.

At last, the Maréchale took Cisy's arm, and pointing towards the Bohemian seated at the table:

"Pray mind him! He's choking himself. I wouldn't want to let his devotion to my pugs be the cause of his death."

The door closed behind him.

"Well?" said Hussonnet.

"Well, what?"

"I thought——"

"What did you think?"

"Were you not——?"

He completed the sentence with a gesture.

"Oh! no—never in all my life!"

Hussonnet did not press the matter further.

He had a reason for inviting himself to dinner. His journal,—which was no longer called *L'Art*, but *Le Flambart*, with the slogan, "Gunners, to your cannons!"—not at all prospering he had a mind to change it into a weekly review, managed by himself, without any assistance from Deslauriers. He again referred to the old project and explained his latest plan.

Frédéric, probably not understanding what he was talking about, replied with some vague words. Hussonnet snatched up several cigars from the tables, said "Good-bye, old chap," and disappeared.

Frédéric called for the bill. It had a long list of items; and the waiter; with his napkin under his arm, was expecting to be paid by Frédéric, when another, a sallow-faced individual, who resembled Martinon, came and said to him:

"Beg pardon; they forgot at the bar to add in the charge for the cab."

"What cab?"

"The cab the gentleman took a short time ago with the little dogs."

And the waiter put on a look of gravity, as if he pitied the poor young man. Frédéric felt inclined to box the fellow's ears. He gave the waiter the twenty francs' change as a tip.

"Thank you, my lord," said the man with the napkin, bowing low.

Frédéric passed the whole of the next day brooding over his anger and humiliation. He reproached himself for not having given Cisy a slap in the face. As for the Maréchale, he swore not to see her again. Others as good-looking could be easily found; and, as money would be required in order to possess these women, he would speculate on the stock market with the money from selling his farm. He would get rich; he would crush the Maréchale and everyone else with his luxury. When the evening came, he was surprised at not having thought of Madame Arnoux.

"So much the better. What's the good of it?"

Two days after, at eight o'clock, Pellerin came to pay him a visit. He began by admiring the furniture and talking flatteringly to Frédéric. Then, abruptly:

"Were you at the races on Sunday?"

"Yes, alas!"

Thereupon the painter decried the anatomy of English horses, and praised the horses of Gericourt and the horses of the Parthenon.

"Rosanette was with you?"

And he artfully proceeded to speak in flattering terms about her.

Frédéric's cold manner disconcerted him.

He did not know how to bring about the question of her portrait. His first idea had been to do a portrait in the style of Titian. But gradually the varied colouring of his model had bewitched him; he had gone on boldly with the work, heaping up brushstroke on brushstroke and light on light. Rosanette, in the beginning, was enchanted. Her appointments with Delmar had interrupted the sittings, and left Pellerin all the time to be bedazzled by his art. Then, as his admiration began to subside, he asked himself whether the picture should not be on a larger scale. He had gone to have another look at the Titians, realised the distance that separated his work from that of the great artist, and saw wherein his own shortcomings lay; and then he began to simplify his outlines. After that, he sought, by scraping them off, to lose there, to mingle there, all the tones of the head and those of the background; and the face had assumed consistency and the shadows vigour—the whole work had a look of greater firmness. At length the Maréchale came back again. She even permitted herself some criticisms. The painter naturally persevered. After a violent outburst at her stupidity, he said to himself that, after all, perhaps she was right.

Then began the era of doubts, twinges of reflection which brought about cramps in the stomach, insomnia, feverishness and disgust with himself. He had the courage to make some retouchings, but without much heart, and with a feeling that his work was bad.

He merely complained of having been refused a place in the Salon; then he reproached Frédéric for not having come to see the Maréchale's portrait.

"What do I care about the Maréchale?"

Such an expression of unconcern emboldened the artist.

"Would you believe that this brute has no interest in the thing any longer?"

What he did not mention was that he had asked her for a thousand crowns. Now the Maréchale did not give herself much bother about ascertaining who was going to pay, and, preferring to screw money out of Arnoux for things of a more urgent nature, had not even spoken to him on the subject.

"Well, what about Arnoux?" asked Frédéric.

She had thrown it over on him. The ex-art-dealer wanted to have nothing to do with the portrait.

"He maintains that it belongs to Rosanette."

"In fact, it is hers."

"How is that? 'Tis she that sent me to you," was Pellerin's answer.

If he had believed in the excellence of his work, he would not have dreamed of exploiting it. But a sum—and a big sum—would be an effective reply to the critics, and would strengthen his own position. Finally, to get rid of him, Frédéric courteously enquired about his terms.

The extravagant figure named by Pellerin quite took away his breath, and he replied:

"Oh! no—no!"

"You, however, are her lover—'tis you gave me the order!"

"Excuse me, I was only an intermediary."

"You can't leave me with this on my hands!"

The artist lost his temper.

"Ha! I didn't imagine you were so greedy!"

"Nor I that you were so stingy! Good-bye!"

He had just gone out when Sénécal appeared.

Frédéric was moving about restlessly, in a state of great agitation.

"What's the matter?"

Sénécal told his story.

"On Saturday, at nine o'clock, Madame Arnoux got a letter which summoned her back to Paris. As there happened to be nobody in the place at the time to go to Creil for carriage, she asked me to go there myself. I refused, for this was not part of my duties. She left, and came back on Sunday evening. Yesterday morning, Arnoux came down to the workshop. The girl from Bordeaux made a complaint to him. I don't know what passed between them; but in front of every one he cancelled the fine I had imposed on her. Some sharp words passed between us. In short, he paid me off, and here I am!"

Then, with a pause between every word:

"Furthermore, I am not sorry. I have done my duty. In any case, it's all your fault."

"How?" exclaimed Frédéric, alarmed lest Sénécal might have guessed his secret.

Sénécal had not, however, guessed anything about it, for he replied:

"That is to say, without you I might have done better."

Frédéric was seized with a kind of remorse.

"In what way can I be of service to you now?"

Sénécal wanted some employment, a situation.

"That is an easy thing for you to manage. You know many people of good position, Monsieur Dambreuse amongst others; at least, so Deslauriers told me."

This allusion to Deslauriers was by no means agreeable to his friend. He scarcely cared to call on the Dambreuses again after his undesirable meeting with them in the Champ de Mars.

"I am not on sufficiently intimate terms with them to recommend anyone."

The democrat endured this refusal stoically, and after a minute's silence:

"All this, I am sure, is due to the girl from Bordeaux, and to your Madame Arnoux."

This "your" had the effect of wiping out of Frédéric's heart the slight modicum of regard he entertained for Sénécal. Nevertheless, out of courtesy he reached for the key of his secretary.

Sénécal anticipated him:

"Thanks!"

Then, forgetting his own troubles, he talked about the affairs of the nation, the crosses of the Légion d' honneur wasted at the Royal Fête, the question of a change of ministry, the Drouillard case and the Bénier case—scandals of the day—denounced the middle class, and predicted a revolution.

His eyes were attracted by a Japanese dagger hanging on the wall. He took hold of it; then he flung it on the sofa with an air of disgust.

"Come, then! good-bye! I must go to Nôtre Dame de Lorette."

"Hold on! Why?"

"The anniversary service for Godefroy Cavaignac is taking place there to-day.[23] He died at work—that man! But all is not over. Who knows?"

And Sénécal, with a show of fortitude, put out his hand:

"Perhaps we shall never see each other again! good-bye!"

This "good-bye," repeated several times, his knitted brows as he gazed at the dagger, his resignation, and the solemnity of his manner, above all, plunged Frédéric into a thoughtful mood, but very soon he ceased to think about Sénécal.

During the same week, his notary at Le Havre sent him the sum realised by the sale of his farm—one hundred and seventy-four thousand francs. He divided it into two portions, invested the first half in government securities, and brought the second half to a stock-broker to gamble on the stock market.

He dined at fashionable restaurants, went to the theatres, and was trying to amuse himself as best he could, when Hussonnet addressed a letter to him announcing happily that the Maréchale had gotten rid of Cisy the very day after the races. Frédéric was delighted at this piece of intelligence, without taking the trouble to ascertain what the Bohemian's motive was in giving him the information.

It so happened that he met Cisy, three days later. That aristocratic young gentleman put on a brave face, and even invited Frédéric to dine on the following Wednesday.

On the morning of that day, Frédéric received a notification from a process-server, in which M. Charles Jean Baptiste Oudry informed him that by the terms of a legal judgment he had become the purchaser of a property situated at Belleville, belonging to M. Jacques Arnoux, and that he was prepared to pay the purchase price of two hundred and twenty-three thousand. But, as this decree also revealed that the amount of the mortgages with which the estate was encumbered exceeded the purchase price, Frédéric's claim was null and void.

The whole trouble arose from not having renewed the registration of the mortgage within the proper time period. Arnoux had undertaken to attend to this matter himself, and had then forgotten all about it. Frédéric got into a rage with him for this, and when the young man's anger had passed:

"Well, what of it?"

"If this can save him, so much the better. It won't kill me! Let us forget about it!"

But, while moving his papers about on the table, he came across Hussonnet's letter, and noticed the postscript, which had not at first attracted his attention. The Bohemian wanted five thousand francs to start his journal.

"Ah! this fellow is getting on my nerves!"

And he sent a curt answer, unceremoniously refusing the request. After that, he dressed himself to go to the Maison d'Or.

Cisy introduced his guests, beginning with the most respectable of them, a big, white-haired gentleman.

"The Marquis Gilbert des Aulnays, my godfather. Monsieur Anselme de Forchambeaux," he said next—(a thin, fair-haired young man, already bald); then, pointing towards a mild-mannered man of forty: "Joseph Boffreu, my cousin; and here is my old tutor, Monsieur Vezou"—a cross between a carter and a seminarist, with large whiskers and a long overcoat fastened at the bottom by a single button, so that it fell over his chest like a shawl.

Cisy was expecting some one else—the Baron de Comaing, who "might perhaps come, but it was not certain." He kept going out every minute, and appeared to be in a restless frame of mind. Finally, at eight o'clock, they proceeded towards a room splendidly lighted and much more spacious than the number of guests required. Cisy had selected it on purpose, out of showiness.

A golden centerpiece laden with flowers and fruit occupied the centre of the table, which was covered with silver dishes, in the old French fashion; small dishes full of salted and spiced meats formed a border all around it. Pitchers of iced rosé wine stood at regular intervals. Five glasses of different sizes were arranged before each plate, with objects whose use was mysterious—a thousand clever dinner utensils. For the first course alone there was a sturgeon's head doused with champagne, a Yorkshire ham with tokay, thrushes au gratin, roast quail, a béchamel vol-au-vent, a stew of red-legged partridges, and at the two ends of all this, stringed potatoes which were mixed with truffles. The room was illuminated by a chandelier and some candelabra, and was hung with red damask.

Four servants in black coats stood behind the armchairs, which were upholstered in morocco leather. At this sight the guests exclaimed in delight—the tutor more emphatically than the rest.

"Upon my word, our host has indulged in a foolishly lavish display of luxury. It is too beautiful!"

"This?" said the Vicomte de Cisy. "Come now!"

And, as they were swallowing the first spoonful:

"Well, my dear old friend Aulnays, have you been to the Palais-Royal to see *Père et Portier*?"

"You know well that I have no time to go!" replied the Marquis.

His mornings were taken up with a course in forestry, his evenings were spent at the Agricultural Club, and all his afternoons were occupied by a study of the production of farming implements. As he resided at Saintonge* for three fourths of the year, he took advantage of his visits to the capital to get fresh information; and his large-brimmed hat, which lay on a side-table, was crammed with pamphlets.

But Cisy, observing that M. de Forchambeaux refused to have wine:

"Go on, dammit, drink! You're not showing much spirit for your last meal as a bachelor!"

At this remark all bowed and congratulated him.

"And the young lady," said the tutor, "is charming, I'm sure?"

"She is indeed!" exclaimed Cisy. "No matter, he is making a mistake; marriage is such a stupid thing!"

"You talk in a thoughtless fashion, my friend!" returned M. des Aulnays, while tears began to gather in his eyes at the recollection of his own dead wife.

---

*Region in western France, on the Atlantic Ocean.

And Forchambeaux repeated several times with a chuckle:

"You'll find out for yourself, you'll find out!"

Cisy protested. He preferred to enjoy himself—to "live in the free-and-easy style of the Regency days." He wanted to learn foot-boxing, so as to visit the seedy cafés of the city, like Rodolphe in the *Mysteries of Paris*;[24] drew out of his pocket a dirty clay pipe, bullied the servants, and drank to excess; then, in order to create a good impression, he criticized all the dishes. He even sent away the truffles; and the tutor, who was exceedingly fond of them, said through servility:

"These are not as good as your grandmother's *oeufs à la neige*."

Then he began to chat with the person sitting next to him, the agriculturist, who found many advantages to living in the country, if it were only to be able to bring up his daughters with simple tastes. The tutor approved of his ideas and flattered him, supposing that this gentleman possessed influence over his former pupil, whose financial adviser he wished to become.

Frédéric had come there filled with hostility towards Cisy; but the young aristocrat's idiocy had disarmed him. However, as the other's gestures, face, and entire person reminded him of the dinner at the Café Anglais, he got more and more irritated; and he listened to the rude remarks made in a low tone by Joseph, the cousin, a fine fellow without any money, who liked hunting and speculating on the stock exchange. Cisy, for the sake of a laugh, called him a "thief" several times; then suddenly:

"Ah! here comes the Baron!"

At that moment, there entered a fellow of thirty, with somewhat rough-looking features and agile limbs, wearing his hat over one ear and a flower in his button-hole. He was the Vicomte's ideal. The young aristocrat was delighted at having him there; and stimulated by his presence, he even attempted a pun; for he said, as they passed a heath-cock:

"There's the best of La Bruyère's characters!"[25]

After that, he asked a lot of questions of M. de Comaing about people unknown to the company; then, as if an idea had suddenly seized him:

"Tell me, pray! have you thought about me?"

The other shrugged his shoulders:

"You are not old enough, my little man. It is impossible!"

Cisy had begged of the Baron to get him admitted into his club. But the other having, no doubt, taken pity on his vanity:

"Ha! I was forgetting! A thousand congratulations on having won your bet, my dear fellow!"

"What bet?"

"The bet you made at the races that you'd spend that very night at that lady's house."

Frédéric felt as if he had got a lash with a whip.

He was speedily appeased by the look of utter confusion in Cisy's face.

In fact, the Maréchale, next morning, was filled with regret when Arnoux, her first lover, her good friend, had presented himself that very day. They both gave the Vicomte the impression that he was in the way, and kicked him out without much ceremony.

He pretended not to have heard what was said.

The Baron went on:

"What has become of her, this fine Rose? Are her legs as pretty as ever?" showing by his manner that he had been on terms of intimacy with her.

Frédéric was annoyed by this discovery.

"There's nothing to blush at," said the Baron, pursuing the topic, " 'tis a good thing!"

Cisy clicked his tongue.

"Whew! not so good!"

"Ah!"

"Good heavens, no! In the first place, I found her to be nothing extraordinary, and then, you can pick up the likes of her as often as you please, for, in fact, she is for sale!"

"Not to everyone!" remarked Frédéric, with some bitterness.

"He imagines that he is different from the others," was Cisy's comment. "What a joke!"

And a laugh went round the table.

Frédéric felt as if the palpitations of his heart would suffocate him. He downed two glasses of water one after the other.

But the Baron had preserved a lively recollection of Rosanette.

"Is she still interested in a fellow named Arnoux?"

"I haven't the faintest idea," said Cisy, "I don't know that gentleman!"

Nevertheless, he suggested that he believed Arnoux was a sort of swindler.

"Just a moment!" exclaimed Frédéric.

"However, there is no doubt about it! Legal proceedings have been taken against him."

"That is not true!"

Frédéric began to defend Arnoux, vouched for his honesty, ended by convincing himself of it, and concocted figures and proofs. The Vicomte, full of spite, and tipsy in addition, persisted in his assertions, so that Frédéric said to him gravely:

"Are you trying to offend me, Monsieur?"

And he looked at him, with eyes as red as his cigar.

"Oh! not at all. I grant you that he possesses something very nice—his wife."

"Do you know her?"

"Faith, I do! Sophie Arnoux; everyone knows her."*

"You mean to tell me that?"

Cisy, who had staggered to his feet, hiccoughed:

"Everyone—knows—her."

"Hold your tongue. It is not with women of her sort you keep company!"

"I—flatter myself—it is."

Frédéric flung a plate at his face. It passed like a flash of lightning over the table, knocked down two bottles, demolished a fruit-dish, and breaking into three pieces, by crashing into the centerpiece, hit the Vicomte in the stomach.

All the other guests arose to hold him back. He struggled and shrieked, possessed by a kind of frenzy.

M. des Aulnays kept repeating:

"Come, be calm, my dear boy!"

"Why, this is abominable!" shouted the tutor.

Forchambeaux, livid as a plum, was trembling. Joseph burst out laughing. The attendants sponged up the traces of the wine, and gathered up the remains of the dinner from the floor; and the Baron

---

*Sophie Arnould (as distinguished from Marie Arnoux) was a singer and an "easy woman" of the time.

went and shut the window, for the uproar, in spite of the noise of carriage-wheels, could be heard on the boulevard.

As all present at the moment the plate had been flung had been talking at the same time, it was impossible to discover the cause of the attack—whether it was on account of Arnoux, Madame Arnoux, Rosanette, or somebody else. One thing only they were certain of, that Frédéric had acted with indescribable brutality. On his part, he positively refused to show the slightest regret for what he had done.

M. des Aulnays tried to soften him. Cousin Joseph, the tutor, and Forchambeaux himself joined in the effort. The Baron, all this time, was cheering up Cisy, who, yielding to weak nerves, began to cry.

Frédéric, on the contrary, was getting more and more angry, and they would have remained there till daybreak if the Baron had not said, in order to bring matters to a close:

"The Vicomte, Monsieur, will send his seconds to call on you to-morrow."

"Your hour?"

"Twelve, if it suits you."

"Perfectly, Monsieur."

Frédéric, as soon as he was out in the open air, drew a deep breath. He had been keeping his feelings too long under restraint; he had satisfied them at last. He felt, so to speak, the pride of virility, a superabundance of energy within him which intoxicated him. He required two seconds. The first person he thought of for the purpose was Regimbart, and he immediately directed his steps towards the Rue Saint-Denis. The shop-front was closed, but some light shone through a pane of glass over the door. It opened and he went in, stooping very low as he passed under the porch.

A candle at the side of the bar lighted up the deserted smoking-room. All the stools, with their feet in the air, were piled on the table. The master and mistress, with their waiter, were at supper in a corner near the kitchen; and Regimbart, with his hat on his head, was sharing their meal, and was even in the way of the waiter, who was forced at every mouthful to turn aside a little. Frédéric, having briefly explained the matter to him, asked Regimbart to assist him. The Citizen at first made no reply. He rolled his eyes, looked as if he were deep in reflection, paced around the room, and at last said:

"Yes, by all means!" and a homicidal smile smoothed his brow when he learned that the adversary was a nobleman.

"Make your mind easy; we'll rout him with flying colours! In the first place, with the sword——"

"But perhaps," broke in Frédéric, "I have not the right."

"I tell you 'tis necessary to take the sword," the Citizen replied roughly. "Do you know how to use one?"

"A little."

"Oh! a little. This is the way with all of them; and yet they have a mania for committing assaults. What does the fencing-school teach? Listen to me: keep a good distance off, always enclose yourself in circles, and give ground, give ground!; that is permitted. Tire him out. Then boldly make a lunge on him! and, above all, no malice, no strokes of the La Fougère kind. No! a simple one-two, and some disengagements. Look here! do you see? turn your wrist as if opening a lock. Père Vauthier, give me your cane. Ha! that will do."

He grasped the rod which was used for lighting the gas, rounded his left arm, bent his right, and began to make some thrusts against the partition. He stamped with his foot, got animated, and pretended to be encountering difficulties, while he exclaimed: "Do you see? Do you follow?" and his enormous silhouette projected itself on the wall with his hat apparently touching the ceiling. The owner of the café shouted from time to time: "Bravo! very good!" His wife, though a little unnerved, was likewise filled with admiration; and Théodore, who had been in the army, remained riveted to the spot with amazement, the fact being, however, that he regarded M. Regimbart with a sort of hero-worship.

Next morning, at an early hour, Frédéric hurried to the establishment in which Dussardier was employed. After having passed through a succession of departments all full of clothing-materials, either adorning shelves or lying on tables, while here and there shawls were fixed on wooden racks shaped like mushrooms, he saw the young man, in a sort of railed cage, surrounded by account-books, and standing in front of a desk at which he was writing. The honest fellow left his work.

The seconds arrived before twelve o'clock.

Frédéric, as a matter of good taste, thought he ought not to be present at the discussion.

The Baron and M. Joseph declared that they would be satisfied with the simplest apology. But Regimbart's principle being never to yield, and his contention being that Arnoux's honour should be vindicated (Frédéric had not spoken to him about anything else), he asked that the Vicomte should apologise. M. de Comaing was indignant at this presumption. The Citizen would not abate an inch. As all conciliation proved impracticable, there was nothing to do but to fight.

Other difficulties arose, for the choice of weapons lay with Cisy, as the insulted party. But Regimbart maintained that by sending the challenge he had constituted himself the offending party. His seconds loudly protested that a slap in the face was the most cruel of offences. The Citizen carped at the words, pointing out that a blow with a plate was not a slap. Finally, they decided to refer the matter to a military man; and the four seconds went off to consult the officers in some of the barracks.

They drew up at the barracks on the Quai d'Orsay. M. de Comaing, having approached two captains, explained to them the question in dispute.

The captains did not understand a word he was saying, due to the confusion caused by the Citizen's incidental remarks. In short, they advised the gentlemen who consulted them to draw up a written statement; after which they would give their decision. Thereupon, they took themselves off to a café; and they even, in order to do things with more discretion, referred to Cisy as H, and Frédéric as K.

Then they returned to the barracks. The officers had gone out. They reappeared, and declared that the choice of arms manifestly belonged to H.

They all returned to Cisy's abode. Regimbart and Dussardier remained on the sidewalk outside.

The Vicomte, when he was informed of the solution of the case, was so upset that they had to repeat for him several times the decision of the officers; and, when M. de Comaing came to deal with Regimbart's contention, he murmured "Nevertheless," not being very reluctant himself to yield to it. Then he let himself sink into an armchair, and declared that he would not fight.

"Eh? What?" said the Baron. Then Cisy launched into a confused flood of words. He wished to fight with firearms—to discharge a single pistol at close range.

"Or else we will put arsenic into a glass, and draw lots to see who must drink it. That's sometimes done. I've read of it!"

The Baron, naturally rather impatient, addressed him in a harsh tone:

"These gentlemen are waiting for your answer. This is indecent, to put it plainly. What weapons are you going to take? Come! is it the sword?"

The Vicomte gave an affirmative reply by merely nodding his head; and it was arranged that the meeting should take place next morning at seven o'clock sharp at the Maillot gate.

Dussardier had to go back to his business, so Regimbart went to inform Frédéric about the arrangement. He had been left all day without any news, and his impatience was becoming unbearable.

"So much the better!" he exclaimed.

The Citizen was satisfied with his reaction.

"Would you believe it? They wanted an apology from us. It was nothing—a mere word! But I sent them off with a flea in their ear. The right thing to do, wasn't it?"

"Undoubtedly," said Frédéric, thinking that it would have been better to choose another second.

Then, when he was alone, he repeated several times in a very loud tone:

"I am going to fight! Hold on, I am going to fight! 'Tis funny!"

And, as he walked up and down his room, while passing in front of the mirror, he noticed that he was pale.

"Does that mean I'm afraid?"

He was seized with a feeling of intolerable misery at the prospect of exhibiting fear on the dueling-ground.

"And yet, suppose I happen to be killed? My father met his death the same way. Yes, I shall be killed!"

And, suddenly, he saw his mother before him in a black dress; incoherent images floated across his mind. His own cowardice exasperated him. A paroxysm of courage, a thirst for human blood, took possession of him. A battalion could not have made him retreat. When this feverish excitement had cooled down, he was overjoyed to feel that his nerves were perfectly steady. In order to distract himself, he went to the opera, where a ballet was being performed. He listened to the music, looked at the *danseuses* through his opera-glass, and drank a glass of punch between the acts. But when he got home again, the sight of his study, of his furniture, in the midst of which he found himself for the last time, made him feel weak.

He went down to the garden. The stars were shining; he gazed up at them. The idea of fighting about a woman gave him a greater importance in his own eyes, and surrounded him with a halo of nobility. Then he went to bed in a tranquil frame of mind.

It was not so with Cisy. After the Baron's departure, Joseph had tried to revive his drooping spirits, but, as the Vicomte remained in the same dull mood:

"However, old boy, if you prefer to drop the whole thing, I'll go and say so."

Cisy did not dare answer "Certainly;" but he would have liked his cousin to do him this service without speaking about it.

He wished that Frédéric would die during the night of a stroke, or that a riot would break out so that next morning there would be enough barricades to shut up all the approaches to the Bois de Boulogne, or that some emergency might prevent one of the seconds from being present; for in the absence of seconds the duel would fall through. He felt a longing to save himself by taking an express train—no matter where. He regretted that he did not understand medicine so as to be able to take something which, without endangering his life, would cause it to look like he was dead. He finally wished to be ill in earnest.

In order to get advice and assistance from someone, he sent for M. des Aulnays. That worthy man had gone back to Saintonge on receiving a letter informing him of the illness of one of his daughters. This appeared an ominous sign to Cisy. Luckily, M. Vezou, his tutor, came to see him. Then he unburdened himself.

"What am I to do? my God! what am I to do?"

"If I were in your place, Monsieur, I should pay some strapping fellow from the market-place to go and give him a thrashing."

"He would still know who brought it about," replied Cisy.

And from time to time he uttered a groan; then:

"But is a man bound to fight a duel?"

" 'Tis a relic of barbarism! What are you to do?"

Out of kindness the pedagogue invited himself to dinner. His pupil did not eat anything, but, after the meal, felt the necessity of taking a short walk.

As they were passing a church, he said:

"Suppose we go in for a little while—to look?"

M. Vezou asked for nothing better, and even offered him holy water.

It was the month of May. The altar was covered with flowers; voices were chanting; the organ was resounding through the church. But he found it impossible to pray, as the pomps of religion inspired him merely with thoughts of funerals. He fancied that he could hear the murmurs of the *De Profundis*.

"Let us leave. I don't feel well."

They spent the whole night playing cards. The Vicomte made an effort to lose in order to exorcise any bad-luck, a thing which M. Vezou turned to his own advantage. At last, at the first streak of dawn, Cisy, who could stand it no longer, sank down on the green cloth, and was soon plunged in sleep, which was disturbed by unpleasant dreams.

If courage, however, consists in wishing to get the better of one's own weakness, the Vicomte was courageous, for in the presence of his seconds, who came to seek him, he stiffened himself up with all the strength he could command, vanity making him realise that to attempt to draw back now would disgrace him. M. de Comaing congratulated him on looking so well.

But, on the way, the jolting of the cab and the heat of the morning sun unnerved him. His energy gave way again. He could not even distinguish any longer where they were. The Baron amused himself by increasing his terror, talking about the "corpse," and of the way they meant to get back clandestinely to the city. Joseph made a reply; both, considering the affair ridiculous, were certain that it would be settled.

Cisy kept his head on his chest; he lifted it up slowly, and drew attention to the fact that they had not taken a doctor with them.

" 'Tis needless," said the Baron.

"Then there's no danger?"

Joseph answered in a grave tone:

"Let us hope so!"

And nobody in the carriage made any further remark.

At ten minutes past seven they arrived in front of the Maillot gate. Frédéric and his seconds were there, the entire group being dressed all in black. Regimbart, instead of a cravat, wore a stiff horsehair collar, like a soldier; and he carried a long violin-case adapted for occasions of this kind. They exchanged frigid bows. Then they all plunged into the Bois de Boulogne, taking the Madrid road, in order to find a suitable place.

Regimbart said to Frédéric, who was walking between him and Dussardier:

"Well, and this dread—what do we care about it? If you need anything, don't worry; I know what to do. Fear is natural to man!"

Then, in a low tone:

"Don't smoke any more; it has a weakening effect."

Frédéric threw away his cigar, which was disturbing him, and went on with a firm step. The Vicomte advanced behind, leaning on the arms of his two seconds. Occasional passers-by crossed their path. The sky was blue, and from time to time they heard rabbits skipping about. At the turn of a path, a woman in a Madras kerchief was chatting with a man in a smock; and in the large avenue under the chestnut-trees some grooms in linen vests were walking horses up and down.

Cisy recalled the happy days when, mounted on his own chestnut horse, and with his monocle in his eye, he had ridden along beside carriage-doors. These recollections intensified his anguish. An intolerable thirst parched his throat. The buzzing of flies mingled with the throbbing of his arteries. His feet sank into the sand. It seemed to him as if he had been walking for an eternity.

The seconds, without stopping, examined with keen glances both sides of the road. They hesitated as to whether they would go to the Catelan Cross or under the walls of the Bagatelle. At last they took a turn to the right; and they drew up in a kind of clearing between some pine-trees.

The spot was chosen in such a way that the level ground was cut equally into two divisions. The two places at which the principals in the duel were to take their stand were marked out. Then Regimbart opened his case. It was lined with red sheep's leather, and contained four charming swords hollowed in the centre, with handles which were adorned with filigree. A ray of light, passing through the leaves, fell on them, and they appeared to Cisy to glitter like silver vipers on a sea of blood.

The Citizen showed that they were of equal length. He took one himself, in order to separate the combatants in case of necessity. M. de Comaing held a walking-stick. There was an interval of silence. They looked at each other. All the faces had in them apprehension or cruelty.

Frédéric had taken off his coat and his waistcoat. Joseph aided Cisy to do the same. When his cravat was removed a religious medal could be seen on his neck. This made Regimbart smile contemptuously.

Then M. de Comaing (in order to allow Frédéric another moment for reflection) tried to raise a quibble. He demanded the right to put on a glove, and to catch hold of his adversary's sword with the left hand. Regimbart, who was in a hurry, made no objection to this. At last the Baron, addressing Frédéric:

"Everything depends on you, Monsieur! There is never any dishonour in acknowledging one's faults."

Dussardier made a gesture of approval. The Citizen gave vent to his indignation:

"Do you think we came here as a mere sham, damn it! Be on your guard, each of you!"

The combatants were facing one another, with their seconds by their sides.

He uttered the single word:

"Go!"

Cisy became dreadfully pale. The end of his blade was quivering like a horsewhip. His head fell back, his hands dropped down helplessly, and he sank unconscious on the ground. Joseph raised him up and while holding a scent-bottle to his nose, gave him a good shaking.

The Vicomte reopened his eyes, then suddenly grasped at his sword like a madman. Frédéric had held his in readiness, and now awaited him with steady eye and uplifted hand.

"Stop! stop!" cried a voice, which came from the road simultaneously with the sound of a horse at full gallop, and the hood of a cab broke the branches. A man leaned out waving a handkerchief, still exclaiming:

"Stop! stop!"

M. de Comaing, believing that this meant the intervention of the police, lifted up his walking-stick.

"Make an end of it. The Vicomte is bleeding!"

"I?" said Cisy.

In fact, he had in his fall skinned his left thumb.

"But this was by falling," observed the Citizen.

The Baron pretended not to understand.

Arnoux had jumped out of the cab.

"Have I arrived too late? No! Thanks be to God!"

He threw his arms around Frédéric, felt him all over, and covered his face with kisses.

"I am the cause of it. You wanted to defend your old friend! That's right—that's right! Never shall I forget it! How good you are! Ah! my own dear boy!"

He gazed at Frédéric and shed tears, while he chuckled with delight. The Baron turned towards Joseph:

"I believe we are in the way at this little family party. It is over, messieurs, is it not ? Vicomte, put your arm into a sling. Hold on! here is my silk handkerchief."

Then, with an imperious gesture: "Come! no spite! This is as it should be!"

The two adversaries shook hands in a very lukewarm fashion. The Vicomte, M. de Comaing, and Joseph disappeared in one direction, and Frédéric left with his friends in the opposite direction.

As the Madrid Restaurant was not far off, Arnoux proposed that they should go and drink a glass of beer there.

"We might even have breakfast."

But, as Dussardier had no time to lose, they confined themselves to having some refreshments in the garden.

They all experienced that sense of satisfaction which follows happy endings. The Citizen, nevertheless, was annoyed at the duel having been interrupted at the most critical stage.

Arnoux had been apprised of it by a person named Compain, a friend of Regimbart; and with an irrepressible outburst of emotion he had rushed to the spot to prevent it, under the impression, however, that he was the cause of it. He begged Frédéric to furnish him with some details about it. Frédéric, touched by these proofs of affection, felt unscrupulous adding to his illusions.

"For mercy's sake, don't say any more about it!"

Arnoux thought that this reserve showed great tact. Then, with his usual levity, he passed on to a fresh subject.

"What news, Citizen?"

And they began talking about banking transactions, and the number of bills that were falling due. In order to be more undisturbed, they went to another table, where they exchanged whispered confidences.

Frédéric could overhear the following words: "You are going to apply for shares for me." "Yes, but mind you!" "I have negotiated it at last for three hundred!" "A nice commission, faith!"

In short, it was clear that Arnoux was mixed up in a great many shady transactions with the Citizen.

Frédéric thought of reminding him about the fifteen thousand francs. But his recent actions forbade any reproachful words even of the mildest description. Besides, he felt tired himself, and this was not a convenient place for talking about such a thing. He put it off to another day.

Arnoux, seated in the shade of an evergreen, was smoking, with a look of joviality in his face. He raised his eyes towards the doors of private rooms looking out on the garden, and said he had often paid visits to the house in former days.

"Probably not by yourself?" returned the Citizen.

"Faith, you're right there!"

"What a rascal you are! you, a married man!"

"Well, and what about yourself?" retorted Arnoux; and, with an indulgent smile: "I am even sure that this rascal here has a room of his own where he entertains young ladies."

The Citizen confessed that this was true by simply raising his eyebrows. Then these two gentlemen proceeded to compare their respective tastes. Arnoux now preferred youth, working girls; Regimbart hated affected women, and went in for the genuine article before anything else. The conclusion which the earthenware-dealer laid down at the close of this discussion was that women were not to be taken seriously.

"Nevertheless, he is fond of his own wife," thought Frédéric, as he made his way home; and he looked on Arnoux as a coarse man. He had a grudge against him on account of the duel, as if it had been for the sake of this individual that he risked his life.

But he felt grateful to Dussardier for his devotedness. Ere long the book-keeper came at his invitation to pay him a visit every day.

Frédéric lent him books—Thiers, Dulaure, Barante, and Lamartine's *Girondins*.*

The honest fellow listened to everything the other said with a thoughtful air, and accepted his opinions as those of a master.

One evening he arrived in a panic.

That morning, on the boulevard, a man who was running so quickly that he was out of breath, had bumped into him, and having recognised him as a friend of Sénécal, had said to him:

"He has just been arrested! I am making my escape!"

There was no doubt about it. Dussardier had spent the day making enquiries. Sénécal was in jail charged with an attempted crime of a political nature.

The son of a foreman, he was born at Lyons, and having had as his teacher a former disciple of Chalier, he had, on his arrival in Paris, obtained admission into the "Society of Families." His ways were known, and the police kept a watch on him. He was one of those who fought in the outbreak of May, 1839, and since then he had stayed in the shadows; but, his self-importance increasing more and more, he became a fanatical follower of Alibaud,[26] mixing up his own grievances against society with those of the people against monarchy, and waking up every morning in the hope of a revolution which in a fortnight or a month would turn the world upside down. At last, disgusted at the inactivity of his brethren, enraged at the obstacles that retarded the realisation of his dreams, and in despair at the state of the country, he used his knowledge as a chemist in the incendiary bomb conspiracy; and he been caught carrying

---

*Adolphe Thiers, Jacques Dulaure, Brugière de Barante, and Alphonse de Lamartine were nineteenth-century liberal historians. Lamartine was also a poet.

gunpowder, which he was going to try at Montmartre—a supreme effort to establish the Republic.

Dussardier was no less attached to the Republican idea, for, from his point of view, it meant emancipation and universal happiness. One day—at the age of fifteen—in the Rue Transnonain,* in front of a grocer's shop, he had seen soldiers' bayonets reddened with blood and with human hairs sticking to their rifle butts. Since that time, the Government had filled him with feelings of rage as the very incarnation of injustice. He confused the assassins with the gendarmes; and in his eyes a police-informer was just as bad as a parricide. All the evil scattered over the earth he naively attributed to Power; and he hated it with a deep-rooted, undying hatred that took possession of his heart and refined his sensibility. He had been dazzled by Sénécal's rhetoric. It was of little consequence whether he happened to be guilty or not, however abominable was his plot! Since he was the victim of Authority, it was only right to help him.

"The Peers will condemn him, certainly! Then he will be taken off in a prison-van, like a convict, and will be shut up in Mont Saint-Michel, where the Government puts them to death! Austen went mad there! Steuben had killed himself! In order to transfer Barbès into a dungeon, they had dragged him by the legs and by the hair.† They trampled on his body, and his head bumped along the staircase with every step they took. What abominable treatment! The wretches!"

He was choking with angry sobs, and he walked about the room overtaken by tremendous anguish.

"In the meantime, something must be done! Let's see, I don't know what to do! Suppose we tried to rescue him, eh? While they are bringing him to the Luxembourg, we could throw ourselves on the escort in the passage! A dozen resolute men—that sometimes is enough to accomplish it!"

There was so much fire in his eyes that Frédéric was a little startled by his look. He recalled Sénécal's sufferings and his austere life. Without feeling the same enthusiasm about him as Dussardier,

---

*The site of a Parisian riot in 1834 that was followed by a random massacre of the rioters by the soldiers.

†Austen, Steuben, and Barbès had been condemned for the May 1839 attack.

he experienced nevertheless that admiration which is inspired by every man who sacrifices himself for an idea. He said to himself that, if he had helped this man, he would not be in his present position; and the two friends anxiously sought to devise some contrivance whereby they could set him free.

It was impossible for them to get access to him.

Frédéric examined the newspapers to try to find out what had become of him, and for three weeks he was a constant visitor at the reading-rooms.

One day several issues of the *Flambard* fell into his hands. The leading article was invariably devoted to taking apart some distinguished man. After that came some society gossip and some scandals. Then there were some wry observations about the Odéon Carpentras, fish-breeding, and prisoners under sentence of death, when there happened to be any. The disappearance of a steamer furnished material for a whole year's jokes. In the third column a chronicle of the arts, in the form of anecdotes or advice, gave some tailors' announcements, together with accounts of evening parties, advertisements of auctions, and analysis of artistic productions, writing in the same strain about a volume of verse and a pair of boots. The only serious portion of it was the criticism of the small theatres, in which fierce attacks were made on two or three managers; and the interests of art were invoked on the subjects of the scenery at the Funambules Theatre or the lead actress at the Délassements.

Frédéric was passing over all these items when his eyes alighted on an article entitled "A Hen with Three Roosters." It was the story of his duel related in a lively style. He had no difficulty in recognising himself, for he was indicated by this little joke, which frequently recurred: "A young man from the College of Sens who has no sense." He was even represented as a poor devil from the provinces, an obscure simpleton trying to mix with persons of high rank. As for the Vicomte, he was given the hero's part, first by having forced his way into the dinner party, then in the affair of the wager, by having carried off the lady, and, finally, by having behaved like a perfect gentleman on the dueling-ground.

Frédéric's courage was not denied exactly, but it was pointed out that an intermediary—the *protector* himself—had come on the scene just in the nick of time. The entire article concluded with this phrase, charged perhaps with sinister meaning:

"What is the reason for their affection? That's the problem! and, as Bazile* says, who the devil is it that is deceived here?"

This was, beyond all doubt, Hussonnet's revenge against Frédéric for having refused him five thousand francs.

What was he to do? If he demanded an explanation from him, the Bohemian would protest that he was innocent, and nothing would be gained by doing this. The best course was to swallow the affront in silence. Nobody, after all, read the *Flambard*.

As he left the reading-room, he saw some people standing in front of an art-dealer's shop. They were staring at the portrait of a woman, with this line written underneath in black letters: "Mademoiselle Rosanette Bron, belonging to M. Frédéric Moreau of Nogent."

It was indeed she—or, at least, like her—her full face displayed, her breasts exposed, with her hair hanging loose, and with a purse of red velvet in her hands, while behind her a peacock leaned his beak over her shoulder, covering the wall with its immense fan of feathers.

Pellerin was exhibiting it in order to compel Frédéric to pay, persuaded that he was a celebrity, and that all Paris, rallying around him, would take an interest in his plight.

Was this a conspiracy? Had the painter and the journalist prepared their attack on him at the same time?

His duel had not put a stop to anything. He had become an object of ridicule, and everyone had been laughing at him.

Three days later, at the end of June, the Northern shares had gone up fifteen francs, and as he had bought two thousand of them within the past month, he found that he had made thirty thousand francs. This stroke of luck gave him renewed self-confidence. He said to himself that he wanted nobody's help, and that all his troubles were the result of his timidity and indecision. He ought to have been tough with the Maréchale from the start and refused Hussonnet the very first day. He should not have compromised himself with Pellerin. And, in order to show that he was not a bit

*Ridiculous character in the comedy *Le Barbier de Séville* (1775; *The Barber of Seville*), by Pierre Caron de Beaumarchais.

embarrassed, he presented himself at one of Madame Dambreuse's regular evening parties.

In the middle of the hall, Martinon, who had arrived at the same time as he had, turned round:

"What! so you are visiting here?" with a look of surprise, and as if displeased at seeing him.

"Why not?"

And, while asking himself what could be the cause of such a display of hostility on Martinon's part, Frédéric made his way into the drawing-room.

The light was dim, in spite of the lamps placed in the corners, for the three windows, which were wide open, made three large squares of black shadow stand parallel with each other. Under the pictures, flower-stands occupied, five or six feet high, the spaces on the walls, and a silver teapot with a samovar cast their reflections in a mirror on the background. There arose a murmur of hushed voices. Shoes could be heard creaking on the carpet. He could distinguish a number of black coats, then a round table lighted up by a large shaded lamp, seven or eight ladies in summer dresses, and at some little distance Madame Dambreuse in a rocking chair. Her dress of lilac taffeta had sleeves with slits, from which emerged puffs of muslin, the charming tint of the material harmonising with the shade of her hair; and she sat leaning back with the tip of her foot on a cushion, with the repose of an exquisitely delicate work of art, or rare flower.

M. Dambreuse and an old gentleman with a white head were walking from one end of the drawing-room to the other. Some of the guests chatted here and there, sitting on the edges of little sofas, while the others, standing up, formed a circle in the centre of the room.

They were talking about votes, amendments, counter-amendments, M. Grandin's speech and M. Benoist's reply. The third party had decidedly gone too far. The Left Centre ought to have been more mindful of its origins. Serious attacks had been made on the minister. It must be reassuring, however, to see that he had no successor. In sort, the situation was completely analogous to that of 1834.

As these things bored Frédéric, he drew near the ladies. Martinon was beside them, standing up, with his hat under his arm, showing himself in three-quarter profile, and looking so neat that he resembled a piece of Sèvres porcelain. He took up a copy of the *Revue des Deux Mondes* which was lying on the table between an *Imitation* and an *Almanach de Gotha*,[27] and spoke of a distinguished poet in a contemptuous tone, said he was going to the "conferences of Saint-Francis," complained of his larynx, swallowed from time to time a lozenge, and in the meantime kept talking about music, and made small talk. Mademoiselle Cécile, M. Dambreuse's niece, who happened to be embroidering a pair of cuffs, gazed at him with her pale blue eyes; and Miss John, the governess, who had a flat nose, laid aside her tapestry on his account. Both of them appeared to be exclaiming internally:

"How handsome he is!"

Madame Dambreuse turned round towards him.

"Please give me my fan which is on that table over there. No, not that one! 'tis the other!"

She arose, and when he came across to her, they met in the middle of the drawing-room face to face. She addressed a few sharp words to him, no doubt of a reproachful character, judging by the haughty expression of her face. Martinon tried to smile; then he went to join the circle in which solemn-looking men were holding discussions. Madame Dambreuse resumed her seat, and, bending over the arm of her chair, said to Frédéric:

"I saw somebody the day before yesterday who was speaking to me about you—Monsieur de Cisy. You know him, don't you?"

"Yes, slightly."

Suddenly Madame Dambreuse uttered an exclamation:

"Oh! Duchesse, what a pleasure to see you!"

And she advanced towards the door to meet a little old lady in a brown taffeta gown and a lace cap with long ribbons. The daughter of a companion in exile of the Comte d'Artois*, and the widow of a marshal of the Empire, who had been created a peer of France in 1830, she had connections to the old court as well as to the new court, and possessed sufficient influence to procure many things. Those who stood talking stepped aside, and then resumed their conversation.

---

*Brother of Louis XVI, and future king Charles X (1757–1836).

It had now centered on extreme poverty, of which, according to these gentlemen, all the descriptions that had been given were grossly exaggerated.

"However," urged Martinon, "let us confess that there is such a thing as poverty! But the remedy depends neither on science nor on power. It is purely an individual question. When the lower classes are willing to get rid of their vices, they will free themselves from their necessities. Let the people be more moral, and they will be less poor!"

According to M. Dambreuse, no good could be attained without a superabundance of capital. Therefore, the only practical method was to entrust, "as the Saint-Simonians proposed (good heavens! there was some merit in their views—let us be just to everybody)—to entrust, I say, the cause of progress to those who can increase the public wealth." Imperceptibly the conversation moved on to the great industrial undertakings—the railways, the coal-mines. And M. Dambreuse, addressing Frédéric, said to him in a low whisper:

"You have not come about that business of ours?"

Frédéric pleaded illness; but, feeling that this excuse was too absurd:

"Besides, I need my money."

"Is it to buy a carriage?" asked Madame Dambreuse, who was brushing past him with a cup of tea in her hand, and for a minute she watched his face with her head tilted slightly to the side.

She believed that he was Rosanette's lover—the allusion was obvious. It seemed even to Frédéric that all the ladies were staring at him from a distance and whispering to one another.

In order to get a better idea as to what they were thinking about, he once more approached them. On the opposite side of the table, Martinon, seated near Mademoiselle Cécile, was turning the pages of an album. It contained lithographs of Spanish costumes. He read the descriptive titles aloud: "A Lady of Seville," "A Valencia Gardener," "An Andalusian Picador"; and once, going down to the bottom of the page, he continued all in one breath:

"Jacques Arnoux, publisher. One of your friends, eh?"

"That is true," said Frédéric, hurt by his tone.

Madame Dambreuse added:

"In fact, you came here one morning—about a house, I believe—a house belonging to his wife." (This meant: "She is your mistress.")

He reddened up to his ears; and M. Dambreuse, who joined them at the same moment, made this additional remark:

"You appear to be deeply interested in them."

These last words had the effect of completely embarrassing Frédéric. His confusion, which, he could not help feeling, was evident to them, was on the point of confirming their suspicions, when M. Dambreuse drew close to him, and, in a tone of great seriousness, said:

"I suppose you don't do business together?"

He protested by repeated shakes of the head, without realising the exact meaning of the capitalist, who wished to give him advice.

He felt a desire to leave. The fear of appearing faint-hearted restrained him. A servant carried away the teacups. Madame Dambreuse was talking to a diplomat in a blue coat. Two young girls, their heads close together, showed each other their jewellery. The others, seated in a semicircle on armchairs, kept moving their white faces crowned with black or fair hair. Nobody, in fact, was paying any attention to them. Frédéric turned on his heels; and, by a succession of long zigzags, he had almost reached the door, when, passing close to a table, he remarked, on the top of it, between a china vase and the panelling, a journal folded up in two. He drew it out a little, and read these words—*The Flambard.*

Who had brought it there? Cisy. Obviously no one else. What did it matter, however? They would believe—already, perhaps, everyone believed—in the article. What was the cause of this vindictiveness? He was enveloped by ironic silence. He felt like one lost in a desert. But suddenly he heard Martinon's voice:

"Talking of Arnoux, I saw in the newspapers, amongst the names of those accused of preparing incendiary bombs, that of one of his *employés*, Sénécal. Is that our Sénécal?"

"The very same!"

Martinon repeated several times in a very loud tone:

"What? our Sénécal! our Sénécal!"

Then questions were asked him about the conspiracy. It was assumed that his connection with the prosecutor's office ought to furnish him with some information on the subject.

He declared that he had none. However, he knew very little about this individual, having seen him only two or three times.

He positively regarded him as a scoundrel. Frédéric exclaimed indignantly:

"Not at all! he is a very honest fellow."

"All the same, Monsieur," said a landowner, "no conspirator can be an honest man."

Most of the men assembled there had served at least four governments; and they would have sold France or the human race in order to preserve their own incomes, to save themselves from any discomfort or embarrassment, or even through sheer baseness, through worship of strength. They all maintained that political crimes were inexcusable. It would be more desirable to pardon those which were provoked by want. And they did not fail to put forward the eternal illustration of the father of a family stealing the eternal loaf of bread from the eternal baker.

A gentleman occupying an administrative office even went so far as to exclaim:

"For my part, Monsieur, if I were told that my brother were a conspirator I would denounce him!"

Frédéric invoked the right of resistance, and recalling some phrases that Deslauriers had used in their conversations, he referred to Delosmes, Blackstone, the English Bill of Rights, and Article 2 of the Constitution of '91.[28] It was even by virtue of this law that the fall of Napoleon had been proclaimed. It had been recognised in 1830, and inscribed at the head of the Charter.* Besides, when the sovereign fails to fulfil the contract, justice requires that he should be overthrown.

"Why, this is abominable!" exclaimed a prefect's wife.

All the rest remained silent, filled with vague terror, as if they had heard the noise of bullets. Madame Dambreuse rocked herself in her chair, and smiled as she listened to him.

A manufacturer, who had formerly been a member of the Carbonari, tried to show that the Orléans family possessed good qualities.[29] No doubt there were some abuses.

"Well, then?"

"But we should not talk about them, my dear Monsieur! If you knew how all these clamourings of the Opposition harm business!"

---

*The constitution "granted" to the French by Louis XVIII in 1814.

"What do I care about business?" said Frédéric.

He was exasperated by the corruption of these old men; and, carried away by the recklessness which sometimes takes possession of even the most timid, he attacked the financiers, the representatives, the government, the king, took up the defence of the Arabs, and said many foolish things. A few of those around him encouraged him in a spirit of irony:

"Go on, pray! continue!" whilst others muttered:

"My word! what enthusiasm!" At last he thought the right thing to do was to withdraw; and, as he was going, M. Dambreuse said to him, alluding to the post of secretary:

"No definite arrangement has been yet arrived at; but hurry up!"

And Madame Dambreuse:

"You'll call again soon, will you not?"

Frédéric considered their parting salutation a final mockery. He had resolved never to come back to this house, or to visit any of these people again. He imagined that he had offended them, not realising what vast reserves of indifference society possesses. These women especially excited his indignation. Not a single one of them had backed him up even with a look of sympathy. He felt angry with them for not having been moved by his words. As for Madame Dambreuse, he found in her something at the same time languid and cold, which prevented him from defining her character with a label. Had she a lover? and, if so, who was her lover? Was it the diplomat or some other? Perhaps it was Martinon? Impossible! Nevertheless, he experienced a sort of jealousy toward Martinon, and an unaccountable ill-will against her.

Dussardier, having called this evening as usual, was awaiting him. Frédéric's heart swelled with bitterness; he unburdened it, and his grievances, though vague and hard to understand, saddened the honest shop-assistant. He even complained of his isolation. Dussardier, after a little hesitation, suggested that they ought to call on Deslauriers.

Frédéric, at the mention of the lawyer's name, was seized with a longing to see him once more. He was now living in the midst of profound intellectual solitude, and found Dussardier's company quite insufficient. In reply to the latter's question, Frédéric told him to arrange matters any way he liked.

Deslauriers had likewise, since their quarrel, felt a void in his life. He yielded without much reluctance to the cordial advances which were made to him. The pair embraced each other, then began chatting about matters of no consequence.

Frédéric's heart was touched by Deslauriers' display of reserve, and in order to make him a sort of reparation, he told the other next day how he had lost fifteen thousand francs without mentioning that these fifteen thousand francs had been originally intended for him. The lawyer, nevertheless, had a shrewd suspicion of the truth; and this misfortune, which justified, in his own mind, his prejudices against Arnoux, entirely disarmed his bitterness; and he did not again refer to the promise made by his friend on a former occasion.

Frédéric, misled by his silence, thought he had forgotten all about it. A few days afterwards, he asked Deslauriers whether there was any way in which he could get back his money.

They might raise the point that the prior mortgage was fraudulent, and might take proceedings against the wife personally.

"No! no! not against her!" exclaimed Frédéric, and, yielding to the ex-law-clerk's questions, he confessed the truth. Deslauriers was convinced that Frédéric had not told him the entire truth, no doubt as a matter of fact. He was hurt by this lack of trust.

They were, however, on the same intimate terms as before, and they even found so much pleasure in each other's society that Dussardier's presence got in the way. Under the pretence that they had appointments, they managed gradually to get rid of him.

There are some men whose only mission amongst their fellowmen is to serve as go-betweens; people use them in the same way as if they were bridges, by stepping over them and going on further.

Frédéric concealed nothing from his old friend. He told him about the coal-mine speculation and M. Dambreuse's proposal. The lawyer grew thoughtful.

"That's strange! For such a post a man with a good knowledge of law would be required!"

"But you could assist me," returned Frédéric.

"Yes!—hold on! faith, yes! certainly."

During the same week Frédéric showed Dussardier a letter from his mother.

Madame Moreau accused herself of having misjudged M. Roque, who had given a satisfactory explanation of his conduct. Then she spoke of his fortune, and of the possibility, later, of a marriage with Louise.

"That would not be a bad match," said Deslauriers.

Frédéric said it was entirely out of the question. Besides, Père Roque was an old swindler. That in no way affected the matter, in the lawyer's opinion.

At the end of July, an inexplicable drop in value made the Northern shares fall. Frédéric had not sold his. He lost sixty thousand francs in one day. His income was considerably reduced. He would have to curtail his expenditure, or take up some profession, or make a brilliant catch in the matrimonial market.

Then Deslauriers spoke to him about Mademoiselle Roque. There was nothing to prevent him from going to see things for himself. Frédéric was rather tired of city life. Provincial existence and the maternal roof would be a sort of respite for him.

The sight of the streets of Nogent, as he passed through them in the moonlight, brought back old memories; and he experienced a kind of pang, like those who have just returned home after a long period of travel.

At his mother's house, all the country visitors had assembled as in former days—MM. Gamblin, Heudras, and Chambrion, the Lebrun family, "those young ladies, the Augers," and, in addition, Père Roque, and, sitting opposite to Madame Moreau at a card-table, Mademoiselle Louise. She was now a woman. She sprang to her feet with a cry of delight. They were all in a flutter of excitement. She remained standing motionless, and the paleness of her face was intensified by the light issuing from four silver candle-sticks.

When she resumed play, her hand was trembling. This emotion was exceedingly flattering to Frédéric, whose pride had been sorely wounded of late. He said to himself: "You, at any rate, will love me!" and, as if he were thus taking his revenge for the humiliations he had endured in the capital, he began to affect the dashing Parisian, recounted all the theatrical gossip, told anecdotes as to the doings of society, which he had borrowed from the columns of the cheap newspapers, and, in short, dazzled his fellow-townspeople.

Next morning, Madame Moreau expatiated on Louise's fine qualities; then she enumerated the woods and farms of which she would be the owner. Père Roque's wealth was considerable.

He had acquired it while making investments for M. Dambreuse; for he had lent money to people who were able to furnish good security in the form of mortgages, whereby he was able to demand additional sums or commissions. The capital, thanks to his active supervision, was in no danger of being lost. Besides, Père Roque never had any hesitation in making a foreclosure. Then he bought up the mortgaged property at a low price, and M. Dambreuse, having got back his money, found his affairs in very good order.

But this manipulation of business matters in a way which was not strictly legal compromised him with his agent. He could refuse Père Roque nothing, and it was owing to the latter's solicitations that M. Dambreuse had received Frédéric so cordially.

The truth was that in the depths of his soul Père Roque cherished a deep-rooted ambition. He wished his daughter to be a countess; and for the purpose of gaining this object, without imperilling the happiness of his child, he knew no other young man than Frédéric through whom he might achieve this.

Through the influence of M. Dambreuse, he could obtain the title of his maternal grandfather, for Madame Moreau was the daughter of a Comte de Fouvens, and was also connected with the oldest families in Champagne, the Lavernades and the D'Etrignys. As for the Moreaus, a Gothic inscription near the mills of Villeneuve-l' Archevèque referred to one Jacob Moreau, who had rebuilt them in 1596; and the tomb of his own son, Pierre Moreau, first esquire of the king under Louis XIV, was to be seen in the chapel of Saint-Nicholas.

So much family distinction fascinated M. Roque, the son of an old servant. If the coronet of a count did not come, he would console himself with something else; for Frédéric might become a representative when M. Dambreuse had been raised to the peerage, and might then be able to assist him in his commercial pursuits, and to obtain for him supplies and grants. He liked the young man personally. In short, he desired to have Frédéric for a son-in-law, because for a long time past he had been smitten with this notion, which only grew all the stronger day by day. Now he went to religious services, and he had won Madame Moreau over to his views, especially by holding before her the prospect of a title.

So it was that, eight days later, without any formal engagement, Frédéric was regarded as Mademoiselle Roque's "intended," and Père Roque, who was not concerned with scruples, often left them alone together.

CHAPTER V

Deslauriers had carried away from Frédéric's house the copy of the deed of subrogation, with a power of attorney in proper form, giving him full authority to act; but, when he had reascended his own five flights of stairs and found himself alone in the midst of his dismal room, in his armchair upholstered in sheep-leather, the sight of the stamped documents disgusted him.

He was tired of these things, and of restaurants at thirty-two sous, of travelling on omnibuses, of enduring want and many struggles. He picked up the documents again; there were others with them. They were prospectuses of the coal-mining company, with a list of the mines and the particulars as to their contents, Frédéric having left all these matters in his hands in order to have his opinion about them.

An idea occurred to him—that of presenting himself at M. Dambreuse's house and applying for the post of secretary. This post, it was perfectly certain, could not be obtained without purchasing a certain number of shares. He recognised the folly of his plan, and said to himself:

"Oh! no, that would be a wrong step."

Then he racked his brains to think of the best way in which he could set about recovering the fifteen thousand francs. Such a sum was a mere trifle to Frédéric. But, if he had it, what a lever it would be in his hands! And the ex-law-clerk was indignant at the other being so well off.

"He makes pitiful use of it. He is a selfish fellow. Ah! what do I care for his fifteen thousand francs!"

Why had he lent the money? For the sake of Madame Arnoux's bright eyes. She was his mistress! Deslauriers had no doubt about it. "There was another way in which money was useful!"

And he was assailed by hateful thoughts.

Then he allowed his thoughts to dwell even on Frédéric's personal appearance. It had always exercised over him an almost feminine charm; and he soon came to admire him for a success which he realised that he was himself incapable of achieving.

"Nevertheless, was not one's will the main element in every enterprise? and, since by its means we may triumph over everything——"

"Ah! that would be funny!"

But he felt ashamed of such treachery, and the next moment:

"Bah! Am I afraid?"

Madame Arnoux—from having heard her spoken about so often—had come to be depicted in his imagination as something extraordinary. The persistency of this passion had irritated him like a problem. Her austerity, which seemed a little theatrical, now annoyed him. Besides, the woman of the world—or, rather, his own conception of her—dazzled the lawyer as the symbol and the epitome of a thousand pleasures unknown to him. Poor though he was, he hankered after luxury in its most glittering form.

"After all, even if he should get angry, it would serve him right! He has behaved too badly for me to care! I have no assurance that she is his mistress! He has denied it. So then I am free to act as I please!"

He could no longer abandon the desire of taking this step. He wished to make a test of his own strength, so that one day, all of a sudden, he polished his boots himself, bought white gloves, and set forth on his way, substituting himself for Frédéric, and almost imagining that he was the other by a singular intellectual evolution, in which there was, at the same time, vengeance and sympathy, imitation and audacity.

He announced himself as "Doctor Deslauriers."

Madame Arnoux was surprised, as she had not sent for any physician.

"Ah! a thousand apologies!—'tis a doctor of law! I have come in Monsieur Moreau's interest."

This name appeared to disturb her.

"So much the better!" thought the ex-law-clerk.

"Since she has a liking for him, she will like me, too!" buoying up his courage with the accepted idea that it is easier to supplant a lover than a husband.

He referred to the fact that he had the pleasure of meeting her on one occasion at the law-court; he even mentioned the date. This remarkable power of memory astonished Madame Arnoux. He went on in an ingratiating tone:

"You were already in difficulty over your financial affairs?"

She made no reply.

"Then it must be true."

He began to chat about one thing or another, about her house, about the factory; then, noticing some miniatures at the sides of the mirror:

"Ah! family portraits, no doubt?"

He noticed that of an old lady, Madame Arnoux's mother.

"She has the appearance of an excellent woman, a southern type."

And, when it was pointed out that she was from Chartres:

"Chartres! pretty town!"

He praised its cathedral and public buildings, and coming back to the portrait, traced resemblances between it and Madame Arnoux, and cast flatteries at her indirectly. She did not appear to be offended at this. He took confidence, and said that he had known Arnoux a long time.

"He is a fine fellow, but one who compromises himself. Take this mortgage, for example—one can't imagine such a reckless act——"

"Yes, I know," said she, shrugging her shoulders.

This involuntary evidence of contempt induced Deslauriers to continue. "That kaolin business of his was near turning out very badly, a thing you may not be aware of, and even his reputation——"

A contraction of the brows made him pause.

Then, falling back on generalities, he expressed his pity for the "poor women whose husbands frittered away their fortunes."

"But in this case, monsieur, the future belongs to him. As for me, I have nothing!"

No matter, one never knows. A man of experience might be useful. He made offers of devoted service, exalted his own merits; and he looked into her eyes through his shining spectacles.

She was seized with a vague inertia; but suddenly said:

"Let us look into the matter, I beg of you."

He exhibited the bundle of papers.

"This is Frédéric's power of attorney. With such a document in the hands of a court officer, who would issue a writ, nothing could be simpler; in twenty-four hours——" (She remained impassive; he changed his tactics.)

"As for me, however, I don't understand what compels him to demand this sum, for, in fact, he doesn't need it."

"How is that? Monsieur Moreau has shown himself to be so kind."

"Oh! granted!"

And Deslauriers began by praising him, then in a mild fashion disparaged him, implying that he was a forgetful individual, and overly fond of money.

"I thought he was your friend, monsieur?"

"That does not prevent me from seeing his flaws. He shows very little appreciation of—how shall I put it?—sympathy——"

Madame Arnoux was turning the pages of the large manuscript.

She interrupted him in order to get him to explain a certain word.

He bent over her shoulder, and his face came so close to hers that he grazed her cheek. She blushed. This heightened colour inflamed Deslauriers, he hungrily kissed her head.

"What are you doing, Monsieur?" And, standing up against the wall, she compelled him to remain perfectly quiet under the glance of her large blue eyes glowing with anger.

"Listen to me! I love you!"

She broke into a laugh, a shrill, discouraging laugh. Deslauriers felt himself suffocating with anger. He restrained his feelings, and, with the look of a vanquished person imploring mercy:

"Ha! you are wrong! As for me, I'm not like him."

"Of whom, pray, are you talking?"

"Of Frédéric."

"Ah! Monsieur Moreau is of little concern to me. I told you that!"

"Oh! forgive me! forgive me!" Then, drawing out his words, in a cutting tone:

"I even imagined that you were sufficiently interested in him personally to learn with pleasure—"

She became quite pale. The ex-law-clerk added:

"He is going to be married."

"He!"

"In a month at latest, to Mademoiselle Roque, the daughter of M. Dambreuse's agent. He has even gone down to Nogent for no other purpose but that."

She placed her hand over her heart, as if at the shock of a great blow; but immediately she rang the bell. Deslauriers did not wait to be ordered to leave. When she turned round he had disappeared.

Madame Arnoux was gasping a little with the strain of her emotions. She drew near the window to get a breath of air.

On the other side of the street, on the sidewalk, a packer in his shirt-sleeves was nailing down a trunk. Hackney-coaches passed. She closed the window-blinds and then sat down again. As the high houses in the vicinity intercepted the sun's rays, the light of day stole coldly into the apartment. Her children had gone out; there was nothing but stillness around her. It seemed as if she were utterly deserted.

"He is going to be married! Is it possible?"

And she was seized with a fit of nervous trembling.

"Why is this? Does it mean that I love him?"

Then all of a sudden:

"Why, yes; I love him—I love him!"

It seemed to her as if she were sinking into endless depths. The clock struck three. She listened to the vibrations of the sounds as they died away. And she remained on the edge of the armchair, with her eyes fixed and an unchanging smile on her face.

The same afternoon, at the same moment, Frédéric and Mademoiselle Louise were walking in the garden belonging to M. Roque at the end of the island.

Old Catherine was watching them, some distance away. They were walking side by side and Frédéric said:

"You remember when I brought you into the country?"

"How good you were to me!" she replied. "You helped me make sand-pies, fill my watering-pot, and rocked me in the swing!"

"All your dolls, who had the names of queens and marquises—what has become of them?"

"Really, I don't know!"

"And your pug Moricaud?"

"He drowned, poor darling!"

"And the *Don Quixote* in which we coloured the engravings together?"

"I have it still!"

He reminded her of the day of her first communion, and how pretty she had been at vespers, with her white veil and her large candle, whilst the girls were all taking their places in a row around the choir, and the bell was ringing.

These memories, no doubt, had little charm for Mademoiselle Roque. She had not a word to say; and, a minute later:

"Naughty fellow! never to have written to me, even once!"

Frédéric made the excuse of his numerous occupations.

"What, then, are you doing?"

He was embarrassed by the question; then he told her that he was studying politics.

"Ah!"

And without questioning him further:

"That keeps you busy; while as for me——!"

Then she spoke to him about the barrenness of her existence, as there was nobody she could go to see, and nothing to amuse her or distract her thoughts. She wished to go horseback riding.

"The vicar maintains that this is improper for a young lady! How stupid these proprieties are! Long ago they allowed me to do whatever I pleased; now, they won't let me do anything!"

"Your father, however, is fond of you!"

"Yes; but——"

She heaved a sigh, which meant: "That is not enough to make me happy."

Then there was silence. They heard only the noise made by their boots in the sand, together with the murmur of falling water; for the Seine, above Nogent, splits into two branches. That which turns the mills discharges in this location the superabundance of its waves in order to unite further down with the natural course of the stream; and a person coming from the bridge could see at the right, on the other bank of the river, a grassy slope on which a white house looks down. At the left, in the meadow, a row of poplar-trees extended, and the horizon opposite was bounded by a curve of the river. The water was smooth as glass. Large insects hovered over the noiseless water. Tufts of reeds and rushes bordered it unevenly; all kinds of plants which happened to spring up there bloomed out in buttercups, trailed yellow clusters, pointed spindly purple flowers, and randomly sprung green spiky leaves. In an inlet of the river white water-lilies displayed themselves; and a row of ancient willows, in which wolf-traps were hidden, formed, on that side of the island, the sole protection of the garden.

In the interior, on this side, four walls with a slate coping enclosed the kitchen-garden, in which the square patches, recently dug up, looked like brown plates. The bell-glasses over the melons shone in a row on their narrow bed. The artichokes, the kidney-beans, the spinach, the carrots and the tomatoes succeeded each other till one reached a background where asparagus grew in such a fashion that it resembled a little forest of feathers.

Under the Directory, this piece of land had been what is called "a folly." The trees had, since then, grown enormously. Clematis obstructed the hornbeams, the walks were covered with moss, brambles abounded on every side. The plaster of statues left crumbled fragments in the grass. Walking through the place one caught one's feet in iron-wire work. There now remained of the pavilion only two rooms on the ground floor, with some blue wall paper hanging in shreds. Before the façade extended an arbour in the Italian style, in which a vine-tree was supported on columns of brick by wooden trellis-work.

Soon they arrived at this spot; and, as the light fell through the irregular gaps on the green hedges, Frédéric, turning his head to speak to Louise, noticed the shadow of the leaves on her face.

She had in her red hair, stuck in her chignon, a needle, terminated by a glass ball in imitation of emerald, and, in spite of her mourning, she wore (so unsophisticated and bad was her taste) straw slippers trimmed with pink satin—a vulgar curiosity probably bought at some fair.

He remarked this, and ironically congratulated her.

"Don't be laughing at me!" she replied.

Then surveying him altogether, from his grey felt hat to his silk stockings:

"How stylish you are!"

After this, she asked him to recommend some books she could read. He gave her the names of several; and she said:

"Oh! how learned you are!"

While yet very small, she had been smitten with one of those childish passions which have, at the same time, the purity of a religion and the violence of a desire. He had been her comrade, her brother, her master, had diverted her mind, made her heart beat more quickly, and, without any desire for such a result, had poured out into the very depths of her being a latent and continuous intoxication. Then he had parted with her at the moment of a tragic crisis in her existence, when her mother had only just died, and these two separations had been mingled together. Absence had idealised him in her memory. He had come back with a sort of halo round his head; and she gave herself up ingenuously to the feelings of bliss she experienced at seeing him once more.

For the first time in his life Frédéric felt himself beloved; and this new pleasure, which did not transcend the ordinary run of agreeable sensations, made him swell with so much emotion that he spread out his two arms and flung back his head.

A large cloud passed across the sky.

"It is going towards Paris," said Louise. "You'd like to follow it—wouldn't you?"

"I! Why?"

"Who knows?"

And surveying him with a sharp look:

"Perhaps you have there" (she searched her mind for the appropriate phrase) "something to engage your affections."

"Oh! I have nothing to engage my affections there."

"Are you perfectly certain?"

"Why, yes, Mademoiselle, perfectly certain!"

In less than a year there had taken place in the young girl an extraordinary transformation, which astonished Frédéric. After a minute's silence he added:

"We ought to address each other less formally, as we used to do long ago—shall we?"

"No."

"Why?"

"Because——"

He persisted. She answered, with downcast face:

"I dare not!"

They had reached the end of the garden, the Livon beach. Frédéric, in a spirit of boyish fun, began to send pebbles skimming over the water. She bade him sit down. He obeyed;

then, looking at the waterfall:

" 'Tis like Niagara!" He began talking about distant countries and long voyages. The idea of making some herself appealed to her. She would not have been afraid either of storms or of lions.

Seated close beside each other, they collected in front of them handfuls of sand, then, while they were chatting, they let it slip through their fingers, and the hot wind, which rose from the plains, carried to them in waves the scent of lavender, together with the smell of tar from a boat behind the lock. The sun's rays fell on the waterfall. The greenish blocks of stone in the little wall over which the water flowed looked as if they were covered with an endless ribbon of silver gauze. Down below a long strip of foam gushed forth with a harmonious murmur. Then it bubbled up, forming whirlpools and a thousand opposing currents, which ended by intermingling in a single limpid stream of water.

Louise said in a musing tone that she envied the life of fishes:

"It must be so delightful to tumble about down there at your ease, and to feel yourself caressed on every side."

She shivered with sensuously enticing movements; but a voice exclaimed:

"Where are you?"

"Your maid is calling you," said Frédéric.

"All right! all right!" Louise did not move.

"She will be angry," he suggested.

"It is all the same to me! and besides——" Mademoiselle Roque gave him to understand by a gesture that the girl was entirely subject to her will.

She arose, however, and then complained of a headache. And, as they were passing in front of a large cart-shed containing some wood:

"Suppose we sat down there, *under shelter*?"

He pretended not to understand this dialectic expression, and even teased her about her accent. Gradually the corners of her mouth turned down, she bit her lips; she stepped aside in order to sulk.

Frédéric came over to her, swore he did not mean to annoy her, and that he was very fond of her.

"Is that true?" she exclaimed, looking at him with a smile which lighted up her entire face, sprinkled with patches of freckles.

He could not resist the sentiment of gallantry which was aroused in him by her fresh youthfulness, and he replied:

"Why should I tell you a lie? Have you any doubt about it, eh?" and, as he spoke, he put his arm around her waist.

A cry, soft as the cooing of a dove, leaped up from her throat. Her head fell back, she was going to faint, when he held her up. And his virtuous scruples were futile. At the sight of this maiden offering herself to him he was seized with fear. He assisted her to take a few steps slowly. He had ceased to address her in soothing words, and no longer caring to talk of anything save the most trifling subjects, he spoke to her about some of the principal figures in the society of Nogent.

Suddenly she pushed him away, and in a bitter tone:

"You would not have the courage to run away with me!"

He remained motionless, with a look of utter amazement in his face. She burst into sobs, and hiding her face in his chest:

"How can I live without you?"

He tried to calm her. She laid her two hands on his shoulders in order to get a better view of his face, and fixing her green eyes on his with an almost fierce tearfulness:

"Will you be my husband?"

"But," Frédéric began, casting about in his inner consciousness for a reply. "Of course, I ask for nothing better."

At that moment M. Roque's cap appeared behind a lilac-tree.

He brought his young friend on a trip through the district for a couple of days in order to show off his property; and when Frédéric returned, he found three letters awaiting him at his mother's house.

The first was a note from M. Dambreuse, containing an invitation to dinner for the previous Tuesday. What was the occasion of this politeness? So, then, they had forgiven his tirade.

The second was from Rosanette. She thanked him for having risked his life on her behalf. Frédéric did not at first understand what she meant; finally, after a considerable amount of digression, while appealing to his friendship, relying on his delicacy, as she put it, and going on her knees to him on account of the pressing necessity of the case, as she needed to eat, she asked him for a loan of five hundred francs. He at once made up his mind to supply her with the amount.

The third letter, which was from Deslauriers, spoke of the power of attorney, and was long and obscure. The lawyer had not yet taken any definite action. He urged his friend to stay where he was: " 'Tis useless for you to come back!" even laying curious stress on this point.

Frédéric got lost in conjectures of every sort; and he felt anxious to return to Paris. This assumption of a right to control his conduct inspired in him a feeling of revolt.

Moreover, he began to experience that nostalgia for the boulevards, and then, his mother was pressing him so much, M. Roque kept revolving about him so constantly, and Mademoiselle Louise was so much in love with him, that it was no longer possible for him to avoid declaring his intentions.

He wanted to think, and he would be better able to judge matters at a distance.

In order to assign a motive for his journey, Frédéric invented a story; and he left home, telling everyone, and believing it himself; that he would soon return.

CHAPTER VI

His return to Paris gave him no pleasure. It was an evening at the close of August. The boulevards seemed empty. The passers-by went past one by one with scowling faces. Here and there a cauldron of tar was smoking; several houses had their blinds entirely drawn. He made his way to his own residence in the city. He found the hangings covered with dust; and, while dining all alone, Frédéric was seized with a strange feeling of forlornness; then his thoughts reverted to Mademoiselle Roque. The idea of being married no longer appeared to him preposterous. They might travel; they might go to Italy, to the East. And he saw her standing on a hillock, or gazing at a landscape, or else leaning on his arm in a Florentine gallery while she looked at the paintings. What a pleasure it would be to him merely to watch this good little creature blossoming under the splendours of Art and Nature! When she had gotten free of the commonplace atmosphere in which she had lived, she would, in a little while, become a charming companion. M. Roque's wealth, moreover, tempted him. And yet he shrank from taking this step, regarding it as a weakness, a degradation.

But he was firmly resolved (whatever he might do) on changing his mode of life—that is to say, to lose his heart no more in fruitless passions; and he even hesitated about carrying out Louise's request. This was to buy for her at Jacques Arnoux's establishment two large-sized statues of many colours representing negroes, like those which were at the Prefecture at Troyes. She knew the manufacturer's number, and would not have any other. Frédéric was afraid that, if he went back to their house, he might once again fall victim to his old passion.

These reflections occupied his mind during the entire evening; and he was just about to go to bed when a woman came in.

" 'Tis I," said Mademoiselle Vatnaz, with a laugh. "I have come on behalf of Rosanette."

So, then, they were reconciled?

"Good heavens, yes! I am not ill-natured, as you are well aware. And besides, the poor girl—it would take too long to tell you all about it."

In short, the Maréchale wanted to see him; she was waiting for an answer, her letter having travelled from Paris to Nogent. Mademoiselle Vatnaz did not know what was in it.

Then Frédéric asked her how the Maréchale was.

He was informed that she was now *with* a very rich man, a Russian, Prince Tzernoukoff, who had seen her at the races in the Champ de Mars last summer.

"He has three carriages, a saddle-horse, livery servants, a groom dressed in the English fashion, a country-house, a box at the Italian opera, and a heap of other things. There you are, my dear friend!"

And Vatnaz, as if she had profited by this change of fortune, appeared livelier and happier. She took off her gloves and examined the furniture and the objects of interest in the room. She mentioned their exact prices like a second-hand dealer. He ought to have consulted her in order to get them cheaper. Then she congratulated him on his good taste:

"Oh! this is pretty, exceedingly charming! Nobody has ideas like you!"

The next moment, as her eyes fell on a door close to the bed in the alcove:

"That's the way you let your little ladies out, eh?"

And, in a familiar fashion, she laid her finger on his chin. He trembled at the contact of her long hands, at the same time thin and soft. Round her cuffs was an edging of lace, and on the body of her green dress lace embroidery, like a hussar's uniform. Her bonnet of black tulle, with a drooping brim, concealed her forehead a little. Her eyes shone underneath; the scent of patchouli escaped from her hair. The oil-lamp placed on a round table, shining up like the footlights of a theatre, made her jaw look prominent; and suddenly before this ugly woman with the little movements of a panther, Frédéric felt an intense longing, a lusty desire.

She said to him, in a buttery tone, while she drew forth from her purse three square slips of paper:

"Will you take these from me?"

They were three tickets for Delmar's benefit performance.

"What! for him?"

"Certainly."

Mademoiselle Vatnaz, without giving a further explanation, added that she adored him more than ever. If she were to be believed, the comedian was now definitely classed amongst "the leading celebrities of the age." And it was not such or such a personage that he represented, but the very genius of France, the People. He had "the humanitarian spirit; he understood the priesthood of Art." Frédéric, in order to put an end to this praise, gave her the money for the three seats.

"You need not say a word about this over there. How late it is, good heavens! I must leave you. Ah! I was forgetting the address—'tis the Rue Grange-Batelier, number 14."

And, at the door:

"Good-bye, beloved man!"

"Beloved by whom?" asked Frédéric. "What a strange woman!"

And he remembered that Dussardier had said to him one day, when talking about her:

"Oh, she's not much!" as if alluding to dishonorable stories.

Next morning he went to the Maréchale's abode. She lived in a new house, with awnings that projected into the street. At the head of each flight of stairs there was a mirror against the wall; before each window there was a flower-stand, and all over the steps extended a carpet of canvas; and when one got inside the door, the coolness of the staircase was refreshing.

It was a man-servant who came to open the door, a footman in a red waistcoat. On a bench in the entrance-hall a woman and two men, tradespeople, no doubt, were waiting as if in a minister's vestibule. At the left, the door of the dining-room, slightly ajar, afforded a glimpse of empty bottles on the sideboards, and napkins on the backs of chairs; and parallel with it ran a corridor in which gold-coloured posts supported an espalier of roses. In the courtyard below, two boys with bare arms were scrubbing a landau. Their voices rose to Frédéric's ears, mingled with the intermittent sounds made by a currycomb knocking against a stone.

The man-servant returned. "Madame will receive Monsieur," and he led Frédéric through a second room, and then into a large drawing-room hung with yellow brocade and rope-mouldings in the corners which were joined in the middle of the ceiling, and which seemed to be continued in the cable-shaped loops of the chandelier. No doubt there had been a party there the night before. Some cigar-ashes had been allowed to remain on the tables.

At last he found his way into a kind of boudoir with stained-glass windows, through which the sun shed a dim light. Trefoils of carved wood adorned the upper portions of the doors. Behind a balustrade, three purple mattresses formed a divan; and the stem of a platinum hookah lay on top of it. Instead of a mirror, there was on the mantelpiece a pyramid-shaped whatnot, displaying on its shelves an entire collection of curiosities, old silver trumpets, Bohemian horns, jewelled clasps, jade studs, enamels, grotesque figures in china, and a little Byzantine virgin with a vermilion cape; and all this was mingled in a golden twilight with the bluish shade of the carpet, the mother-of-pearl reflections of the foot-stools, and the tawny hue of the walls covered with brown leather. In the corners, on little pedestals, there were bronze vases containing clusters of flowers, whose scent made the atmosphere heavy.

Rosanette presented herself, attired in a pink satin jacket with white cashmere trousers, a necklace of piasters, and a red cap encircled with a branch of jasmine.

Frédéric started back in surprise, then said he had brought the thing she had been speaking about, and he handed her the bank-note. She gazed at him in astonishment; and, as he still kept the note in his hand, without knowing where to put it:

"Pray take it!"

She seized it; then, as she flung it on the divan:

"You are very kind."

She wanted it to meet the rent of a piece of ground at Bellevue, which she paid in this way every year. Her offhand manner wounded Frédéric's sensibility. However, so much the better! this would avenge the past.

"Sit down," said she. "There—closer." And in a grave tone: "In the first place, I have to thank you, my dear friend, for having risked your life."

"Oh! that's nothing!"

"What! Why, 'tis a very noble act!"—and the Maréchale exhibited an embarrassing sense of gratitude; for it must have been impressed upon her mind that the duel was entirely on account of Arnoux, as the latter, who believed it himself, was not likely to have resisted the temptation of telling her so.

"She is laughing at me, perhaps," thought Frédéric.

He had nothing more to do, and, pleading that he had an appointment, he rose.

"Oh! no, stay!"

He resumed his seat, and presently complimented her on her costume.

She replied, with an air of dejection:

" 'Tis the Prince who likes me to dress in this fashion! And one must smoke such contraptions as that, too!" Rosanette added, pointing towards the hookah. "Suppose we try it? Have you any objection?"

She procured a light, and, finding it hard to set fire to the tobacco, she began to stamp impatiently with her foot. Then a feeling of languor took possession of her; and she remained motionless on the divan, with a cushion under her arm and her body twisted a little to one side, one knee bent and the other leg straight out.

The long serpent of red morocco, which formed rings on the floor, coiled itself around her arm. She rested the amber mouthpiece on her lips, and gazed at Frédéric while she blinked her eyes in the midst of the cloud of smoke that enveloped her. A gurgling sound came from her throat as she inhaled the fumes, and from time to time she murmured:

"The poor darling! the poor pet!"

He tried to find something of an agreeable nature to talk about. The thought of Vatnaz recurred to his memory.

He remarked that she appeared to him very lady-like.

"Yes, upon my word," replied the Maréchale. "She is very lucky to have me, I'll tell you!"—without adding another word, so much reserve was there in their conversation.

Each of them felt a sense of constraint, something that formed a barrier separating them. In fact, Rosanette's vanity had been flattered by the duel, of which she believed herself to be the cause.

Then, she was very much astonished that he did not hasten to take advantage of his achievement; and, in order to compel him to come back, she had invented this story that she wanted five hundred francs. How was it that Frédéric did not ask for a little love from her in return? This was a piece of refinement that filled her with amazement, and, with a gush of emotion, she said to him:

"Will you come with us to the sea-side?"

"What does 'us' mean?"

"Myself and my friend. I'll make you pass for a cousin of mine, as in the old comedies."

"A thousand thanks!"

"Well, then, you will arrange lodgings near ours." The idea of hiding himself from a rich man humiliated him.

"No! that is impossible."

"Suit yourself!"

Rosanette turned away with tears in her eyes. Frédéric noticed this, and in order to show that he cared for her, he said that he was delighted to see her at last in a comfortable position.

She shrugged her shoulders. What, then, was troubling her? Was it, perchance, that she was not loved.

"Oh! as for me, I always have people to love me!"

She added:

"It remains to be seen in what way."

Complaining that she was "suffocating with the heat," the Maréchale unfastened her vest; and, without anything else underneath except her silk chemise, she leaned her head on his shoulder so as to awaken his tenderness.

A man of less introspective egoism would not have bestowed a thought at such a moment on the possibility of the Vicomte, M. de Comaing, or anyone else appearing on the scene. But Frédéric had been too many times the dupe of these very glances to compromise himself by a fresh humiliation.

She wished to know all about his relationships and his amusements. She even enquired about his financial affairs, and offered to lend him money if he wanted it. Frédéric, unable to stand it any longer, took up his hat.

"I'm off, my pet! I hope you'll enjoy yourself thoroughly down there. *Au revoir!*"

She opened her eyes wide; then, in a dry tone:

"Au revoir!"

He made his way out through the yellow drawing-room, and through the second room. There was on the table, between a vase full of visiting-cards and an inkstand, a chased silver chest. It was Madame Arnoux's. Then he experienced a feeling of tenderness, and, at the same time, as it were, the scandal of a sacrilege. He felt a longing to raise his hands towards it, and to open it. He was afraid of being seen, and went away.

Frédéric was virtuous. He did not go back to the Arnoux's house. He sent his man-servant to buy the two negroes, having given him all the necessary directions; and the case containing them set forth the same evening for Nogent. Next morning, as he was on his way to Deslauriers' lodgings, at the turn where the Rue Vivienne opened out on the boulevard, he met Madame Arnoux face to face.

The first movement of each of them was to draw back; then the same smile came to the lips of both, and they advanced to meet each other. For a minute, neither of them uttered a single word.

The sunlight fell round her, and her oval face, her long eyelashes, her black lace shawl, which showed the outline of her shoulders, her gown of shot silk, the bouquet of violets at the corner of her bonnet; all seemed to him to possess extraordinary magnificence. An infinite softness poured itself out of her beautiful eyes; and in a faltering voice, uttering at random the first words that came to his lips:

"How is Arnoux?"

"Well, thank you!"

"And your children?"

"They are very well!"

"Ah! ah! What fine weather we are having, are we not?"

"Splendid, indeed!"

"You're going out shopping?"

"Yes."

And, with a slow inclination of the head:

"Good-bye!"

She put out her hand, without having spoken one affectionate word, and did not even invite him to dinner at her house. No matter! He would not have given up this chance meeting for the most delightful of adventures; and he pondered over its sweetness as he proceeded on his way.

Deslauriers, surprised at seeing him, concealed his annoyance; for he cherished still through obstinacy some hope with regard to Madame Arnoux; and he had written to Frédéric to prolong his stay in the country in order to be free in his manœuvres.

He informed Frédéric, however, that he had presented himself at her house in order to ascertain if their contract stipulated for a joint estate between husband and wife: in that case, proceedings might be taken against the wife; "and she put on a queer face when I told her about your marriage."

"Now, then! What an invention!"

"It was necessary in order to show that you wanted your own capital! A person who was indifferent would not have been attacked with the fainting fit that she had."

"Really?" exclaimed Frédéric.

"Ha! my fine fellow, you are betraying yourself! Come! be honest!"

A feeling of nervous weakness stole over Madame Arnoux's lover.

"Why, no! I assure you! upon my word of honour!"

These feeble denials ended by convincing Deslauriers. He congratulated his friend, and asked him for some details. Frédéric gave him none, and even resisted a secret yearning to concoct a few. As for the mortgage, he told the other to do nothing about it, but to wait. Deslauriers thought he was wrong on this point, and was cutting in his remonstrances.

He was, besides, more gloomy, malignant, and irascible than ever. In a year, if fortune did not change, he would embark for America or blow out his brains. Indeed, he appeared to be in such a rage against everything, and so uncompromising in his radicalism, that Frédéric could not keep from saying to him:

"Here you are going on in the same way as Sénécal!"

Deslauriers, at this remark, informed him that that individual to whom he alluded had been discharged from Sainte-Pelagie,* the magisterial investigation having failed to supply sufficient evidence, no doubt, to justify his being sent for trial.

---

*Prison in the center of Paris.

Dussardier was so much overjoyed at the release of Sénécal, that he wanted to invite his friends to come and take punch with him, and begged of Frédéric to be one of the party, giving the latter, at the same time, to understand that he would be found in the company of Hussonnet, who had proved himself a very good friend to Sénécal.

In fact, the *Flambard* had just become associated with a business establishment whose prospectus contained the following references: "Vineyard Agency. Office of Publicity. Debt Recovery and Intelligence Office, etc." But the Bohemian was afraid that his connection with trade might be prejudicial to his literary reputation, and he had accordingly taken the mathematician to keep the accounts. Although the situation was a poor one, Sénécal would but for it have died of starvation. Not wishing to mortify the worthy shopman, Frédéric accepted his invitation.

Dussardier, three days beforehand, had himself waxed the red floor of his garret, beaten the armchair, and knocked off the dust from the mantelpiece, on which stood an alabaster clock in a glass case between a stalactite and a cocoanut. As his two chandeliers and his chamber candlestick were not sufficient, he had borrowed two more candlesticks from the concierge; and these five lights shone on the top of the chest of drawers, which was covered with three napkins to provide a decent setting for serving some macaroons, biscuits, a fancy cake, and a dozen bottles of beer. At the opposite side, close to the wall, which was covered with yellow wall paper, there was a little mahogany bookcase containing the *Fables of Lachambeaudie*, the *Mysteries of Paris*, and Norvins' *Napoléon*—and, in the middle of the alcove, the face of Béranger was smiling in a rosewood frame.

The guests (in addition to Deslauriers and Sénécal) were an apothecary who had just qualified, but who had not enough capital to start a business for himself, a young man of his own firm, a wine-merchant, an architect, and a gentleman employed in an insurance office. Regimbart had not been able to come. Regret was expressed at his absence.

They welcomed Frédéric very cordially, as they all knew through Dussardier what he had said at M. Dambreuse's house. Sénécal simply put out his hand in a dignified manner.

He remained standing near the mantelpiece. The others seated, with their pipes in their mouths, listened to him, speak about universal suffrage, from which he predicted as a result the triumph of Democracy and the practical application of the principles of the Gospel. However, the hour was at hand. The banquets of the reform party were becoming more numerous in the provinces.* Piedmont, Naples, Tuscany——

" 'Tis true," said Deslauriers, interrupting him abruptly. "This cannot last much longer!"

And he began to draw a picture of the situation. We had sacrificed Holland to obtain from England the recognition of Louis Philippe; and this precious English alliance was lost, because of the Spanish marriages.[30] In Switzerland, M. Guizot, towed along by the Austrian, supported the treaties of 1815. Prussia, with her Zollverein, was going to spell trouble for us. The Eastern question was still pending.

"The fact that the Grand Duke Constantine sends presents to M. d'Aumale is no reason for placing confidence in Russia. As for home affairs, never have so many blunders, such stupidity, been witnessed. The Government no longer even keeps it majority together. Everywhere, indeed according to the well-known expression, it is nothing! nothing! nothing! And in the face of such public scandals," continued the lawyer, with his hands on his hips, "they declare themselves satisfied!"

The allusion to a notorious vote elicited applause. Dussardier uncorked a bottle of beer; the froth splashed on the curtains. He did not mind it. He filled the pipes, cut the cake, offered each of them a slice of it, and several times went downstairs to see whether the punch was coming up; and ere long they worked themselves up into a state of excitement, as they all felt equally exasperated against Power. Their rage was of a violent character for no other reason save that they hated injustice, and they mixed up with legitimate grievances the most idiotic complaints.

The apothecary groaned over the pitiful state of our fleet. The insurance agent could not tolerate Marshal Soult's two sentinels.

---

*Since freedom of political gathering was restricted, the opposition launched a "campaign of banquets" to propagate its ideas.

Deslauriers denounced the Jesuits, who had just installed themselves publicly at Lille.* Sénécal execrated M. Cousin much more; for eclecticism, by teaching that truth can be deduced from reason, encouraged selfishness and destroyed solidarity. The wine-merchant, knowing very little about these matters, remarked in a very loud tone that he had forgotten many scandals:

"The royal carriage on the Northern railway line must have cost eighty thousand francs. Who'll pay the amount?"

"Aye, who'll pay the amount?" repeated the clerk, as angrily as if this amount had been drawn out of his own pocket.

Then followed recriminations against the crooks of the stock exchange and the corruption of officials. According to Sénécal they ought to go higher up, and lay the blame, first of all, on the princes who had revived the morals of the Regency period.

"Have you not lately seen the Duc de Montpensier's friends coming back from Vincennes, no doubt in a state of intoxication, and disturbing the workmen of the Faubourg Saint-Antoine with their songs?"

"There was even a cry of 'Down with the thieves!' " said the apothecary. "I was there, and I joined in the cry!"

"So much the better! The people are at last waking up since the Teste-Cubières case."

"For my part, that case caused me some pain," said Dussardier, "because it brought dishonour on an old soldier!"

"Do you know," Sénécal went on, "what they have discovered at the Duchesse de Praslin's house——?"

But here the door was sent flying open with a kick. Hussonnet entered.

"Hail, my lords," said he, as he seated himself on the bed.

No allusion was made to his article, which he was sorry, however, for having written, as the Maréchale had sharply reprimanded him on account of it.

---

*The Jesuits had been first banished from France in 1764. Suppressed by Pope Clement XIV in 1773, they were reestablished by Pope Pius VII in 1814 and banished again from France in 1845. Lille is a city in northern France.

He had just seen at the Théâtre de Dumas the *Chevalier de Maison-Rouge*,* and declared that it seemed to him a stupid play.

Such a criticism surprised the democrats, as this drama, by its tendency, or rather by its scenery, appealed to their most passionate beliefs. They protested. Sénécal, in order to bring this discussion to a close, asked whether the play served the cause of Democracy.

"Yes, perhaps; but it is written in a style——"

"Well, then, 'tis a good play. What is style? 'Tis the idea!"

And, without allowing Frédéric to say a word:

"Now, I was pointing out that in the Praslin case——"

Hussonnet interrupted him:

"Ha! that's another worn-out story! I'm sick of hearing it!"

"You aren't the only one," returned Deslauriers.

"It has only gotten five papers suppressed. Listen while I read this paragraph."

And drawing his note-book out of his pocket, he read:

" 'We have, since the establishment of the best of republics, been subjected to twelve hundred and twenty-nine press prosecutions, from which the results to the writers have been imprisonment extending over a period of three thousand one hundred and forty-one years, and the small sum of seven million one hundred and ten thousand five hundred francs by way of fine.' That's charming, eh?"

They all sneered bitterly.

Frédéric, incensed against the others, broke in:

"*The Democratie Pacifique* has had proceedings taken against it on account of its serial, a novel entitled *The Woman's Share*."

"Come now! that's good," said Hussonnet. "Suppose they prevented us from having our share of the women!"

"But what is left that's not prohibited?" exclaimed Deslauriers. "To smoke in the Luxembourg is prohibited; to sing the Hymn to Pius IX is prohibited!"†

"And the printers' banquet has been banned," a soft voice said.

---

*Drama drawn from an Alexandre Dumas novel of the same name (1847) about the French Revolution.

†At the beginning of his papacy (1846–1878), Pius IX appeared to be a liberal.

It was that of an architect, who had sat concealed in the shade of the alcove, and who had remained silent up to that moment. He added that, the week before, a man named Rouget had been convicted of insulting the king.

"That red mullet is fried," said Hussonnet.*

This joke appeared so improper to Sénécal, that he reproached Hussonnet for defending the Juggler of the Hôtel de Ville, the friend of the traitor Dumouriez.[31]

"I? quite the contrary!"

He considered Louis Philippe commonplace, a National Guard type like a grocer in a cotton night-cap! And laying his hand on his heart, the Bohemian uttered the rhetorical phrases:

"It is always with a renewed pleasure. . . . Polish nationality will not perish. . . . Our great enterprises will go on. . . . Give me some money for my little family. . . ."

They all laughed loudly, declaring that he was a delightful fellow, full of wit. Their delight was doubled at the sight of the bowl of punch which was brought in by the keeper of a café.

The flames of the alcohol and those of the wax-candles soon heated the apartment, and the light from the garret, passing across the courtyard, illuminated the side of an opposite roof with the flue of a chimney, whose black outlines could be traced through the darkness of night. They talked in very loud voices all at the same time. They had taken off their coats; they bumped into the furniture; they clinked glasses.

Hussonnet exclaimed:

"Send up some great ladies, in order that this may be more Tour de Nesles,† have more local color, and be more Rembrandtesque!"

And the apothecary, who kept stirring the punch, began bellowing:

"I've two big oxen in my stable,
Two big white oxen——"

Sénécal put his hand over the apothecary's mouth; he did not like rowdiness; and the tenants pressed their faces against the

---

***Rouget* also means red mullet.

†*La Tour de Nesle* (1832; *The Tower of Nesle*) is a historical drama by Alexandre Dumas full of orgies and crimes.

windows, surprised at the unusual uproar that was taking place in Dussardier's room.

The good fellow was happy, and said that this reminded him of their little parties on the Quai Napoléon in days gone by; however, they missed many who used to be present at these reunions, "Pellerin, for instance."

"We can do without him," observed Frédéric. And Deslauriers enquired about Martinon.

"What has become of that interesting gentleman?"

Frédéric, immediately giving vent to the ill-will which he bore to Martinon, attacked his mental capacity, his character, his false elegance, his entire personality. He was a perfect specimen of an upstart peasant! The new aristocracy, the bourgeoisie, was not as good as the old—the nobility. He maintained this, and the democrats expressed their approval, as if he were a member of the one class, and they were in the habit of rubbing elbows with the other. They were charmed by him. The apothecary compared him to M. d'Alton Shée, who, though a peer of France, defended the cause of the people.

The time had come for taking their departure. They all separated with warm handshakes. Dussardier, in a spirit of affection, saw Frédéric and Deslauriers home. As soon as they were in the street, the lawyer assumed a thoughtful air, and, after a moment's silence:

"So you have a grudge, against Pellerin?"

Frédéric did not hide his rancour.

The painter, in the meantime, had withdrawn the notorious picture from the display. A person should not allow a falling out over insignificant matters. What was the use of making an enemy for himself?

"He has given in to a surge of temper, excusable in a man who hasn't a sou. You, of course, can't understand that!"

And, when Deslauriers had gone up to his own rooms, the clerk stayed with Frédéric. He even urged his friend to buy the portrait. In fact, Pellerin, abandoning the hope of being able to intimidate him, had gotten them to use their influence to get him to take the thing.

Deslauriers spoke about it again, and pressed him on the point, urging that the artist's claims were reasonable.

"I am sure that for a sum of, perhaps, five hundred francs——"

"Oh, give it to him! Wait! here it is!" said Frédéric.

The picture was brought the same evening. It appeared to him even more atrocious than when he had first seen it. The half-tints and the shades were darkened under the excessive retouchings, and they seemed obscured when brought into relation with the lights, which, having remained very brilliant here and there, destroyed the harmony of the entire painting.

Frédéric avenged himself for having had to pay for it by bitterly disparaging it. Deslauriers believed in Frédéric's statement on the point, and expressed approval of his conduct, for he had always been ambitious of forming a group of which he would be the leader. Certain men take delight in making their friends do things which are disagreeable to them.

Meanwhile, Frédéric did not renew his visits to the Dambreuses. He lacked the capital for the investment. He would have to enter into endless explanations on the subject; he hesitated about making up his mind. Perhaps he was in the right. Nothing was certain now, the coal-mining business any more than other things. He would have to give up society of that sort. The end of the matter was that Deslauriers succeeded in turning him against the enterprise.

Hatred was making him virtuous, and again he preferred Frédéric in a position of mediocrity. In this way he remained his friend's equal and in more intimate relationship with him.

Mademoiselle Roque's request had been very badly executed. Her father wrote to him, supplying him with the most precise directions, and concluded his letter with this witticism: "At the risk of making you work like a black slave."

Frédéric could not do otherwise than call upon the Arnouxs, once more. He went to the warehouse, where he found nobody. The firm being on shaky ground, the clerks imitated their master's slackness.

He brushed against the shelves laden with earthenware, which filled up the entire space in the centre of the establishment; then, when he reached the lower end, facing the counter, he walked with a more noisy tread in order to make himself heard.

The door curtains parted, and Madame Arnoux appeared.

"What! you here! you!"

"Yes," she faltered, with some embarrassment. "I was looking for——"

He saw her handkerchief near the desk, and guessed that she had come down to her husband's warehouse to have an account given to her as to the business, to clear up some matter that caused her anxiety.

"But perhaps there is something you want?" said she.

"Nothing important, madame."

"These shop-assistants are intolerable! they are never here."

They ought not to be blamed. On the contrary, he was delighted with the circumstances.

She gazed at him in an ironical fashion.

"Well, and this marriage?"

"What marriage?"

"Your own!"

"Mine? I'll never marry as long as I live!"

She made a gesture as if to contradict his words.

"Though, indeed, such things must be, after all? We take refuge in the commonplace, despairing of ever realising the beautiful existence of which we have dreamed."

"All your dreams, however, are not so—innocent!"

"What do you mean?"

"When you drive to races with women!"

He cursed the Maréchale. Then he remembered something.

"But it was you who begged me to see her at one time in the interest of Arnoux."

She replied with a shake of her head:

"And you take advantage of it to amuse yourself?"

"Good God! let us forget all these foolish things!"

" 'Tis right, since you are going to be married."

And she stifled a sigh, while she bit her lips.

Then he exclaimed:

"But I tell you again I am not! Can you believe that I, with my intellectual requirements, my habits, am going to bury myself in the provinces in order to play cards, supervise builders, and walk about in clogs? What reason, pray, could I have for taking such a step? You've been told that she was rich, haven't you? Ah! what do I care about money? Could I, after yearning long for that which is most lovely, tender, enchanting, a sort of Paradise under a human form, and having found this sweet ideal at last, when this vision hides every other from my view——"

And taking her head between his two hands, he began to kiss her on the eyelids, repeating:

"No! no! no! never will I marry! never! never!"

She submitted to these caresses, her mingled amazement and delight leaving her powerless.

The door of the storeroom above the staircase fell back, and she gave a start but remained with her hand outstretched, as if to bid him keep silent. Steps drew near. Then some one said from behind the door:

"Is Madame there?"

"Come in!"

Madame Arnoux had her elbow on the counter, and was calmly rolling a pen between her fingers when the book-keeper threw aside the door curtain.

Frédéric started up, as if on the point of leaving.

"My repects, Madame. The service will be ready—will it not? May I count on it?"

She made no reply. But by thus silently becoming his accomplice in the deception, she made his face flush with the crimson glow of adultery.

On the following day he paid her another visit. She received him; and, in order to follow up the advantage he had gained, Frédéric immediately, without any preamble, attempted to offer some justification for the accidental meeting in the Champ de Mars. It was the merest chance that led to his being in that woman's company. While admitting that she was pretty—which really was not the case—how could she for even a moment absorb his thoughts, seeing that he loved another woman?

"You know it well—I told you it was so!"

Madame Arnoux bowed her head.

"I am sorry you said such a thing."

"Why?"

"The most ordinary proprieties now demand that I should see you no more!"

He protested that his love was innocent. The past ought to be a guaranty as to his future conduct. He had of his own accord made it a point of honour with himself not to disturb her existence, not to deafen her with his pleadings.

"But yesterday my heart overflowed."

"We ought not to let our thoughts dwell on that moment, my friend!"

And yet, where would be the harm in two wretched beings mingling their griefs?

"For, indeed, you are not happy any more than I am! Oh! I know you. You have no one who responds to your craving for affection, for devotion. I will do anything you wish! I will not offend you! I swear to you that I will not!"

And he let himself fall on his knees, in spite of himself, giving way beneath the weight of the feelings that oppressed his heart.

"Get up!" she said; "get up, I insist!"

And she declared in an imperious tone that if he did not comply with her wish, she would never see him again.

"Ha! I defy you to do it!" returned Frédéric. "What is there for me to do in the world? Other men strive for riches, celebrity, power! But I have no profession; you are my exclusive occupation, my whole wealth, the object, the centre of my existence and of my thoughts. I can no more live without you than without the air of heaven! Do you not feel the aspiration of my soul ascending towards yours, and that they must intermingle, and that I am dying on your account?"

Madame Arnoux began to tremble in every limb.

"Oh! leave me, I beg of you"

The look of utter confusion in her face made him pause. Then he advanced a step. But she drew back, with her two hands clasped.

"Leave me in the name of Heaven, for mercy's sake!"

And Frédéric loved her so much that he went away.

Soon afterwards, he was filled with rage against himself, declared in his own mind that he was an idiot, and, after the lapse of twenty-four hours, returned.

Madame was not there. He remained at the head of the stairs, numb with anger and indignation. Arnoux appeared, and informed Frédéric that his wife had, that very morning, gone out to take up her residence at a little country-house of which he had become tenant at Auteuil,* as he had given up possession of the house at Saint-Cloud.

"This is another of her whims. No matter, as long as she is settled at last; and myself, too, for that matter, so much the better. Let us dine together this evening, shall we?"

Frédéric pleaded as an excuse some urgent business; then he hurried off to Auteuil.

Madame Arnoux allowed an exclamation of joy to escape her lips. Then all his bitterness vanished.

He did not say one word about his love. In order to inspire her with confidence in him, he even exaggerated his reserve; and on his asking whether he might call again, she replied: "Why, of course!" putting out her hand, which she withdrew the next moment.

From that time forth, Frédéric increased his visits. He promised extra fares to the cabman who drove him. But often he grew impatient at the slow pace of the horse, and, getting out of the cab, he would make a dash after an omnibus, and climb to the top of it out of breath. Then with what disdain he surveyed the faces of those around him, who were not going to see her!

He could distinguish her house at a distance with an enormous honeysuckle covering, the planks of the roof on one side. It was a kind of Swiss châlet, painted red, with a balcony outside. In the garden there were three old chestnut-trees, and on a mound in the centre was a parasol made of thatch, held up by the trunk of a tree. Under the slate lining the walls, a big vine had come loose and hung down like a rotten cable. The gate-bell, which was rather hard to pull, was slow in ringing, and a long time always elapsed before it was answered. On each occasion he experienced a pang of suspense, an indefinable fear.

Then his ears would be greeted with the pattering of the servant-maid's slippers over the gravel, or else Madame Arnoux herself would make her appearance. One day he came up behind her just as she was stooping down in the act of gathering violets.

Her daughter's temper had made it necessary to send the girl to a convent. Her little son was at school every afternoon. Arnoux was

---

*Village close to Paris, today part of the capital.

now in the habit of taking prolonged lunches at the Palais-Royal with Regimbart and their friend Compain. Nothing could disturb them.

It was clearly understood between Frédéric and her that they should not belong to each other. By this convention they were preserved from danger, and they found it easier to pour out their hearts to each other.

She told him all about her early life at Chartres, which she spent with her mother, her piety at the age of twelve, then her passion for music, when she used to sing till nightfall in her little room, from which the ramparts could be seen.

He related to her how melancholy broodings had haunted him at college, and how a woman's face shone brightly in his poetic imagination, so that, when he first laid eyes upon her, he felt that her features were quite familiar to him.

These conversations, as a rule, covered only the years during which they had been acquainted with each other. He reminisced about insignificant details—the colour of her dress during a certain period, a woman whom they had met on a certain day, what she had said on another occasion; and she replied, quite astonished:

"Yes, I remember!"

Their tastes, their judgments, were the same. Often one of them, when listening to the other, exclaimed:

"So do I!"

And the other replied:

"Me, too!"

Then there were endless complaints about Providence:

"Why was it not the will of Heaven? If we had only met——!"

"Ah! if I had been younger!" she sighed.

"No, but if I had been a little older."

And they pictured a life entirely devoted to love, sufficiently rich to fill up the most vast solitude, surpassing all other joys, defying all sorrows; in which the hours would glide away in a continual outpouring of their own emotions, and which would be as bright and glorious as the shimmering splendour of the stars.

They were nearly always out of doors standing at the top of the stairs. The tops of trees yellowed by the autumn stood before them at unequal heights up to the edge of the pale sky; or else they walked on to the end of the avenue into a summer-house whose only furniture was a couch of grey canvas. Black specks marked the mirror; the walls gave off a mouldy smell; and they remained there chatting freely about all sorts of topics—anything that happened to arise—in a spirit of delight. Sometimes the rays of the sun, passing through the Venetian blind, extended from the ceiling down to the flagstones like the strings of a lyre. Particles of dust whirled amid these luminous bars. She amused herself by dividing them with her hand. Frédéric gently took it in his own; and he gazed on the twinings of her veins, the grain of her skin, and the form of her fingers. Each of those fingers of hers was for him more than a thing—almost a person.

She gave him her gloves, and, the week after, her handkerchief. She called him "Frédéric;" he called her "Marie," adoring this name, which, as he said, was expressly made to be uttered with a sigh of ecstasy, and which seemed to contain clouds of incense and bouquets of roses.

They soon came to an understanding as to the days on which he would call to see her; and, leaving the house as if by mere chance, she walked along the road to meet him.

She made no effort whatever to excite his love, lost in that listlessness which is characteristic of intense happiness. During the whole season she wore a brown silk dressing-gown with velvet borders of the same colour, a large garment, which united the softness of her attitude and her serious expression. Besides, she had just reached the autumnal period of womanhood, in which reflection is combined with tenderness, in which the beginning of maturity colours the face with a more intense flame, when strength of feeling mingles with experience of life, and when, having completely expanded, the entire being overflows with a richness of harmony and beauty. Never had she possessed more sweetness, more leniency. Secure in the thought that she would not err, she abandoned herself to a sentiment which seemed to her won by her sorrows. And, moreover, it was so innocent and fresh! What an abyss lay between the coarseness of Arnoux and the adoration of Frédéric!

He trembled at the thought that by an imprudent word he might lose all that he had gained, saying to himself that an opportunity might be found again, but that a foolish step could never be repaired.

He wished that she should give herself to him rather than that he should take her. The assurance of being loved by her delighted him like a foretaste of possession, and then the charm of her person stirred his heart more than his senses. It was an indefinable feeling of bliss, a sort of intoxication that made him lose sight of the possibility of having his happiness completed. Apart from her, he was consumed with longing.

Ere long the conversations were interrupted by long spells of silence. Sometimes a sort of sexual shame made them blush in each other's presence. All the precautions they took to hide their love only unveiled it; the stronger it grew, the more constrained they became in manner. Living such a lie only served to intensify their sensibility. They experienced a sensation of delight at the odour of moist leaves; they could not endure the east wind; they got irritated without any apparent cause, and had melancholy forebodings. The sound of a footstep, the creaking of a panel, filled them with as much terror as if they had been guilty. They felt as if they were being pushed towards the edge of a chasm. They were surrounded by a tempestuous atmosphere; and when complaints escaped Frédéric's lips, she made accusations against herself.

"Yes, I am doing wrong. I am acting as if I were a coquette! Don't come any more!"

Then he would repeat the same oaths, to which on each occasion she listened with renewed pleasure.

His return to Paris, and the fuss occasioned by New Year's Day, interrupted their meetings to some extent. When he returned, he had an air of greater self-confidence. Every moment she went out of the room to give orders, and in spite of his entreaties she received every visitor that called during the evening.

After this, they engaged in conversations about Léotade, M. Guizot, the Pope, the insurrection at Palermo, and the banquet of the Twelfth Arrondissement, which had caused some anxiety. Frédéric eased his mind by railing against Power, for he longed, like Deslauriers, to turn the whole world upside down, so soured had he now become. Madame Arnoux, for her part, had become sad.

Her husband, indulging in extravagances, was keeping one of the girls in his pottery works, the one who was known as "the girl from Bordeaux." Madame Arnoux was herself informed about it by

Frédéric. He wanted to make use of it as an argument, "inasmuch as she was the victim of deception."

"Oh! I'm not much concerned about it," she said.

This admission on her part seemed to him to strengthen the intimacy between them. Did Arnoux suspect anything?

"No! not now!"

She told him that, one evening, he had left them talking together, and had afterwards come back again and listened behind the door, and as they both were chatting at the time of matters that were of no consequence, he had lived since then in a state of complete security.

"With good reason, too—is that not so?" said Frédéric bitterly.

"Yes, no doubt!"

It would have been better for her not to have ventured such an answer.

One day she was not at home at the hour when he usually called. To him there seemed to be a sort of betrayal in this.

Then, he was upset at seeing the flowers that he brought her always placed in a glass of water.

"Where, then, would you like me to put them?"

"Oh! not there! Though, they are not as cold there as they would be near your heart!"

Not long afterwards he reproached her for having been at the Italian opera the night before without having given him a previous intimation of her intention to go there. Others had seen, admired, fallen in love with her, perhaps; Frédéric clung to his suspicions merely to pick a fight with her, to torment her; for he was beginning to hate her, and the very least he might expect was that she should share in his sufferings!

One afternoon, towards the middle of February, he surprised her in a state of great upset. Eugène had been complaining about his sore throat. The doctor had told her, however, that it was a minor ailment—a bad cold, an attack of influenza. Frédéric was astonished at the child's look of delirium. Nevertheless, he reassured the mother, and brought forward the cases of several children of the same age who had been attacked with similar ailments, and had been speedily cured.

"Really?"

"Why, yes, of course!"

"Oh! how good you are!"

And she took his hand. He clasped hers tightly in his.

"Oh! let me go!"

"What does it matter, when you are offering it for the sake of being consoled? You place every confidence in me for such things, but you distrust me when I talk to you about my love!"

"I don't doubt you on that point, my poor friend!"

"Why this distrust, as if I were a scoundrel capable of taking advantage——"

"Oh! no!——"

"If I only had proof!——"

"What proof?"

"The proof you would give anybody—what you once granted me."

And he reminded her how, on one occasion, they had gone out together, on a winter's evening, when it was foggy. This seemed now a long time ago. What, then, was to prevent her from being seen on his arm before the whole world without any fear on her part, and without any ulterior motive on his, not having anyone around them to trouble them?

"So be it!" she said, with a promptness of decision that at first astonished Frédéric.

But he replied, in a lively fashion:

"Would you like me to wait at the corner of the Rue Tronchet and the Rue de la Ferme?"

"Good heavens, my friend!" faltered Madame Arnoux.

Without giving her time to reflect, he added:

"Next Tuesday, I suppose?"

"Tuesday?"

"Yes, between two and three o'clock."

"I will be there!"

And she turned her face away in shame. Frédéric placed his lips on the nape of her neck.

"Oh! This is not right," she said. "You will face me to repent."

He turned away, dreading the fickleness which is customary with women. Then, on the threshold, he murmured softly, as if it were a thing that was thoroughly understood:

"See you on Tuesday!"

She lowered her beautiful eyes in a cautious and resigned fashion.

Frédéric had a plan arranged in his mind.

He hoped that, because of the rain or the sun, he might get her to stop under some doorway, and that, once there, she would go into the house. The difficulty was to find one that would suit.

He made a search, and about the middle of the Rue Tronchet he read, at a distance on a signboard, "Furnished apartments."

The man at the reception, understanding his intention, showed him immediately above the ground-floor a bedroom and a dressing room with two entrances. Frédéric took it for a month, and paid in advance. Then he went into three shops to buy the rarest of perfumes. He got a piece of imitation lace, which was to replace the horrible red cotton coverlets; he selected a pair of blue satin slippers, only the fear of appearing coarse limited the amount of his purchases. He came back with them; and with more devotion than those who are erecting processional altars, he rearranged the furniture, hung the curtains himself, put heather in the fireplace, and covered the chest of drawers with violets. He would have liked to pave the entire apartment with gold. "To-morrow is the time," said he to himself. "Yes, to-morrow! I am not dreaming!" and he felt his heart throbbing violently under the delirious excitement begotten by his anticipations. Then, when everything was ready, he carried off the key in his pocket, as if the happiness which slept there might have flown away along with it.

A letter from his mother was awaiting him when he reached home:

"Why such a long absence? Your conduct is beginning to look ridiculous. I understand your hesitating more or less at first with regard to this union. However, think well upon it."

And she put the matter before him with the utmost clarity: an income of forty-five thousand francs. However, "people were talking about it;" and M. Roque was waiting for a definite answer. As for the young girl, her position was truly most embarrassing.

"She is deeply in love with you."

Frédéric threw aside the letter even before he had finished reading it, and opened another note which came from Deslauriers.

"Dear Old Boy,—The *pear* is ripe.* In accordance with your promise, we are counting on you. We meet to-morrow at daybreak,

---

*Many caricatures of the time represented Louis-Philippe's head as a pear.

in the Place du Panthéon. Drop into the Café Soufflot. I have to chat with you before the demonstration takes place."

"Oh! I know their demonstrations! Many thanks! I have a more agreeable things to do!"

And on the following morning, at eleven o'clock, Frédéric had left the house. He wanted to give one last glance at the preparations. Then, who could tell but that, by some chance or other, she might be at the place of meeting before him? As he emerged from the Rue Tronchet, he heard a great clamour behind the Madeleine.* He pressed on, and saw at the far end of the square, to the left, a number of men in smocks and well-dressed people.

In fact, a manifesto published in the newspapers had summoned to this spot all who had subscribed to the banquet of the Reform Party. The Ministry had, almost without a moment's delay, posted up a proclamation prohibiting the meeting. The Parliamentary Opposition had, on the previous evening, disclaimed any connection with it; but the patriots, who were unaware of this resolution on the part of their leaders, had come to the meeting-place, followed by a great crowd of spectators. A deputation from the schools had made its way, a short time before, to the house of Odillon Barrot.† It was now at the residence of the Minister for Foreign Affairs; and nobody could tell whether the banquet would take place, whether the Government would carry out its threat, and whether the National Guards would make their appearance. People were as much enraged against the representatives as against Power. The crowd was growing bigger and bigger, when suddenly the strains of the "Marseillaise" rang through the air.

It was the column of students which had just arrived on the scene. They marched along at an ordinary walking pace, in double file and in good order, with angry faces, bare hands, and all exclaiming at intervals:

"Long live Reform! Down with Guizot!"

---

*Eighteenth-century church in the form of a Greek temple not far from the Place de la Concorde in Paris.

†Lawyer and royalist politician opposed to Louis-Philippe.

Frédéric's friends were there, sure enough. They would have noticed him and dragged him along with them. He quickly sought refuge in the Rue de l'Arcade.

When the students had gone twice around the Madeleine, they went down in the direction of the Place de la Concorde. It was full of people; and, at a distance, the crowd pressed close together, had the appearance of a field of black corn swaying to and fro.

At the same moment, some army soldiers lined up in battle-array at the left-hand side of the church.

The groups remained standing there, however. In order to put an end to this, some police-officers in civilian dress brutally seized the most riotous of them, and carried them off to the guardhouse. Frédéric, in spite of his indignation, remained silent; he might have been arrested along with the others, and he would have missed Madame Arnoux.

A little while afterwards the helmets of the Municipal Guards appeared. They kept striking around them with the flat side of their swords. A horse fell down. The people made a rush forward to save him, and as soon as the rider was back in the saddle, they all ran away.

Then there was a great silence. The thin rain, which had moistened the asphalt, was no longer falling. Clouds floated past, gently swept on by the west wind.

Frédéric began running through the Rue Tronchet, looking before him and behind him.

Finally the clock struck two.

"Ah! now is the time!" said he to himself. "She is leaving her house; she is approaching," and a minute later, "she could have been here by now."

Up until three he tried to keep calm. "No, she is not late—a little patience!"

With nothing better to do he examined the most interesting shops that he passed—a bookseller's, a saddler's and a mourning outfitters. Soon he knew the names of the different books, the various kinds of harnesses, and every sort of material. The shopkeepers from seeing him continually pacing back and forth, were at first surprised, and then alarmed, and they closed up their shop-fronts.

No doubt she had met with some obstacle, and she also must be suffering on account of it. But what delight would be his in a very short time! For she would come—that was certain. "She has given me her promise!" In the meantime an intolerable feeling of anxiety was gradually seizing hold of him. Impelled by an absurd idea, he returned to his hotel, as if he expected to find her there. At the same moment, she might have reached the street in which their meeting was to take place. He rushed out. Was there no one? And he resumed tramping up and down the sidewalk.

He studied the gaps in the pavement, the mouths of the gutters, the candelabra, and the numbers above the doors. The most trivial objects became his companions, or rather, mocking spectators, and the regular fronts of the houses seemed to him to be pitiless. His feet were cold. He felt as if he were about to succumb to the dejection which was crushing him. The reverberation of his footsteps vibrated through his brain.

When he saw by his watch that it was four o'clock, he experienced, a sort of dizziness and a feeling of dismay. He tried to repeat some verses to himself, to make a calculation, no matter of what sort, to invent some kind of story. Impossible! He was beset by the image of Madame Arnoux; he felt a longing to run to meet her. But what road should he take so that they might not miss each other?

He went up to a messenger, put five francs into his hand, and ordered him to go to the Rue de Paradis to Jacques Arnoux's residence to enquire "if Madame were at home." Then he stationed himself at the corner of the Rue de la Ferme and of the Rue Tronchet, so as to be able to look down both of them at the same time. On the boulevard, in the background of the scene in front of him, confused masses of people were gliding past. He could distinguish, every now and then, a dragoon's helmet or a woman's hat; and he strained his eyes in an effort to recognise the wearer. A child in rags, exhibiting a jack-in-the-box, asked him, with a smile, for money.

The man with the velvet jacket reappeared. "The concierge had not seen her going out." What had kept her in? If she were ill he would have been told about it. Was it a visitor? Nothing was easier than to say that she was not at home. He struck his forehead.

"Ah! I am stupid! Of course, 'tis this political outbreak that prevented her from coming!"

He was relieved by this apparently natural explanation. Then, suddenly: "But her quarter of the city is quiet." And a horrible doubt seized hold of his mind: "Suppose she was not coming at all, and merely gave me a promise in order to get rid of me? No, no!" What had prevented her from coming was, no doubt, some extraordinary stroke of bad luck, one of those occurrences that baffled all one's anticipations. In that case she would have written to him.

And he sent the hotel errand-boy to his residence in the Rue Rumfort to find out whether there happened to be a letter waiting for him there.

No letter had been brought. This absence of news reassured him.

He drew omens from the random number of coins in his hand, from the facial expressions of the passers-by, and from the colour of different horses; and when the omen was unfavourable, he forced himself to disbelieve in it. In his sudden outbursts of rage against Madame Arnoux, he abused her in muttering tones. Then came fits of weakness that nearly made him faint, followed, all of a sudden, by renewed hopefulness. She would make her appearance soon! She was there, behind his back! He turned round—there was nobody there! Once he perceived, about thirty feet away, a woman of the same height, with a dress of the same kind. He came up to her—it was not she. It struck five—half-past five—six. The gas-lamps were lighted. Madame Arnoux had not come.

The night before, she had dreamed that she had been, for some time, on the sidewalk of the Rue Tronchet. She was waiting there for something the nature of which was not quite clear, but which, nevertheless, was of great importance; and, without knowing why, she was afraid of being seen. But an accursed little dog kept barking at her furiously and biting at the hem of her dress. He kept stubbornly coming back again and again, always barking more violently than before. Madame Arnoux woke up. The dog's barking continued. She strained her ears to listen. It came from her son's room. She rushed there in her bare feet. It was the child himself who was coughing. His hands were burning, his face flushed, and his voice strangely hoarse. Every minute he found it more difficult to breathe freely. She waited there till daybreak, bent over the coverlet watching him.

At eight o'clock the drum of the National Guard gave warning to M. Arnoux that his comrades were expecting his arrival.

He dressed himself quickly and went off, promising that he would immediately go by the house of their doctor, M. Colot.

At ten o'clock, when M. Colot did not make his appearance, Madame Arnoux dispatched her chambermaid for him. The doctor was away in the country; and the young man who was taking his place had gone out on some business.

Eugène kept his head on one side of the bolster with knitted eyebrows and dilated nostrils. His pale little face had become whiter than the sheets; and there escaped from his larynx a wheezing with each intake of breath, which was becoming gradually shorter, dryer, and more metallic. His cough resembled the noise made by those barbarous mechanisms which enable toy-dogs to bark.

Madame Arnoux was seized with terror. She rang the bell violently, calling out for help, and exclaiming:

"A doctor! a doctor!"

Ten minutes later came an elderly gentleman in a white tie, and with grey whiskers well trimmed. He asked several questions as to the habits, the age, and the constitution of the young patient, then examined his throat, listened to his breathing by pressing his ear against Eugène's back and wrote out a prescription.

The calm manner of this old man was intolerable. He smelt of embalming. She would have liked to hit him. He said he would come back in the evening.

The horrible coughing soon began again. Sometimes the child sat up suddenly. Convulsive movements shook the muscles of his chest; and in his efforts to breathe his stomach contracted as if he were gasping for air after running too hard. Then he sank down, with his head thrown back and his mouth wide open. With infinite pains, Madame Arnoux tried to make him swallow the contents of the medicine bottles, ipacacuanha syrup, and an antimony potion. But he pushed away the spoon, groaning in a feeble voice. He seemed to be blowing out his words.

From time to time she re-read the prescription. The formula frightened her. Perhaps the apothecary had made some mistake. Her powerlessness filled her with despair. M. Colot's pupil arrived.

He was a young man of modest demeanour, new to medical work, and he made no attempt to conceal his opinions. He was at first undecided as to what he should do, for fear of committing himself, and finally he ordered pieces of ice to be applied to the sick child. It took a long time to get ice. The bladder containing the ice burst. It was necessary to change the little boy's shirt. This disturbance brought on an attack even more dreadful than any of the previous ones.

The child began tearing off the bandages round his neck, as if he wanted to remove the obstacle that was choking him; and he scratched the walls and grabbed onto the curtains of his bedstead, trying to get a point of support to assist him in breathing.

His face was now of a bluish hue, and his entire body, steeped in a cold perspiration, appeared to be growing thinner. His haggard eyes were fixed with terror on his mother. He threw his arms round her neck, and hung there in a desperate fashion; and, repressing her rising sobs, she whispered loving words to him in a broken voice:

"Yes, my pet, my angel, my treasure!"

Then came intervals of calm.

She went to look for some toys—a doll, a picture book, and spread them out on the bed in order to amuse him. She even made an attempt to sing.

She began to sing a little ballad which she used to sing years before, when she was nursing him wrapped up in swaddling-clothes in this same little upholstered chair. But a shiver ran all over his frame, just as when a wave is agitated by the wind. His eyeballs protruded. She thought he was going to die, and turned away to avoid seeing him.

The next moment she felt strength enough in her to look at him. He was still alive. The hours succeeded each other—dull, mournful, interminable, hopeless, and she no longer counted the minutes, save by the progress of this agony. The shakings of his chest threw him forward as if to shatter his body. Finally, he vomited something strange, which was like a tube of parchment. What was this? She imagined that he had thrown up one end of his entrails. But he now began to breathe freely and regularly. This appearance of well-being frightened her more than anything else that had happened. She was standing there petrified, her arms hanging by her sides, her eyes fixed, when M. Colot suddenly made his appearance. The child, in his opinion, was saved.*

---

*The child's disease was the croup, which affects the larynx.

She did not realise what he meant at first, and made him repeat the words. Was not this one of those consoling phrases which were customary with medical men? The doctor went away with an air of tranquillity. Then it seemed as if the cords that squeezed her heart were loosened.

"Saved! Is this possible?"

Suddenly the thought of Frédéric entered her mind clearly and inexorably. It was a warning sent to her by Providence. But the Lord in His mercy had not wished to punish her completely. What expiation could she offer hereafter if she were to persevere in this love-affair? No doubt insults would be flung at her son on her account; and Madame Arnoux saw him a young man, wounded in a duel, carried off on a stretcher, dying. In a single bound, she threw herself on the little chair, and, lifting up her soul towards the heights of heaven, she vowed to God that she would sacrifice her first real passion, her only weakness as a woman.

Frédéric had returned home. He remained in his armchair, without even possessing enough energy to curse her. A sort of slumber fell upon him, and, in the midst of his nightmare, he could hear the rain falling, still under the impression that he was there outside on the sidewalk.

Next morning, unable to resist the temptation, he again sent a messenger to Madame Arnoux's house.

Whether the true explanation happened to be that the fellow did not deliver his message, or that she had too many things to say to explain herself in a word or two, the same answer was brought back. This insolence was too great! A feeling of angry pride took possession of him. He swore in his own mind that he would never again cherish a desire; and, like a group of leaves carried away by a hurricane, his love disappeared. He experienced a sense of relief, a feeling of stoic joy, then a need of violent action; and he walked on randomly through the streets.

Men from the faubourgs were marching past armed with guns and old swords, some of them wearing red caps, and all singing the "Marseillaise" or the "Girondins." Here and there a National Guard was hurrying to his local town hall. Drums could be heard rolling in the distance. A conflict was going on at Porte Saint-Martin. There was something lively and warlike in the air. Frédéric kept walking on without stopping. The excitement of the great city raised his spirits.

In the vicinity of the Frascati gambling parlor he caught sight of the Maréchale's windows: a wild idea occurred to him, a youthful impulse. He crossed the boulevard.

The yard-gate was just being closed; and Delphine, who was in the act of writing on it with a piece of charcoal, "Arms handed over," said to him in an eager tone:

"Ah! Madame is in such a state! She dismissed a groom who insulted her this morning. She thinks there's going to be looting everywhere. She is frightened to death! and all the more so since Monsieur has gone!"

"What Monsieur?"

"The Prince!"

Frédéric entered the boudoir. The Maréchale appeared in her petticoat, and her hair hanging down her back in disorder.

"Ah! thank you! You have come to save me! 'tis the second time! You are one of those who never count the cost!"

"A thousand pardons!" said Frédéric, catching her round the waist with both hands.

"Hey! What are you doing?" stammered the Maréchale, at the same time, surprised and cheered up by his manner.

He replied:

"I am following the fashion! I'm reforming myself!"

She let herself fall back on the divan, and continued laughing under his kisses.

They spent the afternoon looking out through the window at the people in the street. Then he brought her to dinner at the Trois Frères Provençaux. The meal was long and exquisite. They walked back since they had no carriage.

At the announcement of a change of Ministry,* Paris had changed. Everyone was in a state of delight. People kept promenading about the streets, and every floor was illuminated with lamps, so that it seemed as if it were broad daylight. The soldiers made their way back to their barracks, worn out and looking quite

*Louis-Philippe replaced Guizot with Comte Molé (1781–1855).

depressed. The people saluted them with exclamations of "Long live the infantry!"

They continued on without making any response.

Among the National Guard, on the contrary, the officers, flushed with enthusiasm, brandished their sabres, crying out:

"Long live Reform!"

And every time the two lovers heard this word they laughed.

Frédéric told droll stories, and was quite elated.

Making their way through the Rue Duphot, they reached the boulevards. Venetian lanterns hanging from the houses formed wreaths of flame. Underneath, a confused swarm of people kept in constant motion. In the midst of those moving shadows could be seen, here and there, the steely glitter of bayonets. A great din arose. The crowd was too compact, and it was impossible to make one's way back in a straight line. They were entering the Rue Caumartin, when suddenly there burst forth behind them a noise like the sound of a huge piece of silk being torn in two. It was the firing of muskets on the Boulevard des Capucines.[32]

"Ah! They're killing off some bourgeois," said Frédéric calmly; for there are situations in which the least cruel of men is so detached from his fellow-men that he would see the entire human race perish without a single throb of the heart.

The Maréchale was clinging to his arm with her teeth chattering. She declared that she would not be able to walk even twenty more steps. Then, through a refined hatred, in order to desecrate the memory of Madame Arnoux, he led Rosanette to the house in the Rue Tronchet, and brought her up to the room which he had prepared for the other.

The flowers were not withered. The lace was spread out on the bed. He drew forth from the cupboard the little slippers. Rosanette considered this thoughtfulness on his part very delicate. About one o'clock she was awakened by distant rumblings, and she saw that he was sobbing with his head buried in the pillow.

"What's the matter with you now, my darling?"

" 'Tis too much happiness," said Frédéric. "I have been yearning for you too long!"

PART THREE

CHAPTER I

He was abruptly roused from sleep by the noise of musket fire; and, in spite of Rosanette's entreaties, Frédéric was fully determined to go and see what was happening. He hurried down to the Champs-Elysées, where the shots were fired. At the corner of the Rue Saint-Honoré some men in smocks ran past him, exclaiming:

"No! not that way! to the Palais-Royal!"

Frédéric followed them. The railings of the church of the Assumption had been torn down. A little further on he noticed three paving-stones in the middle of the street, the beginning of a barricade, no doubt; then fragments of bottles and bundles of iron-wire, to obstruct the cavalry; and, at the same moment, there rushed suddenly out of a lane a tall young man of pale complexion, with his black hair flowing over his shoulders, and wearing a sort of singlet with colored dots. In his hand he held a long military musket, and he dashed along on the tips of his slippers with the air of a sleep-walker and with the agility of a tiger. At intervals detonations could be heard.

On the evening of the day before, the spectacle of the wagon containing five corpses picked up from amongst those that were lying on the Boulevard des Capucines had changed the mood of the people; and, while at the Tuileries the aides-de-camp came and went, and M. Molé, having set about the composition of a new Cabinet, did not return, and M. Thiers was making efforts to constitute another, and while the King picked fights, hesitated, and finally assigned the post of commander-in-chief to Bugeaud* only

---

*Marshall Bugeaud, who had conquered Algeria, ordered the massacre at Rue Transnonain (see footnote on p. 260).

to prevent him from using it, the insurrection was organising itself formidably, as if directed by a single hand.

Men with a kind of frantic eloquence harangued the mob at the street-corners, others were in the churches ringing the bells as loudly as they could. Lead was cast for bullets, cartridges were rolled. The trees on the boulevards, the public urinals, the benches, the railings, the gas-lamps, everything was torn out or overturned. Paris, that morning, was covered with barricades. The resistance which was offered was of short duration, so that at eight o'clock the people, by voluntary surrender or by force, had taken possession of five barracks, nearly all the municipal buildings, the most favourable strategic points. Of its own accord, without any effort, the Monarchy was melting away in rapid dissolution, and now an attack was made on the guard-house of the Château d'Eau, in order to liberate fifty prisoners, who were not there.

Frédéric was forced to stop at the entrance to the square.* It was filled with groups of armed men. The Rue Saint-Thomas and the Rue Fromanteau were occupied by infantry companies. The Rue de Valois was blocked by an enormous barricade. The smoke hanging on it was breaking up. Men kept running towards it, making violent gestures; they vanished from sight; then the firing began again. It was answered from the guard-house without anyone being seen inside. Its windows, protected by oaken window-shutters, were pierced with loop-holes; and the monument with its two storys, its two wings, its fountain on the first floor and its little door in the centre, was beginning to be speckled with white spots under the shock of the bullets. The three steps in front remained empty.

At Frédéric's side a man in a Greek cap, with a cartridge-box over his knitted vest, was having a dispute with a woman with a Madras kerchief on her head. She said to him:

"Come back! Come back!"

"Leave me alone!" replied the husband. "You can easily mind the concierge's lodge by yourself. I ask, citizen, is this fair? I have on every occasion done my duty—in 1830, in '32, in '34, and in '39! To-day they're fighting again. I must fight! Go away!"

---

*"Square" refers to the Palais-Royal (see footnote on p. 30).

And the concierge's wife ended by yielding to his protests and to those of a National Guard near them—a man of forty, whose kindly face was adorned with a circle of blond beard. He loaded his gun and fired while talking to Frédéric, as cool in the midst of the outbreak as a horticulturist in his garden. A young lad in an apron was trying to coax this man to give him a few caps, so that he might make use of a gun he had, a fine fowling-piece which a "gentleman" had made him a present of.

"Grab some behind my back," said the good man, "and keep yourself from being seen, or you'll get yourself killed!"

The drums beat for the charge. Sharp cries, hurrahs of triumph burst forth. A continual ebbing to and fro made the multitude sway back and forth. Frédéric, caught between two thick masses of people, did not move an inch, all the time fascinated and exceedingly amused by the scene around him. The wounded who sank to the ground, the dead lying at his feet, did not seem like persons really wounded or really dead. The impression left on his mind was that he was watching a show.

In the midst of the surging throng, above the sea of heads, could be seen an old man in a black coat, mounted on a white horse with a velvet saddle. He held in one hand a green bough, in the other a paper, and he kept shaking them persistently; but at length, giving up all hope of being heard, he withdrew from the scene.

The soldiers of the infantry had gone, and only the municipal troops remained to defend the guard-house. A wave of dauntless spirits dashed up the steps; they were flung down; others came on to replace them, and the door resounded under blows from iron bars. The municipal guards did not give way. But a wagon, stuffed full of hay, and burning like a gigantic torch, was dragged up against the walls. Bundles of sticks were speedily brought, then straw, and a barrel of alcohol. The fire mounted up to the stones along the wall; the building began to send forth smoke on all sides like the crater of a volcano; and at its summit, between the balustrades of the terrace, huge roaring flames escaped with a harsh noise. The first story of the Palais-Royal was occupied by National Guards. Shots were fired through every window in the square; the bullets whizzed, the water of the fountain, which had been broken, was mingled with the blood, forming little pools on the ground. People slipped in the mud over clothes, military caps, and weapons. Frédéric felt something soft under his foot. It was the hand of a sergeant in a grey over-coat, lying face-down in the stream that ran along the street. Fresh bands of people were continually coming up, pushing the combatants towards the guard-house. The firing became more rapid. The wine-shops were open; people went into them from time to time to smoke a pipe and drink a glass of beer, and then came back again to fight. A lost dog began to howl. This made the people laugh.

Frédéric was shaken by the impact of a man falling on his shoulder groaning with a bullet through his back. At this shot, perhaps directed at himself, he felt enraged; and he was plunging forward when a National Guard stopped him.

" 'Tis useless! the King has just gone! Ah! if you don't believe me, go and see for yourself!"

This assurance calmed Frédéric. The Place du Carrousel looked tranquil. The Hôtel de Nantes stood there as fixed as ever; and the houses in the rear; the dome of the Louvre in front, the long wooden gallery at the right, and the wasteland that ran unevenly as far as the sheds of the stall-keepers were, so to speak, steeped in the grey hues of the atmosphere, where indistinct murmurs seemed to mingle with the fog; while, at the opposite side of the square, a harsh light, falling through the parting of the clouds on the façade of the Tuileries, made all its windows look like white patches. Near the Arc de Triomphe a dead horse lay on the ground. Behind the railings groups consisting of five or six people were talking. The doors of the château were open, and the servants on the threshold allowed the people to enter.

Below stairs, in a kind of little parlour, bowls of *café au lait* were being served. A few of spectators sat down at the table jokingly; others remained standing, and amongst the latter was a hackney-coachman. He snatched up with both hands a jar full of powdered sugar, cast a restless glance right and left, and then began to eat voraciously, with his nose stuck right into the jar.

At the bottom of the great staircase a man was writing his name in a register.

Frédéric was able to recognise him by his back. "Hello, Hussonnet!"

"Yes, 'tis I," replied the Bohemian. "I am introducing myself at Court. This is a good joke, isn't it?"

"Suppose we go upstairs?"

And they went up to the Salle des Maréchaux. The portraits of those illustrious generals, save that of Bugeaud, which had been pierced through the stomach, were all intact. They were represented leaning on their sabres with a gun-carriage behind each of them, and in majestic postures in contrast with the circumstances. A large clock proclaimed it was twenty minutes past one.

Suddenly the "Marseillaise" resounded. Hussonnet and Frédéric bent over the banisters. It was the mob. They rushed up the stairs, shaking with a dizzying, wave-like motion bare heads, helmets, red caps, bayonets, shoulders with such impetuosity that some people disappeared in this swarming mass, which was mounting up like a river compressed by an equinoctial tide, driven by an irresistible impulse with a continuous roar. When they got to the top of the stairs, they scattered, and their chant died away. Nothing more could be heard but the tramp of all the shoes intermingled with the babble of many voices. The crowd contented themselves with looking about them inoffensively. But, from time to time, an elbow, cramped for room, broke through a pane of glass, or else a vase or a statue rolled from a table down on the floor. The wall panelling creaked under the pressure of people against it. Every face was flushed; the perspiration was rolling down their faces in large beads. Hussonnet made this remark:

"Heroes don't smell very nice."

"Ah! you are annoying," returned Frédéric.

And, pushed forward in spite of themselves, they entered a room in which a canopy of red velvet stretched across the ceiling. On the throne below sat a worker with a black beard, his shirt gaping open, a jolly air, and the stupid look of a baboon. Others climbed up the platform to sit in his place.

"What a myth!" said Hussonnet. "There you see the sovereign people!"

The armchair was lifted up on the hands of a number of people and passed across the hall, swaying from one side to the other.

"By Jove, 'tis like a boat! The Ship of State is tossing about in a stormy sea! Let it dance the cancan! Let it dance the cancan!"

They had drawn it towards a window, and in the midst of hisses, they launched it out.

"Poor old chap!" said Hussonnet, as he saw it falling into the garden, where it was speedily picked up in order to be carried to the Bastille and burned.

Then a frenzied joy burst forth, as if, instead of the throne, a future of boundless happiness had appeared; and the people, less through a spirit of vindictiveness than to assert their right of possession, broke or tore the mirrors, the curtains, the chandeliers, the sconces, the tables, the chairs, the stools, all of the furniture, including the albums of drawings, and the needlework baskets. Since they had triumphed, they were entitled to amuse themselves! The common herd ironically wrapped themselves up in lace and cashmere. Gold fringe was twined round smock sleeves. Hats with ostrich feathers adorned blacksmiths' heads, and ribbons of the Légion d'honneur served as waistbands for prostitutes. Each person satisfied his or her whim; some danced, others drank. In the queen's apartment a woman gave a gloss to her hair with pomade. Behind a folding-screen two lovers were playing cards. Hussonnet pointed out to Frédéric an individual who was smoking a clay pipe with his elbows resting on a balcony; and the delirious frenzy resounded with a continuous crash of broken porcelain and pieces of crystal, which, as they rebounded, made sounds like the keys of a harmonica.

Then their fury took on a darker note. An obscene curiosity made them rummage through all the dressing-rooms, all the alcoves and open all the drawers. Ex-convicts thrust their arms into the beds in which princesses had slept, and rolled around on the top of them, as consolation for not being able to rape them. Others, with sinister faces, roamed about silently, looking for something to steal, but too great a multitude was there. Through the doorways of the suites of apartments could be seen only a dark mass of people between the gilding of the walls under a cloud of dust. Everyone was panting. The heat became more and more suffocating; and the two friends, afraid of being stifled, seized the opportunity of making their way out.

In the antechamber, standing on a heap of garments, appeared a prostitute as a statue of Liberty, motionless, her grey eyes wide open—a fearful sight.

They had taken three steps outside the château when a company of the National Guards, in greatcoats, advanced towards them, and, taking off their policemen's-caps, and, at the same time, uncovering their heads, which were slightly bald, bowed very low to the people. The ragged victors were delighted with this show of respect. Hussonnet and Frédéric were not without experiencing a certain pleasure from it as well.

They were filled with excitement. They went back to the Palais-Royal. In front of the Rue Fromanteau, soldiers' corpses were heaped up on the straw. They passed close to the dead without a single quiver of emotion, feeling a certain pride in being able to keep their composure.

The Palais overflowed with people. In the inner courtyard seven piles of wood were flaming. Pianos, chests of drawers, and clocks were hurled out through the windows. Fire-engines sent streams of water up to the roofs. Some vagabonds tried to cut the hose with their sabres. Frédéric urged a pupil of the Polytechnic School to interfere. The latter did not understand him, and, moreover, appeared to be half-witted. All around, in the two galleries, the populace, having taken possession of the wine-cellars, gave themselves up to a horrible drunken orgy. Wine flowed in streams and wetted people's feet; ragamuffins drank out of the bottoms of bottles, and shouted as they staggered along.

"Come away out of this," said Hussonnet; "I am disgusted with the people."

All over the Orléans Gallery the wounded lay on mattresses on the ground, with purple curtains folded round them as coverlets; and the small shopkeepers' wives and daughters from the quarter brought them broth and bandages.

"I don't care what you think!" said Frédéric; "I consider the people sublime."

The great vestibule was filled with a whirlwind of furious individuals. Men tried to ascend to the upper storys in order to complete its total destruction. National Guards, on the steps, strove to keep them back. The bravest was a guard who had a bare head, disheveled hair, and straps torn to pieces. His shirt was sticking out between his trousers and his coat, and he struggled desperately in the midst of the others. Hussonnet, who had sharp sight, recognised Arnoux from a distance.

Then they went into the Tuileries garden, so as to be able to breathe more freely. They sat down on a bench; and they remained for some minutes with their eyes closed, so much stunned that they had not the energy to say a word. The people who were passing came up to them and informed them that the Duchesse d'Orléans had been appointed Regent,[1] and that it was all over. Everybody was experiencing that feeling of well-being which follows quick resolutions to crises, when at the windows of the attics in the château appeared men-servants tearing their liveries to pieces. They flung their torn clothes into the garden, as a mark of renunciation. The people hooted at them, and then they withdrew.

Frédéric and Hussonnet's attention was distracted by a tall fellow who was walking quickly between the trees with a musket on his shoulder. A cartridge-belt was strapped around his red tunic; a handkerchief was wound round his forehead under his cap. He turned his head to one side. It was Dussardier; and casting himself into their arms:

"Ah! what good fortune, my poor old friends!" without being able to say another word, so much out of breath was he with fatigue.

He had been on his legs for the last twenty-four hours. He had been engaged at the barricades of the Latin Quarter, had fought in the Rue Rambuteau, had saved three dragoons' lives, had entered the Tuileries with Colonel Dunoyer, and, after that, had gone to the Chamber, and then to the Hôtel de Ville.

"I have come from there! all goes well! the people are victorious! the workmen and the employers are embracing one another. Ha! if you knew what I have seen! what brave fellows! what a fine sight it was!"

And without noticing that they were unarmed:

"I was quite certain of finding you there! It was a bit rough for a moment there—but it's all over now!"

A drop of blood ran down his cheek, and in answer to the questions put to him by the two others:

"Oh! 'tis nothing! a slight scratch from a bayonet!"

"Still, you really ought to take care of yourself."

"Pooh! I am sturdy! What does this signify? The Republic is proclaimed! We'll be happy now! Some journalists, who were talking just now in front of me, said they were going to liberate Poland

and Italy! No more kings! You understand? The entire land free! the entire land free!"

And with one comprehensive glance at the horizon, he spread out his arms in triumph. But a long line of men rushed over the terrace beside the water.

"Ah, dammit! I was forgetting. The forts are still occupied. I must be off. Good-bye!"

He turned round to cry out to them while brandishing his musket:

"Long live the Republic!"

From the chimneys of the château escaped enormous whirlwinds of black smoke which bore sparks along with them. The ringing of the bells sent out over the city a wild and startling alarm. Right and left, in every direction, the conquerors discharged their weapons.

Frédéric, though he was not a warrior, felt his Gallic blood leaping in his veins. The magnetism of the public enthusiasm had seized hold of him. He inhaled with delight the stormy atmosphere filled with the odour of gunpowder; and, in the meantime, he quivered with the consciousness of an immense love, a supreme and universal tenderness, as if the heart of all humanity were throbbing in his chest.

Hussonnet said with a yawn:

"It is time, perhaps, to go and educate the masses."

Frédéric followed him to his correspondence-office on the Place de la Bourse; and he began to compose for the Troyes newspaper an account of the events in a lyrical style—a veritable masterpiece—to which he signed his name. Then they dined together at a tavern. Hussonnet was pensive; the eccentricities of the Revolution exceeded his own.

After leaving the café, when they went to the Hôtel de Ville in search of news, the boyish impulses which were natural to him had gotten the upper hand once more. He scaled the barricades like a chamois, and answered the sentinels with patriotic jokes.

They heard the Provisional Government proclaimed by torchlight. At last, Frédéric got back to his house at midnight, overcome with fatigue.

"Well," said he to his man-servant, while the latter was undressing him, "are you satisfied?"

"Yes, no doubt, Monsieur; but I don't like to see the mob marching in step."

Next morning, when he awoke, Frédéric thought of Deslauriers. He hastened to his friend's lodgings. He ascertained that the lawyer had just left Paris, having been appointed as a provincial commissioner. The evening before, he had managed to see Ledru-Rollin, and by pestering him in the name of the Law Schools, had obtained from him a post, a mission.[2] However, the concierge explained, he was going to write and give his address the following week.

After this, Frédéric went to see the Maréchale. She gave him a chilly reception. She resented his desertion of her. Her bitterness disappeared when he gave her repeated assurances that peace was restored.

All was quiet now. There was no reason to be afraid. He kissed her, and she declared herself in favour of the Republic, as his lordship the Archbishop of Paris had already done, and as the magistrature, the Council of State, the Institute, the marshals of France, Changarnier, M. de Falloux, all the Bonapartists, all the Legitimists, and a considerable number of Orléanists were about to do with a swiftness indicative of marvellous zeal.

The fall of the Monarchy had been so rapid that, as soon as the first moment of stupefaction had passed, there was amongst the middle class a feeling of astonishment at the fact that they were still alive. The summary execution of some thieves, who were shot without a trial, was regarded as an admirable act of justice. For a month Lamartine's phrase was repeated with reference to the red flag, "which had only been carried round the Champ de Mars, whereas the tricoloured flag . . ." etc.;[3] and all placed themselves under its shade, each party seeing amongst the three colours only its own, and firmly determined, as soon as it would be the most powerful, to tear away the two others.

As business was suspended, anxiety and curiosity drove everyone into the street. The casual style of dress blurred differences of social position. Hatred masked itself; high hopes were expressed; the multitude seemed full of good-nature. The pride of having gained their rights shone in the people's faces. They exhibited the gaiety of a carnival, a camp-fire mood. Nothing could have been more enchanting than Paris during the days that followed the Revolution.

Frédéric gave the Maréchale his arm, and they strolled along through the streets together. She was highly distracted by the display of rosettes in every buttonhole, by the banners hung from every window, and the bills of every colour that were posted upon the walls, and threw some money here and there into the collection-boxes for the wounded, which were placed on chairs in the middle of the sidewalk. Then she stopped before some caricatures representing Louis Philippe as a pastry-cook, as an acrobat, as a dog, or as a leech. But she was a little frightened at the sight of Caussidière's men with their sabres and scarves.* At other times it was a tree of Liberty that was being planted. The clergy vied with each other in blessing the Republic, escorted by servants in gold lace; and the masses thought this very fine. The most frequent spectacle was that of deputations of everything under the sun, going to demand something at the Hôtel de Ville, for every trade, every industry, was looking to the Government to put a complete end to its problems. Some of them, it is true, went to offer advice or congratulations, or merely to pay a little visit, and to see the government machine performing its functions. One day, about the middle of the month of March, as they were passing the Pont d'Arcole, having to do some errand for Rosanette in the Latin Quarter, Frédéric saw approaching a column of individuals with oddly-shaped hats and long beards. At its head, beating a drum, walked a negro who had formerly been an artist's model; and the man who bore the banner, on which this inscription floated in the wind, "Artist-Painters," was no other than Pellerin.

He made a sign to Frédéric to wait for him, and then reappeared five minutes later, having some time to spare; for the Government was, at that moment, receiving a deputation from the stone-cutters. He was going with his colleagues to ask for the creation of a Forum of Art, a kind of Exchange where the interests of Æsthetics would be discussed. Sublime masterpieces would be produced, inasmuch as the workers would amalgamate their talents. Ere long Paris would be covered with gigantic monuments. He would decorate them. He had even begun a figure of the Republic. One of his comrades had

*Under the Provisional Government, Caussidière formed a police force that comprised active opponents to the previous regime.

come to get him, for the deputation from the poulterers was hard on their heels.

"What stupidity!" growled a voice in the crowd. "Always some nonsense, nothing significant!"

It was Regimbart. He did not greet Frédéric, but took advantage of the occasion to vent his own bitterness.

The Citizen spent his days wandering about the streets, pulling his moustache, rolling his eyes about, accepting and propagating any dismal news that was communicated to him; and he had only two phrases: "Look out! we're going to be out flanked!" or else, "Why, dammit! The Republic is being double-crossed!" He was dissatisfied with everything, and especially with the fact that we had not taken back our natural frontiers.

The very name of Lamartine made him shrug his shoulders. He did not consider Ledru-Rollin "sufficient for the problem," referred to Dupont (of the Eure) as an old numbskull, Albert as an idiot, Louis Blanc as an Utopist, and Blanqui as an exceedingly dangerous man; and when Frédéric asked him what would be the best thing to do, he replied, gripping his arm till he nearly bruised it:

"To take the Rhine, I tell you! to take the Rhine, dammit!"

Then he blamed the Reactionaries. They were taking off their mask. The sack of the château of Neuilly and Suresne, the fire at Batignolles, the troubles at Lyons, all the excesses and all the grievances, were now being exaggerated by adding Ledru-Rollin's circular, the forced currency of bank-notes, the fall of the government stock to sixty francs, and, to top it all off, as the supreme iniquity, a final blow, a culminating horror, the tax of forty-five centimes! And over and above all these things, there was Socialism too! Although these theories, as new as love and war, had been discussed sufficiently for forty years to fill a number of libraries, they terrified the wealthier citizens, as if they had been a hailstorm of meteorites; and they expressed indignation at them by virtue of that hatred which the advent of every idea provokes, simply because it is an idea—a hatred from which it derives subsequently its glory, and which causes its enemies to be always beneath it, however lowly it may be.

Now Property rose to the level of Religion, and was indistinguishable from God. The attacks made on it appeared to them a sacrilege; almost a species of cannibalism. In spite of the most humane legislation that ever existed, the spectre of '93* reappeared, and the sound of the guillotine vibrated in every syllable of the word "Republic," which did not prevent them from despising it for its weakness. France, no longer having a master, was beginning to shriek with terror, like a blind man without his stick or an infant that had lost its nurse.

Of all Frenchmen, M. Dambreuse was the most alarmed. The new condition of things threatened his fortune, but, more than anything else, it contradicted his experience. A system so good! a king so wise! was it possible? The ground was giving way beneath their feet! Next morning he dismissed three of his servants, sold his horses, bought a soft hat to go out into the streets, thought even of letting his beard grow; and he remained at home, prostrated, reading over and over again newspapers most hostile to his own ideas, and plunged into such a gloomy mood that even the jokes about the pipe of Flocon† failed to make him smile.

As a supporter of the last reign, he was dreading the vengeance of the people so far as concerned his estates in Champagne when Frédéric's journalistic effusion‡ fell into his hands. Then it occurred to him that his young friend was a very useful person, and that he might be able, if not to serve him, at least to protect him, so that, one morning, M. Dambreuse presented himself at Frédéric's residence, accompanied by Martinon.

This visit, he said, had no object save that of seeing him for a little while, and having a chat with him. In short, he rejoiced at the events that had happened, and with his whole heart adopted "our sublime motto, *Liberty, Equality, and Fraternity*," having always been at heart a Republican. If he voted under the other *régime* with the Ministry, it was simply in order to accelerate an inevitable downfall. He even inveighed against M. Guizot, "who has gotten us into a fine mess, we must admit!" By way of retaliation, he spoke in an enthusiastic fashion about Lamartine, who had shown himself

---

*1793 was the French Revolution's year of the Terror.

†Ferdinand Flocon, a minister in the Provisional Government, always sported a pipe.

‡The article that Frédéric wrote for the Troyes newspaper.

"magnificent, upon my word of honour, when, with reference to the red flag——"

"Yes, I know," said Frédéric. After which he declared that his sympathies were on the side of the workingmen.

"For, in fact, more or less, we are all workingmen!" And he carried his impartiality so far as to acknowledge that Proudhon* had a certain amount of logic in his views. "Oh, a great deal of logic, dammit!"

Then, with the detachment of a superior mind, he chatted about the exhibition of paintings, at which he had seen Pellerin's work. He considered it original and well-painted.

Martinon backed up all he said with expressions of approval; and likewise was of his opinion that it was necessary to rally boldly to the side of the Republic. And he talked about labour, his father, and assumed the part of the peasant, the man of the people. They soon came to the question of the elections for the National Assembly, and the candidates in the arrondissement of La Fortelle.† The Opposition candidate had no chance.

"You should take his place!" said M. Dambreuse. Frédéric protested.

"But why not?" For he would obtain the vote of the Ultras‡ owing to his personal opinions, and that of the Conservatives on account of his family. "And perhaps also," added the banker, with a smile, "thanks to my influence, in some measure."

Frédéric protested that he did not know how to go about it.

There was nothing easier if he only got himself recommended to the patriots of the Aube by one of the Paris clubs. All he had to do was to read out, not a profession of faith such as might be seen every day, but a serious statement of principles.

"Bring it to me; I know what they like down there; and you can, I say again, render great services to the country—to us all—to myself."

In such times people ought to aid each other, and, if Frédéric was in need of anything, he or his friends——

---

*Socialist theoretician Pierre-Joseph Proudhon (1809–1865) was a founder of anarchism and a promoter of economic and political federalism.

†The district in the *département* of Aube where M. Dambreuse has his property.

‡That is, of the ultra-royalists.

"Oh, a thousand thanks, my dear Monsieur!"

"You'll do as much for me in return, mind!"

Decidedly, the banker was a decent man.

Frédéric could not refrain from pondering over his advice; and soon he was dazzled by a kind of dizziness.

The great figures of the Convention passed before his mental vision. It seemed to him that a splendid dawn was about to rise. Rome, Vienna, and Berlin were in a state of insurrection, and the Austrians had been driven out of Venice. All Europe was agitated. Now was the time to make a plunge into the movement, and perhaps to accelerate it; and then he was fascinated by the costume which it was said the members of the Assembly would wear. Already he saw himself in a waistcoat with lapels and a tricoloured sash; and this itching, this hallucination, became so violent that he opened his mind to Dambreuse.

The honest fellow's enthusiasm had not abated.

"Certainly—sure enough! Offer yourself!"

Frédéric, nevertheless, consulted Deslauriers.

The idiotic opposition which trammelled the commissioner in his province had augmented his Liberalism. He at once replied, exhorting Frédéric with the utmost vehemence to come forward as a candidate. However, as Frédéric needed the approval of a greater number of people, he confided the thing to Rosanette one day, when Mademoiselle Vatnaz happened to be present.

She was one of those Parisian spinsters who, every evening when they have given their lessons or tried to sell little sketches, or to place their poor manuscripts, return to their own homes with mud on their petticoats, make their own dinner, which they eat by themselves, and then, with their soles resting on a foot-warmer, by the light of a filthy lamp, dream of a love, a family, a hearth, wealth—all that they lack. So it was that, like many others, she had hailed in the Revolution the advent of vengeance, and she delivered herself up to unbridled Socialistic propaganda.

The enfranchisement of the proletariat, according to Vatnaz, was only possible by the enfranchisement of women. She wished to have her own sex admitted to every kind of employment, to have an enquiry made into the paternity of children, a different legal code, the abolition, or at least a more intelligent regulation, of marriage.

In that case every Frenchwoman would be bound to marry a Frenchman, or to adopt an old man. Nurses and midwives should be civil servants receiving salaries from the State.

There should be a jury to examine the works of women, special editors for women, a polytechnic school for women, a National Guard for women, everything for women! And, since the Government ignored their rights, they ought to overcome force with force. Ten thousand citizenesses with good guns ought to make the Hôtel de Ville quake!

Frédéric's candidature appeared to her favourable for carrying out her ideas. She encouraged him, pointing out the glory that shone on the horizon. Rosanette was delighted at the notion of having a man who would make speeches at the Chamber.

"And then, perhaps, they'll give you a good post?"

Frédéric, a man prone to every foible, was infected by the universal mania. He wrote an address and went to show it to M. Dambreuse.

At the sound made by the great door falling back, a curtain gaped open a little behind a window, and a woman appeared. He had not time to find out who she was; but, in the hall, a picture caught his attention—Pellerin's picture—which lay on a chair, no doubt temporarily.

It represented the Republic, or Progress, or Civilisation, under the form of Jesus Christ driving a locomotive, which was passing through a virgin forest. Frédéric, after a minute's contemplation, exclaimed:

"How appalling!"

"Is it not—eh?" said M. Dambreuse, coming in unexpectedly just at the moment when this opinion was uttered, and thinking that it made reference, not so much to the picture as to the doctrine glorified by the work. Martinon presented himself at the same time. They made their way into the study, and Frédéric was drawing a paper out of his pocket, when Mademoiselle Cécile, entering suddenly, said, with an innocent air:

"Is my aunt here?"

"You know well she is not," replied the banker. "No matter! make yourself at home, Mademoiselle."

"Oh! no thanks! I am going!"

Scarcely had she left when Martinon seemed to be searching for his handkerchief.

"I forgot to take it out of my overcoat—excuse me!"

"Of course!" said M. Dambreuse.

Evidently he was not deceived by this manœuvre, and even seemed to regard it with favour. Why? But Martinon soon reappeared, and Frédéric began reading his address.

At the second page, which pointed towards the preponderance of financial interests as a disgrace, the banker made a grimace. Then, touching on reforms, Frédéric demanded free trade.

"What? Allow me, now!"

The other paid no attention, and went on. He called for a tax on yearly incomes, a progressive tax, a European federation, and the education of the people, the encouragement of the fine arts on the liberal scale.

"If the country could provide men like Delacroix or Hugo with incomes of a hundred thousand francs, what would be the harm?"

At the close of the address advice was given to the upper classes.

"Spare nothing, ye rich; but give! give!"

He stopped, and remained standing. The two who had been listening to him did not utter a word. Martinon opened his eyes wide; M. Dambreuse was quite pale. At last, concealing his emotion under a bitter smile:

"That address of yours is simply perfect!" And he praised the style exceedingly in order to avoid giving his opinion as to the content of the address.

This virulence on the part of an inoffensive young man frightened him, especially as a sign of the times.

Martinon tried to reassure him. The Conservative party, in a little while, would certainly be able to take its revenge. In several cities the commissioners of the provisional government had been driven away; the elections were not to occur till the twenty-third of April; there was plenty of time. In short, it was necessary for M. Dambreuse to present himself personally in the Aube; and from that time forth, Martinon no longer left his side, became his secretary, and was as attentive to him as any son could be.

Frédéric arrived at Rosanette's house very happy with himself. Delmar happened to be there, and told him of his intention to stand as a candidate at the Seine elections. In a poster addressed to the people, in which he addressed them in a familiar tone, the actor boasted of being able to understand them, and of having, in order to save them, gotten himself "crucified for the sake of art," so that he was the incarnation, the ideal of the popular spirit. He believed that he had, in fact, such enormous power over the masses that he proposed, when he was in a Ministry office, to quell any outbreak single-handedly; and, with regard to the means he would employ, he gave this answer: "Never fear! I'll show them my face!"

Frédéric, in order to mortify him, gave him to understand that he was himself a candidate. The showman, from the moment he realized that his future colleague aspired to represent the province, declared himself his servant, and offered to be his guide to the various clubs.

They visited them, or nearly all, the red and the blue, the furious and the tranquil, the puritanical and the licentious, the mystical and the intemperate, those that had voted for the death of kings, and those in which the frauds in the grocery trade had been denounced; and everywhere the tenants cursed the landlords; the smock was full of spite against the tailcoat; and the rich conspired against the poor. Many wanted compensation on the ground that they had formerly been martyrs of the police; others appealed for money in order to carry out certain inventions, or else there were plans of phalansteria, projects for village bazaars, systems of universal happiness; then, here and there a flash of genius amid these clouds of folly, sudden as splashes, the law formulated by an oath, and flowers of eloquence on the lips of some soldier-boy, with a shoulder-belt strapped over his bare, shirtless chest. Sometimes, too, a gentleman made his appearance—an aristocrat of humble demeanour, talking in a plebeian strain, and with his hands unwashed, so as to make them look calloused. A patriot recognised him; the most fanatical members insulted him; and he went off with rage in his soul. On the pretext of good sense, it was desirable to be always criticizing the lawyers, and to make use as often as possible of these expressions: "To carry one's stone to the building," "social problem," "workshop."

Delmar did not miss the opportunities afforded him for getting in a word; and when he no longer found anything to say, his device was to plant himself in some conspicuous position with one of his hands on his hip and the other in his waistcoat, turning himself round abruptly in profile, so as to give a good view of his head. Then there were outbursts of applause, which came from Mademoiselle Vatnaz at the lower end of the hall.

Frédéric, in spite of the weakness of orators, did not dare to try the experiment of speaking. All those people seemed to him too unpolished or too hostile.

But Dussardier made enquiries, and informed him that there existed in the Rue Saint-Jacques a club which bore the name of the "Club of Intellect." Such a name gave good reason for hope. Besides, he would bring some friends there.

He brought those whom he had invited to have punch with him—the bookkeeper, the wine-merchant, and the architect; even Pellerin had offered to come, and Hussonnet would probably form one of the party, and on the pavement before the door stood Regimbart, with two individuals, the first of whom was his faithful Compain, a rather heavy-set man with pock-marks and bloodshot eyes; and the second, an ape-like negro, exceedingly hairy, and whom he knew only as "a patriot from Barcelona."

They passed through an alley, and were then introduced into a large room, no doubt a carpenter's workshop with walls still fresh and smelling of plaster. Four oil-lamps were hanging parallel to each other, and shed an unpleasant light. On a platform, at the end of the room, there was a desk with a bell; below a table, representing the rostrum, and on each side two others, somewhat lower, for the secretaries. The audience that lined the benches consisted of old painters, school monitors, and literary men who could not get their works published.

In the midst of those lines of overcoats with greasy collars could be seen here and there a woman's cap or a workman's linen smock. The back of the room was full of workmen, who had in all likelihood come there to pass an idle hour, and who had been brought along by some speakers in order that they might applaud.

Frédéric took care to place himself between Dussardier and Regimbart, who was scarcely seated when he leaned both hands on his walking-stick and his chin on his hands and shut his eyes, whilst at the other end of the room Delmar stood looking down at the assembly. Sénécal appeared at the president's desk.

The worthy bookkeeper thought Frédéric would be pleased at this unexpected discovery. It only annoyed him.

The crowd showed great deference to the president. He was one who, on the twenty-fifth of February, had desired an immediate organisation of labour. On the following day, at the Prado, he had declared himself in favour attacking the Hôtel de Ville; and, as every person at that time modeled himself after someone, one copied Saint-Just, another Danton, another Marat; as for him, he tried to be like Blanqui, who imitated Robespierre.[4] His black gloves, and his hair brushed back, gave him a severe look exceedingly becoming.

He opened the proceedings with the declaration of the Rights of Man and of the Citizen—a customary act of faith. Then, a vigorous voice struck up Béranger's "Souvenirs du Peuple."

Other voices were raised:

"No! no! not that!"

" 'La Casquette!' " the patriots at the back began to howl.

And they sang in chorus the favourite lines of the period:

"Doff your hat before my cap—
Kneel before the working-man!"

At a word from the president the audience became silent.

One of the secretaries proceeded to open the letters.

Some young men announced that they burned a copy of the *Assemblée Nationale** every evening in front of the Panthéon, and they urged all patriots to follow their example.

"Bravo! adopted!" responded the audience.

The Citizen Jean Jacques Langreneux, a printer on the Rue Dauphin, would like to have a monument raised to the memory of the martyrs of Thermidor.†

Michel Evariste Népomucène, ex-professor, gave expression to the wish that the European democracy should adopt unity of language. A dead language might be used for that purpose—as, for example, improved Latin.

"No; no Latin!" exclaimed the architect.

"Why?" said the school master.

---

*Newspaper that supported the July Monarchy.

†Maximilien Robespierre, Louis de Saint-Just, and their friends who were guillotined by their enemies in July (Thermidor in the revolutionary calendar) 1794.

And these two gentlemen engaged in a discussion, in which the others also took part, each putting in a word of his own for effect; and the conversation on this topic soon became so tedious that many left. But a little old man, who wore below his prodigiously high forehead a pair of green spectacles, asked permission to speak in order to make an important communication.

It was a memorandum on the assessment of taxes. The figures flowed on in a continuous stream, as if they were never going to end. The impatience of the audience was expressed at first in murmurs, in whispered talk. He allowed nothing to bother him. Then they began hissing and calling out. Sénécal called the persons who were interrupting to order. The orator went on like a machine. It was necessary to take him by the elbow in order to stop him. The old fellow looked as if he were waking out of a dream, and, placidly lifting his spectacles, said:

"Pardon me, citizens! pardon me! I am going—a thousand pardons!"

Frédéric was disconcerted by the failure of the old man's attempts to read this written statement. He had his own address in his pocket, but an extemporaneous speech would have been preferable.

Finally the president announced that they were about to pass on to the important matter, the question of elections. They would not discuss the big Republican lists. However, the "Club of Intellect" had every right, like every other, to form its own list, "with all respect for the pashas of the Hôtel de Ville," and the citizens who sought the popular mandate might state their qualifications.

"Go on, now!" said Dussardier.

A man in a cassock, with woolly hair and a petulant expression on his face, had already raised his hand. He said, with a stutter, that his name was Ducretot, priest and agriculturist, and that he was the author of a work entitled "Manure." He was told to send it to a horticultural club.

Then a patriot in a smock climbed up onto the platform. He was a man of the people, with broad shoulders, a big face, very gentle-looking, with long black hair. He cast on the assembly an almost voluptuous glance, flung back his head, and, finally, spreading out his arms:

"You have repelled Ducretot, O my brothers! and you have done right; but it was not through irreligion, for we are all religious."

Many of those present listened open-mouthed, with the ecstatic air of catechumens.

"It is not either because he is a priest, for we, too, are priests! The workman is a priest, just as the founder of Socialism was—the Master of us all, Jesus Christ!"

The time had arrived to inaugurate the Kingdom of God. The Gospel led directly to '89. After the abolition of slavery, the abolition of the proletariat. They had had the age of hate—the age of love was about to begin.

"Christianity is the keystone and the foundation of the new edifice——"

"Are you making fun of us?" exclaimed the wine merchant. "Who has given me such a priest's cap?"

This interruption gave great offense. Nearly all the audience got on benches, and, shaking their fists, shouted: "Atheist! aristocrat! devil!" whilst the president's bell kept ringing, and the cries of "Order! order!" multiplied. But, aimless, and, moreover, fortified by three cups of coffee which he had consumed before coming to the meeting, he struggled in the midst of the others:

"What? I an aristocrat? Come, now!"

When, at length, he was permitted to give an explanation, he declared that he would never be at peace with the priests; and, since something had just been said about economic measures, it would be a splendid one to put an end to the churches, the sacred vessels, and finally all creeds.

Somebody raised the objection that he was going too far.

"Yes! I am going too far! But, when a ship is caught suddenly in a storm——"

Without waiting for the conclusion of this comparison, another made a reply to his observation:

"Granted! But this is to demolish at a single stroke, like a mason devoid of judgment——"

"You are insulting the masons!" yelled a citizen covered with plaster. And persisting in the belief that provocation had been offered to him, he spewed forth insults, and wished to fight, clinging tightly to the bench whereon he sat. It took no less than three men to throw him out.

Meanwhile the workman still remained on the platform. The two secretaries gave him an intimation that he should come down. He protested against the injustice done to him.

"You shall not prevent me from crying out, 'Eternal love to our dear France! eternal love all to the Republic!' "

"Citizens!" said Compain—"Citizens!"

And, by repeating "Citizens," having obtained a little silence, he leaned on the rostrum with his two red hands, which looked like stumps, bent forward, and blinking his eyes:

"I believe that it would be necessary to give a larger extension to the calf's head."

All who heard him kept silent, thinking that they had misunderstood his words.

"Yes! the calf's head!"

Three hundred laughs burst forth at the same time. The ceiling shook.

At the sight of all these faces convulsed with laughter, Compain shrank back. He continued in an angry tone:

"What! you don't know what the calf's head is!"

This brought on a fit of hysterics and delirium. They held their sides. Some of them even tumbled off the benches to the ground with convulsions of laughter. Compain, not being able to stand it any longer, took refuge beside Regimbart, and wanted to drag him away.

"No! I am remaining till it is all over!" said the Citizen.

This reply caused Frédéric to make up his mind; and, as he looked about to the right and the left to see whether his friends were prepared to support him, he saw Pellerin on the rostrum in front of him.

The artist assumed a haughty tone in addressing the crowd.

"I would like to get some notion as to who is the candidate amongst all these that represents art. I myself have painted a picture."

"We have nothing to do with painting pictures!" was the churlish remark of a thin man with red spots on his cheeks.

Pellerin protested against this interruption.

But the other, in a tragic tone:

"Shouldn't the Government have already, by decree, abolished prostitution and poverty?"

And this phrase having promptly gained him the good will of the audience, he thundered against the corruption of the great cities.

"Shame and infamy! We ought to grab hold of wealthy citizens on their way out of the Maison d'Or and spit in their faces—unless it be that the Government encourages debauchery! But the collectors of the city dues exhibit towards our daughters and our sisters an indecency——"

A voice exclaimed, some distance away:

"This is comical! Throw him out!"

"They extract taxes from us to pay for licentiousness! Consider the high salaries paid to actors——"

"I can answer to that!" cried Delmar.

He leaped from the rostrum, pushed everybody aside, and declaring that he was disgusted by such stupid accusations, expatiated on the civilising mission of the actor. Inasmuch as the theatre was the focus of national education, he would vote for the reform of the theatre; and to begin with, no more managers, no more privileges!

"Yes; of any sort!"

The actor's performance excited the audience, and subversive motions came from all parts of the hall.

"No more academies! No more Institut!"

"No missions!"

"No more baccalauréat! Down with University degrees!"

"Let us preserve them," said Sénécal; "but let them be conferred by universal suffrage, by the people, the only true judge!"

Besides, these things were not the most urgent. It was necessary to bring down the wealthy. And he represented them as wallowing in crime under their gilded ceilings; while the poor, writhing in their garrets with famine, cultivated every virtue. The applause became so vehement that he had to break off. For several minutes he remained with his eyes closed, his head thrown back, and, as it were, lulling himself to sleep over the fury which he had aroused.

Then he began to talk in a dogmatic fashion, in phrases as imperious as laws. The State should take possession of the banks and of the insurance offices. Inheritances should be abolished. A social fund should be established for the workers. Many other measures were desirable in the future. For the time being, these would suffice, and, returning to the question of the elections: "We want pure citizens, men entirely fresh. Let some one come forward."

Frédéric arose. There was a buzz of approval made by his friends. But Sénécal, assuming the attitude of a Fouquier-Tinville,* began to ask questions as to his Christian name and surname, his antecedents, life, and morals.

Frédéric answered succinctly, and bit his lips. Sénécal asked whether anyone saw any impediment to this candidature.

"No! no!"

But, for his part, he saw some. All around him bent forward and strained their ears to listen. The citizen who was seeking their support had not delivered a certain sum promised by him to the foundation of a democratic journal. Moreover, on the twenty-second of February, though he had had sufficient notice on the subject, he had failed to be at the meeting-place in the Place de Panthéon.

"I swear that he was at the Tuileries!" exclaimed Dussardier.

"Can you swear to having seen him at the Panthéon?"

Dussardier bowed his head. Frédéric was silent. His friends, scandalised, looked at him anxiously.

"In any case," Sénécal went on, "do you know a patriot who will answer to us on your principles?"

"I will!" said Dussardier.

"Oh! this is not enough; another!"

Frédéric turned round to Pellerin. The artist replied to him with a great number of gestures, which meant:

"Ah! my dear boy, they have rejected me! What do you want me to do?"

Thereupon Frédéric gave Regimbart a nudge.

"Yes, that's true; 'tis time! I'm going."

And Regimbart stepped upon the platform; then, pointing towards the Spaniard, who had followed him:

"Allow me, citizens, to present to you a patriot from Barcelona!"

---

*Antoine-Quentin Fouquier-Tinville was the pitiless prosecutor of the Revolutionary Tribunal during the French Revolution's Year of Terror.

The patriot made a low bow, rolled his silvery eyes about, and with his hand on his heart:

"Ciudadanos! mucho aprecio el honor que me dispensáis, y si grande es vuestra bondad, mayor vuestra atención!"

"I demand the right to speak!" cried Frédéric.

"Desde que se proclamo la constitución de Cadiz, ese pacto fundamental of las libertades Españolas, hasta la ultima revolución, nuestra patria cuenta numerosos y heroicos mártires."

Frédéric once more made an effort to obtain a hearing:

"But, citizens!——"

The Spaniard went on: "El martes proximo tendra lugar en la iglesia de la Magdelena un servicio fúnebre."

"This is ridiculous! Nobody understands him!"

This observation exasperated the audience.

"Throw him out! Throw him out!"

"Who? I?" asked Frédéric.

"Yes, you!" said Sénécal, majestically. "Out with you!"

He rose to leave, and the voice of the Iberian pursued him:

"Y todos los Españoles descarien ver alli reunidas las disputaciónes de los clubs y de la milicia nacional. Una oración fúnebre en honor de la libertad Española y del mundo entero serà pronunciada por un miembro del clero de Paris en la sala Bonne Nouvelle. Honor al pueblo francés que llamaria yo el primero pueblo del mundo, sino fuese ciudadano de otra nación!"

"Aristo!" screamed one lout, shaking his fist at Frédéric, as the latter, boiling with indignation, rushed out into the courtyard adjoining the place where the meeting was held.

He reproached himself for his devotedness, without reflecting that, after all, the accusations brought against him were just.

What fatal idea was this candidature! But what asses! what idiots! He drew comparisons between himself and these men, and soothed his wounded pride with the thought of their stupidity.

Then he felt the need of seeing Rosanette. After such an exhibition of ugliness, and so much maliciousness, her sweetness would be a relief. She was aware that he had intended to present himself at a club that evening. However, she did not even ask him a single question when he came in. She was sitting near the fire, ripping open the lining of a dress. He was surprised to find her thus occupied.

"Hello! what are you doing?"

"You can see for yourself," said she, dryly. "I am mending my clothes! So much for this Republic of yours!"

"Why do you call it mine?"

"Oh, it's mine then!"

And she began to blame him for everything that had happened in France for the last two months, accusing him of having brought about the Revolution and with having ruined her prospects by making everybody that had money leave Paris, and that she would by-and-by be dying in a hospital.

"It is easy for you to talk lightly about it, with your yearly income! However, at the rate at which things are going, you won't have your yearly income long."

"That may be," said Frédéric. "The most devoted are always misunderstood, and if one were not sustained by one's conscience, the brutes that you mix yourself up with would make you feel disgusted with your own self-sacrifice!"

Rosanette gazed at him with knitted brows.

"Eh? What? What self-sacrifice? Monsieur has not succeeded, it would seem? So much the better! It will teach you to make patriotic donations. Oh, don't lie! I know you have given them three hundred francs, for this Republic of yours has to be kept like a mistress. Well, amuse yourself with her, my good man!"

Under this avalanche of abuse, Frédéric passed from his former disappointment to a more painful disillusion.

He withdrew to the other end of the room. She came over to him.

"Look here! Think it out a bit! In a country as in a house, there must be a master, otherwise, everyone pockets something out of the household money. At first, everybody knows that Ledru-Rollin is upto his ears in debt. As for Lamartine, how can you expect a poet to understand politics? Ah! 'tis all very well for you to shake your head and to presume that you have more brains than the others; all the same, what I say is true! But you are always quibbling; a person can't get in a word with you! For instance, there's Fournier-Fontaine, who had stores at Saint-Roch! do you know how much he lost? Eight hundred thousand francs! And Gomer, the packer opposite to him—another Republican, that one—he smashed the tongs on his wife's head, and he drank so much absinthe that he is going to be put into an asylum. That's the way with the whole of them—the Republicans! A Republic at twenty-five percent. Ah! yes! it's something you can be proud of!"

Frédéric went off. He was disgusted at the foolishness of this girl, which was expressed in such common, low-class language. He felt himself even becoming a little patriotic once more.

The ill-temper of Rosanette only worsened. Mademoiselle Vatnaz irritated her with her enthusiasm. Believing that she had a mission, she felt a furious desire to make speeches, to carry on disputes, and—sharper than Rosanette in matters of this sort—overwhelmed her with arguments.

One day she made her appearance burning with indignation against Hussonnet, who had just indulged in some smutty remarks at the Woman's Club. Rosanette approved of this conduct, declaring even that she would put on men's clothes to go and "give them a bit of her mind, and to give them a whipping, the entire lot of them.

Frédéric entered just at that moment.

"You'll accompany me—won't you?"

And, in spite of his presence, a bickering match took place between them, one of them acting like a citizen's wife and the other a female philosopher.

According to Rosanette, women were born exclusively for love, or in order to bring up children, to be housekeepers.

According to Mademoiselle Vatnaz, women ought to have a position in the Government. In former times, the Gaulish women, and also the Anglo-Saxon women, took part in the legislation; the squaws of the Hurons formed a portion of the Council. The work of civilisation was common to both. It was necessary that all should contribute towards it, and that fraternity should be substituted for egoism, association for individualism, and cultivation on a large scale for minute subdivision of land.

"Come, now that is good! you know a great deal about agriculture now!"

"Why not? Besides, it is a question of humanity, of its future!"

"Mind your own business!"

"This is my business!"

They got into a fight. Frédéric intervened. Vatnaz became very hot under the collar, and went so far as to defend Communism.

"What nonsense!" said Rosanette. "How could such a thing ever come to pass?"

The other gave, in support of her theory, the examples of the Essenes, the Moravian Brethren, the Jesuits of Paraguay, the family of the Pingons near Thiers in Auvergne; and, as she gestured a great deal, her watch chain got entangled in her bunch of charms, one of which was a gold sheep.

Suddenly, Rosanette turned exceedingly pale.

Mademoiselle Vatnaz continued extricating her charms.

"Don't give yourself so much trouble," said Rosanette. "Now, I know your political opinions."

"What?" replied Vatnaz, with a blush on her face like that of a virgin.

"Oh! oh! you understand me."

Frédéric did not understand. There had evidently been something taking place between them of a more important and personal nature than Socialism.

"And even though it should be so," said Vatnaz in reply, rising up unflinchingly. " 'Tis a loan, my dear—set off one debt against the other."

"Faith, I don't deny my own debts. I owe some thousands of francs—a nice sum. I borrow, at least; I don't rob anyone."

Mademoiselle Vatnaz made an effort to laugh.

"Oh! I would put my hand in the fire for him."

"Take care! it is dry enough to burn."

The spinster held out her right hand to her, and keeping it raised in front of her:

"But there are friends of yours who find it attractive enough."

"Andalusians, I suppose? as castanets?"

"You wench!"

The Maréchale gave a low bow.

"There's nobody more charming!"

Mademoiselle Vatnaz made no reply. Beads of perspiration appeared on her temples. Her eyes fixed themselves on the carpet. She panted for breath. At last she reached the door, and slamming it vigorously: "Good night! You'll hear from me!"

"I can hardly wait!" said Rosanette. The effort of self-constraint had shattered her nerves. She sank down on the divan, shaking all over, stammering forth words of abuse, shedding tears. Was it this threat on the part of Vatnaz that had caused so much agitation in her mind? Oh, no! what did she care? It was the golden sheep, a present; and in the midst of her tears the name of Delmar escaped her lips. So, then, she was in love with the actor?

"In that case, why did she take up with me?" Frédéric asked himself. "How is it that he has come back again? Who compels her to stay with me? What is the sense of all of this?"

Rosanette was still sobbing. She remained all the time stretched at the edge of the divan, with her right cheek resting on her two hands, and she seemed a being so dainty, helpless, and so sorely troubled, that he drew closer to her and softly kissed her on the forehead.

Thereupon she gave him assurances of her affection for him; the Prince had just left her, they would be free. But she was for the time being short of money. "You saw yourself that this was so, the other day, when I was trying to turn my old linings to use." No more carriages now! And this was not all; the upholsterer was threatening to take back the bedroom and the large drawing-room furniture. She did not know what to do.

Frédéric had a mind to answer:

"Don't worry yourself about it. I will pay."

But the lady knew how to lie. Experience had enlightened him. He confined himself to mere expressions of sympathy.

Rosanette's fears were not in vain. It was necessary to give up the furniture and to move out of the handsome apartment in the Rue Drouot. She took another on the Boulevard Poissonnière, on the fourth floor.

The curiosities of her old boudoir were quite sufficient to give the three rooms a coquettish air. There were Chinese blinds, an awning over the terrace, and in the drawing-room a second-hand carpet still perfectly new, with ottomans covered in pink silk. Frédéric had contributed largely to these purchases. He had felt the joy of a newly-married man who possesses at last a house of his own, a wife of his own—and, being much pleased with the place, he used to sleep there nearly every evening.

One morning, as he was passing out through the hall, he saw, on the third floor, on the staircase, the shako of a National Guard who was ascending it. Where in the world was he going?

Frédéric waited. The man continued his progress up the stairs, with his head down. He raised his eyes. It was Arnoux!

The situation was clear. They both reddened simultaneously, overcome by a feeling of embarrassment common to both.

Arnoux was the first to find a way out of it.

"She is better—isn't she?" as if Rosanette were ill, and he had come to learn how she was.

Frédéric took advantage of this opening.

"Yes, certainly! at least, so I was told by her maid," wishing to convey that he had not been allowed to see her.

Then they stood facing each other, both undecided as to what they would do next, and eyeing one another intently. The question now was, which of the two was going to remain. Arnoux once more solved the problem.

"Oh, well! I'll come back another time. Where are you going? I'll go with you!"

And, when they were in the street, he chatted as naturally as usual. Unquestionably he was not a man of jealous disposition, or else he was too good-natured to get angry. Besides, his time was devoted to serving his country. He never took off his uniform now. On the twenty-ninth of March he had defended the offices of the *Presse*. When the Chamber was invaded, he distinguished himself by his courage, and he was at the banquet given for the National Guard at Amiens.

Hussonnet, who was still on duty with him, availed himself of his flask and his cigars; but, irreverent by nature, he delighted in contradicting him, putting down the somewhat ungrammatical style of the government's decrees; the conferences at the Luxembourg, the woman known as the "Vésuviennes," the political section bearing the name of "Tyroliens"; everything, in fact, down to the chariot of Agriculture, drawn by horses to the ox-market, and escorted by ugly girls. Arnoux, on the other hand, was the upholder of authority, and dreamed of uniting the different parties. However, his own affairs had taken an unfavourable turn, and he was more or less anxious about them.

He was not much troubled about Frédéric's relations with the Maréchale; for this discovery made him feel justified (in his conscience) in withdrawing the allowance which he had renewed since the Prince had left her. He pleaded financial difficulties, and uttered many lamentations—and Rosanette was generous. The result was that M. Arnoux regarded himself as the lover who appealed entirely to the heart, an idea that raised him in his own estimation, and made him feel young again. Having no doubt that Frédéric was paying the Maréchale, he fancied that he was "playing a nice trick" on the young man, even called at the house in such a stealthy fashion as to keep the other in the dark about it, and when they happened to meet, left the coast clear for him.

Frédéric was not pleased with sharing Rosanette with Arnoux and his rival's politeness seemed only an elaborate joke. But by taking offence at it, he would have removed from his path every opportunity of ever finding his way back to Madame Arnoux; and then, this was the only means whereby he could hear about her movements. The earthenware-dealer, in accordance with his usual practice, or perhaps with some cunning design, mentioned her readily in the course of conversation, and asked him why he no longer came to see her.

Frédéric, having exhausted every excuse he could think of, assured him that he had called several times to see Madame Arnoux, but without success. Arnoux was convinced that this was so, for he had often referred in an eager tone at home to the absence of their friend, and she had invariably replied that she was out when he called, so that these two lies, instead of contradicting, corroborated each other.

The young man's gentle ways and the pleasure of finding a dupe in him made Arnoux like him all the better. He carried familiarity to its extreme limits, not through disdain, but through assurance. One day he wrote saying that very urgent business compelled him to be away in the country for twenty-four hours. He begged the young man to mount guard in his stead. Frédéric dared not refuse, so he took himself to the guard-house in the Place du Carrousel.

He had to put up with the company of the National Guards, and, with the exception of a sugar-refiner, a witty fellow who drank an inordinate amount, they all appeared to him more stupid than their cartridge-belts. The principal subject of conversation amongst them was the substitution of sashes for belts. Others railed against the national workshops.[5]

One man said:

"Where are we going?"

The man to whom the words had been addressed opened his eyes as if he were standing on the verge of an abyss.

"Where are we going?"

Then, one who was more daring than the rest exclaimed:

"It cannot last! It must come to an end!"

And as the same kind of talk went on till evening, Frédéric was bored to death.

Great was his surprise when, at eleven o'clock, he suddenly beheld Arnoux, who immediately explained that he had hurried back to set him free, having taken care of his own business.

The fact was that he had no business to transact. The whole thing was an invention to enable him to spend twenty-four hours alone with Rosanette. But the worthy Arnoux had placed too much confidence in his own powers, so that, now in the state of exhaustion which was the result, he was seized with remorse. He had come to thank Frédéric, and to invite him to have some supper.

"A thousand thanks! I'm not hungry. All I want is to go to bed."

"All the more reason for having a snack together. How lazy you are! One does not go home at such an hour as this. It is too late! It would be dangerous!"

Frédéric once more yielded. Arnoux was quite a favorite with his brethren-in-arms, who had not expected to see him—and he was a particular crony of the refiner. They were all fond of him, and he was such a good fellow that he was sorry Hussonnet was not there. But he wanted to shut his eyes for one minute, no longer.

"Sit down beside me!" said he to Frédéric, stretching himself on the camp-bed without taking off his belt and straps. Through fear of an alert, in spite of the regulations, he even kept his gun in his hand, then stammered out some words:

"My darling! my little angel!" and ere long was fast asleep.

Those who had been talking to each other became silent; and gradually there was a deep silence in the guard-house. Frédéric, tormented by the fleas, kept looking around. The wall, painted yellow, had, half-way up, a long shelf, on which the knapsacks formed a succession of little humps, while underneath, the muskets, which were the colour of lead, rose up side by side; and there could be heard a succession of snores, produced by the National Guards, whose stomachs were outlined through the darkness. On the top of the stove stood an empty bottle and some plates. Three straw chairs were drawn around the table, with a pack of cards on it. There was a drum, in the middle of the bench, with its strap hanging down.

A warm breeze coming through the door caused the lamp to smoke. Arnoux slept with his two arms wide apart; and his gun was placed in a slightly crooked position, with the butt on the floor, the mouth of the barrel up right under his arm. Frédéric noticed this, and was alarmed.

"But, no, I'm wrong, there's nothing to be afraid of! And yet, what if he were to die!"

And immediately images passed through his mind in endless succession.

He saw himself with her at night in a coach, then on a river's bank on a summer's evening, and under the reflection of a lamp at home in their own house. He even fixed his attention on household expenses and domestic arrangements, contemplating, feeling already his happiness between his hands; and in order to realise it, all that was needed was that the cock of the gun should rise. The end of it could be pushed with one's toe, the gun would go off—it would be a mere accident—nothing more!

Frédéric brooded over this idea like a playwright in the creative act. Suddenly it seemed to him that it was not far from being carried into practical operation, and that he was going to contribute to that result—that, in fact, he was yearning for it; and then a feeling of absolute terror took possession of him. In the midst of this mental distress he experienced a sense of pleasure, and he allowed himself to sink deeper and deeper into it, with a dreadful consciousness all the time that his scruples were vanishing. In the wildness of his reverie the rest of the world vanished, and he was no longer conscious of himself except for an unbearable tightness in his chest.

"Let us have a drop of white wine!" said the refiner, as he awoke.

Arnoux sprang to his feet, and, as soon as the white wine was swallowed, he wanted to relieve Frédéric of his sentry duty.

Then he brought him to have breakfast in the Rue de Chartres, at Parly's, and as he needed to recuperate his energies, he ordered two dishes of meat, a lobster, an omelet with rum, a salad, etc., and finished this off with a brand of Sauterne of 1819 and one of '42 Romanée, not to speak of the champagne at dessert and the liqueurs.

Frédéric let him have his way. He was disturbed in mind as if by the thought that the other might somehow trace on his face the idea that had lately flitted before his imagination. With both elbows on the table and his head bent forward, so that he annoyed Frédéric by his fixed stare, he confided some of his hobbies to the young man.

He wanted to lease for farming purposes all the embankments on the Northern line, in order to plant potatoes there, or else to organise on the boulevards a gigantic procession in which the celebrities of the day would take part. He would rent all the windows, which would, at an average rate of three francs produce a handsome profit. In short, he dreamed of a great stroke of fortune by means of a monopoly. He assumed a moral tone, nevertheless, found fault with excesses and all sorts of misconduct, spoke about his "poor father," and every evening, as he said, made an examination of his conscience before offering his soul to God.

"A little curaçao, eh?"

"Just as you please."

As for the Republic, things would right themselves; in fact, he looked on himself as the happiest man on earth; and forgetting himself, he exalted Rosanette's attractive qualities, and even compared her with his wife. It was quite a different thing. You could not imagine a lovelier person!

"Your health!"

Frédéric touched glasses with him. He had, out of politeness, drunk a little too much. Besides, the strong sunlight dazzled him; and when they went up the Rue Vivienne together again, their shoulders touched each other in a fraternal fashion.

When he got home, Frédéric slept till seven o'clock. After that he called on the Maréchale. She had gone out with somebody—with Arnoux, perhaps! Not knowing what to do with himself, he continued his promenade along the boulevard, but could not get past the Porte Saint-Martin, because of the great crowd that blocked the way.

Poverty had left a considerable number of workmen to their own devices, and they used to come there every evening, no doubt to take stock of the situation and await a signal.

In spite of the law against riotous assemblies, these clubs of despair increased frightfully, and many citizens went along every day to the spot through bravado, and because it was the fashion.

All of a sudden Frédéric caught a glimpse, three yards away, of M. Dambreuse along with Martinon. He turned his head away, for since M. Dambreuse had gotten himself nominated as a representative of the people, he bore a grudge against him. But the capitalist stopped him.

"One word, my dear monsieur! I owe you an explanation."

"I am not asking you for any."

"Pray listen to me!"

It was not his fault in any way. Appeals had been made to him; pressure had, to a certain extent, been placed on him. Martinon immediately endorsed all that he had said. Some of the electors of Nogent had presented themselves in a deputation at his house.

"Besides, I expected to be free as soon as——"

A crush of people on the sidewalk forced M. Dambreuse to get out of the way. A minute after he reappeared, saying to Martinon:

"This is a great service you have done for me, really, and you won't have any reason to regret——"

All three stood leaning against a shop in order to be able to chat more easily.

From time to time there was a cry of, "Long live Napoléon! Long live Barbès! Down with Marie!"[6]

The countless throng kept talking very loudly and all these voices, echoing off of the houses, made, a noise like the continuous ripple of waves in a harbour. At intervals they ceased; and then voices could be heard singing the "Marseillaise."

Under the carriage-gates, mysterious men offered sword-sticks to those who passed. Sometimes two individuals, passing one another, would wink, and then quickly hurry away. The sidewalks were filled with groups of staring idlers. A dense crowd swayed to and fro on the pavement. Entire bands of police-officers, emerging from the alleys, had scarcely made their way into the midst of the multitude when they were swallowed up in the mass of people. Little red flags here and there looked like flames. Coachmen high up on their boxes waved their arms energetically, and then turned to go back. It was a case of perpetual movement—one of the strangest sights that could be imagined.

"How all this," said Martinon, "would have amused Mademoiselle Cécile!"

"My wife, as you are aware, does not like my niece to come with us," returned M. Dambreuse with a smile.

One could scarcely recognise in him the same man. For the past three months he had been crying, "Long live the Republic!" and he had even voted in favour of the banishment of Orleans. But there should be an end of concessions. He exhibited his rage so far as to carry a tomahawk in his pocket.

Martinon had one, too. Judicial posts no longer being a lifetime appointment, he had withdrawn from the Public Prosecutor's Office and surpassed M. Dambreuse in his show of violence.

The banker especially hated Lamartine (for having supported Ledru-Rollin) and, at the same time, Pierre Leroux, Proudhon, Considérant, Lamennais,[7] and all the cranks, all the Socialists.

"For in fact, what is it they want? The duty on meat has been abolished and so has imprisonment for debt. Now plans for a mortgage bank are under consideration; the other day it was a national bank; and there are five millions in the Budget for the workingmen! But luckily, it is over, thanks to Monsieur de Falloux!* Good-bye to them! let them go!"

In fact, not knowing how to maintain the three hundred thousand men in the national workshops, the Minister of Public Works had that very day signed an order inviting all citizens between the ages of eighteen and twenty to serve as soldiers, or else head to the provinces to cultivate the ground there.

They were indignant at the alternative thus put before them, convinced that the object was to destroy the Republic. They were

---

*A royalist deputy in 1848, Count Frédéric de Falloux voted for the dissolution of the national workshops.

aggrieved by the thought of having to live at a distance from the capital, as if it were a kind of exile. They saw themselves dying of fevers in desolate parts of the country. To many of them, moreover, who had been accustomed to work of a refined nature, agriculture seemed a degradation; it was, in short, a mockery, a decisive breach of all the promises which had been made to them. If they offered any resistance, force would be employed against them. They had no doubt of it, and made preparations to anticipate it.

About nine o'clock the riotous assemblies which had formed at the Bastille and at the Châtelet ebbed back towards the boulevard. From the Porte Saint-Denis to the Porte Saint-Martin nothing could be seen save an enormous swarm of people, a single mass of a dark blue shade, nearly black. The men of whom one caught a glimpse all had burning eyes, pale complexions, faces emaciated with hunger and excited with a sense of wrong.

Meanwhile, some clouds had gathered. The stormy sky electrified the people, and they kept whirling about of their own accord with the great swaying movements of a swelling sea, and one felt that there was an incalculable force in the depths of this excited throng, and as it were, the energy of force of nature. Then they all began exclaiming: "Lights! Lights!" Many windows had no illumination, and stones were flung at the panes. M. Dambreuse deemed it prudent to withdraw from the scene. The two young men accompanied him home. He predicted great disasters. The people might once more invade the Chamber, and on this point he told them how he would have been killed on the fifteenth of May had it not been for the devotion of a National Guardsman.

"But I had forgotten! he is a friend of yours—your friend the earthenware manufacturer—Jacques Arnoux!" The rioters had been actually throttling him, when that brave citizen caught him in his arms and put him safely out of their reach.

So it was that, since then, there had been a kind of intimacy between them.

"It would be necessary, one of these days, to dine together, and, since you often see him, give him the assurance that I like him very much. He is an excellent man, and has, in my opinion, been slandered; and he has his wits about him in the morning. My compliments once more! A very good evening!"

Frédéric, after he had left M. Dambreuse, went back to the Maréchale, and, in a very gloomy fashion, said that she should choose between him and Arnoux. She replied sweetly that she did not understand "talk of this sort," that she did not care about Arnoux, and had no attachment to him. Frédéric was thirsting to get out of Paris. She did not offer any opposition to this whim; and next morning they set out for Fontainebleau.[8]

The hotel at which they stayed could be distinguished from others by a fountain splashing in the middle of its courtyard. The doors of the various rooms opened out on a corridor, as in monasteries. The room assigned to them was large, well-furnished, hung with chintz, and quiet, due to the scarcity of tourists. Alongside the houses, people who had nothing to do kept passing up and down; then, under their windows, when the day was declining, children in the street were running races; and this tranquillity, following so soon the tumult they had witnessed in Paris, filled them with astonishment and exercised over them a soothing influence.

Every morning at an early hour, they went to pay a visit to the château. As they passed in through the gate, they had a view of its entire front, with the five pavilions covered with pointed roofs, and its horseshoe-shaped staircase at the far end of the courtyard, which is flanked by two lower buildings. On the paved ground lichens blended their colours with the tawny hue of bricks, and the entire appearance of the palace, rust-coloured like old armour, had about it something of the impassiveness of royalty—a sort of melancholy military grandeur.

At last, a man-servant made his appearance with a bunch of keys in his hand. He first showed them the apartments of the queen, the Pope's oratory, the gallery of Francis I, the mahogany table on which the Emperor signed his abdication, and in one of the rooms cut in two the old Galerie des Cerfs, the place where Christine had Monaldeschi assassinated.* Rosanette listened to this narrative attentively, then, turning towards Frédéric:

"No doubt it was jealousy? Better watch out!" After this they passed through the Council Chamber, the Guards' Room, the

---

*Alleging her equerry Gian Rinaldo Monaldeschi had revealed her secret political plans, Queen Christina of Sweden had him executed at Fontainebleau in the seventeenth century.

Throne Room, and the drawing-room of Louis XIII. The uncurtained windows sent forth a white light. The handles of the window-latches and the brass feet of the consoles were slightly tarnished and dusty. The armchairs were hidden under coarse linen covers. Above the doors could be seen hunting-scenes of Louis XIV, and here and there hangings representing the gods of Olympus, Psyche, or the battles of Alexander.

As she was passing in front of the mirrors, Rosanette stopped for a moment to smooth her hair.

After passing through the Turret-Court and the Saint-Saturnin Chapel, they reached the Banqueting Hall.

They were dazzled by the magnificence of the ceiling, which was divided into octagonal sections set off with gold and silver, more finely chiselled than a jewel, and by the vast number of paintings covering the walls, from the immense fireplace, where the arms of France were surrounded by crescents and quivers, down to the musicians' gallery, which had been erected at the other end along the entire width of the hall. The ten arched windows were wide open; the sun made the pictures gleam; the blue sky continued the ultramarine of the arches in an endless curve; and from the depths of the forest, where the lofty summits of the trees filled up the horizon, there seemed to come an echo of flourishes blown by ivory trumpets, and mythological ballets, princesses and nobles gathering together under the foliage disguised as nymphs or satyrs—an epoch of primitive science, of violent passions, and sumptuous art, when the ideal was to sweep away the world in a vision of the Hesperides, and when the mistresses of kings mingled their glory with the stars. There was a portrait of one of the most beautiful of these celebrated women in the form of Diana the huntress, and even the Infernal Diana, no doubt in order to indicate the power which she possessed even beyond the limits of the tomb. All these symbols confirmed her glory, and there remained about the spot something of her, an indistinct voice, a radiation that stretched out indefinitely. A mysterious feeling of retrospective lust took possession of Frédéric.

In order to divert these passionate longings he began to gaze tenderly on Rosanette, and asked her would she not like to have been this woman?

"What woman?"

"Diane de Poitiers!"*

He repeated:

"Diane de Poitiers, the mistress of Henry II."

She uttered a little "Ah!" that was all.

Her silence clearly demonstrated that she knew nothing about the matter, and had failed to comprehend his meaning, so that out of kindness he said to her:

"Perhaps you are getting tired of this?"

"No, no—quite the opposite." And lifting up her chin, and casting around her a vague glance Rosanette let these words escape her lips:

"It brings back memories!"

Meanwhile, it was easy to trace on her face a strained expression, a certain sense of awe; and, as this air of gravity made her look all the prettier, Frédéric overlooked it.

The carps' pond amused her more. For a quarter of an hour she kept flinging pieces of bread into the water in order to see the fishes skipping about.

Frédéric had seated himself by her side under the linden-trees. He saw in imagination all the people who had haunted these walls—Charles V, the Valois Kings, Henry IV, Peter the Great, Jean Jacques Rousseau, and "the beautiful ladies who wept in the stage-boxes," Voltaire, Napoléon, Pius VII, and Louis Philippe; and he felt himself surrounded, jostled, by these tumultuous dead. He was stunned by such a confusion of images, even though he found a certain fascination in contemplating them.

At last they descended into the flower-garden.

It is a vast rectangle, which presents to the spectator, at the first glance, its wide yellow walks, its square grass-plots, its ribbons of box-wood, its yew-trees shaped like pyramids, its low-lying green shrubs, and its narrow borders, in which scattered flowers stood out in spots on the grey soil. At the end of the garden is a park along whose entire length stretches a canal.

Royal residences have attached to them a peculiar kind of melancholy, due, no doubt, to their dimensions being much too large for the limited number of guests entertained within them, to the silence

---

*Favorite of Henry II in the sixteenth century.

which one feels astonished to find in them after so many flourishes of trumpets, to the unchanging luxury, which attests by its antiquity to the transitory character of dynasties, the eternal misery of all things; and this emanation of the centuries, overwhelming and funereal, like the scent of a mummy, makes itself felt even in the simplest minds. Rosanette yawned greatly. They went back to the hotel.

After their breakfast an open carriage came round for them. They started from Fontainebleau at a point where several roads diverged, then went up at a walking pace a gravelly road leading towards a little pine-wood. The trees became larger, and, from time to time, the driver would say, "This is the Frères Siamois, the Pharamond, the Bouquet de Roi," not forgetting a single one of these notable sites, sometimes even drawing up to enable them to admire the scene.

They entered the forest of Franchard. The carriage glided over the grass like a sleigh; pigeons which they could not see began cooing. Suddenly, the waiter of a café made his appearance, and they got down in front of the gate of a garden full of round tables. Then, passing the walls of a ruined abbey, they made their way over some big boulders, and soon reached the lower part of the gorge.

It is covered on one side with sandstones and juniper-trees tangled together, while on the other side the ground, almost quite bare, slopes towards the hollow of the valley, where a path makes a pale line through the purple heather; and far above could be traced a flat cone-shaped summit with a telegraph-tower behind it.

Half-an-hour later they stepped out of the vehicle once more, in order to climb the heights of Aspremont.

The roads form zigzags between the thick-set pine-trees under rocks with angular outlines. All this corner of the forest has a sort of muffled, wild and solitary look. It brings up thoughts of hermits—companions of huge stags with fiery crosses between their horns, who welcomed with paternal smiles the good kings of France when they knelt before their grottoes. The warm air was filled with a resinous odour, and roots of trees crossed one another like veins close to the soil. Rosanette stumbled over them, grew dejected, and wanted to cry.

But, at the very top, she became joyous once more on finding, under a roof made of branches, a sort of tavern where carved wood was sold. She drank a bottle of lemonade, and bought a holly-stick; and, without one glance towards the landscape which disclosed itself from the plateau, she entered the Brigands' Cave, with a waiter carrying a torch in front of her. Their carriage was awaiting them in the Bas Breau.

A painter in a blue smock was working at the foot of an oak-tree with his box of colours on his knees. He raised his head and watched them as they passed.

In the middle of the hill of Chailly, the sudden breaking of a cloud caused them to pull up the hoods of their cloaks. Almost immediately the rain stopped, and the paving-stones of the street glistened under the sun when they were re-entering the town.

Some travellers, who had recently arrived, informed them that a terrible battle had stained Paris with blood.[9] Rosanette and her lover were not surprised. Then everybody left; the hotel became quiet, the gas was put out, and they were lulled to sleep by the murmur of the fountain in the courtyard.

On the following day they went to see the Wolf's Gorge, the Fairies' Pool, the Long Rock, and the *Marlotte*. Two days later, they began again at random, just as their coachman thought fit to drive them, without asking where they were, and often even neglecting the famous sites.

They felt so comfortable in their old landau, low as a sofa, and covered with a rug made of a striped material which was quite faded. The ditches, filled with brushwood, stretched out under their eyes with a gentle, continuous movement. White rays passed like arrows through the tall ferns. Sometimes a road that was no longer used appeared straight in front of them, and here and there was a feeble growth of weeds. In the centre between four cross-roads, a crucifix extended its four arms. In other places, stakes were bending down like dead trees, and little curved paths, which were lost under the leaves, made them feel a longing to pursue them. At the same moment the horse turned round; they entered there; they plunged into the mud. Further down moss had sprouted out at the edges of the deep ruts.

They believed that they were far away from all other people, quite alone. But suddenly a game-keeper with his gun, or a band of women in rags with big bundles of sticks on their backs, would hurry past them.

When the carriage stopped, there was a universal silence. The only sounds that reached them were the breathing of the horse in the shafts with the faint, repeated cry of a bird.

The light at certain points illuminating the outskirts of the wood, left the interior in deep shadow, or else, dimmed in the foreground by a sort of dusk, it exhibited in the background a violet mist, a white radiance. The midday sun, falling directly on wide tracts of greenery, made splashes of light over them, hung gleaming drops of silver from the ends of the branches, streaked the grass with long lines of emeralds, and flung gold spots on the beds of dead leaves. When they let their heads fall back, they could distinguish the sky through the tops of the trees. Some of them, which were enormously high, looked like patriarchs or emperors, or, touching one another at their extremities formed with their long shafts, as it were, triumphal arches; others, growing obliquely from their base, looked like falling columns. Occasionally this array of vertical lines would open out. Then, enormous green waves rolling away in unequal curves to the bottom of the valleys, towards which advanced the crests of other hills looking down on blond plains, which ended by losing themselves in a misty paleness.

Standing side by side, on some rising ground, they felt, as they drank in the air, the pride of a life more free penetrating into the depths of their souls, with an abundance of energy and joy which they could not explain.

The variety of trees furnished a diversified spectacle. The beeches with their smooth white bark twisted their tops together. Ash trees softly curved their bluish branches. In the tufts of the hornbeams rose up holly stiff as bronze. Then came a row of thin birches, bent into elegiac attitudes; and the pine-trees, symmetrical as organ pipes, seemed to be singing a song as they swayed to and fro. There were gigantic guarled oaks which writhed as they strained upward from the ground pressed close against each other, and with firm torso-like trunks launched forth to heaven desperate appeals with their bare arms like a group of Titans struck motionless in their rage. An atmosphere of gloom, a feverish languor, brooded over the pools, whose sheets of water were overshadowed by thorn-trees. The lichens on their banks, where the wolves come to drink, are of the colour of sulphur, burnt, as it were, by the footprints of witches, and the incessant croaking of the frogs responds to the cawing of the crows as they wheel through the air. After this they passed through the monotonous glades, planted here and there with saplings. The sound of iron falling with a succession of rapid blows could be heard. On the side of the hill a group of quarrymen were breaking the rocks. These rocks became more and more numerous and finally filled up the entire landscape, cube-shaped like houses, flat like flag-stones, propping up, overhanging, and became intermingled with each other, as if they were the ruins, unrecognisable and monstrous, of some vanished city. But the wild chaos they exhibited made one rather dream of volcanoes, of deluges, of great unknown cataclysms. Frédéric said they had been there since the beginning of the world, and would remain so till the end. Rosanette turned aside her head, declaring that this would drive her out of her mind, and went off to collect sweet heather. The little violet blossoms, packed close together grew in patches, and the soil, which came away from their roots, made a soft dark fringe on the sand spangled with quartz.

One day they reached a point half-way up a hill, where the soil was full of sand. Its surface, untrodden till now, was streaked resembling symmetrical waves. Here and there, like promontories on the dry bed of an ocean, rose rocks with the vague outlines of animals, tortoises thrusting forward their heads, crawling seals, hippopotami, and bears. Not a soul around them. Not a single sound. The sand glowed under the dazzling rays of the sun, and all at once in this vibration of light the animals seemed to move. They hurried away quickly, flying from the dizziness that had seized hold of them, almost frightened.

The solemnity of the forest exercised an influence over them, and hours passed in silence, during which, allowing themselves to yield to the lulling effects of springs, they remained as it were sunk in a calm intoxication. With his arm around her waist, he listened to her talking while the birds were warbling, noticed with the same glance the black grapes on her bonnet and the juniper-berries, the folds of her veil, and the spiral forms assumed by the clouds, and when he bent towards her the freshness of her skin mingled with the strong perfume of the woods. They found amusement in everything. They showed one another, as a curiosity, cobwebs hanging from bushes, holes in the middle of stones full of water, a squirrel on the branches, the way in which two butterflies kept flying after them; or else, twenty yards from them, under the trees, a doe strode on peacefully, with an air of nobility and gentleness, its fawn walking by its side.

Rosanette would have liked to run after it to embrace it.

She got very much alarmed once, when a man suddenly appeared and showed her three vipers in a box. She wildly flung herself into Frédéric's arms. He felt happy at the thought that she was weak and that he was strong enough to defend her.

That evening they dined at an inn on the banks of the Seine. The table was near the window, Rosanette sitting opposite him, and he contemplated her little fine white nose, her upturned lips, her bright eyes, the cascading tresses of her chestnut hair, and her pretty oval face. Her dress of raw silk clung to her slightly sloping shoulders, and her two hands, emerging from their cuffs—cut up her food, poured out wine, moved over the table-cloth. The waiters placed before them a chicken with its four limbs stretched out, a stew of eels in a clay dish, bad wine, bread that was too hard, and knives with notches in them. All these things increased their pleasure, added to the illusion. It was as if they were travelling in Italy on their honeymoon. Before starting again they went for a walk along the bank of the river.

The soft blue sky, rounded like a dome, leaned on the horizon over the jagged outline of the woods. On the opposite side, at the end of the meadow, there was a village steeple; and further away, to the left, the roof of a house made a red spot on the river, which wound its way without any apparent motion. Some rushes bent over it, however, and the water lightly shook some poles with nets fixed at its edge. A wicker trap and two or three old fishing-boats there. Near the inn a girl in a straw hat was drawing buckets of water out of a well. Every time they came up again, Frédéric heard the grating sound of the chain with a feeling of inexpressible delight.

He had no doubt that he would be happy till the end of his days, so natural did his contentment feel to him, so much a part of his life, and so intimately associated with this woman's being. He was irresistibly impelled to address her with endearments. She answered with affectionate words, light taps on the shoulder, displays of tenderness that charmed him by their unexpectedness. He discovered in her quite a new sort of beauty, in fact, which was perhaps only the reflection of surrounding things, unless it happened to blossom from their hidden potential.

When they were resting in the open country, he would stretch himself out with his head on her lap, under the shelter of her parasol; or else they'd lie flat on their stomachs in the grass, face to face, gazing at each other so that their pupils seemed to intermingle, thirsting for one another and ever satiating their thirst, and then with half-closed eyelids they lay side by side without uttering a single word.

Now and then the distant rolling of a drum reached their ears. It was the signal-drum which was being beaten in the different villages calling on people to go and defend Paris.

"Oh! yes! 'tis the riots!" said Frédéric, with a disdainful pity, all this agitation seemed like misery to him compared to their love and eternal nature.

And they talked about whatever happened to come into their heads, things that were perfectly familiar to them, persons in whom they took no interest, a thousand trivialities. She chatted with him about her chambermaid and her hairdresser. One day she forgot herself to the point that she told him her age—twenty-nine years. She was becoming quite an old woman.

Several times, without intending it, she gave him some particulars with reference to her own life. She had been a "shop girl," had taken a trip to England, and had begun studying for the stage; all this she told without any explanation of how these changes had come about; and he found it impossible to reconstruct her entire history.

She related to him more about herself one day when they were seated side by side under a plane-tree at the back of a meadow. At the road-side, further down, a little barefooted girl, standing amid a heap of dust, was leading a cow to pasture. As soon as she caught sight of them she came up to beg, and while with one hand she held up her tattered petticoat, she kept scratching with the other her black hair, which, like a wig of Louis XIV's time, curled round her dark face, lighted by a magnificent pair of eyes.

"She will be very pretty one day," said Frédéric.

"How lucky she is, if she has no mother!" remarked Rosanette.

"Eh? How is that?"

"Certainly. I, if it were not for mine——"

She sighed, and began to speak about her childhood. Her parents were weavers in the Croix-Rousse.* She acted as an apprentice to her father. In vain did the poor man wear himself out with hard work; his wife was continually abusing him, and sold everything for drink. Rosanette could see, as if it were yesterday, the room they occupied with the looms arranged lengthwise against the windows, the pot boiling on the stove, the bed painted like fake mahogany, a cupboard facing it, and the obscure loft where she used to sleep up to the time when she was fifteen years old. At last a gentleman made his appearance on the scene—a fat man with a face of the colour of boxwood, a pious look, and a suit of black clothes. Her mother and this man had a conversation together, with the result that three days later—Rosanette stopped, and with a look in which there was as much bitterness as shamelessness:

"It was done!"

Then, in response to a gesture of Frédéric:

"As he was married (he would have been afraid of compromising himself in his own house), I was brought to a private room in a restaurant, and told that I would be happy, that I would get a handsome present.

"At the door, the first thing that struck me was a golden candelabra on a table, laid for two. A mirror on the ceiling showed their reflections, and the blue silk hangings on the walls made the entire room look like an alcove; I was seized with astonishment. You understand—a poor creature who had never seen anything before. In spite of my dazed mental condition, I got frightened. I wanted to leave. However, I remained.

"The only seat in the room was a sofa close beside the table. It was so soft that it gave way under me. The heating vent in the middle of the carpet sent out towards me warm air, and there I sat without touching a thing. The waiter, who was standing near me, urged me to eat. He poured out for me immediately a

---

*The Croix-Rousse was a neighborhood of silk weavers and workers in Lyons.

large glass of wine. My head began to swim, I wanted to open the window. He said to me:

" 'No, Mademoiselle! that is forbidden.' "

"And he left me.

"The table was covered with lots of things that I had never seen before. Nothing there seemed good to me. Then I decided to try the pot of jam, and patiently waited. I did not know what prevented him from coming. It was very late—midnight at least—I couldn't bear the fatigue any longer. While pushing aside one of the pillows, in order to hear better, I found under my hand a kind of album—a book of engravings, they were vulgar pictures. I was sleeping on top of it when he entered the room."

She bowed her head and remained pensive.

The leaves rustled around them. Amid the tangled grass a great foxglove was swaying to and fro. The sunlight flowed like a wave over the green expanse, and the silence was interrupted at intervals by the grazing of the cow, which they could no longer see.

Rosanette kept her eyes fixed on a particular spot, three feet away from her, her nostrils heaving, and her mind absorbed in thought. Frédéric caught hold of her hand.

"How you suffered, poor darling!"

"Yes," said she, "more than you imagine! So much so that I wanted to put an end to it all—they had to fish me out of the river!"

"What?"

"Ah! think no more about it! I love you, I am happy! kiss me!"

And she picked off, one by one, the sprigs of the thistles which clung to the hem of her gown.

Frédéric was thinking mostly about what she had not told him. What were the means by which she had gradually emerged from such misery? To what lover did she owe her education? What had occurred in her life down to the day when he first came to her house? Her latest admission forbade these questions. All he asked her was how she had made Arnoux's acquaintance.

"Through Vatnaz."

"Wasn't it you that I once saw with both of them at the Palais-Royal?"

He referred to the exact date. Rosanette made a movement which showed a sense of deep pain.

"Yes, it is true! I was not very happy during that time!"

But Arnoux had proved himself a very good fellow. Frédéric had no doubt of it. However, their friend was an odd character, full of faults. He took pains to remind her of them. She quite agreed with him on this point.

"Never mind! He is likeable, all the same, the rascal!"

"Still—even now?" said Frédéric.

She began to redden, half smiling, half angry.

"Oh, no! that's an old story. I don't keep anything hidden from you. Even though it might be so, with him it is different. Besides, I don't think you are nice towards your victim!"

"My victim!"

Rosanette caught hold of his chin.

"No doubt!"

And changing into baby talk:

"Haven't always been so good! Never went night-night with his wife?"

"I! never at any time!"

Rosanette smiled. He felt hurt by this smile of hers, which seemed to him a proof of indifference.

But she went on gently, and with one of those looks which seem to appeal for a denial of the truth:

"Are you perfectly certain?"

"Not a doubt of it!"

Frédéric solemnly declared on his word of honour that he had never bestowed a thought on Madame Arnoux, as he was too much in love with another woman.

"With whom, pray?"

"Why, with you, my beauty!"

"Ah! don't laugh at me! I don't like it!"

He thought it a prudent course to invent a story—to pretend that he was swayed by a passion. He manufactured some circumstantial details. This woman, however, had made him very unhappy.

"You certainly have not been lucky," said Rosanette.

"Oh! oh! I may have been!" wishing to convey in this way that he had been often fortunate in his love-affairs, so that she might have a better opinion of him, just as Rosanette did not avow how many lovers she had had, in order that he might have more respect for her—for there will always be found in the midst of the most intimate confidences restrictions, false shame, delicacy, and pity. You divine either in the other or in yourself precipices or muddy paths which prevent you from penetrating any farther; moreover, you feel that you will not be understood. It is hard to express accurately the thing you mean, whatever it may be; and this is the reason why perfect unions are rare.

The poor Maréchale had never known one better than this. Often, when she gazed at Frédéric, tears came into her eyes; then she would raise them or cast a glance towards the horizon, as if she saw there some bright dawn, perspectives of boundless happiness. At last, she confessed one day to him that she wished to have a mass said, "so that it might bring a blessing on our love."

How was it, then, that she had resisted him so long? She herself could not say. He repeated his question a great many times; and she replied, as she clasped him in her arms:

"It was because I was afraid, my darling, of loving you too much!"

On Sunday morning, Frédéric read, amongst the list of the wounded given in a newspaper, the name of Dussardier. He let out an exclamation, and showing the paper to Rosanette, declared that he was going to leave at once for Paris.

"For what purpose?"

"In order to see him, to take care of him!"

"You are not going to leave me by myself, are you?"

"Come with me!"

"To poke my nose in a brawl like that? Oh, no, thanks!"

"Well, I cannot——"

"Oh, la, la! as if they had need of nurses in the hospitals! And then, what concern is he of yours any longer? Everyone for himself!"

He was roused to indignation by this egoism on her part, and he reproached himself for not being in the capital with the others. Such indifference to the misfortunes of the nation had something petty and bourgeois about it. And now, all of a sudden, his love weighed on him as if it were a crime. For an hour they were quite cool towards each other.

Then she appealed to him to wait, and not expose himself to danger.

"Suppose you happen to be killed?"

"Well, I should only have done my duty!"

Rosanette jumped to her feet. His first duty was to love her; but, no doubt, he did not care about her any longer. There was no common sense in what he was going to do. Good heavens! what an idea!

Frédéric rang for his bill. But to get back to Paris was not an easy matter. The Leloir mail-coach had just left; the Lecomte berlins were not running; the stage-coach from Bourbonnais would not be passing till a late hour that night, and perhaps it might be full, one could never tell. After he had lost a great deal of time in making enquiries about the various modes of transportation, the idea occurred to him to travel by post-horse. The post master refused to supply him with horses, as Frédéric had no passport. Finally, he hired an open carriage—the same one in which they had driven about the country—and at about five o'clock they arrived in front of the Hôtel du Commerce at Melun.*

The market-place was covered with piles of arms. The prefect had forbidden the National Guards to proceed towards Paris. Those who did not belong to his department wished to continue on. There was a great deal of shouting, and the inn was packed with a noisy crowd.

Rosanette, seized with terror, said she would not go a step further, and once more begged him to stay. The innkeeper and his wife joined in her entreaties. A decent sort of man who happened to be dining there intervened, and observed that the fighting would be over in a very short time. Besides, one ought to do his duty. This made the Maréchale cry even harder. Frédéric got exasperated. He handed her his purse, kissed her quickly, and disappeared.

On reaching Corbeil, he learned at the station that the insurgents had cut the rails at regular intervals, and the coachman refused to drive him any farther; he said that his horses were "overspent."

Through his influence, however, Frédéric managed to procure an old cabriolet, which, for the sum of sixty francs, without taking into account the tip for the driver, was to take him as far as the Barriere d'Italie.† But a hundred yards from the barrier his coachman made him get out and he turned back. Frédéric was walking along the

---

*City east of Paris.

†A southern limit of Paris.

pavement, when suddenly a sentinel thrust out his bayonet. Four men seized him, exclaiming:

"This is one of them! Look out! Search him! Brigand! scoundrel!"

And he was so thoroughly stupefied that he let himself be dragged to the guard-house of the barrier, at the very point where the Boulevard des Gobelins and Boulevard de l'Hôpital meet the Rue Godefroy and Rue Mouffetard.

Four barricades at the ends of four different routes formed enormous sloping ramparts of paving-stones. Torches were glimmering here and there. In spite of the rising clouds of dust he could distinguish infantrymen and National Guards, all with their faces blackened, disheveled, and haggard. They had just captured the square, and had shot a number of men. Their rage had not yet cooled. Frédéric said he had come from Fontainebleau to the relief of a wounded comrade who lodged in the Rue Bellefond. Not one of them would believe him at first. They examined his hands; they even put their noses to his ear to make sure that he did not smell of powder.

However, after repeating over and over the same thing, he finally satisfied a captain, who directed two fusiliers to take him to the guard-house of the Jardin des Plantes. They descended the Boulevard de l'Hôpital. A strong breeze was blowing. It revived him.

After this they turned up the Rue du Marché aux Chevaux. The Jardin des Plantes at the right formed a long black mass, whilst at the left the entire front of the Hôpital de la Pitié,* with every window lit up, blazed like it was on fire, and shadows passed rapidly behind the window-panes.

The two men charged with escorting Frédéric went off. Another accompanied him to the Polytechnic School. The Rue Saint-Victor was quite dark, without a gas-lamp or a light in any of the houses. Every ten minutes could be heard the words:

"Sentries! Attention!"

And this exclamation, cast into the midst of the silence, was prolonged like the repeated striking of a stone against the side of a chasm as it falls through space.

---

*A hospital.

Every now and then the stamp of heavy footsteps could be heard drawing nearer. This was a patrol consisting of at least a hundred men. From this confused mass escaped whisperings and the dull clanking of iron; and, moving away with a rhythmic swing, it melted into the darkness.

In the middle of the crossing, where several streets met, a dragoon sat motionless on his horse. From time to time a dispatch rider passed at a rapid gallop; then the silence fell once more. Cannons, which were being drawn along the streets, made, on the pavement, a heavy rolling sound that seemed full of menace—a sound different from every ordinary sound—which struck fear in the heart. The sound seemed to intensify the silence, which was profound, unlimited—a black silence. Men in white smocks accosted the soldiers, spoke one or two words to them, and then vanished like phantoms.

The guard-house of the Polytechnic School overflowed with people. The doorway was blocked by women, who had come to see their sons or their husbands. They were sent on to the Panthéon, which had been transformed into a morgue; and nobody paid any attention to Frédéric. He pressed forward resolutely, solemnly declaring that his friend Dussardier was waiting for him, that he was dying. At last they sent a corporal to accompany him to the top of the Rue Saint-Jacques, to the Mayor's office in the twelfth arrondissement.

The Place du Panthéon was filled with soldiers lying asleep on straw. The day was breaking; the camp-fires were going out.

The insurrection had left terrible traces in this quarter. The surface of the streets, from one end to the other, was churned up. Against the wrecked barricades, omnibuses, gas-pipes, and cart-wheels were piled up. In certain places there were little dark pools, which must have been blood. The houses were riddled with bullets, and their framework could be seen through the holes in the plaster. Window-blinds, attached only by a single nail, hung like rags. The staircases having fallen in, doors opened on to vacant space. The interiors of rooms could be perceived with their wallpaper in shreds. In some instances delicate objects had remained intact. Frédéric noticed a clock, a parrot's perch, and some engravings.

When he entered town hall, the National Guards were incessantly chattering about the deaths of Bréa and Négrier, about the deputy Charbonnel, and about the Archbishop of Paris. He heard them saying that the Duc d'Aumale had landed at Boulogne, that Barbès had fled from Vincennes, that artillery was coming from Bourges,[10] and that abundant aid was arriving from the provinces. About three o'clock some one brought good news.

Spokesmen for the insurgents were in conference with the President of the Assembly.

They all rejoiced; and as he had a dozen francs left, Frédéric sent for a dozen bottles of wine, hoping by this means to hasten his deliverance. Suddenly musket fire was heard. The drinking stopped. They peered with distrustful eyes into the unknown—it might be Henry V.*

To be free of all responsibility, they took Frédéric to the town hall of the eleventh arrondissement, which he was not permitted to leave till nine o'clock in the morning.

He started at a running pace from the Quai Voltaire. At an open window an old man in his shirtsleeves was crying, with his eyes raised. The Seine glided peacefully along. The sky was of a clear blue; and in the trees round the Tuileries birds were singing.

Frédéric was just crossing the Place du Carrousel when a stretcher happened to be passing by. The soldiers at the guard-house immediately presented arms; and the officer, putting his hand to his shako, said: "Honour to unfortunate bravery!" This phrase seemed to have almost become a matter of duty. He who pronounced it appeared to be, on each occasion, filled with profound emotion. A group of people in a state of fierce excitement followed the stretcher, exclaiming:

"We will avenge you! we will avenge you!"

The vehicles kept moving about on the boulevard, and women in front of their doors were shredding linen. Meanwhile, the outbreak had been quelled, or very nearly so. A proclamation from Cavaignac,† just posted up, announced the fact. At the top of the

---

*The Comte de Chambord (1820–1883), Legitimist contender to the throne.

†The minister of war in the Provisional Government, General Louis-Eugène Cavaignac crushed the June rebellion in 1848.

Rue Vivienne, a company of the Garde Mobile appeared. Then the prosperous citizens shouted enthusiastically. They raised their hats, applauded, danced, wanted to kiss them, and to offer them a drink; and flowers, flung by ladies, fell from the balconies.

At last, at ten o'clock, at the moment when the cannon was booming as an attack was being made on the Faubourg Saint-Antoine, Frédéric reached the abode of Dussardier. He found the bookkeeper in his garret, lying asleep on his back. From the adjoining apartment a woman tiptoed—Mademoiselle Vatnaz.

She took Frédéric aside and explained to him how Dussardier had gotten wounded.

On Saturday, on the top of a barricade in the Rue Lafayette, a boy wrapped in a tricoloured flag cried out to the National Guards: "Are you going to shoot your brothers?" As they advanced, Dussardier threw down his gun, pushed away the others, sprang over the barricade, and, with a kick, knocked down the young insurgent, from whom he tore the flag. He had afterwards been found under a heap of debris with a slug of copper in his thigh. It was necessary to make an incision in order to extract the bullet. Mademoiselle Vatnaz arrived the same evening, and since then had not left his side.

She intelligently prepared everything that was needed for the dressings, assisted him in taking his medicine or other liquids, attended to his slightest wishes, left and returned again with footsteps more light than those of a fly, and gazed at him with eyes full of tenderness.

Frédéric, during the two following weeks, did not fail to come back every morning. One day, while he was speaking about the devotion of Vatnaz, Dussardier shrugged his shoulders:

"Oh! no! she does this out of self-interest."

"Do you think so?"

He replied: "I am sure of it!" without seeming disposed to give any further explanation.

She smothered him with kindnesses, carrying her attentions so far as to bring him the newspapers in which his gallant action was extolled. He even confessed to Frédéric that his conscience bothered him.

Perhaps he ought to have put himself on the other side with the smocks; for, indeed, a heap of promises had been made to them which had not been carried out. Their conquerors hated the Republic; and, then, they had treated them very harshly. No doubt they were in the wrong—not entirely, however; and the honest fellow was tormented by the thought that he might have fought against the righteous cause. Sénécal, who was imprisoned in the Tuileries, under the terrace at the water's edge,* had none of this mental anguish.

There were nine hundred men in the place, huddled together in the midst of filth, without the slightest order, their faces blackened with powder and coagulated blood, shivering with fever and breaking out into cries of rage, and those who were brought there to die were not separated from the rest. Sometimes, on hearing the sound of an explosion, they believed that they were all going to be shot. Then they threw themselves against the walls, and after that fell back again into their places, so much numbed by suffering that it seemed to them that they were living in a nightmare, a mournful hallucination. The lamp, which hung from the arched roof, looked like a stain of blood, and little green and yellow flames fluttered about, caused by the vapors from the cellar. Through fear of epidemics, a commission was established. When he had advanced a few steps, the president recoiled, frightened by the stench from the excrement and the corpses.

As soon as the prisoners drew near a vent-hole, the National Guards who were on sentry, in order to prevent them from shaking the bars of the grating, prodded them indiscriminately with their bayonets.

As a rule they showed no pity. Those who had not taken part in the fighting wished to distinguish themselves. There was an outbreak of fear. They avenged themselves at the same time for the newspapers, the clubs, the mobs, the doctrines for everything that had exasperated them during the last three months, and in spite of the victory that had been achieved, equality (as if punishing its defenders and ridiculing its enemies) manifested itself triumphantly—an equality of brute beasts, a same level of bloody turpitude; for the fanaticism of self-interest balanced the frenzy of the poor, aristocracy had the same fits of fury as the mob, and the cotton cap did not

---

*Since prisons were full, insurgents were incarcerated in these improvised cells.

prove less hideous than the red cap. The public psyche was disturbed just as it would be after great natural disasters. Sensible men lost their sanity for the rest of their lives on account of it.

Père Roque had become very courageous, almost foolhardy. Having arrived on the 26th at Paris with some of the inhabitants of Nogent, instead of going back with them, he had gone to give his assistance to the National Guard encamped at the Tuileries; and he was quite satisfied to be placed on sentry duty in front of the terrace at the water's side. There, at least, he had these brigands under his thumb! He was delighted at their defeat and degradation, and he could not refrain from hurling abuse at them.

One of them, a young lad with long fair hair, put his face to the bars, and asked for bread. M. Roque ordered him to hold his tongue. But the young man repeated in a mournful tone:

"Bread!"

"Have I any to give you?"

Other prisoners presented themselves at the vent-hole, with their bristling beards, their burning eyeballs, all pushing forward, and yelling:

"Bread!"

Père Roque was indignant at seeing his authority slighted. In order to frighten them he took aim at them; and, borne upwards towards the ceiling by the crush that nearly smothered him, the young man, with his head thrown backward, once more exclaimed:

"Bread!"

"Hold on! here it is!" said Père Roque, firing a shot from his gun. There was a fearful howl—then, silence. At the side of the trough something white was left lying on the ground.

After this, M. Roque returned horne, for he had a house in the Rue Saint-Martin, which he used as a temporary residence; and the damage done to the front of the building during the riots had in no small degree contributed to his rage. It seemed to him, seeing it again, that he had exaggerated how bad it was. His recent act had a soothing effect on him, as if it compensated him for his loss.

It was his daughter who opened the door for him. She immediately said that she had been worried because of his excessively prolonged absence. She was afraid that he had met with some misfortune—that he had been wounded.

This manifestation of filial love softened Père Roque. He was astonished that she should have set out on a journey without Catherine.

"I sent her out on an errand," was Louise's reply.

And she made enquiries about his health, about one thing or another; then, with an air of indifference, she asked him whether he had happened to come across Frédéric:

"No; I didn't see him!"

It was on his account alone that she had come up from the country.

Some one was walking at that moment in the corridor.

"Oh! excuse me——"

And she disappeared.

Catherine had not found Frédéric. He had been away several days, and his intimate friend, M. Deslauriers, was now living in the provinces.

Louise reappeared, shaking all over, without being able to utter a word. She leaned against the furniture.

"What's the matter with you? Tell me—what's the matter with you?" exclaimed her father.

She indicated by a wave of her hand that it was nothing, and with a great effort of will she regained her composure.

The caterer on the opposite side of the street brought them soup. But Père Roque had experienced too much violent emotion. "It wouldn't go down," and at dessert he had a sort of fainting fit. A doctor was sent for at once, and he prescribed a potion. Then, when M. Roque was in bed, he asked to be covered with as many blankets as possible in order to make him sweat. He sighed; he moaned.

"Thanks, my good Catherine! Kiss your poor father, my pet! Ah! these revolutions!"

And, when his daughter scolded him for having made himself ill by worrying on her account, he replied:

"Yes! you are right! But I couldn't help it! I am too sensitive!"

CHAPTER II

Madame Dambreuse, in her boudoir, between her niece and Miss John, was listening to M. Roque as he described the hardships of his military life.

She was biting her lips, and appeared to be in pain.

"Oh! 'tis nothing! it will pass!"

And, with a gracious air:

"We are going to have an acquaintance of yours at dinner with us,—Monsieur Moreau."

Louise gave a start.

"And then just a few intimate friends—amongst others, Alfred de Cisy."

And she praised his manners, his personal appearance, and especially his moral character.

Madame Dambreuse was being less untruthful than she thought; the Vicomte was contemplating marriage. He said so to Martinon, adding that Mademoiselle Cécile was certain to like him, and that her parents would accept him.

To dare to confide such a thing, he must have had satisfactory information with regard to her dowry. Now Martinon had a suspicion that Cécile was M. Dambreuse's natural daughter; and it is probable that it would have been a very bold move on his part to ask for her hand. Such audacity, of course, was not unaccompanied by danger; and for this reason Martinon had, up to the present, acted in a way that would not compromise him. Besides, he did not see how he could get rid of the aunt. Cisy's confidence induced him to make up his mind; and he had formally made his proposal to the banker, who, seeing no obstacle to it, had just informed Madame Dambreuse about the matter.

Cisy presently made his appearance. She arose and said:

"We thought you had forgotten us. Cécile, shake hands!"

At the same moment Frédéric entered the room.

"Ah! at last we have found you!" exclaimed Père Roque. "I have been to your house three times this week with Louise."

Frédéric had carefully avoided them. He explained that he spent all his days beside a wounded comrade.

Apart from that he had been tied up with lots of things for a long time, and he tried to invent stories to explain his conduct. Luckily the guests arrived in the midst of his explanation. First of all M. Paul de Grémonville, the diplomat whom he met at the ball; then Fumichon, that manufacturer whose conservative zeal had scandalised him one evening. After them came the old Duchesse de Montreuil Nantua.

But then two loud voices could be heard in the entrance-hall. "I am certain of it," said one. "Dear lady! Dear lady!" the other responded, "Please calm yourself." It was M. de Nonancourt, an old buck with the air of a mummy preserved in cold cream, and that of Madame de Larsillois, the wife of a prefect of Louis Philippe. She was terribly frightened, for she had just heard an organ playing a polka which was a signal amongst the insurgents. Many of the wealthy class of citizens had similar apprehensions; they thought that men in the catacombs were going to blow up the Faubourg Saint-Germain. Strange noises escaped from cellars, and suspicious things were happening behind windows.

Everyone in the meantime made an effort to calm Madame de Larsillois. Order was re-established. There was no longer anything to fear.

"Cavaignac has saved us!"

As if the horrors of the insurrection had not been sufficiently numerous, they exaggerated them. There had been twenty-three thousand convicts on the side of the Socialists—no less!

They had no doubt whatever that food had been poisoned, that Gardes Mobiles had been sawn in half between two planks, and that there had been inscriptions on flags inciting pillage and arson.

"And something more!" added the ex-prefect.

"Oh, dear!" said Madame Dambreuse, whose modesty was shocked, while she gave a warning glance towards the three young girls in the room.

M. Dambreuse came forth from his study accompanied by Martinon. She turned her head round and responded to a bow from Pellerin, who was advancing towards her. The artist gazed in a restless fashion towards the walls. The banker took him aside, and conveyed to him that it was desirable for the moment to conceal his revolutionary painting.

"No doubt," said Pellerin, the rebuff which he received at the Club of Intellect having modified his opinions.

M. Dambreuse let it slip out very politely that he would give him orders for other works.

"But excuse me. Ah! my dear friend, what a pleasure!"

Arnoux and Madame Arnoux stood before Frédéric.

He felt dizzy. Rosanette had been irritating him all afternoon with her display of admiration for soldiers, and his old passion was reawakened.

The steward came to announce that dinner was on the table. With a look she directed the Vicomte to take Cécile's arm, while she said in a low voice to Martinon, "You scoundrel!" And then they proceeded into the dining-room.

Under the green leaves of a pineapple, in the middle of the tablecloth, lay a dorade, with its head pointing towards a haunch of venison and its tail just grazing a mound of crayfish. Figs, huge cherries, pears, and grapes (the first fruits from Parisian hothouses) rose like pyramids in trays of old Saxon china. Here and there a bunch of flowers mingled with the shining silver. The white silk blinds, drawn down in front of the windows, filled the room with a soft light. It was cooled by two fountains, in which there were pieces of ice; and tall men-servants, in short breeches, waited on them. All these luxuries seemed more precious after the emotion of the past few days. They felt a fresh delight at possessing things which they had been afraid of losing; and Nonancourt expressed the general sentiment when he said:

"Ah! let us hope that these Republican gentlemen will allow us to dine!"

"In spite of their fraternity!" Père Roque added, with an attempt at wit.

These two personages were placed respectively at the right and at the left of Madame Dambreuse, her husband being exactly opposite her, between Madame Larsillois, at whose side was the diplomat and the old Duchesse, who was elbow to elbow with Fumichon. Then came the painter, the earthenware dealer, and Mademoiselle Louise; and, thanks to Martinon, who had taken his place to be near Cécile, Frédéric found himself beside Madame Arnoux.

She wore a black barège gown, a gold bracelet on her wrist, and, as on the first day that he dined at her house, something red in her hair, a branch of fuchsia twisted round her chignon. He could not help saying:

" 'Tis a long time since we saw each other."

"Ah!" she returned coldly.

He went on, in a mild tone, which mitigated the impertinence of his question:

"Have you thought of me on occasion?"

"Why should I think of you?"

Frédéric was hurt by these words.

Perhaps, "You are right, after all."

But very soon, regretting what he had said, he swore that he had not lived a single day without being ravaged by the memory of her.

"I don't believe a single word of it, Monsieur."

"And yet, you know that I love you!"

Madame Arnoux made no reply.

"You know that I love you!"

She still kept silent.

"Well, then, go to blazes!" said Frédéric to himself.

And, as he raised his eyes, he caught sight of Mademoiselle Roque at the other side of Madame Arnoux.

She thought it gave her a coquettish look to dress entirely in green, a colour which contrasted horribly with her red hair. The buckle of her belt was too high and her collar cramped her neck. This lack of elegance had, no doubt, contributed to the coldness which Frédéric at first displayed towards her. She watched him from where she sat, some distance away from him, with curious glances; and Arnoux, close to her side, in vain lavished his gallantries—he could not get three words out of her, so that, finally giving up on trying to please, he listened to the conversation which was now on the subject of pineapple purées at the Luxembourg.

Louis Blanc, according to Fumichon, owned a large house in the Rue Saint-Dominique, which he refused to rent to the workers.

"For my part, what I find funny," said Nonancourt, "is Ledru-Rollin hunting on the royal estates."

"He owes twenty thousand francs to a gold-smith!" Cisy interposed, "and 'tis said that——"

Madame Dambreuse stopped him.

"Ah! how dreadful to be getting hotheaded over politics! and for such a young man, too! Pay attention rather to your fair neighbour!"

After this, the serious-minded guests attacked the newspapers. Arnoux took it upon himself to defend them. Frédéric mixed himself up in the discussion, describing them as commercial establishments just like any other house of business. Those who wrote for them were, as a rule, imbeciles or jokers; he claimed to be acquainted with journalists, and combatted his friend's generous sentiments with sarcasm.

Madame Arnoux did not notice that this was said through a feeling of spite against her.

Meanwhile, the Vicomte was racking his brain to find a way to conquer Mademoiselle Cécile. He began by finding fault with the shape of the decanters and the engraving on the knives, in order to show his artistic tastes. Then he talked about his stables, his tailor and his shirtmaker. Finally, he took up the subject of religion, and seized the opportunity of conveying to her that he fulfilled all his duties.

Martinon set to work in an even better fashion. Talking at a monotonous pace and without taking his eyes off of her, he praised, her birdlike profile, her dull blond hair, and her hands, which were unusually short and stubby. The plain-looking young girl was delighted at this shower of flatteries.

It was impossible to hear anything, as all present were talking at the tops of their voices. M. Roque wanted "an iron hand" to govern France. Nonancourt even regretted that the death penalty was abolished for political crimes. They ought to have all these scoundrels put to death together. "They're cowards too," said Fumichon. "I don't see anything brave about taking shelter behind a barricade."

"Speaking of that, tell us about Dussardier," said M. Dambreuse, turning towards Frédéric.

The worthy shop-assistant was now a hero, like Sallesse, the brothers Jeanson, the wife of Pequillet, etc.

Frédéric, without waiting to be pressed, related his friend's story, which shed a reflected glory on him.

Then they came quite naturally to refer to various acts of courage.

According to the diplomat, it was not hard to face death, witness the case of men who fight duels.

"We might take the Vicomte's testimony on that point," said Martinon.

The Vicomte's face got very flushed.

The guests stared at him, and Louise, more astonished than the rest, murmured:

"What is it, pray?"

"He *sank* before Frédéric," returned Arnoux, in a very low tone.

"Do you know anything about it, Mademoiselle?" said Nonancourt quickly, and he related her reply to Madame Dambreuse, who, bending forward a little, began to fix her gaze on Frédéric.

Martinon did not wait for Cécile's questions. He informed her that this affair concerned a woman of questionable character. The young girl drew back slightly in her chair, as if to escape from contact with such a libertine.

The conversation started up again. The great wines of Bordeaux were sent round, and the guests became animated. Pellerin had a grudge against the Revolution, because he attributed to it the complete loss of the Spanish Museum.

This is what grieved him most as a painter.

As he made the latter remark, M. Roque asked:

"Are you not the painter of a very notable picture?"

"Perhaps! What is it?"

"It shows a lady in a costume—faith!—a little skimpy, with a purse, and a peacock behind her."

Frédéric, in his turn, reddened. Pellerin pretended that he had not heard the words.

"Nevertheless, it is certainly by you! For your name is written at the bottom of it, and there is a line on it stating that it is Monsieur Moreau's property."

One day, when Père Roque and his daughter were waiting at his residence to see him, they saw the Maréchale's portrait. The old gentleman had even taken it for "a Gothic painting."

"No," said Pellerin rudely, " 'tis a woman's portrait."

Martinon added:

"And a woman who is very much alive! Isn't that so, Cisy?"

"Oh! I know nothing about it."

"I thought you were acquainted with her. But, since it makes you uncomfortable, I must beg a thousand pardons!"

Cisy lowered his eyes, proving by his embarrassment that he must have played a sorry part in connection with this portrait. As for Frédéric, the model could only be his mistress. It was one of those convictions which are immediately formed, and the faces of the assembly revealed it with the utmost clarity.

"How he lied to me!" said Madame Arnoux to herself.

"It is for her, then, that he left me," thought Louise.

Frédéric had an idea that these two stories might compromise him; and when they were in the garden, he reproached Martinon with his indiscretion. Mademoiselle Cécile's wooer burst out laughing in his face.

"Oh, not at all! it will do you good! Go ahead!"

What did he mean? Besides, what was the cause of this good nature, so contrary to his usual conduct? Without giving any explanation, he proceeded towards the far end, where the ladies were seated. The men were standing round them, and, in their midst, Pellerin was spouting his ideas. The form of government most favourable for the arts was an enlightened monarchy. He was disgusted with modern times, "if only on account of the National Guard"—he looked back regretfully to the Middle Ages and the days of Louis XIV. M. Roque congratulated him on his opinions, confessing that they overcame all his prejudices against artists. But almost without a moment's delay he went off when the voice of Fumichon caught his attention.

Arnoux tried to prove that there were two Socialisms—a good one and a bad one. The manufacturer saw no difference whatsoever between them, his head becoming dizzy with rage at the mere mention of the word "property."

" 'Tis a law written on the face of Nature! Children cling to their toys. All peoples, all animals share my opinion. The lion even, if he were able to speak, would declare himself a landowner! Thus I myself, messieurs, began with capital of fifteen thousand francs. Would you be surprised to hear that for thirty years I used to get up at four o'clock every morning? I've had as much pain as five hundred devils in making my fortune! And people will come and tell me I'm not the master, that my money is not my money; in short, that property is theft!"

"But Proudhon——"

"Let me alone with your Proudhon! if he were here I think I'd strangle him!"

He would have strangled him. After the intoxicating drink he had swallowed Fumichon did not know what he was talking about any longer, and his apoplectic face was on the point of exploding like a bombshell.

"Good day, Arnoux," said Hussonnet, who was walking briskly across the grass.

He brought M. Dambreuse the first sheet of a pamphlet, bearing the title of "The Hydra," the Bohemian defending the interests of a reactionary club, and in that capacity he was introduced by the banker to his guests.

Hussonnet amused them by relating how the candlemakers hired three hundred and ninety-two street urchins to bawl out every evening "Light up!" and then by ridiculing the principles of '89, the emancipation of the negroes, and the orators of the Left; and he even went so far as to do a skit on "Prudhomme on a Barricade,"[11] perhaps under the influence of a kind of simple-minded jealousy of these rich people who had enjoyed a good dinner. The caricature did not please them too much. Their faces grew long.

This, however, was not a time for joking, so Nonancourt observed, as he recalled the death of Monseigneur Affre and that of General de Bréa. These events were being constantly alluded to, and arguments were made about them. M. Roque described the archbishop's conduct in his final moments as "everything that one could call sublime." Fumichon gave the palm to the soldier, and instead of simply expressing regret for these two murders, they discussed them with a view to determining which excited the greatest indignation. A second comparison came next, namely, between Lamoricière and Cavaignac, M. Dambreuse glorifying Cavaignac, and Nonancourt, Lamoricière.*

Not one of the persons present, with the exception of Arnoux, had ever seen either of them at work. None the less, everyone formulated an irrevocable judgment with reference to their activities.

Frédéric, however, declined to give an opinion on the matter, confessing that he had not served as a soldier. The diplomat and M. Dambreuse gave him an approving nod of the head. In fact, to have fought against the insurrection was to have defended the Republic. The result, although favourable, strengthened the republican cause; and now that they had gotten rid of the vanquished, they also wanted to be rid of the conquerors.

As soon as they had gone out into the garden, Madame Dambreuse, taking Cisy aside, chided him for his awkwardness. When she caught sight of Martinon, she sent him away, and then tried to learn from her future nephew the cause of his witticisms at the Vicomte's expense.

"There isn't any."

"And all this, as it were, for the glory of M. Moreau. What is the reason for it?"

"There's no reason. Frédéric is a charming fellow. I am very fond of him."

"And so am I. Bring him here. Go and look for him!"

After two or three commonplace remarks, she began by lightly criticizing her guests, and in this way she placed him on a higher level than the others. He did not fail to put down the rest of the ladies a little, which was a subtle way of paying her compliments. But she left his side from time to time, as it was a reception-night, and ladies were constantly arriving; then she returned to her seat, and the fortuitous arrangement of the chairs enabled them to avoid being overheard.

She showed herself to be playful and yet serious, melancholy and yet quite rational. Her daily occupations interested her very

---

*Christophe Lamoricière was a general under the orders of Cavaignac during the June repression (see footnote on p. 375).

little—there was a whole category of feelings of a more lasting nature. She complained about poets, who misrepresent the facts of life, then she raised her eyes towards heaven, asking him the name of a star.

Two or three Chinese lanterns had been suspended from the trees; the wind shook them, and rays of coloured light flickered across her white dress. She sat, in her usual fashion, a little back in her armchair, with a footstool in front of her. The tip of a black satin shoe could be seen; and at intervals Madame Dambreuse allowed a louder word than usual, and sometimes even a laugh, to escape her.

These coquetries did not affect Martinon, who was occupied with Cécile; but they were bound to make an impression on M. Roque's daughter, who was chatting with Madame Arnoux. She was the only member of her own sex present whose manners did not appear disdainful. Louise came and sat beside her; then, yielding to the desire to open her heart:

"Does he not speak well—Frédéric Moreau, I mean?"

"Do you know him?"

"Oh! very well! We are neighbours; and he used to play with me when I was quite a little girl."

Madame Arnoux cast at her a sidelong glance, which meant:

"You aren't in love with him, are you?"

The young girl's face replied with an untroubled look:

"Yes."

"You see him often, then?"

"Oh, no! only when he comes to his mother's house. 'Tis ten months now since he came. He promised, however, to come more often."

"The promises of men are not to be too much relied on, my child."

"But he has not deceived me!"

"As he did others!"

Louise shivered: "Can it be by any chance that he promised something to her;" and her face became puckered with distrust and hate.

Madame Arnoux was almost afraid of her; she would have gladly withdrawn what she had said. Then both became silent.

As Frédéric was sitting opposite them on a folding-stool, they kept staring at him, the one discreetly out of the corner of her eye, the other boldly, with parted lips, so that Madame Dambreuse said to him:

"Come, now, turn round, and let her have a good look at you!"

"Whom do you mean?"

"Why, Monsieur Roque's daughter!"

And she teased him on having won the heart of this young girl from the provinces. He denied that this was so, and tried to laugh.

"Is it believable, I ask you? Such an ugly creature!"

However, he experienced an intense feeling of gratified vanity. He remembered the other party which he had left, his heart filled with bitter humiliation, and he drew a deep breath, for it seemed to him that he was now in the environment that really suited him, as if all these things, including the Dambreuse mansion, belonged to him. The ladies formed a semicircle around him while they listened to him, and in order to create an effect, he declared that he was in favor of the re-establishment of divorce,* which he maintained should be easily procurable, so as to enable people to leave and come back to one another without any limit as often as they liked. They uttered loud protests; a few of them began to talk in whispers. Little exclamations every now and then burst forth from the shadows at the foot of the creeper-covered wall. It was like the excited cackling of hens; and he went on developing his theory with that self-confidence which is generated by the awareness of success. A man-servant brought into the arbour a tray laden with ices. The gentlemen drew close together and began to chat about the recent arrests.

Thereupon Frédéric took his revenge on the Vicomte by making him believe that he might be prosecuted as a Legitimist. The other objected saying he had not stirred outside of his own room. His adversary enumerated the chances against him. MM. Dambreuse and Grémonville found the discussion very amusing. Then they complimented Frédéric, while expressing regret at the same time that he did not employ his abilities in the defence of order. They grasped his hand with the utmost warmth; he might for the future

---

*The right of divorce was recognized by the French revolutionary government and subsequently abolished during the Restoration.

count on them. At last, just as everyone was leaving, the Vicomte made a low bow to Cécile:

"Mademoiselle, I have the honour of wishing you a very good evening."

She replied coldly:

"Good evening." But she gave Martinon a parting smile.

Pére Roque, in order to continue the conversation between himself and Arnoux, offered to see him home, "as well as Madame"—they were going the same way. Louise and Frédéric walked in front of them. She had caught hold of his arm; and, when she was some distance away from the others she said:

"Ah! at last! at last! I've suffered enough all evening! How nasty those women were! What haughty airs they had!"

He made an effort to defend them.

"First of all, you might certainly have spoken to me the moment you came in, after being away a whole year!"

"It was not a year," said Frédéric, glad to be able to give some sort of rejoinder on this point in order to avoid the other questions.

"Be it so; the time appeared very long to me, that's all. But, during this horrid dinner, one would think you felt ashamed of me. Ah! I understand—I don't possess what is needed to please a man as they do."

"You are mistaken," said Frédéric.

"Really! Swear to me that you don't love any of them."

He did swear.

"You love nobody but me alone?"

"Good lord!"

This assurance filled her with delight. She would have liked to lose her way in the streets, so that they might walk about together the whole night.

"I have been so much tormented down there! Nothing was talked about but barricades. I imagined I saw you falling on your back covered with blood! Your mother was confined to her bed with rheumatism. She knew nothing about what was happening. I had to hold my tongue. I could stand it no longer, so I took Catherine with me."

And she related to him all about her departure, her journey, and the lie she told her father.

"He's bringing me back in two days. Come tomorrow evening, as if you were merely paying a casual visit, and take advantage of the opportunity to ask for my hand in marriage."

Never had Frédéric been further from the idea of marriage. Besides, Mademoiselle Roque appeared to him a rather absurd little person. How different she was from a woman like Madame Dambreuse! A very different future was in store for him. He had found reason today to feel perfectly certain on that point; and, therefore, this was not the time to involve himself, from mere sentimental motives, in a step of such momentous importance. It was necessary now to be decisive—and then he had seen Madame Arnoux once more. Nevertheless he was rather embarrassed by Louise's candour.

He said in reply to her last words:

"Have you considered this matter?"

"What?" she exclaimed, frozen with astonishment and indignation.

He said that to marry at such a time as this would be folly.

"So you don't want me?"

"But, you don't understand me!"

And he launched into a complicated speech in order to impress upon her that he was held back by more serious considerations; that he had business on hand which would take a long time to deal with; that even his inheritance had been placed in jeopardy (Louise cut all these explanations short with one simple word); that, last of all, the present political situation made the thing undesirable. So, then, the most reasonable course was to wait patiently for some time. Matters would, no doubt, right themselves—at least, he hoped so; and, as he couldn't think of any more excuses, he pretended to have suddenly remembered that he should have been with Dussardier two hours ago.

Then, bowing to the others, he darted down the Rue Hauteville, took a turn round the Gymnase Theatre, returned to the boulevard, and quickly rushed up Rosanette's four flights of stairs.

M. and Madame Arnoux left Père Roque and his daughter at the entrance of the Rue Saint-Denis. Husband and wife returned home without exchanging a word, as he was unable to continue chattering any longer, feeling quite worn out. She even leaned against his shoulder. He was the only man who had displayed any honourable sentiments during the evening. She felt full of indulgence towards him. Meanwhile, he was still feeling spite against Frédéric.

"Did you notice his face when a question was asked about the portrait? When I told you that he was her lover, you did not wish to believe what I said!"

"Oh! yes, I was wrong!"

Arnoux, gratified with his triumph, pressed the matter even further.

"I'd even make a bet that when he left us, a little while ago, he went to see her again. He's with her at this moment, you may be sure! He's finishing the evening with her!"

Madame Arnoux had pulled down her hat very low.

"Why, you're shaking all over!"

"That's because I feel cold!" was her reply.

As soon as her father was asleep, Louise made her way into Catherine's room, and, taking her by the shoulders, shook her.

"Get up—quick! as quick as you can! and go and fetch a cab for me!"

Catherine replied that there was not one to be had at such an hour.

"Will you come with me yourself there, then?"

"Where, might I ask?"

"To Frédéric's house!"

"Impossible! What do you want to go there for?"

It was in order to have a talk with him. She could not wait. She must see him immediately.

"Just think of what you're about to do! To present yourself this way at a house in the middle of the night! Besides, he's asleep by this time!"

"I'll wake him up!"

"But this is not a proper thing for a young girl to do!"

"I am not a young girl—I'm his wife! I love him! Come—put on your shawl!"

Catherine, stood at the side of the bed, thinking. She said at last:

"No! I won't go!"

"Well, stay behind then! I'll go there by myself!"

Louise glided like a snake down the staircase. Catherine rushed after her, and joined her on the sidewalk outside the house. Her remonstrances were fruitless; and she followed the girl, fastening her jacket as she hurried along in the rear. The walk appeared to her exceedingly tedious. She complained that her legs were getting weak from age.

"After all, I haven't the same thing to drive me on that you have!"

Then she grew softened.

"Poor soul! You haven't anyone now but your Cathy do you?"

From time to time scruples took hold of her.

"Ah, this is a nice thing you're making me do! Suppose your father happened to wake and miss you! Lord God, let us hope nothing terrible happens!"

In front of the Théâtre des Variétés, a patrol of National Guards stopped them.

Louise immediately explained that she was going with her servant to look for a doctor in the Rue Rumfort. The patrol allowed them to pass on.

At the corner of the Madeleine they came across a second patrol, and, Louise having given the same explanation, one of the National Guards asked in return:

"Is it for a nine months' ailment, deary?"

"Oh, damn it!" exclaimed the captain, "no foul language in the ranks! Pass on, ladies!"

In spite of the captain's orders, they still kept cracking jokes.

"Have a good time!"

"My respects to the doctor!"

"Look out for the big bad wolf!"

"They like laughing," Catherine remarked in a loud tone. "That's the way it is to be young."

At last they reached Frédéric's house.

Louise gave the bell a vigorous pull, which she repeated several times. The door opened a little, and, in answer to her inquiry, the concierge said:

"No!"

"But he must be in bed!"

"I tell you he's not. Why, for nearly three months he has not slept at home!"

And the little window of the lodge dropped back down sharply, like the blade of a guillotine.

They remained in the darkness under the archway.

An angry voice cried out to them:

"Be off with you!"

The door was again opened; they went out.

Louise had to sit down on a gate-stone; and clasping her face with her hands, she wept copious tears welling up from her full heart. The day was breaking, and carts were making their way into the city.

Catherine led her back home, holding her up, kissing her, and offering her every sort of consolation that she could extract from her own experience. She need not give herself so much trouble about a lover. If this one failed her, she could find others.

CHAPTER III

When Rosanette's enthusiasm for the Mobile Guards had calmed down, she became more charming than ever, and Frédéric gradually glided into the habit of living with her.

The best portion of the day was the morning on the terrace. In a light gauze dress, and with slippers on her bare feet, she kept moving about him—went and cleaned her canaries' cage, gave her gold-fish some water, and with a coal shovel did a little gardening in the window-box filled with soil, from which arose a trellis of nasturtiums, climbing up the wall. Then, leaning, on the balcony, they stood side by side, gazing at the vehicles and the passers-by; and they warmed themselves in the sunlight, and made plans for the evening. He would go out for only two hours at most, and, after that, they would go to some theatre, where they would get seats in front of the stage; and Rosanette, with a large bouquet of flowers in her hand, would listen to the instruments, while Frédéric, leaning close to her ear, would whisper funny stories or loving words. At other times they took an open carriage to the Bois de Boulogne and would drive until late at night. At last they made their way home through the Arc de Triomphe and the grand avenue, inhaling the breeze, with the stars above their heads, and with all the gas-lamps aligned in the background like a double string of luminous pearls.

Frédéric always waited for her when they were going out together. She took a very long time fastening the two ribbons of her bonnet; and she smiled at herself in the mirror set in the wardrobe; then she would slip her arm through his, and, make him look at himself in the glass beside her:

"We look nice this way, the two of us side by side. Ah! my poor darling, I could eat you up!"

He was now her chattel, her property. She wore on her face a continuous radiance, while at the same time she seemed softer and more tender, more rounded in figure; and, without being able to explain in what way, he found her changed, nevertheless.

One day she informed him, as if it were a very important bit of news, that Arnoux had lately set up a linen-draper's shop for a woman who was formerly employed in his factory. He used to go there every evening—"he spent a great deal on it no less than a week ago; he had even given her a set of rosewood furniture."

"How do you know that?" said Frédéric.

"Oh! I'm sure of it."

Delphine, while carrying out some orders for her, had made enquiries about the matter. She must, then, be much attached to Arnoux to take such a deep interest in his movements. He contented himself with saying to her in reply:

"What does this matter to you?"

Rosanette looked surprised at this question.

"Why, the rascal owes me money. Isn't it atrocious to see him keeping beggars?"

Then, with an expression of triumphant hate in her face:

"Besides, she is having a nice laugh at him. She has three others on hand. So much the better; and I'll be glad if she squeezes every last penny out of him!"

Arnoux had, in fact, let himself be used by the girl from Bordeaux with the indulgence of an infatuated old fool. His factory had closed down. The entire state of his affairs was pitiful; so that, in order to set them afloat again, he first thought of opening a *café chantant*, at which only patriotic songs would be sung. With a grant from the Minister, this establishment would become at the same time a focus for the purpose of propagandism and a source of profit. Now that power had been directed into a different channel, the thing was impossible.

His next idea was a big military hat-making business. He lacked the capital, however, to give it a start.

He was not more fortunate in his domestic life. Madame Arnoux was less agreeable in manner towards him, sometimes even a little rude. Marthe always took her father's side. This increased the discord, and the house was becoming an intolerable place. He often went out in the morning, spent his day making long excursions out of the city, in order to divert his thoughts, then dined at a rustic tavern, abandoning himself to his reflections.

The prolonged absence of Frédéric disturbed him. Then he presented himself one afternoon, begged him to come and see him as in former days, and obtained from him a promise to do so.

Frédéric was afraid to go back to Madame Arnoux's house. He felt as if he had betrayed her. But this conduct was very cowardly. There was no excuse for it. There was only one way of ending the matter, and so, one evening, he set out on his way.

As the rain was falling, he had just turned up the Passage Jouffroy, when, under the light shed from the shop-windows, a fat little man accosted him. Frédéric had no difficulty in recognising Compain, that orator whose motion had excited so much laughter at the club. He was leaning on the arm of an individual in a zouave's red cap, with a very long upper lip, a complexion as yellow as an orange, a tuft of beard, and was gazing at Compain with big eyes filled with admiration.

Compain was, no doubt, proud of him, for he said:

"Let me introduce you to this good fellow! He is a bootmaker and a patriot whom I include amongst my friends. Come, let us have a drink together."

Frédéric having declined his offer, he immediately thundered against Rateau's motion, which he described as a manœuvre of the aristocrats. In order to put an end to it, it would be necessary to begin '93 over again! Then he enquired about Regimbart and some others, who were also well known, such as Masselin, Sanson, Lecornu, Maréchal, and a certain Deslauriers, who had been implicated in the case of the carbines lately intercepted at Troyes.

All this was news to Frédéric. Compain knew nothing more about the subject. He left the young man with these words:

"You'll come soon, will you not? for you're a member, aren't you?"

"Of what?"

"The calf's head!"

"What calf's head?"

"Ha, you joker!" returned Compain, giving him a tap on the stomach.

And the two terrorists dived into a café.

Ten minutes later Frédéric was no longer thinking of Deslauriers. He was on the sidewalk of the Rue de Paradis in front of a house; and he was staring at the light which came from a lamp in the second floor behind a curtain.

Finally, he ascended the stairs.

"Is Arnoux in?"

The chambermaid answered:

"No; but come in all the same."

And, abruptly opening a door:

"Madame, it is Monsieur Moreau!"

She arose, whiter than the collar round her neck.

"To what do I owe the honour—of a visit—so unexpected?"

"Nothing. The pleasure of seeing old friends once more."

And as he took a seat:

"How is Arnoux?"

"Very well. He has gone out."

"Ah, I understand! still following his old nightly practices. A little distraction!"

"And why not? After a day spent in making calculations, the head needs a rest."

She even praised her husband as a hard-working man. Frédéric was irritated at hearing this; and pointing towards a piece of black cloth with a narrow blue braid which lay on her lap:

"What is it you are doing there?"

"A jacket which I am trimming for my daughter."

"Now that you remind me of it, I have not seen her. Where is she?"

"At a boarding-school," was Madame Arnoux's reply.

Tears came into her eyes. She held them back, while she rapidly plied her needle. To keep his composure, he picked up an issue of *L'Illustration* which had been lying on the table close to where she sat.

"These caricatures by Cham* are very funny, aren't they?"

"Yes."

Then they relapsed into silence once more.

All of a sudden, a fierce gust of wind shook the windows.

"What weather!" said Frédéric.

---

*Surname of a famous French caricaturist.

"It was very good of you, indeed, to come here in the midst of this dreadful rain."

"Oh! what do I care about that? I'm not like those whom it prevents, no doubt, from going to keep their appointments."

"What appointments?" she asked with an innocent air.

"Don't you remember?"

A shudder ran through her and she hung her head.

He gently laid his hand on her arm.

"I assure you that you have given me great pain."

She replied, with a sort of wail in her voice:

"But I was frightened about my child."

She told him about Eugène's illness, and all the tortures which she had endured on that day.

"Thank you! Thank you! I doubt you no longer. I love you as much as ever."

"Ah! no; it is not true!"

"Why so?"

She glanced at him coldly.

"You forget the other! the one you took with you to the races! the woman whose portrait you have—your mistress!"

"Well, yes!" exclaimed Frédéric, "I don't deny anything! I am a scoundrel! Just listen to me!"

If he had had her, it was through despair, as one commits suicide. However, he had made her very unhappy in order to avenge himself on her with his own shame.

"What mental anguish! Do you not realise what this means?"

Madame Arnoux turned away her beautiful face while she held out her hand to him; and they closed their eyes, absorbed in a kind of sweet, infinite intoxication. Then they stood face to face, gazing at one another.

"Could you believe it possible that I no longer loved you?"

She replied in a low voice, full of caressing tenderness:

"No! in spite of everything, I felt at the bottom of my heart that it was impossible, and that one day the obstacle between us would disappear!"

"So did I; and I was dying to see you again."

"I once passed close by you in the Palais-Royal!"

"Did you really?"

And he spoke to her of the happiness he experienced at coming across her again at the Dambreuses' house.

"But how I hated you that evening as I was leaving the place!"

"Poor boy!"

"My life is so sad!"

"And mine, too! If it were only the sorrows, the anxieties, the humiliations, all that I endure as a wife and mother, since everyone must die one day, I would not complain; the dreadful part is my loneliness, without anyone."

"But you have me here with you!"

"Oh! yes!"

A sob of deep emotion made her bosom swell. She spread out her arms, and they embraced as their lips met in a long kiss.

The floor creaked. There was a woman standing close to them; it was Rosanette. Madame Arnoux had recognised her. Her eyes, opened wide with astonishment and indignation, stared at her. Finally, Rosanette said to her:

"I have come to see Monsieur Arnoux about a business matter."

"As you can see, he is not here."

"Ah! that's true," returned the Maréchale. "Your maid was right! A thousand apologies!"

And turning towards Frédéric:

"So here you are!"

The familiar tone in which she addressed him, and in her own presence, too, made Madame Arnoux flush as if she had received a slap right across the face.

"I tell you again, he is not here!"

Then the Maréchale, who was looking this way and that, said quietly:

"Let us go home together! I have a cab waiting outside."

He pretended not to hear.

"Come! let's go!"

"Ah! yes! now's your chance! Go! go!" said Madame Arnoux.

They went off together, and she stooped over the banister in order to see them once more, and a laugh—piercing, heart-rending, reached them from the top of the stairs. Frédéric pushed Rosanette into the cab, sat down opposite her, and during the entire drive did not utter a word.

The disgrace and its appalling consequences had been brought about by himself alone. He experienced at the same time the dishonour of a crushing humiliation and the regret caused by the loss of his new-found happiness. Just when, at last, he had it in his grasp, it had for ever more become impossible, and all because of this loose woman, this harlot. He would have liked to strangle her. He was choking with rage. When they had gotten into the house he flung his hat on a piece of furniture and tore off his cravat.

"Ha! that was a nice thing you did just now, admit it!"

She planted herself boldly in front of him.

"Ah! well, what of it? Where's the harm?"

"What! Are you spying on me?"

"Is that my fault? Why do you go to amuse yourself with virtuous women?"

"That's beside the point! I won't have you insulting her!"

"How have I insulted her?"

He had no answer to make to this, and in a more spiteful tone:

"But on the other occasion, at the Champ de Mars——"

"Ah! you bore us to death with your old flames!"

"You bitch!"

He raised his fist.

"Don't kill me! I'm pregnant!"

Frédéric staggered back.

"You are lying!"

"Why, just look at me!"

She seized a candlestick, and pointing at her face:

"Don't you recognise the signs?"

Little yellow spots dotted her skin, which was strangely swollen. Frédéric did not deny the evidence. He went to the window, and opened it, took a few steps up and down the room, and then sank into an armchair.

This event was a calamity which, in the first place, put off their separation, and, next, upset all his plans. The notion of being a father, moreover, appeared to him grotesque, unthinkable. But why? If, in place of the Maréchale——And his reverie became so deep that he had a kind of hallucination. He saw there, on the carpet, in front of the fireplace, a little girl. She resembled Madame Arnoux and himself a little—dark, and yet fair, with two black eyes, thick eyebrows, and a red ribbon in her curly hair. (Oh, how he would have loved her!) And he seemed to hear her voice saying: "Papa! papa!"

Rosanette, who had just undressed herself, came across to him, and noticing a tear in his eyelids, kissed him gravely on the forehead.

He arose, saying:

"By Jove, we mustn't kill this little one!"

Then she talked a lot of nonsense. To be sure, it would be a boy, and its name would be Frédéric. It would be necessary for her to begin making its clothes; and, seeing her so happy, he was moved to pity for her. As he no longer felt any anger towards her, he wanted to know the reason for the step she had just taken. She said it was because Mademoiselle Vatnaz had sent her that day a bill which had fallen due a long time ago; and so she hastened to Arnoux to get the money from him.

"I'd have given it to you!" said Frédéric.

"It is a simpler course for me to get over there what belongs to me, and to pay back to the other one her thousand francs."

"Is this really all you owe her?"

She answered:

"Of course!"

On the following day, at nine o'clock in the evening (the hour recommended by the concierge), Frédéric went to Mademoiselle Vatnaz's residence.

In the hallway, he bumped into the furniture, which was heaped together. But the sound of voices and of music guided him. He opened a door, and tumbled into the middle of a party. Standing up before a piano, which a young lady in spectacles was playing, Delmar, as serious as a pontiff, was reciting a humanitarian poem on prostitution; and his hollow voice rolled to the accompaniment of the sustained chords. A row of women sat close to the wall, attired, as a rule, in dark colours without collars or sleeves. Five or six men, all intellectuals, occupied seats here and there. In an armchair was seated a former writer of fables, a wreck of a man now; and the pungent odour of the two lamps was intermingled with the aroma of the chocolate which filled a number of bowls placed on the card-table.

Mademoiselle Vatnaz, with an Oriental shawl thrown over her shoulders, sat at one side of the fireplace. Dussardier sat facing her at the other side. He looked a bit embarrassed by his position. Besides, he was rather intimidated by his artistic surroundings. Had Vatnaz, then, broken off with Delmar? Perhaps not. However, she seemed to be keeping a jealous watch on the worthy shop-assistant; and Frédéric having asked to have a word with her, she made a sign to him to join them in her room. When the thousand francs were put down before her, she asked, in addition, for interest.

"It isn't worth while," said Dussardier.

"Hold your tongue!"

This cowardice on the part of so brave a man pleased Frédéric as a justification of his own conduct. He brought back the bill with him, and never again referred to the scandal at Madame Arnoux's house. But from that time forth he saw clearly all the defects in the Maréchale's character.

She possessed incurable bad taste, incomprehensible laziness, the ignorance of a savage, so much so that she regarded Doctor Derogis as a person of great celebrity, and she felt proud of entertaining him and his wife, because they were "married people."

She lectured with a pedantic air on the affairs of daily life to Mademoiselle Irma, a poor little creature endowed with a little voice, who had as a protector a gentleman "very well off," an ex-clerk in the Custom-house, who had a rare talent for card tricks. Rosanette used to call him "My big sweetie-pie." Frédéric could no longer endure the repetition of her stupid words, such as "Nothing doing," "Get lost," "One can never tell," etc.; and her habit of wiping off the dust in the morning from her trinkets with a pair of old white gloves. He was above all disgusted by her treatment of her servant, whose wages were constantly in arrears, and who even lent her money. On the days when they settled their accounts, they used to wrangle like two fish-wives; and then, on becoming reconciled, used to embrace each other. It was a relief to him when Madame Dambreuse's evening parties began again.

There, at any rate, he found something to amuse him. She was well versed in the intrigues of society, the changes of ambassadors, the personnel of the fashion houses, and, if commonplace remarks escaped her lips, it was done in such a becoming fashion, that one could take it ironically or as pure politeness. It was worthwhile to watch the way in which, in the midst of twenty people chatting around her, she would, without overlooking anyone, elicit the answers she desired and avoid those that were dangerous. Things of a very simple nature, when related by her, seemed like confidences. Her slightest smile gave rise to dreams; in short, her charm, like the exquisite scent which she usually wore, was complex and indefinable.

While he was with her, Frédéric experienced on each occasion the pleasure of a new discovery, and, nevertheless, he always found her equally serene the next time they met, like the reflection of limpid waters.

But why was there such coldness in her manner towards her niece? At times she even darted strange looks at her.

As soon as the question of marriage was raised, she objected to it, when discussing the matter with M. Dambreuse, based on the state of "the dear child's" health, and had at once taken her off to the baths of Balaruc.* On her return other excuses were raised by her—that the young man was not in a good position, that this ardent passion did not appear to be a very serious attachment, and that no risk would be run by waiting. Martinon had replied, when the suggestion was made to him, that he would wait. His conduct was sublime. He sang Frédéric's praises. He did more. He enlightened him on the best way to please Madame Dambreuse, insinuating that he knew the aunt's feeling through her niece.

As for M. Dambreuse, far from exhibiting jealousy, he treated his young friend with the utmost attention, consulted him about various things, and even showed anxiety about his future, so that one day, when they were talking about Père Roque, he whispered with a sly air:

"You have done well."

And Cécile, Miss John, the servants and the porter, every one of them in the house was charming to him. He came there every evening, leaving Rosanette. Her approaching maternity rendered her more serious, and even a little melancholy, as if she were tormented by worry. To every question put to her she replied:

"You are mistaken; I am quite well."

She had, in fact, signed five IOUs, and not having the courage to tell Frédéric after the first had been paid, she had gone back to the

---

*Spa on the French Riviera.

home of Arnoux, who had promised her, in writing, a third of his profits in a company providing gaslight in the towns of Languedoc (a marvellous undertaking!), while requesting her not to make use of this note before the meeting of shareholders. The meeting was postponed from week to week.

Meanwhile the Maréchale needed money. She would have died sooner than ask Frédéric for any. She did not want to get it from him; it would spoil their love. He contributed a great deal to the household expenses; but a little carriage, which he hired by the month, and other sacrifices, which were indispensable since he had begun to visit the Dambreuses, prevented him from doing more for his mistress. On two or three occasions, when he came back to the house at a different time than usual, he imagined he could see men's backs disappearing behind the door, and she often went out without wishing to state where she was going. Frédéric did not attempt to enquire into these matters. One of these days he would make up his mind as to his future course of action. He dreamed of another life which would be more amusing and more noble. Such an ideal made him partial to the Dambreuse mansion.

It was an informal branch of the Rue de Poitiers club.* There he met the great M. A., the illustrious B., the profound C., the eloquent Z., the immense Y., the old mouthpieces of the Left Centre, the paladins of the Right, the stalwart middle-of-the-roaders; the eternal characters of the political comedy. He was astonished at their abominable style of talking, their pettiness, their spite, their dishonesty—all these people, after voting for the Constitution, now striving to destroy it; and they got into a state of great agitation, and launched forth manifestoes, pamphlets, and biographies. Hussonnet's biography of Fumichon was a masterpiece. Nonancourt devoted himself to the work of propagandism in the country districts; M. de Grémonville worked on the clergy; and Martinon brought together the young men of the wealthy class. Each helped to the best of his ability, including Cisy. With his thoughts now all day long absorbed in serious matters, he made excursions here and there in a cab on party business.

*The conservatives held meetings in an apartment on the Rue de Poitiers in Paris.

M. Dambreuse was like a barometer, constantly indicating its latest direction. Lamartine could not be alluded to without eliciting from this gentleman the quotation of a famous phrase of the man of the people: "We've had enough poetry!" Cavaignac was, from this time forth, nothing better in his eyes than a traitor. The President,* whom he had admired for a period of three months, was beginning to go down in his estimation (as he did not appear to exhibit the "necessary energy"); and, as he always wanted a savior, his gratitude, since the affair of the Conservatoire, belonged to Changarnier:† "Thank God for Changarnier . . . Let us hope Changarnier . . . Oh, there's nothing to fear as long as Changarnier——"

M. Thiers was praised, above all, for his volume against Socialism, in which he showed that he was quite as much of a thinker as a writer. There was an immense laugh at Pierre Leroux, who had quoted passages from the philosophers to the Chamber. Jokes were made about the phalansterian tail.[12] They went to applaud the vaudeville show "The Market of Ideas" and its authors were compared to Aristophanes. Frédéric went to see it like the rest.

Political verbiage and good food had a dulling effect on his morality. Mediocre as these persons appeared to him, he felt proud to know them, and inwardly longed for their respect. A mistress like Madame Dambreuse would give him a position in society.

He set about taking the necessary steps for achieving that goal.

He made it his business to cross her path when she went for a walk, did not fail to go and greet her in her box at the theatre, and, being aware of the hours when she went to church, he would plant himself behind a pillar in a melancholy attitude. There was a continual interchange of little notes between them with regard to curiosities to which they drew each other's attention, preparations for a concert, or the borrowing of books or reviews. In addition to his visit each night, he sometimes made a call in the late afternoon; and he experienced an intensification of pleasure in successively passing through the large front entrance, through the courtyard,

---

*Louis-Napoléon Bonaparte (1808–1873), running against General Cavaignac, was elected by a vast majority (see footnote on p. 375).

†Nicolas Changarnier was a general who in June 1849 liberated the Conservatoire des Arts et Métiers, which was occupied by demonstrators.

through the entrance hall and through the two reception-rooms. Finally, he reached her boudoir, which was as quiet as a tomb, as warm as an alcove, and in which one brushed up against the upholstered furniture in the midst of objects of every sort placed here and there—lingerie chests, screens, bowls, and trays made of lacquer, or shell, or ivory, or malachite, expensive objects which were frequently replaced. Amongst them were simple things too: three pebbles from the beach at Etretat which were used as paper-weights, and a Frisian cap hung from a Chinese screen. Nevertheless, there was a harmony among all of these objects, and one was even impressed by the grandeur of the entire place, which was, no doubt, due to the loftiness of the ceiling, the richness of the door curtains, and the long silk fringe that floated over the gold legs of the stools.

She nearly always sat on a little sofa, close to the flower-stand in the recess of the window. Frédéric, seating himself on the edge of a large ottoman on castors, addressed compliments to her of the most appropriate kind that he could conceive; and she looked at him, with her head a little to one side, and a smile on her lips.

He read her poetry, into which he threw his whole soul in order to move her and inspire her admiration. She would now and then interrupt him with a disparaging remark or a practical observation; and their conversation relapsed incessantly into the eternal question of Love. They discussed the circumstances that produced it, whether women felt it more than men, and in what way they differed on that point. Frédéric tried to express his opinion, and, at the same time, to avoid being coarse or insipid. This became a sort of battle between them, sometimes enjoyable and at other times tedious.

Whilst at her side, he did not experience that ravishment of his entire being which drew him towards Madame Arnoux, nor the feeling of voluptuous delight with which Rosanette had, at first, inspired him. But he felt a passion for her as a thing that was unique and difficult to attain, because she was of aristocratic rank, because she was wealthy, because she was devout—imagining that she had a delicacy of sentiment as rare as the lace she wore, together with amulets against her skin, and modesty even in her depravity.

He made a certain use of his old passion, uttering in his new flame's ear all those amorous sentiments which Madame Arnoux had caused him to feel in earnest, and pretending that it was Madame Dambreuse herself who inspired them. She received all this like one accustomed to such things, and, without giving him a formal refusal, did not yield in the slightest degree; and he came no nearer to seducing her than Martinon did to getting married. In order to bring matters to an end with her niece's suitor, she accused him of having money as his motive, and even begged her husband to put the matter to the test. M. Dambreuse then declared to the young man that Cécile, being the orphan child of poor parents, had neither expectations nor a dowry.

Martinon, not believing that this was true, or feeling that he had gone too far to draw back, or through idiotic obstinacy which turns out to be an act of genius, replied that his patrimony, amounting to fifteen thousand francs a year, would be sufficient for them. The banker was touched by this unexpected display of altruism. He promised the young man the post of tax-inspector, undertaking to obtain it for him; and in the month of May, 1850, Martinon married Mademoiselle Cécile. There was no ball to celebrate the event. The young couple started the same evening for Italy. Frédéric came the next day to pay a visit to Madame Dambreuse. She appeared to him paler than usual. She sharply contradicted him about two or three matters of no importance. However, she went on to observe, all men were egoists.

There were, however, some devoted men, though he might happen himself to be the only one.

"Pooh, pooh! you're just like the rest of them!"

Her eyelids were red; she had been weeping.

Then, forcing a smile:

"Pardon me; I am in the wrong. Sad thoughts have taken possession of my mind."

He could not understand what she meant to convey by the last words.

"No matter! she is weaker than I imagined," he thought.

She rang for a glass of water, drank a mouthful of it, sent it away again, and then began to complain of the wretched way in which her servants waited on her. In order to amuse her, he offered to become her servant himself, pretending that he knew how to hand round plates, dust furniture, and announce visitors—in fact, to do the duties of a *valet-de-chambre*, or, rather, of a footman, although the latter was now out of fashion. He would have liked to cling on behind her carriage with a hat adorned with cock's feathers.

"And how I would follow you with majestic stride, carrying your little dog on my arm!"

"You are funny," said Madame Dambreuse.

Was it not foolish, he returned, to take everything seriously? There were enough miseries in the world without creating more. Nothing was worth the cost of a single pang. Madame Dambreuse raised her eyelids with a sort of vague approval.

This agreement in their views of life impelled Frédéric to take a bolder course. His former miscalculations now gave him insight. He went on:

"Our grandfathers lived better. Why not follow our impulses?" After all, love was not a thing of such importance in itself.

"But what you have just said is immoral!"

She had resumed her seat on the little sofa. He sat down at the side of it, near her feet.

"Don't you see that I am lying! For in order to please women, one must exhibit the levity of a buffoon or all the wild passion of tragedy! They only laugh at us when we simply tell them that we love them! For my part, I consider the exaggeration which tickles their fancy a profanation of true love, so that it is no longer possible to give expression to it, especially when addressing women who possess more than ordinary intelligence."

She gazed at him from under half-closed eye-lids. He lowered his voice, while he bent his head closer to her face.

"Yes! you frighten me! Perhaps I am offending you? Forgive me! I did not intend to say all that I have said! 'Tis not my fault! You are so beautiful!"

Madame Dambreuse closed her eyes, and he was astonished at his easy victory. The tall trees in the garden stopped their gentle quivering. Motionless clouds streaked the sky with long strips of red, and on every side everything seemed to come to a standstill. Then he remembered, in a blurry sort of way, evenings just the same as this, filled with the same unbroken silence. Where was it that he had known them?

He sank upon his knees, seized her hand, and swore that he would love her for ever. Then, as he was leaving her, she beckoned to him to come back, and said to him in a low tone:

"Come back to dinner! We'll be all alone!"

It seemed to Frédéric, as he descended the stairs, that he had become a different man, that he was surrounded by the balmy temperature of hot-houses, and that he was without question entering into the higher sphere of patrician adulteries and lofty intrigues. In order to reach the top all he required was a woman like this. Greedy, no doubt, for power and success, and married to a man of inferior calibre, for whom she had done prodigious services, she longed for some one strong who she could guide. Nothing was impossible now. He felt himself capable of riding two hundred leagues on horseback, of travelling for several nights in succession without fatigue. His heart overflowed with pride.

Just in front of him, on the pavement, a man wrapped in a seedy overcoat was walking with downcast eyes, and with such an air of dejection that Frédéric, as he passed, turned around to have a better look at him. The other raised his head. It was Deslauriers. He hesitated. Frédéric threw his arms around him.

"Ah! my poor old friend! What! Is it really you?"

And he dragged Deslauriers into his house, asking his friend a lot of questions all at the same time.

Ledru-Rollin's ex-commissioner commenced by describing the tortures to which he had been subjected. As he preached fraternity to the Conservatives, and respect for the laws to the Socialists, the former tried to shoot him, and the latter brought ropes to hang him with. After June he had been brutally dismissed. He found himself involved in a charge of conspiracy—that which was connected with the seizure of arms at Troyes. He had subsequently been released for lack of evidence. Then the action committee had sent him to London, where he had come to blows with his colleagues in the middle of a banquet. On his return to Paris——

"Why did you not call here, then, to see me?"

"You were always out! Your concierge had mysterious airs—I did not know what to think; and, besides, I had no desire to reappear before you as a defeated man."

He had knocked at the portals of Democracy, offering to serve it with his pen, with his voice, with all his energies. He had been rejected everywhere. They had mistrusted him; and he had sold his watch, his library, and even his linen.

"It would be much better to die on the prison-ships of Belle Isle with Sénécal!"*

Frédéric, who had been fastening his cravat, did not appear to be much affected by this news.

"Ha! so he has been deported, this good Sénécal?"

Deslauriers replied, while he surveyed the walls with an envious air:

"Not everybody has your luck!"

"Excuse me," said Frédéric, without noticing the allusion to his own circumstances, "but I am dining in the city. We must get you something to eat; order whatever you like. You can even take my bed!"

This cordial reception dissipated Deslauriers' bitterness.

"Your bed? But that might inconvenience you!"

"Oh, no! I have others!"

"Oh, all right!" returned the lawyer, with a laugh. "Pray, where are you dining?"

"At Madame Dambreuse's."

"Can it be that you are—perhaps——?"

"You are too inquisitive," said Frédéric, with a smile, which confirmed this hypothesis.

Then, after a glance at the clock, he sat down again.

"That's how it is! and we mustn't despair, my ex-defender of the people!"

"Mercy! let others worry about the people for a change!"

The lawyer detested the working-men, because he had suffered so much on their account in his province, a coal-mining district. Every pit had appointed a provisional government, from which he received orders.

"Besides, their conduct has been charming everywhere—at Lyons, at Lille, at Havre, at Paris! For, following the example of the

---

*A number of June insurgents were transported to Belle-Île, an island in Brittany.

manufacturers, who would exclude foreign products, these gentlemen call on us to banish the English, German, Belgian, and Savoyard workmen. As for their intelligence, what was the use of that precious trades' union of theirs which they established under the Restoration? In 1830 they joined the National Guard, without having the common sense to get control of it. Is it not a fact that, after '48, the various trade-unions reappeared with their banners? They even demanded representatives in the Chamber for themselves, who only speak on their behalf. All this is the same as if the beetroot representatives were to concern themselves about nothing save beetroot. Ah! I've had enough of these dodgers who in turn prostrate themselves before the scaffold of Robespierre, the boots of the Emperor, and the umbrella of Louis Philippe—a rabble who always yield allegiance to the person that flings bread into their mouths. They are always crying out against the venality of Talleyrand and Mirabeau;[13] but the messenger downstairs would sell his country for fifty centimes if they'd only promise him a tariff of three francs for every erand he ran. Ah! what a wretched state of affairs! We ought to set the four corners of Europe on fire!"

Frédéric said in reply:

"The spark was missing! You were simply a lot of shopboys, and even the best of you were nothing better than penniless students. As for the workmen, they may well complain; for, apart from a million taken from the civil list, of which you granted them with the vilest flattery, you have given them nothing, save fine phrases! The workman's certificate remains in the hands of the employer, and the person who is paid wages remains (even in the eye of the law), the inferior of his master, because his word is not believed. In short, the Republic seems to me a worn-out institution. Who knows? Perhaps Progress can be realised only through an aristocracy or through a single man? The initiative always comes from the top, and whatever may be the people's pretensions, they are lower than those placed over them!"

"That may be true," said Deslauriers.

According to Frédéric, the vast majority of citizens aimed only at a life of peace (he had been listening during his visits to the Dambreuses), and the odds were all on the side of the Conservatives. That party, however, was lacking new men.

"If you came forward, I am sure——"

He did not finish the sentence. Deslauriers saw what Frédéric meant, and passed his two hands over his forehead; then, all of a sudden:

"But what about yourself? Is there anything to prevent you from doing it? Why shouldn't you be a representative?"

Following a double election in the Aube there was a vacancy for a candidate. M. Dambreuse, who had been re-elected as a member of the Legislative Assembly, belonged to a different arrondissement.

"Would you like me to see what I can do?" He was acquainted with many publicans, schoolmasters, doctors, notaries' clerks and their employers. "Besides, you can make the peasants believe anything you like!"

Frédéric felt his ambition rekindling.

Deslauriers added:

"You ought to find a job for me in Paris."

"Oh! it would not be hard to manage it through Monsieur Dambreuse."

"As we happened to have been talking just now about coal-mines," the lawyer went on, "what has become of his big company? This is the sort of employment that would suit me, and I could make myself useful to them while preserving my own independence."

Frédéric promised that he would introduce him to the banker in the next few days.

The dinner, which he enjoyed alone with Madame Dambreuse, was a delightful affair. She sat facing him with a smile on her face at the opposite side of the table, whereon was placed a basket of flowers, while a lamp suspended above their heads shed its light on them; and, as the window was open, they could see the stars. They talked very little, distrusting themselves, no doubt; but, the moment the servants had turned their backs, they blew each other kisses. He told her about his idea of becoming a candidate. She approved, promising even to get M. Dambreuse to help.

As the evening advanced, some of her friends appeared to congratulate and sympathize with her; she must be so much pained at the loss of her niece. Besides, it was all very well for newly-married people to go on a trip; later there would be incumbrances, children. But really, Italy did not live up to one's expectations.

They were still at the age of illusions; and, the honeymoon made everything look beautiful. The last two who stayed behind were M. de Grémonville and Frédéric. The diplomat was not inclined to leave. At last he departed at midnight. Madame Dambreuse beckoned to Frédéric to go with him, and thanked him for this compliance with her wishes by giving him a gentle squeeze of the hand more delightful than anything before.

The Maréchale uttered an exclamation of joy on seeing him again. She had been waiting for him for the last five hours. He gave as an excuse for the delay an indispensable step which he had to take in the interests of Deslauriers. His face wore a look of triumph, a halo which dazzled Rosanette.

" 'Tis perhaps on account of your black coat, which fits you well; but I have never seen you look so handsome! How handsome you are!"

Carried away by tenderness, she made a vow inwardly never again to belong to any other man, no matter what might be the consequence, even if she were to die of hunger.

Her pretty eyes sparkled with such intense passion that Frédéric took her upon his knees and said to himself:

"What a swine I am!" while admiring his own wickedness.

CHAPTER IV

Dambreuse, when Deslauriers presented himself at his house, was thinking of reviving his great coal-mining scheme. But this fusion of all the companies into one was looked upon unfavourably; there was an outcry against monopolies, as if immense capital were not needed for carrying out enterprises of this kind!

Deslauriers, who had read for the purpose the work of Gobet and the articles of M. Chappe in the *Journal des Mines*, understood the question perfectly. He demonstrated that the law of 1810 established for the benefit of the grantee a privilege which could not be transferred. Besides, a democratic colour might be given to the undertaking. To interfere with the formation of coal-mining companies was an attack on the very principle of association.

M. Dambreuse gave him some notes for the purpose of drawing up a memorandum. As for the way in which he meant to pay for the work, his promises were all the more attractive for being vague.

Deslauriers called again at Frédéric's house, and gave him an account of the interview. Moreover, he had caught a glimpse of Madame Dambreuse at the bottom of the stairs, just as he was going out.

"My compliments, old boy!"

Then they had a chat about the election. Some plan would have to be devised.

Three days later Deslauriers reappeared with a sheet of paper covered with handwriting, intended for the newspapers, and which was nothing less than a friendly letter from M. Dambreuse, expressing approval of their friend's candidature. Supported by a Conservative and praised by a Red, he ought to succeed. How was it that the capitalist had put his signature to such a document?

The lawyer had, of his own initiative, and without the least appearance of embarrassment, gone and shown it to Madame Dambreuse, who, thinking it quite appropriate, had taken the rest of the business on her own shoulders.

Frédéric was astonished at this proceeding. Nevertheless, he approved of it; then, as Deslauriers was in touch with M. Roque, his friend explained to him how he stood with regard to Louise.

"Tell them anything you like; that my affairs are in an unsettled state, that I am putting them in order. She is young enough to wait!"

Deslauriers set forth, and Frédéric looked upon himself as a very able man. He experienced, moreover, a feeling of gratification, a profound satisfaction. His delight at being the possessor of a rich woman was an unmitigated pleasure. The sentiment harmonised with the surroundings. His life would now be full of joy in every sense.

Perhaps the most delicious sensation of all was to gaze at Madame Dambreuse in the midst of a number of other ladies in her drawing-room. The propriety of her manners made him dream of other postures. While she was talking in a tone of coldness, he would recall to mind the loving words which she had murmured in his ear. All the respect which he felt for her virtue gave him a thrill of pleasure, as if it were a homage which was reflected back on himself; and at times he felt a longing to exclaim:

"But I know her better than you! She is mine!"

It was not long ere their relations came to be socially recognised as an established fact. Madame Dambreuse, during the whole winter, brought Frédéric with her into fashionable society.

He nearly always arrived before her; and he watched her as she entered the house they were visiting with her arms bare, a fan in her hand, and pearls in her hair. She would pause on the threshold (the doorway surrounded her like a frame), and with a certain air of indecision, she half-closed her eyes in order to see whether he was there.

She drove him back in her carriage; the rain lashed the carriage-blinds. The passers-by seemed merely shadows wavering in the mire of the street; and, pressed close to each other, they observed all these things vaguely with a calm disdain. Under various pretexts, he would linger in her room for an entire additional hour.

It was chiefly through a feeling of boredom that Madame Dambreuse had yielded. But this latest experience was not going to be wasted. She desired to give herself up to a great passion; and so she began to heap on him adulations and caresses.

She sent him flowers; she had an upholstered chair made for him. She made presents to him of a cigar-holder, an inkstand, a thousand little things for daily use, so that every act of his life should remind him of her. These kind attentions charmed him at first, and soon after he took them for granted.

She would step into a cab, get rid of it at the opening of an alley-way, and come out at the other end; and then, gliding along by the walls, with a double veil on her face, she would reach the street where Frédéric, who had been keeping watch, would take her arm quickly to lead her towards his house. His two men-servants would have gone out for a walk, and the concierge would have been sent on some errand. She would throw a glance around her—nothing to fear!—and she would breathe forth the sigh of an exile who beholds his country once more. Their luck emboldened them. Their appointments became more frequent. One evening, she even presented herself, all of a sudden, in full ball-dress. These surprises could be dangerous. He reproached her for her lack of prudence. Nevertheless, he thought she looked unattractive. The low body of her dress exposed her meager bosom.

It was then that he discovered what he had hitherto hidden from himself—the disillusionment of his senses. None the less he made professions of ardent love; but in order to call up such emotions he found it necessary to evoke the images of Rosanette and Madame Arnoux.

This sentimental atrophy left his head entirely clear; and he was more ambitious than ever of attaining a high position in society. Inasmuch as he had such a stepping-stone, the very least he could do was to make use of it.

One morning, about the middle of January, Sénécal entered his study, and in response to his exclamation of astonishment, announced that he was Deslauriers' secretary. He even brought Frédéric a letter. It contained good news, and yet it took him to task for his negligence; he would have to come to see his constituency. The future representative said he would set out on his way there in two days' time.

Sénécal gave no opinion on the other's merits as a candidate. He spoke about his own concerns and about the affairs of the country.

Miserable as the state of things happened to be, it gave him pleasure, for they were advancing in the direction of Communism. In the first place, the Administration moved towards it of its own accord, since every day a greater number of things were controlled by the Government. As for Property, the Constitution of '48, in spite of its weaknesses, had not spared it. The State might, in the name of public utility, henceforth take whatever it thought would suit it. Sénécal declared himself in favour of authority; and Frédéric noticed in his remarks the exaggeration which characterised what he had said himself to Deslauriers. The Republican even inveighed against the masses for their inadequacy.

"Robespierre, by upholding the right of the minority, had brought Louis XVI before the National Convention, and saved the people. The end justifies the means. A dictatorship is sometimes indispensable. Long live tyranny, provided that the tyrant promotes the public welfare!"

Their discussion lasted a long time; and, as he was taking his departure, Sénécal confessed (perhaps it was the real reason for his visit) that Deslauriers was getting very impatient at M. Dambreuse's silence.

But M. Dambreuse was ill. Frédéric saw him every day, as an intimate friend of the family.

General Changarnier's dismissal* had powerfully affected the capitalist's mind. He was, on the evening of the occurrence, seized with a burning sensation in his chest, together with a breathlessness that prevented him from lying down. The application of leeches gave him immediate relief. The dry cough disappeared; the respiration became more easy; and, eight days later, he said, while swallowing some broth:

"Ah! I'm better now—but I was near going on my last long journey!"

---

*He was dismissed by President Bonaparte in 1851 because he was an Orleanist (see the second footnote on p. 407).

"Not without me!" exclaimed Madame Dambreuse, intending by this remark to convey that she could not survive without him.

Instead of replying, he cast upon her and upon her lover a singular smile, in which there was at the same time resignation, indulgence, irony, and even, as it were, a touch of humour, a sort of secret satisfaction almost amounting to actual joy.

Frédéric wished to start for Nogent. Madame Dambreuse objected to this; and he unpacked and repacked his luggage according to the changes in the invalid's condition.

Suddenly M. Dambreuse spat forth a considerable amount of blood. The "princes of medical science," on being consulted, could not think of any new remedy. His legs swelled, and his weakness increased. He had several times expressed a desire to see Cécile, who was at the other end of France with her husband, now a collector of taxes, a position to which he had been appointed a month ago. M. Dambreuse gave express orders to send for her. Madame Dambreuse wrote three letters, which she showed him.

Without trusting him even to the care of the nun, she did not leave him for one second, and no longer went to bed. People who left their names with the concierge made enquiries about her admiringly, and the passers-by were filled with respect on seeing the quantity of straw which was placed in the street under the windows.

On the 12th of February, at five o'clock, a frightful hæmoptysis came on. The doctor on duty pointed out that the case had taken a dangerous turn. They sent in haste for a priest.

While M. Dambreuse was making his confession, Madame kept gazing curiously at him some distance away. After this, the young doctor applied a blister, and awaited the result.

The flame of the lamps, obscured by some of the furniture, lit up the room unevenly. Frédéric and Madame Dambreuse, at the foot of the bed, watched the dying man. In the recess of a window the priest and the doctor chatted in low voices. The good sister on her knees kept mumbling prayers.

At last came a rattling in the throat. The hands grew cold; the face began to turn white. Now and then he drew a deep breath; but gradually this became rarer and rarer. Two or three confused words escaped him. He turned his eyes upward, and at the same moment his respiration became so feeble that it was almost imperceptible. Then his head sank to one side on the pillow.

For a minute, all present remained motionless.

Madame Dambreuse advanced towards the dead body of her husband, and, without an effort—with the unaffectedness of one discharging a duty—she drew down the eyelids. Then she spread out her arms, her figure writhing as if in a spasm of repressed despair, and left the room, supported by the physician and the nun.

A quarter of an hour afterwards, Frédéric made his way up to her room.

There was an indefinable odour there, emanating from some delicate things which filled the place. In the middle of the bed lay a black dress, in glaring contrast to the pink coverlet.

Madame Dambreuse was standing at the corner of the mantelpiece. Without attributing to her any passionate regret, he thought she looked a little sad; and, in a mournful voice, he said:

"Are you suffering?"

"I? No—not at all."

As she turned around, her eyes fell on the dress, which she inspected. Then she told him not to stand on ceremony.

"Smoke, if you like! You can make yourself at home with me!"

And, with a great sigh:

"Ah! Blessed Virgin!—what a relief to be rid of him!"

Frédéric was astonished at this exclamation. He replied, as he kissed her hand:

"All the same, we were free enough!"

This allusion to the facility with which the intrigue between them had been carried on hurt Madame Dambreuse.

"Ah! you don't know the services that I did for him, or the misery in which I lived!"

"What!"

"Why, certainly! How could I feel secure always having that bastard of his around? A daughter, whom he introduced into the house after five years of married life, and who, were it not for me, might have led him to do something foolish?"

Then she explained how her affairs stood. The arrangement on the occasion of her marriage was that the property of each party should be separate. The amount of her inheritance was three hundred thousand francs. M. Dambreuse had guaranteed by the marriage contract that in the event of her surviving him, she should have an income of fifteen thousand francs a year, together with the ownership of the mansion. But a short time afterwards he had made a will by which he gave her all he possessed, and this she estimated, so far as it was possible to ascertain at the moment, at over three million.

Frédéric opened his eyes wide.

"It was worth the trouble, wasn't it? However, I contributed to it! It was my own property I was protecting; Cécile would have unjustly robbed me of it."

"Why did she not come to see her father?"

As he asked her this question Madame Dambreuse eyed him attentively; then, in a dry tone:

"I haven't the least idea! Sheer heartlessness, probably! Oh! I know what she is! And for that reason she won't get a penny from me!"

She had not been very troublesome, he pointed out; at any rate, since her marriage.

"Ha! her marriage!" said Madame Dambreuse, with a sneer. And she blamed herself for having treated only too well this stupid creature, who was jealous, self-interested, and hypocritical. "All the faults of her father!" She disparaged him more and more. There was never a person with such profound duplicity, and with such a merciless disposition, as hard as a stone—"a bad man, a bad man!"

Even the wisest people make mistakes. Madame Dambreuse had just made a serious one through this overflow of hatred on her part. Frédéric, sitting opposite her in an easy chair, was reflecting deeply, scandalised by the language she had used.

She arose and knelt down beside him.

"To be with you is the only real pleasure! You are the only one I love!"

While she gazed at him her heart softened, a nervous reaction brought tears into her eyes, and she murmured:

"Will you marry me?"

At first he thought he had not understood what she meant. He was dizzy with the thought of all this wealth.

She repeated in a louder tone:

"Will you marry me?"

At last he said with a smile:

"Have you any doubt about it?"

Then he had a pang of conscience, and in order to make a kind of reparation to the dead man, he offered to watch over him himself. But, feeling ashamed of this pious sentiment, he added, in a flippant tone:

"It would be perhaps more seemly."

"Perhaps so, indeed," she said, "on account of the servants."

The bed had been drawn completely out of the alcove. The nun was near the foot of it, and at the head of it sat a priest, a different one, a tall, thin, Spanish-looking man, with a fanatical air about him. On the night-table, covered with a white cloth, three candles were burning.

Frédéric took a chair, and gazed at the corpse.

The face was as yellow as straw. At the corners of the mouth there were traces of blood-stained foam. He had a silk handkerchief tied around his head, a knitted waistcoat, and a silver crucifix on his chest between his folded arms.

It was over, this life full of anxieties! How many visits had he not made to various offices? How many rows of figures calculated? How many deals hatched? How many reports read? What schemes, what smiles and bows! For he had acclaimed Napoleon, the Cossacks, Louis XVIII, 1830, the working-men, every *régime*, loving power so dearly that he would have paid in order to have the opportunity of selling himself.

But he had left behind him the estate of La Fortelle, three factories in Picardy, the woods of Crancé in the Yonne, a farm near Orleans, and a great deal of stocks and bonds.

Frédéric thus made an estimate of her fortune; and it would soon belong to him! First of all, he thought of "what people would say"; of what present he ought to make to his mother, of his future carriages, and of an old coachman belonging to his own family who he'd like to make his concierge. Of course, the livery would not be the same. He would convert the large reception-room into his own study. There was nothing to prevent him from knocking down three walls to set up a picture-gallery on the second-floor. Perhaps there might be an opportunity to set up a Turkish bath downstairs. As for M. Dambreuse's office, a disagreeable spot, what use could he make of it?

These reflections were from time to time rudely interrupted by the sounds made by the priest in blowing his nose, or by the good sister in stoking the fire.

But reality confirmed them. The corpse was still there. The eyelids had reopened, and the pupils, although steeped in a cloudy, glutinous film, had an enigmatic expression which Frédéric found intolerable.

Frédéric imagined that he saw there a judgment directed at himself, and he felt almost a sort of remorse, for he had never any complaint to make against this man, who, on the contrary——

"Come, now! an old scoundrel" and he looked at the dead man more closely in order to strengthen his mind, mentally addressing him thus:

"Well, what? Have I killed you?"

Meanwhile, the priest read his breviary; the nun, who sat motionless, had fallen asleep. The wicks of the three candles had grown longer.

For two hours the heavy rolling of carts could be heard making their way to the markets. The windows grew whiter. A cab passed; then a group of donkeys went trotting along the road. Then came the noise of hammering, cries of itinerant vendors and blasts of horns. Already every other sound was blended with the great voice of awakening Paris.

Frédéric went out to perform the duties assigned to him. He first went to the Mayor's office to make the necessary declaration; then, when the medical officer had given him a certificate of death, he called a second time at the municipal buildings in order to name the cemetery which the family had selected, and to make arrangements with the undertakers.

The clerk in the office showed him a plan which indicated the different classes of interment, and a programme giving full particulars with regard to the aesthetic details of the funeral. Would he like to have an open funeral-car or a hearse with plumes, ribbons on the horses, and aigrettes on the footmen, initials or a coat-of-arms, funeral-lamps, a man to display the family distinctions? and what number of carriages would he require?

Frédéric did not economise in the slightest degree. Madame Dambreuse was determined to spare no expense.

After this he made his way to the church.

The curate in charge of burials found fault with the waste of money on an ornate funeral.

For instance, the officer for the display of armorial distinctions was really useless. It would be far better to have a goodly display of candles. A low mass accompanied by music would be appropriate.

Frédéric gave written directions to have everything that was agreed upon carried out, with a solid commitment to pay all the expenses.

He went next to the Hôtel de Ville to purchase a burial plot. A plot which was two metres in length and one in breadth cost five hundred francs. Did he want a grant for fifty years or forever?

"Oh, forever!" said Frédéric.

He took the matter seriously and went to a lot of trouble over it. In the courtyard of the mansion a marble-cutter was waiting to show him estimates and plans of Greek, Egyptian, and Moorish tombs; but the family architect had already been in consultation with Madame; and on the table in the vestibule there were all sorts of prospectuses with reference to the cleaning of mattresses, the disinfection of rooms, and the various processes of embalming.

After dining, he went back to the tailor's shop to order mourning clothes for the servants; and he had still to discharge another function, for the gloves that he had ordered were of beaver, whereas the right kind for a funeral were floss-silk.

When he arrived next morning, at ten o'clock, the large reception-room was filled with people, and nearly everyone said, on encountering the others, in a melancholy tone:

"It is only a month ago since I saw him! Good heavens! it will be the same way with us all!"

"Yes; but let us try to keep it as far away as possible!"

Then there were little smiles of satisfaction; and they even engaged in conversations entirely unsuited to the occasion. Finally, the master of the ceremonies, in a black coat in the French fashion and short breeches, with a cloak, mourning-bands, a long sword by his side, and a three-cornered hat under his arm, spoke, with a bow, the customary words:

"Messieurs, if you please."

The funeral started. It was the market-day for flowers on the Place de la Madeleine. The weather was clear and mild; and the breeze, which shook the canvas tents, puffed out the edges of the enormous black cloth which was hung over the portal. M. Dambreuse's coat of arms, which covered a square piece of velvet, was repeated there three times. It was: *Sable, with an arm sinister and a clenched hand with a glove argent*; with the coronet of a count, and this motto: *By every path.*

The bearers lifted the heavy coffin to the top of the staircase, and they entered the building. The six chapels, the apse, and the seats were hung with black. The catafalque at the bottom of the choir formed, with its large candles, a single blaze of yellow lights. At the two corners, over the candelabra, flames of spirits of wine were burning.

The persons of highest rank took up their position in the sanctuary, and the rest in the nave; and then the Mass began.

With the exception of a few, the religious ignorance of all was so profound that the master of the ceremonies had, from time to time, to make signs to them to rise, to kneel, or to resume their seats. The organ and the two double-basses could be heard alternately with the voices. In the intervals of silence, the only sounds that reached the ear were the mumblings of the priest at the altar; then the music and the chanting went on again.

The daylight shone dimly through the three cupolas, but the open door let in a stream of white radiance, which, entering in a horizontal direction, fell on every uncovered head; and in the air, half-way towards the ceiling of the church, floated a shadow, which was penetrated by the reflection of the gilding that decorated the ribs of the pendentives and the foliage of the capitals.

Frédéric, in order to pass the time, listened to the *Dies iræ*. He gazed at those around him, or tried to catch a glimpse of the pictures hanging too far above his head, wherein the life of Mary Magdalen was represented. Luckily, Pellerin came to sit down beside him, and immediately plunged into a long dissertation on the subject of frescoes. The bell began to toll. They left the church.

The hearse, adorned with hanging draperies and tall plumes, set out for Père-Lachaise* drawn by four black horses, with their manes braided with ribbons, their heads decked with tufts of feathers, and with large trappings embroidered with silver flowing down to their hooves. The driver of the vehicle, in Hessian boots, wore a three-cornered hat with a long crape ribbon. The ropes were held by four people: a treasurer of the Chamber of Deputies, a member of the General Council of the Aube, a delegate from the coal-mining company, and Fumichon, as a friend. The carriage of the deceased and a dozen mourning-coaches followed. The guests came in the rear, filling up the middle of the boulevard.

The passers-by stopped to look at the mournful procession. Women, with their children in their arms, got up on chairs, and people, who had been drinking glasses of beer in the cafés, came to the windows with billiard-cues in their hands.

The route was long, and, as at formal meals where people are at first reserved and then expansive, the general atmosphere soon relaxed. They talked of nothing but the refusal of a grant by the Chamber to the President. M. Piscatory had shown himself to be too harsh; Montalembert had been "magnificent, as usual,"† and MM. Chamballe, Pidoux, Creton, in short, the entire committee would be compelled perhaps to follow the advice of MM. Quentin-Bauchard and Dufour.

This conversation was continued as they passed through the Rue de la Roquette, with shops on each side, in which could be seen only chains of coloured glass and black discs covered with patterns and gold letters—which made them look like caves full of stalactites and china shops. But, when they had reached the cemetery-gate, every-one instantly stopped speaking.

The tombs among the trees: broken columns, pyramids, temples, dolmens, obelisks, and Etruscan vaults with doors of bronze. Some contained a sort of funereal boudoir, with rustic armchairs and folding-stools. Spider webs hung like rags from the little chains of

---

*Cemetery laid out in 1804 in eastern Paris; many illustrious people are buried there.

†Initially an opponent, Count Charles de Montalembert (1810–1870), a liberal Catholic journalist, came around to the cause of Louis-Napoléon.

the urns; and the bouquets of satin ribbons and the crucifixes were covered with dust. Everywhere, between the balustrades on the tombstones, were crowns of immortelles and candle sticks, vases, flowers, black discs set off with gold letters, and plaster statuettes—little boys or little girls or little angels suspended in the air by brass wires; several of them even had a zinc roof overhead. Huge cables made of glass strung together, black, white, or blue, descended from the tops of the monuments to the ends of the flagstones in long coils, like boas. The rays of the sun, striking them, made them glitter in the midst of the black wooden crosses. The hearse advanced along the broad paths, which are paved like the streets of a city. From time to time the axles creaked. Women, kneeling down, with their dresses trailing in the grass, addressed the dead in tones of tenderness. Little white plumes of smoke arose through the green leaves of the yew trees. These came from offerings that had been left behind, waste material that had been burnt.

M. Dambreuse's grave was close to the graves of Manuel and Benjamin Constant.* The soil in this place slopes with an abrupt decline. One has a lofty view of the tops of green trees, further down the chimneys of steam-pumps, then the entire great city.

Frédéric found an opportunity of admiring the scene while the various speeches were being delivered.

The first was in the name of the Chamber of Deputies, the second in the name of the General Council of the Aube, the third in the name of the coal-mining company of Saone-et-Loire, the fourth in the name of the Agricultural Society of the Yonne, and there was another in the name of a Philanthropic Society. Finally, just as everyone was leaving, a stranger began reading a sixth address, in the name of the Amiens Society of Antiquaries.

And thereupon they all took advantage of the occasion to denounce Socialism, of which M. Dambreuse had died a victim. It was the effect produced on his mind by the exhibitions of anarchy, together with his devotion to order, that had shortened his days. They praised his intellectual powers, his integrity, his generosity, and even his silence as a representative of the people, "for, if he was not an orator, he possessed instead those solid qualities a thousand

---

*Two liberal politicians; the latter was also a Romantic writer.

times more useful," etc., with all the requisite phrases—"Premature end; eternal regrets; the better land; farewell, or rather no, *au revoir!*"

The clay, mingled with stones, fell on the coffin, and he would never again be a subject for discussion in society.

They did still continue talking about him as they left the cemetery and they were not embarrassed to say what they really thought about him. Hussonnet, who would have to give an account of the interment in the newspapers, joked about the speeches, for, in truth, the worthy Dambreuse had been one of the most notable palm-greasers of the last reign. Then the citizens were driven in the mourning-coaches to their places of business; the ceremony had not lasted very long, thank God.

Frédéric returned to his own home quite worn out.

When he presented himself next day at Madame Dambreuse's residence, he was informed that she was busy below stairs in the room where M. Dambreuse had kept his papers.

The filing cabinets, the different drawers were open in disarray, and the account-books had been flung about right and left. A roll of papers which were labelled "Bad debts" lay on the ground. He was near falling over it, and picked it up. Madame Dambreuse had sunk back in the armchair, so that he did not see her.

"Well? where are you? What is the matter!"

She sprang to her feet with a bound.

"What is the matter? I am ruined, ruined! do you understand?"

M. Adolphe Langlois, the notary, had sent her a message to call at his office, and had informed her about the contents of a will made by her husband before their marriage. He had bequeathed everything to Cécile; and the other will was lost. Frédéric turned very pale. No doubt she had not made a sufficient search.

"Well, then, look yourself!" said Madame Dambreuse, pointing at the objects around the room.

The two strong-boxes were gaping wide, having been broken open with blows of a cleaver, and she had turned over the desk, rummaged in the cupboards, and shaken the straw-mattings, when, all of a sudden, letting out a piercing cry, she dashed into a corner where she had just noticed a little box with a brass lock. She opened it—nothing!

"Ah! the swine! I, who took such devoted care of him!"

Then she burst into sobs.

"Perhaps it is somewhere else?" said Frédéric.

"Oh! no! it was there! in that strong-box. I saw it there lately. 'Tis burned! I'm certain of it!"

One day, in the early stage of his illness, M. Dambreuse had gone down to this room to sign some documents.

" 'Tis then he must have done the deed!"

And she fell back on a chair, crushed. A mother grieving beside an empty cradle was not more woeful than Madame Dambreuse was at the sight of the open strong-boxes. Indeed, her sorrow, in spite of the baseness of the motive which inspired it, appeared so deep that he tried to console her by reminding her that, after all, she was not reduced to sheer poverty.

"It is poverty, when I am not in a position to offer you a large fortune!"

She had not more than thirty thousand francs a year, without taking into account the mansion, which was worth from eighteen to twenty thousand, perhaps.

Although to Frédéric this would have been opulence, he felt, none the less, a certain amount of disappointment. Farewell to his dreams and to the grand life he would have led! Honour compelled him to marry Madame Dambreuse. For a minute he reflected; then, in a tone of tenderness:

"I'll always have you!"

She threw herself into his arms, and he clasped her to his chest with an emotion in which there was a slight element of admiration for himself.

Madame Dambreuse, whose tears had ceased to flow, raised her face, beaming all over with happiness, and seizing his hand:

"Ah! I never doubted you! I knew I could count on you!"

This anticipated certainty with regard to what he considered a noble action annoyed the young man.

Then she brought him into her own room, and they began to make plans for the future. Frédéric should now consider the best way of advancing himself in life. She even gave him excellent advice with reference to his candidature.

The first point was to learn two or three phrases on political economy. It was necessary to take up a specialty, such as horse-breeding, for example; to write a number of notes on questions of local interest, to have always at his disposal post-office appointments or tobacco licenses and to do a host of small services. In this respect M. Dambreuse had shown himself a true model. Thus, on one occasion, in the country, he had drawn up his wagonette, full of friends of his, in front of a cobbler's stall, and had bought a dozen pairs of shoes for his guests and for himself a dreadful pair of boots, which he had the heroism to wear for an entire fortnight. This anecdote put them into a good humour. She related others, with a renewal of grace, youthfulness, and wit.

She approved of his notion of taking a trip immediately to Nogent. Their parting was an affectionate one; then, on the threshold, she murmured once more:

"You do love me—don't you?"

"Eternally," was his reply.

A messenger was waiting for him at his own house with a line written in lead-pencil informing him that Rosanette was about to give birth. He had been so preoccupied for the past few days that he had not bestowed a thought upon the matter.

She had been placed in a special establishment at Chaillot.

Frédéric took a cab and set out for this institution.

At the corner of the Rue de Marbeuf he read on a board in big letters: "Private Lying-in-Hospital, kept by Madame Alessandri, first-class midwife, ex-pupil of the Maternity, author of various works, etc." Then, in the centre of the street, over the door—a little side-door—there was another sign-board: "Private Hospital of Madame Alessandri," with all her titles.

Frédéric gave a knock. A saucy-looking maid brought him into the reception-room, which was adorned with a mahogany table, armchairs of garnet colored velvet, and a clock in a glass case.

Almost immediately Madame appeared. She was a tall brunette of forty, with a slender waist, fine eyes, and the manners of good society. She apprised Frédéric of the mother's happy delivery, and brought him up to her room.

Rosanette broke into a smile of unutterable bliss, and, as if drowned in the floods of love that overwhelmed her, she said in a low tone:

"A boy—there, there!" pointing towards a cradle close to her bed.

He flung open the curtains, and saw, wrapped up in linen, a yellowish-red object, exceedingly shrivelled-looking, which had a bad smell, and was bawling.

"Embrace him!"

He replied, in order to hide his repugnance:

"But I am afraid of hurting him."

"No! no!"

Then, very gingerly he kissed his child.

"How like you he is!"

And with her two weak arms, she clung to his neck with an outburst of feeling which he had never witnessed on her part before.

The remembrance of Madame Dambreuse came back to him. He reproached himself as a monster for having deceived this poor creature, who loved and suffered with all the sincerity of her nature. For several days he kept her company until the evening.

She felt happy in this quiet place; the window-shutters in front of it remained always closed. Her room, hung with bright chintz, looked out on a large garden. Madame Alessandri, whose only shortcoming was that she liked to talk about her intimate acquaintanceship with eminent physicians, showed her the utmost attention. Her associates, nearly all provincial young ladies, were exceedingly bored, as they had nobody to come to see them. Rosanette saw that they looked upon her with envy, and told this to Frédéric with pride. It was desirable to speak low, nevertheless. The partitions were thin, and everyone tried to eavesdrop, in spite of the constant noise of the pianos.

At last, he was about to take his departure for Nogent, when he got a letter from Deslauriers. Two fresh candidates had offered themselves, one a Conservative, the other a Red; a third, whatever he might be, would have no chance. It was all Frédéric's fault; he had let the lucky moment pass by; he should have come sooner and gotten himself moving.

"You have not even been seen at the agricultural assembly!" The lawyer blamed him for not having any newspaper connections.

"Ah! if you had followed my advice long ago! If we had only a paper of our own!"

He laid special stress on this point. However, many people who would have voted for him out of consideration for M. Dambreuse, abandoned him now. Deslauriers was one of them. Not having anything more to expect from the capitalist, he had thrown over his *protégé*.

Frédéric took the letter to show it to Madame Dambreuse.

"You have not been to Nogent, then?" said she.

"Why do you ask?"

"Because I saw Deslauriers three days ago."

Having learned that her husband was dead, the lawyer had come to make a report about the coalmines, and to offer his services to her as a man of business. This seemed strange to Frédéric; and what was his friend doing down there?

Madame Dambreuse wanted to know how he had spent his time since they had parted.

"I have been ill," he replied.

"You ought at least to have told me about it."

"Oh! it wasn't worth while;" besides, he had to settle a number of things, to keep appointments and to pay visits.

From that time forth he led a double life, spending every night at the Maréchale's and passing the afternoon with Madame Dambreuse, so that there was scarcely a single hour of freedom left to him in the middle of the day.

The infant was in the country at Andilly.* They went to see it once a week.

The wet-nurse's house was in the upper part of the village, at the back of a little yard as dark as a pit, with straw on the ground, hens here and there, and a vegetable-cart in the shed.

Rosanette would begin by frantically kissing her baby, and, seized with a kind of delirium, moved about constantly, trying to milk the she-goat, eating farmhouse bread, and sniffing at the manure; she even wanted to put a little of it into her handkerchief.

Then they took long walks, in the course of which she went into the nursery gardens, tore off branches from the lilac-trees which hung down over the walls, and exclaimed, "Gee up, donkey!" to the asses that were drawing cars along, and stopped to gaze through the gate into the interior of one of the lovely gardens; or else the wet-nurse would take the child and place it under the shade of a

---

*Village a few miles north of Paris.

walnut-tree; and for hours the two women would keep talking about the most tiresome nonsense.

Frédéric, not far away from them, gazed at the beds of vines on the slopes, with a clump of trees here and there, at the dusty paths resembling strips of grey ribbon; at the houses, which looked like white and red spots in the midst of the greenery; and sometimes the smoke of a locomotive stretched out horizontally across the bases of the hills, covered with foliage, like a gigantic ostrich feather, the thin end of which was disappearing from view.

Then his eyes once more rested on his son. He imagined the child grown into a young man; he would make a companion of him; but perhaps he would be a blockhead, a failure, in any event. His illegitimate birth would always be a burden to him; it would have been better if he had never been born! And Frédéric would murmur, "Poor child!" his heart swelling with unutterable sadness.

They often missed the last train. Then Madame Dambreuse would scold him for his lack of punctuality. He would invent some falsehood.

It was necessary to invent some explanations, too, to satisfy Rosanette. She could not understand how he spent all his evenings; and when she sent a messenger to his house, he was never there! One day, when he happened to be at home, the two women made their appearance almost at the same time. He got the Maréchale to go away, and concealed Madame Dambreuse, pretending that his mother was coming up to Paris.

Soon, he found these lies amusing. He would repeat to one the oath which he had just uttered to the other, send them both identical bouquets, write to them at the same time, and then would make comparisons between them. There was a third always present in his thoughts. The impossibility of possessing her seemed to him a justification of his duplicity, which intensified his pleasure with the spice of variety; and the more he deceived one of the two, no matter which, the fonder of him she grew, as if the love of one of them added heat to that of the other, and, as if by a sort of rivalry, each of them were seeking to make him forget the other.

"See how I trust you!" said Madame Dambreuse one day to him, opening a sheet of paper, in which she was informed that M. Moreau and a certain Rose Bron were living together as husband and wife.

"Can it be that this is the lady from the races?"

"Don't be absurd!" he returned. "Let me have a look at it!"

The letter, written in capitals, had no signature. Madame Dambreuse, in the beginning, had tolerated this mistress, who served as a cover for their adultery. But, as her passion became stronger, she had insisted that he give her up—a thing which had been effected long since, according to Frédéric's account; and when he had ceased to protest, she replied, narrowing her eyes, in which shone a look as sharp as the point of a stiletto under a muslin robe:

"Well—what about the other one?"

"What other one?"

"The earthenware-dealer's wife!"

He shrugged his shoulders disdainfully. She did not press him on the matter.

But, a month later, while they were talking about honour and loyalty, and he was boasting about his own (in a casual sort of way, for safety's sake), she said to him:

"It is true—are you being honest—you don't go back there any more?"

Frédéric, who was at the moment thinking of the Maréchale, stammered:

"Where, pray?"

"To Madame Arnoux's."

He implored her to tell him from whom she got the information. It was through her second dressmaker, Madame Regimbart.

So, she knew all about his life, and he knew nothing about hers!

In the meantime, he had found in her dressing-room the miniature of a gentleman with a long moustache—was this the same person about whose suicide a vague story had been told him at one time? But there was no way of learning any more about it!

What was the use of it? The hearts of women are like little cabinets, full of secret drawers fitted one inside the other; you hurt yourself, break your nails in opening them, and then find within only some dried flowers, a few grains of dust—or nothing! And then perhaps he felt afraid of learning too much about the matter.

She made him refuse invitations where she was unable to accompany him, stuck to his side, was afraid of losing him; and, in spite of this union which was becoming stronger every day, all of a sudden, abysses opened up between them about the most trivial matters—appreciating a certain person or a work of art.

She had a style of playing on the piano which was precise and heavy-handed. Her spiritualism (Madame Dambreuse believed in the transmigration of souls into the stars) did not prevent her from taking the utmost care of her finances. She was haughty towards her servants; her eyes remained dry at the sight of the rags of the poor. An unconscious egoism revealed itself in her everyday expressions: "What concern is that of mine? I'd be a fool if I did! What need have I?" and a thousand little acts incapable of analysis revealed hateful qualities in her. She would have been capable of listening behind doors: she could not help lying to her confessor. Out of a spirit of domination, she insisted on Frédéric going to the church with her on Sunday. He obeyed, and carried her prayer-book.

The loss of her inheritance had changed her considerably. These marks of grief, which people attributed to the death of M. Dambreuse, made her more interesting, and, as in former times, she had a great number of visitors. Since Frédéric's defeat at the election, she was ambitious of obtaining for both of them a diplomatic post in Germany; therefore, the first thing they should do was to follow the current trends of ideas.

Some people were in favour of the Empire, others of the Orléans family, and others of the Comte de Chambord; but they were all of one opinion as to the urgency of decentralisation, and several methods were proposed with that view, such as to cut up Paris into many large streets in order to establish villages there, to transfer the seat of government to Versailles, to have the schools set up at Bourges, to do away with the libraries, and to entrust everything to the generals; and they glorified a rustic existence on the assumption that the uneducated man had naturally more sense than other men! Hatreds increased—hatred of primary teachers and wine-merchants, of philosophy classes, of history courses, of novels, red waistcoats, long beards, of independence in any shape, or any manifestation of individuality, for it was necessary "to restore the principle of authority"—let it be exercised in the name of no matter whom; let it come from no matter where, as long as it was Force, Authority! The Conservatives now talked in the very same way as Sénécal. Frédéric was completely puzzled, and once more he found at the house of his former mistress the same remarks made by the same men.

The salons of unmarried women (it was from this period that their importance dates) were a sort of neutral ground where reactionaries of different kinds met. Hussonnet, who was engaged in criticizing the great men of the day (a good thing for the restoration of Order), inspired Rosanette with a longing to have evening parties of her own. He said he would publish accounts of them, and first of all he brought Fumichon, a serious-minded man, then came Nonancourt, M. de Grémonville, the Sieur de Larsilloix, ex-prefect, and Cisy, who was now an agriculturist in Lower Brittany, and more devoutly Christian than ever.

In addition, men who had at one time been the Maréchale's lovers came, such as the Baron de Comaing, the Comte de Jumillac, and others, and Frédéric was annoyed by their free-and-easy behaviour.

In order to make himself look like the master of the house, he improved their style of living. So he hired a groom, moved to a new house, and got new furniture. These displays of extravagance were useful for the purpose of making his upcoming marriage appear less out of proportion with his fortune. The result was that his fortune was soon alarmingly reduced—and Rosanette didn't understand any of it!

A woman of the middle-class, who had come down in the world, she adored a domestic life, a quiet little home. All the same, it gave her pleasure to have "an at home day." Referring to persons of her own class, she called them "Those women!" She wished to be a society lady, and believed herself to be one. She begged of him not to smoke in the drawing-room any more, and for the sake of good form tried to make him observe fast days.

She played her part badly, after all; for she grew serious, and even before going to bed always exhibited a certain melancholy. It was like finding cypress trees at the door of a tavern.*

He found out the cause of it; she was dreaming of marriage—she, too! Frédéric was exasperated at this. Besides, he remembered her appearance at Madame Arnoux's house, and then he held onto a certain spite towards her for having resisted him for so long.

---

*Cypresses were commonly associated with mourning.

He made enquiries none the less as to who her lovers had been. She denied having had any relations with any of them. A sort of jealous feeling took possession of him. He irritated her by asking questions about presents that had been made to her, and were still being made to her; and in proportion to the annoyance which her personality produced in him more and more, he was still drawn to her by a bestial and violent lust, momentary illusions which ended in hate.

Her words, her voice, her smile, all had an unpleasant effect on him, and especially her glances with that female gaze forever limpid and foolish. Sometimes he felt so tired of her that he could have watched her die without being moved by it. But how could he get into a fight with her? She was so sweet and even-tempered that there was no hope of picking a quarrel.

Deslauriers reappeared, and explained his sojourn at Nogent by saying that he was making arrangements to buy a lawyer's office. Frédéric was glad to see him again. It was somebody else! and as a third person in the house, he helped to break the monotony.

The lawyer dined with them from time to time, and whenever any little disputes arose, always took Rosanette's side, so that Frédéric, on one occasion, said to him:

"Eh! go to bed with her if you like!" so much did he long for some chance of getting rid of her.

About the middle of the month of June, she was served with an order from the law courts in which Maître Athanase Gautherot, bailiff, called upon her to pay four thousand francs due to Mademoiselle Clémence Vatnaz; if not, he would come the next day to seize her belongings.

In fact, of the four bills which she had signed at various times, only one had been paid; the money which she managed to get since then had been spent on other things.

She rushed off at once to see Arnoux. He lived now in the Faubourg Saint-Germain, and the porter was unable to tell her the name of the street. She made her way next to the houses of several friends of hers, could not find one of them at home, and came back in a state of utter despair.

She did not wish to tell Frédéric anything about it, fearing that this new incident might damage the chances of a marriage between them.

On the following morning, Maître Athanase Gautherot presented himself with two assistants, one of them pale and sly-looking and an envious air about him, the other wearing a detachable collar and tight trouser-straps, with a stall of black taffeta on his index-finger—and both revoltingly dirty, with greasy necks, and the sleeves of their coats too short.

Their employer, on the contrary, a very good-looking man, began by apologising for the disagreeable duty he had to perform, while at the same time he threw a look round the room, "full of pretty things, upon my word of honour!" He added, "Apart from the things that can't be seized." At a gesture the two bailiff's men disappeared.

Then he became twice as polite as before. Could anyone believe that a lady so charming would not have a genuine friend! A sale of her goods under an order of the courts would be a real misfortune. One never gets over a thing like that. He tried to frighten her; then, seeing that she was very upset, suddenly assumed a paternal tone. He knew the world. He had dealings with all these ladies—and as he mentioned their names, he examined the frames of the pictures on the walls. They were old paintings from the worthy Arnoux, sketches by Sombary, water-colours by Burieu, and three landscapes by Dittmer. It was evident that Rosanette was ignorant of their value. Maître Gautherot turned round to her:

"Look here! to show that I am a decent fellow, do one thing: give me those Dittmers there—and I will pay your debt. Do you agree?"

At that moment Frédéric, who had been informed about the matter by Delphine in the hall, and who had just seen the two assistants, barged in with his hat still on his head. Maître Gautherot resumed his dignified air; and, as the door had been left open:

"Come on, gentlemen—write this down! In the second room, let us say—an oak table with its two leaves, two sideboards——"

Frédéric stopped him, asking whether there was not some way of preventing the seizure.

"Oh! certainly! Who paid for the furniture?"

"I did."

"Well, draw up a claim—you still have time to do it."

Maître Gautherot did not take long in writing out his official report, citing Mademoiselle Bron in his report to the court, and having done this he left.

Frédéric uttered no reproach. He gazed at the traces of mud left on the floor by the bailiff's shoes, and, speaking to himself:

"We must go and find some money!"

"Ah! my God, how stupid I am!" said the Maréchale.

She ransacked a drawer, took out a letter, and made her way rapidly to the Languedoc Gas Lighting Company, in order to get the transfer of her shares.

She came back an hour later. The interest in the shares had been sold to another. The clerk had said, in answer to her demand, while examining the sheet of paper containing Arnoux's written promise to her: "This document in no way establishes you as the proprietor of the shares. The company has no cognisance of the matter." In short, he sent her away unceremoniously, while she choked with rage; and Frédéric would have to go to Arnoux's house at once to have the matter cleared up.

But Arnoux would perhaps imagine that he had come to recover in an indirect fashion the fifteen thousand francs due on the mortgage which he had lost; and then this claim from a man who had been his mistress's lover seemed despicable.

Choosing another route, he went to the Dambreuse mansion to get Madame Regimbart's address, sent a messenger to her residence, and in this way ascertained the name of the café which the Citizen now frequented.

It was the little café on the Place de la Bastille, in which he sat all day in the corner to the right at the back, never moving any more than if he were part of the building.

After having gone successively through the half-cup of coffee, the glass of grog, the "bishop," the glass of mulled wine, and even the red wine and water, he fell back on beer, and every half hour he let fall this word, "Bock!" having reduced his language to the bare minimum. Frédéric asked him if he saw Arnoux occasionally.

"No!"

"Really?—Why not?"

"An imbecile!"

Politics, perhaps, kept them apart, and so Frédéric thought it wise to enquire about Compain.

"What a brute!" said Regimbart.

"How is that?"

"His calf's head!"

"Ah! explain to me what the calf's head is!"

Regimbart's face wore a contemptuous smile.

"Some nonsense!"

After a long interval of silence, Frédéric went on to ask:

"So, then, has he changed his address?"

"Who?"

"Arnoux!"

"Yes—Rue de Fleurus!"

"What number?"

"Do I associate with the Jesuits?"

"What do you mean, Jesuits!"

The Citizen replied angrily:

"With the money of a patriot whom I introduced to him, this pig has set up as a dealer in rosary beads!"

"It isn't possible!"

"Go there, and see for yourself!"

It was perfectly true; Arnoux, weakened by an illness, had turned religious; besides, he had always been religious at heart, and (with that mixture of commercialism and ingenuity which was natural to him), in order to gain his salvation and a fortune, he had become a dealer of religious objects.

Frédéric had no difficulty in finding his establishment, on whose signboard appeared these words: "*Emporium of Gothic Art*—Restoration of articles used in ecclesiastical ceremonies—Church ornaments—Polychrome sculpture—Frankincense of the Magi, Kings, &c., &c."

At the two corners of the shop-window rose two wooden statues, streaked with gold, vermilion, and azure, a Saint John the Baptist with his sheepskin, and a Saint Genevieve with roses in her apron and a distaff under her arm; next, groups in plaster, a good sister teaching a little girl, a mother on her knees beside a little bed, and three schoolboys at the communion table. The prettiest object there was a kind of châlet representing the stable of Bethlehem with the donkey, the ox, and the child Jesus lying on straw—real straw. From the top to the bottom of the shelves were medals by the dozen, rosaries of every sort, holy-water basins in the form of shells, and portraits of ecclesiastical dignitaries, amongst whom shone the smiling faces of Monsignor Affre and the Holy Father.

Arnoux sat asleep at his counter with his head down. He had aged terribly. He even had round his temples red pimples, and the reflection of the gold crosses touched by the rays of the sun shone on them.

Frédéric was filled with sadness at the sight of such a decline. Through devotion to the Maréchale, however, he steeled himself and stepped forward. At the far end of the shop Madame Arnoux appeared; thereupon, he turned on his heel.

"I couldn't find him," he said, when he got back to Rosanette.

And in vain he went on to promise that he would write at once to his notary at Le Havre for some money—she flew into a rage. She had never seen a man so weak, so spineless. While she was enduring a thousand sacrifices, other people were enjoying themselves.

Frédéric was thinking about poor Madame Arnoux, and picturing to himself the heart-rending impoverishment of her surroundings. He had seated himself before the writing-desk; and, as Rosanette's voice still kept up its bitter complaining:

"Ah! in the name of Heaven, hold your tongue!"

"You are not going to defend them, are you?"

"Well, yes!" he exclaimed. "What's the cause of such constant ill-will towards them?"

"But why is it that you don't want to make them pay up? 'Tis for fear of hurting your old flame—confess it!"

He felt like hitting her over the head with the clock. Words failed him. He relapsed into silence.

Rosanette, while pacing the room, continued:

"I am going to hurl a law suit at this Arnoux of yours. Oh! I don't want your assistance. I'll get legal advice."

Three days later, Delphine rushed abruptly into the room where her mistress sat.

"Madame! madame! there's a man here with a pot of glue who frightens me!"

Rosanette made her way down to the kitchen, and saw there a vagabond whose face was pitted with pock marks. Moreover, one of his arms was paralysed, and he was three fourths drunk, and slurring his words.

This was Maître Gautherot's bill-sticker. The objections to the seizure having been overruled, the sale followed as a matter of course.

For his trouble in getting up the stairs he demanded, in the first place, a half-glass of brandy; then he wanted another favour, namely, tickets for the theatre, on the assumption that the lady of the house was an actress. After this he spent some minutes winking unintelligibly. Finally, he declared that for forty sous he would tear off the corners of the poster which he had already affixed to the door down-stairs. Rosanette found herself referred to by name in it—a piece of exceptional severity which showed Vatnaz's spite.

She had at one time exhibited sensitivity, and had even, while suffering from the effects of a heartache, written to Béranger for his advice.* But under the ravages of life's storms, her spirit had become soured, for she had been forced, in turn, to give piano lessons, to run a boarding house, to write for the fashion journals, to let rooms, and to traffic in lace in the world of loose women, her relations with whom enabled her to be of service to many people, and amongst others to Arnoux. She had formerly been employed in a commercial establishment.

There it was one of her functions to pay the working girls; and for each of them there were two account books, one of which always remained in her hands. Dussardier, who, through kindness, kept the account of a girl named Hortense Baslin, happened to come one day to the cash-office at the moment when Mademoiselle Vatnaz was presenting this girl's acccount, 1,682 francs, which the cashier paid her. Now, on the very evening before this, Dussardier had only entered the sum as 1,082 in the girl Baslin's book. He asked to have the book back on some pretext; then, anxious to cover up this theft, he stated that he had lost it. The working girl innocently repeated this falsehood to Mademoiselle Vatnaz, and the latter, in order to satisfy her mind about the matter, casually asked the shop assistant about it. He simply replied: "I have burned it!" A little while later she left the house, without believing that the book had been really destroyed, and filled with the idea that Dussardier had kept it.

---

*Pierre-Jean de Béranger (1780–1857) was a very popular poet and chansonnier.

On hearing that he had been wounded, she rushed to his home, in the interest of getting it back. Then, having discovered nothing, in spite of the most thorough search, she was seized with respect, and presently with love, for this youth, so loyal, so gentle, so heroic and so strong! At her age such good fortune in an affair of the heart was a thing that one would not expect. She threw herself into it with the appetite of an ogress; and she gave up literature, Socialism, "the consoling doctrines and the generous Utopias," the course of lectures which she had projected on the "De-subordination of Woman"—everything, even Delmar himself; finally she offered to unite herself to Dussardier in marriage.

Although she was his mistress, he was not at all in love with her. Besides, he had not forgotten her theft. And then she was too wealthy for him. He refused her offer. Thereupon, with tears in her eyes, she told him about what she had dreamed—it was to have for both of them a confectioner's shop. She possessed the capital that was required for the purpose, and next week this would be increased to the extent of four thousand francs. By way of explanation, she referred to the proceedings she had taken against the Maréchale.

Dussardier was annoyed at this on account of his friend. He remembered the cigar-case that had been presented to him at the guard-house, the evenings spent in the Quai Napoléon, the many pleasant chats, the books lent to him, the thousand acts of kindness which Frédéric had done on his behalf. He begged Vatnaz to abandon the proceedings.

She laughed at his good nature, while exhibiting a loathing for Rosanette which he could not understand. She longed for wealth, in fact, in order to crush her, only, with her four-wheeled carriage.

Dussardier was terrified by these black abysses of hate, and once he knew the date fixed for the sale, he hurried out. On the following morning he made his appearance at Frédéric's house with a look of embarrassment on his face.

"I owe you an apology."

"For what?"

"You must take me for an ingrate, I, whom she is the—" He faltered.

"Oh! I'll see no more of her. I am not going to be her accomplice!" And as the other was gazing at him in astonishment:

"Isn't your mistress's furniture to be sold in three days' time?"

"Who told you that?"

"Herself—Vatnaz! But I am afraid of offending you—"

"Impossible, my dear friend!"

"Ah! that is true—you are so good!"

And he held out to him, in a cautious fashion, a hand in which he clasped a little wallet made of sheep-leather.

It contained four thousand francs—all his savings.

"What! Oh! no! no!——"

"I knew well I would hurt your feelings," returned Dussardier, with a tear in the corner of his eye.

Frédéric pressed his hand, and the honest fellow went on in a plaintive voice:

"Take the money! Give me that much pleasure! I am in such a state of despair. Can it be, furthermore, that all is over ? I thought we should be happy when the Revolution had come. Do you remember what a beautiful thing it was? how freely we breathed! But here we are flung back into a worse condition than ever.

"Now, they are killing our Republic, just as they killed the other one—the Roman one! ay, and poor Venice! poor Poland! poor Hungary![14] What abominable deeds! First of all, they knocked down the trees of Liberty, then they restricted the right to vote, shut down the clubs, re-established censorship and surrendered to the priests the power of teaching, so that we now wait for the Inquisition. Why not? The Conservatives would like to see the Cossacks back*. The newspapers are punished merely for speaking out against the death-penalty. Paris is overflowing with bayonets; sixteen departments are in a state of siege; and then the demand for amnesty is again rejected!"

He placed both hands on his forehead, then, spreading out his arms as if in great distress:

"If, however, we only made the effort! if we were only sincere, we might understand each other. But no! The workmen are no

---

*The Cossacks had occupied Paris in the wake of Napoléon I's defeat in 1815.

better than the capitalists, you see! At Elbœuf recently they refused to help at a fire! There are wretches who treat Barbès as an aristocrat! In order to ridicule the people, they want to nominate Nadaud for the presidency, a mason—just imagine! And there is no way out of it—no remedy! Everybody is against us! For my part, I have never done any harm; and yet this is like a weight pressing down on my stomach. If this state of things continues, I'll go mad. I have a mind to kill myself. I tell you I don't need my money! You'll pay it back to me, dammit! I am lending it to you."

Frédéric, who felt himself constrained by necessity, ended by taking the four thousand francs from him. And so they had no more worries as far as Vatnaz was concerned.

But it was not long before Rosanette was defeated in her suit against Arnoux; and through sheer obstinacy she wished to appeal.

Deslauriers exhausted his energies in trying to make her understand that Arnoux's promise constituted neither a gift nor a proper transfer. She did not even pay the slightest attention to him, her notion being that the law was unjust—it was because she was a woman; men backed up each other amongst themselves. In the end, however, she followed his advice.

He made himself so much at home in the house, that on several occasions he brought Sénécal to dine there. Frédéric, who had advanced him money, and even got his own tailor to supply him with clothes, did not like this lack of ceremony; and the lawyer gave his old clothes to the Socialist, whose means were now exceedingly uncertain.

He was, however, anxious to be of service to Rosanette. One day, when she showed him a dozen shares in the Kaolin Company (that enterprise which had resulted in Arnoux paying thirty thousand francs in damages), he said to her:

"But this is a shady transaction! This is splendid!"

She had the right to sue him for the reimbursement of her shares. In the first place, she could prove that he was jointly bound to pay all the company's liabilities, since he had certified personal debts as collective debts—in short, he had embezzled sums which were payable only to the company.

"All this renders him guilty of fraudulent bankruptcy under articles 586 and 587 of the Commercial Code, and you may be sure, my pet, we'll send him packing."

Rosanette threw her arms around his neck. He entrusted her case next day to his former employer, not having time to devote attention to it himself, as he had business at Nogent. In case of any urgency, Sénécal could write to him.

His negotiations for the purchase of an office were a mere pretext. He spent his time at M. Rogue's house, where he had begun not only by singing the praises of their friend, but by imitating his manners and language as much as possible; and in this way he had gained Louise's confidence, while he won over her father by making an attack on Ledru-Rollin.

If Frédéric did not return, it was because he mingled in aristocratic society, and gradually Deslauriers led them to understand that he was in love with somebody, that he had a child, and that he was keeping a fallen woman.

Louise's despair was intense. The indignation of Madame Moreau was just as strong. She saw her son whirling towards the bottom of a gulf the depth of which could not be determined, was wounded in her religious ideas as to propriety, and as it were, experienced a sense of personal dishonour; then all of a sudden her expression changed. To the questions which people put to her with regard to Frédéric, she replied in a sly fashion:

"He is well, quite well."

She was aware that he was about to be married to Madame Dambreuse.

The date of the event had been set, and he was even trying to think of some way of making Rosanette swallow it.

About the middle of autumn she won her suit relative to the kaolin shares. Frédéric was informed about it by Sénécal, whom he met at his own door, on his way back from the courts.

It had been held that M. Arnoux was an accomplice to all the fraudulent transactions, and the ex-tutor had such an air of delight over it that Frédéric prevented him from coming further, assuring Sénécal that he would convey the news to Rosanette. He entered her house with a look of irritation on his face.

"Well, now you are satisfied!"

But, without minding what he had said:

"Look!"

And she pointed towards her child, which was lying in a cradle close to the fire. She had found it so sick at the house of the wet-nurse that morning that she had brought it back with her to Paris.

All the infant's limbs were exceedingly thin, and the lips were covered with white specks, which in the interior of the mouth looked like clots of milk.

"What did the doctor say?"

"Oh! the doctor! He pretends that the journey has increased his—I don't know what it is, some name ending in 'itis'—in short, that he has thrush. Do you know what that is?"

Frédéric replied without hesitation: "Certainly," adding that it was nothing.

But in the evening he was alarmed by the child's debilitated look and by the progress of these whitish spots, resembling mould, as if life, already abandoning this little frame, had left now nothing but matter from which vegetation was sprouting. His hands were cold; he was no longer able to drink anything; and the nurse, another woman, whom the porter had gone and gotten at random in an agency, kept repeating:

"It seems to me he's very bad, very bad!"

Rosanette was up all night with the child.

In the morning she went to look for Frédéric.

"Just come and look at him. He isn't moving."

In fact, he was dead. She took him up, shook him, clasped him in her arms, calling him most tender names, covered him with kisses, broke into sobs, turned on herself in a frenzy, screamed and tore her hair, and then let herself sink into the divan, where she lay with her mouth open and a flood of tears rushing from her wildly-glaring eyes.

Then a torpor fell upon her, and all became still in the apartment. The furniture was overturned. Two or three napkins were lying on the floor. The clock struck six. The night-light had gone out.

Frédéric, as he gazed at the scene, almost felt like he was dreaming. His heart was overcome with anguish. It seemed to him that this death was only a beginning, and that behind it was a worse calamity, which was just about to come on.

Suddenly, Rosanette said in an appealing tone:

"We'll preserve the body—shall we not?"

She wished to have the dead child embalmed. There were many objections to this. The principal one, in Frédéric's opinion, was that the thing was impractical in the case of children so young. A portrait would be better. She adopted this idea. He wrote a line to Pellerin, and Delphine hastened to deliver it.

Pellerin arrived speedily, anxious by this display of zeal to efface all recollection of his former conduct. The first thing he said was:

"Poor little angel! Ah, my God, what a tragedy!"

But gradually (the artist in him getting the upper hand) he declared that nothing could be made out of those darkened eyes, that livid face, that it was a real case of still-life, and would, therefore, require very great talent to treat it effectively; and so he murmured:

"Oh, it isn't easy—it isn't easy!"

"No matter, as long as it is life-like," urged Rosanette.

"Pooh! what do I care about a thing being lifelike? Down with Realism! 'Tis the spirit that must be portrayed by the painter! Leave me alone! I am going to try to conjure up what it ought to be!"

He reflected, with his left hand clasping his brow, and with his right hand clutching his elbow; then, all of a sudden:

"Ah, I have an idea! a pastel! With coloured half-tints, almost spread out flat, a lovely model could be obtained with the outer surface alone!"

He sent the chambermaid to look for his box of colours; then, having a chair under his feet and another by his side, he began to throw out great touches as calmly as if he were copying a bust. He praised the little Saint John of Correggio, the Infanta Rosa of Velasquez, the milk-white flesh-tints of Reynolds, the distinction of Lawrence, and especially the child with long hair that sits in Lady Gower's lap.[15]

"Besides, could you find anything more charming than these little toads? The most sublime (Raphael has proved it by his Madonnas) is probably a mother with her child?"

Rosanette, who felt herself suffocating, went away; and presently Pellerin said:

"Well, about Arnoux; you know what has happened?"

"No! What?"

"In any case, it was bound to end that way!"

"What has happened, might I ask?"

"Perhaps by this time he is—Excuse me!"

The artist got up in order to raise the head of the little corpse higher.

"You were saying—" Frédéric resumed.

And Pellerin, half-closing his eyes, in order to take his dimensions better:

"I was saying that our friend Arnoux is perhaps by this time locked up!"

Then, in a tone of satisfaction:

"Just take a look. Have I got it?"

"Yes, 'tis quite right. But about Arnoux?"

Pellerin laid down his pencil.

"As far as I could understand, he was sued by one Mignot, an intimate friend of Regimbart—now there's a brain, for you, eh? What an idiot! Just imagine! one day—"

"What! it's not Regimbart that's in question, is it?"

"That's true! Well, yesterday evening, Arnoux had to produce twelve thousand francs; if not, he was a ruined man."

"Oh! this is perhaps exaggerated," said Frédéric.

"Not a bit. It looked to me a very serious business, very serious!"

At that moment Rosanette reappeared, with red eyelids, which glowed like dabs of rouge. She sat down near the drawing and gazed at it. Pellerin made a sign to the other to hold his tongue on account of her. But Frédéric, without minding her:

"Nevertheless, I can't believe——"

"I tell you I met him yesterday," said the artist, "at seven o'clock in the evening, in the Rue Jacob. He had even taken the precaution to have his passport with him; and he spoke about embarking from Le Havre, he and his whole camp."

"What! with his wife?"

"No doubt. He is too much of a family man to live by himself."

"And are you sure of this?"

"Certain, faith! Where do you expect him to find twelve thousand francs?"

Frédéric took two or three turns round the room. He panted for breath, bit his lips, and then snatched up his hat.

"Where are you going now?" said Rosanette.

He made no reply, and disappeared.

CHAPTER V

Twelve thousand francs should be procured, or, if not, he would see Madame Arnoux no more; and until now there had lingered in his heart an unconquerable hope. Did she not, as it were, constitute the very substance of his heart, the very basis of his life? For some minutes he went staggering along the footpath, his mind tortured with anxiety, and nevertheless gladdened by the thought that he was no longer by the other's side.

Where was he to get the money? Frédéric was well aware from his own experience how hard it was to obtain it immediately, no matter at what cost. There was only one person who could help him in the matter—Madame Dambreuse. She always kept a good supply of bank-notes in her desk. He called at her house; and asked her straight out:

"Have you twelve thousand francs to lend me?"

"What for?"

That was another person's secret. She wanted to know who this person was. He would not give way on this point. They were equally determined not to yield. Finally, she declared that she would give nothing until she knew the reason.

Frédéric's face became very flushed; and he stated that one of his comrades had committed a theft. It was necessary to replace the sum this very day. "Let me know his name? His name? Come! what's his name?"

"Dussardier!"

And he threw himself on his knees, imploring of her to say nothing about it.

"What idea have you got into your head about me?" Madame Dambreuse replied. "One would imagine that you were the guilty party yourself. Be done with your tragic airs! Hold on! here's the money! and much good may it do him!"

He hurried off to see Arnoux. That worthy merchant was not in his shop. But he was still residing in the Rue de Paradis, for he had two addresses.

In the Rue de Paradis, the concierge said that M. Arnoux had been away since the evening before. As for Madame, he ventured to say nothing; and Frédéric, having rushed like an arrow up the stairs, put his ear to the keyhole. Finally, the door was opened. Madame had gone out with Monsieur. The servant could not say when they would be back; her wages had been paid, and she was leaving herself.

Suddenly he heard the door creaking.

"But is there anyone in the room?"

"Oh, no, Monsieur! it is the wind."

Thereupon he withdrew. There was something inexplicable in such a rapid disappearance.

Regimbart, being Mignot's intimate friend, could perhaps enlighten him? And Frédéric got himself driven to that gentleman's house at Montmartre in the Rue l'Empereur.

Attached to the house there was a small garden shut in by a gate which was reinforced by sheets of iron. Three front steps set off the white façade; and a person passing along the sidewalk could see the two rooms on the ground-floor, the first of which was a parlour with ladies' dresses lying all over the furniture, and the second the workshop for Madame Regimbart's dress-making assistants.

They were all convinced that Monsieur had important occupations, distinguished connections, that he was a man altogether beyond comparison. When he was passing through the lobby with his hat turned up at the sides, his long grave face, and his green over-coat, the girls stopped in the midst of their work. Besides, he never failed to address to them a few words of encouragement, some observation which showed his ceremonious courtesy; and, afterwards, in their own homes they felt unhappy, because they had him held up as their ideal.

No one, however, was so devoted to him as Madame Regimbart, an intelligent little woman, who supported him with her business.

As soon as M. Moreau had given his name, she came out quickly to meet him, knowing through the servants what his relations were with Madame Dambreuse. Her husband would be back in a moment; and Frédéric, while he followed her, admired the appearance of the house and the profusion of oil-cloth that was displayed in it. Then he waited a few minutes in a kind of office, into which the Citizen was in the habit of retiring, in order to be alone with his thoughts.

When they met, Regimbart's manner was less cranky than usual.

He related Arnoux's recent story. The ex-earthenware-manufacturer had excited the vanity of Mignot, a patriot who owned a hundred shares in the *Siècle*,* by professing to show that it would be necessary from the democratic standpoint to change the management and the editorship of the newspaper; and under the pretext of making his views prevail in the next meeting of shareholders, he had given the other fifty shares, telling him that he could pass them on to reliable friends who would back up his vote. Mignot would have no personal responsibility, and need not annoy himself about anyone; then, when he had achieved success, he would be able to secure a good place in the administration of at least five to six thousand francs. The shares had been delivered. But Arnoux had at once sold them, and with the money had entered into partnership with a dealer in religious articles. Thereupon came complaints from Mignot, to which Arnoux sent evasive answers. At last the patriot had threatened to bring against him a charge of cheating if he did not restore his share certificates or pay an equivalent sum—fifty thousand francs.

Frédéric's face wore a look of despondency.

"That is not the whole of it," said the Citizen. "Mignot, who is an honest fellow, has reduced his claim to one fourth. New promises on the part of the other, and, of course, new dodges. In short, on the morning of the day before yesterday Mignot sent him a written application to pay up, within twenty-four hours, twelve thousand francs, without prejudice to the balance."

"But I have the amount!" said Frédéric.

The Citizen slowly turned round:

"You're joking!"

**Le Siècle* was a leftist newspaper.

"Excuse me! I have the money in my pocket. I brought it with me."

"How do you do it! I'll be darned! However, it's too late now—the complaint has been lodged, and Arnoux is gone."

"Alone?"

"No! along with his wife. They were seen at the Le Havre station."

Frédéric grew exceedingly pale. Madame Regimbart thought he was going to faint. He regained his self-possession with an effort, and had even sufficient presence of mind to ask two or three questions about the occurrence. Regimbart was grieved at the affair, considering that it would injure the cause of Democracy. Arnoux had always been lax in his conduct and disorderly in his life.

"A regular hare-brained fellow! He burned the candle at both ends! His skirt-chasing has ruined him! It's not he that I pity, but his poor wife!" For the Citizen admired virtuous women, and had a great esteem for Madame Arnoux.

"She must have suffered a lot!"

Frédéric felt grateful to him for his sympathy; and, as if Regimbart had done him a service, shook his hand effusively.

"Did you see to everything?" was Rosanette's greeting to him when she saw him again.

He had not been able to pluck up courage, he answered, and walked about the streets at random trying to forget.

At eight o'clock, they passed into the dining-room; but they remained seated face to face in silence, each let out deep sigh every now and then, and pushed away their plates.

Frédéric drank some brandy. He felt quite shattered, crushed, annihilated, no longer conscious of anything except a sensation of extreme fatigue.

She went to look at the portrait. The red, the yellow, the green, and the indigo made glaring stains that jarred with each other, so that it looked hideous—almost ridicuous.

Besides, the dead child was now unrecognisable. The purple hue of his lips made the whiteness of his skin more remarkable. His nostrils were more drawn than before, his eyes more hollow; and his head rested on a pillow of blue taffeta, surrounded by petals of camelias, autumn roses, and violets. This was an idea suggested by the chambermaid, and both of them had thus with pious care arranged the little corpse. The mantelpiece, covered with a lace cloth, supported silver-gilt candlesticks interspersed with bouquets of holly-box. At the corners there were a pair of vases in which incense was burning. All these things, taken in conjunction with the cradle, looked like an altar; and Frédéric remembered the night when he had watched beside M. Dambreuse's death-bed.

Nearly every quarter of an hour Rosanette drew aside the curtains in order to take a look at her child. She saw him in her imagination, a few months hence, beginning to walk; then at college, in the middle of the recreation-ground, running races; then at twenty years a full-grown young man; and all these pictures conjured up by her brain made her feel that she had lost so many sons, the excess of her grief intensifying the maternal instinct in her.

Frédéric, sitting motionless in another armchair, was thinking of Madame Arnoux.

No doubt she was at that moment in a train, with her face leaning against a carriage window, while she watched the country disappearing behind her in the direction of Paris, or else on the deck of a steamboat, as on the occasion when they first met; but this vessel carried her away into distant countries, from which she would never return. He next saw her in a room at an inn, with trunks covering the floor, the wallpaper hanging in shreds, and the door shaking in the wind. And after that—what would become of her? Would she have to become a schoolmistress or a lady's companion, or perhaps a chambermaid? She was exposed to all the vicissitudes of poverty. His utter ignorance as to what her fate might be tortured his mind. He ought either to have opposed her departure or to have followed her. Was he not her real husband? And as the thought impressed itself on his consciousness that he would never meet her again, that it was all over forever, that she was lost to him beyond recall, he felt, so to speak, a rending of his entire being, and the tears that had been gathering since morning in his heart overflowed.

Rosanette noticed the tears in his eyes.

"Ah! You are crying just like me! You are grieving, too?"

"Yes! Yes! I am——"

He pressed her to his heart, and they both sobbed, locked in each other's arms.

Madame Dambreuse was weeping too, as she lay, face downwards, on her bed, with her head in her hands.

Olympe Regimbart having come that evening to try on her first coloured gown after mourning, had told her about Frédéric's visit, and even about the twelve thousand francs which he was ready to transfer to M. Arnoux.

So, then, this money, her very own money, was intended to be used simply for the purpose of preventing the other from leaving Paris—for the purpose, in fact, of preserving a mistress!

At first, she broke into a violent rage, and was determined to dismiss him like a lackey. A copious flow of tears produced a soothing effect upon her. It was better to keep it all to herself, and say nothing about it.

Frédéric brought her back the twelve thousand francs on the following day.

She begged of him to keep the money lest he might require it for his friend, and she asked a number of questions about this gentleman. Who, then, had tempted him to such a breach of trust? A woman, no doubt! Women drag you into every kind of crime.

This mocking tone disconcerted Frédéric. He felt deep remorse for the calumny he had invented. He was reassured by the reflection that Madame Dambreuse could not be aware of the facts. All the same, she was very persistent about the subject; for, two days later, she again made enquiries about his young friend, and, after that, about another—Deslauriers.

"Is this young man trustworthy and intelligent?"

Frédéric spoke highly of him.

"Ask him to call on me one of these mornings; I want to consult him about a business matter."

She had found a roll of old papers in which there were some bills of Arnoux, which had been duly protested, and which had been signed by Madame Arnoux. It was about these very bills Frédéric had called on M. Dambreuse on one occasion while the latter was at breakfast; and, although the capitalist had not sought to enforce repayment of this outstanding debt, he had not only gotten a judgment from the Tribunal of Commerce against Arnoux, but also against his wife, who knew nothing about the matter, as her husband had not thought fit to give her any information on the point.

Here was a weapon placed in Madame Dambreuse's hands—she had no doubt about it. But her notary would advise her to take no step in the affair. She would have preferred to act through some obscure person, and she thought of that big fellow with such an impudent expression of face, who had offered her his services.

Frédéric innocently performed this commission for her.

The lawyer was enchanted at the idea of having business relations with such an aristocratic lady.

He hurried to Madame Dambreuse's house.

She informed him that the inheritance belonged to her niece, a further reason for setting the debts owed to her husband in order to kill the Martinons with kindness.

Deslauriers guessed that there was some hidden design underlying all this. He reflected while he was examining the bills. Madame Arnoux's name, traced by her own hand, brought once more before his eyes her entire person, and the insult which he had received at her hands. Since vengeance was offered to him, why should he not snatch at it?

He accordingly advised Madame Dambreuse to have the bad debts which went with the inheritance sold at auction. An agent whose name would not be divulged, would buy them up, and would exercise the legal rights thus given him to realise them. He would take it on himself to provide a man to discharge this function.

Towards the end of the month of November, Frédéric, happening to pass through the street in which Madame Arnoux had lived, raised his eyes towards the windows of her house, and saw posted on the door a sign on which was printed in large letters:

"Sale of valuable furniture, consisting of kitchen utensils, personal and table linen, shirts and chemises, lace, petticoats, trousers, French and Indian cashmeres, an Erard piano, two Renaissance oak chests, Venetian mirrors, Chinese and Japanese porcelain."

"It's their furniture!" said Frédéric to himself, and his suspicions were confirmed by the concierge.

As for the person who had given instructions for the sale, he could get no information. But perhaps the auctioneer, Maître Berthelmot, might be able to throw light on the subject.

The official did not at first want to tell what creditor was having the sale carried out. Frédéric pressed him on the point. It was a gentleman named Sénécal, an agent; and Maître Berthelmot even carried his politeness so far as to lend his newspaper—the *Petites Affiches*—to Frédéric.

The latter, on reaching Rosanette's house, flung down this paper on the table spread wide open.

"Read that!"

"Well, what?" said she with a face so calm that he was revolted.

"Ah! keep up that air of innocence!"

"I don't understand what you mean."

" 'Tis you who are selling out Madame Arnoux yourself!"

She read over the announcement again.

"Where is her name?"

"Oh! 'tis her furniture. You know that as well as I do."

"What does that matter to me?" said Rosanette, shrugging her shoulders.

"What does it matter to you? But you are taking your revenge, that's all. This is the consequence of your persecutions. Haven't you outraged her so far as to call at her house?—you, a worthless creature! and this to the most saintly, the most charming, the best woman that ever lived! Why do you set your heart on ruining her?"

"I assure you, you are mistaken!"

"Come now! As if you had not put Sénécal forward to do this!"

"What nonsense!"

Then he was carried away with rage.

"You lie! you lie! you bitch! You are jealous of her! You have obtained judgment against her husband! Sénécal is already mixed up in your affairs. He detests Arnoux; and your two hatreds have joined together. I saw how delighted he was when you won that action of yours about the kaolin shares. Are you going to deny this?"

"I give you my word——"

"Oh, I know what that's worth—your word!"

And Frédéric reminded her of her lovers, giving their names and circumstantial details. Rosanette drew back, all the colour fading from her face.

"You are astonished at this. You thought I was blind because I shut my eyes. Now I have had enough of it. We do not die through the treacheries of a woman of your sort. When they become too monstrous we get out of the way. To inflict punishment on account of them would be only to degrade oneself."

She wrung her hands.

"My God, who can it be that has changed him?"

"Nobody but yourself."

"And all this for Madame Arnoux!" exclaimed Rosanette, weeping.

He replied coldly:

"I have never loved any woman but her!"

At this insult her tears ceased to flow.

"That shows your good taste! A woman of mature years, with a complexion like liquorice, a thick waist, big eyes like the ventholes of a cellar, and just as empty! As you like her so much, go and join her!"

"This is just what I expected. Thank you!"

Rosanette remained motionless, stupefied by this extraordinary behaviour.

She even allowed the door to be shut; then, with a bound, she pulled him back into the hall, and flinging her arms around him:

"Why, you are mad! you are mad! this is absurd! I love you!" She implored him:

"Good heavens! for the sake of our dead infant!"

"Confess that you were behind this affair!" said Frédéric.

She still protested that she was innocent.

"You will not acknowledge it?"

"No!"

"Well, then, farewell!—forever!"

"Listen to me!"

Frédéric turned round:

"If you understood me better, you would know that my decision is irrevocable!"

"Oh! oh! you will come back to me again!"

"Never as long as I live!"

And he slammed the door behind him violently.

Rosanette wrote to Deslauriers saying that she wanted to see him at once.

He called one evening, about five days later; and, when she told him about the quarrel:

"That's all! What's the fuss?"

She thought at first that he would have been able to bring back Frédéric; but now all was lost. She ascertained through the concierge that he was about to be married to Madame Dambreuse.

Deslauriers gave her a lecture, and was curiously happy and high-spirited and, as it was very late, asked permission to spend the night in an armchair.

Then, next morning, he set out again for Nogent, informing her that he was unable to say when they would meet again. In a little while, there would perhaps be a great change in his life.

Two hours after his return, the town was in a state of revolution. The news went round that M. Frédéric was going to marry Madame Dambreuse.

Finally the three Mesdemoiselles Auger, unable to stand it any longer, made their way to the house of Madame Moreau, who with an air of pride confirmed this piece of intelligence. Père Roque became quite ill when he heard it. Louise locked herself up; it was even rumoured that she had gone mad.

Meanwhile, Frédéric was unable to hide his dejection. Madame Dambreuse, in order to divert his mind, no doubt, was more attentive than ever. Every afternoon they went out for a drive in her carriage; and, on one occasion, as they were passing along the Place de la Bourse, she had the idea of paying a visit to the public auction-rooms for a bit of amusement.

It was the 1st of December, the very day on which the sale of Madame Arnoux's furniture was to take place. He remembered the date, and expressed his repugnance, declaring that this place was intolerable on account of the crush and the noise. She only wanted to get a peep at it. The brougham drew up. He had no alternative but to accompany her.

In the open space could be seen washhand-stands without basins, the wooden portions of armchairs, old hampers, pieces of porcelain, empty bottles, mattresses; and men in smocks or in dirty frock-coats, all grey with dust, and mean-looking faces, some with canvas sacks over their shoulders, were chatting in separate groups or greeting each other in a disorderly fashion.

Frédéric pointed out the drawbacks to going on any further.

"Nonsense!"

And they ascended the stairs. In the first room, at the right, gentlemen, with catalogues in their hands, were examining pictures; in another, a collection of Chinese weapons were being sold. Madame Dambreuse wanted to go downstairs again. She looked at the numbers over the doors, and she led him to the end of the corridor towards a room which was crowded with people.

He immediately recognised the two whatnots belonging to the office of *L'Art Industriel*, her worktable, all her furniture. Heaped up at the end of the room according to their respective heights, they formed a long slope from the floor to the windows, and at the other sides of the room, the carpets and the curtains hung down straight along the walls. There were underneath steps occupied by old men who had fallen asleep. At the left rose a sort of counter at which the auctioneer, in a white cravat, was lightly swinging a little hammer. By his side a young man was writing, and below him stood a sturdy fellow, looking like a cross between a commercial traveller and a ticket vendor crying out: "Furniture for sale." Three attendants placed the articles on a table, at the sides of which sat in a row second-hand and old-clothes dealers. The general public at the auction kept walking in a circle behind them.

When Frédéric came in, the petticoats, the handkerchiefs, and even the chemises were being passed on from hand to hand, and then given back. Sometimes they were flung some distance, and suddenly strips of whiteness went flying through the air. After that her gowns were sold, and then one of her hats, the broken feather of which was hanging down, then her furs, and then three pairs of boots; and the disposal by sale of these relics, wherein he could trace in a confused sort of way the very outlines of her form, appeared to him an atrocity, as if he had seen crows mangling her corpse. The atmosphere of the room, heavy with human breath, made him feel sick. Madame Dambreuse offered him her smelling-bottle. She said that she found all this highly amusing.

The bedroom furniture was now exhibited. Maître Berthelmot named a price. The crier immediately repeated it in a louder voice, and the three auctioneer's assistants quietly waited for the stroke of the hammer, and then carried off the article sold to an adjoining room. In this way disappeared, one after the other, the large blue carpet spangled with camellias, which her dainty feet used to touch so lightly as she advanced to meet him, the little upholstered easy-chair, in which he used to sit facing her when they were alone together, the two screens belonging to the mantelpiece, the ivory of which had been rendered smoother by the touch of her hands, and a velvet pincushion, which was still bristling with pins. It was as if portions of his heart had been carried away with these things; and the monotony of the same voices and the same gestures numbed him with fatigue, and caused within him a mournful torpor, a sensation like that of death itself.

There was a rustle of silk close to his ear. Rosanette touched him.

It was through Frédéric himself that she had learned about this auction. When her first feelings of vexation were over, the ideà of deriving profit from it occurred to her. She had come to see it in a white satin vest with pearl buttons, a flounced gown, tight-fitting gloves on her hands, and a look of triumph on her face.

He grew pale with anger. She stared at the woman who was by his side.

Madame Dambreuse had recognised her, and for a minute they examined each other from head to foot with scrupulous attention, in order to discover same defect, or blemish—one perhaps envying the other's youth, and the other filled with spite at the extreme good taste, the aristocratic simplicity of her rival.

At last Madame Dambreuse turned her head round with a smile of unspeakable insolence.

The crier had opened a piano—her piano! While he remained standing before it he ran the fingers of his right hand over the keys, and put up the instrument at twelve hundred francs; then he brought down the figures to one thousand, then to eight hundred, and finally to seven hundred.

Madame Dambreuse, in a playful tone, laughed at the old tin can.

The next thing placed before the second-hand dealers was a little chest with medallions and silver corners and clasps, the same one which he had seen at the first dinner in the Rue de Choiseul, which had subsequently been in Rosanette's house, and again transferred back to Madame Arnoux's residence. Often during their conversations his eyes wandered towards it. He was bound to it by the dearest memories, and his soul was melting with tender emotions about it, when suddenly Madame Dambreuse said:

"Look here! I am going to buy that!"

"But it is not a very rare article," he returned.

She considered it, on the contrary, very pretty, and the appraiser commended its delicacy.

"A gem of the Renaissance! Eight hundred francs, messieurs! Almost entirely of silver! With a little polish it can be made to shine brilliantly."

And, as she was pushing forward through the crush of people:

"What an odd ideal!" said Frédéric.

"You are annoyed at this!"

"No! But what can be done with a fancy article of that sort?"

"Who knows? Love-letters might be kept in it, perhaps!"

She gave him a look which made the allusion very clear.

"There's another reason for not robbing the dead of their secrets."

"I did not think she was as dead as all that." And then in a loud voice she went on to bid:

"Eight hundred and eighty francs!"

"What you're doing is not right," murmured Frédéric.

She began to laugh.

"But this is the first favour, dear, that I am asking from you."

"Come, now! doesn't it strike you that at this rate you won't be a very considerate husband?"

Some one had just at that moment made a higher bid.

"Nine hundred francs!"

"Nine hundred francs!" repeated Maître Berthelmot.

"Nine hundred and ten—fifteen—twenty—thirty!" squeaked the auctioneer's crier, with jerky shakes of his head as he cast a sweeping glance at those assembled around him.

"Show me that I am going to have a wife who is open to reason," said Frédéric.

And he gently drew her towards the door.

The auctioneer proceeded:

"Come, come, messieurs; nine hundred and thirty. Is there any bidder at nine hundred and thirty?"

Madame Dambreuse, just as she had reached the door, stopped, and raising her voice to a high pitch: "One thousand francs!"

There was a thrill of astonishment, and then a dead silence.

"A thousand francs, messieurs, a thousand francs! Anyone else? Very well, then—one thousand francs! going!—gone!"

And down came the ivory hammer. She passed in her card, and the little chest was handed over to her. She thrust it into her muff.

Frédéric felt a great chill penetrating his heart.

Madame Dambreuse had not let go her hold of his arm; and she had not the courage to look up at his face in the street, where her carriage was awaiting her.

She flung herself into it, like a thief flying away after a robbery, and then turned towards Frédéric. He had his hat in his hand.

"Are you not going to come in?"

"No, Madame!"

And, bowing to her frigidly, he shut the carriage-door, and then made a sign to the coachman to drive away.

The first feeling that he experienced was one of joy at having regained his independence. He was filled with pride at the thought that he had avenged Madame Arnoux by sacrificing a fortune to her; then, he was amazed at his own act, and he felt overwhelmed with extreme physical exhaustion.

Next morning his man-servant brought him the news.

The city had been declared to be in a state of siege; the Assembly had been dissolved; and a number of the representatives of the people had been imprisoned at Mazas.* Public affairs had become utterly unimportant to him, so deeply preoccupied was he by his private troubles.

He wrote to several tradesmen cancelling various orders which he had given for the purchase of articles in connection with his projected marriage, which now appeared to him a rather shabby speculation; and he cursed Madame Dambreuse, because, due to her, he had been very near dishonoring himself. He had forgotten the Maréchale, and did not even worry about Madame Arnoux—he thought only of himself, himself alone—lost amid the wreck of his dreams, sick at heart, full of grief and disappointment, and in his hatred of the artificial atmosphere wherein he had suffered so much, he longed for the freshness of green fields, the repose of provincial life, a sleepy life spent

---

*On December 2, 1851, Louis-Napoléon Bonaparte led his coup d'état. Mazas was a prison in Paris.

beneath the roof of the house where he was born, in the midst of innocent hearts. At last, when Wednesday evening arrived, he went out.

On the boulevard numerous groups had stationed themselves. From time to time a patrol came and dispersed them; they only gathered together again behind it. They talked freely and in loud tones, insulted and joked about the soldiers, without anything further happening.

"What! are they not going to fight?" said Frédéric to a workman.

"We're not such fools as to get ourselves killed for the rich! Let them take care of themselves!"

And a gentleman muttered, as he glanced across at the people of the faubourgs:

"Socialist rascals! If it were only possible, this time, to exterminate them!"

Frédéric could not, for the life of him, understand the necessity of so much hatred and stupidity. His feelings of disgust for Paris were intensified, and two days later he set out for Nogent on the first train.

The houses soon became lost to view; the country stretched out before him. Alone in the train car, with his feet on the seat in front of him, he pondered over the events of the last few days, and then on his entire past. The recollection of Louise came back to him.

"She, indeed, loved me truly! I was wrong not to snatch this chance of happiness. So what? let's forget it."

Then, five minutes afterwards: "Who knows, after all? Why not, later on?"

His reverie, like his eyes, wandered off towards vague horizons.

"She was naïve, a peasant girl, almost a savage; but so good!"

In proportion as he drew nearer to Nogent, her image drew closer to him. As they were passing through the meadows of Sourdun, he saw her once more in his imagination under the poplar-trees, as in the old days, cutting rushes beside the pools. And now they had reached their destination; he stepped out of the train.

Then he leaned with his elbows on the bridge, to gaze again at the isle and the garden where they had walked together one sunny day, and the dizzy sensation caused by travelling and the country air, together with the weakness brought on by his recent emotions, arousing in his chest a sort of exaltation, he said to himself:

"She has gone out, perhaps; suppose I were to go and meet her!"

The bell of Saint-Laurent was ringing, and in the square in front of the church there was a crowd of poor people around an open carriage, the only one in the district—the one which was always hired for weddings. And all of a sudden, under the churchgate, accompanied by a number of well-dressed people in white cravats, a newly-married couple appeared.

He thought he must be hallucinating. But no! It was, indeed, Louise! covered with a white veil which flowed from her red hair down to her heels; and with her was no other than Deslauriers, attired in a blue coat embroidered with silver—the uniform of a prefect.

What was the meaning of all this?

Frédéric concealed himself at the corner of a house to let the procession pass.

Shamefaced, vanquished, crushed, he retraced his steps to the railway-station, and returned to Paris.

The cabman who drove him assured him that the barricades were erected from the Château d'Eau to the Gymnase Theatre, and turned down the Faubourg Saint-Martin. At the corner of the Rue de Provence, Frédéric stepped out in order to reach the boulevards on foot.

It was five o'clock. A thin drizzle was falling. A number of citizens blocked the sidewalk close to the Opera House. The houses opposite were closed. No one at any of the windows. Taking up the whole width of the boulevard, dragoons were galloping at full speed, leaning over their horses; with swords drawn and, the plumes of their helmets, and their large white cloaks, billowing behind them, could be seen under the glare of the gas-lamps, which shook in the wind and mist. The crowd gazed at them mute with fear.*

In the intervals between the cavalry-charges, squads of policemen arrived on the scene to keep back the people in the streets.

---

*On the night of December 3, resistance to the coup was bloodily crushed.

But on the steps of Tortoni's,* a man—Dussardier—who could be distinguished at a distance by his great height, remained standing as still as a statue.

One of the police-officers, marching at the head of his men, with his three-cornered hat drawn over his eyes, threatened him with his sword.

The other thereupon took one step forward, and shouted:

"Long live the Republic!"

The next moment he fell on his back with his arms crossed.

A yell of horror arose from the crowd. The police-officer looked all around him; and Frédéric, stupefied, recognised Sénécal.

---

†Famous café on the boulevards.

CHAPTER VI

He travelled.

He came to know the melancholy of steamboats, the chill one feels on waking up in tents, the dizzy effect of landscapes and ruins, and the bitterness of ruptured friendships.

He returned home.

He mingled in society, and had other loves. But the constant recollection of his first love made these appear insipid; and besides the vehemence of desire, the very flower of the feeling had vanished. In like manner, his intellectual ambitions had grown weaker. Years passed; and he endured the idleness of his intelligence and the inertia of his heart.

Towards the end of March, 1867, just as it was getting dark, one evening, he was sitting all alone in his study, when a woman suddenly came in.

"Madame Arnoux!"

"Frédéric!"

She took hold of his hands, and drew him gently towards the window, and, as she gazed into his face, she kept repeating:

" 'Tis he! Yes, indeed—'tis he!"

In the growing shadows of the twilight, he could see only her eyes under the black lace veil that hid her face.

Once she had put down on the edge of the mantelpiece a little wallet of garnet velvet, she seated herself in front of him, and they both remained silent, unable to utter a word, smiling at one another.

At last he asked her a number of questions about herself and her husband.

They had gone to a remote part of Brittany to live cheaply, so as to be able to pay their debts. Arnoux, now almost always ill, had become quite an old man. Her daughter was married and living in Bordeaux, and her son was garrisoned at Mostaganem.*

Then she raised her head to look at him again:

"But now I've seen you again! I am happy!"

He did not fail to let her know that, as soon as he heard of their misfortune, he had hastened to their house.

"Yes, I know!"

"How?"

She had seen him in the street outside the house, and had hidden herself.

"Why did you do that?"

Then, in a trembling voice, and with long pauses between her words:

"I was afraid! Yes—afraid of you and of myself!"

This disclosure gave him, as it were, a shock of delight. His heart began to throb wildly. She went on:

"Excuse me for not having come sooner." And, pointing towards the little wallet covered with golden palm-branches:

"I embroidered it specially for you. It contains the amount for which the Belleville property was supposed to be the security."

Frédéric thanked her for letting him have the money, while chiding her at the same time for having given herself any trouble over it.

"No! 'tis not for this I came! I was determined to pay you this visit—then I will return . . . there."

And she spoke about the place where they lived.

It was a low-built house of only one story; and there was a garden full of huge box-trees, and a double avenue of chestnut-trees, reaching up to the top of the hill, from which there was a view of the sea.

"I go there and sit down on a bench, which I have called 'Frédéric's bench.' "

Then she proceeded to fix her gaze on the furniture, the ornaments, the pictures, greedily, so that she might be able to carry

*City in northern Algeria.

away the impressions of them in her memory. The Maréchale's portrait was half-hidden behind a curtain. But the golds and the whites, which showed their outlines through the midst of the surrounding darkness, attracted her attention.

"It seems to me I knew that woman?"

"Impossible!" said Frédéric. "It is an old Italian painting."

She confessed that she would like to take a walk through the streets on his arm.

They went out.

The light from the shop-windows fell, every now and then, on her pale profile; then once more she was wrapped in shadow, and in the midst of the carriages, the crowd, and the din, they walked on without paying any heed to what was happening around them, without hearing anything, like those who walk together in the countryside over beds of dead leaves.

They talked about the days which they had formerly spent in each other's company, the dinners at the time when *L'Art Industriel* flourished, Arnoux's various fads, his habit of tugging at the points of his collar and of smearing pomade over his moustache, and other matters of a more intimate and serious nature. What delight he experienced on the first occasion when he heard her singing! How lovely she looked on her feast-day at Saint-Cloud! He reminded her of the little garden at Auteuil, evenings at the theatre, a chance meeting on the boulevard, and some of her old servants, including her negress.

She was astonished at his vivid recollection of these things.

"Sometimes your words come back to me like a distant echo, like the sound of a bell carried on by the wind, and when I read love passages in books, it is as if you were here before me."

"All that people have found fault with as exaggerated in fiction you have made me feel," said Frédéric. "I can understand Werther,* who felt no disgust at his Charlotte for serving bread and butter."

"Poor, dear friend!"

She heaved a sigh; and, after a prolonged silence:

"No matter; we will have loved each other so much!"

---

*Goethe's hero of *Die Leiden des jungen Werther* (1774; *The Sorrows of Young Werther*), the tragic lover of Lotte.

"And still without having ever belonged to each other!"

"This perhaps is all the better," she replied.

"No, no! What happiness we might have enjoyed!"

"Oh, I am sure of it with a love like yours!"

And it must have been very strong to endure after such a long separation.

Frédéric wished to know from her how she first discovered that he loved her.

"It was when you kissed my wrist one evening between the glove and the cuff. I said to myself, 'Ah! yes, he loves me—he loves me;' nevertheless, I was afraid of finding out if it was true. So charming was your discretion, that I delighted in it as an unconscious and continuous homage."

He regretted nothing now. He was compensated for all he had suffered in the past.

When they came back to the house, Madame Arnoux took off her bonnet. The lamp, placed on a console table threw its light on her white hair. Frédéric felt as if some one had given him a blow in the middle of the chest.

In order to conceal from her his sense of disillusion, he flung himself on the floor at her feet, and seizing her hands, began to whisper in her ear words of tenderness:

"Your person, your slightest movements, seemed to me to have a superhuman importance in the world. My heart was stirred like dust under your feet. You affected me like moonlight on a summer's night, when around us we find nothing but perfume, soft shadows, pale light infinity; and all the delights of the flesh and of the spirit were for me embodied in your name, which I kept repeating to myself while I tried to kiss it with my lips. I thought of nothing beyond that. It was Madame Arnoux such as you were with your two children, tender, serious, dazzlingly beautiful, and yet so good! This image erased every other. Did I not think of it alone? for I had always in the very depths of my soul the music of your voice and the brightness of your eyes!"

She accepted rapturously these tributes of adoration to the woman whom she could no longer claim to be. Frédéric, becoming intoxicated with his own words, came to believe what he was saying. Madame Arnoux, with her back turned to the light of the lamp, stooped towards him. He felt the caress of her breath on his forehead, and the undefined touch of her entire body through the garments that kept them apart. Their hands were clasped; the tip of her bootee peeped out from beneath her gown, and feeling faint he said to her:

"The sight of your foot is disturbing me."

An impulse of modesty made her rise. Then, without any further movement, she said, with the strange intonation of a sleepwalker:

"At my age!—he—Frédéric! Ah! no woman has ever been loved as I have been. No! what is the use of being young? What do I care about that? I despise them—all those women who come here!"

"Oh! very few women come to this place," he returned, kindly.

Her face brightened up, and then she asked him whether he would marry.

He swore that he never would.

"Are you perfectly sure? Why should you not?"

" 'Tis on your account!" said Frédéric, clasping her in his arms.

She remained thus pressed to his heart, with her head thrown back, her lips parted, and her eyes raised. Suddenly she pushed him away from her with a look of despair, and when he implored her to say something to him in reply, she bent forward and whispered:

"I would have liked to make you happy!"

Frédéric had a suspicion that Madame Arnoux had come to offer herself to him, and once more he was seized with a desire to possess her—stronger, fiercer, more desperate than he had ever experienced before. And yet he felt, the next moment, an unaccountable repugnance to the thought of such a thing, like the guilt of committing incest. Another fear, too stopped him, the fear of being disgusted later. Besides, what an inconvenience it would be!—and, abandoning the idea, partly through prudence, and partly through a resolve not to degrade his ideal, he turned on his heel and proceeded to roll a cigarette between his fingers.

She watched him with admiration.

"How considerate you are! There is no one like you! There is no one like you!"

The clock struck eleven.

"Already!" she exclaimed; "at a quarter-past I must go."

She sat down again, but she kept looking at the clock, and he paced the room, puffing at his cigarette. Neither of them could think of anything further to say to the other. There is a moment at the hour of parting when the person that we love is already with us no longer.

At last, when the hands of the clock passed the twenty-five minute mark, she slowly took up her bonnet, holding it by the strings.

"Good-bye, my friend—my dear friend! I shall never see you again! This is the closing page in my life as a woman. My soul shall remain with you even when you see me no more. May all the blessings of Heaven be yours!"

And she kissed him on the forehead, like a mother.

But she appeared to be looking for something, and then she asked him for a pair of scissors.

She unfastened her comb, and all her white hair fell down.

With an abrupt movement of the scissors, she cut off a long lock from the roots.

"Keep it! Good-bye!"

When she was gone, Frédéric rushed to the window and threw it open. There on the sidewalk he saw Madame Arnoux beckoning towards a passing cab. She stepped into it. The vehicle disappeared.

And that was all.

CHAPTER VII

About the beginning of this winter, Frédéric and Deslauriers were chatting by the fireside, destined by nature, to always reunite and become friends again.

Frédéric briefly explained his quarrel with Madame Dambreuse, who had married again, her second husband being an Englishman.

Deslauriers, without telling how he had come to marry Mademoiselle Roque, related to his friend how his wife had one day eloped with a singer. In order to wipe away to some extent the ridicule that this brought upon him, he had compromised himself by an excess of zeal for the government in his functions as prefect. He had been dismissed. After that, he had been an agent for colonisation in Algeria, secretary to a pasha, editor of a newspaper, and an advertising agent, his latest employment being the office of legal counsil for a manufacturing company.

As for Frédéric, having squandered two thirds of his fortune, he was now living a middle-class life.

Then they brought each other up-to-date on their friends.

Martinon was now a member of the Senate.

Hussonnet occupied a high position, in which he was fortunate enough to have control of all the theatres and the entire press.

Cisy, deeply religious, and the father of eight children, was living in the château of his ancestors.

Pellerin, after turning his hand to Fourrièrism, homœpathy, table-turning, Gothic art, and humanitarian painting, had become a photographer; and he was to be seen on every wall in Paris, where he was represented in a black coat with a very small body and a big head.

"And what about your chum Sénécal?" asked Frédéric.

"Disappeared—I can't tell you where! And yourself—what about the woman you were so passionately attached to, Madame Arnoux?"

"She must be in Rome with her son, a cavalry lieutenant."

"And her husband?"

"He died a year ago."

"You don't say," exclaimed the lawyer. Then, striking his forehead:

"Now that I think of it, the other day in a shop I met that dear old Maréchale, holding by the hand a little boy whom she has adopted. She is the widow of a certain M. Oudry, and is now enormously stout. What a change for the worse!—she who formerly had such a slender waist!"

Deslauriers did not deny that he had taken advantage of her despair to find this out for himself.

"After all you gave me permission."

This admission was a compensation for the silence he had maintained with reference to his attempt to seduce Madame Arnoux.

Frédéric would have forgiven him, inasmuch as he had not succeeded in the attempt.

Although a little annoyed at the discovery, he pretended to laugh at it; and the allusion to the Maréchale brought back Vatnaz to his recollection.

Deslauriers had never seen her, any more than the others who used to come to the Arnoux's house; but he remembered Regimbart perfectly.

"Is he still living?"

"He is barely alive. Every evening regularly he drags himself from the Rue de Grammont to the Rue Montmartre, to the cafés, weak, bent in two, emaciated, a ghost of a man!"

"Well, and what about Compain?"

Frédéric uttered a cry of joy, and begged the ex-delegate of the provisional government to explain to him the mystery of the calf's head.

"It's an idea imported from England. In order to parody the ceremony which the Royalists celebrated on the thirtieth of January, some Independents threw on annual banquet, at which they ate calves' heads, and drank red wine out of calves' skulls while toasting the extermination of the Stuarts. After Thermidor, some Terrorists organized a brotherhood of a similar description, which proves how contagious stupidity is."

"You seem to have lost you passion for politics?"

"Effect of age," said the lawyer.

And then they each proceeded to summarise their lives.

They had both failed in their plans—the one who dreamed only of love, and the other of power.

What was the reason for this?

" 'Tis perhaps from not having kept to a steady course," said Frédéric.

"In your case that may be so. I, on the contrary, have sinned through excess rigidity, without taking into account a thousand secondary things more important than any other. I had too much logic, and you too much sentiment."

Then they blamed bad luck, circumstances, the times in which they were born.

Frédéric went on:

"We have never done what we thought of doing long ago at Sens, when you wished to write a critical history of Philosophy and I a great mediæval romance about Nogent, the subject of which I had found in Froissart:* 'How Messire Brokars de Fenestranges and the Bishop of Troyes attacked Messire Eustache d'Ambrecicourt.' Do you remember?"

And, exhuming their youth with every sentence, they said to each other:

"Do you remember?"

They saw once more the school playground, the chapel, the parlour, the fencing room at the bottom of the staircase, the faces of the school monitors and of the pupils—one named, Angelmarre, from Versailles, who used to make himself trousers-straps from old boots, M. Mirbal and his red whiskers, the two professors of geometric and artistic drawing, who were always wrangling, and the Pole, the fellow-countryman of Copernicus, with his planetary system on cardboard, an itinerant astronomer whose lecture had been paid for by a free dinner in the refectory, then a drunken escapade

---

*See footnote on p. 17.

while they were out on a walking excursion, the first pipes they had smoked, the distribution of prizes, and the delightful sensation of going home for the holidays.

It was during the vacation of 1837 that they had called at the house of the Turkish woman.

This was the phrase used to designate a woman whose real name was Zoraide Turc; and many people believed her to be a Muslim, a Turk, which added to the poetic charm of her establishment, situated at the water's edge behind the ramparts. Even in the middle of summer there was shade around her house, which could be recognised by a glass bowl of goldfish near a pot of mignonette on the windowsill. Young ladies in white nightdresses, with painted cheeks and long earrings, used to tap at the panes as the students passed; and as it grew dark, their custom was to hum softly in their husky voices standing on the doorstep.

This den of iniquity spread its fantastic notoriety over all the arrondissement. Allusions were made to it indirectly: "The place you know—a certain street—below the Bridges." It made the farmers' wives of the district tremble for their husbands, and the bourgeois ladies grow apprehensive about their servants' virtue, because the sub-prefect's cook had been caught there; and, it was, of course, the secret obsession of every adolescent.

One Sunday, when everyone was at Vespers, Frédéric and Deslauriers, having previously curled their hair, gathered some flowers in Madame Moreau's garden, then made their way out through the gate leading into the fields, and, after taking a long detour through the vineyards, came back through the Fishery, and stole into the Turkish woman's house with their big bouquets still in their hands.

Frédéric presented his as a lover does to his betrothed. But the great heat, the fear of the unknown, and even the very pleasure of seeing at one glance so many women placed at his disposal, affected him so strangely that he turned exceedingly pale, and remained there without taking a single step or uttering a single word. All the girls burst out laughing, amused at his embarrasment. Thinking that they were making fun of him, he ran away; and, as Frédéric had the money, Deslauriers was obliged to follow him.

They were seen leaving the house; and the episode furnished material for a bit of local gossip which was still remembered three years later.

They related the story to each other at great length, each completing the narrative where the other's memory failed; and, when they had finished:

"That was the best we ever got!" said Frédéric.

"Yes, perhaps so, indeed! It was the best time we ever had," said Deslauriers.

ENDNOTES

Part One

1. (p. 5) *15th of September, 1840*: We are in the middle of the reign of the "bourgeois king" Louis-Philippe, brought to power by the revolution of 1830.
2. (p. 5) *Quai St. Bernard*: This wharf is in the center of Paris, on the left bank. The boat *Ville de Montereau* will steam up the Seine to the town of Montereau.
3. (p. 5) *receiving an inheritance*: Frédéric Moreau has made an excursion to Le Havre, at the estuary of the Seine on the English Channel; after a halt in Paris, he is returning to his native town of Nogent-sur-Seine.
4. (p. 15) *Madame Lafarge*: Accused of poisoning her husband, Madame Lafarge had just been condemned to forced labor but never ceased to claim her innocence.
5. (p. 16) *an army recruiter at Troyes*: Every twenty-year-old Frenchman could be drafted by lottery for a seven-year stint of military service; those with a called-up number and sufficient means could "buy" a substitute. People like M. Deslauriers acted as middlemen in these transactions.
6. (p. 17) *Jouffroy, Cousin, Laromiguière, Malebranche, and the Scotch metaphysicians*: Théodore Jouffroy, Victor Cousin, and Pierre Laromiguière were eclectic nineteenth-century French philosophers. Around 1680 Nicolas Malebranche attempted to reconcile Cartesianism and Christianity. And in the eighteenth century and the beginning of the nineteenth, Scots Thomas Reid and Dugald Stewart founded their metaphysics on the certainty of common sense.
7. (p. 17) *the Walter Scott of France*: Scott, the prolific author of *Waverley* (1814) and *Ivanhoe* (1819), was extraordinarily popular in France during the Romantic period, a fact that explains the durable success of the historical novel.
8. (p. 22) *Rastignac in the* Comédie Humaine: The young protagonist of *Le Père Goriot* (1835; *Father Goriot*), by Honoré de Balzac, starts as a poor provincial student in Paris and finds success in later novels largely through his connections with rich women.

9. (p. 26) *But he left off studying the Civil Code . . . and he gave up the Institutes at the* Summa Divisio Personarum: The French Civil Code (the Napoleonic Code) was established under Napoléon I in 1804 and is still in use today. The *Institutes* is one of four books comprising the Justinian code composed under the Byzantine emperor Justinian in the sixth century A.D.

10. (p. 32) *he perceived a large gathering around the Panthéon*: A temple to France's illustrious men, in the Latin Quarter, the Panthéon went back to its initial function as a church under the Second Empire.

11. (p. 32) *some other events*: The Reform asked for was that of the electoral system, which allowed only citizens paying a certain level of taxes to vote. The National Guard was a civic militia created by the French Revolution to maintain public order; it was abolished in 1871. The census of finance minister Jean-Georges Humann, falsely perceived as an instrument to increase taxes, raised a lot of protest.

12. (p. 33) *like Frédéric Lemaître in* Robert Macaire: Frédéric Lemaître was a well-known Romantic actor in the mid-nineteenth century; Robert Macaire was a thief in a melodrama of the same name.

13. (p. 34) *"Down with Guizot!" "Down with Pritchard!"*: The influence of George Pritchard, an English Protestant missionary in Tahiti, a French protectorate since 1843, created tensions between France and Great Britain. Pritchard, a British consul, had argued that Tahiti should become a British protectorate. The conservative government minister François Guizot (see the introduction) placated him with a large monetary compensation, which was a very unpopular measure.

14. (p. 35) *the "Marseillaise" . . . to Béranger's house . . . Laffitte's house . . . Chateaubriand's house . . . "To Voltaire's house!" yelled the young man with the fair moustache*: Under the restored kings, the "Marseillaise" was not the national hymn but a revolutionary song. Pierre-Jean de Béranger (1780–1857), a popular poet and chansonnier, Jacques Laffitte (1767–1844), a rich banker, and even François de Chateaubriand (1768–1848), a Legitimist and well-known writer, all had liberal tendencies. The Enlightenment philosopher Voltaire (1694–1778) was dead by this time.

15. (p. 39) *noticing . . . a volume of Hugo and another of Lamartine . . . criticisms of the romantic school*: Although far from revolutionary in their poetic practices, Alphonse de Lamartine (1790–1869), Victor Hugo (1802–1885), and the other Romantics were accused by the Classicists of distorting the French language. Lamartine and Hugo were both "engagés" writers of leftist leaning.

16. (p. 59) *Louis Blanc*: Louis Blanc, a historian and socialist theoretician, was very active in the provisional government of 1848. His *Histoire de dix ans* (1841–1844; *The History of Ten Years*) violently attacks the July Monarchy.

17. (p. 65) *The "Bastillization" of Paris, the September laws, Pritchard, Lord Guizot*: "The 'Bastillization' of Paris" refers to the construction of fortifications in progress around the capital. The laws of September government's control of the press and the theaters. For P the latter suspected of anglophilia, see note 13 to part one.

18. (p. 74) *The July Column glittered . . . the dome of the Tuile lines . . . one great round mass of blue*: The July Column had b Louis-Philippe on the site of the destroyed Bastille to comm the revolutions of 1789 and July 1830. The Renaissance-era royal palace of the Tuileries, next to the Louvre, was burned down during the Commune of 1871.

Part Two

1. (p. 127) *"the Franks will no longer oppress the Gauls"*: According to certain theories, the Frank warriors who invaded Roman Gaul in the fifth century A.D. gave birth to the nobility and the conquered Gauls to the plebeians.
2. (p. 128) *"who are electors, perhaps eligible as candidates"*: In the electoral system then in effect, in order to be an elector one had to have enough means to pay a certain level of taxes; paying yet higher taxes could make one eligible to serve in Parliament.
3. (p. 129) *"Camille Desmoulins . . . drove the people on to the Bastille"*: Camille Desmoulins, a republican lawyer and influential journalist, gave important speeches two days before the storming of the Bastille in July 1789 that helped lead to that event.
4. (p. 153) *he hoped to reach the* Conseil d'Etat *with the help of . . . the representative*: The Conseil d'Etat examines laws before they are presented to the Parliament and serves as the supreme administrative court.
5. (p. 154) *He had annotated the* Contrat Social . . . *crammed himself with the* Revue Indépendante . . . *acquainted with Mably, Morelly, Fourier, Saint-Simon, Comte, Cabet, Louis Blanc: The Social Contract* (1762), by Jean-Jacques Rousseau, is a treatise in favor of democracy. The *Revue Indépendante* (1841–1848), a publication produced by George Sand and Pierre Leroux, was also democratic in inspiration. Gabriel de Mably and Morelly were eighteenth-century Enlightenment philosophers; Charles Fourier, Henri de Saint-Simon, Étienne Cabet, and Louis Blanc were nineteenth-century utopian socialists; the philosopher Auguste Comte was the creator of "Positivism."
6. (p. 156) *murders of Buzançais and the crisis arising from a shortage of food*: This is an allusion to the murder of a rich farmer by hungry rioters in Buzançais, and to the execution of the culprits.
7. (p. 156) *"Are we to follow the advice of the infamous Malthus?"*: The British economist Thomas Malthus (1766–1834) saw population growth as a threat to the survival of the nations; he recommended the voluntary restriction of births as the solution.

(p. 156) *listening to the Phalansterians talking. . . . Fourier was a great man*: The utopian socialist Charles Fourier (1772–1837) advocated a social system based on small communities, "phalanxes," in which total freedom of passions and activities would prevail. Members lived in buildings called phalansteries.

9. (p. 157) *"Saint-Simon and his church, with his hatred of the French Revolution"*: Henri de Saint-Simon (1760–1825) promoted the "religion of Science" and a socialism based on productivity, technocracy, and the collaboration of the social classes. He was very influential in the nineteenth century.

10. (p. 158) *Barbès had his sympathy*: The republican leader and conspirator Barbès was in prison when the February 1848 revolution liberated him; he was incarcerated again shortly afterward and died in exile.

11. (p. 158) *"For my part, the thing I blame Louis Philippe for is abandoning the Poles"*: Louis-Philippe did nothing to support Poland, which, after its insurrection of 1830 against Russian occupation, suffered severe repression.

12. (p. 159) *"'tis an invention of Lafayette! The Poles . . . the real ones having been drowned with Poniatowski"*: The Marquis de Lafayette (1757–1834), the general who helped American revolutionaries and who was a politician during the French Revolution, had pleaded the cause of Poland against Russia. After 1830 a number of Poles emigrated to Paris. Józef Poniatowski, a Polish general who led a Polish brigade in Napoleon's army, died heroically in battle in 1813 when he attempted to cross a river on horseback while wounded.

13. (p. 159) *"the revocation of the Edict of Nanes, and that antiquated nonsense about the Saint-Bartholomew massacre!"*: The Edict of Nantes, which ended the French Wars of Religion in 1598 by granting rights to the Protestants, was revoked by Louis XIV in 1685. The massacre of Saint Bartholomew's Night, in August 1572, is an episode of those wars, in which many Huguenots were killed by Catholic fanatics.

14. (p. 159) *tableaux vivants at the Gymnase Theatre, which at that time attracted a great number of people*: In *tableaux vivants*, living men and women reproduce on stage famous paintings or scenes. The Gymnase Theatre specialized in lightweight theatrical fare.

15. (p. 178) *"What would you expect . . . when we see M. de Genoude giving his assistance to* Le Siècle?: In his opposition to the Orleanist monarchy, the Legitimist journalist Genoude shared positions with the leftist newspaper *Le Siècle*.

16. (p. 196) *comparing him to Saint Vincent de Paul with a dash of Brutus and Mirabeau*: Saint Vincent de Paul was a seventeenth-century priest famous for his charity. Lucius Junius Brutus was the Roman who in the sixth century B.C. ousted an Etruscan king and established the Roman Republic. For Mirabeau, see the footnote on p. 22.

17. (p. 199) *their Prefect*: In a system instituted by Napoleon, a prefect represents the central government in every *département* (administrative territory). The general council is the elected assembly of a *département*.

18. (p. 200) *Père Enfantin gives his blessing . . . Pierre Leroux wishes people . . . Louis Blanc inclines toward a State religion*: Prosper Enfantin (1796–1864) was the most vocal and eccentric of Saint-Simon's disciples (see note 9 to part two). Pierre Leroux (1797–1871) was a Christian socialist. For Louis Blanc, see note 16 to part one.

19. (p. 201) *the Academy, the École Normale, the Conservatoire, the Comédie Française, everything that resembled an institution*: The French Academy, founded in 1634, assembles forty writers in charge of composing an "official" dictionary. The École Normale (Normal School), founded in 1794, trains future professors and researchers, and the Conservatoire, founded in 1795, trains musicians. The Comédie-Française, the national theater of France, created in 1680 and publicly subsidized, performs plays from a classical repertory.

20. (p. 227) *in the middle of the Champ de Mars, near some other vehicles . . . in the Hippodrome*: The Champ-de-Mars, on the west side of Paris, was once used for military parades and is now the site of the Eiffel Tower. The Hippodrome, at the Champ-de-Mars, was the site of horse races at the time of the July Monarchy.

21. (p. 235) *he enquired about the College of France, from which Edgar Quinet and Mickiewicz had been barred*: The Collège de France is a prestigious institution of higher learning founded in the sixteenth century. Edgar Quinet (1803–1875), a historian and Romantic writer, lost his teaching chair at the Collège in 1847 because of his anticlericalism. Several years before, Adam Mickiewicz (1798–1855), a Polish Romantic poet and patriot, had also been suspended from the Collège because of the content of his teachings.

22. (pp. 236–237)*"Not Orléans, pray! . . . "Would you prefer a turbot* à la *Chambord?"*: "D'Orléans" is the title of the younger branch of the Bourbon dynasty, which came to power with Louis-Philippe. The Legitimists were in favor of the older branch that had been in power from the reign of Louis XIV to that of Charles X (with the interruption of the Revolution and the Empire); the last representative of this branch was the Count of Chambord.

23. (p. 243) *"The anniversary service for Godefroy Cavaignac is taking place there today"*: Godefroy Cavaignac (1801–1845)—not to be confused with his brother the general—was a popular republican leader whose funeral cortege comprised thousands of sympathizers.

24. (p. 246) *Rodolphe in the* Mysteries of Paris: In the famous serial novel by Eugène Sue, *Les Mystères de Paris* (1842–1843), Prince Rodolphe visits the dregs of the Parisian populace in order to practice his philanthropy.

25. (p. 246) *he even attempted a pun; for he said, as they passed a heath-cock: "There's the best of La Bruyère's characters!"*: A heath-cock is a *coq de bruyère* in French; hence the pun on the name Jean de La Bruyère, seventeenth-century author of *Les Caractères . . . ou les moeurs de ce siècle* (1688; *The Characters, or the Manners of the Age*).

26. (p. 259) *had as his teacher a former disciple of Chalier . . . admission into the "Society of Families." . . . he became a fanatical follower of Alibaud*: Marie-Joseph Chalier was a Jacobin leader in Lyons during the Revolution. The Society of Families was a secret society directed by Barbès and Louis-Auguste Blanqui that in May 1839 organized a failed insurrection. Alibaud was executed for attempting to kill Louis-Philippe.

27. (p. 264) *He took a copy of the* Revue des Deux Mondes . . . *between an* Imitation *and an* Almanach de Gotha: For the *Revue des Deux Mondes*, see the footnote on p. 30. The *Imitation of Christ*, originally in Latin, is an anonymous spiritual guide that has been widely read since the fifteenth century. The *Almanach de Gotha*, an annual publication in French and German, provides the genealogies of royal families.

28. (p. 267) *the English Bill of Rights, and Article 2 of the Constitution of '91*: The English Bill of Rights of 1689 limited royal power. The French Constitution of 1791 defined the natural and inalienable rights of men, which included the right to resist oppression.

29. (p. 267) *A manufacturer, who had formerly been a member of the Carbonari, tried to show that the Orléans family possessed good qualities*: The Carbonari was a secret society in Italy, France, and Spain. In France its members were opponents of the Restoration; most were republicans, some Orleanists.

30. (p. 293) *this precious English alliance was lost, because of the Spanish marriages*: Following Great Britain's position, France supported Belgium's independence from Holland in 1830. But the marriage of Isabel of Spain to a son of Louis-Philippe displeased the English crown.

31. (p. 296) *the Juggler of the Hôtel de Ville, the friend of the traitor Dumouriez*: These phrases are derogatory references to Louis-Philippe, who had been proclaimed king at the Hôtel de Ville (City Hall) in Paris and had served during the revolution under General Charles Dumouriez (1739–1823), who later switched his allegiance to the enemy.

32. (p. 317) *It was the firing of muskets on the Boulevard des Capucines*: On the evening of February 23, 1848, soldiers opened fire on demonstrators on the Boulevard des Capucines, killing around a hundred people. The corpses were paraded in carts all night long on the streets of Paris. This atrocity fired up the revolution of 1848.

Part Three

1. (p. 328) *The people . . . informed them that the Duchesse d'Orléans had been appointed Regent*: As a result of the revolution of 1848, Louis-Philippe abdicated in favor of his nine-year-old grandson, whose mother, the Duchess of Orleans, was to become regent. But the revolution did not let this come to pass.

2. (p. 330) *he had managed to see Ledru-Rollin, and . . . had obtained from him a post, a mission*: The provincial commissioners replaced Louis-Philippe's prefects. The lawyer Alexandre Ledru-Rollin was a minister in the provisional government until June 1848.

3. (p. 330) *in reference to the red flag, "which had only been carried round the Champ de Mars, whereas the tri-colored flag . . ."*: This refers to lines from the famous speech that Lamartine made in February 1848: ". . . while the tricolored flag had made its way around the world upholding the name, the glory and the liberty of the homeland," following which the blue, white, and red flag of the French Revolution was adopted.
4. (p. 340) *one copied Saint-Just, another Danton, another Marat . . . he tried to be like Blanqui, who imitated Robespierre*: Louis de Saint-Just, Georges Danton, Jean-Paul Marat, and Maximilien Robespierre were leaders of the French Revolution. Louis-Auguste Blanqui was a socialist theoretician and militant active in the workers' movement of 1848.
5. (p. 353) *the national workshops*: Proposed by Louis Blanc, who was active in the provisional government of 1848, these workshops were organized to guarantee labor for the workers, but turned out to be closer to welfare centers.
6. (p. 356) *"Long live Napoléon! Long live Barbès! Down with Marie!"*: "Napoléon" refers to Louis-Napoléon Bonaparte, who pretended to support the provisional government of 1848. For Barbès, see note 10 to part two. The government minister Alexandre Marie implemented the national workshops (see the preceding note).
7. (p. 357) *Considérant, Lamennais*: Victor-Prosper Considérant, a disciple of the utopian Charles Fourier, was active in the June rebellion. The priest Félicité Lamennais, whose views evolved from royalism and support for papal authority to democracy, was elected as a representative to the Constituent Assembly after the 1848 revolution.
8. (p. 359) *Fontainebleau*: In the forest of Fontainebleau sits François I's imposing Renaissance castle. There Napoléon I signed his first abdication in 1814.
9. (p. 363) *a terrible battle had stained Paris with blood*: The decision to dissolve the national workshops triggered an insurrection in Paris that was pitilessly repressed by the army and national guards from June 23 through June 26, 1848.
10. (p. 375) *deaths of Bréa and Négrier, about the Deputy Charbonnel . . . Archbishop of Paris . . . Duc d'Aumale had landed at Boulogne . . . Barbès had fled. from Vincennes . . . artillery was coming from Bourges*: General Bréa, General Négrier, Deputy Charbonnel, and the Archbishop of Paris were killed by the insurgents. The Duc d'Aumale, a son of Louis-Philippe, fled to England. For Barbès, see note 10 to part two. Vincennes was a prison in a southern suburb of Paris. Bourges is a city in central France.
11. (p. 387) *"Light up! . . . Prudhomme on a Barricade"*: During demonstrations, lanterns were usually lighted and placed in windows as a sign of solidarity. Prudhomme, a fictional creation of Henri Monnier (1805–1877), is a caricature of the self-satisfied petit bourgeois.

12. (p. 407) *Thiers was praised. . . . There was an immense laugh at Pierre Leroux. . . . Jokes were made about the phalansterian tail*: For Thiers, see the footnote on p. 179, and for Leroux, see note 18 to part two. A caricature by Cham represented the Fourierist Victor-Prosper Considérant with a tail, a joke inspired by Fourier's delirious utopianism (see note 8 to part two).

13. (p. 413) *the venality of Talleyrand and Mirabeau*: Charles Talleyrand was a politician and diplomat who served all regimes from the 1789 Revolution to the July Monarchy. The revolutionary leader the Comte de Mirabeau accepted bribery from Louis XVI (1754–1793).

14. (p. 445) *they are killing our Republic, just as they killed the other one—the Roman . . . poor Venice! poor Poland! poor Hungary!*: The Roman Republic was proclaimed by a popular insurrection in 1849; but Louis-Napoléon Bonaparte helped the Pope return to power in 1850. (Concerning the bloody repression of Poland's 1830 rebellion against Russian domination, see notes 11 and 12 to part two above.) In 1849 Austria reestablished its hegemony over Venice and crushed the rebellion in Hungary.

15. (p. 449) *Saint John of Correggio, the Infanta Rose of Velasquez. . . . Reynolds . . . Lawrence . . . the child . . . that sits in Lady Gower's lap*: Correggio was a sixteenth-century Italian artist; Diego Velázquez was a seventeenth-century Spanish artist; Sir Joshua Reynolds and Sir Thomas Lawrence (who painted Lady Gower's portrait) were eighteenth- and nineteenth-century English artists.

INSPIRED BY *SENTIMENTAL EDUCATION*

> One thing admits of little doubt: Flaubert created the modern realistic novel and directly or indirectly has influenced all writers of fiction since his day. Thomas Mann when he wrote *Buddenbrooks*, Arnold Bennett when he wrote *The Old Wives' Tale*, Theodore Dreiser when he wrote *Sister Carrie* were following a trail that Flaubert blazed.
>
> —W. Somerset Maugham

Realism and Guy de Maupassant

Gustave Flaubert is widely credited with having had a primary influence on literary Realism. Following in the footsteps of the French masters Stendhal and Honoré de Balzac and paving the way for Alphonse Daudet, Edmond and Jules de Goncourt, and Émile Zola, Flaubert codified for French literature a style that blended finely observed detail about human society with historical accuracy and detached narration, a style commonly referred to as Realism—a term first applied to realistic, representational painting. (Zola coined "Naturalism" to describe his own literary efforts, and many writers who came after preferred this term.) The rejection of merely subjective—and what Flaubert would have deemed escapist—literature was quickly taken up by writers the world over. Realism was embraced in Germany by Gerhart Hauptmann, Arno Holz, Johannes Schlaf, and Thomas Mann; in England by George Gissing, Arnold Bennett, Thomas Hardy, Samuel Butler, and W. Somerset Maugham; and in America by William Dean Howells, Henry James, Stephen Crane, Frank Norris, Jack London, and Theodore Dreiser.

Arguably the Realist writer who benefited most from Flaubert's influence was the latter's fellow Frenchman, Guy de Maupassant.

A young law student whose schooling was interrupted by his military service in the Franco-Prussian War, Maupassant returned to Paris in 1871 and found himself under the tutelage of Flaubert. This quickly became a literary apprenticeship that would become Maupassant's most life-defining experience. Flaubert introduced Maupassant to the leading authors of the day—Edmond de Goncourt, Henry James, Ivan Turgenev, Émile Zola—encouraging Maupassant in his own writing. In his study of Maupassant, Pol Neveux observed:

> Without ever becoming despondent, silent and persistent, [Maupassant] accumulated manuscripts, poetry, criticisms, plays, romances and novels. Every week he docilely submitted his work to the great Flaubert, the childhood friend of his mother and his uncle Alfred Le Poittevin. The master had consented to assist the young man, to reveal to him the secrets that make *chefs-d'oeuvre* immortal. It was he who compelled him to make copious research and to use direct observation and who inculcated in him a horror of vulgarity and a contempt for facility. . . . The worship of Flaubert was a religion from which nothing could distract him, neither work, nor glory, nor slow moving waves, nor balmy nights (*Oeuvres completes de Guy de Maupassant*, vol. 3, Paris: Louis Conard, 1908–1910).

Maupassant adopted from Flaubert his class sensibility, his French nationalism, and his brutal realism, including the frank portrayal of sexuality that characterizes *Madame Bovary.* "The sexual impulse," wrote Henry James in the *Fortnightly Review* (March 1888), "is . . . the wire that moves almost all M. de Maupassant's puppets, and as he has not hidden it, I cannot see that he has eliminated analysis or made a sacrifice to discretion. His pages are studded with that particular analysis; he is constantly peeping behind the curtain, telling us what he discovers there." Joseph Conrad, who described Maupassant as "a very splendid sinner," championed Flaubert's disciple in *Notes on Life and Letters* (1921): "He looks with an eye of profound pity upon [mankind's] troubles, deceptions and misery. But he looks at them all. He sees—and does not turn his head."

"I am always thinking of my poor Flaubert," wrote Maupassant, "and I say to myself that I should like to die if I were sure that anyone would think of me in the same manner." Maupassant wrote novels, plays, travel sketches, and more than 300 short stories; of the latter, among the best known are "Boule de suif" ("Tallow Ball"), "La Ficelle" ("The Piece of String"), and "La Parure" ("The Necklace"). Maupassant's masterful short fiction—his most memorable legacy—has itself inspired the work of Kate Chopin, W. Somerset Maugham, and O. Henry, among others.

Flaubert's Parrot

"Why does the writing make us chase the writer? Why can't we leave well enough alone? Why aren't the books enough?" So wrote British novelist Julian Barnes in *Flaubert's Parrot* (1984). Described as a "puzzler," *Flaubert's Parrot* is narrated by Geoffrey Braithwaite, a retired English doctor, who embarks on a desperate search for a stuffed parrot Flaubert is thought to have kept on his desk for inspiration. As Braithwaite embarks on a detail-embroidered historical adventure, he compulsively attempts to discover the real Flaubert: "Gustave imagined he was a wild beast—he loved to think of himself as a polar bear, distant, savage and solitary. I went along with this, I even called him a wild buffalo of the American prairie; but perhaps he was really just a parrot." As Braithwaite delves more deeply, he begins to analyze his process of discovery, realizing that his eccentric obsessions are a way of quantifying and documenting human life—an impulse provoked by his wife's suicide.

In a review of *Flaubert's Parrot*, Frank Kermode remarked "Wit, charm, fantasy are [Barnes's] instruments"; add to this an adroit juggling of historical facts and insight, as well as a distinctly British sensibility. *Flaubert's Parrot* was shortlisted for the Booker McConnell Prize in 1984, and it won the Geoffrey Faber Memorial Prize in 1985 and the Prix Médicis in 1986. In addition to his numerous novels, Barnes has written *Something to Declare* (2002), a book of essays, including many about Gustave Flaubert.

COMMENTS & QUESTIONS

In this section, we aim to provide the reader with an array of perspectives on the text, as well as questions that challenge those perspectives. The commentary has been culled from sources as diverse as comments contemporaneous with the work, literary criticism of later generations, and appreciations written throughout the work's history. Following the commentary, a series of questions seeks to filter Sentimental Education *through a variety of points of view and bring about a richer understanding of this enduring work.*

Comments

HENRY JAMES

"L'Éducation Sentimentale" is a strange, an indescribable work, about which there would be many more things to say than I have space for, and all of them of the deepest interest. It is moreover, to simplify my statement, very much less satisfying a thing, less pleasing whether in its unity or its variety, than its specific predecessor. But take it as we will, for a success or a failure—M. Faguet indeed ranks it, by the measure of its quantity of intention, a failure, and I on the whole agree with him—the personage offered us as bearing the weight of the drama, and in whom we are invited to that extent to interest ourselves, leaves us mainly wondering what our entertainer could have been thinking of. He takes Frédéric Moreau on the threshold of life and conducts him to the extreme of maturity without apparently suspecting for a moment either our wonder or our protest—"Why, why *him*?" Frédéric is positively too poor for his part, too scant for his charge; and we feel with a kind of embarrassment, certainly with a kind of compassion, that it is somehow the business of a protagonist to prevent in his designer an excessive waste of faith . . .

We meet Frédéric first, we remain with him long, as a *moyen*, a provincial bourgeois of the mid-century, educated and not without fortune, thereby with freedom, in whom the life of his day reflects itself. Yet the life of his day, on Flaubert's showing, hangs together with the poverty of Frédéric's own inward or for that matter outward life; so that, the whole thing being, for scale, intention and extension, a sort of epic of the usual (with the Revolution of 1848 introduced indeed as an episode), it affects us as an epic without air, without wings to lift it; reminds us in fact more than anything else of a huge balloon, all of silk pieces strongly sewn together and patiently blown up, but that absolutely refuses to leave the ground. The discrimination I here make as against our author is, however, the only one inevitable in a series of remarks so brief. What it really represents—and nothing could be more curious—is that Frédéric enjoys his position not only without the aid of a single "sympathetic" character of consequence, but even without the aid of one with whom we can directly communicate. Can we communicate with the central personage? Or would we really if we could? A hundred times no, and if he himself can communicate with the people shown us as surrounding him this only proves him of their kind. Flaubert on his "real" side was in truth an ironic painter, and ironic to a tune that makes his final accepted state, his present literary dignity and "classic" peace, superficially anomalous. There is an explanation to which I shall immediately come; but I find myself feeling for a moment longer in presence of "L'Éducation" how much more interesting a writer may be on occasion by the given failure than by the given success. Successes pure and simple disconnect and dismiss him; failures—though I admit they must be a bit qualified—keep him in touch and in relation. Thus it is that as the work of a "gran écrivain" "L'Éducation," large, laboured, immensely "written," with beautiful passages and a general emptiness, with a kind of leak in its stored sadness, moreover, by which its moral dignity escapes—thus it is that Flaubert's ill-starred novel is a curiosity for a literary museum. Thus it is also that it suggests a hundred reflections, and suggests perhaps most of them directly to the intending labourer in the same field. If in short, as I have said, Flaubert is the novelist's novelist, this performance does more than any other toward making him so.

—from *Notes on Novelists* (1914)

JAMES HUNEKER

Flaubert's realism was of a vastly superior sort to pierce behind appearances, and while his surfaces are extraordinary in finish, exactitude, and detail, the aura of persons and things is never wanting. His visualizing power has never been excelled, not even by Balzac; a stroke or two and a man or woman peers from behind the type. He ambushed himself in the impersonal, and thus his criticism seems hard, cold, and cruel to those readers who look for the occasional personal fillip of Fielding, Thackeray, and Dickens. The frigid withdrawal of self behind the screen of his art gave him all the more freedom to set moving his puppets. For those who mortise the cracks in their imagination with romanticism, Flaubert will never captivate. He seems too remote. He regards his characters too dispassionately. This objectivity is carried to dangerous lengths in "Sentimental Education," for the book is in the minor key, without much exciting incident; that is, exciting in the Dumas or Stevenson sense; and it is very long . . .

The list is not large, but every figure is painted by a master. And the vanity, the futility, the barrenness of it all. It is the concentrated philosophy of disenchantment—as Edgar Saltus would say—and about the book hangs the inevitable atmosphere of mortification, of defeat, of unheroic resignation. But it is genuine life, commonplace, quotidian life, and Truth is stamped on its portals. All is vanity and vexation of spirit. The tragedy of the petty has never before been so mockingly, so menacingly, so absolutely displayed. Tchekoff, with his gray-in-gray miniatures of misery, comes nearer to the French story than any other modern. Perhaps Henry James is right in declaring that "Sentimental Education" (a misleading title; it was to have been "Withered Fruits") is like the mastication of sawdust and ashes. A pitiless book, you will say! Yes, and it proves nothing, except that life is but a rope of sand. Read it, if you care for art in its quintessence; but if you are better pleased with the show and bravery of things external, avoid this novel for it is as bitter as a page from Ecclesiastes.

—from *Puck* (September 9, 1916)

GEORGE SAINTSBURY

That there was no danger of Flaubert's merely palming off, in his novel work, replicas with a few superficial differences, had now been shown. It was further established by his third and longest book, *L'Éducation Sentimentale.* This was not only, as the other had been, violently attacked, but was comparatively little read—indeed it is the only one of his books, with the usual exception of *Bouvard et Pécuchet*, which has been called, by any rational creature, dull. I do not find it so; but I confess that I find its intrinsic interest, which to me is great, largely enhanced by its unpopularity . . .

It is simply a panorama of human folly, frailty, feebleness, and failure—never permitted to rise to any great heights or to sink to any infernal depths, but always maintained at a probable human level. We start with Frédéric Moreau as he leaves school at the correct age of eighteen. I am not sure at what actual age we leave him, though it is at some point or other of middle life, the most active part of the book filling about a decade. But "vanity is the end of all his ways," and vanity has been the beginning and middle of them—a perfectly quiet and everyday kind of vanity, but vain from centre to circumference and entire surface. He (one cannot exactly say "tries," but) is brought into the possibility of trying love of various kinds—illegitimate-romantic, legitimate-not-unromantic, illegitimate-professional but not disagreeable, illegitimate-conventional. Nothing ever "comes off" in a really satisfactory fashion. He is "exposed" (in the photographic-plate sense) to all, or nearly all, the influences of a young man's life in Paris—law, literature, art, insufficient means, quite sufficient means, society, politics—including the Revolution of 1848—enchantments, disenchantments—*tout ce qu'il faut pour vivre*—to alter a little that stock expression for "writing materials" which is so common in French. But he never can get any real "life" out of any of these things. He is neither a fool, nor a cad, nor anything discreditable or disagreeable. He is "only an or'nary person," to reach the rhythm of the original by adopting a slang form in not quite the slang sense. And perhaps it is not unnatural that other ordinary persons should find him too faithful to their type to be welcome. In this respect at least I may claim not to be ordinary. One goes down so many empty wells, or wells with mere rubbish at the bottom of them, that to find Truth at last is to be happy with her (without prejudice to the convenience of another well or two here and there, with an agreeable Falsehood waiting for one). I do not know that *L'Éducation Sentimentale* is a book to be read very often; one has the substance in one's own experience, and in the contemplation of other people's, too readily at hand for that to be necessary or perhaps desirable. But a great work of art which is also a great record of nature is not too common—and this is what it is.

—from *History of the French Novel* (1917–1919)

JOHN MIDDLETON MURRY

Of the faculty which employs visual imagery to differentiate the subtler emotions of the soul, Flaubert had little or nothing at all. The true faculty of metaphor was denied him.

Lacking this, a writer cannot be reckoned among the great masters of style. But Flaubert lacked something more fundamental still. If we consider his works in the order they were written we are chiefly struck by the strange absence of inward growth which they reveal. The surface texture of L'Éducation Sentimentale is more closely woven than that of Madame Bovary, but the scope of the story itself is, if anything, less significant. Flaubert's vision of life had not deepened in the long interval which separates the two works. He saw a larger extent of life, perhaps, but he saw no further into it; he had acquired more material, but no greater power of handling it; he manipulated more characters, but he could not make them more alive. Though the epicure of technical effects may find more to interest him in the later book, it is impossible not to endorse the general verdict that Madame Bovary is Flaubert's masterpiece. Undoubtedly the choice lies between those books, for La Tentation de St Antoine and Salammbô are set-pieces which will not kindle, and Bouvard et Pécuchet (which de Gourmont declared the equal of Don Quixote!) cannot be redeemed from dullness by the mildly amusing bubbles which float to the surface of its viscous narrative.

We may suspect that a writer who does not really develop, the vitality and significance of whose latest work is less than that of his first, has not the root of the matter in him. And Flaubert had not. It may not be given to mortal men to understand life more deeply at the end than at the beginning of their share of it; but they can more keenly feel its complexity and its wonder; they can attain to an eminence from which they contemplate it calmly and undismayed.

The great writers do this, and convey the issue of their contemplation to us through the created world which they devise. But of this unmortified detachment Flaubert was incapable. He lived and died indignant at the stupidity of the human race. As he was at thirty, so he was at sixty; in stature of soul he was a child.

—from *The Dial* (December 1921)

Questions

1. Given everything that happens in *Sentimental Education*, is Flaubert's pessimism justified? Even if it is internally justified, can it possibly correspond with external reality? Is his pessimism directed toward the times, the historical moment, or the nature of human life?

2. In *Sentimental Education* we get something more like a process than a plot. No governess marries a great lord. No young hero finds the Holy Grail stuffed with bank notes. No lofty hero or heroine suffers a fall because of a fatal flaw. Does Flaubert sacrifice too much, does he have difficulty holding the readers' attention, by not having a clearly articulated plot to order his incidents and create suspense? What does he gain?

3. What should Frédéric have done to create for himself a satisfying and meaningful life? If *Sentimental Education* is a novel of education, what exactly does Frédéric learn?

4. What is Flaubert's view of love between the sexes? Is it redemptive? An irresistible biological urge? Projected narcissism? Contaminated by ulterior motives? The best thing in life? A spark of the divine in mortal flesh? A swindle? A delusion?

FOR FURTHER READING

Other Works by Gustave Flaubert

Madame Bovary (1857)
Salammbô (1862)
L'Éducation sentimentale (1869; *A Sentimental Education*)
La Tentation de Saint Antoine (1874; *The Temptation of Saint Anthony*)
Le Candidat (performed 1874, published 1904; *The Candidate*)
Trois Contes (1877; *Three Tales*)
Bouvard et Pécuchet (1881)
Par les Champs et par les grèves (1886; *Over the Fields and Over the Shores*)

Biography

Bart, Benjamin. *Flaubert*. Syracuse, NY: Syracuse University Press, 1967.

Le Calvez, Eric, ed. *Gustave Flaubert: A Documentary Volume*. Detroit, MI: Gale, 2004.

Lottman, Herbert. *Flaubert: A Biography*. New York: Fromm International, 1990.

Sartre, Jean-Paul. *The Family Idiot: Gustave Flaubert, 1821–1857*. Translated by Carol Cosman. Chicago: University of Chicago Press, 1981.

Wall, Geoffrey. *Flaubert: A Life*. London: Faber, 2001.

Criticism

Bernheimer, Charles. *Flaubert and Kafka: Studies in Psychopoetic Structure*. New Haven, CT: Yale University Press, 1982.

Bourdieu, Pierre. *The Rules of Art: Genesis and Structure of the Literary Field*. Stanford, CA: Stanford University Press, 1995.

Brombert, Victor H. *The Novels of Flaubert: A Study of Themes and Techniques*. Princeton, NJ: Princeton University Press, 1966.

Cortland, Peter. *The Sentimental Adventure: An Examination of Flaubert's* Éducation sentimentale. The Hague and Paris: Mouton, 1967.

Culler, Jonathan D. *Flaubert: The Uses of Uncertainty*. Ithaca, NY: Cornell University Press, 1974.

Donato, Eugenio. *The Script of Decadence: Essays on the Fictions of Flaubert and the Poetics of Romanticism*. New York: Oxford University Press, 1993.

Giraud, Raymond. *The Unheroic Hero in the Novels of Stendhal, Balzac, and Flaubert*. New York: Octagon Books, 1969.

Haig, Sterling. *Flaubert and the Gift of Speech: Dialogue and Discourse in Four "Modern" Novels*. Cambridge and New York: Cambridge University Press, 1986.

Knight, Diana. *Flaubert's Characters: The Language of Illusion*. Cambridge and New York: Cambridge University Press, 1985.

LaCapra, Dominick. *History, Politics, and the Novel*. Ithaca, NY: Cornell University Press, 1987.

Lukács, György. *The Theory of the Novel: A Historico-Philosophical Essay on the Forms of Great Epic Literature*. Translated by Anna Bostock. Cambridge, MA: MIT Press, 1971.

Paulson, William. *Sentimental Education: The Complexity of Disenchantment*. New York: Twayne; Toronto: Maxwell Macmillan Canada; New York: Maxwell Macmillan International, 1992.

Sherrington, R. J. *Three Novels by Flaubert: A Study of Techniques*. Oxford: Clarendon Press, 1970.

Williams, D. A. *'The Hidden Life at Its Source': A Study of Flaubert's* L'Éducation Sentimentale. Hull, UK: Hull University Press, 1987.

Works Cited in the Introduction

Flaubert, Gustave. *Correspondance*. 4 vols. Paris: Gallimard (Pléiade), 1973–1998. In the introduction, translations of quotations from these volumes are by the author of the introduction, Claudie Bernard.

Flaubert, Gustave. *The Letters of Gustave Flaubert, 1857–1880.* Selected, edited, and translated by Francis Steegmuller. Cambridge, MA: Harvard University Press, 1982.
Marx, Karl. *The Eighteenth Brumaire of Louis Bonaparte.* New York: International Publishers, 1963.
Proust, Marcel. *Against Sainte-Beuve and Other Essays.* Translated by John Sturrock. London: Penguin, 1994.

TIMELESS WORKS. NEW SCHOLARSHIP. EXTRAORDINARY VALUE.

Look for the following titles, available now and forthcoming from BARNES & NOBLE CLASSICS.

Visit your local bookstore for these and more fine titles.
Or to order online go to: WWW.BN.COM/CLASSICS

Title	Author	ISBN	Price
Aesop's Fables	Aesop	1-59308-062-X	$5.95
The Age of Innocence	Edith Wharton	1-59308-143-X	$5.95
Agnes Grey	Anne Brontë	1-59308-323-8	$5.95
Alice's Adventures in Wonderland and Through the Looking-Glass	Lewis Carroll	1-59308-015-8	$5.95
Anna Karenina	Leo Tolstoy	1-59308-027-1	$8.95
The Art of War	Sun Tzu	1-59308-017-4	$7.95
The Awakening and Selected Short Fiction	Kate Chopin	1-59308-113-8	$6.95
Babbitt	Sinclair Lewis	1-59308-267-3	$7.95
Barchester Towers	Anthony Trollope	1-59308-337-8	$7.95
The Beautiful and Damned	F. Scott Fitzgerald	1-59308-245-2	$7.95
Beowulf	Anonymous	1-59308-266-5	$4.95
Bleak House	Charles Dickens	1-59308-311-4	$9.95
The Bostonians	Henry James	1-59308-297-5	$7.95
The Brothers Karamazov	Fyodor Dostoevsky	1-59308-045-X	$9.95
The Call of the Wild and White Fang	Jack London	1-59308-200-2	$5.95
Candide	Voltaire	1-59308-028-X	$4.95
A Christmas Carol, The Chimes and The Cricket on the Hearth	Charles Dickens	1-59308-033-6	$5.95
The Collected Poems of Emily Dickinson	Emily Dickinson	1-59308-050-6	$5.95
Common Sense and Other Writings	Thomas Paine	1-59308-209-6	$6.95
The Communist Manifesto and Other Writings	Karl Marx and Friedrich Engels	1-59308-100-6	$5.95
The Complete Sherlock Holmes, Vol. I	Sir Arthur Conan Doyle	1-59308-034-4	$7.95
The Complete Sherlock Holmes, Vol. II	Sir Arthur Conan Doyle	1-59308-040-9	$7.95
A Connecticut Yankee in King Arthur's Court	Mark Twain	1-59308-210-X	$7.95
The Count of Monte Cristo	Alexandre Dumas	1-59308-151-0	$7.95
The Country of the Pointed Firs and Selected Short Fiction	Sarah Orne Jewett	1-59308-262-2	$6.95
Daisy Miller and Washington Square	Henry James	1-59308-105-7	$4.95
Daniel Deronda	George Eliot	1-59308-290-8	$8.95
David Copperfield	Charles Dickens	1-59308-063-8	$7.95
Dead Souls	Nikolai Gogol	1-59308-092-1	$7.95
The Death of Ivan Ilych and Other Stories	Leo Tolstoy	1-59308-069-7	$7.95
The Deerslayer	James Fenimore Cooper	1-59308-211-8	$7.95
Don Quixote	Miguel de Cervantes	1-59308-046-8	$9.95
Dracula	Bram Stoker	1-59308-114-6	$6.95
Emma	Jane Austen	1-59308-152-9	$6.95
The Enchanted Castle and Five Children and It	Edith Nesbit	1-59308-274-6	$6.95
Essays and Poems by Ralph Waldo Emerson		1-59308-076-X	$6.95
Essential Dialogues of Plato		1-59308-269-X	$9.95
The Essential Tales and Poems of Edgar Allan Poe		1-59308-064-6	$7.95
Ethan Frome and Selected Stories	Edith Wharton	1-59308-090-5	$5.95

(continued)

Far from the Madding Crowd	Thomas Hardy	1-59308-223-1	$7.95
The Federalist	Hamilton, Madison, Jay	1-59308-282-7	$7.95
The Four Feathers	A. E. W. Mason	1-59308-313-0	$6.95
Frankenstein	Mary Shelley	1-59308-115-4	$4.95
Germinal	Émile Zola	1-59308-291-6	$7.95
The Good Soldier	Ford Madox Ford	1-59308-268-1	$6.95
Great American Short Stories: from Hawthorne to Hemingway	Various	1-59308-086-7	$7.95
Great Expectations	Charles Dickens	1-59308-116-2	$6.95
Grimm's Fairy Tales	Jacob and Wilhelm Grimm	1-59308-056-5	$7.95
Gulliver's Travels	Jonathan Swift	1-59308-132-4	$5.95
Hard Times	Charles Dickens	1-59308-156-1	$5.95
The Histories	Herodotus	1-59308-102-2	$6.95
The House of Mirth	Edith Wharton	1-59308-153-7	$6.95
The House of the Dead and Poor Folk	Fyodor Dostoevsky	1-59308-194-4	$7.95
Howards End	E. M. Forster	1-59308-022-0	$6.95
The Idiot	Fyodor Dostoevsky	1-59308-058-1	$7.95
The Iliad	Homer	1-59308-232-0	$7.95
The Importance of Being Earnest and Four Other Plays	Oscar Wilde	1-59308-059-X	$6.95
Incidents in the Life of a Slave Girl	Harriet Jacobs	1-59308-283-5	$5.95
The Inferno	Dante Alighieri	1-59308-051-4	$6.95
The Interpretation of Dreams	Sigmund Freud	1-59308-298-3	$8.95
Ivanhoe	Sir Walter Scott	1-59308-246-0	$7.95
Jane Eyre	Charlotte Brontë	1-59308-117-0	$7.95
Journey to the Center of the Earth	Jules Verne	1-59308-252-5	$4.95
Jude the Obscure	Thomas Hardy	1-59308-035-2	$6.95
The Jungle	Upton Sinclair	1-59308-118-9	$6.95
The Jungle Books	Rudyard Kipling	1-59308-109-X	$5.95
Kim	Rudyard Kipling	1-59308-192-8	$4.95
King Solomon's Mines	H. Rider Haggard	1-59308-275-4	$4.95
Lady Chatterley's Lover	D. H. Lawrence	1-59308-239-8	$6.95
The Last of the Mohicans	James Fenimore Cooper	1-59308-137-5	$5.95
Leaves of Grass: First and "Death-bed" Editions	Walt Whitman	1-59308-083-2	$9.95
The Legend of Sleepy Hollow and Other Writings	Washington Irving	1-59308-225-8	$6.95
Les Liaisons Dangereuses	Pierre Choderlos de Laclos	1-59308-240-1	$7.95
Les Misérables	Victor Hugo	1-59308-066-2	$9.95
The Life of Charlotte Brontë	Elizabeth Gaskell	1-59308-314-9	$7.95
Little Women	Louisa May Alcott	1-59308-108-1	$6.95
Madame Bovary	Gustave Flaubert	1-59308-052-2	$6.95
Maggie: A Girl of the Streets and Other Writings about New York	Stephen Crane	1-59308-248-7	$6.95
The Magnificent Ambersons	Booth Tarkington	1-59308-263-0	$7.95
Man and Superman and Three Other Plays	George Bernard Shaw	1-59308-067-0	$7.95
The Man in the Iron Mask	Alexandre Dumas	1-59308-233-9	$8.95
Mansfield Park	Jane Austen	1-59308-154-5	$5.95
The Mayor of Casterbridge	Thomas Hardy	1-59308-309-2	$5.95
The Metamorphoses	Ovid	1-59308-276-2	$7.95
The Metamorphosis and Other Stories	Franz Kafka	1-59308-029-8	$6.95

Title	Author	ISBN	Price
Middlemarch	George Eliot	1-59308-023-9	$8.95
Moby-Dick	Herman Melville	1-59308-018-2	$9.95
Moll Flanders	Daniel Defoe	1-59308-216-9	$5.95
The Moonstone	Wilkie Collins	1-59308-322-X	$7.95
My Ántonia	Willa Cather	1-59308-202-9	$5.95
My Bondage and My Freedom	Frederick Douglass	1-59308-301-7	$6.95
Nana	Émile Zola	1-59308-292-4	$6.95
Narrative of Sojourner Truth		1-59308-293-2	$6.95
Narrative of the Life of Frederick Douglass, an American Slave		1-59308-041-7	$4.95
Nicholas Nickleby	Charles Dickens	1-59308-300-9	$8.95
Night and Day	Virginia Woolf	1-59308-212-6	$7.95
Northanger Abbey	Jane Austen	1-59308-264-9	$5.95
Nostromo	Joseph Conrad	1-59308-193-6	$7.95
O Pioneers!	Willa Cather	1-59308-205-3	$5.95
The Odyssey	Homer	1-59308-009-3	$5.95
Oliver Twist	Charles Dickens	1-59308-206-1	$6.95
The Origin of Species	Charles Darwin	1-59308-077-8	$7.95
Paradise Lost	John Milton	1-59308-095-6	$7.95
Père Goriot	Honoré de Balzac	1-59308-285-1	$7.95
Persuasion	Jane Austen	1-59308-130-8	$5.95
Peter Pan	J. M. Barrie	1-59308-213-4	$4.95
The Picture of Dorian Gray	Oscar Wilde	1-59308-025-5	$4.95
The Pilgrim's Progress	John Bunyan	1-59308-254-1	$7.95
Poetics and Rhetoric	Aristotle	1-59308-307-6	$9.95
The Portrait of a Lady	Henry James	1-59308-096-4	$7.95
A Portrait of the Artist as a Young Man and Dubliners	James Joyce	1-59308-031-X	$6.95
The Possessed	Fyodor Dostoevsky	1-59308-250-9	$9.95
Pride and Prejudice	Jane Austen	1-59308-201-0	$5.95
The Prince and Other Writings	Niccolò Machiavelli	1-59308-060-3	$5.95
The Prince and the Pauper	Mark Twain	1-59308-218-5	$4.95
Pudd'nhead Wilson and Those Extraordinary Twins	Mark Twain	1-59308-255-X	$5.95
The Purgatorio	Dante Alighieri	1-59308-219-3	$7.95
Pygmalion and Three Other Plays	George Bernard Shaw	1-59308-078-6	$7.95
The Red and the Black	Stendhal	1-59308-286-X	$7.95
The Red Badge of Courage and Selected Short Fiction	Stephen Crane	1-59308-119-7	$4.95
Republic	Plato	1-59308-097-2	$6.95
The Return of the Native	Thomas Hardy	1-59308-220-7	$7.95
Robinson Crusoe	Daniel Defoe	1-59308-360-2	$5.95
A Room with a View	E. M. Forster	1-59308-288-6	$5.95
Sailing Alone Around the World	Joshua Slocum	1-59308-303-3	$6.95
Scaramouche	Rafael Sabatini	1-59308-242-8	$6.95
The Scarlet Letter	Nathaniel Hawthorne	1-59308-207-X	$4.95
The Scarlet Pimpernel	Baroness Orczy	1-59308-234-7	$5.95
The Secret Garden	Frances Hodgson Burnett	1-59308-277-0	$5.95
Selected Stories of O. Henry		1-59308-042-5	$5.95
Sense and Sensibility	Jane Austen	1-59308-125-1	$5.95
Sentimental Education	Gustave Flaubert	1-59308-306-8	$6.95
Silas Marner and Two Short Stories	George Eliot	1-59308-251-7	$6.95

(continued)

Sister Carrie	Theodore Dreiser	1-59308-226-6	$7.95
Six Plays by Henrik Ibsen		1-59308-061-1	$8.95
Sons and Lovers	D. H. Lawrence	1-59308-013-1	$7.95
The Souls of Black Folk	W. E. B. Du Bois	1-59308-014-X	$5.95
The Strange Case of Dr. Jekyll and Mr. Hyde and Other Stories	Robert Louis Stevenson	1-59308-131-6	$4.95
Swann's Way	Marcel Proust	1-59308-295-9	$8.95
A Tale of Two Cities	Charles Dickens	1-59308-138-3	$5.95
Tao Te Ching	Lao Tzu	1-59308-256-8	$5.95
Tess of d'Urbervilles	Thomas Hardy	1-59308-228-2	$7.95
This Side of Paradise	F. Scott Fitzgerald	1-59308-243-6	$6.95
Three Lives	Gertrude Stein	1-59308-320-3	$6.95
The Three Musketeers	Alexandre Dumas	1-59308-148-0	$8.95
Thus Spoke Zarathustra	Friedrich Nietzsche	1-59308-278-9	$7.95
Tom Jones	Henry Fielding	1-59308-070-0	$8.95
Treasure Island	Robert Louis Stevenson	1-59308-247-9	$4.95
The Turn of the Screw, The Aspern Papers and Two Stories	Henry James	1-59308-043-3	$5.95
Twenty Thousand Leagues Under the Sea	Jules Verne	1-59308-302-5	$5.95
Uncle Tom's Cabin	Harriet Beecher Stowe	1-59308-121-9	$7.95
Utopia	Sir Thomas More	1-59308-244-4	$5.95
Vanity Fair	William Makepeace Thackeray	1-59308-071-9	$7.95
The Varieties of Religious Experience	William James	1-59308-072-7	$7.95
Villette	Charlotte Brontë	1-59308-316-5	$7.95
The Virginian	Owen Wister	1-59308-236-3	$7.95
The Voyage Out	Virginia Woolf	1-59308-229-0	$6.95
Walden and Civil Disobedience	Henry David Thoreau	1-59308-208-8	$5.95
War and Peace	Leo Tolstoy	1-59308-073-5	$12.95
Ward No. 6 and Other Stories	Anton Chekhov	1-59308-003-4	$7.95
The Waste Land and Other Poems	T. S. Eliot	1-59308-279-7	$4.95
The Way We Live Now	Anthony Trollope	1-59308-304-1	$9.95
The Wind in the Willows	Kenneth Grahame	1-59308-265-7	$4.95
The Wings of the Dove	Henry James	1-59308-296-7	$7.95
Wives and Daughters	Elizabeth Gaskell	1-59308-257-6	$7.95
The Woman in White	Wilkie Collins	1-59308-280-0	$7.95
Women in Love	D. H. Lawrence	1-59308-258-4	$8.95
The Wonderful Wizard of Oz	L. Frank Baum	1-59308-221-5	$6.95
Wuthering Heights	Emily Brontë	1-59308-128-6	$5.95